The Complete Fairy Tales
of the
BROTHERS GRIMM

The Complete Fairy Tales
of the
BROTHERS GRIMM

Translated and With an Introduction by
Jack Zipes

Illustrations by John B. Gruelle

BANTAM BOOKS
TORONTO · NEW YORK · LONDON · SYDNEY · AUCKLAND

THE COMPLETE FAIRY TALES OF THE BROTHERS GRIMM
A Bantam Book / February 1987

The present translation is based in part on the first edition
of the KINDER- UND HAUSMÄRCHEN published in two volumes in
1812 and 1815. The first 211 tales in this translation are based
on the seventh and final edition published in 1857.

The inside illustrations by John B. Gruelle first appeared in
Grimms Fairy Tales, translated by Margaret Hunt in 1914.

Library of Congress Cataloging-in-Publication Data

Kinder- und Hausmärchen.   English.
The complete fairy tales of the Brothers Grimm.

Translation of: Kinder- und Hausmärchen.
Summary: A new translation of 242 fairy tales collected
by the Brothers Grimm. Also includes a listing of their
oral and/or literary sources.
1. Fairy tales—Germany. [1. Fairy tales. 2. Folklore—
Germany] I. Grimm, Jacob, 1785–1863. II. Grimm,
Wilhelm, 1786–1859. III. Zipes, Jack David. IV. Gruelle,
Johnny, 1880?–1938, ill. V. Title.
PT921.K5613   1987   398.2'1'0943   86–47724
ISBN 0-553-05184-9

Published simultaneously in the United States and Canada

Bantam Books are published by Bantam Books, Inc. Its trademark, consisting of
the words "Bantam Books" and the portrayal of a rooster, is Registered in
U.S. Patent and Trademark Office and in other countries. Marca Registrada.
Bantam Books, Inc., 666 Fifth Avenue, New York, New York 10103.

PRINTED IN THE UNITED STATES OF AMERICA

DH   0 9 8 7 6 5 4 3 2 1

For my daughter,
Hanna,
and for her grandparents,
Celia and Phil, Bette and Dave,
who share the spirit of
once upon a time

Contents

Once There Were Two Brothers Named Grimm
by Jack Zipes

MANY ARE THE FAIRY TALES and myths that have been spread about the Brothers Grimm, Jacob and Wilhelm. For a long time it was believed that they had wandered about Germany and gathered their tales from the lips of doughty peasants and that all their tales were genuinely German. Although much of what had been believed has been disproven by recent scholarship, new rumors and debates about the Grimms keep arising. For instance, one literary scholar has recently charged them with manufacturing the folk spirit of the tales in order to dupe the general public in the name of nationalism. Other critics have found racist and sexist components in the tales that they allege need expurgation, while psychologists and educators battle over the possible harmful or therapeutic effects of the tales. Curiously, most of the critics and most of the introductions to the English translations of the Grimms' tales say very little about the brothers themselves or their methods for collecting the tales—as though the Grimms were incidental to their tales. Obviously, this is not the case, and in view of their 200th birthdays, celebrated in 1985 and 1986, it is time to set the record straight.

Just who were the Brothers Grimm and how did they discover those tales, which may be the most popular in the world today? Why and how did the brothers change the tales? And what is the significance of the magic of those tales today?

A fairy-tale writer could not have created a more idyllic and propitious setting for the entrance of the Brothers Grimm into the world. Their father, Philipp Wilhelm Grimm, a lawyer, was ambitious, diligent, and prosperous, and their mother Dorothea (née Zimmer), daughter of a city councilman in Kassel, was a devoted and caring housewife, even though she tended at times to be melancholy. Initially they settled in the quaint village of Hanau, and during the first twelve years of their marriage, there were nine births, out of which six children survived: Jacob Ludwig Grimm (1785–1863), Wilhelm Carl Grimm (1786–1859), Carl Friedrich Grimm (1787–1852), Ferdinand Philipp Grimm (1788–1844), Ludwig Emil Grimm (1790–1863), and

Charlotte Amalie (Lotte) Grimm (1793–1833). By 1791 the family had moved to Steinau, near Kassel, where Philipp Grimm had obtained an excellent position as district judge (*Amtmann*) and soon became the leading figure of the town. He and his family lived in a large comfortable home there and had servants to help with the domestic chores. As soon as the children were of age, they were sent to a local school, where they received a classical education. They also received strict religious training in the Reform Calvinist Church. Both Jacob and Wilhelm were bright, hardworking pupils and were distinctly fond of country life. Their familiarity with farming, nature, and peasant customs and superstitions would later play a major role in their research and work in German folklore. At first, though, both boys appeared destined to lead comfortable lives, following in the footsteps of their father, whose seal was *Tute si recte vixeris*—"honesty is the best policy in life." To be sure, this was the path that Jacob and Wilhelm took, but it had to be taken without the guidance of their father.

Philipp Grimm died suddenly in 1796 at the age of forty-four, and his death was traumatic for the entire family. Within weeks after his death, Dorothea Grimm had to move out of the large house and face managing the family of six children without servants or much financial support. From this point on, the family was totally dependent on outside help, particularly on Henriette Zimmer, Dorothea's sister, who was a lady-in-waiting for the princess of Hessia-Kassel. Henriette arranged for Jacob and Wilhelm to study at the prestigious Lyzeum (high school) in Kassel and obtained provisions and funds for the family.

Although the brothers were different in temperament—Jacob was more introverted, serious, and robust; Wilhelm was outgoing, gregarious, and asthmatic—they were inseparable and totally devoted to each other. They shared the same room and bed and developed the same work habits: in high school the Grimms studied more than twelve hours a day and were evidently bent on proving themselves to be the best students at the Lyzeum. That they were treated by some teachers as socially inferior to the other "highborn" students only served to spur their efforts. In fact, the Grimms had to struggle against social slights and financial deprivation during a good part of their lives, but they never forgot their father's motto, *Tute si recte vixeris,* and they became famous not only because of their remarkable scholarship but also because of their great moral integrity.

Although each one was graduated from the Lyzeum at the head of his class, Jacob in 1802 and Wilhelm in 1803, they both had to obtain special dispensations to study law at the University of Marburg because their social standing was not high enough to qualify them. Once at the university they had to confront yet another instance of injustice, for most of the students from wealthier families received stipends, while the Grimms had to pay for their own education and live on a small budget. This inequity made them feel even more compelled to prove themselves, and at Marburg they drew the attention of Professor Friedrich Karl von Savigny, the genial founder of the historical school of law. Savigny argued that the spirit of a law can be comprehended only by tracing its origins to the development of the customs and language of the people and by paying attention to the changing historical context in which laws developed. Ironically, it was Savigny's emphasis on the philological aspect of law that led Jacob and Wilhelm to dedicate themselves to the study of ancient German literature and folklore. This decision was made in 1805 after Savigny had taken Jacob to Paris to assist him in research on the history of Roman law. Upon returning to Germany in 1806, Jacob left the university and rejoined his mother, who had moved to Kassel. Given the pecuniary situation of the family, it was Jacob's duty, as head of the family now, to support his brothers and sister, and he found a position as secretary for the Kassel War Commission, which made decisions pertaining to the war with France. Fortunately for Jacob, he was able to pursue his study of old German literature and customs on the side while Wilhelm remained in Marburg to complete his legal studies.

The correspondence between Jacob and Wilhelm during this time reflects their great concern for the welfare of their family. With the exception of Ludwig, who later became an accomplished painter and also illustrated the fairy tales, the other children had difficulty establishing careers for themselves. Neither Carl nor Ferdinand displayed the intellectual aptitude that the two oldest brothers did or the creative talents of Ludwig. Carl eventually tried his hand at business and ended up destitute as a language teacher, while Ferdinand tried many different jobs in publishing and later died in poverty. Lotte's major task was to assist her mother, who died in 1808. After that, Lotte managed the Grimm household until she married a close friend of the family, Ludwig Hassenpflug, in 1822. Hassenpflug became an important politician in Germany and eventually had a falling out with Jacob and Wilhelm because of his conservative and opportunistic actions as statesman.

While Ludwig, Carl, Ferdinand, and Lotte were young, they were chiefly the responsibility of Jacob, who looked after them like a stern father. Even Wilhelm regarded him as such and acknowledged his authority, not only in family matters, but also in scholarship. It was during the period 1806–1810, when each of the siblings was endeavoring to make a decision about a future career and concerned about the stability of their home, that Jacob and Wilhelm began systematically gathering folk tales and other materials related to folklore. Clemens Brentano, a gifted romantic writer and friend, had requested that the Grimms help him collect tales for a volume that he intended to publish some time in the future. The Grimms responded by selecting tales from old books and recruiting the help of friends and acquaintances in Kassel. The Grimms were unable to devote all their energies to their research, though. Jacob lost his job on the War Commission in 1807, when Kassel was invaded by the French and became part of the Kingdom of Westphalia under the rule of Jérôme Bonaparte. Soon thereafter, the Grimms' mother died, and it was imperative that Jacob find some new means of supporting the family. Although he had a strong antipathy to the French, he applied for the position of King Jérôme's private librarian in Kassel, and was awarded the post in 1808. This job enabled him to pursue his studies and help his brothers and sister. Meanwhile, Wilhelm had to undergo a cure for a heart disease in Halle. Ludwig began studying art at the Art Academy in Munich, and Carl began working as a businessman in Hamburg. From 1809 to 1813 there was a period of relative stability and security for the Grimm family, and Jacob and Wilhelm began publishing the results of their research on old German literature: Jacob wrote *On the Old German Meistergesang,* and Wilhelm, *Old Danish Heroic Songs,* both in 1811. Together they published in 1812 a study of the *Song of Hildebrand* and the *Wessobrunner Prayer.* Of course, their major publication at this time was the first volume of the *Kinder- und Hausmärchen (Children's and Household Tales)* with scholarly annotations, also in 1812.

The Napoleonic Wars and French rule had been upsetting to both Jacob and Wilhelm, who were dedicated to the notion of German unification. Neither wanted to see the restoration of oppressive German princes, but they did feel a deep longing to have the German people united in one nation through customs and laws of their own making. Thus, in 1813 they celebrated when the French withdrew from Kassel and the French armies were defeated throughout Central Europe. Jacob was appointed a member of the Hessian Peace Delegation and did diplomatic work in Paris and Vienna. During his absence Wilhelm was able to procure the position as secretary to the royal librarian in Kassel and to concentrate on bringing out the second volume of the *Children's and Household Tales* in 1815. When the peace treaty with the French was concluded in Vienna, Jacob returned home and was disappointed to find that the German princes were seeking to reestablish their narrow, vested interests in different German principalities, and to discard the broader notion of German unification.

After securing the position of second librarian in the royal library of Kassel, Jacob joined Wilhelm in editing the first volume of *German Legends* in 1816. During the next thirteen years, the Grimms enjoyed a period of relative calm and prosperity. Their work as librarians was not demanding, and they could devote themselves to scholarly research and the publication of their findings. Together they published the second volume of *German Legends* (1818), and *Irish Elf Tales* (1826), while Jacob wrote the first volume of *German Grammar* (1819) and *Ancient German Law* (1828) by himself, and Wilhelm produced *The German Heroic Legend* (1829).

In the meantime, there were changes in the domestic arrangement of the Grimms. Lotte moved out of the house to marry Ludwig Hassenpflug in 1822, and a few years later, in 1825, Wilhelm married Dortchen Wild, who was the daughter of a druggist in Kassel. She had known both brothers for over twenty years and had been part of a group of storytellers who had provided the Grimms with numerous tales. Now it became her task to look after the domestic affairs of the brothers, for Jacob did not leave the house. Indeed, he remained a bachelor for his entire life and had very little time for socializing. The Grimms insisted on a quiet atmosphere and a rigid schedule at home so that they could conduct their research without interruptions. Although Wilhelm continued to enjoy company and founded a family— he had three children with Dortchen—he was just as much married to his work as Jacob. Since Dortchen had been well-acquainted with the brothers before her marriage, when she assumed her role in the family she fully supported their work and customary way of living.

In 1829, however, when the first librarian died and his position in Kassel became vacated, the Grimms' domestic tranquility was broken. Jacob, who had already become famous for his scholarly publications, had expected to be promoted to this position. But he did not have the right connections or the proper conservative politics and was overlooked. In response to this, he and Wilhelm resigned their posts, and one year later they traveled to Göttingen, where Jacob became professor of old German literature and head librarian, and Wilhelm, librarian and, eventually, professor in 1835. Both were considered gifted teachers, and they broke new ground in the study of German literature, which had only recently become an accepted field of study at the university. Aside from their teaching duties, they continued to write and publish important works: Jacob wrote the third volume of *German Grammar* (1831) and a major study entitled *German Mythology* (1835), while Wilhelm prepared the third edition of *Children's and Household Tales*. Though their positions were secure, there was a great deal of political unrest in Germany due to the severely repressive political climate since 1819. By 1830 many revolts and peasant uprisings had erupted, and a group of intellectuals known as Young Germany (*Jungdeutschland*) pushed for more democratic reform in different German principalities. For the most part, however, their members were persecuted and silenced, just as the peasants too were vanquished. Some leading writers, such as Ludwig Börne, Heinrich Heine, and Georg Büchner, took refuge in exile. The Brothers Grimm were not staunch supporters of the Young Germany movement, but they had always supported the liberal cause throughout Germany and were greatly affected by the political conflicts.

In 1837, when King Ernst August II succeeded to the throne of Hannover, he revoked the constitution of 1833 and dissolved parliament. In his attempt to restore absolutism to the Kingdom of Hannover, of which Göttingen was a part, he declared that all civil servants must pledge an oath to serve him personally. Since the king was nominally the rector of the University of Göttingen, the Grimms were obligated to take an oath of allegiance, but instead they, along with five other professors, led a protest against the king and were summarily dismissed. Jacob was compelled to leave Göttingen immediately and returned to Kassel, where Wilhelm joined him a few months later.

Once again, they were in desperate financial straits. Despite the fact that they received funds and support from hundreds of friends and admirers who supported their stand on academic freedom, the ruling monarchs of the different principalities prevented them from teaching at another university. It was during this time that Jacob and Wilhelm decided to embark on writing the *German Dictionary,* one of the most ambitious lexicographical undertakings of the nineteenth century. Though the income from this project would be meager, they hoped to support themselves through other publishing ventures as well. In the meantime, Bettina von Arnim, Friedrich Karl von Savigny, and other influential friends were trying to convince the new king of Prussia, Friedrich Wilhelm IV, to bring the brothers to Berlin. Finally, in November 1840 Jacob and Wilhelm received offers to become professors at the University of Berlin and to do research at the Academy of Sciences. It was not until March 1841, however, that the Grimms took up residence in Berlin and were able to continue their work on the *German Dictionary* and their scholarly research on other subjects. In addition to teaching, the Grimms played an active role in the institutionalization of German literature as a field of study at other universities and entered into political debates. When the Revolution of 1848 occurred in Germany, the Grimms were elected to the civil parliament, and Jacob was considered to be one of the most prominent men among the representatives at the National Assembly held in Frankfurt am Main. However, the brothers' hopes for democratic reform and the unification of the German principalities dwindled as one compromise after another was reached with the German monarchs. Both brothers retired from active politics after the demise of the revolutionary movement. In fact, Jacob resigned from his position as professor in 1848, the same year he published his significant study entitled *The History of the German Language.* Wilhelm retired from his post as professor in 1852. For the rest of their lives, the Grimms devoted most of their energy to completing the monumental *German Dictionary*, but they got only as far as the letter *F*. Though they did not finish the *Dictionary*, a task that had to be left to scholars in the twentieth century, they did produce an astonishing number of remarkable books during their lifetimes: Jacob published twenty-one, and Wilhelm, fourteen. Together they produced eight. In addition, there are another twelve volumes of their essays and notes and thousands of important letters. The Grimms made scholarly contributions to the areas of folklore, history, ethnology, religion, jurisprudence, lexicography, and literary criticism. Even when they did not work as a team, they shared their ideas and discussed all their projects together. When Wilhelm died in 1859, the loss affected Jacob deeply; he became even more solitary but did not abandon the projects he had held in common with his brother. In addition, the more he realized that his hopes for democratic reform were being dashed in Germany, the more he voiced his criticism of reactionary trends in Germany. Both Jacob and Wilhelm regarded their work as part of a social effort to foster a sense of justice among the German people and to create pride in the folk tradition. Jacob died in 1863 after completing the fourth volume of his book *German Precedents*. In German the title, *Deutsche Weistümer,* connotes a sense of the wisdom of the ages that he felt should be passed on to the German people.

Though the Grimms made important discoveries in their research on ancient German literature and customs, they were neither the founders of folklore as a study in Germany, nor were they the first to begin collecting and publishing folk and fairy tales. In fact, from the beginning their principal concern was to uncover the etymological and linguistic truths that bound the German people together and were expressed in their laws and customs. The fame of the Brothers Grimm as collectors of folk and fairy tales must be understood in this context, and even here, chance played a role in their destiny.

In 1806 Clemens Brentano, who had already published an important collection of folk songs entitled *Des Knaben Wunderhorn* (*The Boy's Magic Horn,* 1805) with Achim von Arnim, was advised to seek out the aid of Jacob and Wilhelm Grimm because they were known to have a vast knowledge of old German literature and folklore. They were also considered to be conscientious and indefatigable workers. Brentano hoped to use whatever tales they might send him in a future publication of folk tales, and he was able to publish some of the songs they gathered in the second and third volumes of *Des Knaben Wunderhorn* in 1808. The Grimms believed strongly in sharing their research and findings with friends and congenial scholars, and between 1807 and

1812 they began collecting tales with the express purpose of sending them to Brentano, as well as of using them as source material for gaining a greater historical understanding of the German language and customs.

Contrary to popular belief, the Grimms did not collect their tales by visiting peasants in the countryside and writing down the tales that they heard. Their primary method was to invite storytellers to their home and then have them tell the tales aloud, which the Grimms either noted down on first hearing or after a couple of hearings. Most of the storytellers during this period were educated young women from the middle class or aristocracy. For instance, in Kassel a group of young women from the Wild family (Dortchen, Gretchen, Lisette, and Marie Elisabeth), and their mother (Dorothea), and from the Hassenpflug family (Amalie, Jeanette, and Marie) used to meet regularly to relate tales they had heard from their nursemaids, governesses, and servants. In 1808 Jacob formed a friendship with Werner von Haxthausen, who came from Westphalia, and in 1811 Wilhelm visited the Haxthausen estate and became acquainted there with a circle of young men and women (Ludowine, Marianne, and August von Haxthausen, and Jenny and Annette von Droste-Hülfshoff), whose tales he noted down. Still, the majority of the storytellers came from Hessia: Dorothea Viehmann, a tailor's wife from nearby Zwehrn who used to sell fruit in Kassel, would visit the Grimms and told them a good many significant tales; and Johann Friedrich (*Wachtmeister*) Krause, an old retired soldier, gave the brothers tales in exchange for some of their old clothes. Many of the tales that the Grimms recorded had French origins because the Hassenpflugs were of Huguenot ancestry and spoke French at home. Most of the brothers' informants were familiar with both oral tradition and literary tradition and would combine motifs from both sources. In addition to the tales of these storytellers and others who came later, the Grimms took tales directly from books and journals and edited them according to their taste.

In 1810, when Brentano finally requested the Grimms' collection of tales, the brothers had copies made and sent forty-nine texts to him. They had copies made because they felt Brentano would take great poetic license and turn them into substantially different tales, whereas they were intent on using the tales to document basic truths about the customs and practices of the German people and on preserving their authentic ties to the oral tradition. Actually, the Grimms need not have worried about Brentano's use of their tales, for he never touched them but abandoned them in the Ölenberg Monastery in Alsace. Only in 1920 were the handwritten tales rediscovered, and they were published in different editions in 1924, 1927, and 1974. The last publication by Heinz Rölleke is the most scholarly and useful, for he has carefully shown how the Grimms' original handwritten manuscripts can help us to document their sources and reveal the great changes the brothers made in shaping the tales.

As it happened, after the Grimms sent their collected texts to Brentano, who was unreliable and was going through great personal difficulties, they decided to publish the tales themselves and began changing them and preparing them for publication. They also kept adding new tales to their collection. Jacob set the tone, but the brothers were very much in agreement about how they wanted to alter and stylize the tales. This last point is significant because some critics have wanted to see major differences between Jacob and Wilhelm. These critics have argued that there was a dispute between the brothers after Wilhelm assumed major responsibility for the editing of the tales in 1815 and that Wilhelm transformed them against Jacob's will. There is no doubt that Wilhelm was the primary editor after 1815, but Jacob established the framework for their editing practice between 1807 and 1812 and even edited the majority of the tales for the first volume. A comparison of the way Jacob and Wilhelm worked both before and after 1815 does not reveal major differences, except that Wilhelm did take more care to refine the style and make the contents of the tales more acceptable for a children's audience, or, really, for adults who wanted the tales censored for children. Otherwise, the editing of Jacob and Wilhelm exhibits the same tendencies from the beginning to the end of their project: the endeavor to make the tales stylistically smoother; the concern for clear sequential structure; the desire to make the stories more lively and pictorial by adding adjectives, old proverbs, and direct dialogue; the reinforcement of motives for action in the plot; the infusion of psychological motifs; and the elimination of elements that might detract from a rustic tone. The model for a good many of their tales was the work of the gifted artist Philipp Otto Runge, whose two stories in dialect, *The Fisherman and His Wife* and *The Juniper Tree,* represented in tone, structure, and content the ideal narrative that the Grimms wanted to create.

And create they did. The Grimms were not merely collectors. In fact, their major accomplishment in publishing their two volumes of 156 tales in 1812 and 1815 was to *create* an ideal type for the literary fairy tale, one that sought to be as close to the oral tradition as possible, while incorporating stylistic, formal, and substantial thematic changes to appeal to a growing middle-class audience. By 1819, when the second edition of the tales, now in one volume that included 170 texts, was published and Wilhelm assumed complete charge of the revisions, the brothers had established the form and manner through which they wanted to preserve, contain, and present to the German public what they felt were profound truths about the origins of civilization. Indeed, they saw the "childhood of humankind" as embedded in customs that Germans had cultivated, and the tales were to serve as reminders of such rich, natural culture.

After 1819 there were five more editions and sixty-nine new texts added to the collection and twenty-eight omitted. By the time the seventh edition appeared in 1857, there were 211 texts in all. Most of the additions after 1819 were from literary sources, and the rest were either sent to the brothers by informants or recorded from a primary source. Indeed, the chief task after 1819 was largely one of refinement: Wilhelm often changed the original texts by comparing them to different versions that he had acquired. While he evidently tried to retain what he and Jacob considered the essential message of the tale, he tended to make the tales more proper and prudent for bourgeois audiences. Thus it is crucial to be aware of the changes both brothers made between the original handwritten manuscript and the last edition of 1857. Compare the following, for example:

"Snow White"—Ölenberg Manuscript
When Snow White awoke the next morning, they asked her how she happened to get there. And she told them everything, how her mother, the queen, had left her alone in the woods and gone away. The dwarfs took pity on her and persuaded her to remain with them and do the cooking for them when they went to the mines. However, she was to beware of the queen and not to let anyone into the house.

"Snow White"—1812 Edition
When Snow White awoke, they asked her who she was and how she happened to get into the house. Then she told them how her mother had wanted to have her put to death, but the hunter had spared her life, and how she had run the entire day and finally arrived at their house. So the dwarfs took pity on her and said, "If you keep house for us and cook, sew, make the beds, wash and knit, and keep everything tidy and clean, you may stay with us, and you will have everything you want. In the evening, when we come home, dinner must be ready. During the day we are in the mines and dig for gold, so you will be alone. Beware of the queen and let no one into the house."

"Rapunzel"—1812 Edition
At first Rapunzel was afraid, but soon she took such a liking to the young king that she made an agreement with him: he was to come every day and be pulled up. Thus they lived merrily and joyfully for a certain time, and the fairy did not discover anything until one day when Rapunzel began talking to her and said, "Tell

me, Mother Gothel, why do you think my clothes have become too tight for me and no longer fit?"

"Rapunzel"—1857 Edition

When he entered the tower, Rapunzel was at first terribly afraid, for she had never laid eyes on a man before. However, the prince began to talk to her in a friendly way and told her that her song had touched his heart so deeply that he had not been able to rest until he had seen her. Rapunzel then lost her fear, and when he asked her whether she would have him for her husband, and she saw that he was young and handsome, she thought, He'll certainly love me better than old Mother Gothel. So she said yes and placed her hand in his.

"I want to go with you very much," she said, "but I don't know how I can get down. Every time you come, you must bring a skein of silk with you, and I'll weave it into a ladder. When it's finished, then I'll climb down, and you can take me away on your horse."

They agreed that until then he would come to her every evening, for the old woman came during the day. Meanwhile, the sorceress did not notice anything, until one day Rapunzel blurted out, "Mother Gothel, how is it that you're much heavier than the prince? When I pull him up, he's here in a second."

"The Three Spinners"—1812 Edition

In olden times there lived a king who loved flax spinning more than anything in the world, and his queen and daughters had to spin the entire day. If he did not hear the wheels humming, he became angry. One day he had to take a trip, and before he departed, he gave the queen a large box with flax and said, "I want this flax spun by the time I return."

"The Three Spinners"—1857 Edition

There once was a lazy maiden who did not want to spin, and no matter what her mother said, she refused to spin. Finally, her mother became so angry and impatient that she beat her, and her daughter began to cry loudly. Just then the queen happened to be driving by, and when she heard the crying, she ordered the carriage to stop, went into the house, and asked the mother why she was beating her daughter, for her screams could be heard out on the street. The woman was too ashamed to tell the queen that her daughter was lazy and said, "I can't get her to stop spinning. She does nothing but spin and spin, and I'm so poor that I can't provide the flax."

"Well," the queen replied, "there's nothing I like to hear more than the sound of spinning, and I'm never happier than when I hear the constant humming of the wheels. Let me take your daughter with me to my castle. I've got plenty of flax, and she can spin as much as she likes."

As is evident from the above examples, the Grimms made major changes while editing the tales. They eliminated erotic and sexual elements that might be offensive to middle-class morality, added numerous Christian expressions and references, emphasized specific role models for male and female protagonists according to the dominant patriarchal code of that time, and endowed many of the tales with a "homey" or *biedermeier* flavor by the use of diminutives, quaint expressions, and cute descriptions. Moreover, though the collection was not originally printed with children in mind as the primary audience—the first two volumes had scholarly annotations, which were later published separately—Wilhelm made all the editions from 1819 on more appropriate for children, or rather, to what he thought would be proper for children to learn. Indeed, some of the tales, such as *Mother Trudy* and *The Stubborn Child,* are intended to be harsh lessons for children. Such didacticism did not contradict what both the Grimms thought the collection should be, namely an *Erziehungsbuch,* an educational manual. The tendency toward attracting a virtuous middle-class audience is most evident in the so-called *Kleine Ausgabe* (*Small Edition*), a selection of fifty tales from the *Grosse Ausgabe* (*Large Edition*). This *Small Edition* was first published in 1825 in an effort to popularize the larger work and to create a best-seller. There were ten editions of this book, which contained the majority of the *Zaubermärchen* (the magic fairy tales), from 1825 to 1858. With such tales as *Cinderella, Snow White, Sleeping Beauty, Little Red Riding Hood,* and *The Frog King,* all of which underline morals in keeping with the Protestant ethic and a patriarchal notion of sex roles, the book was bound to be a success.

The magic fairy tales were the ones that were the most popular and acceptable in Europe and America during the nineteenth century, but it is important to remember that the Grimms' collection also includes unusual fables, legends, anecdotes, jokes, and religious tales. The variety of their tales is often overlooked because only a handful have been selected by parents, teachers, publishers, and critics for special attention. This selective process is generally neglected when critics talk about the effects of the tales and the way they should be conveyed or not conveyed to children.

The Grimms' collection *Children's and Household Tales* was not an immediate success in Germany. In fact, Ludwig Bechstein's *Deutsches Märchenbuch* (*German Book of Fairy Tales,* 1845) was more popular for a time. However, by the 1870s the Grimms' tales had been incorporated into the teaching curriculum in Prussia and other German principalities, and they were also included in primers and anthologies for children throughout the western world. By the beginning of the twentieth century, the *Children's and Household Tales* was second only to the Bible as a best-seller in Germany, and it has continued to hold this position. Furthermore, there is no doubt that the Grimms' tales, published either together in a single volume or individually as illustrated books, enjoy the same popularity in the English-speaking world.

Such popularity has always intrigued critics, and advocates of various schools of thought have sought to analyze and interpret the "magic" of the Grimms' tales. Foremost among the critics are the folklorists, educators, psychologists, and literary critics of different persuasions, including structuralists, literary historians, semioticians, and Marxists. Each group has made interesting contributions to the scholarship on the Grimms' tales, although there are times when historical truths about the Grimms' work are discarded or squeezed to fit into a pet theory.

The efforts made by folklorists to categorize the Grimms' tales after the nineteenth century were complicated by the fact that numerous German folklorists used the tales to explain ancient German customs and rituals, under the assumption that the tales were authentic documents of the German people. This position, which overlooked the French and other European connections, led to an "Aryan" approach during the 1920s, 1930s, and 1940s, which allowed many German folklorists to interpret the tales along racist and elitist lines. Such an approach had always been contested by folklorists outside Germany, who viewed the tales as part of the vast historical development of the oral tradition, wherein the Grimms' collection is given special attention because of the mixture of oral and literary motifs. These motifs have been related by folklorists to motifs in other folk tales in an effort to find the origin of a particular motif or tale type and its variants. By doing this kind of research, folklorists have been able to chart distinctions in the oral traditions and customs of different countries.

Educators have not been interested in motifs so much as in the morals and the types of role models in the tales. Depending on the country and the educational standards in a particular historical period, teachers and school boards have often dictated which Grimms' tales are to be used or abused. Generally speaking, such tales as *The Wolf and the Seven Young Kids, Cinderella, Little Red Cap,* and *Snow White* have always been deemed acceptable because they instruct children through explicit warnings and lessons, even though some of the implicit messages may be harmful to children. Most of the great pedagogical debates center around the brutality and cruelty in some tales, and the tendency among publishers and adapters of the tales has been to eliminate the harsh scenes. Consequently, Cinderella's sisters will not have their eyes pecked out; Little Red Cap and her grandmother will not be gobbled up by the wolf; the witch in *Snow White* will not be forced to dance in red-hot shoes; and the witch in *Hansel and Gretel* will not be shoved into an oven.

Such changes have annoyed critics of various psychoanalytical orientations, because they believe that the violence and conflict in the tales derive from profound instinctual developments in the human psyche and hence represent symbolical modes by which children and adults deal with sexual problems. Most psychoanalytical critics take their cues from Freud, even if they have departed from his method and have joined another school of analysis. One of the first important books about the psychological impact of the Grimms' tales was Josephine Belz's *Das Märchen und die Phantasie des Kindes* (*The Fairy Tale and the Imagination of the Child,* 1919) in which she tried to establish important connections between children's ways of fantasizing and the symbols in the tales. Later, Carl Jung, Erich Fromm, and Gerza Roheim wrote valuable studies of fairy tales that sought to go beyond Freud's theories. In the period following World War II, Aniela Jaffé, Joseph Campbell, and Maria von Franz charted the links between archetypes, the collective unconscious, and fairy tales, while Julius Heuscher and Bruno Bettelheim focused on oedipal conflicts from neo-Freudian positions in their analyses of some Grimms' tales. Finally, André Favat published an important study, *Child and the Tale* (1977), which uses Piaget's notions of child development, interests, and stages of understanding to explore the tales and their impact. Although the various psychoanalytical approaches have shed light on the symbolical meanings of the tales from the point of view of particular schools of thought, the tales have often been taken out of context to demonstrate the value of a psychoanalytical theory rather than to render a cultural and aesthetic appreciation and evaluation of the text.

Literary critics have reacted to the psychoanalytical approach in different ways. Influenced by the theories of Vladimir Propp (*Morphology of the Folktale,* 1968) and Max Lüthi (*Once Upon a Time,* 1970), formalists, structuralists, and semioticians have analyzed individual texts to discuss the structure of the tale, its aesthetic components and functions, and the hidden meanings of the signs. Literary historians and philologists such as Ludwig Denecke and Heinz Rölleke have tried to place the Grimms' work in a greater historical context in order to show how the brothers helped develop a mixed genre, often referred to as the *Buchmärchen* (book tale), combining aspects of the oral and literary tradition. Sociological and Marxist critics such as Dieter Richter, Christa Bürger, and Bernd Wollenweber have discussed the tales in light of the social and political conditions in Germany during the nineteenth century and have drawn attention to the racist and sexist notions in the tales. In the process, they have added fuel to the debate among educators, and the use and abuse of the Grimms' tales remains a key issue even today—among educators, psychologists, folklorists, and literary critics.

Though there were debates about the value of the tales during the Grimms' own lifetime, if they were alive today, they would probably be surprised to see how vigorous and violent some of the debates are and how different the interpretations tend to be. To a certain extent, the intense interest in their tales by so many different groups of critics throughout the world is a tribute to the Grimms' uncanny sense of how folk narratives inform cultures. They were convinced that their tales possessed essential truths about the origins of civilization, and they selected and revised those tales that would best express these truths. They did this in the name of humanity and *Kultur:* the Grimms were German idealists who believed that historical knowledge of customs, mores, and laws would increase self-understanding and social enlightenment. Their book is not so much a book of magic as it is a manual for education that seeks to go beyond the irrational. It is in their impulse to educate, to pass on the experiences of a variety of people who knew the lore of survival, that we may find the reasons why we are still drawn to the tales today. Though the Grimms imbued the tales with a heavy dose of Christian morality, the Protestant work ethic, and patriarchalism, they also wanted the tales to depict social injustices and possibilities for self-determination. Their tales reflect their concerns and the contradictions of their age. Today we have inherited their concerns and contradictions, and their tales still read like innovative strategies for survival. Most of all they provide hope that there is more to life than mastering the art of survival. Their "once upon a time" keeps alive our utopian longing for a better world that can be created out of our dreams and actions.

A Note on the Translation

This translation is based on the seventh, or final, edition of the *Kinder- und Hausmärchen* (*Children's and Household Tales*), published in 1857. In addition, I have translated thirty-two tales that appeared in some of the other editions before 1857 but were eventually omitted by the Grimms for one reason or another. These tales are appearing in English for the first time, and thus the present edition provides readers with the most comprehensive translation of the Grimms' tales to date.

Although a great commotion was made in the press in 1983 when a tale by the Grimms was discovered in a letter and subsequently purchased and printed by an American publisher, this tale is not legitimately a Grimms' tale, for the brothers did not consider it significant enough to include in their collection. It is very much like the other posthumous tales, which Heinz Rölleke gathered and published in *Märchen aus dem Nachlass der Brüder Grimm* (Bonn: Bouvier, 1977)—interesting, but not appealing enough for the Grimms to stamp their own imprint on it. On the other hand, all of the tales in the present collection were shaped and refined by the Grimms, even those that they eventually omitted.

The tales of the Brothers Grimm have been translated numerous times, and some readers might justly raise the question: Why publish another translation? However, with the exception of the work by Ralph Mannheim, David Luke, and Brian Alderson, the available translations are lacking on two accounts: either they are too anachronistic and imitative of Victorian models, or they seek to streamline the language according to present-day usage and often negate the historical features of the tales. In preparing the present translation, I have endeavored to respect the historical character and idioms of each tale and to retain a nineteenth-century flavor while introducing contemporary vocabulary and terms when they were, in my estimation, more apropos. Furthermore, I have tried to let the different voices within the Grimms' collection speak for themselves.

Although Wilhelm Grimm (more than Jacob) revised and altered most of the tales over a period of approximately forty years to make them more graceful and suitable for children and a proper Christian upbringing, many of the tales are still mixed with coarse and naive expressions of their original lower-class storytellers. In fact, a good number of the tales were printed in German dialect and possess the rustic, natural tone that the Grimms admired and attempted to imitate in their refined, high German renditions. The unevenness and variety in tone and expression are actually qualities that I too have sought to convey without destroying the flow of a tale.

The Grimms tended to make their tales more dramatic and colorful in their revisions, especially by shifting indirect speech to direct speech. I have emphasized the dramatic qualities of the tales even more by indenting the direct speech and creating more paragraphs. In many instances, I have provided smoother transition by adding phrases, but I have not departed radically from the texts. The Grimms had a fine ear for unusual idioms and proverbs and often invented their own. These expressions appeared odd and quaint in their own time, and I have retained them because they continue to be striking today.

If there were inconsistencies in the narrative structure, I have endeavored to resolve them without changing the meaning of the tale or incident. In some cases, I have left the contradictions because they were too minor to change. Here and there the translations of the titles will differ with those in other translations. My purpose in doing so has been to make the titles historically more accurate. The Grimms hoped to find great truths about the German people and their laws and customs by collecting their tales, for they believed that language was what created national bonds and stamped the national character of a people. Little did they know that their "German" collection would transcend their own country and through translations create universal bonds of understanding.

This project was originally conceived with the help of LuAnn Walther, whose advice and gentle prodding enabled me to dare a new translation. Deborah Futter assumed charge of the manuscript at a crucial time and supported me with fine suggestions and encouragement. Cecilia Hunt did a remarkable job of editing the translation and catching my errors, while Anne Greenberg made certain that our productive efforts would reach fruition. During the entire process, my wife, Carol Dines, helped me revise many of the translations, and I am most grateful for the understanding and criticism she has given me.

JACK ZIPES
Gainesville, 1986

The Complete Fairy Tales
of the
BROTHERS GRIMM

❖ 1 ❖

The Frog King, or Iron Heinrich

IN OLDEN TIMES, when wishing still helped, there lived a king whose daughters were all beautiful, but the youngest was so beautiful that the sun itself, which had seen so many things, was always filled with amazement each time it cast its rays upon her face. Now, there was a great dark forest near the king's castle, and in this forest, beneath an old linden tree, was a well. Whenever the days were very hot, the king's daughter would go into this forest and sit down by the edge of the cool well. If she became bored, she would take her golden ball, throw it into the air, and catch it. More than anything else she loved playing with this ball.

One day it so happened that the ball did not fall back into the princess's little hand as she reached out to catch it. Instead, it bounced right by her and rolled straight into the water. The princess followed it with her eyes, but the ball disappeared, and the well was deep, so very deep that she could not see the bottom. She began to cry, and she cried louder and louder, for there was nothing that could comfort her. As she sat there grieving over her loss a voice called out to her, "What's the matter, Princess? Your tears could move even a stone to pity."

She looked around to see where the voice was coming from and saw a frog sticking his thick, ugly head out of the water. "Oh, it's you, you old water-splasher!" she said. "I'm crying because my golden ball has fallen into the well."

"Be quiet and stop crying," the frog responded. "I'm sure I can help you. But what will you give me if I fetch your plaything?"

"Whatever you like, dear frog," she said. "My clothes, my pearls and jewels, even the golden crown I'm wearing on my head."

"I don't want your clothes, your pearls and jewels, or your golden crown," the frog replied. "But if you will love me and let me be your companion and playmate, and let me sit beside you at the table, eat from your little golden plate, drink out of your little cup, and sleep in your little bed—if you promise me all that, I'll dive down and retrieve your golden ball."

"Oh, yes," she said. "I'll promise you anything you want if only you'll bring back the ball!" However, she thought, What nonsense that stupid frog talks! He just sits in the water croaking with the rest of the frogs. How can he expect a human being to accept him as a companion?

Once the frog had her promise, he dipped his head under the water, dived downward, and soon came paddling back to the surface with the ball in his mouth. When he threw it onto the grass, the princess was so delighted to see her beautiful plaything again that she picked it up and ran off with it.

"Wait, wait!" cried the frog. "Take me with you. I can't run like you."

He croaked as loudly as he could, but what good did it do? She paid no attention to him. Instead, she rushed home and soon forgot about the poor frog, who had to climb back down into his well.

The next day, as she sat at the table with the king and his courtiers and ate from her little golden plate, something came crawling *splish, splash, splish, splash* up the marble steps. When it reached the top, it knocked at the door and cried out, "Princess, youngest daughter, open up!"

She ran to see who was outside. But when she opened the door and saw the frog, she quickly slammed the door shut and went back to the table in a state of fright. The king could clearly see her heart was thumping and said, "My child, what are you afraid of? Has a giant come to get you?"

"Oh, no," she answered. "It's not a giant, but a nasty frog."

"What does a frog want from you?"

"Oh, dear Father, yesterday when I was sitting and playing near the well in the forest, my golden ball fell into the water, and because I cried so much, the frog fetched it for me, and because he insisted, I had to promise he could be my companion. But I never thought he'd get out of the water. Now he's outside and wants to come in and be with me."

Just then there was a second knock at the door, and a voice cried out:

"Princess, Princess, youngest daughter,
open up and let me in.
Have you forgotten
what you promised
down by the well's cool water?
Princess, Princess, youngest daughter,
open up and let me in."

Then the king said, "If you've made a promise, you must keep it. Go and let him in."

After she went and opened the door, the frog hopped into the room and followed her right to her chair, where he plopped himself down and cried out, "Lift me up beside you!"

She refused until the king finally ordered her to do so. Once the frog was on the chair, he wanted to climb onto the table, and when he made it to the table, he said, "Now push your little golden plate nearer to me so we can eat together."

To be sure, she did this, but it was quite clear that she did not like it. The frog enjoyed his meal, while each bite the princess took got stuck in her throat. Finally he said, "I've had enough, and now I'm tired. Carry me upstairs to your room and get your silken bed ready so we can go to sleep."

The princess began to cry because the cold frog frightened her. She did not even have enough courage to touch him, and yet, now she was supposed to let him sleep in her beautiful, clean bed. But the king gave her an angry look and said, "It's not proper to scorn someone who helped you when you were in trouble!"

So she picked up the frog with her two fingers, carried him upstairs, and set him down in a corner. Soon after she had got into bed, he came crawling over to her and said, "I'm tired and want to sleep as much as you do. Lift me up, or I'll tell your father!"

This made the princess extremely angry, and after she picked him up, she threw him against the wall with all her might.

"Now you can have your rest, you nasty frog!"

However, when he fell to the ground, he was no longer a frog but a prince with kind and beautiful eyes. So, in keeping with her father's wishes, she accepted him as her dear companion and husband, whereupon the prince told her that a wicked witch had cast a spell over him and no one could have got him out of the well except her, and now he intended to take her to his kingdom the next day. Then they fell asleep, and in the morning, when the sun woke them, a coach drawn by eight white horses came driving up. The horses had ostrich plumes on their heads and harnesses with golden chains. At the back of the coach stood Faithful Heinrich, the young king's servant. He had been so distressed when he had learned his master had been turned into a frog that he had ordered three iron bands be wrapped around his heart to keep it from bursting from grief and sadness. But now the coach had come to bring the young king back to his kingdom, and Faithful Heinrich helped the prince and princess into it and then took his place at the back again. He was overcome by joy because his master had been saved.

When they had traveled some distance, the prince heard a cracking noise behind him, as if something had broken. He turned around and cried out:

"Heinrich, the coach is breaking!"
"No, my lord, it's really nothing
but the band around my heart,
for it nearly fell apart
when the witch did cast her spell
and made you live as a frog in a well."

The cracking noise was heard two more times along the way, and the prince thought each time that the coach was breaking, but the noise was only the sound of the bands snapping from Faithful Heinrich's heart, for he knew his master was safe and happy.

◈ 2 ◈

The Companionship of the Cat and the Mouse

A CAT HAD MADE the acquaintanceship of a mouse and had talked so much about his great love and friendship for her that he eventually convinced her to live with him in the same house and set up a common household.

"But we must get supplies for the winter," said the cat, "or else we'll starve. A little mouse like you can't venture just anywhere, for one of these days you might get caught in a trap."

They acted on his good advice and bought a little jar of fat, but they did not know where to put it. Finally, after long deliberation, the cat said, "I can't think of a safer place than the church. No one would dare take anything away from there. Let's put it under the altar, and we won't touch it unless we really need it."

The little jar was safely stored away, but it was not long before the cat felt a craving for it and said to the mouse, "I've been meaning to tell you, little mouse. My cousin gave birth to a baby boy, white with brown spots, and I've been asked to be godfather. I'm to hold him at the christening. Would you mind letting me go out today and looking after the house by yourself?"

"No, of course not," answered the mouse. "Go, for God's sake. If you get something good to eat, think of me. I sure would like to have a drink of that sweet, red christening wine."

Naturally, none of what the cat had said was true. He did not have a cousin, nor had he been asked to be godfather. He went straight to the church, crept to the little jar of fat, and began licking and licking until he had licked the skin off the top. Then he strolled over the roofs of the city and contemplated his opportunities. After a while he stretched himself out in the sun and wiped his whiskers whenever he thought about the little jar of fat. It was not until evening that he returned home.

"Well, you're back," the mouse said. "I'm sure you had a wonderful day."

"It wasn't bad," the cat responded.

"What name did they give the child?" the mouse asked.

"*Skin-Off,*" the cat said dryly.

"Skin-Off?" exclaimed the mouse. "That's a strange and unusual name. Is it common in your family?"

"What's there to it?" the cat said. "It's no worse than Crumb-Thief, as your godchildren are called."

Shortly after that the cat felt another great craving and said to the mouse, "You've got to do me a favor again and look after the house by yourself. I've been asked to be godfather once more, and since the child has a white ring around his neck, I can't refuse."

The good mouse consented, and the cat went slinking behind the city wall to the church, where he ate up half the jar of fat.

"Nothing tastes better," he said, "than what you eat yourself," and

The Cat and Mouse in Partnership ~

he was very satisfied with his day's work. When he returned, the mouse asked, "What was this child christened?"

"*Half-Gone*," answered the cat.

"Half-Gone! You don't say! I've never heard of such a name in all my life. I'll bet it's not on the list of proper names."

Soon the cat's mouth began watering once more for the delicacy.

"All good things come in threes," he said to the mouse. "I've been asked to be godfather again. This child's all black and has white paws. Aside from that there's not a white hair on his body. That only happens once every few years. You'll let me go, won't you?"

"Skin-Off! Half-Gone!" the mouse responded. "Those are really curious names. I'm beginning to wonder about them."

"Look, you sit at home in your dark gray fur coat and your long pigtail," the cat said, "and you begin imagining things. That's because you don't go out during the day."

While the cat was gone, the mouse cleaned the house and put it in order. Meanwhile the greedy cat ate up the rest of the jar.

"It's only after everything's all gone," the cat said to himself, "that you can really begin to rest."

It was very late at night by the time the cat returned home, and he was fat and stuffed. The mouse asked right away what name had been given to the third child.

"You won't like this one either," the cat said. "It's *All-Gone*."

"All-Gone!" exclaimed the mouse. "That's the most suspicious of all the names. I've never seen it in print. All-Gone! What's it supposed to mean?" She shook her head, rolled herself up into a ball, and fell asleep.

From then on, no one asked the cat to be a godfather. But, when winter came and there was nothing more to be found outside, the mouse thought about their supply of fat and said, "Come, cat, let's go to our jar that we've been saving. It'll taste good."

"Yes," said the cat. "You'll enjoy the taste just as much as if you stuck your dainty tongue out the window."

They set out on their way, and when they got there, the jar of fat was still in its place, but it was empty.

"Oh," said the mouse. "Now I know what's happened! It's as clear as day. Some nice friend you are! You ate it all up when you went to be a godfather. First the skin, then half, then . . ."

"You better be quiet!" yelled the cat. "One more word, and I'll eat you up!"

"All gone" was already on the tip of the mouse's tongue. No sooner did she say it than the cat jumped on her, grabbed her, and devoured her.

You see, that's the way of the world.

❖ 3 ❖

The Virgin Mary's Child

A POOR WOODCUTTER and his wife lived at the edge of a large forest, and their only child was a little girl who was three years old. They were so poor they could not have daily meals anymore and did not know how they would provide food for their daughter. One morning the woodcutter, who was distressed by all this, went into the forest to work. As he began chopping wood a tall, beautiful woman suddenly appeared before him. She was wearing a crown of shining stars on her head and said to him, "I am the Virgin Mary, mother of the Christ Child. Since you are poor and needy, bring me your child. I'll take her with me and be her mother and look after her."

The woodcutter obeyed her. He brought his child and gave her to the Virgin Mary, who took her up to heaven. Everything went well for the girl there: she ate cake and drank sweet milk. Her clothes were made of gold, and the little angels played with her. One day, when she turned fourteen, the Virgin Mary summoned her and said, "Dear child, I intend to go on a long journey, and I want you to take care of the keys to the thirteen doors of the kingdom of heaven. You may open twelve of the doors and look at all the marvelous things inside, but I forbid you to open the thirteenth door that this little key unlocks. Be on your guard and don't open it. If you do, you'll be unhappy."

The maiden promised to be obedient, and when the Virgin Mary had departed, she began to explore the rooms of the kingdom of heaven. Every day she opened a new room until she had unlocked twelve of them. In each one there was an apostle in dazzling light, and she was delighted by the glory and splendor, and the little angels who always accompanied her were delighted too. Now the forbidden door was the only one left, and she felt a great desire to know what was inside, and she said to the little angels, "I won't open it all the way, and I won't go inside. I'll only unlock it so we can peek through the crack a little."

"Oh, no!" said the little angels. "That would be a sin. The Virgin Mary's forbidden it, and something awful could happen to you."

So the maiden said nothing more about this, but she could not still the urge in her heart. Her desire kept gnawing and pecking away at her and gave her no peace. One day when the angels had all gone out, she thought, Now I'm all alone and can take a peek. No one will know if I do.

She looked for the key, and when she got it in her hand, she put it in the lock and turned it. Suddenly the door sprang open, and there she saw the Holy Trinity sitting in fire and splendor. She stood still for a while and looked at everything in amazement. Then she touched the light just a little with her finger, and the finger turned golden. All at once she was overcome by a tremendous fear, and she slammed the door and ran away. The fear would not abate, no matter what she did, and her heart pounded constantly and could not be calmed. Moreover, the gold stayed on her finger and would not go away even though she washed and rubbed it as much as she could.

Soon after, the Virgin Mary returned from her journey. She summoned the maiden and asked her to return the keys of heaven to her. When the maiden handed her the bunch of keys, the Virgin looked into her eyes and said, "Didn't you also open the thirteenth door?"

"No," she answered.

Then the Virgin Mary put her hand on the maiden's heart and could feel it pounding and pounding. Now she knew the maiden had disobeyed her command and had opened the door. Once again she asked, "You opened the door, didn't you?"

"No," said the maiden for a second time.

When the Virgin Mary glanced at the finger that had become golden from touching the heavenly fire, she knew the maiden had sinned.

"Didn't you?" she asked for a third time.

"No," the maiden replied for the third time.

Then the Virgin Mary said, "You've disobeyed me, and you've even lied. You're no longer worthy enough to stay in heaven."

The maiden sank then into a deep sleep, and when she awoke, she was lying on earth in the middle of a wilderness. She wanted to cry out, but she could not utter a sound. She jumped up and wanted to run away, but wherever she turned, she encountered thick hedges of thorns and could not make her way through them. She was imprisoned in this desolate spot and had to make an old hollow tree her dwelling place. When night came, she crawled inside and fell asleep. If it rained and there was stormy weather, she found shelter there. But it was a miserable life, and whenever she thought about how beautiful it had been in heaven and how the angels had played with her, she shed bitter tears. Roots and wild berries were her only food, and she went out looking for them as far as she could walk. In the fall she gathered the nuts and leaves that fell to the ground and carried them into the hollow tree. The nuts were her food in the winter and, when snow and ice came, she crawled into the leaves like a poor little animal so she would not freeze. Before long her clothes became tattered, and one piece after the other fell off her body. As soon as the sun began to shine again, she went out and sat in front of the tree. Her long hair covered her on all sides like a cloak. She spent year after year like this and felt the sorrow and misery of the world.

One day, when the trees were fresh and green again, the king of the country came to hunt in the forest and began chasing a deer. When it fled into the bushes that surrounded the maiden's dwelling spot in the forest, he got off his horse, pulled the bushes apart, and cut a path for himself with his sword. When he finally got through, he saw a wonderful-looking maiden sitting under a tree, and her golden hair covered her down to her toes. He stood still and gazed at her full of amazement. Then he addressed her and said, "Who are you? Why are you sitting in this desolate spot?"

However, she did not answer because she could not open her mouth.

So the king continued to speak. "Would you like to come to my castle with me?"

She nodded her head just a little. Then the king took her in his arms, carried her to his horse, and rode home with her. When he reached the royal castle, he had her dressed in beautiful garments and gave her plenty of everything. Even though she could not speak, she was so sweet and beautiful that he fell in love with her, and it was not long before he married her.

When about a year had passed, the queen gave birth to a son. Immediately following this, in the night as she lay alone in bed, the Virgin Mary appeared before her and said, "If you'll tell me the truth and confess that you unlocked the forbidden door, I'll open your mouth and give you back the power of speech. If you persist in your sin and stubbornly deny it, I shall take your newborn baby away with me."

The queen was given the power to answer, but she remained stubborn and said, "No, I didn't open the forbidden door."

So the Virgin Mary took the newborn baby out of her arms and disappeared with him. The next morning, when the child could not be found, a rumor began circulating among the people that the queen was an ogress and had killed her own child. She heard all this but could do nothing to deny it. However, the king refused to believe it because he loved her so much.

After a year had passed, the queen gave birth to another son. Once more the Virgin Mary came to her and said, "If you'll confess that you opened the forbidden door, I'll give you back your child and loosen your tongue. But if you persist in your sin and deny it, I'll take this newborn baby away with me too."

Once again the queen said, "No, I didn't open the forbidden door."

So the Virgin Mary took the child out of her arms and went away with him to heaven. The next morning, when this baby had also vanished, the people said quite openly that the queen had devoured it, and the king's councillors demanded that she be executed. However, the king loved her so much that he would not believe it and ordered his councillors to stop talking about it on pain of death.

The following year the queen gave birth to a beautiful little daughter, and at night the Virgin Mary appeared before her for the third time and said, "Follow me."

She took her by the hand and led her to heaven, where she showed her how her two oldest children were laughing and playing with a globe of the earth. When the queen expressed her delight, the Virgin Mary asked, "Hasn't your heart softened yet? If you'll confess that you opened the forbidden door, I'll give you back your two little sons."

But the queen answered for a third time, "No, I didn't open the forbidden door."

Then the Virgin Mary let her sink down to earth again and took away her third child too. The next morning, when it became known, everyone cried out openly, "The queen is an ogress! She must be sentenced to death!"

The king could no longer restrain his councillors, and the queen was brought to trial. Since she could not answer or defend herself, she was condemned to die at the stake. The wood was gathered, and when she was bound to the stake and the fire began to burn all around her, the hard ice of her pride melted, and her heart was moved by repentance. If only I could confess before I die that I opened the door! she thought. Suddenly her voice came back, and she cried aloud, "Yes, Mary, I did it!"

All at once rain poured from the sky and put out the flames. A light erupted above her, and the Virgin Mary descended with the two little sons at either side and the newborn daughter in her arms. She said to the queen kindly, "Those who repent their sins and confess will be forgiven."

Then she handed the queen her three children, loosened her tongue, and bestowed happiness on her for the rest of her life.

◈ 4 ◈

A Tale About the Boy Who Went
Forth to Learn What Fear Was

A FATHER had two sons. The older was smart and sensible and could cope in any situation, while the younger was stupid and could neither learn nor understand anything. Whenever people encountered him, they said, "He'll always be a burden to his father!"

If there were things to be done, the older son was always the one who had to take care of them. Yet, if the father asked the older son to fetch something toward evening or during the night, and if that meant he would have to pass through the churchyard or some other scary place, he would answer, "Oh, no, Father, I won't go there. It gives me the creeps!" Indeed, he was afraid.

Sometimes stories that would send shivers up your spine were told by their fireside at night, and the listeners would say: "Oh, it gives me the creeps!" Often the younger son would be sitting in the corner and listening, but he never understood what they meant. "They're always saying 'It gives me the creeps! It gives me the creeps!' But it doesn't give me the creeps. It's probably some kind of a trick that I don't understand."

One day his father happened to say to him, "Listen, you over there in the corner, you're getting too big and strong. It's time you learned how to earn your living. Look how hard your brother works, while you're just a hopeless case."

"Oh, no, Father," he responded. "I'd gladly learn something. If possible, I'd like to learn how to get the creeps. That's something I know nothing about."

When the older son heard that, he laughed and thought to himself, Dear Lord, my brother's really a dumbbell! He'll never amount to anything. You've got to start young to get anywhere.

The father sighed and answered, "You're sure to learn all about getting the creeps in due time, but it won't help you earn a living."

Shortly after this, the sexton came to the house for a visit, and the father complained about his younger son, that he was incapable of doing anything, much less learning and knowing anything. "Just think, when I asked him what he wanted to do to earn a living, he actually said he wanted to learn how to get the creeps."

"If that's all he wants," the sexton replied, "he can learn it at my place. Just hand him over to me, and I'll smooth over his rough edges."

The father was pleased to do this because he thought, The boy needs some shaping up.

So the sexton took him to his house, where the boy was assigned the task of ringing the church bell. After a few days had passed, the sexton woke him at midnight and told him to get up, climb the church steeple, and ring the bell.

Now you'll learn what the creeps are, the sexton thought, and secretly went up ahead of him. When the boy reached the top and turned around to grab hold of the bell rope, he saw a white figure standing on the stairs across from the sound hole.

"Who's there?" he cried out, but the figure did not answer, nor did it move an inch. "Answer me," the boy shouted, "or get out of here! You've no business being here at night."

However, the sexton did not move, for he wanted to make the boy think he was a ghost.

The boy shouted a second time, "What do you want? If you're an honest man, say something, or I'll throw you down the stairs!"

He really can't be as mean as that, the sexton thought, and he kept still, standing there as if he were made of stone.

The boy shouted at him a third time, and when that did not help, he lunged at the ghost and pushed him down the stairs. The ghost fell ten steps and lay in a corner. The boy then rang the bell, went home, got into bed without saying a word, and fell asleep. The sexton's wife waited for her husband for a long time, but he failed to return. Finally, she became anxious, woke the boy, and asked, "Do you know where my husband is? He climbed the steeple ahead of you."

"No," replied the boy. "But someone was standing across from the sound hole. When he refused to answer me or go away, I thought he was some sort of scoundrel and pushed him down the stairs. Why don't you go and see if it wasn't him? I'd feel sorry if it was."

The wife ran off and found her husband, who was lying in a corner and moaning because of a broken leg. She carried him down the stairs and then rushed off to the boy's father screaming as she went.

"Your boy has caused a terrible accident!" she cried out. "He threw my husband down the stairs and made him break a leg. Get that good-for-nothing out of our house!"

The father was mortified and ran straight to the sexton's house, where he began scolding the boy. "What kind of godless tricks have you been playing? The devil must have put you up to it!"

"Father," he replied, "just listen to me. I'm completely innocent.

He was standing there in the dark like someone who had evil designs. I didn't know who he was and warned him three times to say something or go away."

"Ah," said the father, "you'll never be anything but trouble for me! Get out of my sight. I don't want to see you anymore."

"All right, Father. Gladly. Just give me until daylight, and I'll go away and learn how to get the creeps. Then I'll know a trick or two and be able to earn a living."

"Learn what you want," the father said. "It's all the same to me. Here's fifty talers. Take them and go out into the wide world, but don't tell anyone where you come from or who your father is because I'm ashamed of you."

"Yes, Father, as you wish. If that's all you desire, I can easily bear that in mind."

At daybreak the boy put the fifty talers in his pocket, went out on the large highway, and kept saying to himself, "If I could only get the creeps! If I could only get the creeps!"

As the boy was talking to himself a man came along and overheard him. When they had gone some distance together, they caught sight of the gallows, and the man said to him, "You see the tree over there. That's where seven men were wedded to the ropemaker's daughter. Now they're learning how to fly. Sit down beneath the tree and wait till night comes. Then you'll certainly learn how to get the creeps."

"If that's all it takes," the boy responded, "I can do it with ease. And, if I learn how to get the creeps as quickly as that, you shall have my fifty talers. Just come back here tomorrow morning."

The boy went to the gallows, sat down beneath it, and waited until evening came. Since he was cold, he made a fire. Nevertheless, at midnight the wind became colder, and he could not get warm in spite of the fire. When the wind knocked the hanged men against each other and they swung back and forth, he thought, If you're freezing down here by the fire, they must really be cold and shivering up there. Since he felt sorry for them, he took a ladder, climbed up, untied one hanged man after the other, and hauled all seven down to the ground. Then he stirred the fire, blew on it, and set them all around it so they might warm themselves. However, they sat there without moving, and their clothes caught on fire.

"Be careful," he said, "otherwise I'll hang you all back up there."

The dead men did not hear. Indeed, they just remained silent and let their rags continue to burn. Then the boy became angry and said, "If you won't take care, I can't help you, and I surely won't let you burn me."

So he hung them up again, all in a row, sat down by his fire, and fell asleep. Next morning the man came and wanted his fifty talers.

"Well," he said, "now you know what the creeps are?"

"No," answered the boy. "How should I know? Those men up there didn't open their mouths. They're so stupid they let the few old rags they're wearing get burned."

The man realized he would never get the fifty talers that day. So he went off saying, "Never in my life have I met anyone like that!"

The boy also went his way, and once again he began talking to himself. "Oh, if I could only get the creeps! If I could only get the creeps!"

A carter, who was walking behind him, overheard him and asked, "Who are you?"

"I don't know," answered the boy.

"Where do you come from?" the carter continued questioning him.

"I don't know."

"Who's your father?"

"I'm not allowed to tell."

"What's that you're always mumbling to yourself?"

"Oh," the boy responded, "I want to get the creeps, but nobody can teach me how."

"Stop your foolish talk," said the carter. "Come along with me, and I'll see if I can find a place for you to stay."

The boy went with the carter, and in the evening they reached an inn, where they intended to spend the night. As they entered the main room the boy spoke loudly once more. "If I could only get the creeps! If I could only get the creeps!"

The innkeeper heard this and laughed. "If that's what you desire," he remarked, "there'll be ample opportunity for you to get it here."

"Oh, be quiet!" the innkeeper's wife said. "There have already been enough foolish fellows who've lost their lives. It would be a mighty shame if that boy with such pretty eyes never saw the light of day again."

But the boy said, "It doesn't matter how hard it may be. I want to get the creeps. That's why I left home."

He kept bothering the innkeeper until the man told him about the haunted castle nearby, where one could really learn how to get the creeps. All he had to do was to spend three nights in it. The king had promised his daughter to anyone who would undertake the venture, and she was the most beautiful maiden under the sun. There were also great treasures in the castle guarded by evil spirits. Once the treasures were set free, they would be enough to make a poor man rich. Many men had already gone into the castle, but none had ever come out again.

The next morning the boy appeared before the king and said, "If I may have your permission, I'd like to spend three nights in the haunted castle."

The king looked at him and found the boy to his liking, so he said, "You may request three things to take with you into the castle, but they must be lifeless objects."

"Well then," he answered, "I'd like to have a fire, a lathe, and a carpenter's bench with a knife."

The king had these things carried into the castle for him during the day. Just before nightfall the boy himself went up to the castle, made a bright fire in one of the rooms, set up the carpenter's bench with the knife next to it, and sat down on the lathe.

"Oh, if I could only get the creeps!" he said. "But I don't think I'll learn it here either."

Toward midnight he wanted to stir the fire again, but just as he was blowing it, he suddenly heard a scream coming from a corner. "*Meow! Meow!* We're freezing!"

"You fools!" he cried out. "What are you screaming for? If you're freezing, come sit down by the fire and warm yourselves."

No sooner had he said that than two big black cats came over with a tremendous leap, sat down beside him, and glared ferociously at him with their fiery eyes. After a while, when they had warmed themselves, they said, "Comrade, let's play a round of cards."

"Why not?" he responded. "But first show me your paws."

They stretched out their claws.

"My goodness!" he said. "What long nails you have! Wait, I've got to give them a good clipping."

Upon saying that, he grabbed them by the scruffs of their necks, lifted them onto the carpenter's bench, and fastened their paws in a vise.

"I was keeping a sharp eye on you two," he said, "and now I've lost my desire to play cards."

Then he beat them to death and threw them into the water. But, after he had put an end to those two and was about to sit down at his fire again, black cats and black dogs on glowing chains came out of all the nooks and crannies, and they kept coming and coming so it was impossible for him to flee. They made a gruesome noise, stamped on his fire, tore it apart, and tried to put it out. He watched them calmly for a while, but when it became so awful that he could no longer stand it, he grabbed his knife and yelled, "Get out of here, you lousy creatures!" And he started swinging the knife. Some of them ran away while he killed the rest and threw them into the pond. When he returned to his place, he built up his fire again by blowing on the sparks and proceeded to warm himself. As he was sitting there, his eyelids grew heavy, and he felt a strong desire to sleep. Then he looked around and saw a large bed in the corner.

"That's just what I was looking for," he said and lay down on it.

But just as he was about to shut his eyes, the bed began to move by itself and raced all around the castle.

"Keep it up," he said. "But go a little faster."

The bed sped on as though it were being drawn by six horses. It rolled through doorways and up and down stairs. Then all of a sudden, *bing-bang!* it turned upside down and lay on top of him like a mountain. But he flung the blankets and pillows in the air, climbed out, and said, "Now, anyone else who wants a ride can have one." He lay down by the fire and slept until it was day.

In the morning the king came, and when he saw the boy lying on the ground, he thought that he was dead and that the ghosts had killed him.

"What a pity! He was such a handsome fellow," the king said.

Upon hearing this, the boy sat up and said, "It's not over yet!"

The king was astonished but also glad and asked him how things had gone.

"Very well," he answered. "One night's over and done with. The other two will pass also."

Then he went to the innkeeper, who gaped at him in amazement.

"I never expected to see you alive again," he said. "Have you learned now what the creeps are?"

"No," he said. "It's no use. If only someone could tell me!"

The second night he went up to the old castle, sat down at the fire, and repeated his old refrain. "If I could only get the creeps!"

Toward midnight he heard a lot of noise and rumbling, first softly, then louder and louder. Soon it became quiet for a while until suddenly, with a loud cry, half a man came tumbling down the chimney and fell right at his feet.

"Hey there!" cried the boy. "There's a half missing. This isn't enough."

Once again the noise began. There was a roaring and howling, and the other half came tumbling down.

"Wait," the boy said. "I'll just give the fire a little stir for you."

After he had done that, he looked around and saw that the two pieces had joined together to form a gruesome-looking man who was now sitting in his place.

"That wasn't part of the bargain," said the boy. "The bench is mine."

The man tried to push him away, but the boy did not let him. Instead, he gave the man a mighty shove and sat back down in his place.

Suddenly more men came tumbling down the chimney, one after the other, and they brought nine dead men's bones and two dead men's skulls, set them up, and began to play a game of ninepins.

The boy felt a desire to play as well and asked, "Hey, can I play too?"

"Yes, if you have money."

"Money enough," he answered, "but your balls aren't round."

He took the skulls, put them in the lathe, and turned them until they were round.

"Now they'll roll much better," he said. "Hurray! Let's have some fun!"

He joined their game and lost some of his money, but when the clock struck twelve, everything disappeared before his eyes, and he lay down and fell asleep in peace.

The next morning the king came to inquire about him, and he asked, "How did things go for you this time?"

"I played a game of ninepins," he said, "and I lost a few hellers."

"Didn't you get the creeps?"

"Not at all!" he responded. "I had a lot of fun. If I only knew what the creeps were!"

The third night he sat down on his bench again and said quite sadly, "If I could only get the creeps!"

When it grew late, six huge men came in carrying a coffin. Then he said, "Aha, that must be my cousin who died just a few days ago." He signaled to them with his finger and cried out, "Come here, little cousin, come here!"

They set the coffin on the ground, and he went over and lifted the lid. There was a dead man lying inside, and the boy felt his face, which was as cold as ice.

"Wait," he said. "I'll warm you up a bit."

He went to the fire, warmed his hand, and placed it on the dead man's face, but it remained cold. So he took the dead man out and set him near the fire, then put him on his lap and rubbed his arms until his blood began circulating again. When that did not work either, the boy recalled that two people can warm each other up when they lie in bed together. So he brought the man to the bed, covered him, and lay down beside him. After a while the dead man got warm and began to move.

"You see, cousin," said the boy. "What if I hadn't warmed you?"

But the dead man shouted, "Now I'm going to strangle you!"

"What?" the boy responded. "Is that my thanks? I'm going to put you right back into your coffin."

He lifted him up, tossed him inside, and shut the lid. Then the six men returned and carried the coffin away.

"I can't get the creeps," the boy said. "I'll never learn it here no matter how long I live."

Just then a ghastly-looking man entered. He was old and larger than the others and had a long white beard.

"Oh, you scoundrel!" the man cried out. "Now you'll learn what the creeps are, for you're about to die."

"Not so fast!" said the boy. "If I'm about to die, you'll have to get me first."

"Don't worry, I'll get you," said the monster.

"Easy does it. Don't talk so big! I'm just as strong as you are if not stronger."

"We'll see about that," said the old man. "If you're stronger than I am, I'll let you go. Come, let's give it a try."

He led the boy through dark passages to a smithy, picked up an ax, and drove an anvil right into the ground with one blow.

"I can do better than that," the boy said, and he went to the other anvil. The old man, with his white beard hanging down, drew near him to watch. The boy grabbed the ax, split the anvil in two with one blow, and wedged the old man's beard in the middle.

"Now I've got you!" the boy said. "It's your turn to die!"

He seized an iron and beat the old man until he whimpered and begged the boy to stop and promised to give him great treasures. The boy pulled out the ax and let him go. The old man led him back into the castle and showed him three chests full of gold in a cellar.

"One of them," he said, "belongs to the poor, the second to the king, and the third is yours."

Just then the clock struck twelve, and the ghost vanished, leaving the boy standing in the dark.

"I'll find my way out of here all the same," he said, and groped about until he found the way back to his room, where he fell asleep by the fire.

In the morning the king came and said, "Now you must have learned what the creeps are."

"No," he answered. "What are they? My dead cousin was here, and a bearded man came. He showed me a great deal of money down in the cellar, but nobody told me what the creeps are."

Then the king said, "You've saved the castle and shall marry my daughter."

"That's all fine and good," he answered, "but I still don't know what the creeps are."

Now the gold was brought up from the cellar, and the wedding was celebrated. The boy loved his wife dearly and was very happy, but he still kept saying, "If I could only get the creeps! If I could only get the creeps!"

After a while his wife became annoyed by that, but her chambermaid said, "Don't worry. I'll make sure he gets to know what the creeps are."

She went out to a brook that ran through the garden and fetched a bucket full of minnows. That night, when the young king was sleeping, his wife pulled the covers off him and poured the bucket full of cold water and minnows on him. Then the little fish began flapping all over him, causing him to wake up and exclaim, "Oh, I've got the creeps! I've got the creeps! Now I know, dear wife, just what the creeps are."

◈ 5 ◈

The Wolf and the Seven Young Kids

ONCE UPON A TIME there was an old goat who had seven young kids, and she loved them as any mother loves her children. One day she decided to go into the forest to fetch some food. So she called all seven of them to her and said, "Dear children, I'm going into the forest, and I want you to be on your guard against the wolf. If he gets in here, he'll eat you all up, skin and bones. That villain often disguises himself, but you can recognize him right away by his gruff voice and black feet."

"Dear Mother," the kids said, "we'll take good care of ourselves. Just go and don't worry about leaving us here."

The old goat bleated and went on her way with an easy mind, but it was not long before someone knocked at the door and called out, "Open up, dear children, your mother's back and has brought something for each one of you."

But the kids knew it was the wolf by his gruff voice.

"We're not opening up," they cried out. "You're not our mother. She has a lovely, soft voice, and yours is gruff. You're the wolf!"

The wolf went away to a shopkeeper and bought a big piece of chalk, which he ate, and it made his voice soft. Then he returned, knocked at the door, and called out, "Open up, dear children. Your mother's back and has brought something for each one of you."

But the wolf had put his black paw on the windowsill, and when the children saw it, they cried out, "We're not opening up. Our mother doesn't have a black paw like yours. You're the wolf!"

The wolf ran to a baker and said, "I've stubbed my toe. Put some dough on it for me." After the baker covered his paw, he ran to the miller and said, "Sprinkle some white flour on my paw."

The miller thought, The wolf wants to trick someone. So he refused. But the wolf said, "If you don't do it, I'll eat you up!"

This frightened the miller, so he made the wolf's paw white. Yes, indeed, that's the way people are.

Now the villain went to the house for a third time, knocked, and said, "Open up, children, your dear mother's back and has brought something from the forest for each one of you."

The kids called out, "First show us your paw so we know that you're really our dear mother."

He put his paw on the windowsill, and when they saw that it was white, they believed him and opened the door. Yet, who else but the wolf stepped inside! The kids were terrified and tried to hide themselves. The first kid ran and jumped under the table, the second into the bed, the third into the oven, the fourth into the kitchen, the fifth into the cupboard, the sixth under the washbasin, and the seventh into the clock case. However, the wolf began to find them and make short shrift of them. He swallowed one after the other down his throat, but he was unable to find the youngest in the clock case. When the wolf had satisfied his desire, he tottered off, lay down beneath a tree on a green meadow, and fell asleep.

Shortly after, the old goat came home from the forest, and oh, what a sight met her eyes! The door to her house was wide open. The table, chairs, and benches were turned over. The washbasin lay on the ground in pieces. The cover and pillows were stripped off the bed. She looked for her children, but they were nowhere to be found. Finally, when she got near the youngest, she heard a soft voice calling, "Dear Mother, I'm in the clock case!"

She drew him out, and he told her that the wolf had come and had eaten up all the others. Well, you can imagine how she wept over her poor children.

At length she went outside, still grieving, while the youngest kid ran beside her. When they reached the meadow, she found the wolf snoring so loudly that the tree branches above him were trembling. She examined him from all sides and saw that something was moving and wriggling in his stuffed stomach. Oh, God! she thought. Could it be that my poor children that he gobbled up for his supper are still alive?

She sent the little kid home to fetch scissors, needle, and thread. Then she cut the monster's belly open, and no sooner did she make the first cut than a kid stuck out his head. As she cut some more all six of them jumped out, one after the other. They were all still alive and had not suffered the least bit of harm, for the monster's gluttony had been so great that he had swallowed them whole. What joy there was! They hugged their dear mother and hopped about like a tailor at his own wedding. But the old goat said, "Now go and look for some stones in the field. We'll fill the godless beast's belly with them while he's still asleep."

The seven kids quickly fetched some stones and put as many as they could into his stomach. Then the old goat sewed him up again with such speed that he did not notice a thing, nor did he even stir. When the wolf had slept to his content, he stood up, and since the stones in his stomach had made him very thirsty, he wanted to go to a well and have a drink. However, as he began to walk, he swayed back and forth, and the stones in his body knocked against each other and rattled. Then he cried out:

"What's that in my belly rumbling?
Could it be my bones are crumbling?
Six little kids I thought I ate;
they're more like stones with all their weight."

When he reached the well and leaned over to drink the water, the heavy stones pulled him in, and he was drowned in a miserable way. Upon seeing this, the seven kids ran up to the well and cried aloud, "The wolf is dead! The wolf is dead!"

Then they took their mother and danced for joy around the well.

◆ 6 ◆

Faithful Johannes

ONCE UPON A TIME there was an old king who was sick, and he thought, This will surely be my deathbed. Then he said aloud, "Tell Faithful Johannes to come to me."

Faithful Johannes, his most cherished servant, had been given this name because of his lifelong loyalty to the king. When he reached the old man's bedside, the king said to him, "Most Faithful Johannes, I feel that my end is drawing near, but I am not worried about anything except my son. He is still young in years and doesn't always know what's best for him. You must promise to teach him everything he should know and be his foster father, or I shall not be able to close my eyes in peace."

"I will not forsake him," Faithful Johannes reassured him, "and I will serve him faithfully even if it costs me my life."

"Now I can die in comfort and in peace," the old king said, and then added, "After my death you're to show him the entire castle—all the rooms, halls, and vaults, along with the treasures that are in them. But I do not want you to show him the room at the end of the long hallway, where the portrait of the Princess of the Golden Roof is hidden. If he sees that portrait, he'll fall passionately in love with her and lose consciousness for a while, and then he'll be obliged to undertake great risks because of her. You must protect him against this."

Once again Faithful Johannes assured the old king he would keep his promise. The king then became silent, laid his head on his pillow, and died. After the old king was buried, Faithful Johannes told the young king what he had promised the old king on his deathbed and said, "I intend to keep my promise and remain just as faithful to you as I was to your father, even if it costs me my life."

When the mourning period ended, Faithful Johannes said to him, "It's now time for you to see what you've inherited. So I shall show you the castle of your forefathers."

He led the young king all around the castle, upstairs and down, and let him see all the treasures and splendid rooms. But there was one room he did not open, for it contained the dangerous portrait, which was placed in such a way that one would see it the moment the door was opened. Furthermore, it was such a wonderful painting that it appeared to be real and alive, and there was nothing more beautiful or more lovely in the whole world. Now, the young king quickly noticed that Faithful Johannes kept passing by one door, and therefore he said, "Why don't you ever open this door for me?"

"There's something in there that would horrify you," Faithful Johannes replied.

"I've seen the entire castle," the king said, "and I also want to know what's in there."

He went and tried to open the door by force, but Faithful Johannes restrained him and said, "I promised your father before his death that you would not see what is inside this room. It could cause great misfortune for you and me."

"No, that can't be!" the young king responded. "If I *don't* get in, it will certainly be the end of me, because I won't be able to rest day or night until I've seen the room with my own eyes. You won't get me to move from this spot unless you unlock the door."

When Faithful Johannes saw there was nothing he could do, he picked out the key from the large bunch he was carrying. His heart was heavy, and he heaved many sighs as he opened the door. He made sure that he entered first, because he intended to cover the portrait with his body so the king would not see it. But what good did that do? The king stood on his tiptoes and looked over his shoulder. When he glimpsed the maiden's magnificent portrait, which glistened with gold and jewels, he fell to the ground unconscious. Faithful Johannes lifted him up, carried him to his bed, and was very concerned.

Disaster has struck, he thought. Good Lord, what will come of it all? Then he gave the king some wine to refreshen him, whereupon he regained consciousness. The first words he spoke were, "Oh, who is that beautiful maiden in the picture?"

"That's the Princess of the Golden Roof," answered Faithful Johannes.

"My love for her is so great," continued the king, "that even if all the leaves on all the trees were tongues, they wouldn't be able to express how I feel. I intend to risk my life to win her, and since you're my most Faithful Johannes, you must help me."

It took the faithful servant a long time to determine how they might proceed, for it was difficult to gain access to the princess. Finally, he thought of a way and said to the king, "Everything she has around her is made of gold—the tables, chairs, dishes, cups, bowls, and all the household utensils. There are five tons of gold in your treasury. Have the goldsmiths of your kingdom make one ton of it into different kinds of vessels and utensils and into all sorts of birds, wild game, and marvelous animals that will please her. Then we'll take all this and travel there to try our luck."

The king had all the goldsmiths summoned to him, and they had to work day and night until the most magnificent things were ready. When the golden objects were all loaded on board a ship, Faithful Johannes put on the clothes of a merchant, as did the king so that he would not be recognized. Then they sailed across the sea, and they kept sailing until they came to the city where the Princess of the Golden Roof made her home.

Faithful Johannes told the king to stay on board the ship and to wait for him. "I may come back with the princess," he said. "So make sure that everything's in order. Have the golden vessels set out on display and have your men decorate the entire ship."

He then gathered together all kinds of golden trinkets in his apron, went ashore, and began walking toward the royal castle. When he reached the courtyard, a beautiful maiden was standing at the well. She had two golden buckets in her hands and was drawing water. Just as she turned around and got ready to carry the sparkling water away, she noticed the stranger and asked him who he was.

"I'm a merchant," he answered, while opening his apron so she could see what was in it.

"Goodness, what beautiful golden trinkets!" she exclaimed. Then she put the buckets down and examined the treasures, one after the other. "The princess must see these things," she remarked. "She takes so much pleasure in golden objects that I'm certain she'll buy all you have."

She took him by the hand and led him up to the palace, for she was the chambermaid. When the princess saw the wares, she was delighted and said, "They're so beautifully wrought that I'll buy everything you have."

But Faithful Johannes said, "I'm only a rich merchant's servant.

What I have here is nothing compared to what my master has on his ship. Indeed, he has the most artful and precious things that have ever been made in gold."

The princess wanted everything brought up to the castle, but he said, "There is such a huge number of objects that it would take many days to do this. Besides, your palace is not large enough, for you would need many more rooms to display all the articles."

Now her curiosity and desire were roused even more, so that she finally said, "Take me to the ship. I'll go there myself to look over your master's treasures."

So, feeling very happy, Faithful Johannes conducted her to the ship. When the king caught sight of the princess and saw that she was even more beautiful than her portrait, he felt as though his heart would burst. After she climbed aboard the ship and the king led her inside the cabin, Faithful Johannes remained behind with the helmsman and ordered the ship to cast off. "Set all sails so that our ship will fly like a bird!"

Inside the cabin the king showed the princess the golden vessels, each and every piece: the dishes, the cups, the bowls, the birds, the wild game, and the marvelous animals. She looked at everything for many hours, and in her joy she did not notice that the ship had sailed. After she had examined the last piece, she thanked the merchant and wanted to go home. But, when she stepped out on deck, she saw that the ship was on the high seas, far from land, and racing forward at full sail.

"Oh!" she cried out in horror. "You've deceived me! I'm being kidnapped, and I'm in the hands of a merchant no less! I'd rather die!"

But the king seized her hand and said, "I'm not a merchant. I'm a king, and I'm not inferior to you in birth. I tricked you and carried you off by stealth because I was overwhelmed by my love for you. The first time I saw your portrait, I fainted and fell to the ground."

When the Princess of the Golden Roof heard this, she felt more at ease, and her heart went out to him in such a way that she consented to be his wife.

While they were sailing on the high seas, however, Faithful Johannes saw three ravens flying through the air as he was sitting and playing music in the bow of the ship. When they approached, he stopped playing and listened, for he understood their language quite well. One of them cried out, "My, he's bringing the Princess of the Golden Roof home with him!"

"Yes," responded the second, "but he doesn't have her yet."

"You're wrong, he does," the third said. "She's sitting right beside him in the ship."

Then the first raven began to speak again. "What good will that do him? When they reach land, a horse as red as a fox will come trotting up to him, and the king will want to mount it. But, if he does, the horse will ride off with him and soar into the air, so he'll never be able to see his maiden again."

"Is there no way he can be saved?" asked the second.

"Oh, yes, if someone else jumps on the horse quickly, takes out the gun that's bound to be in the saddle holster, and shoots the horse dead. This way the young king will be saved. But who knows that? And, even if someone knows it and tells it to the king, that person will be turned into stone from the tips of his toes to his knees."

"I know still more," the second raven said. "Even if the horse is killed, the young king will not keep his bride. When they go to the castle together, he will find a ready-made bridal outfit in a basin. It will look as if it were woven out of gold and silver, yet it's nothing but sulfur and pitch. If he puts it on, it will burn him down to the very bone and marrow."

"Is there no way he can be saved?" asked the third raven.

"Oh, yes," said the second. "Someone must grab the shirt with gloves, throw it into the fire, and let it burn. Then the young king will be saved. But what good will that do? Whoever knows this and tells the king will be turned to stone from his knees to his heart."

"I know still more," said the third raven. "Even if the bridal outfit is burned, the king will still not be able to keep his bride. After the wedding, there will be a ball, and when the young queen begins to dance, she will suddenly turn pale and fall down as if she were dead. If no one lifts her up, draws three drops of blood from her right breast, and spits them out, she will die. But whoever reveals what he knows will have his entire body turned to stone from top to bottom."

After having talked about all this, the ravens flew away. Faithful Johannes had understood everything they had said, and from then on he became silent and sad. For if he did not tell his master what he had heard, the young king would be doomed; but, if he did reveal everything to his master, he himself would have to pay with his life. At length he said to himself, "I must and shall save my master even if it means my own destruction."

When they went ashore, everything started to happen the way the ravens had predicted. A splendid horse, red as a fox, came galloping toward them.

"Well now, what's this?" said the king. "This horse will carry me to my castle."

As the king was about to mount it Faithful Johannes jumped in front of him and swung himself quickly into the saddle. Then he pulled the gun out of the saddle holster and shot the horse dead. The king's other servants disliked Faithful Johannes and cried out, "What a crime! Why did he have to kill that beautiful creature that was to carry the king to his castle?"

But the king declared, "Be quiet and let him go! He's Johannes, my most faithful servant, and who knows what good may come of this?"

Now they went into the castle, and there was a basin in the hall. The ready-made bridal outfit was lying in it and looked as though it were made of gold and silver. The young king went over and was about to pick it up when Faithful Johannes shoved him aside, grabbed it with gloves, tossed it into the fire, and let it burn. Once again the other servants began to murmur and say, "Just look! Now he's even burned the king's bridal outfit."

But the young king declared, "Who knows what good may come of this? Let him go. He's Johannes, my most faithful servant."

After the wedding was celebrated, the dance began, and the bride took part in it. Faithful Johannes paid close attention and kept looking at her face. All of a sudden she turned pale and fell to the ground as if she were dead. Then he rushed over to her, lifted her up, and carried her into a room, where he laid her on a bed, then knelt down and sucked three drops of blood from her right breast and spat them out. No sooner had he done this than she began breathing again and regained consciousness. The young king had seen all this, but he was puzzled by Faithful Johannes's actions and became angry.

"Throw him into prison!" he declared.

The next morning Faithful Johannes was condemned to death and led to the gallows. As he stood there and was about to be executed, he said, "Every condemned man is usually allowed to say one last word before he dies. May I also have this right?"

"Yes," answered the king. "I shall grant you this right."

Then Faithful Johannes said, "I've been unjustly sentenced to death, for I've always served you faithfully," and he told him how he had heard the ravens' conversation on the sea and how he had been compelled to do all those things to save his master.

The king then cried out, "Oh, my most Faithful Johannes, pardon! Pardon! Bring him down!"

But the moment after Faithful Johannes had uttered his last words, he had fallen down and then turned into stone. The king and queen were greatly grieved by this, and the king said, "Oh, how poorly I've rewarded such great fidelity!"

He ordered the stone figure to be carried up to his bedroom and placed beside his bed. Whenever he looked at it, he would weep and say, "Oh, if only I could bring you back to life, my most Faithful Johannes!"

After some time had passed, the queen gave birth to twins, two little boys, who grew up and became the queen's delight. One day, when the queen was at church and the two children were sitting and playing near their father, the king looked at the stone figure and sighed.

"Oh, if only I could bring you back to life, my most faithful Johannes!" he exclaimed.

Then the stone began to speak and said, "Yes, you can bring me back to life if you're willing to sacrifice what you love most."

"I'd give everything I have in this world for you!" the king responded.

The stone continued, "If you cut off the heads of your two children with your own two hands and rub their blood on me, I shall be brought back to life."

The king was horrified when he heard that he himself would have to kill his precious children. He recalled, nevertheless, the great fidelity of Faithful Johannes and how he had died for him. So the king drew his sword and cut off his children's heads with his own hand. And, after he had rubbed the stone with their blood, it came to life, and Faithful Johannes stood before him once again, alive and well.

"Your loyalty shall not go unrewarded," he said to the king, and he took the children's heads, put them back in place, and rubbed the wounds with their blood. Within seconds they were whole again and were running around and playing as if nothing had happened to them. The king was overjoyed, and when he saw the queen coming, he hid Faithful Johannes and the two children in a large closet. After she entered, he said to her, "Did you pray while you were in church?"

"Yes," she answered, "but I could only think of Faithful Johannes and how unfortunate he was because of us."

"Dear wife," he said. "We can bring him back to life, but it will cost our two little sons, whom we shall have to sacrifice."

The queen became pale, and her heart trembled greatly. However, she said, "We owe this to him because of his great fidelity."

The king rejoiced when he saw that she felt as he did. He went over to the closet, opened it, and brought out the children and Faithful Johannes.

"God be praised!" he said. "He's been saved, and our sons have been restored to us as well."

Then he told her what had happened, and they all lived happily together until the end of their days.

◆ 7 ◆

The Good Bargain

A FARMER DROVE his cow to the market and sold it for seven talers. On his way home he had to pass a pond, and even though he was a good distance from the pond, he was able to hear the frogs croaking *"Aat, aat, aat, aat."*

"What nonsense!" he said to himself. "I got seven talers in the bargain, not *eight*." When he reached the water, he called out to the frogs, "You're nothing but stupid creatures, that's what you are! Don't you know any better than that? It was seven talers not eight."

But the frogs held to their *"aat, aat, aat, aat."*

"Well, if you won't believe me, I can count them out in front of you," and he took the money out of his pocket and counted the seven talers, twenty-four groschen to the taler. But the frogs paid no attention to his calculations and kept croaking *"Aat, aat, aat, aat."*

"That does it!" the farmer exclaimed quite angrily. "If you think you know everything, count it yourselves!"

He tossed the money right at them, and it landed in the water. He remained standing there and intended to wait until they were finished counting and had returned his money to him. Yet the frogs continued to be stubborn and kept on croaking *"aat, aat, aat, aat."* Nor did they return the money to him. He waited for quite some time, until finally it became dark and he had to go home. Now he cursed the frogs and called out to them, "Water-splashers! Thickheads! Goggle-eyes! The only thing you can do with your big mouths is to make loud sounds and hurt people's ears. But you can't count seven talers. Do you think you can keep me waiting here forever?"

Upon saying this he went away, but the frogs kept croaking *"aat, aat, aat, aat"* after him, and he was in a very bad mood when he got home.

After some time he bought another cow, and when he had slaughtered it, he calculated that, if he could get a good price for the meat, he could earn as much as the two cows were worth together and still have the hide left in the bargain. When he got to the city with the meat, he encountered a whole pack of dogs outside the city gate. At the head of the pack was a big greyhound who jumped around the meat and kept sniffing and barking *"Wuff, wuff, wuff, wuff!"* Since the dog would not stop barking, the farmer said to him, "All right, I understand. You're saying '*wuff, wuff, wuff, wuff*' because you want a whiff of the meat. But I'd be in a fine pickle if I gave it to you."

The dog's only response was *"Wuff, wuff!"*

"Will you promise not to eat it and to vouch for your companions over there?"

"Wuff, wuff," said the dog.

"Well, if you insist, you can have it. After all, I know you and I know your masters. But let me tell you one thing: I want my money in three days, or else you'll be in for trouble! You can just bring it out to my place."

Thereupon he set the meat on the ground and turned back home.

The dogs scrambled for the meat and barked loudly, *"Wuff, wuff!"* When the farmer heard this from afar, he said to himself, "Just listen! Now they all want some of the meat. But I'll hold that big dog responsible for whatever happens."

After three days had passed, the farmer thought, Tonight you'll have the money in your pocket. And he was quite delighted. However, nobody came, and nobody paid him. "You just can't depend on anyone anymore," he said. Finally his patience gave out, and he went to the butcher in the city and demanded his money. The butcher thought he was joking, but the farmer said, "It's no joke. I want my money. Didn't that big dog bring you all the meat from the cow I slaughtered three days ago?"

This remark made the butcher angry, and he grabbed a broomstick and drove the farmer out of his shop.

"Just wait!" the farmer yelled. "There's still some justice in the world!"

Now he went to the royal castle and requested an audience. So he was led before the king, who was sitting there with his daughter, and the king asked the farmer what wrong had been committed against him.

"Ah," he said, "the frogs and dogs have taken things that rightfully belong to me, and the butcher paid me for some of it with a broomstick."

Then he proceeded to tell them in great detail everything that had happened. The king's daughter burst out laughing, and the king said to him, "I can't provide you with justice in this case, but you shall have my daughter for your wife. This is the first time in her life that she has laughed like this, and you're the cause. You can thank God for your good fortune because I promised to give her to whoever might make her laugh."

"Oh, no," responded the farmer. "I definitely don't want her. I've already got one wife at home, and she's much too much for me. Whenever I come home, it seems as if I have a wife standing in every corner."

Then the king got angry and said, "What a stupid boor!"

"Ah, Your Majesty, what else can you expect from an ox but beef?" the farmer replied.

"Wait," the king declared. "I shall give you another reward, but for the time being, I want you out of here. Come back in three days, and I'll pay you five hundred in full measure."

As the farmer was going through the gate, the sentry said, "The king must have given you a really fine reward, since you made his daughter laugh."

"Well, I should think so," answered the farmer. "I'm going to get five hundred."

"Listen," the soldier said, "give me some of it. What can you do with all that money?"

"Since it's you," the farmer said, "I'll give you two hundred. Report to the king in three days and let them pay it out to you."

A Jew had been standing nearby and had overheard the conversation. He ran after the farmer, seized him by the coattails, and said, "Wonder of God! What a lucky fellow you are! Let me change the money for you. I'll give you small coins for it. What do you want with those hard talers?"

"Yid," the farmer said, "I'll give you three hundred, but I want the coins right now. In three days you can go to the king, and he will give you my payment."

The Jew was happy about the little profit he was making and gave him the sum in bad groschen, three of which were worth two good ones. After the three days had passed, the farmer followed the king's orders and appeared before the king, who said, "Take off his coat. He shall receive his five hundred!"

"Oh," the farmer said. "They don't belong to me anymore. I've given away two hundred to the sentry, and the Jew changed three hundred for me. According to the law, there's nothing due me anymore."

Meanwhile, the soldier and the Jew had entered and demanded what they had won from the farmer. Indeed, they were soon dealt their just measure of blows. The soldier bore the lashing patiently, for he already knew how the whip tasted. But the Jew reacted terribly. "*Ow, ow,* it hurts! Are these the hard talers?"

The king could not help laughing at what the farmer had done, and when all his anger had vanished, he said, "Since you lost your reward before you even received it, I'm going to make it up to you. Go into my treasure chamber and take as much money as you want."

The farmer did not have to be asked twice, and he filled his large pockets with whatever he could fit inside. Afterward he went to the tavern and began counting his money. The Jew had sneaked after him and heard him muttering to himself, "Well, that scoundrel of a king really cheated me! If he'd have doled out the money himself, I'd know exactly what I have. Now, since I had to stuff my pocket any way I could, I don't know whether I've got the right amount."

"God help us!" the Jew said to himself. "He's speaking disrespectfully about our king. I'm going to run and report him. Then I'll get a reward, and he'll be punished in the bargain."

When the king heard about the farmer's remarks, he was infuriated and ordered the Jew to go and fetch the slanderer. The Jew ran to the farmer and said, "Our Majesty, the king, wants you to report to him at once, just as you are."

"That's not proper, and I know better," said the farmer. "First I'll have a new coat made for me. Do you think that a man who has so much money like me should appear before the king in an old tattered coat?"

When the Jew realized that the farmer would not budge without another coat, he feared the king's anger would subside, and this would prevent him from getting his reward, and the farmer would also go unpunished.

"I'll lend you my beautiful coat," he said. "It's just for a short time and out of friendship. Just think of how much one will do out of kindness!"

The farmer was pleased by the offer, so he put on the Jew's coat and departed with him. Now the king reprimanded the farmer for his bad remarks, which the Jew had conveyed to him behind the farmer's back.

"Come now!" said the farmer. "Jews always tell lies. There's not a word of truth that comes out of his mouth. Why, that fellow's even capable of claiming that I'm wearing his coat."

"What's this?" the Jew screamed. "That's my coat! I lent it to you out of sheer friendship so you could appear before the king!"

When the king heard that, he said, "The Jew has certainly deceived someone, either me or the farmer."

So he had the Jew given his due again in *hard* talers. Meanwhile, the farmer went home in the good coat with good money in his pocket, and he said, "This time I made a good bargain!"

◈ 8 ◈

The Marvelous Minstrel

ONCE UPON A TIME there was a marvelous minstrel who walked through a forest all alone and thought about all kinds of things. When there was nothing more to think about, he said to himself, "I'm getting bored here in the forest, and I need to get myself a good companion."

He took his fiddle from his back and began playing a tune that resounded through the trees. It was not long before a wolf came trotting through the thicket.

"Ah, here comes a wolf! I don't have any desire to see a wolf," said the musician.

But the wolf came closer and said to him, "Oho, dear musician, what's that lovely tune you're playing? I'd like to learn to play that way too."

"You can easily do it," responded the minstrel. "You only have to do as I say."

"Oh, minstrel," the wolf said, "I'll obey you just as a pupil obeys his teacher."

The minstrel told him to come along, and after they had walked some distance together, they came to an old oak tree that was hollow inside and split down the middle.

"Look here," said the minstrel, "if you want to learn how to fiddle, you must put your front paws into this crack."

The wolf obeyed, but the minstrel quickly picked up a stone, and with one blow he wedged the wolf's front paws in so tightly that the beast was forced to stay there like a prisoner.

"Wait here until I get back," the minstrel said, and he went his way.

After a while he said to himself once more, "I'm getting bored here in the forest, and I need to get myself another companion."

He took his fiddle and played another tune that was heard throughout the forest. It was not long before a fox came slinking through the trees.

"Ah, here comes a fox!" said the minstrel. "I don't have any desire to see a fox."

The fox came up to him and said, "Oho, dear minstrel, what's that lovely tune you're playing? I'd like to learn to play that way too."

"You can easily do it," said the minstrel. "You only have to do as I say."

"Oh, minstrel," the wolf said, "I'll obey you just as a pupil obeys his teacher."

"Follow me," said the minstrel.

After they had walked some distance, they came to a footpath with tall bushes on either side. The minstrel stopped, grabbed hold of a little hazel tree, and bent it down to the ground. Then he held the top down with his foot while he bent another little hazel tree down from the other side.

"Well now, my little fox," he said, "if you want to learn something, give me your left front paw."

The fox obeyed, and the minstrel bound the paw to the tree on the left.

"Little fox," he said, "now give me your right paw."

He bound this one to the tree on the right. After he made sure that the knots were tight enough, he let go, and the little trees shot up into the air and jerked the fox up high so he was left dangling in the air.

"Wait here till I get back," said the minstrel, and he went his way.

Once again he said to himself, "I'm getting bored in the forest and need to get another companion."

So he took his fiddle, and the sounds reverberated through the forest. Then a little hare came hopping toward him.

"Ah, here comes a hare!" said the minstrel. "I didn't want a hare."

"Oho, dear minstrel," the little hare said, "what's that lovely tune you're playing? I'd like to play that way too."

"You can easily do it," said the minstrel. "You only have to do as I say."

"Oh, minstrel," the little hare answered, "I'll obey you just as a pupil obeys his teacher."

They walked some distance together until they came to a clearing in the forest where an aspen tree was standing. The minstrel tied a long cord around the little hare's neck and attached the other end to the tree.

"Move lively, little hare," the minstrel cried out. "I want you to run around the tree twenty times."

The little hare obeyed, and after he had done that twenty times, the cord was wrapped around the tree twenty times, and the little hare was trapped. No matter how much he pulled or tugged, he only made the cord cut deeper into his soft neck.

"Wait here till I get back," said the minstrel, and he went off.

In the meantime, the wolf had yanked and pulled and bitten on the stone. He kept working at it until he finally freed his paws and drew them out of the crack. Bursting with anger and fury, he rushed after the minstrel, intending to tear him to pieces. When the fox saw him running along, he began to wail and scream with all his might, "Brother wolf, come help me! The minstrel has tricked me!"

The wolf pulled the little trees down to the ground, bit the rope in two, and freed the fox, who went with him to get revenge on the minstrel. They found the little hare tied up and released him as well. Now all three began searching for their enemy.

As the minstrel walked along his way he played his fiddle once again, but this time he was more fortunate. The sounds reached the ears of a poor woodcutter who was instantly compelled to stop working whether he wanted to or not, and he went to listen to the music with his ax under his arm.

"Here comes the right companion at last!" said the minstrel. "I never wanted beasts in the first place, just humans."

Now he began to play so beautifully and so delightfully that the poor man stood there as if he were under a magic spell, and his heart leapt for joy. As he was standing there, the wolf, the fox, and the little hare came running up, and he could see that they had something evil in mind. So he raised his glittering ax and stood in front of the minstrel as if to say, "Whoever wants him had better watch out, because he'll have to deal with me first."

The animals were frightened by this and ran back into the forest, while the minstrel played one more tune for the woodcutter out of gratitude. Then he moved on his way.

◈ 9 ◈

The Twelve Brothers

ONCE UPON A TIME a king and a queen lived together peacefully and had twelve children, all boys. One day the king said to his wife, "When you give birth to our thirteenth child and it's a girl, the twelve boys shall die so she may have all the wealth and the kingdom for herself."

He even had twelve coffins made and filled with wood shavings. Each was fitted with a death pillow, and all the coffins were locked in a room. The king gave the key to the queen and ordered her never to say one word about this to anyone. She then sat and lamented the entire day. Her youngest son, Benjamin, whose name she had taken from the Bible, was always with her, and he asked, "Dear Mother, why are you so sad?"

"Dearest child," she replied. "I'm not allowed to tell you."

But he gave her no peace until she opened the room and showed him the twelve coffins already filled with wood shavings. She then said, "My dearest Benjamin, your father had these coffins made for you and your eleven brothers. If I give birth to a girl, all of you shall be killed and buried in them."

As she was telling him this, she wept, and her son consoled her by saying, "Don't weep, dear Mother. We'll find a way to help ourselves and get away from here."

Then she said, "Go into the forest with your eleven brothers. I want you to find the tallest tree and take turns sitting on top. You're to keep watch and look toward the castle tower. If I give birth to a little boy, I'll raise a white flag, and then you'll be able to return. If I give birth to a little girl, I'll raise a red flag, and then you're to flee as fast as you can. And may the good Lord protect you. I'll get up every night and pray that you're able to warm yourselves by a fire in the winter and that you don't suffer from the heat during the summer."

After she gave her blessing to her sons, they went out into the forest, where they took turns keeping watch. Each one sat on top of the tallest oak tree and looked toward the tower. When eleven days had passed and it was Benjamin's turn, he saw a flag being raised. However, it was not a white one but a bloodred flag announcing that they were to die. When the brothers heard that, they became angry and said, "Why should we suffer death because of a girl? We swear we'll get our revenge. Wherever we find a girl, her red blood shall flow."

Then they went deeper into the forest, where it was darkest. There they found an empty little cottage, which was bewitched.

"We shall dwell here," they said, "and you, Benjamin, since you're the youngest and weakest, shall stay home and keep house. We others shall go out and search for food."

So they went off into the forest and shot hares, wild deer, birds, little pigeons, and whatever was fit to eat. They brought this to Benjamin, who had to prepare it nicely for them so they could still their hunger. They lived together for ten years in this little cottage, and the time passed quickly for them.

Meanwhile, the daughter that their mother, the queen, had brought into the world had grown to be a little girl. She had a kind heart and beautiful features and a gold star on her forehead. One time when there was a great deal of washing to do, she saw twelve boy's shirts among the things to be washed and asked her mother, "Whose shirts are these? They're much too small for Father."

Her mother answered her with a heavy heart. "Dear child, they belong to your twelve brothers."

"Where are my twelve brothers?" the girl asked. "I've never heard of them until now."

"Only God knows where they are," she answered. "They're wandering around somewhere in the world." She took the girl, opened the room, and showed her the twelve coffins with the wood shavings and the death pillows. "These coffins were destined for your brothers," she said, "but the boys departed secretly before you were born." And then she told her everything that had happened.

"Dear Mother," the girl said, "don't weep. I'm going to look for my brothers."

So she took the twelve shirts and went straight into the great forest. She walked the whole day, and by evening she came to the bewitched cottage. When she entered, she found a young boy who asked, "Where have you come from and where are you going?" He was astonished by her beauty, her royal garments, and the star on her forehead.

"I'm a princess," she responded, "and I'm looking for my twelve brothers. I'm prepared to continue walking as far as the sky is blue until I find them."

She showed him the twelve shirts, and Benjamin realized she was his sister.

"I'm Benjamin," he said, "your youngest brother."

She began to cry for joy, and they kissed and lovingly hugged each other. But then he said, "Dear sister, there's still a problem. We agreed that any maiden who came our way would have to die, for we had to leave our kingdom on account of a girl."

"I'll gladly die," she said, "if I can save my twelve brothers by doing this."

"No," he responded. "You shall not die. Sit down under this tub and wait till our eleven brothers come back. Then I'll settle everything with them."

She did as he said, and when it was night, the others came back from the hunt and found their meal ready. After they sat down at the table and began eating, they asked, "What's new?"

"You don't know?" Benjamin said.

"No," they replied.

"You're in the forest the whole day," he continued, "while I stay at home. Yet, I still know more than you."

"Then tell us!" they cried out.

"Only if you promise me that the first girl we meet shall not be killed," he said.

"Yes!" they all exclaimed. "Now tell us."

"Our sister is here!" he said, and he lifted up the tub, and the princess came crawling out in her royal garments. She had the gold star on her forehead and was very beautiful, gentle, and delicate. In their joy they embraced and kissed her, for they loved her with all their hearts.

Now she stayed at home with Benjamin and helped him with the work. The eleven brothers went into the forest, caught wild game, deer, birds, and pigeons so they would have something to eat, and their sister and Benjamin made sure that their meals were prepared. They fetched the wood for cooking, herbs to go along with the vegetables, and put the pots on the fire so dinner was always ready when the eleven brothers came home. Moreover, they kept the little cottage in order and put nice clean white sheets on the little beds. All this kept the brothers satisfied, and they lived with her in great harmony.

One day the two at home had prepared a wonderful meal, and when they were all together, they sat down, ate, drank, and were full of joy. Now, there was a small garden next to the bewitched cottage, and in it were twelve lilies, also called students. Since she wanted to please her brothers, the sister plucked the twelve flowers with the intention of giving one to each brother at the end of the meal. But right after she had plucked the flowers, the twelve brothers were instantly changed into twelve ravens and flew away over the forest, while the cottage and the garden vanished as well. Now the maiden

was all alone in the wild forest, and when
she looked around, an old woman was
standing near her and she said, "My
child, what have you done? Why
didn't you leave those twelve
white flowers alone? They
were your brothers, and
you've changed them
into ravens forever."

"Is there no way
to save them?" the
maiden asked as
she wept.

"No," the old woman said. "That is—there's only one way in the
entire world, but it's so hard you won't be able to free them. You see,
you would have to remain silent for seven years and neither speak nor
laugh. If you utter but a single word and there is just an hour to go in
the seven years, everything will be in vain, and your brothers will be
killed by that one word."

"I know for sure," the maiden spoke with her whole heart, "that I
shall save my brothers."

She went and searched for a tall tree. After climbing it, she sat
down and began spinning and did not say a word or laugh. Now, it
so happened that a king was hunting in the forest. He had a big
greyhound that ran·up to the tree where the maiden was sitting. The
dog began jumping around, yelping and barking at her. The king then
went over to the tree and saw the beautiful princess with the gold star
on her forehead. He was so enraptured by her beauty that he called up

to her and asked her if she would be his wife. She did not respond but nodded a little with her head. Then he climbed up the tree himself, carried her down, put her on his horse, and took her home. The wedding was celebrated with great splendor and joy, but the bride did not speak or laugh.

After they lived together for a few years, the king's mother, who was an evil woman, began to slander the young queen and said to the king, "The maiden you brought home with you is nothing but a common beggar girl! Who knows what godless mischief she's been secretly plotting? If she's mute and can't talk, she could at least laugh every now and then. Anyone who doesn't laugh must have a bad conscience."

At first the king did not want to believe this, but the old woman kept at it so long and accused the maiden of so many wicked things that the king finally let himself be convinced and sentenced her to death. A huge fire was made in the courtyard, and the young queen was to be burned in it. The king stood upstairs at a window and watched everything with tears in his eyes, since he still loved her. When she was already bound to the stake and the fire was licking her clothes with its red tongues, the last second of the seven years expired. Suddenly a whirring noise could be heard in the air, and twelve ravens came flying toward the yard and swooped down. Then, just as they touched the ground, they turned into her twelve brothers whom she had saved. They tore apart the fire, put out the flames, freed their dear sister, and hugged and kissed her. Now that she was allowed to open her mouth and talk, she told the king why she had been silent and had never laughed. The king was glad to hear she was innocent, and they all lived together in harmony until their death. The evil mother was brought before the court and put into a barrel that was filled with boiling oil and poisonous snakes. Indeed, she died a horrible death.

◆ 10 ◆

Riffraff

THE ROOSTER SAID TO THE HEN, "Now's the time the nuts are ripe. Let's go up to the hill and for once eat our fill before the squirrel hauls them all away."

"All right," responded the hen. "Let's go and have a good time."

They went up the hill, and since it was such a bright cheery day, they stayed till evening. Now, I do not know whether it was because they had stuffed themselves too much, or whether they had become too high and mighty, but they did not want to return home on foot. so the rooster had to build a small carriage out of nut shells. When it was finished, the hen got in and said to the rooster, "Now you can just harness yourself to it."

"You have some nerve!" said the rooster. "I'd rather go home by foot than let myself be harnessed to this carriage. No, that wasn't part of our bargain. I'd gladly be coachman and sit on the box, but I refuse to pull the carriage!"

As they were quarreling, a duck came by quacking "You thieves! Who said you could come up on my nut hill? Just you wait! You'll pay for this!"

She charged at the rooster with a wide-open beak, but the rooster was on his toes and threw himself at the duck nice and hard. Then he dug his spurs into her so violently that the duck begged for mercy and willingly let herself be harnessed to the carriage as punishment. Now the rooster sat down on the box as coachman, and when they set out, he shouted, "Giddyap, duck! Run as fast as you can!"

After they had gone some distance, they encountered two travelers on foot, a needle and a pin.

"Stop! Stop!" the two cried out. It would soon be very dark, they said, and they would not be able to go one step further. Besides, the road was dirty. So they asked if they could have a ride. They had been at the tailor's tavern outside the town gate and had had one beer too many, which made them late as well.

Since they were thin and did not take up much room, the rooster let them both get in, but they had to promise not to step on his or the hen's feet. Later that evening they came to an inn, and as they did not want to travel any farther, and as the duck was not walking well but swayed from side to side, they decided to stop there. At first the innkeeper raised a lot of objections and said his inn was already full. Moreover, he thought they were not a very distinguished looking group. However, they used some sweet talk and offered him the egg that the hen had laid along the way and told him that he could also keep the duck, who laid an egg a day. So finally he relented and said they could spend the night.

Now they ordered some good hot food and had a merry time of it. Early the next morning, as the sun was rising and everyone was asleep, the rooster woke the hen, fetched the egg, pecked it open, and together they devoured it. After throwing the shells on the hearth, they went to the needle, who was still asleep, grabbed him by the head, and stuck him into the innkeeper's easy chair. Then they stuck the pin into his towel. Finally, without much ado, they flew away over the heath.

The duck, who liked to sleep in the open air and had spent the night in the yard, heard the flapping of their wings. So she roused herself, found a brook, and swam off. That went much faster than being harnessed to a carriage. A few hours later the innkeeper got out of bed, washed himself, and took the towel to dry himself. However, the pin scratched his face, leaving a red mark from ear to ear. Then he went into the kitchen and wanted to light his pipe. But, as he leaned over the hearth, the eggshells popped into his eyes.

"Everything's after my head this morning," he said, and went to sit down in his easy chair to settle his bad mood, but he jumped up immediately and screamed, *"Oww!"* The needle stuck him worse than the pin and not in the head. Now he was completely angry and suspected the guests who had arrived so late the night before. But when he went looking for them, they were gone. Then he swore he would never again let riffraff stay at his inn, especially when they eat so much, pay nothing, and play mean tricks on top of it all.

◆ 11 ◆

Brother and Sister

A LITTLE BROTHER took his little sister by the hand and said, "Since our mother died, we've not had one moment of happiness. Our step-mother beats us every day, and when we come near her, she kicks us away with her foot. We get nothing but hard crusts of bread, just leftovers for food, and the dog under the table is better off. At least he gets a good chunk of meat to eat every now and then. Lord have mercy on us, if our mother only knew! Come, let's go off together into the wide world."

They walked over meadows, fields, and stones the entire day, and when it began to rain, the sister said, "God and our hearts are weeping at the same time."

In the evening they came to a great forest and were so exhausted from their grief, hunger, and long journey that they crept into a hollow tree and fell asleep. When they woke up the next morning, the sun was already high in the sky and warmed the tree with its rays.

"Sister," said the brother, "I'm thirsty. If only I knew where to find a spring, I'd go and have a drink right away. Listen, I think I hear one gurgling."

The brother stood up, took his sister by the hand, and set out to look for the spring. However, the evil stepmother, who was a witch, had noticed that the children had run away. She had gone slinking after them in secret, as witches often slink, and had put a curse on all the springs in the forest. So, when they found a spring rushing and leaping over stones, the brother wanted to take a drink, but the sister heard the gurgling spring say, "Whoever drinks of me will be turned into a tiger."

Then the sister exclaimed, "Please, brother, don't drink, or else you'll turn into a wild beast and tear me to pieces!"

Even though he was very thirsty, the brother did not drink. Instead he said, "I'll wait until we reach the next spring."

When they reached the next spring, once again the sister heard what it was babbling. "Whoever drinks of me will be turned into a wolf. Whoever drinks of me will be turned into a wolf."

"Brother!" the sister exclaimed. "Please don't drink, or else you'll be turned into a wolf and eat me up."

The brother did not drink and said, "I'll wait until we reach the next spring, but then I must drink no matter what you say. My thirst is much too great."

When they came to the third spring, the sister heard the babbling of the spring. "Whoever drinks of me will be turned into a deer. Whoever drinks of me will be turned into a deer."

"Oh, brother!" the sister exclaimed. "Please don't drink, or else you'll be turned into a deer and run away from me."

But the brother, who was already kneeling at the spring, leaned over and drank some of the water. Immediately after a few drops had touched his lips, he lay there in the form of a fawn. The sister began weeping over her poor bewitched brother, sitting sadly at her side, and the little fawn wept too. Finally, the girl said, "Hush, my dear little fawn. I shall never forsake you."

She took off her golden garter and put it around the fawn's neck. Then she pulled up some rushes and wove them into a soft rope, which she attached to the little animal. Afterward she led him onward and deeper into the forest. When they had gone a long, long way, they came to a little house, and the girl looked inside. Since it was empty, she thought, We might as well stay and live right here. So she looked for leaves and moss and made a soft bed for the fawn. Every morning she went out and gathered roots, berries, and nuts for herself, and for the fawn she brought back tender grass, which he ate out of her hand. This made him content, and he would romp around her in a playful fashion. At night, when the sister was tired and had said her prayers, she would lay her head on the back of the fawn. That was her pillow, and she would fall into a sweet sleep. If only the brother could have regained his human form, it would have been a wonderful life.

For a long time they lived like this, all alone in the wilderness. However, it came to pass that the king of the country held a great hunt in the forest, and soon horns could be heard along with the barking of dogs and the merry cries of the huntsmen. The fawn listened to the sounds and longed very much to be a part of it all.

"Ah," he said to his sister, "let me go and join the hunt. I can't bear it any longer!" He kept pleading until she gave her consent.

"But make sure you're back here by evening," she said to him. "I'm going to lock the door to keep the brutal hunters out, and when you return, I want you to knock on the door and say, 'My little sister, let me in.' That way I'll recognize you. If you don't say this, I won't open the door."

Then the fawn ran off, glad and merry to be out in the open air. The king and his huntsmen saw the beautiful creature and set out in pursuit, but they could not catch up with him. Whenever they thought they had him for sure, he would burst through the bushes and disappear. When it got dark, he ran back to the little house, knocked, and said, "My little sister, let me in."

The little door was opened for him, and he jumped inside. Then he rested the entire night on his bed. The next morning the hunt began anew, and when the fawn heard the horn again and the *"Tallyho!"* of the huntsmen, he became very restless and said, "Sister, open the door. I must be off!"

The sister opened the door for him and said, "Remember, you must be back by evening and say the passwords."

When the king and his huntsmen saw the fawn with the golden collar once more, they all pursued him, but he was still too swift and nimble for them. All day long they chased him, but finally by evening they had surrounded him. Then one huntsman wounded him slightly on his foot, and as the fawn slowly ran away he was limping. This allowed a huntsman to trail him all the way to the house, and he heard the fawn cry out, "My little sister, let me in." He watched the door open and close quickly and took note of all that happened. Then the huntsman went back to the king and told him about everything he had seen and heard.

"Tomorrow we shall hunt again," the king said.

Meanwhile, the sister was greatly distressed when she saw her little fawn was wounded. She washed off the blood, placed herbs on the wound, and said, "Now, go to bed, my dear fawn. You must let your wound heal."

Actually the wound was so slight that the fawn did not even feel it the next morning. And, once again, when he heard the merry cries of the hunt outside, he said, "I can't bear it. I've got to be there! I won't make it easy for them to catch me."

The sister wept and said, "Now they'll kill you, and I'll be left alone in the forest, forsaken by the whole world. I'm not going to let you out."

"Then I'll die of misery," responded the fawn. "Whenever I hear the sounds of the hunting horn, I feel as if I were going to burst out of my skin."

After he said that, his sister could no longer refuse, and with a heavy heart she opened the door for him. The fawn bounded cheerfully and sprightfully into the forest. When the king caught sight of him, he said to his huntsmen, "Now, I want you to chase him the whole day long and into the night, but make sure that you don't harm him."

Later, as the sun began to set, the king turned to the huntsman and said, "All right, take me and show me the little house in the forest."

After the king arrived at the front door, he knocked and called out, "Dear little sister, let me in."

The door opened, and upon entering, the king stood face-to-face with the most beautiful maiden he had ever seen in his life. The maiden was frightened when she saw it was a man with a golden crown on his head and not her fawn. Yet, he looked at her in a kind way, and after extending his hand, he said, "Would you like to come with me to my castle and be my dear wife?"

"Oh, yes," responded the maiden. "But the fawn must come with me too. I won't ever forsake him."

"He can stay with you as long as you live," said the king, "and he shall want for nothing."

Just then the little fawn came running in, and the sister attached the rope of rushes to him, took the rope in her own hand, and led him out of the house. The king lifted the beautiful maiden onto his horse and brought her to his castle, where the wedding was celebrated with great splendor. Now the sister was queen, and for a long time they all lived together in happiness. The fawn was well tended and ran about the castle garden.

In the meantime, the evil stepmother, who had caused the children to run away in the first place, thought that the sister had been torn to pieces by wild beasts and that the brother, as a fawn, had been shot to death by huntsmen. When she learned instead how happy they were and how well everything was going for them, jealousy and resentment stirred in her heart and gave her no peace. Her one and only thought now was to find a way to bring about their misfortune again. Her own daughter, who was as ugly as sin and had only one eye, reproached her by saying, "I'm the one who should be queen! Why don't I have any luck?"

"Just be quiet!" said the old woman, who gave her reason to be satisfied. "When the right time comes, I'll know what to do."

Finally, the right time came: the queen gave birth one day to a baby boy while the king was out hunting. So the old witch assumed the form of the chambermaid, went into the room where the queen was lying, and said to the convalescent, "Come, your bath is ready. It will make you feel better and give you fresh strength. Quick, before it gets cold."

The witch's daughter had come too. Together they carried the frail queen into the bathroom, put her into the tub, locked the door, and ran away, for they had made such a terrible fire in the bathroom that the queen was soon suffocated to death.

When that was done, the old woman took her daughter, put a nightcap on her, and laid her in bed in place of the queen. She also gave her the shape and features of the queen. However, she could not replace the eye that the daughter had lost. Therefore, the daughter had to lie on the side where she had no eye. That way the king would not notice anything amiss. In the evening, when he returned home and heard his wife had given birth to a baby boy, he was very happy and wanted to go to his dear wife's bedside and see how she was doing. But the old woman cried out quickly, "For goodness sake, keep the curtains closed! The queen must not be exposed to light. She needs peace and quiet."

The king stepped back and was thus prevented from discovering the false queen lying in the bed. However, at midnight, when everyone was asleep except the nurse, who was sitting by the cradle in the nursery and watching over the baby all by herself, the door opened, and the true queen entered. She lifted the baby out of the cradle, took him in her arms, and suckled him. Then she puffed up his little pillow, put him back in the cradle, and covered him with a little blanket. Nor did she forget the fawn. She went to the corner where he was lying and stroked his back. Then she silently left the room, and when morning came, the nurse asked the guards whether they had seen anyone enter the castle during the night.

"No, we didn't see a soul," they replied.

Thereafter the queen came many nights and never uttered a word. The nurse always saw her, but she did not dare tell anyone about it.

After some time had passed, the queen began to speak, and one night she said:

"How's my child? How's my fawn?
Twice more I'll come, then I'll be gone."

The nurse did not answer her, but when the queen disappeared, she went to the king and told him everything.
"Oh, God!" he exclaimed. "What's going on? Tonight I'll keep watch over the child myself."
In the evening he went into the nursery, and at midnight the queen reappeared and said:

"How's my child? How's my fawn?
Once more I'll come, then I'll be gone."

She nursed the child as she usually did and then disappeared. The king did not dare to speak to her, but he kept watch the following night as well. Once again she said:

"How's my child? How's my fawn?
There's no more time. Soon I'll be gone."

The king could no longer restrain himself. He sprang forward and said, "You can be no one else but my dear wife!"
At that very moment life was restored to her by the grace of God. Indeed, she was alive and well, and the rosy color came back to her cheeks. She then told the king how the evil witch and her daughter had committed cruel crimes against her. So the king had them led before the court, and they received their sentences. The daughter was taken into the forest, where wild beasts tore her to pieces, while the witch was thrown into a fire and miserably burned to death. When there was nothing left of her but ashes, the fawn was transformed and regained his human form. From then on sister and brother lived happily until the end of their days.

◈ 12 ◈

Rapunzel

ONCE UPON A TIME there was a husband and wife who for quite some time had been wishing in vain for a child. Finally, the dear Lord gave the wife a sign of hope that their wish would be fulfilled. Now, in the back of their house the couple had a small window that overlooked a splendid garden filled with the most beautiful flowers and herbs. The garden, however, was surrounded by a high wall, and nobody dared enter it because it belonged to a sorceress who was very powerful and feared by all. One day when the wife was standing at the window and looking down into the garden, she noticed a bed of the finest rapunzel lettuce. The lettuce looked so fresh and green that her mouth watered, and she had a great craving to eat some. Day by day this craving increased, and since she knew she could not get any, she began to waste away and look pale and miserable.

Her husband became alarmed and asked, "What's wrong with you, dear wife?"

"Ah," she responded, "I shall certainly die if I don't get any of that rapunzel from the garden behind our house."

Her husband, who loved her, thought, Before I let my wife die, I'll do anything I must to make sure she gets some rapunzel.

That day at dusk he climbed over the wall into the garden of the sorceress, hastily grabbed a handful of rapunzel, and brought them to his wife. Immediately she made them into a salad and ate it with great zest. But the rapunzel tasted so good to her, so very good, that her desire for them was three times greater by the next day. If she was to have any peace, her husband knew he had to climb into the garden once more. So at dusk he scaled the wall again, and just as he landed on the other side, he was given a tremendous scare, for he stood face-to-face with the sorceress.

"How dare you climb into my garden and steal my rapunzel like a thief?" she said with an angry look. "You'll pay for this!"

"Oh," he cried. "Please, let mercy prevail over justice. I did this only because I was in a predicament: my wife noticed your rapunzel from our window, and she developed such a great craving for it that she would have died if I hadn't brought her some to eat."

Upon hearing that, the anger of the sorceress subsided, and she said to him, "If it's truly as you say, then I shall permit you to take as many rapunzel as you like, but only under one condition: when your wife gives birth, I must have the child. You needn't fear about the child's well-being, for I shall take care of it like a mother."

In his fear the man agreed to everything, and when his wife had the baby, the sorceress appeared at once. She gave the child the name Rapunzel and took her away.

Rapunzel grew to be the most beautiful child under the sun. But when she was twelve years old, the sorceress locked her in a tower that was in a forest. It had neither door nor stairs, only a little window high above. Whenever the sorceress wanted to get in, she would stand below and call out:

"Rapunzel, Rapunzel,
let down your hair for me."

Rapunzel's hair was long and radiant, as fine as spun gold. Every time she heard the voice of the sorceress, she unpinned her braids and wound them around a hook on the window. Then she let her hair drop twenty yards, and the sorceress would climb up on it.

A few years later a king's son happened to be riding through the forest and passed by the tower. Suddenly, he heard a song so lovely that he stopped to listen. It was Rapunzel, who passed the time in her solitude by letting her sweet voice resound in the forest. The prince wanted to climb up to her, and he looked for a door but could not find one. So he rode home. However, the song had touched his heart so deeply that he rode out into the forest every day and listened. One time, as he was standing behind a tree, he saw the sorceress approach and heard her call out:

"Rapunzel, Rapunzel,
let down your hair."

Then Rapunzel let down her braids, and the sorceress climbed up to her.

"If that's the ladder one needs to get up there, I'm also going to try my luck," the prince declared.

The next day, as it began to get dark, he went to the tower and called out:

"Rapunzel, Rapunzel,
let down your hair."

All at once the hair dropped down, and the prince climbed up. When he entered the tower, Rapunzel was at first terribly afraid, for she had never laid eyes on a man before. However, the prince began to talk to her in a friendly way and told her that her song had touched his heart so deeply that he had not been able to rest until he had seen her. Rapunzel then lost her fear, and when he asked her whether she would have him for her husband, and she saw that he was young and handsome, she thought, He'll certainly love me better than old Mother Gothel. So she said yes and placed her hand in his.

"I want to go with you very much," she said, "but I don't know how I can get down. Every time you come, you must bring a skein of silk with you, and I'll weave it into a ladder. When it's finished, then I'll climb down, and you can take me away on your horse."

They agreed that until then he would come to her every evening, for the old woman came during the day. Meanwhile, the sorceress did not notice anything, until one day Rapunzel blurted out, "Mother Gothel, how is it that you're much heavier than the prince? When I pull him up, he's here in a second."

"Ah, you godless child!" exclaimed the sorceress. "What's this I hear? I thought I had made sure you had no contact with the outside world, but you've deceived me!"

In her fury she seized Rapunzel's beautiful hair, wrapped it around her left hand several times, grabbed a pair of scissors with her right hand, and *snip, snap* the hair was cut off, and the beautiful braids lay on the ground. Then the cruel sorceress took Rapunzel to a desolate land where she had to live in great misery and grief.

On the same day that she had banished Rapunzel, the sorceress fastened the braids that she had cut off to the hook on the window, and that evening, when the prince came and called out:

"Rapunzel, Rapunzel,
let down your hair,"

she let the hair down.

The prince climbed up, but instead of finding his dearest Rapunzel on top, he found the sorceress, who gave him vicious and angry looks.

"Aha!" she exclaimed with contempt. "You want to fetch your darling wife, but the beautiful bird is no longer sitting in the nest, and she won't be singing anymore. The cat has got her, and it will also scratch out your eyes. Rapunzel is lost to you, and you will never see her again!"

The prince was beside himself with grief, and in his despair he jumped off the tower. He escaped with his life, but the thorns he fell into pierced his eyes, so he became blind. Now he strayed about in the forest, ate nothing but roots and berries, and did nothing but mourn and weep about the loss of his dearest wife. Thus he wandered for many years in misery. Eventually, he made his way to the desolate land where Rapunzel was leading a wretched existence with the twins, a boy and a girl, to whom she had given birth. When he heard a voice that he thought sounded familiar, he went straight toward it, and when he reached her, Rapunzel recognized him. She embraced him and wept, and as two of her tears dropped on his eyes they became clear, and he could see again. Then he escorted her back to his kingdom, where he was received with joy, and they lived happily and contentedly for a long time thereafter.

◆ 13 ◆

The Three Little Gnomes in the Forest

THERE WAS A MAN WHOSE WIFE DIED, and a woman whose husband died; and the man had a daughter, and the woman also had a daughter. The girls knew each other and one day took a walk together. Afterward they went to the woman's house, and she said to the man's daughter, "Listen, tell your father I want to marry him. Then you shall wash yourself in milk every morning and drink wine, while my daughter will wash herself in water and drink water."

The maiden went home and told her father what the woman had said. The man responded, "What shall I do? Marriage is both joy and torture." Finally, since he could not reach a decision, he took off a boot and said, "Take this boot. It's got a hole in the sole. Carry it up to the loft, hang it on a big nail, and pour water into it. If it holds the water, I'll get married again. But if it leaks, I won't."

The maiden did as she was told, but the water drew the hole together, and the boot became full to the brim. The daughter informed her father how everything turned out. Then he climbed up into the loft to see for himself, and when he saw she was right, he went to the widow and courted her. Soon after, the wedding took place.

On the day after the wedding when the two girls got up, the man's daughter had milk to wash herself and wine to drink, while the woman's daughter had water to wash herself and water to drink. On the second morning both the girls had water to wash themselves and water to drink. On the third morning the man's daughter had water to wash herself and water to drink, while the woman's daughter had milk to wash herself and wine to drink. And that's the way it remained. The woman became her stepdaughter's most bitter enemy and tried to think of ways to make it worse for her from one day to the next. Moreover, she was envious because her stepdaughter was beautiful and lovely, and her own daughter was ugly and gruesome.

Once, when it was winter, everything was frozen over as hard as rock, and hill and dale were covered with snow. The woman made a dress out of paper, called her stepdaughter to her, and said, "Now put on this dress, go into the forest, and fetch me a basket of strawberries. I've got a craving for them."

"Good Lord!" the girl said. "Strawberries don't grow in winter.

The ground is frozen, and everything's covered with snow. Besides, why do you want me to go in a paper dress? It's so cold outside that my breath will freeze. The wind will blow right through the dress, and the thorns will tear it off my body."

"You have some nerve talking back to me!" the stepmother said. "Get going, and don't show your face around here again until you have the basket filled with strawberries." Then she gave her a little piece of hard bread and said, "You can use this as food for the day."

All the while she thought, She'll starve and freeze to death out there, and I won't ever have to lay eyes on her again.

The maiden was obedient, so she put on the paper dress and went out with the little basket. There was nothing but snow as far as the eye could see, not even a blade of green grass.

When she reached the forest, she saw a small cottage, and three little gnomes were looking out the window. She wished them a good day and knocked politely at the door.

"Come in," they cried out.

She entered the room and sat down on the bench near the stove, since she wanted to warm herself and eat her breakfast. The three gnomes said, "Give us some too."

"Gladly," she replied. She divided the bread in two and gave them half.

"What are you doing out here in the forest during the winter walking about in such a little dress?" they asked.

"Oh," she answered, "I'm supposed to look for strawberries, and I'm not supposed to return home until I've gathered a basketful."

After she had eaten her bread, they gave her a broom and said, "Sweep the snow away from the back door."

Once she was outside, the three gnomes began talking among themselves. "What should we give her for being so polite and kind and sharing her bread with us?"

"She shall become more and more beautiful each day that passes. This is my gift," said the first one.

"Each time she utters a word, gold pieces shall fall out of her mouth. This is my gift," said the second.

"A king shall come and take her for his wife. This is my gift," said the third.

Meanwhile, the maiden did as the gnomes had asked and swept the snow away from the back of the house, and what do you think she found? There were lots of ripe, dark red strawberries shooting out of the ground. In her joy she filled her basket with them. Then she thanked the little men by shaking hands with each of them and ran home to her stepmother, bringing her what she had demanded. As the maiden entered the house and said "Good evening" a piece of gold fell right out of her mouth. Then she explained what had happened to her in the forest, and with each word she uttered, gold pieces fell out of her mouth until soon the entire room was covered with gold.

"Just look at how arrogant she is!" her stepsister exclaimed. "The way she throws money around!"

But secretly the stepsister was envious and wanted to go into the forest and look for strawberries too.

"No, no, my dear little daughter," her mother said. "It's too cold, and you could freeze to death."

However, her daughter gave her no peace, and finally her mother had to yield. She sewed her a magnificent fur coat to wear and gave her bread and butter and cake to take with her.

The maiden went into the forest and headed straight for the little cottage. The three gnomes were looking out the window once again, but she did not greet them. Instead, she tramped right into their house, sat down by the stove, and began eating her cake without even glancing at them or saying good day.

"Give us some," the little men cried out.

But she answered, "It's not even enough for me, so how can you expect me to give you anything?"

When she had finished eating, they said to her, "Here's a broom. Go outside and sweep around the back door so it's clean."

"Do your own sweeping!" she responded. "I'm not your maid."

When she saw that they were not going to give her anything, she went out the door, and the three gnomes began talking among themselves. "What should we give her for being so naughty and having such a wicked and greedy heart that makes her so stingy?"

"She shall grow uglier with each day that passes. This is my gift," said the first one.

"Each time she utters a word, a toad shall spring out of her mouth. This will be my gift," said the second.

"She will die a miserable death. This will be my gift," said the third.

Meanwhile, the maiden looked for strawberries outside, and when she could not find any, she went home in a bad mood. As she opened her mouth to tell her mother what had happened in the forest a toad sprang out of her mouth with each word she uttered, causing everyone to be repulsed by her.

Now the stepmother was even more disturbed than before and could only think of how she might be able to hurt her husband's daughter, who was getting more beautiful day by day. Finally she took a kettle, put it on the fire, and boiled some yarn in it. When the yarn was boiled, she hung it on the poor maiden's shoulders, gave her an ax, and ordered her to go to the frozen river, where she was to chop a hole and rinse the yarn. Since she was obedient, the maiden went to the river and began chopping the hole in the ice. While she was in the middle of chopping the hole, a splendid coach with a king inside came driving by. The coach stopped, and the king asked, "Who are you, my child, and what are you doing here?"

"I'm a poor maiden, and I'm rinsing yarn."

The king felt sorry for her, and when he saw how beautiful she was, he said, "Would you like to ride with me in my coach?"

"Oh, yes, with all my heart!" she replied, for she was glad to get as far away as possible from her mother and sister.

So she climbed into the coach and drove away with the king, and when they got to his castle, the wedding was celebrated with great pomp, and this would not have happened were it not for the gifts of the three gnomes.

After a year had passed, the young queen gave birth to a son, and when the stepmother heard about her great fortune, she went to the castle with her daughter as if she wanted to pay a visit. However, when the king left the castle and no one else was there, the evil woman seized the queen by her head, and the daughter grabbed her by the feet. They lifted her from the bed and threw her right out the window into the river flowing by the castle. Then the ugly daughter lay down in the bed, and the old woman pulled the covers over her head. When the king came back home and wanted to speak to his wife, the old woman cried out, "Hush, hush! Now's not the time. She's in a terrible sweat. You must let her rest today."

The king did not suspect any mischief and came again the next day. When he began talking with his wife and she answered, there were toads springing out of her mouth with each word she uttered, not the pieces of gold that usually fell out. So he asked what all this meant, and the old woman said this came from the terrible sweating and would soon go away.

During the night, however, a kitchen boy saw a duck swimming through the drain, and it said:

"King, my king, what are you doing?
Are you awake, or might you be sleeping?"

When the boy did not answer, the duck said:

"And are all my guests now sound asleep?"

Then the kitchen boy answered:

"Yes, indeed, you can't hear a peep."

Then she asked again:

"How about that baby of mine?"

He replied:

"Oh, he's asleep and doing just fine."

Finally the duck assumed the shape of the queen, went upstairs, nursed the baby, plumped up his little bed, covered him, and returned to the drain, where she swam away as a duck. This happened the next night too, and on the third night, she said to the kitchen boy, "Go and tell the king to take his sword and swing it three times over my head on the threshold."

The kitchen boy ran and told the king, who came with his sword and swung it three times over the ghost. At the third time his wife appeared before him alive and as well as ever before.

Now the king was exceedingly happy, but he kept the queen hidden in a room until Sunday, when their child was to be baptized. When he was baptized, the king said, "What does a person deserve who drags someone out of his bed and throws him into the water?"

"The scoundrel deserves nothing better than to be put into a barrel studded with nails on the inside," said the old woman. "And then he should be rolled down the hill into the water."

"You have pronounced your own sentence," said the king.

He ordered a barrel like that to be fetched, and the old woman and her daughter were put inside. The lid was hammered on, and the barrel was rolled down the hill into the river.

◈ 14 ◈

The Three Spinners

THERE ONCE WAS A LAZY MAIDEN who did not want to spin, and no matter what her mother said, she refused to spin. Finally, her mother became so angry and impatient that she beat her, and her daughter began to cry loudly. Just then the queen happened to be driving by, and when she heard the crying, she ordered the carriage to stop, went into the house, and asked the mother why she was beating her daughter, for her screams could be heard out on the street. The woman was too ashamed to tell the queen that her daughter was lazy and said, "I can't get her to stop spinning. She does nothing but spin and spin, and I'm so poor that I can't provide the flax."

"Well," the queen replied, "there's nothing I like to hear more than the sound of spinning, and I'm never happier than when I hear the constant humming of the wheels. Let me take your daughter with me to my castle. I've got plenty of flax, and she can spin as much as she likes."

The mother was delighted to give her consent, and the queen took the maiden with her. After they reached the castle, she led the maiden upstairs to three rooms that were filled with the finest flax from floor to ceiling.

"Now, spin this flax for me," she said. "And if you finish all this, you shall have my oldest son for your husband. It doesn't matter to me that you're poor. You work industriously and you never stop. That in itself is dowry enough."

The maiden was deeply frightened, for she could not have spun the flax even if she were to live three hundred years and sit there every day from morning till night. Therefore, when she was left alone, she began to weep and sat there for three days without lifting a finger. On the third day the queen came back to the room, and when she saw that nothing had been spun, she was puzzled. But the maiden made up an excuse and said she had been so tremendously upset about leaving her mother's house that she had been unable to begin working. The queen accepted this excuse, but upon leaving she said, "Tomorrow you must begin your work for me."

When the maiden was alone again, she did not know what to do or where to turn. In her distress she went over to the window and saw three women coming in her direction: the first had a broad flat foot, the second had such a large lower lip that it hung down over her chin, and the third had an immense thumb. They stopped in front of her window, looked up, and asked the maiden what the matter was. She told them about her predicament, and they offered to help her.

"We'll spin your flax for you in no time at all," they said. "But only if you invite us to your wedding and are not ashamed of us. Moreover, you must call us your cousins, and let us eat at your table."

"With all my heart," she responded. "Just come in and get to work right away."

She let the three odd women in and cleared a place for them in the first room where they could sit down and begin their spinning. One drew out the thread and began treading the treadle, the other wet the thread, and the third twisted it and struck the table with her finger. Whenever she struck it, a reel of yarn dropped to the ground, and it was always most delicately spun. The maiden concealed the three spinners from the queen, and every time the queen came, the maiden showed her such a large amount of spun yarn that there was no end to the queen's praise for her. When the first room was empty of flax, they moved on to the second and then the third until it too was cleared of flax. Now the three women took their leave and said to the maiden, "Don't forget what you've promised us. It will determine your good fortune."

When the maiden showed the queen the empty rooms and the large piles of yarn, the queen arranged for the wedding, and the bridegroom was happy to get such a skillful and industrious wife and gave her tremendous praise.

"I have three cousins," said the maiden, "and since they've done so many good things for me, I'd like to remember them in my happiness by inviting them to the wedding. Please allow me to do this and let them sit at our table."

The queen and the bridegroom said, "Why, of course, we'll allow this."

When the feast was just about to begin, the three women entered in bizarre costumes, and the bride said, "Welcome, dear cousins."

"Ahh!" said the bridegroom. "How did you ever come by such ghastly-looking friends?"

Then he went to the one with a broad flat foot and asked, "How did you get such a flat foot?"

"From treading," she answered. "From treading."

Next the bridegroom went to the second and asked, "How did you get such a drooping lip?"

"From licking," she answered. "From licking."

Then he asked the third one, "How did you get such an immense thumb?"

"From twisting thread," she answered. "From twisting thread."

Upon hearing this the prince was alarmed and said, "Never ever shall my beautiful wife touch a spinning wheel again."

Thus she was able to rid herself of the terrible task of spinning flax.

◈ 15 ◈

Hansel and Gretel

A POOR WOODCUTTER lived with his wife and his two children on the edge of a large forest. The boy was called Hansel and the girl Gretel. The woodcutter did not have much food around the house, and when a great famine devastated the entire country, he could no longer provide enough for his family's daily meals. One night, as he was lying in bed and thinking about his worries, he began tossing and turning. Then he sighed and said to his wife, "What's to become of us? How can we feed our poor children when we don't even have enough for ourselves?"

"I'll tell you what," answered his wife. "Early tomorrow morning we'll take the children out into the forest where it's most dense. We'll build a fire and give them each a piece of bread. Then we'll go about our work and leave them alone. They won't find their way back home, and we'll be rid of them."

"No, wife," the man said. "I won't do this. I don't have the heart to leave my children in the forest. The wild beasts would soon come and tear them apart."

"Oh, you fool!" she said. "Then all four of us will have to starve to death. You'd better start planing the boards for our coffins!" She continued to harp on this until he finally agreed to do what she suggested.

"But still, I feel sorry for the poor children," he said.

The two children had not been able to fall asleep that night either. Their hunger kept them awake, and when they heard what their stepmother said to their father, Gretel wept bitter tears and said to Hansel, "Now it's all over for us."

"Be quiet, Gretel," Hansel said. "Don't get upset. I'll soon find a way to help us."

When their parents had fallen asleep, Hansel put on his little jacket, opened the bottom half of the door, and crept outside. The moon was shining very brightly, and the white pebbles glittered in front of the house like pure silver coins. Hansel stooped down to the ground and stuffed his pocket with as many pebbles as he could fit in. Then he went back and said to Gretel, "Don't worry, my dear little sister. Just sleep in peace. God will not forsake us." And he lay down again in his bed.

At dawn, even before the sun began to rise, the woman came and woke the two children: "Get up, you lazybones! We're going into the forest to fetch some wood." Then she gave each one of them a piece of bread and said, "Now you have something for your noonday meal, but don't eat it before then because you're not getting anything else."

Gretel put the bread under her apron because Hansel had the pebbles in his pocket. Then they all set out together toward the forest. After they had walked a while, Hansel stopped and looked back at the house. He did this time and again until his father said, "Hansel, what are you looking at there? Why are you dawdling? Pay attention, and don't forget how to use your legs!"

"Oh, Father," said Hansel, "I'm looking at my little white cat that's sitting up on the roof and wants to say good-bye to me."

"You fool," the mother said. "That's not a cat. It's the morning sun shining on the chimney."

But Hansel had not been looking at the cat. Instead, he had been taking the shiny pebbles from his pocket and constantly dropping them on the ground. When they reached the middle of the forest, the father said, "Children, I want you to gather some wood. I'm going to make a fire so you won't get cold."

Hansel and Gretel gathered together some brushwood and built quite a nice little pile. The brushwood was soon kindled, and when the fire was ablaze, the woman said, "Now, children, lie down by the fire, and rest yourselves. We're going into the forest to chop wood. When we're finished, we'll come back and get you."

Hansel and Gretel sat by the fire, and when noon came, they ate their pieces of bread. Since they heard the sounds of the ax, they thought their father was nearby. But it was not the ax. Rather, it was a branch that he had tied to a dead tree, and the wind was banging it back and forth. After they had been sitting there for a long time, they became so weary that their eyes closed, and they fell sound asleep. By the time they finally awoke, it was already pitch black, and Gretel began to cry and said, "How are we going to get out of the forest?"

But Hansel comforted her by saying, "Just wait awhile until the moon has risen. Then we'll find the way."

And when the full moon had risen, Hansel took his little sister by the hand and followed the pebbles that glittered like newly minted silver coins and showed them the way. They walked the whole night long and arrived back at their father's house at break of day. They knocked at the door, and when the woman opened it and saw it was Hansel and Gretel, she said, "You wicked children, why did you sleep so long in the forest? We thought you'd never come back again."

But the father was delighted because he had been deeply troubled by the way he had abandoned them in the forest.

Not long after that the entire country was once again ravaged by famine, and one night the children heard their mother talking to their father in bed. "Everything's been eaten up again. We only have half a loaf of bread, but after it's gone, that will be the end of our food. The children must leave. This time we'll take them even farther into the forest so they won't find their way back home again. Otherwise, there's no hope for us."

All this saddened the father, and he thought, It'd be much better to share your last bite to eat with your children. But the woman would not listen to anything he said. She just scolded and reproached him. Once you've given a hand, people will take your arm, and since he had given in the first time, he also had to yield a second time.

However, the children were still awake and had overheard their conversation. When their parents had fallen asleep, Hansel got up, intending to go out and gather pebbles as he had done the time before, but the woman had locked the door, and Hansel could not get out. Nevertheless, he comforted his little sister and said, "Don't cry, Gretel. Just sleep in peace. The dear Lord is bound to help us."

Early the next morning the woman came and got the children out of bed. They each received little pieces of bread, but they were smaller than the last time. On the way into the forest Hansel crumbled the bread in his pocket and stopped as often as he could to throw the crumbs on the ground.

"Hansel, why are you always stopping and looking around?" asked the father. "Keep going!"

"I'm looking at my little pigeon that's sitting on the roof and wants to say good-bye to me," Hansel answered.

"Fool!" the woman said. "That's not your little pigeon. It's the morning sun shining on the chimney."

But little by little Hansel managed to scatter all the bread crumbs on the path. The woman led the children even deeper into the forest until they came to a spot they had never in their lives seen before. Once again a large fire was made, and the mother said, "Just keep sitting here, children. If you get tired, you can sleep a little. We're going into the forest to chop wood, and in the evening, when we're done, we'll come and get you."

When noon came, Gretel shared her bread with Hansel, who had scattered his along the way. Then they fell asleep, and evening passed, but no one came for the poor children. Only when it was pitch black did they finally wake up, and Hansel comforted his little sister by saying," Just wait until the moon has risen, Gretel. Then we'll see the little bread crumbs that I scattered. They'll show us the way back home."

When the moon rose, they set out but could not find the crumbs, because the many thousands of birds that fly about in the forest and fields had devoured them.

"Don't worry, we'll find the way," Hansel said to Gretel, but they could not find it. They walked the entire night and all the next day as well, from morning till night, but they did not get out of the forest. They were now also very hungry, for they had had nothing to eat except some berries that they had found growing on the ground. Eventually they became so tired that their legs would no longer carry them, and they lay down beneath a tree and fell asleep.

It was now the third morning since they had left their father's house. They began walking again, and they kept going deeper and deeper into the forest. If help did not arrive soon, they were bound to perish of hunger and exhaustion. At noon they saw a beautiful bird as white as snow sitting on a branch. It sang with such a lovely voice that the children stood still and listened to it. When the bird finished its song, it flapped its wings and flew ahead of them. They followed it until they came to a little house that was made of bread. Moreover, it had cake for a roof and pure sugar for windows.

"What a blessed meal!" said Hansel. "Let's have a taste. I want to eat a piece of the roof. Gretel, you can have some of the window, since it's sweet."

Hansel reached up high and broke off a piece of the roof to see how it tasted, and Gretel leaned against the windowpanes and nibbled on them. Then they heard a shrill voice cry out from inside:

"Nibble, nibble, I hear a mouse.
Who's that nibbling at my house?"

The children answered:

"The wind, the wind; it's very mild,
blowing like the Heavenly Child."

And they did not bother to stop eating or let themselves be distracted. Since the roof tasted so good, Hansel ripped off a large piece and pulled it down, while Gretel pushed out a round piece of the windowpane, sat down, and ate it with great relish. Suddenly the door opened, and a very old woman leaning on a crutch came slinking out of the house. Hansel and Gretel were so tremendously frightened that they dropped what they had in their hands. But the old woman wagged her head and said, "Well now, dear children, who brought you here? Just come inside and stay with me. Nobody's going to harm you."

She took them both by the hand and led them into her house. Then she served them a good meal of milk and pancakes with sugar and apples and nuts. Afterward she made up two little beds with white sheets, whereupon Hansel and Gretel lay down in them and thought they were in heaven.

The old woman, however, had only pretended to be friendly. She was really a wicked witch on the lookout for children, and had built the house made of bread only to lure them to her. As soon as she had any children in her power, she would kill, cook, and eat them. It would be like a feast day for her. Now, witches have red eyes and cannot see very far, but they have a keen sense of smell, like animals, and can detect when human beings are near them. Therefore, when Hansel and Gretel had come into her vicinity, she had laughed wickedly and scoffed, "They're mine! They'll never get away from me!"

Early the next morning, before the children were awake, she got up and looked at the two of them sleeping so sweetly with full rosy cheeks. Then she muttered to herself, "They'll certainly make for a tasty meal!"

She seized Hansel with her scrawny hands and carried him into a small pen, where she locked him up behind a grilled door. No matter how much he screamed, it did not help. Then she went back to Gretel, shook her until she woke up, and yelled, "Get up, you lazybones! I want you to fetch some water and cook your brother something nice. He's sitting outside in a pen, and we've got to fatten him up. Then, when he's fat enough, I'm going to eat him."

Gretel began to weep bitter tears, but they were all in vain. She had to do what the wicked witch demanded. So the very best food was cooked for poor Hansel, while Gretel got nothing but crab shells. Every morning the old woman went slinking to the little pen and called out, "Hansel, stick out your finger so I can feel how fat you are."

However, Hansel stuck out a little bone, and since the old woman had poor eyesight, she thought the bone was Hansel's finger. She was puzzled that Hansel did not get any fatter, and when a month had gone by and Hansel still seemed to be thin, she was overcome by her impatience and decided not to wait any longer.

"Hey there, Gretel!" she called to the little girl. "Get a move on and fetch some water! I don't care whether Hansel's fat or thin. He's going to be slaughtered tomorrow, and then I'll cook him."

Oh, how the poor little sister wailed as she was carrying the water, and how the tears streamed down her cheeks!

"Dear God, help us!" she exclaimed. "If only the wild beasts had eaten us in the forest, then we could have at least died together!"

Early the next morning Gretel had to go out, hang up a kettle full of water, and light the fire.

"First we'll bake," the old woman said. "I've already heated the oven and kneaded the dough." She pushed poor Gretel out to the oven, where the flames were leaping from the fire. "Crawl inside," said the witch, "and see if it's properly heated so we can slide the bread in."

The witch intended to close the oven door once Gretel had climbed inside, for the witch wanted to bake her and eat her too. But Gretel sensed what she had in mind and said, "I don't know how to do it. How do I get in?"

"You stupid goose," the old woman said. "The opening's large enough. Watch, even I can get in!"

She waddled up to the oven and stuck her head through the oven door. Then Gretel gave her a push that sent her flying inside and shut the iron door and bolted it. *Whew!* The witch began to howl dreadfully, but Gretel ran away, and the godless witch was miserably burned to death.

Meanwhile, Gretel ran straight to Hansel, opened the pen, and cried out, "Hansel, we're saved! The old witch is dead!"

Then Hansel jumped out of the pen like a bird that hops out of a cage when the door is opened. My how happy they were! They hugged each other, danced around, and kissed. Since they no longer had anything to fear, they went into the witch's house, and there they found chests filled with pearls and jewels all over the place.

"They're certainly much better than pebbles," said Hansel, and he put whatever he could fit into his pockets, and Gretel said, "I'm going to carry some home too," and she filled her apron full of jewels and pearls.

"We'd better be on our way now," said Hansel, "so we can get out of the witch's forest."

When they had walked for a few hours, they reached a large river.

"We can't get across," said Hansel. "I don't see a bridge or any way over it."

"There are no boats either," Gretel responded, "but there's a white duck swimming over there. It's bound to help us across if I ask it." Then she cried out:

"Help us, help us, little duck!
It's Hansel and Gretel, and we're really stuck.
We can't get over, try as we may.
Please take us across right away!"

The little duck came swimming up to them, and Hansel got on top of its back and told his sister to sit down beside him.

"No," Gretel answered. "That will be too heavy for the little duck. Let it carry us across one at a time."

The kind little duck did just that, and when they were safely across and had walked on for some time, the forest became more and more familiar to them, and finally they caught sight of their father's house from afar. They began to run at once, and soon rushed into the house and threw themselves around their father's neck. The man had not had a single happy hour since he had abandoned his children in the forest, and in the meantime his wife had died. Gretel opened and shook out her apron so that the pearls and jewels bounced about the room, and Hansel added to this by throwing one handful after another from his pocket. Now all their troubles were over, and they lived together in utmost joy.

My tale is done. See the mouse run. Catch it, whoever can, and then you can make a great big cap out of its fur.

◆ 16 ◆

The Three Snake Leaves

ONCE UPON A TIME there was a poor man who could no longer provide enough food for his only son. Therefore, the son said, "Dear Father, you're having such a hard time and I'm becoming such a burden that I'd prefer to go away and try to earn a living by myself." The father gave him his blessing but was greatly saddened to see him depart.

The king of a powerful country was waging war when all this occurred, and the young man enlisted in the king's army and went out to fight. When he approached enemy territory, a battle was being fought, and there was a great deal of danger. The air was filled with bullets striking his comrades, who fell dead on all sides. When the commander as well was killed, the survivors wanted to flee the field, but the young man stepped forward and encouraged them to keep fighting.

"We shall not let our fatherland be destroyed!" he cried out.

The others followed him as he charged forward, and they defeated the enemy. When the king heard that he owed this victory to the young man alone, he promoted him above all the others, gave him great treasures, and made him the most important person in his kingdom.

The king had a daughter who was very beautiful but also very strange, for she had made a vow that she would accept as her lord and master only a man who would let himself be buried alive with her if she should die first.

"If he really loves me with all his heart," she said, "why would he want to continue living?"

She was prepared to do the same in return, and if he were to die first, she would let herself be buried in the grave with him. This strange vow had scared away all suitors up to that time, but the young man was so infatuated by her beauty that he did not care about anything else and asked her father for her hand.

"Do you know what you must promise?" the king asked.

"I shall have to be buried alive in her grave if I survive her," the young man said. "But my love for her is so great that I don't care about the danger."

The king gave his consent, and the wedding was celebrated with great splendor. After this the couple lived happily and were contented with each other for some time. But then the young queen fell seriously ill, and no doctor could help her. When she lay dead, the young king remembered the promise he had been obliged to make, and he shuddered at the thought of being buried alive. However, there was no escape. The old king had had all the gates posted with guards, and it was impossible for his son-in-law to avoid what fate had in store for him. When the day came for the queen's body to be buried in the royal vault, he was led down into the crypt with it, and the door was bolted and locked behind him.

In the vault, next to the coffin, was a table, and on it were four candles, four loaves of bread, and four bottles of wine. As soon as the provisions were used up, the young man would perish from starvation. So there he sat, full of sorrow and grief. Each day he ate just a little bit of bread and drank just a swig of wine. Yet, he saw death coming closer and closer. Once, as he was staring into space, he saw a snake crawling from a corner of the vault and heading toward the dead body. Since he thought the snake was coming to gnaw at the body, he drew his sword and said, "As long as I live, you shall not touch her." And he cut the snake into three pieces. After a while another snake came crawling out of the corner, but when it saw the first one lying dead and cut to pieces, it went back to where it came from. It returned shortly, however, with three green leaves in its mouth, and it proceeded to take the three pieces of the snake, put them in their proper places, and set one leaf on each of the wounds. All at once the pieces that had been severed came back to life, and both snakes hurried off together. The leaves remained on the ground, and it occurred to the unfortunate young man, who had witnessed the whole thing, that the miraculous power of the leaves that had brought the snake back to life might also be able to help a human being. So he picked up the leaves and placed one on his dead wife's mouth, and the other two on her eyes. No sooner had he done this than the blood began to stir in her veins, rose up into her pale face, and gave her cheeks a rosy color. Then she took a deep breath, opened her eyes, and said, "Oh, God, where am I?"

"You're with me, dear wife," he answered, and he told her how everything had happened and how he had brought her back to life. Then he handed her some of the wine and bread, and when she had regained her strength, she stood up, and they went to the door. There they knocked and yelled so loudly that the guards heard them and reported it to the king. The king himself then came and opened the door. When he found them alive and well, he rejoiced with them and was glad that their troubles were over.

The young king took the three snake leaves, gave them to a servant, and said, "Take good care of them for me and carry them with you at all times. If we find ourselves in a predicament, they might be able to help us."

Meanwhile, a change had come over his wife after she had been restored to life. It was as if all the love she had felt for her husband had been drained from her. When some time had gone by and he wished to make a voyage overseas to visit his old father, they boarded a ship, but she, having forgotten the great love and devotion he had shown her at the time of her rescue, gave in to her wicked passion for the ship's captain. Then one night, when the young king was lying asleep, she called the captain. After she took her sleeping husband by the head, she ordered the captain to take his feet, and they threw him overboard into the sea. Once they had done their shameful deed, she said, "Now let us return home and say he died on the way. I'll rave about you and praise you so much that my father will let you marry me and make you heir to his crown."

However, the faithful servant had witnessed everything. He unfastened a small boat from the ship without their noticing it, got into it, and sailed after his master, while the traitors continued their voyage. He fished the dead man out of the sea, and with the help of the snake leaves, which he was carrying with him, and which he put on his master's eyes and mouth, he succeeded in bringing him back to life.

Now the two of them rowed day and night with all their might, and their little boat sailed so swiftly over the sea that they reached the old king before the others. The king was puzzled when he saw them coming back alone, and he asked what had happened to them. When he learned about his daughter's treachery, he said, "I can't believe she would do such an awful thing, but the truth will soon come to light."

He ordered the young king and his servant to hide in a secret chamber and not to let themselves be seen by anyone. Soon after, the big ship came sailing home, and the godless woman appeared before her father with a troubled expression.

"Why have you come home alone?" he asked. "Where's your husband?"

"Ah, dear Father," she answered. "I'm returning home in great sorrow. My husband suddenly took sick and died during the voyage, and if it had not been for the support of the good captain, things would have gone badly for me. He was present at my husband's death and can tell you everything."

But the king said, "I'm going to bring the dead man back to life," and he opened the chamber door and told the two to come out.

When the king's daughter caught sight of her husband, she was thunderstruck, and falling to her knees, she begged for mercy.

"There will be no mercy," said the old king. "He was ready to die with you and brought you back to life, but you killed him in his sleep, and now you shall receive your just reward."

Then she and her accomplice were put aboard a ship peppered with holes and sent out to sea, where they soon sank beneath the waves.

◈ 17 ◈

The White Snake

A LONG TIME AGO there lived a king who was famous throughout the entire country for his wisdom. Nothing remained hidden from him, and it seemed as if he could obtain news of the most secret things through the air. However, he had one strange custom. Every day at noon, after the table was cleared of food and nobody else was present, a trusted servant had to bring him one more dish. This dish was always covered, and the servant himself did not know what was in it, nor did anyone else, for the king did not take the cover from the dish and eat until he was all alone. The king continued this custom for quite some time, until one day the servant, while removing the dish, was overcome by curiosity. He took it into his room, and after he had carefully locked the door, he lifted the cover and found a white snake lying inside. Once he laid eyes on it, though, he had an irresistible desire to taste it. So he cut off a little piece and put it in his mouth. No sooner did his tongue touch it than he heard a strange whispering of exquisite voices outside his window. He went over to it to listen and noticed some sparrows talking to one another, telling what they had seen in the fields and forest. Tasting the snake had given him the power to understand the language of animals.

Now, it so happened that on this very day the queen lost her most beautiful ring, and the trusted servant was suspected of committing the theft because he had access to everything. The king summoned the servant and with harsh words threatened him, saying that if he was not able to name the guilty person by morning, he himself would be considered the thief and would be executed. It was to no avail that the servant protested his innocence, for he was given a curt dismissal.

Distressed and afraid, he went down into the courtyard and tried to think of a way out of his predicament. Some ducks were peacefully sitting and resting by a running brook, preening themselves and chatting in a confidential tone. The servant stopped and listened to them as they told each other where they had been waddling about all morning and what good pickings they had found. But one of the ducks was irritable and said, "There's something heavy in my stomach. I was eating too fast and swallowed a ring that was lying under the king's window."

Right away the servant grabbed the duck by its neck, carried it into the kitchen, and said to the cook, "This one's well-fed. It's time you killed it!"

"All right," said the cook, weighing it in his hands. "It certainly hasn't been shy about stuffing itself. Besides, it's been waiting long enough for its roasting."

So he cut off the duck's neck, and when it was being cleaned, the queen's ring was found in its stomach. Now the servant could easily prove his innocence, and since the king wanted to make amends for having wronged his servant, he granted him a favor and promised him whatever royal post of honor he desired. The servant declined all of this. His only request was for a horse and some travel money, for he had a desire to travel about for a while and see the world.

When his wish had been granted, he set out on his way, and one day, as he was passing a pond, he noticed three fish trapped in the reeds and gasping for water. Though it is said that fish cannot talk, he heard them crying in distress and wailing that they had to die so miserably. Since he felt sorry for them, he got down from his horse and put the three trapped fish back into the water. They wriggled for joy, stuck their heads out of the water, and cried out to him, "We'll remember you for saving our lives, and one day we'll repay you."

He rode on, and a while later it seemed to him that he heard a voice in the sand at his feet. He listened and heard an ant king complaining, "If only people with their clumsy beasts would keep away from us! That stupid horse is mercilessly trampling my people to death with his heavy hooves!"

The servant turned his horse onto a side path, and the ant king cried out to him, "We'll remember this, and one day we'll repay you."

The servant's path led into a forest, and there he saw a father and mother raven standing near their nest and pushing their young ones out of the nest.

"Get out! You're nothing but freeloaders!" they were exclaiming. "We can't find enough food to feed you anymore, and now you're big enough to feed yourselves."

The poor young birds lay on the ground, flapped their wings, and began crying, "We're just helpless children! How are we supposed to feed ourselves when we can't fly? All we can do is stay here and starve."

Then the kind young man dismounted, killed his horse with his sword, and left it for the young ravens to feed on. They hopped over to the horse, ate their fill, and cried out, "We'll remember this, and one day we'll repay you."

Now the servant had to use his own legs. After he had walked a long way, he reached a big city where there was a great deal of noise and a large crowd in the streets. A man on horseback rode by and announced that the king's daughter was looking for a husband, but whoever declared himself a suitor would have to perform a difficult task, and if he did not complete it successfully, he would forfeit his life. Many men had already tried and had risked their lives in vain. When the young man saw the princess, he was so dazzled by her great beauty that he forgot all about the danger, went before the king, and declared himself a suitor. He was promptly led to the sea, and a gold ring was thrown into it before his eyes. The king told him that he was to fetch the ring from the depths of the sea, and he added, "If you come up without it, you'll be continually pushed back down until you perish in the waves."

Everyone felt sorry for the handsome young man and left him alone by the sea. He was standing on the shore thinking about what to do when he suddenly saw three fish swimming toward him. They were none other than the three fish whose lives he had saved. The one in the middle held a shell in its mouth, which it set down on the beach at the feet of the young man, who picked it up. When he opened the shell, he found the gold ring, and bursting with joy, he brought it to the king expecting that he would receive the promised reward. But when the proud king's daughter discovered that he was not her equal in birth, she scorned him and demanded that he first perform another task. She went down into the garden, and she herself scattered ten sacks full of millet in the grass.

"He must pick them all up before the sun rises tomorrow," she said. "And not a single grain may be missing."

The young man sat down in the garden and tried to think of a way to accomplish the task, but nothing occurred to him, and he sat there quite sadly, expecting to be led to his death at the break of dawn. But when the first rays of the sun fell on the garden, he saw ten sacks all filled to the top and standing side by side. Not a single grain was missing. The ant king had come during the night with thousands and thousands of ants, and the grateful insects had picked up the millet seeds with great diligence and gathered them into the sacks. The princess herself went down to the garden and was amazed to see that the young man had accomplished the task. But her proud heart could not be tamed, and she said, "Even if he has accomplished the first two tasks, he shall not become my husband until he has brought me an apple from the Tree of Life."

The young man did not know where the Tree of Life was. Therefore, he set out with the intention of going as far as his legs could carry him, even though he had no hope of finding it. One evening, after he had traveled through three kingdoms and reached a forest, he sat down beneath a tree and wanted to sleep. But he heard a noise in the tree, and a golden apple fell into his hand. At the same time three ravens flew down to him, landed on his knees, and said, "We're the three young ravens whom you saved from starvation. When we grew up, we heard you were looking for the golden apple. So we flew across the sea to the end of the world, where the Tree of Life is standing, and we've fetched the apple."

Now the young man was full of joy and started on his way home. He brought the golden apple to the beautiful princess, who no longer had any excuses to make. They divided the apple of life and ate it together, and her heart filled with love for him. In time they reached a ripe old age in peace and happiness.

◆ 18 ◆

The Straw, the Coal, and the Bean

THERE ONCE WAS A POOR OLD WOMAN who lived in a village, and she had gathered a bunch of beans that she wanted to cook. So she prepared a fire on her hearth, lighting it with a handful of straw to make it burn faster. As she was emptying the beans into the pot, one of them slipped to the floor unnoticed and lay next to a straw. Soon after, a glowing coal jumped from the hearth and joined the other two. Then the straw began to speak. "Dear friends, where have you come from?"

"Fortunately, I jumped out of the fire," responded the coal. "If I hadn't used sheer force, it would have been the end of me. I would have been burned to ashes."

"I also escaped by the skin of my teeth," said the bean. "If the old woman had thrown me into the pot, I'd have been cooked into a soup without mercy like my comrades."

"Do you think my fate would have been any better?" said the straw. "The old woman let all my brothers burn up in smoke. She grabbed sixty all at once and put them to death. Fortunately, I slipped through her fingers."

"Well, what should we do now?" asked the coal.

"Since we were so lucky to escape death, I think we should stick together like good comrades," the bean said. "Also we'd better begin heading for a foreign country before there's a new fatality."

This proposal pleased the other two, and they set out on their way. However, they soon came to a small brook, and since there was no bridge or way over it, they did not know how they would manage to cross it. Then the straw came up with a good idea and said, "I'll lay myself across, and then you'll be able to walk over me like a bridge."

So the straw stretched itself from one bank to the other, and the coal, who had a fiery temperament, marched boldly onto the newly built bridge. Yet, when it was halfway across and heard the water murmuring below, it got frightened, stopped in its tracks, and did not dare go any further. But now the straw began to burn, broke in two pieces, and fell into the brook. The coal tumbled after, and as it hit the water, it gave up the ghost. The bean, which had cautiously stayed behind, had to laugh when it saw what happened, but it was unable to stop and kept laughing so hard that it burst. Now, it would have been all over for the bean were it not for a traveling tailor who had been resting near the brook. He felt so sorry for the bean that he took out his needle and thread and sewed the bean together. The bean thanked him most kindly, but because the tailor had used black thread, all beans since then have had a black seam.

◆ 19 ◆

The Fisherman and His Wife

ONCE UPON A TIME there was a fisherman who lived with his wife in a dirty hovel near the sea. Every day the fisherman went out to fish, and all he did was fish and fish. One day he was sitting with his line and gazing into the clear water. And all he did was sit and sit. Suddenly his line sank deep down to the bottom, and when he pulled it up, he had a large flounder on the line, and the flounder said to him, "Listen here, fisherman, I beg of you, let me live. I'm not a real flounder but an enchanted prince. So what would it benefit you to kill me? I certainly wouldn't taste very good. Put me back into the water, and let me go."

"Hold on," said the man. "You don't have to waste your words on me. I would have thrown a talking fish back into the water anyway."

He then put the fish back into the clear water, and the flounder swam to the bottom, leaving behind a long streak of blood. Then the fisherman stood up and went to the hovel to be with his wife.

"Husband," asked the wife, "didn't you catch anything today?"

"No," said the man. "I caught a flounder, but he said he was an enchanted prince, and I let him go."

"Didn't you wish for anything?" asked the wife.

"No," said the husband. "What should I have wished for?"

"Ah," said the wife. "Don't you think it's awful that we've got to keep living in such a hovel? It stinks, and it's disgusting. You should have wished for a little cottage. Go back and call him. Tell him we want a little cottage. I'm sure he'll give us one."

"But there's no reason to go back," said the husband.

"Of course there is," said the wife. "Look, you caught him and let him go. That's why he's bound to give it to us. Now go at once!"

The man really did not want to go, but neither did he want to oppose his wife. So he went back to the sea.

When he got there, the sea was very green and yellow and no longer so clear. He stood on the shore and said:

"Flounder, flounder, in the sea,
if you're a man, then speak to me.
Though I do not care for my wife's request,
I've come to ask it nonetheless."

The flounder came swimming up to him and said, "Well, what does she want?"

"Oh," said the man. "My wife thinks I should have wished for something because I caught you. Since she doesn't want to live in a hovel, she'd like to have a cottage."

"Just go home," said the flounder. "She's already got it."

When the fisherman arrived at home, his wife was no longer sitting in a hovel. Instead, she was sitting on a bench before the door to a little cottage. His wife took him by the hand and said, "Come inside, husband. Look! Now, isn't this better?"

They went inside, and in the house he found a little hallway, a splendid parlor, and a bedroom. There was also a kitchen and a pantry furnished with all the best dishware and utensils, tinware and brass, everything that one could possibly need. Behind the cottage was a little yard with chickens and ducks and a garden with vegetables and fruit.

"You see," said the wife, "isn't this nice?"

"Yes," said the husband. "Hopefully, it will stay that way. Now we can live quite happily."

"That's something we've got to think about," said the wife.

Thereupon they had something to eat and went to bed.

Everything went well for about a week or two, and then the wife said, "Listen, husband, the cottage is much too cramped, and the yard and garden are too small. The flounder could have given us a larger house. I'd very much like to live in a great stone castle. Go back to the flounder and tell him to give us a castle."

"Ah, wife," the husband said, "the cottage is good enough. Why should we want to live in a castle?"

"My goodness!" said the wife. "Just go back to him! The flounder can do this without any trouble."

"No, wife," said the husband. "The flounder has just given us a cottage, and I don't want to go back again so soon. He might be insulted."

"Just go!" said the wife. "He can easily do it, and he'll be glad to do it. Just go back to him!"

The husband's heart grew heavy, and he did not want to go. He said to himself, "It just isn't right." Nevertheless, he went.

When he got to the sea, the water was purple, dark blue, gray, and dense. It was no longer green and yellow, though it was still calm. Then he stood there and said:

"Flounder, flounder, in the sea,
if you're a man, then speak to me.
Though I do not care for my wife's request,
I've come to ask it nonetheless."

"Well, what does she want?" the flounder asked.

"Oh," said the man, somewhat distressed. "She wants to live in a great stone castle."

"Just go home. She's already standing at the gate," the flounder said.

The man went back, thinking he was going home, but as he approached the spot where the house had been, he found a great stone palace, and his wife was standing on the steps just about to enter. She took him by the hand and said, "Come inside."

He went in with her and found a big front hall with a marble floor and numerous servants who opened the large doors for them. The walls were all bright and covered with beautiful tapestries. All of the chairs and tables in the rooms were made of gold. Crystal chandeliers hung from the ceilings, and all the rooms and chambers had carpets. Furthermore, the tables sagged under the weight of food and bottles of the very best wine. Behind the palace was a huge yard with stables for horses and cows and the finest carriages. There was also a wonderful large garden with the most beautiful flowers and fine fruit trees, as well as a pleasure park about half a mile long, which had stags, deer, hares, and everything else in it that one could wish for.

"Well," said the wife, "isn't that beautiful?"

"Oh, yes," said the husband. "Hopefully, it will stay that way. Now let's live in the beautiful castle and be content."

"We'll have to think about that," said the wife, "and sleep on it."

Then they went to bed.

The next morning the wife woke up first. It was just daybreak, and from her window she could see the glorious countryside lying before her. As her husband began stretching she poked him in the side with her elbow and said, "Husband, get up and look out the window. Listen, don't you think you can be king over all this country? Go to the flounder and tell him that we want to be king."

"Ah, wife," said the husband. "Why should we be king? I don't want to be king."

"Well," said the wife, "you may not want to be king, but I do. Go to the flounder, and tell him I want to be king."

"Oh, wife," said the husband, "why do you want to be king? I don't want to tell him that."

"Why not?" said the wife. "Go to him at once and tell him I must be king!"

The husband went but was most distressed that his wife wanted to be king. It's not right. It's just not right, he thought, and he did not want to go but went just the same.

When he got to the sea, it was completely gray and black, and the water was twisting and turning from below and smelled putrid. The fisherman stood there and said:

"Flounder, flounder, in the sea,
if you're a man, then speak to me.
Though I do not care for my wife's request,
I've come to ask it nonetheless."

"Well, what does she want?" asked the flounder.
"Oh," said the man. "She wants to be king."
"Go back home," said the flounder. "She's already king."

Then the man went home, and as he approached the palace, he saw that the castle had become much larger, with a huge tower and glistening ornaments on it. There were sentries standing in front of the gate, along with many soldiers, drums, and trumpets. When he entered the palace, he found that everything was made of pure marble and gold and had velvet covers with large golden tassles. The doors to the hall were opened, and he could see the whole court. His wife was sitting on a high throne of gold and diamonds, and on her head she had a big golden crown and in her hand a scepter of pure gold and jewels. Two rows of ladies-in-waiting were standing on either side of her, each lady a head shorter than the next. The fisherman stepped forward and said, "Oh, wife, now you're king, aren't you?"

"Yes," said his wife, "now I am king."

He stood there and looked at her, and after he had gazed at her for some time, he said, "Oh, wife, it's wonderful that you're king! Now let's not wish for anything more."

"No, husband," the wife said as she became very restless. "I have too much time on my hands, and I can't stand it anymore. Go back to the flounder and tell him I'm king, but now I must become emperor as well."

"Oh, wife," said the husband, "why do you want to become emperor?"

"Husband," she said. "Go to the flounder. I want to be emperor!"

"Oh, wife," the husband said. "He can't make you emperor. I don't want to tell that to the flounder. There's only one emperor in the empire. The flounder can't make you emperor. He definitely can't do that."

"What!" said the wife. "I'm king, and you're just my husband. I want you to go there at once! And I mean, at once! If he can make a king, he can also make an emperor. Go to there at once!"

The husband had to return, but as he walked along, he became scared and thought to himself, This won't turn out well at all. Such arrogance, to want to be emperor! The flounder's going to get sick and tired of this.

When he got to the sea, it was all black and dense, and it began to twist and turn from below so that bubbles rose up, and a strong wind

whipped across the surface and made the water curdle. The man became frightened, but he stepped forward and said:

"Flounder, flounder, in the sea,
if you're a man, then speak to me.
Though I do not care for my wife's request,
I've come to ask it nonetheless."

"Well, what does she want?" asked the flounder.

"Oh, flounder," he said. "My wife wants to be emperor."

"Go back home," said the flounder. "She's already emperor."

Then the man went home, and when he arrived, the entire castle was made of polished marble with alabaster figures and golden ornaments. Soldiers were marching in front of the gate, and they were blowing trumpets and beating cymbals and drums. Meanwhile, barons, counts, and dukes were inside the palace walking around like servants. They opened the doors of pure gold for him, and as he entered, he saw his wife sitting on a two-mile-high throne made from a single piece of gold. She was wearing a golden crown three yards tall and covered with diamonds and garnets. In one hand she held the scepter and in the other the imperial globe. She was flanked on either side by two rows of bodyguards, each man shorter than the next, beginning with a tremendous giant two miles tall and ending with the tiniest dwarf, who was no bigger than my pinky. There were also many princes and dukes standing before her, and her husband stepped up and said, "Wife, now you're emperor, aren't you?"

"Yes," she said, "I'm emperor."

Then he stood there and took a good look at her, and after gazing at her for some time, he said, "Oh, wife, it's wonderful that you're emperor. Let's keep it that way."

"Husband," she said. "Why are you standing there? It's true that I'm emperor, but now I want to be pope. Go and tell this to the flounder."

"Oh, wife," said the husband. "What, in heaven's name, don't you want? You can't be pope. There's only one pope in Christendom. The flounder can't make you pope."

"Husband," she said. "I want to be pope! Go there at once and tell him I must be pope."

"No, wife," said the husband. "I don't want to tell him that. It won't turn out well. That's too much to ask. The flounder can't make you pope."

"Stop talking nonsense, husband!" said the wife. "If he can make me emperor, he can also make me pope. Go there at once! I'm the emperor, and you're just my husband. So, do as I say!"

The man became frightened and went, but he felt rather queasy. He was trembling and shaking, and his knees began to wobble. A strong wind swept across the land. Dark clouds flew by as evening came. Leaves were falling from the trees, and the sea rose up in waves and roared as if it were boiling, and the waves splashed against the shore. In the distance the fisherman could see ships firing guns in distress as they were tossed up and down by the waves. Though there was still a little blue in the middle of the sky, the horizon was completely red, as if a heavy thunderstorm were coming. Then he stepped forward, filled with fear and dread, and said:

"Flounder, flounder, in the sea
if you're a man, then speak to me.
Though I do not care for my wife's request,
I've come to ask it nonetheless."

"Well, what does she want?" asked the flounder.

"Oh," the man said, "she wants to be pope."

"Go back home," said the flounder. "She's already pope."

Then the man went home, and when he arrived, he found a great church with nothing but palaces surrounding it. He forced his way through crowds of people and found everything inside illuminated by thousands and thousands of candles. His wife was sitting on a throne even higher than the one before, and she was dressed in pure gold with three big golden crowns on her head. Numerous bishops and priests were standing around her, and there were two rows of candles on either side of her. The biggest candle was as thick and as large as the highest tower, and the tiniest was a church candle. And all the emperors and kings were taking their turn kneeling before her and kissing her slipper.

"Wife," the man said as he looked at her carefully, "now you're pope, aren't you?"

"Yes," she said, "I'm pope."

Then he stepped forward and took a good look at her, and it was as if he were looking into the bright sun. After gazing at her for some time, he said, "Oh, wife, it's wonderful that you're pope. Let's keep it that way."

But she sat stiff as a board and neither stirred nor moved. Then he said, "Wife, be satisfied. Now that you're pope, you can't become anything greater."

"I'll think about it," said the wife.

Then they both went to bed, but she was not satisfied, and her ambition did not let her sleep. She kept thinking of ways she might become greater than she was, while her husband slept soundly, for he had run around a good deal that day. She could not get to sleep at all and tossed and turned from side to side the whole night, trying to think of ways she might become greater than she was. However, nothing whatsoever occurred to her. When the sun began to rise and she saw the red glow of the dawn, she sat up in bed and watched the sun rise from her window. Then the thought occurred to her: Aha, I could also make the sun and the moon rise! She poked her husband in the ribs with her elbow and said, "Husband, wake up and go to the flounder. Tell him I want to be like God."

The husband was still half asleep, but he was so shocked by what she had said that he fell out of the bed. He thought that he had misheard her and rubbed his eyes.

"Oh, wife," he said. "What did you say?"

"Husband," she said, "if I can't make the sun and the moon rise, I won't be able to bear it. Do you think I want to just watch? No, I won't have any more peace until I myself can make them rise."

She gave her husband such an awful look that a shudder ran through his bones.

"Go there at once! I want to be like God."

"Oh, wife!" the husband said, and fell down on his knees. "The flounder can't do that. He can make you an emperor and pope, but I beg you, be content and stay pope."

She immediately became furious, and her hair flew wildly about her head. She tore open her bodice, gave him a kick with her foot, and screamed, "I won't stand for it and can't stand it any longer! I want you to go at once!"

He slipped into his trousers then and ran off like a madman. Outside a great storm was raging, so he could barely keep on his feet. Houses and trees were falling, mountains were trembling, and large boulders were rolling into the sea from the cliffs. The sky was completely pitch black, and there was thunder and lightning. Black waves rose up in the sea as high as church steeples and mountains, and they all had crests of white foam on top. Then the fisherman screamed, but he could not even hear his own words:

"Flounder, flounder, in the sea,
if you're a man, then speak to me.
Though I do not care for my wife's request,
I've come to ask it nonetheless."

"Well, what does she want?" the flounder asked.

"Oh," he said, "she wants to be like God."

"Go back home. She's sitting in your hovel again."

And there they are still living this very day.

The Brave Little Tailor

ONE SUMMER MORNING a little tailor was sitting on his table by his window. He was in good spirits and was sewing with all his might. Just then a peasant woman came down the street and cried out, "Good jam for sale! Good jam for sale!"

That sounded lovely to the little tailor's ears. He stuck his tiny head out the window and called, "Up here, my dear woman, you're sure to make a good sale with me!"

The woman, with her heavy basket, climbed the three flights of stairs to the tailor's place and had to unpack all her jars in front of him. He inspected each one of them by lifting and sniffing the jam. Finally, he said, "The jam seems good to me. I'll take three ounces, dear woman, but if it comes to a quarter of a pound, it won't matter."

The woman, who had hoped to sell a great deal, gave him what he wanted but went away very annoyed and grumbling.

"Now, may God bless my jam!" the little tailor exclaimed. "Let it give me energy and strength!" He fetched a loaf of bread from the cupboard, cut a full slice for himself, and spread it with the jam. "This certainly won't have a bitter taste," he said. "But first I want to finish the jacket before I take a bite."

He put the bread down beside him and continued sewing, making bigger and bigger stitches due to his joy. Meanwhile, the smell of the sweet jam rose to the wall, where lots of flies had gathered and were now enticed by the smell to swarm and settle on the jam.

"Hey, who invited you?" the little tailor said, and chased the unwelcome guests away. But the flies did not understand German, nor would they let themselves be deterred. Rather, they kept coming back in even larger numbers. Finally, the little tailor had been needled enough, as they say, and he grabbed a piece of cloth from under his worktable.

"Wait, I'll give you something!" he said, swinging at them mercilessly. When he let up and counted, there were no less than seven flies lying dead before him with their legs stretched out.

"You're quite a man!" he said to himself, and could not help but admire his bravery. "The entire city should know about this!" And the little tailor hastily cut out a belt for himself, stitched it, and embroidered large letters on it: "Seven with one blow!"

"But why just the city?" he continued. "Why shouldn't the whole world know about it?" And his heart wagged with joy like a lamb's tail.

The tailor tied the belt around his waist, and since he now thought that his bravery was too great for his workshop, he decided to go out into the world. Before he left, he searched his house for something to take with him, but he found only a piece of old cheese, which he put in his pocket. Outside the city gate he noticed a bird caught in the bushes, and the bird too found its way into his pocket. Now he bravely hit the road with his legs and pushed on. Since he was light and nimble, he did not become tired. His way led him up a mountain, and when he reached the highest peak, he came across a powerful giant who was sitting there comfortably and gazing about. The little tailor went up to him, addressed him fearlessly, and said, "Good day, friend, you're sitting there and gazing at the great wide world, right? Well, I happen to be on my way into the world to try my luck. Would you like to come along?"

The giant looked at the tailor contemptuously and said, "You crumb! You miserable creature!"

"Is that so!" the little tailor responded, and opened his coat to show the giant his belt. "You can read for yourself what kind of man I am!"

The giant read "Seven with one blow!" and thought that it meant the tailor had slain seven men. Therefore, he began to show some respect for the little fellow. Nevertheless, he wanted to test him first. So he took a stone in his hand and squeezed it until water began to drip from it.

"Do the same," said the giant, "if you have the strength."

"Is that all?" the little tailor said. "That's just child's play for a man like me."

He reached into his pocket, took out the soft cheese, and squeezed it until the liquid ran out.

"That beats yours, doesn't it?" the tailor declared.

The giant did not know what to say, for he could not believe that such a little man was so strong. Next he picked up a stone and threw it so high that it could barely be seen with the naked eye.

"Now, you do the same, you midget!"

"That was a good throw," said the tailor, "but even so, the stone had to return to the ground in the end. Now, I'm going to throw one that won't ever come back."

He reached into his pocket, took out the bird, and threw it into the air. The bird was glad to be free and just kept climbing high in the sky and never returned.

"How did you like that little show, friend?" the tailor asked.

"You certainly can throw," the giant said. "But let's see if you can carry a decent load."

He led the little tailor to a tremendous oak tree that had been cut down and was lying on the ground.

"If you're strong enough," he said, "help me carry the tree out of the forest."

"Gladly," answered the little man. "You take the trunk on your shoulder, and I'll carry the branches and the twigs. After all, they're the heaviest."

The giant lifted the trunk onto his shoulder, while the tailor sat down on a branch. Since the giant could not turn to look around, he had to carry the entire tree and the little tailor as well. Of course, the tailor was feeling good and was quite merry in the rear, so he began to whistle a little song called "Three Little Tailors Who Went Out for a Ride," as if carrying a tree were child's play. After the giant had carried the heavy load a good part of the way, he could go no further and cried out, "Listen, I've got to let the tree drop."

The tailor quickly jumped down, grabbed the tree with both his arms as if he had been carrying it, and said to the giant, "You're such a huge fellow, and yet you can't even carry the tree!"

They walked on together, and when they came to a cherry tree, the giant seized the top, where the fruit was ripest. He bent it down, handed it to the tailor, and told him to eat some of the fruit. But the little tailor was much too weak to hold on to the treetop, and when the giant let go of it, the tailor was catapulted into the air. After he came down again, unharmed, the giant said, "What's this? Don't tell me that you're not strong enough to hold on to that measly twig!"

"Don't worry, I've got plenty of strength," the tailor responded. "Do you think that something like that is really difficult for a man who's slain seven with one blow? I jumped over the tree because some huntsmen were shooting there in the bushes. Let's see if you can jump over it yourself."

The giant tried but could not make it over the tree. He got stuck in the branches, so the little tailor got the better of him once again.

"Well, if you're such a brave fellow," the giant said, "come along with me to our cave and spend the night with us."

The little tailor agreed and followed him. When they arrived in the cave, the other giants were still sitting by the fire, and each one had a roasted sheep in his hand and was eating it. The little tailor looked around and thought, It's certainly roomier in here than in my workshop.

The giant showed him to a bed and told him to lie down and have a good sleep. But the bed was too big for the little tailor, so he did not get into it but crept into a corner of the cave. When midnight came and the giant thought the little tailor was sound asleep, he got up, took a large iron bar, smashed the bed in two with one stroke, and thought he had put an end to the grasshopper. At dawn the next day the giants went into the forest and forgot all about the little tailor. But all of a sudden he came walking along quite merrily and boldly. The giants were horrified, for they feared he might slay them all. So they ran away as fast as they could.

The tailor just followed his pointed nose and kept going. After he had traveled about for a long time, he came to the courtyard of a royal palace. Since he felt tired, he lay down in the grass and fell asleep. While he was lying there, some people came, examined him from all sides, and read on his belt "Seven with one Blow."

"Ah!" they said. "What can a great warrior be doing here during peacetime? He must be a mighty lord."

They went and reported it to the king and advised him that the warrior would be an important and useful man to have if war broke out and that the king should try to keep him there at all costs. The king appreciated the advice, and he sent one of his courtiers to the little tailor to offer him, after he woke up, a military position. The envoy remained standing near the sleeper until the tailor stretched his limbs and opened his eyes. Then the courtier made him the proposal.

"That's exactly why I've come here," answered the little tailor. "I am prepared to enter the king's service."

So he was honorably received and given special living quarters. However, the soldiers were jealous of the little tailor and wished him a thousand miles away.

"What will come of all this?" they began saying among themselves. "If we quarrel with him and he starts swinging, seven of us will fall with one blow. None of us can stand up to him."

Once they had reached a decision, they all went to the king and asked for their discharge. "We can't hold our own with a man who can slay seven with one blow," they said.

The king was sad to lose all his faithful servants on account of one man, and he wished he had never laid eyes on him. He actually wanted to get rid of him, but he dared not dismiss him for fear that the tailor might kill him and all his people and take over the royal throne. The king thought about this for a long time, going back and forth in his mind until he hit upon a plan. Then he sent a message to the little tailor that contained a proposal for him—since he was such a great warrior. There were two giants living in a forest in the king's country, and they were causing great damage by robbing, murdering, ravaging, and burning. Anyone who came near the giants would be placing his life in danger. However, if the tailor could conquer these two giants and kill them, he would receive the king's only daughter for his wife and half the kingdom as dowry. Moreover, one hundred knights were to accompany him and lend him assistance.

That would be just right for a man like you! thought the little tailor. It's not every day somebody offers you a princess and half a kingdom. So he answered, "Yes, indeed, I'll soon tame the giants, but I won't need the hundred knights. A man who's already slain seven with one blow does not need to be afraid of two."

The little tailor set out, followed by the hundred knights. When he came to the edge of the forest, he said to his escorts, "Just stay right here. I'll take care of the giants all by myself."

After he scampered into the forest, he looked to the right and to the left. Soon he caught sight of the two giants, who were lying asleep under a tree and snoring so hard that the branches bobbed up and down. Since the little tailor was no slouch, he filled his pockets full of stones and carried them up a tree. When he got halfway up the tree, he slid out on a branch until he was perched right over the sleepers. Then he dropped one stone after another on the chest of one of the giants. It took some time before the giant felt anything. However, he finally woke up, shoved his companion, and said, "Why are you hitting me?"

"You're dreaming," the other said. "I haven't been hitting you."

They lay down to sleep again, and the tailor threw a stone at the other giant.

"What's the meaning of that?" the second giant cried out. "Why are you throwing things at me?"

"I'm not throwing things at you," the first one replied and growled.

They quarreled for a while, but since they were tired, they let it pass, and their eyes closed again. Now the little tailor began his game anew. He took out his largest stone and threw it with all his might at the chest of the first giant.

"That does it!" he screamed, jumping up like a madman, and he slammed his companion against the tree so hard that it shook. The other giant paid him back in kind, and they both became so furious that they tore up trees and beat each other for some time until together they fell down dead. Then the little tailor jumped down from the tree.

"Lucky for me that they didn't tear up the tree I was sitting on," he said. "Otherwise, I'd have had to jump like a squirrel from one tree to another. Still, a man like me is always nimble."

He drew his sword, gave the giants a few hearty blows on their chests, and went out of the forest to the knights.

"The work's done," he said. "I've put an end to the two of them. But the battle was a hard one. They became so desperate that they tore up trees to defend themselves. Yet, there's nothing anyone can do against a man like me who can slay seven with one blow."

"Didn't they wound you?" the knights asked.

"It'll take more than two giants before that happens," he answered. "They couldn't even touch the hair on my head."

The knights would not believe him and rode into the forest, where they found the giants swimming in their own blood, with uprooted trees lying all around them. Meanwhile, the little tailor went and demanded the reward promised by the king, but the king regretted his promise and thought up a new way to get rid of the hero.

"Before you can have my daughter and half the kingdom," he said to the tailor, "you must put your heroism on display again and perform one more deed. There's a unicorn running around and causing great damage in the forest, and I want you to capture it."

"Do you expect me to be afraid of a unicorn after facing two giants?" the tailor asked. "Seven with one blow is more my style."

He took some rope and an ax with him, went to the forest, and ordered his escorts once again to remain outside. He did not have to search long, for the unicorn did not keep him waiting: it charged right at him with its horn lowered, as if it meant to gore him without much ado.

"Easy does it, easy does it!" the tailor said. "You won't get anywhere by doing things too hastily."

The little tailor stood still and waited until the unicorn was very close. Then he jumped nimbly behind a tree, while the animal ran with all its might into the tree, thrusting its horn into the trunk so hard that it did not have the strength to pull it out again. This was the way the unicorn was caught.

"Now I've got the little bird," the tailor said, and he came out from behind the tree, put the rope around the unicorn's neck, and chopped the horn free of the tree with the ax. When everything was all set, he led the unicorn away and took it to the king.

The king, however, still refused to give him the promised reward and made a third demand. Before the wedding could take place, the tailor was to capture a wild boar that was causing great damage in the forest, and the king's huntsmen were to lend him assistance.

"Gladly," said the tailor. "This is child's play."

He did not take the huntsmen with him into the forest, and they were pleased, for the wild boar had already given them such rough treatment that they had no desire to chase it. When the boar caught sight of the tailor, it charged at him, foaming at the mouth and gnashing its teeth. The beast tried to trample him to the ground, but the nimble hero ducked into a nearby chapel and jumped right out again through one of the windows. The boar followed him inside, while the tailor ran around on the outside to shut the front door. Thus the raging beast was trapped, because it was much too heavy and clumsy to jump out the window. The little tailor called the huntsmen to see the prisoner with their own eyes, while the hero went to the king, who had to keep his promise this time, whether he liked it or not. So he gave the tailor his daughter and half the kingdom. If he had known that he had been dealing with a mere tailor and not a hero from the wars, the entire affair would have caused him even more grief than it did. As it was, the wedding was celebrated with great splendor but little joy, and a king was made out of a tailor.

After some time had passed, the young queen heard her husband talking in his sleep one night. "Boy, finish that jerkin and mend the trousers fast, or else I'll give you a whack on your head with my yardstick!"

Now she knew the young lord was of humble origins, and the next morning she went to her father to complain and begged him to help her get rid of this husband who was nothing but a tailor. The king comforted her and said, "Leave the door of your bedroom open tonight. My servants shall be waiting outside, and when he's asleep, they'll go inside, tie him up, and take him aboard a ship that will carry him out into the wide world."

The king's daughter was content with this plan. But the king's armor-bearer had overheard everything, and since he was kindly disposed toward the young king, he told him all about the plot.

"I'm going to have to throttle their plans," said the little tailor.

That evening he went to bed with his wife at the usual time. When she thought he had fallen asleep, she got up, opened the door, and returned to the bed. The little tailor, who was only pretending to be asleep, began to cry out in a clear voice, "Boy, finish that jerkin and mend the trousers fast, or else I'll give you a whack on your head with my yardstick! I've slain seven with one blow, killed two giants, captured a unicorn, and trapped a wild boar. Do you think those fellows waiting outside my door could ever scare me?"

When the men heard the tailor talking like that, they were petrified and ran off as if the wild host of hell were after them, and none of them ever dared to do anything to him after this. Thus the tailor reigned as king and remained king for the rest of his life.

◈ 21 ◈

Cinderella

THE WIFE OF A RICH MAN FELL ILL, and as she felt her end approaching, she called her only daughter to her bedside and said, "Dear child, be good and pious. Then the dear Lord shall always assist you, and I shall look down from heaven and take care of you." She then closed her eyes and departed.

After her mother's death the maiden went every day to visit her grave and weep, and she remained good and pious. When winter came, snow covered the grave like a little white blanket, and by the time the sun had taken it off again in the spring, the rich man had a second wife, who brought along her two daughters. They had beautiful and fair features but nasty and wicked hearts. As a result a difficult time was ahead for the poor stepsister.

"Why should the stupid goose be allowed to sit in the parlor with us?" they said. "Whoever wants to eat bread must earn it. Out with this kitchen maid!"

They took away her beautiful clothes, dressed her in an old gray smock, and gave her wooden shoes.

"Just look at the proud princess and how decked out she is!" they exclaimed with laughter, and led her into the kitchen.

They expected her to work hard there from morning till night. She had to get up before dawn, carry the water into the house, make the fire, cook, and wash. Besides this, her sisters did everything imaginable to cause her grief and make her look ridiculous. For instance, they poured peas and lentils into the hearth ashes so she had to sit there and pick them out. In the evening, when she was exhausted from working, they took away her bed, and she had to lie next to the hearth in the ashes. This is why she always looked so dusty and dirty and why they all called her Cinderella.

One day it happened that her father was going to the fair and asked his two stepdaughters what he could bring them.

"Beautiful dresses," said one.

"Pearls and jewels," said the other.

"And you, Cinderella?" he asked. "What do you want?"

"Father," she said, "just break off the first twig that brushes against your hat on your way home and bring it to me."

So he bought beautiful dresses, pearls, and jewels for the two stepsisters, and as he was riding through some green bushes on his return journey, a hazel twig brushed against him and knocked off his hat. So he broke off that twig and took it with him. When he arrived home, he gave his stepdaughters what they had requested, and Cinderella received the twig from the hazel bush. She thanked him, went to her mother's grave, planted the twig on it, and wept so hard that the tears fell on the twig and watered it. Soon the twig grew and quickly became a beautiful tree. Three times every day Cinderella would go and sit beneath it and weep and pray, and each time, a little white bird would also come to the tree. Whenever Cinderella expressed a wish, the bird would throw her whatever she had requested.

In the meantime, the king had decided to sponsor a three-day festival, and all the beautiful young girls in the country were invited so that his son could choose a bride. When the two stepsisters learned that they too had been summoned to make an appearance, they were in good spirits and called Cinderella.

"Comb our hair, brush our shoes, and fasten our buckles!" they said. "We're going to the wedding at the king's castle."

Cinderella obeyed but wept, because she too would have liked to go to the ball with them, and so she asked her stepmother for permission to go.

"You, Cinderella!" she said. "You're all dusty and dirty, and yet you want to go to the wedding? How can you go dancing when you've got no clothes or shoes?"

When Cinderella kept pleading, her stepmother finally said, "I've emptied a bowlful of lentils into the ashes. If you can pick out all the lentils in two hours, you may have my permission to go."

The maiden went through the back door into the garden and cried out, "Oh, you tame pigeons, you turtledoves, and all you birds under heaven, come and help me pick

the good ones for the little pot,
the bad ones for your little crop."

Two white pigeons came flying to the kitchen window, followed by the turtledoves. Eventually, all the birds under heaven swooped down, swarmed into the kitchen, and settled around the ashes. The pigeons bobbed their heads and began to peck, peck, peck, peck, and all the other birds also began to peck, peck, peck, peck, and they put all the good lentils into the bowl. It did not take longer than an hour for the birds to finish the work, whereupon they flew away. Happy, because she thought she would now be allowed to go to the wedding, the maiden brought the bowl to her stepmother. But her stepmother said, "No, Cinderella. You don't have any clothes, nor do you know how to dance. Everyone would only laugh at you."

When Cinderella started crying, the stepmother said, "If you can pick two bowlfuls of lentils out of the ashes in one hour, I'll let you come along." But she thought, She'll never be able to do it.

Then the stepmother dumped two bowlfuls of lentils into the ashes, and the maiden went through the back door into the garden and cried out, "Oh, you tame pigeons, you turtledoves, and all you birds under heaven, come and help me pick

the good ones for the little pot,
the bad ones for your little crop."

Two white pigeons came flying to the kitchen window, followed by the turtledoves. Eventually, all the birds under heaven swooped down, swarmed into the kitchen, and settled around the ashes. The pigeons bobbed their heads and began to peck, peck, peck, peck, and all the other birds also began to peck, peck, peck, peck, and they put all the good lentils into the bowl. Before half an hour had passed, they finished their work and flew away. Happy, because she thought she would now be allowed to go to the wedding, the maiden carried the bowls to her stepmother. But her stepmother said, "Nothing can help you. I can't let you come with us because you don't have any clothes to wear and you don't know how to dance. We'd only be ashamed of you!"

Then she turned her back on Cinderella and hurried off with her two haughty daughters. When they had all departed, Cinderella went to her mother's grave beneath the hazel tree and cried out:

"Shake and wobble, little tree!
Let gold and silver fall all over me."

The bird responded by throwing her a gold and silver dress and silk slippers embroidered with silver. She hastily slipped into the dress and went to the wedding. She looked so beautiful in her golden dress that her sisters and stepmother did not recognize her and thought she must be a foreign princess. They never imagined it could be Cinderella; they thought she was sitting at home in the dirt picking lentils out of the ashes.

Now, the prince approached Cinderella, took her by the hand, and danced with her. Indeed, he would not dance with anyone else and would not let go of her hand. Whenever someone came and asked her to dance, he said, "She's my partner."

She danced well into the night, and when she wanted to go home, the prince said, "I'll go along and escort you," for he wanted to see whose daughter the beautiful maiden was. But she managed to slip away from him and got into her father's dovecote. Now the prince waited until her father came, and he told him that the unknown maiden had escaped into his dovecote. The old man thought, Could that be Cinderella? And he had an ax and pick brought to him so he could chop it down. However, no one was inside, and when they went into the house, Cinderella was lying in the ashes in her dirty clothes, and a dim little oil lamp was burning on the mantel of the chimney. Cinderella had swiftly jumped out the back of the dovecote and run to the hazel tree. There she had taken off the beautiful clothes and laid them on the grave. After the bird had taken them away, she had made her way into the kitchen, where she had seated herself in the gray ashes wearing her gray smock.

The next day when the festival had begun again and her parents and sisters had departed, Cinderella went to the hazel tree and cried out:

"Shake and wobble, little tree!
Let gold and silver fall all over me."

The bird responded by throwing her a dress that was even more splendid than the one before. And when she appeared at the wedding in this dress, everyone was amazed by her beauty. The prince had been waiting for her, and when she came, he took her hand right away and danced with no one but her. When others went up to her and asked her to dance, he said, "She's my partner."

When evening came and she wished to leave, the prince followed her, wanting to see which house she went into, but she ran away from him and disappeared into the garden behind the house. There she went to a beautiful tall tree covered with the most wonderful pears, and she climbed up into the branches as nimbly as a squirrel. The prince did not know where she had gone, so he waited until her father came and said, "The unknown maiden has slipped away from me, and I think she climbed the pear tree."

The father thought, Can that be Cinderella? And he had an ax brought to him and chopped the tree down, but there was no one in it. When they went into the kitchen, Cinderella was lying in the ashes as usual, for she had jumped down on the other side of the tree, brought the beautiful clothes back to the bird, and put on her gray smock.

On the third day, when her parents and sisters had departed, Cinderella went to her mother's grave again and cried out to the tree:

"Shake and wobble, little tree!
Let gold and silver fall all over me."

The bird responded by throwing her a dress that was more magnificent and radiant than all the others she had received, and the slippers were pure gold. When she appeared at the wedding in this dress, the people were so astounded they did not know what to say. The prince danced with no one but her, and whenever someone asked her to dance, he said, "She's my partner."

When it was evening and Cinderella wished to leave, the prince wanted to escort her, but she slipped away from him so swiftly that he could not follow her. However, the prince had prepared for this with a trick: he had all the stairs coated with pitch, and when Cinderella went running down the stairs, her left slipper got stuck there. After the prince picked it up, he saw it was small and dainty and made of pure gold.

Next morning he carried it to Cinderella's father and said, "No one else shall be my wife but the maiden whose foot fits this golden shoe."

The two sisters were glad to hear this because they had beautiful feet. The oldest took the shoe into a room to try it on, and her mother stood by her side. However, the shoe was too small for her, and she could not get her big toe into it. So her mother handed her a knife and said, "Cut your toe off. Once you become queen, you won't have to walk anymore."

The maiden cut her toe off, forced her foot into the shoe, swallowed the pain, and went out to the prince. He took her on his horse as his bride and rode off. But they had to pass the grave where the two pigeons were sitting on the hazel tree, and they cried out:

"Looky, look, look
at the shoe that she took.
There's blood all over, and her foot's too small.
She's not the bride you met at the ball."

He looked down at her foot and saw the blood oozing out. So he turned his horse around, brought the false bride home again, and said that she was definitely not the right one and the other sister should try on the shoe. Then the second sister went into a room and was fortunate enough to get all her toes in, but her heel was too large. So her mother handed her a knife and said, "Cut off a piece of your heel. Once you become queen, you won't have to walk anymore."

The maiden cut off a piece of her heel, forced her foot into the shoe, swallowed the pain, and went out to the prince. He took her on his horse as his bride, and rode off with her. As they passed the hazel tree the two pigeons were sitting there, and they cried out:

"Looky, look, look
at the shoe that she took.
There's blood all over, and her foot's too small.
She's not the bride you met at the ball."

He looked down at her foot and saw the blood oozing out of the shoe and staining her white stockings all red. Then he turned his horse around and brought the false bride home again.

"She isn't the right one either," he said. "Don't you have any other daughters?"

"No," said the man. "There's only little Cinderella, my dead wife's daughter, who's deformed, but she can't possibly be the bride."

The prince told him to send the girl to him, but the mother responded, "Oh, she's much too dirty and really shouldn't be seen."

However, the prince demanded to see her, and Cinderella had to be called. First she washed her hands and face until they were clean, and then she went and curtsied before the prince, who handed her the golden shoe. She sat down on a stool, took her foot out of the heavy wooden shoe, and put it into the slipper that fit her perfectly. After she stood up and the prince looked her straight in the face, he recognized the beautiful maiden who had danced with him.

"This is my true bride!" he exclaimed.

The stepmother and the two sisters were horrified and turned pale with rage. However, the prince took Cinderella on his horse and rode away with her. As they passed the hazel tree the two white pigeons cried out:

"Looky, look, look
at the shoe that she took.
Her foot's just right, and there's no blood at all.
She's truly the bride you met at the ball."

After the pigeons had made this known, they both came flying down and landed on Cinderella's shoulders, one on the right, the other on the left, and there they stayed.

On the day that the wedding with the prince was to take place, the two false sisters came to ingratiate themselves and to share in Cinderella's good fortune. When the bridal couple set out for the church, the oldest sister was on the right, the younger on the left. Suddenly the pigeons pecked out one eye from each of them. And as they came back from the church later on the oldest was on the left and the youngest on the right, and the pigeons pecked out the other eye from each sister. Thus they were punished with blindness for the rest of their lives due to their wickedness and malice.

◆ 22 ◆

The Riddle

ONCE UPON A TIME there was a prince who was overcome by a desire to travel about the world, and the only person he took with him was his faithful servant. One day he found himself in a great forest when evening came. He had not found a place to spend the night and did not know what to do. Then he noticed a maiden going toward a small cottage, and when he came closer, he saw that she was young and beautiful. So he spoke to her and said, "Do you think, dear girl, that my servant and I could spend the night in the cottage?"

"Why, yes," said the maiden with a sad voice. "You certainly can, but I wouldn't advise it. Don't go in."

"Why not?" asked the prince.

The maiden sighed and said, "My stepmother practices evil arts and is not well-disposed toward strangers."

He realized then that he had come to the house of a witch. However, it was dark and he could not continue, and since he was fearless, he decided to go in. The old woman was sitting in an easy chair by the fire and looked at the strangers with her red eyes.

"Good evening!" she snarled, and then she pretended to be quite friendly. "Have a seat and rest yourselves!"

She was cooking something in a little pot on the fire, and she stoked the coals. The daughter had warned the two men to be careful not to drink or eat anything, for the old woman brewed deadly potions. The two men slept peacefully until early in the morning. When they were getting ready to depart and the prince was seated on his horse, the old woman said, "Wait a minute! I want to offer you a parting drink."

While she went to fetch it, the prince rode off, and the servant, who was still trying to strap his saddle on tight, was the only one there when the evil witch came back with the drink.

"Bring this to your master," she said, but at that moment the glass broke, the poison splattered on the horse, and it was so lethal that the animal fell down dead on the spot. The servant ran after his master and told him what had happened, but he did not want to abandon his saddle and so went back to fetch it. When he came to the dead horse, a raven was already sitting there and eating it.

"Who knows if we'll be able to find anything better to eat today?" said the servant, and so he killed the raven and took it with him.

They went on traveling the whole day in the forest but could not find their way out. At nightfall they came upon an inn and went inside. The servant gave the raven to the innkeeper and told him to prepare it for their supper. However, what they had stumbled on was a den of murderers, and when it was dark, twelve murderers arrived and wanted to kill and rob them. But before getting down to their work, they sat down at the table, and the innkeeper and the witch joined them. They all ate out of the same bowl of soup filled with the chopped meat of the raven. No sooner did they swallow a few bites than they fell down dead, for the raven had been infected by the poisoned horsemeat. Now there was nobody left in the big house except the innkeeper's daughter, who was honest and had not taken any part in the wicked deeds of the murders. She opened all the doors in the inn and showed the prince the vast treasures the murderers had accumulated. However, he wanted none of it and told her that she could keep it all, and he rode off with his servant.

After they had traveled about for a long time, they came to a city inhabited by a beautiful but haughty princess. She had proclaimed that she would wed any man who could give her a riddle she could not solve, but a man who offered a riddle that she was able to solve would have his head chopped off. She was allowed three days to think about the riddle, but she was so smart that she always solved it before the end of the time. In fact, nine men had already lost their lives by the time the prince arrived. Nevertheless, he was so bedazzled by her great beauty that he was willing to risk his life, and he appeared before her and posed his riddle.

"Can you guess this?" he asked. "One slew nobody and yet slew twelve."

The princess did not know what that could mean, and she thought and thought but could not come up with the answer. She consulted her riddle books, but there was nothing in them about this. In short, her wisdom had reached its limits, and she was at a loss as to what to do. So, on the first night, she ordered her maid to sneak into the prince's bedroom and listen to his dreams, for she thought he might talk in his sleep and reveal the riddle. But the clever servant took his master's place in the bed, and when the maid came in, he ripped off the cloak she had wrapped herself in and sent her running with a good beating. On the second night, the princess sent her chambermaid, to see if she might succeed better in eavesdropping, but again the servant took her cloak away and sent her running with a good beating. Now, on the third night, the prince thought he would be safe and lay down in his own bed. However, this time the princess herself came. She was wearing a misty gray cloak and sat down beside him. When she thought he was sleeping and dreaming, she spoke to him and hoped he would answer in his dreams as many do. But he was awake and understood and heard everything quite perfectly.

"One slew nobody," she said. "What does that mean?"

"A raven that ate a dead poisoned horse and died of it," he said.

Then she asked again, "And yet slew twelve. What does that mean?"

"Those are the twelve murderers who ate the raven and died of it."

When she knew the answer to the riddle, she wanted to sneak away, but he held her cloak so tightly, she had to leave it behind her. The next morning the princess announced she had solved the riddle and ordered the twelve judges to come. Then she explained the riddle in front of them, but the young prince asked for a hearing and declared, "She crept into my room during the night and questioned me all about the riddle. Otherwise she never would have solved it."

"Bring us proof!" the judges said.

Then the prince's servant brought in the three cloaks, and when the judges saw the misty gray one that the princess usually wore, they said, "Have the cloak embroidered with gold and silver, for it will be your wedding cloak."

◆ 23 ◆

The Mouse, the Bird, and the Sausage

ONCE UPON A TIME a mouse, a bird, and a sausage came together and set up house. For a long time they lived together in peace and happiness, and they managed to increase their possessions by a considerable amount. The bird's job was to fly into the forest every day and bring back wood. The mouse had to carry water, light the fire, and set the table, while the sausage did the cooking.

Yet, those who lead the good life are always looking for ways to make it even better. And, one day, as the bird was flying about, he met another bird and boasted about how wonderful his life was. But the other bird called him a poor sap because he had to do all the hard work, while his companions just enjoyed themselves at home. Indeed, after the mouse started the fire and carried the water into the house, she generally went to her little room and rested until she was called to set the table. The sausage always stayed by the pot and kept an eye on the cooking, and right before mealtime he usually slid through the stew or vegetables to make sure everything was salted and seasoned properly. And that was all he did. When the bird came home and laid down his load, they would sit down at the table, and after finishing the meal they would sleep soundly until the next morning. Such was their glorious life.

However, the bird had been disturbed by what the other bird had said, and next day he refused to fly into the forest. He told his companions that he had been their slave long enough, and that they must have taken him for a fool. He demanded that they try another arrangement. The mouse and the sausage argued against this, but the bird would not be denied, and he insisted that they try a new way. So they drew lots, and it fell upon the sausage to get the wood from then on, while the mouse became cook, and the bird was to fetch water.

What happened?

After the sausage went to fetch the wood, the bird started the fire, and the mouse put the kettle on the stove. Then they waited for the sausage to return with the wood for the next day. However, the sausage was gone so long that the other two had an uneasy feeling, and the bird flew out a little way to meet him. Not far from their home, however, he encountered a dog, and he learned that this dog had considered the sausage free game and had grabbed him and swallowed him down. The bird was furious and accused the dog of highway robbery, but it was of no use, for the dog maintained he had found forged letters on the sausage, and therefore the sausage had had to pay for this with his life.

Now the bird sadly picked up the wood and carried it back home. He told the mouse what he had seen and heard, and they were very distressed. Nevertheless, they agreed to do the best they could and stay together. Meanwhile, the bird set the table, and the mouse prepared the meal. She intended to put the finishing touches on it by seasoning it and sliding through the vegetables the way the sausage used to do, but before she even reached the middle, she got stuck and had to pay for it with her life.

When the bird came to serve the meal, there was no cook. He became so upset that he scattered wood all over the place, calling and searching for the mouse. But his cook was no longer to be found. Due to the bird's distraction the wood soon caught fire, and the house went up in flames. When the bird rushed to fetch some water, however, the bucket slipped and fell into the well, dragging the bird along. Since he could not get himself out, he was left to drown.

❖ 24 ❖

Mother Holle

A WIDOW HAD TWO DAUGHTERS, one who was beautiful and industrious, the other ugly and lazy. But she was fonder of the ugly and lazy one because she was her own daughter. The other had to do all the housework and carry out the ashes like a cinderella. Every day the poor maiden had to sit near a well by the road and spin and spin until her fingers bled.

Now, one day it happened that the reel became quite bloody, and when the maiden leaned over the well to rinse it, it slipped out of her hand and fell to the bottom. She burst into tears, ran to her stepmother, and told her about the accident. But the stepmother gave her a terrible scolding and was very cruel. "If you've let the reel fall in," she said, "then you'd better get it out again."

The maiden went back to the well but did not know where to begin. She was so distraught that she jumped into the well to fetch the reel, but she lost consciousness. When she awoke and regained her senses, she was in a beautiful meadow where the sun was shining and thousands of flowers were growing. She walked across this meadow, and soon she came to a baker's oven full of bread, but the bread was yelling, "Take me out! Take me out, or else I'll burn. I've been baking long enough!"

She went up to the oven and took out all the loaves one by one with the baker's peel. After that she moved on and came to a tree full of apples.

"Shake me! Shake me!" the tree exclaimed. "My apples are all ripe."

She shook the tree till the apples fell like raindrops, and she kept shaking until they had all come down. After she had gathered them and stacked them in a pile, she moved on. At last she came to a small cottage where an old woman was looking out of a window. She had such big teeth that the maiden was scared and wanted to run away. But the old woman cried after her, "Why are you afraid, my dear child? Stay with me, and if you do all the housework properly, everything will turn out well for you. Only you must make my bed nicely and carefully and give it a good shaking so the feathers fly. Then it will snow on earth, for I am Mother Holle."*

Since the old woman had spoken so kindly to her, the maiden plucked up her courage and agreed to enter her service. She took care of everything to the old woman's satisfaction and always shook the bed so hard that the feathers flew about like snowflakes. In return, the woman treated her well: she never said an unkind word to the maiden, and she gave her roasted or boiled meat every day. After the maiden had spent a long time with Mother Holle, she became sad. At first she did not know what was bothering her, but finally she realized she was homesick. Even though everything was a thousand times better there than at home, she still had a desire to return. At last she said to Mother Holle, "I've got a tremendous longing to return home, and even though everything is wonderful down here, I've got to return to my people."

"I'm pleased that you want to return home," Mother Holle responded, "and since you've served me so faithfully, I myself shall bring you up there again."

She took the maiden by the hand and led her to a large door. When it was opened and the maiden was standing right beneath the doorway, an enormous shower of gold came pouring down, and all the gold stuck to her so that she became completely covered with it.

"I want you to have this because you've been so industrious," said Mother Holle, and she also gave her back the reel that had fallen into the well. Suddenly the door closed, and the maiden found herself back

---

*Whenever it showed in olden days, people in Hessia used to say Mother Holle is making her bed.

up on earth, not far from her mother's house. When she entered the yard, the cock was sitting on the well and crowed:

"*Cock-a-doodle-doo!*
My golden maiden, what's new with you?"

She went inside to her mother, and since she was covered with so much gold, her mother and sister gave her a warm welcome. Then she told them all about what had happened to her, and when her mother heard how she had obtained so much wealth, she wanted to arrange it so her ugly and lazy daughter could have the same good fortune. Therefore, her daughter had to sit near the well and spin, and she made the reel bloody by sticking her fingers into a thornbush and pricking them. After that she threw the reel down into the well and jumped in after it. Just like her sister, she reached the beautiful meadow and walked along the same path. When she came to the oven, the bread cried out again, "Take me out! Take me out, or else I'll burn! I've been baking long enough!"

But the lazy maiden answered, "I've no desire to get myself dirty!"

She moved on, and soon she came to the apple tree that cried out, "Shake me! Shake me! My apples are all ripe."

However, the lazy maiden replied, "Are you serious? One of the apples could fall and hit me on my head."

Thus she went on, and when she came to Mother Holle's cottage, she was not afraid because she had already heard of the old woman's big teeth, and she hired herself out to her right away. On the first day she made an effort to work hard and obey Mother Holle when the old woman told her what to do, for the thought of gold was on her mind. On the second day she started loafing, and on the third day she loafed even more. Indeed, she did not want to get out of bed in the morning, nor did she make Mother Holle's bed as she should have, and she certainly did not shake it hard so the feathers flew. Soon Mother Holle became tired of this and dismissed the maiden from her service. The lazy maiden was quite happy to go and expected that now the shower of gold would come. Mother Holle led her to the door, but as the maiden was standing beneath the doorway, a big kettle of pitch came pouring down over her instead of gold.

"That's a reward for your services," Mother Holle said, and shut the door. The lazy maiden went home covered with pitch, and when the cock on the well saw her, it crowed:

"Cock-a-doodle-doo!
My dirty maiden, what's new with you?"

The pitch did not come off the maiden and remained on her as long as she lived.

◈ 25 ◈

The Seven Ravens

THERE ONCE WAS A MAN who had seven sons, and no matter how much he wished for a little daughter, his wish remained unfulfilled. Then one day his wife gave him hope of another child, and when the baby was born, it was indeed a girl. Their joy was great, but the child was sickly and small, and because she was so weak, she had to be baptized at home. The father sent one of the boys to run quickly to the well for some baptismal water. The other six ran along with him, and since each of them scrambled to be the first to draw the water, the pitcher fell into the well. There they stood, not knowing what to do, nor did any of them dare go home. When they failed to return, their father grew impatient and said, "Those wicked boys must have forgotten what I sent them to do! They're probably playing games again." He was afraid that his daughter might die without being baptized, and in his anger he exclaimed "I wish those boys would all be turned into ravens!"

No sooner had he uttered those words than he heard a whirring over his head, and when he looked up, he saw seven ravens, black as coal, flying up and away. It was too late for the parents to revoke the curse, and even though they were sad about the loss of their seven sons, they were comforted to a certain extent by their dear little daughter, who grew stronger and more beautiful with each day that passed. For a long time she was unaware that she had brothers, because her parents took great care not to mention them. But one day she overheard some people talking about her and saying that though she was indeed beautiful, she was actually the one who had caused the misfortune that had struck her seven brothers. Upon hearing this she was greatly distressed. She went to her father and mother and asked whether she had brothers and what had happened to them. Her parents could no longer keep the secret from her. However, they said the will of heaven had been responsible for her brothers' fate and not her own birth. Nonetheless, their fate weighed heavily on the maiden's conscience, and she believed it was up to her to rescue them. From then on she had no peace of mind, and finally she secretly set out into the wide world to find some trace of her brothers and free them, no matter what it might cost. The only things she took with her were a little ring as a memento to remind her of her parents, a loaf of bread to still her hunger, a jug of water to quench her thirst, and a little stool to rest on when she became tired.

She set out, walking straight ahead, and went far, far away until she reached the end of the world. She came to the sun, but it was too hot and terrible, and it ate little children. So she turned away from there as quickly as she could and ran to the moon, but it was too cold, not to mention gruesome and wicked. When it saw the girl, it said, "I smell something! I smell human flesh!" Immediately she scampered away and went to the stars, which were friendly and kind to her. Each one was sitting on its own little chair, but the morning star stood up, handed her the drumstick of a chicken, and said, "If you don't have this drumstick, you won't be able to open the glass mountain, and that's where you'll find your brothers."

The girl took the drumstick, wrapped it carefully in a piece of cloth, and continued traveling until she reached the glass mountain. The gate was locked, but she was prepared to take out the drumstick. Yet, when she began unfolding the cloth, she found it was empty. Indeed, she had lost the gift of the good, kind stars. What was she to do now? She wanted to rescue her brothers but did not have a key to the glass mountain. So the good sister took a knife, cut off a little finger, stuck it in the gate, and was fortunate enough to unlock it. After she entered, a little dwarf came toward her and said, "What are you looking for, my child?"

"I'm looking for my brothers, the seven ravens," she replied.

"The lord ravens are not at home," the dwarf said. "But, if you wish to wait here until they return, come right in."

Then the dwarf brought in the ravens' meal on seven little plates, along with seven little cups, and their sister ate a tiny morsel from each one of the plates and took a little sip from each one of the cups. When she came to the last cup, she took the ring that she had been carrying with her and dropped it into the cup.

All at once there was a whirring and fluttering noise in the air, and the dwarf said, "Now the lord ravens will soon be home."

When they arrived, they wanted to eat and drink and went straight to their plates and cups. Then each one in his turn cried out, "Who's been eating from my plate? Who's been drinking from my cup? It was a human mouth."

And when the seventh brother got to the bottom of his cup, a little ring rolled out. He looked at it and recognized it as the ring that belonged to his parents.

"God grant us that our little sister may be here. Then we'd be saved!" he said.

The maiden was standing behind the door, and when she heard that, she came out, and all the ravens regained their human form. They hugged and kissed each other and went happily home.

◈ 26 ◈

Little Red Cap

ONCE UPON A TIME there was a sweet little maiden. Whoever laid eyes upon her could not help but love her. But it was her grandmother who loved her most. She could never give the child enough. One time she made her a present, a small, red velvet cap, and since it was so becoming and the maiden insisted on always wearing it, she was called Little Red Cap.

One day her mother said to her, "Come, Little Red Cap, take this piece of cake and bottle of wine and bring them to your grandmother. She's sick and weak, and this will strengthen her. Get an early start, before it becomes hot, and when you're out in the woods, be nice and good and don't stray from the path, otherwise you'll fall and break the

glass, and your grandmother will get nothing. And when you enter her room, don't forget to say good morning, and don't go peeping in all the corners."

"I'll do just as you say," Little Red Cap promised her mother. Well, the grandmother lived out in the forest, half an hour from the village, and as soon as Little Red Cap entered the forest, she encountered the wolf. However, Little Red Cap did not know what a wicked sort of an animal he was and was not afraid of him.

"Good day, Little Red Cap," he said.

"Thank you kindly, wolf."

"Where are you going so early, Little Red Cap?"

"To Grandmother's."

"What are you carrying under your apron?"

"Cake and wine. My grandmother's sick and weak, and yesterday we baked this so it will help her get well."

"Where does your grandmother live, Little Red Cap?"

"Another quarter of an hour from here in the forest. Her house is under the three big oak trees. You can tell it by the hazel bushes," said Little Red Cap.

The wolf thought to himself, This tender young thing is a juicy morsel. She'll taste even better than the old woman. You've got to be real crafty if you want to catch them both. Then he walked next to Little Red Cap, and after a while he said, "Little Red Cap, just look at the beautiful flowers that are growing all around you! Why don't you look around? I believe you haven't even noticed how lovely the birds are singing. You march along as if you were going straight to school, and yet it's so delightful out here in the woods!"

Little Red Cap looked around and saw how the rays of the sun were dancing through the trees back and forth and how the woods were full of beautiful flowers. So she thought to herself, If I bring Grandmother a bunch of fresh flowers, she'd certainly like that. It's still early, and I'll arrive on time.

So she ran off the path and plunged into the woods to look for flowers. And each time she plucked one, she thought she saw another even prettier flower and ran after it, going deeper and deeper into the forest. But the wolf went straight to the grandmother's house and knocked at the door.

"Who's out there?"

"Little Red Cap. I've brought you some cake and wine. Open up."

"Just lift the latch," the grandmother called. "I'm too weak and can't get up."

The wolf lifted the latch, and the door sprang open. Then he went straight to the grandmother's bed without saying a word and gobbled her up. Next he put on her clothes and her nightcap, lay down in her bed, and drew the curtains.

Meanwhile, Little Red Cap had been running around and looking for flowers, and only when she had as many as she could carry did she remember her grandmother and continue on the way to her house again. She was puzzled when she found the door open, and as she entered the room, it seemed so strange inside that she thought, Oh, my God, how frightened I feel today, and usually I like to be at Grandmother's. She called out, "Good morning!" But she received no answer. Next she went to the bed and drew back the curtains. There lay her grandmother with her cap pulled down over her face giving her a strange appearance.

"Oh, Grandmother, what big ears you have!"

"The better to hear you with."

"Oh, Grandmother, what big hands you have!"

"The better to grab you with."

"Oh, Grandmother, what a terribly big mouth you have!"

"The better to eat you with!"

No sooner did the wolf say that than he jumped out of bed and gobbled up poor Little Red Cap. After the wolf had satisfied his desires, he lay down in bed again, fell asleep, and began to snore very loudly. The huntsman happened to be passing by the house and thought to himself, The way the old woman's snoring, you'd better see if anything's wrong. He went into the room, and when he came to the bed, he saw the wolf lying in it.

"So I've found you at last, you old sinner," said the huntsman. "I've been looking for you for a long time."

He took aim with his gun, and then it occurred to him that the wolf could have eaten the grandmother and that she could still be saved. So he did not shoot but took some scissors and started cutting open the sleeping wolf's belly. After he made a couple of cuts, he saw the little red cap shining forth, and after he made a few more cuts, the girl jumped out and exclaimed, "Oh, how frightened I was! It was so dark in the wolf's body."

Soon the grandmother came out. She was alive but could hardly breathe. Little Red Cap quickly fetched some large stones, and they filled the wolf's body with them. When he awoke and tried to run away, the stones were too heavy so he fell down at once and died.

All three were quite delighted. The huntsman skinned the fur from the wolf and went home with it. The grandmother ate the cake and drank the wine that Little Red Cap had brought, and soon she regained her health. Meanwhile, Little Red Cap thought to herself, Never again will you stray from the path by yourself and go into the forest when your mother has forbidden it.

There is also another tale about how Little Red Cap returned to her grandmother one day to bring some baked goods. Another wolf spoke to her and tried to entice her to leave the path, but this time Little Red Cap was on her guard. She went straight ahead and told her grandmother that she had seen the wolf, that he had wished her good day, but that he had had such a mean look in his eyes that "he would have eaten me up if we hadn't been on the open road."

"Come," said the grandmother. "We'll lock the door so he can't get in."

Soon after, the wolf knocked and cried out, "Open up, Grandmother. It's Little Red Cap, and I've brought you some baked goods."

But they kept quiet and did not open the door. So Grayhead circled the house several times and finally jumped on the roof. He wanted to wait till evening when Little Red Cap would go home. He intended to sneak after her and eat her up in the darkness. But the grandmother realized what he had in mind. In front of the house was a big stone trough, and she said to the child, "Fetch the bucket, Little Red Cap. I cooked sausages yesterday. Get the water they were boiled in and pour it into the trough."

Little Red Cap kept carrying the water until she had filled the big, big trough. Then the smell of sausages reached the nose of the wolf. He sniffed and looked down. Finally, he stretched his neck so far that he could no longer keep his balance on the roof. He began to slip and fell right into the big trough and drowned. Then Little Red Cap went merrily on her way home, and no one harmed her.

❖ 27 ❖

The Bremen Town Musicians

A MAN HAD A DONKEY who had diligently carried sacks of grain to the mill for many years. However, the donkey's strength was reaching its end, and he was less and less fit for the work. His master thought it was time to dispense with him and save on food, but the donkey got wind of what was in store for him. So he ran away and set out for Bremen, where he thought he could become a town musician. After traveling some distance he came across a hunting dog lying on the roadside and panting as if he had run himself ragged.

"Why are you panting so hard, you old hound dog?" asked the donkey.

"Ah," the dog said, "because I'm old and getting weaker every day. Now I can't even hunt anymore, and my master wanted to kill me. Naturally, I cleared out, but how am I going to earn a living now?"

"You know what," said the donkey, "I'm going to Bremen to become a town musician, and you can come with me and also join the town band. I'll play the lute, and you, the drums."

The dog agreed, and they continued on their way. Soon after, they encountered a cat sitting on the roadside, making a long and sorry face.

"Well, what's gone wrong with you, old whiskers?" asked the donkey.

"How can I be cheerful when my neck's in danger?" the cat replied. "My mistress wanted to drown me because I'm getting on in years. Moreover, my teeth are dull, and I'd rather sit behind the stove and spin than chase after mice. Anyway, I managed to escape, but now I don't know what to do or where to go."

"Why don't you come along with us to Bremen? You know a great deal about night serenades, and you can become a town musician."

The cat thought that was a good idea and went along. Then the three fugitives passed a farmyard where a rooster was perched on the gate and crowing with all his might.

"Your crowing gives me the chills," said the donkey. "Why are you screaming like this?"

"I've predicted good weather for today," said the rooster, "because it's Our Lady's Day, when she washes the Christ Child's shirts and sets them out to dry. Still, my mistress has no mercy. Tomorrow's Sunday, and guests are coming. So she told the cook to cut off my head tonight because she wants to eat me in the soup tomorrow. Now you know why I'm screaming my lungs out, while there's still time to scream."

"That's foolish, redhead!" said the donkey. "You'd be smarter if you'd come along with us. We're off to Bremen where there are better things than death. You've got a good voice, and if we make music together, it's sure to be a good thing."

The rooster liked the proposal, and all four of them continued the journey together. However, they could not reach the town of Bremen in one day, and by evening they came to a forest, where they decided to spend the night. The donkey and the dog lay down under a big tree, while the cat and rooster climbed up and settled down in the branches. To be on the safe side, the rooster flew to the top. Before he went to sleep, he looked around in all directions, and it seemed to him he saw a light burning in the distance. He called to his companions and told them there must be a house nearby, since he could see something shining.

"Well, this place is not all that comfortable, so let's get moving," said the donkey.

The dog thought some bones and meat would be just right for him, and they all set out toward the light. Soon it began to grow brighter, and it got even more so once they reached a brightly lit robber's den. Since the donkey was the tallest, he went up to the window and looked inside.

"What do you see, gray steed?" the rooster asked.

"What do I see?" replied the donkey. "I see a table covered with wonderful food and drinks and some robbers sitting there and enjoying themselves."

"That would be just the thing for us!" said the rooster.

"You're right!" said the donkey. "If only we could get in!"

Then the animals discussed what they would have to do to drive the robbers away. Finally they hit upon a plan. The donkey was to stand upright and place his forefeet on the windowsill. The dog was to jump on the donkey's back, and the cat was to climb upon the dog. When that was done, the rooster was to fly up and perch on the cat's head. After they put their plan into action, the signal was given, and they all started to make music together: the donkey brayed, the dog barked, the cat meowed, and the rooster crowed. Then they crashed into the room, shattering the window. Startled by the horrible cries, the robbers were convinced that a ghost had burst into the room, and they fled in great fright into the forest. Then the four companions sat down at the table, delightedly gathered up the leftovers, and ate as if there were no tomorrow.

When the four minstrels were finished, they put out the light and looked for a place to sleep, each according to his nature and custom. The donkey lay down on the dung heap in the yard, the dog behind the door, the cat on the hearth near the warm ashes, and the rooster on the beam of the roof. Since they were tired from their long journey, they soon fell asleep.

When it was past midnight and the robbers saw from the distance that there was no light in the house and everything seemed peaceful, the leader of the band said, "We shouldn't have let ourselves be scared out of our wits."

He ordered one of the robbers to return and check out the house. When he found everything quiet, the robber went into the kitchen to light a candle and mistook the cat's glowing fiery eyes for live coals. So he held a match to them to light a fire, but the cat did not appreciate the joke. He jumped into the robber's face, spitting and scratching, and the robber was so terribly frightened that he ran out the back door. However, the dog was lying there and bit him in the leg. When the robber raced across the yard, he passed the dung heap, and here the donkey gave him a solid kick with his hind foot. All this noise woke the rooster from his sleep, and he became lively again and crowed *"Cock-a-doodle-doo!"* from his beam.

The robber ran back to the leader as fast as he could and said, "There's a gruesome witch in the house! She spat on me and scratched my face with her long claws. At the door there's a man with a knife, and he stabbed my leg. In the yard there's a black monster who beat me with a wooden club. And on top of the roof the judge was sitting and screaming 'Bring me the rascal!' I got out of there as fast as I could!"

Since that time the robbers have never dared return to the house, but the four Bremen Town musicians liked the place so much that they stayed on forever.

And the last person who told this tale has still got warm lips.

◈ 28 ◈

The Singing Bone

ONCE UPON A TIME there was a country in great distress because a wild boar was devastating the farmers' fields, killing cattle, and ripping people apart with its tusks. The king promised a large reward to anyone who could rid the country of this plague. However, the beast was so big and so strong that no one dared go near the forest in which it dwelled. At last the king proclaimed that whoever caught or killed the wild boar would receive his only daughter for a wife.

Now, there were two brothers, sons of a poor man, who were living in that country, and they declared themselves willing to take on the dangerous challenge. The older brother, a cunning and smart fellow, was doing it out of pride, while the younger, innocent and naive, was doing it out of the goodness of his heart.

"You must enter the forest from opposite sides," said the king. "That way you'll be more sure of finding the beast."

So the older entered from the west and the younger from the east. After the younger had walked for a while, a little dwarf with a black spear approached him and said, "I'm giving you this spear because you have a good and pure heart. With this you can attack the wild boar, and you won't have to worry about his harming you."

He thanked the dwarf, set the spear on his shoulder, and continued walking without fear. Shortly after, he caught sight of the beast, and when it charged him, he stuck out the spear, and in its blind fury the boar ran into it with such force that its heart was cut in two. The young man swung the monster over his shoulder and headed home with the intention of bringing the boar to the king.

When he came out at the other side of the forest, he saw a house where people were dancing, drinking, and having a good time. His older brother had gone there thinking that the boar was not about to run away, and he had also wanted to pump himself up with courage first by having a few drinks. When he saw his younger brother coming out of the forest and carrying his prize, his jealous and wicked heart gave him no peace.

"Come inside, dear brother," he called to him. "Take a rest and refresh yourself with a glass of wine."

Since the younger brother did not suspect anything evil, he went inside and told him about the good dwarf who had given him a spear so he could kill the boar. The older brother kept him there till evening, and then they departed together. In the darkness they came to a bridge that spanned a brook, and the older brother let the younger go ahead of him, and when the younger was halfway across, his brother gave him such a hard blow from behind that he fell down dead. After the older brother buried him under the bridge, he took the boar and brought it to the king, pretending he was the one who had killed it. So the king gave him his daughter for his wife. When the younger brother never returned, the older said, "The boar probably ripped him apart." And everyone believed him.

However, nothing remains hidden from God, and this evil deed was bound to come to light.

After many years had passed, a shepherd was driving his flock across the bridge and saw a little bone, as white as snow, lying beneath it. He thought it would make a good mouthpiece for his horn, so he climbed down, picked it up, and carved a mouthpiece out of it. When he blew on it for the first time, the shepherd was startled to find that the little bone began to sing on its own accord:

"Oh, shepherd, shepherd, don't you know
you're blowing on my bone!
My brother killed me years ago,
buried me by the brook that flows,
carried off the dead wild boar,
and married the king's fine daughter."

"What a remarkable horn!" said the shepherd. "It sings by itself! I've got to take it to the king."

When he went to the king, the little horn began to sing its song again. The king understood it full well and had the ground under the bridge dug up. After the entire skeleton of the murdered man was revealed, the wicked brother could not deny the deed, and he was sewn up in a sack and drowned. However, the bones of his murdered brother were laid to rest in a beautiful grave in the churchyard.

◆ 29 ◆

The Devil With the Three Golden Hairs

ONCE UPON A TIME there was a poor woman who gave birth to a little son, and since he was born with a caul, it was prophesied he would marry the king's daughter by the time he was fourteen. Soon after, the king happened to come to the village, but no one knew that he was the king. When he asked the people about the latest news, they answered, "Just recently a child was born with a caul. Now fortune will shine on him in all his endeavors. Indeed, it's been prophesied that he'll marry the king's daughter by the time he's fourteen."

Since the king had an evil heart and was disturbed by the prophecy, he went to the boy's parents and pretended to be friendly.

"I know that you're very poor people," he said. "So let me have your child, and I'll take good care of him."

At first they refused, but when the stranger offered them a great deal of gold for him, they thought, Since he's fortune's favorite, it's bound to turn out well for him. Therefore, they finally agreed and gave the child to the stranger.

The king laid him in a box and rode away with him until he came to a deep river. Then he threw the box into the water and thought, Well, now I've rid my daughter of an undesirable suitor. But the box did not sink. Instead, it floated like a little boat, and not a single drop of water got into it. The box drifted to within two miles of the king's capital city, where it was blocked from going any further by a mill dam. Fortunately, the miller's apprentice was standing on the bank and saw it. Thinking he had found a great treasure, he used a hook to pull the box ashore. However, when he opened it, he discovered a lovely-looking boy who was alive and well. So he took the boy to the miller and his wife because they did not have any children. Indeed, they were delighted and said, "God has blessed us with this gift."

They took good care of the foundling and made sure that he was raised with all the best virtues. Now, one day the king happened to get caught in a thunderstorm and arrived at the mill. There he asked the miller and his wife whether the big boy was their son.

"No," they answered. "He's a foundling. Fourteen years ago he floated down to the mill dam, and our apprentice fished him out of the water."

The king realized that it was no one else but fortune's favorite, whom he had thrown into the water.

"My good people," he said, "would it be possible for the young boy to carry a letter to the queen? I'll give him two gold coins as a reward."

"As Your Majesty commands," they answered and told the young boy to get ready. Then the king wrote a letter to the queen, which said, "As soon as the boy arrives with this letter, he's to be killed and buried. All this is to be done before my return."

The boy set out with this letter but lost his way, and at night he came to a great forest. When he saw a small light in the darkness, he began walking toward it and soon reached a little cottage. Upon

entering, he discovered an old woman sitting all alone by the fire. She
was startled by the sight of him and asked, "Where did you come
from and where are you going?"

"I'm coming from the mill," he answered, "and I'm on my way to
deliver a letter to the queen. But since I've lost my way, I'd like to
spend the night here."

"You poor boy," said the woman. "You've stumbled on a robbers'
den. When they come home, they'll kill you."

"I don't care if they come," the young boy said. "I'm not afraid. Besides, I'm too tired to go any further."

He stretched himself out on a bench and fell asleep. Soon after, the robbers arrived and angrily asked who the strange boy was that was lying there.

"Oh," said the old woman, "he's just an innocent child who's lost his way in the forest, and I've taken him in out of pity. He's carrying a letter to the queen."

The robbers opened the letter and read it, and they discovered that the boy was to be killed immediately upon arrival. The hard-hearted robbers felt sorry for him, and the leader of the band tore up the letter and wrote another one, which said that the boy was to wed the king's daughter immediately upon arrival. They let him sleep peacefully on the bench until morning, and when he awoke, they showed him the right path out of the forest.

Once the queen received the letter and read it, she did as it said: she prepared a splendid wedding feast, and the king's daughter was married to fortune's favorite. Since the boy was handsome and friendly, she was quite happy and content to live with him. After some time passed, the king returned to the castle and saw that the prophecy had been fulfilled and that fortune's favorite had married his daughter.

"How did it happen?" he asked. "I gave entirely different orders in my letter."

The queen handed him the letter and told him to see what it said for himself. The king read the letter and realized right away that it had been switched for the one he wrote. He asked the young boy what had happened to the letter he had been entrusted to carry and why he had delivered another instead.

"I know nothing about it," he answered. "It must have been switched while I was asleep in the forest."

"Well, you're not going to get things as easily as you think!" said the king in a rage. "Whoever wants to have my daughter must first travel to hell and fetch three golden hairs from the devil's head. If you bring me what I want, you may keep my daughter."

This way the king hoped to get rid of him forever, but fortune's favorite answered, "You can count on me to fetch the golden hairs. I'm not afraid of the devil."

He then took his leave and began the journey. His way led him to a big city, where the watchman at the gate asked him what kind of trade he practiced and what he knew.

"I know everything," fortune's favorite said.

"Then you can do us a favor," the watchman responded, "and tell us why the fountain at our marketplace, which used to gush with wine, has run dry and doesn't even provide us with water anymore."

"Just wait until I return," he answered, "and you shall learn the reason why."

He continued on his way, and when he came to another city, the watchman at the gate again asked him what trade he practiced and what he knew.

"I know everything," he said.

"Then you can do us a favor and tell us why a tree in our city that used to bear golden apples doesn't produce even leaves anymore."

"Just wait until I return," he answered, "and you shall learn the reason why."

He went further and came to a big river that he had to cross. The ferryman asked him what kind of trade he practiced and what he knew.

"I know everything," he said.

"Then you can do me a favor," said the ferryman, "and tell me why I must take people back and forth without relief."

"Just wait until I return," he answered, "and you shall learn the reason why."

When fortune's favorite reached the other side of the river, he found the entrance to hell. It was dark and sooty inside, and the devil was not at home. However, his grandmother was sitting in a large easy chair.

"What do you want?" she asked him, but she did not look very wicked.

"I'd like to have three golden hairs from the devil's head," he replied, "or else I won't be able to keep my wife."

"That's a lot to ask," she said. "If the devil comes home and finds you, it will cost you your neck. But, since I feel sorry for you, I'll see if I can help."

She changed him into an ant and said, "Crawl into the folds of my skirt. You'll be safe there."

"All right," he answered. "That's fine, but there are still three things I'd like to know: Why has a fountain that used to gush with wine become dry and why doesn't it produce even water now? Why has a tree that used to bear golden apples no longer bear even leaves anymore? And, why must a ferryman take people back and forth without relief?"

"Those are difficult questions," she replied. "But keep still and quiet, and pay attention to what the devil says when I pull out the three golden hairs."

At nightfall the devil came home. No sooner did he enter the house than he noticed the air was not pure.

"I smell, I smell the flesh of a man," he said. "Something's wrong here."

Then he looked in all the nooks and crannies and searched around but could not find anything. The grandmother scolded him. "I've just swept," she said, "and put everything in order. Now you're messing it all up again. You're always smelling the flesh of men. Just sit down and eat your supper!"

After he had something to eat and drink, he was tired and laid his head in his grandmother's lap. Then he told her to pick the lice from his head for a while. Soon after, he fell asleep and began to snore and wheeze. Now the old woman grabbed hold of a golden hair, ripped it out, and put it down beside her.

"Ouch!" screamed the devil. "What are you doing to me?"

"I had a bad dream," the grandmother said, "and grabbed hold of your hair."

"What did you dream?" the devil asked.

"I dreamed there was a fountain at the marketplace that used to gush with wine, and it ran dry. It even stopped providing water. Why do you think that happened?"

"Ha!" the devil replied. "If they only knew! There's a toad

sitting underneath a stone in the fountain. If they kill it, the wine will flow again."

The grandmother began lousing him again until he fell asleep and snored so loudly that the windows trembled. Then she tore out a second hair.

"*Hey!* What are you doing?" the devil screamed angrily.

"I didn't mean it," she said. "I did it in a dream."

"What did you dream this time?" he asked.

"I dreamed that in a kingdom there was an apple tree that used to bear golden apples, and now it can't produce even leaves. Why do you think that happened?"

"Ha!" the devil replied. "If they only knew! There's a mouse gnawing at the roots. When they kill the mouse, the tree will bear golden apples again. If it continues to gnaw much longer, the tree will wither completely away. Now leave me alone with your dreams! If you disturb me in my sleep one more time, I'll give you a good hard slap!"

The grandmother spoke softly to him and loused him again until he fell asleep and began snoring. Then she grabbed hold of the third golden hair and tore it out. The devil jumped up, screamed, and was about to teach her a lesson, but she calmed him down again and said,

"What can you do against dreams?"

"What did you dream?" he asked and was curious in spite of himself.

"I dreamed of a ferryman who complained that he had to take people back and forth without relief. Why do you think he's got to do this?"

"Ha! The fool!" the devil replied. "He just has to put the pole into the hand of someone who wants to get across, and this person will have to do the ferrying, and the ferryman will be free."

Since the grandmother had now torn out the three golden hairs and the three questions had been answered, she let the old snake rest peacefully and sleep until daybreak. Thereupon the devil departed, and the old woman took the ant from the fold in her skirt and restored fortune's favorite to his human form.

"Here are the three golden hairs," she said. "You undoubtedly heard what the devil said to your three questions."

"Yes," he answered. "I heard everything, and I'll certainly remember it all."

"Then you have what you need," she said, "and now you can move on."

He thanked the old woman for helping him out of his predicament and left hell in a happy mood, for he had achieved what he had set out to do. When he came to the ferryman, he was obliged to keep his promise.

"Take me across first," said fortune's favorite, "and I'll tell you how you can be relieved of your work."

When he was on the other side, he gave him the devil's advice. "When someone comes and wants to be taken across, just put the pole in his hands."

Then fortune's favorite moved on, and when he came to the city where the barren tree stood, the watchman was also expecting his answer. So fortune's favorite told him what he had heard from the devil. "Kill the mouse that's been gnawing on the roots, then the tree will bear apples again."

The watchman thanked him and rewarded him with two donkeys laden with gold. Next fortune's favorite went to the city where the fountain had run dry and told the watchman what the devil had said. "There's a toad in the fountain sitting underneath a stone. You must find it and kill it. Then the fountain will gush with plenty of wine again."

The watchman thanked him and also gave him two donkeys laden with gold. Finally, fortune's favorite returned home to his wife, who was very happy to see him again and to hear how successful he had been. He brought the king what he had demanded, the three golden hairs, and when the king saw the four donkeys laden with gold, he was very pleased and said, "Now all the conditions have been fulfilled, and you may keep my daughter. But, my dear son-in-law, tell me, where did you get all this gold? It's such a great treasure!"

"I found it on the ground and picked it up after I crossed a river," he replied. "The bank is completely covered with gold instead of sand."

"Can I also get some?" asked the king, who was very greedy.

"As much as you like," he answered. "There's a ferryman at the river. Just let him take you across, and you'll be able to fill your sacks to the brim."

The greedy king set out as fast as he could, and when he came to the river, he signaled the ferryman to take him across. The ferryman came and told him to get into the boat, and when they reached the other side, the ferryman put the pole into his hand and ran away. From then on the king was compelled to ferry people back and forth as punishment for his sins.

"Is he still ferrying?"

"Why, of course. Do you think someone's about to take the pole away from him?"

◈ 30 ◈

The Louse and the Flea

A LOUSE AND A FLEA KEPT HOUSE TOGETHER and were brewing beer in an eggshell when the louse fell in and was scalded. Then the flea began to scream as loud as he could, and the little door to the room asked, "Why are you screaming, flea?"

"Because louse has been scalded."

Then the door began to creak, and a little broom in the corner asked, "Why are you creaking, door?"

"Why shouldn't I creak?"

Louse has just got scalded.
Flea is weeping."

Then the broom began to sweep in a frenzy, and when a little cart came driving by, it asked, "Why are you sweeping, broom?"

"Why shouldn't I sweep?

Louse has just got scalded.
Flea is weeping.
Door is creaking."

"Well, then I'm going to race around," said the cart, and it began racing around furiously, and the dung heap, which it passed, asked, "Why are you racing around, cart?"

"Why shouldn't I race around?

Louse has just got scalded.
Flea is weeping.
Door is creaking.
Broom is sweeping."

"Then I'm going to burn with fury," said the dung heap, and it began to burn in bright flames. Then a little tree nearby asked, "Why are you burning, dung heap?"

"Why shouldn't I burn?

Louse has just got scalded.
Flea is weeping.
Door is creaking.
Broom is sweeping.
Cart is racing."

"Well, then I'm going to shake myself," said the tree, and it shook itself so hard that all its leaves began to fall. Then a maiden with a water jug came by and asked, "Tree, why are you shaking?"
"Why shouldn't I shake?

Louse has just got scalded.
Flea is weeping.
Door is creaking.
Broom is sweeping.
Cart is racing.
Dung heap is burning."

"Well, then I'm going to break my water jug," said the maiden, and as she was breaking it, the spring from which the water came asked, "Maiden, why are you breaking the water jug?"
"Why shouldn't I break it?

Louse has just got scalded.
Flea is weeping.
Door is creaking.
Broom is sweeping.
Cart is racing.
Dung heap is burning.
Tree is shaking."

"Goodness gracious!" said the spring. "Then I'm going to flow," and it began to flow so violently that they were all drowned in the water—the maiden, the tree, the dung heap, the cart, the door, the flea, and the louse, every last one of them.

◆ 31 ◆

The Maiden Without Hands

A MILLER HAD BEEN FALLING little by little into poverty, and soon he had nothing left but his mill and a large apple tree behind it. One day, as he was on his way to chop wood in the forest, he met an old man whom he had never seen before.

"There's no reason you have to torture yourself by cutting wood," the old man said. "I'll make you rich if you promise to give me what's behind your mill."

What else can that be but my apple tree, thought the miller, and he gave the stranger his promise in writing.

"In three years I'll come and fetch what's mine," the stranger said with a snide laugh, and he went away.

When the miller returned home, his wife went out to meet him and said, "Tell me, miller, how did all this wealth suddenly get into our house? All at once I've discovered our chests and boxes are full. Nobody's brought anything, and I don't know how it's all happened."

"It's from a stranger I met in the forest," he said. "He promised me great wealth if I agreed in writing to give him what's behind our mill. We can certainly spare the large apple tree."

"Oh, husband!" his wife exclaimed in dread. "That was the devil! He didn't mean the apple tree but our daughter, who was behind the mill sweeping out the yard."

The miller's daughter was a beautiful and pious maiden who went through the next three years in fear of God and without sin. When the time was up and the day came for the devil to fetch her, she washed herself clean and drew a circle around her with chalk. The devil appeared quite early, but he could not get near her, and he said angrily to the miller, "I want you to take all the water away from her so she can't wash herself anymore. Otherwise, I have no power over her."

Since the miller was afraid of the devil, he did as he was told. The next morning the devil came again, but she wept on her hands and made them completely clean. Once more he could not get near her and said furiously to the miller, "Chop off her hands. Otherwise, I can't touch her."

The miller was horrified and replied, "How can I chop off the hands of my own child!"

But the devil threatened him and said, "If you don't do it, you're mine, and I'll come and get you myself!"

The father was so scared of him that he promised to obey. He went to his daughter and said, "My child, if I don't chop off both your hands, the devil will take me away, and in my fear I promised I'd do it. Please help me out of my dilemma and forgive me for the injury I'm causing you."

"Dear Father," she answered, "do what you want with me. I'm your child."

Then she extended both her hands and let him chop them off. The devil came a third time, but she had wept so long and so much on the stumps that they too were all clean. Then he had to abandon his game and lost all claim to her.

Now the miller said to his daughter, "I've become so wealthy because of you that I shall see to it you'll live in splendor for the rest of your life."

But she answered, "No, I cannot stay here. I'm going away and shall depend on the kindness of people to provide me with whatever I need."

Then she had her maimed arms bound to her back, and at dawn she set out on her way and walked the entire day until it became dark. She was right outside a royal garden, and by the glimmer of the moon she could see trees full of beautiful fruit. She could not enter the garden, though because it was surrounded by water. Since she had traveled the entire day without eating, she was very hungry. Oh, if only I could get in! she thought. I must eat some of the fruit or else I'll perish! Then she fell to her knees, called out to the Lord, and prayed. Suddenly an angel appeared who closed one of the locks in the stream so that the moat became dry and she could walk through it. Now she went into the garden accompanied by the angel. She caught sight of a beautiful tree full of pears, but the pears had all been counted. Nonetheless, she approached the tree and ate one of the pears with her mouth to satisfy her hunger, but only this one. The gardener was watching her, but since the angel was standing there, he was afraid, especially since he thought the maiden was a spirit. He kept still and did not dare to cry out or speak to her. After she had eaten the pear, and her hunger was stilled, she went and hid in the bushes.

The next morning the king who owned the garden came and counted the pears. When he saw one was missing, he asked the gardener what had happened to it, for the pear was not lying under the tree and had somehow vanished.

"Last night a spirit appeared," answered the gardener. "It had no hands and ate one of the pears with its mouth."

"How did the spirit get over the water?" asked the king. "And where did it go after it ate the pear?"

"Someone wearing a garment as white as snow came down from heaven, closed the lock, and dammed up the water so the spirit could walk through the moat. And, since it must have been an angel, I was afraid to ask any questions or to cry out. After the spirit had eaten the pear, it just went away."

"If it's as you say," said the king, "I shall spend the night with you and keep watch."

When it became dark, the king went into the garden and brought a priest with him to talk to the spirit. All three sat down beneath the tree and kept watch. At midnight the maiden came out of the bushes, walked over to the tree, and once again ate one of the pears with her mouth, while the angel in white stood next to her. The priest stepped forward and said to the maiden, "Have you come from heaven or from earth? Are you a spirit or a human being?"

"I'm not a spirit, but a poor creature forsaken by everyone except God."

"You may be forsaken by the whole world, but I shall not forsake you," said the king.

He took her with him to his royal palace, and since she was so beautiful and good, he loved her with all his heart, had silver hands made for her, and took her for his wife.

After a year had passed, the king had to go to war, and he placed the young queen under the care of his mother and said, "If she has a child, I want you to protect her and take good care of her, and write me right away."

Soon after, the young queen gave birth to a fine-looking boy. The king's mother wrote to him immediately to announce the joyful news. However, on the way the messenger stopped to rest near a brook, and since he was exhausted from the long journey, he fell asleep. Then the devil appeared. He was still trying to harm the pious queen, and so he exchanged the letter for another one that said that the queen had given birth to a changeling. When the king read the letter, he was horrified and quite distressed, but he wrote his mother that she should protect the queen and take care of her until his return. The messenger started back with the letter, but he stopped to rest at the same spot and fell asleep. Once again the devil came and put a different letter in his pocket that said that they should kill the queen and her child. The old mother was tremendously disturbed when she received the letter and could not believe it. She wrote the king again but received the same answer because the devil kept replacing the messenger's letters with false letters each time. The last letter ordered the king's mother to keep the tongue and eyes of the queen as proof that she had done his bidding.

But the old woman wept at the thought of shedding such innocent blood. During the night she had a doe fetched and cut out its tongue and eyes and put them away. Then she said to the queen, "I can't let you be killed as the king commands. However, you can't stay here any longer. Go out into the wide world with your child and never come back."

She tied the child to the queen's back, and the poor woman went off with tears in her eyes. When she came to a great wild forest, she fell down on her knees and prayed to God. The Lord's angel appeared before her and led her to a small cottage with a little sign saying "Free Lodging for Everyone." A maiden wearing a snow white garment came out of the cottage and said, "Welcome, Your Highness," and took her inside. She untied the little boy from her back and offered him her breast so he could have something to drink. Then she laid him down in a beautifully made bed.

"How did you know that I'm a queen?" asked the poor woman.

"I'm an angel sent by God to take care of you and your child," replied the maiden in white.

So the queen stayed seven years in the cottage and was well cared for. By the grace of God and through her own piety her hands that had been chopped off grew back again.

When the king finally returned from the wars, the first thing he wanted to do was to see his wife and child. However, his old mother began to weep and said, "You wicked man, why did you write and order me to kill two innocent souls?" She showed him the two letters that the devil had forged and resumed talking. "I did as you ordered," and she displayed the tongue and eyes.

At the sight of them the king burst into tears and wept bitterly over his poor wife and little son. His old mother was aroused and took pity on him.

"Console yourself," she said. "She's still alive. I secretly had a doe killed and kept its tongue and eyes as proof. Then I took the child and tied him to your wife's back and ordered her to go out into the wide world, and she had to promise me never to return here because you were so angry with her."

"I shall go as far as the sky is blue, without eating or drinking, until I find my dear wife and child," the king said. "That is, unless they have been killed or have died of hunger in the meantime."

The king wandered for about seven years and searched every rocky cliff and cave he came across. When he did not find her, he thought she had perished. During this time he neither ate nor drank, but God kept him alive. Eventually, he came to a great forest, where he discovered the little cottage with the sign "Free Lodging for Everyone." Then the maiden in white came out, took him by the hand, and led him inside.

"Welcome, Your Majesty," she said, and asked him where he came from.

"I've been wandering about for almost seven years looking for my wife and child, but I can't find them."

The angel offered him food and drink, but he refused and said he only wanted to rest awhile. So he lay down to sleep and covered his face with a handkerchief. Then the angel went into the room where the queen was sitting with her son, whom she was accustomed to calling Sorrowful, and said, "Go into the next room with your child. Your husband has come."

So the queen went to the room where he was lying, and the handkerchief fell from his face.

"Sorrowful," she said, "pick up your father's handkerchief and put it over his face again."

The child picked the handkerchief up and put it over his face. The king heard all this in his sleep and took pleasure in making the handkerchief drop on the floor again. The boy became impatient and said, "Dear Mother, how can I cover my father's face when I have no father on earth. I've learned to pray to 'our Father that art in heaven,' and you told me that my father was in heaven and that he was our good Lord. How am I supposed to recognize this wild man? He's not my father."

When the king heard this, he sat up and asked her who she was.

"I'm your wife," she replied, "and this is your son, Sorrowful."

When the king saw that she had real hands, he said, "My wife had silver hands."

"Our merciful Lord let my natural hands grow again," she answered.

The angel went back into the sitting room, fetched the silver hands, and showed them to him. Now he knew for certain that it was his dear wife and dear son, and he kissed them and was happy.

"A heavy load has been taken off my mind," he said.

After the Lord's angel ate one more meal with them, they went home to be with the king's old mother. There was rejoicing everywhere, and the king and queen had a second wedding and lived happily ever after.

◈ 32 ◈

Clever Hans

"WHERE ARE YOU GOING, Hans?" his mother asked.

"To Gretel's," Hans replied.

"Take care, Hans."

"Don't worry. Good-bye, Mother."

Hans arrived at Gretel's place.

"Good day, Gretel."

"Good day, Hans. Have you brought me anything nice?"

"Didn't bring anything. Want something from you."

Gretel gave him a needle.

"Good-bye, Gretel," Hans said.

"Good-bye, Hans."

Hans took the needle, stuck it in the hay wagon, and walked home behind the wagon.

"Good evening, Mother."

"Good evening, Hans. Where have you been?"

"At Gretel's."

"What did you bring her?"

"Didn't bring her a thing. Got something."

"What did Gretel give you?"

"Got a needle."

"Where'd you put the needle, Hans?"

"Stuck it in a hay wagon."

"That was stupid of you, Hans. You should have stuck it in your sleeve."

"Doesn't matter. I'll do better next time."

"Where are you going, Hans?"

"To Gretel's, Mother."

"Take care, Hans."

"Don't worry. Good-bye, Mother."

Hans arrived at Gretel's place.

"Good day, Gretel."

"Good day, Hans. Have you brought me anything nice?"

"Didn't bring anything. Want something from you."

Gretel gave Hans a knife.

"Good-bye, Gretel."

"Good-bye, Hans."

Hans took the knife, stuck it in his sleeve, and went home.

"Good evening, Mother."

"Good evening, Hans. Where have you been?"

"At Gretel's."

"What did you bring her?"

"Didn't bring her a thing. Got something."

"What did Gretel give you?"

"Got a knife."

"Where'd you put the knife, Hans?"

"Stuck it in my sleeve."

"That was stupid of you, Hans. You should have put it in your pocket."

"Doesn't matter. I'll do better next time."

"Where are you going, Hans?"

"To Gretel's, Mother."

"Take care, Hans."

"Don't worry. Good-bye, Mother."

Hans arrived at Gretel's place.

"Good day, Gretel."

"Good day, Hans. Have you brought me anything nice?"

"Didn't bring anything. Want something from you."
Gretel gave Hans a kid goat.
"Good-bye, Gretel."
"Good-bye, Hans."
Hans took the goat, tied its legs together, and stuck it in his pocket. By the time he got home, the goat had suffocated.
"Good evening, Mother."
"Good evening, Hans. Where have you been?"
"At Gretel's."
"What did you bring her?"
"Didn't bring a thing. Got something."
"What did Gretel give you?"
"Got a goat."
"Where'd you put the goat, Hans?"
"Stuck it in my pocket."
"That was stupid of you, Hans. You should have tied the goat to a rope."
"Doesn't matter. I'll do better next time."

"Where are you going, Hans?"
"To Gretel's, Mother."
"Take care, Hans."
"Don't worry. Good-bye, Mother."
"Good-bye, Hans."
Hans arrived at Gretel's place.
"Good day, Gretel."
"Good day, Hans. Have you brought me anything nice?"
"Didn't bring anything. Want something from you."
Gretel gave Hans a piece of bacon.
Hans took the bacon, tied it to a rope, and dragged it along behind him. The dogs came and ate the bacon. By the time Hans arrived home, he had the rope in his hand but nothing attached to it anymore.
"Good evening, Mother."
"Good evening, Hans. Where have you been?"
"At Gretel's."
"What did you bring her?"
"Didn't bring her a thing. Got something."
"What did Gretel give you?"
"Got a piece of bacon."
"What have you done with the bacon, Hans?"
"Tied it to a rope. Dragged it home. Dogs got it."
"That was stupid of you, Hans. You should have carried the bacon on your head."
"Doesn't matter. I'll do better next time."

"Where are you going, Hans?"

"To Gretel's, Mother."

"Take care, Hans."

"Don't worry. Good-bye, Mother."

"Good-bye, Hans."

Hans arrived at Gretel's place.

"Good day, Gretel."

"Good day, Hans. Have you brought me anything nice?"

"Didn't bring anything. Want something from you."

Gretel gave Hans a calf.

"Good-bye, Gretel."

"Good-bye, Hans."

Hans took the calf, set it on his head, and the calf kicked him in his face.

"Good evening, Mother."

"Good evening, Hans. Where have you been?"

"At Gretel's."

"What did you bring her?"

"Didn't bring her a thing. Got something."

"What did Gretel give you?"

"Got a calf."

"What have you done with the calf?"

"Put it on my head. Kicked me in my face."

"That was stupid of you, Hans. You should have led the calf to the stable and put it in the stall."

"Doesn't matter. I'll do better next time."

"Where are you going, Hans?"

"To Gretel's, Mother."

"Take care, Hans."

"Don't worry. Good-bye, Mother."

"Good-bye, Hans."

Hans arrived at Gretel's place.

"Good day, Gretel."

"Good day, Hans. Have you brought me anything nice?"

"Didn't bring anything. Want something from you."

"I'll come along with you," Gretel said.

Hans took Gretel, put a rope around her, led her into the stable, tied her to a stall, and threw her some grass. Then he went to his mother.

"Good evening, Mother."

"Good evening, Hans. Where have you been?"

"At Gretel's."

"What did you bring her?"

"Didn't bring her a thing."

"What did Gretel give you?"

"Got nothing. She came along."

"Where have you left Gretel?"

"Led her by a rope and tied her up in the stall and threw her some grass."

"That was stupid of you, Hans. You should have thrown friendly looks at her with the eyes."

Hans went into the stable, cut out the eyes of all the cows and sheep, and threw them in Gretel's face. Then Gretel got angry, tore herself loose, and ran away. That was how Hans lost his bride.

◆ 33 ◆

The Three Languages

THERE WAS ONCE AN OLD COUNT who lived in Switzerland, and he had an only son, who was quite stupid and could not learn anything.

"Listen, my son," the father said, "I can't get anything to sink into your head, no matter how much I try. So I'm sending you away from here and placing you under the care of a famous master. Let's see what he can do with you."

The young man was sent to a strange city and stayed with the master for a whole year. At the end of this time he came home, and his father asked, "Well, my son, what have you learned?"

"Father," he responded, "I've learned to understand the barking of dogs."

"May God have mercy on us!" the father exclaimed. "Is that all you've learned? Well, now I'm going to send you to a master in another city."

The young man was taken there and stayed one year with this master as well. When he came back home, his father asked again, "My son, what have you learned?"

"Father," he responded, "I've learned to understand the language of birds."

The father became infuriated and said, "You're hopeless! Why, you've wasted all this valuable time and have learned nothing! And you're not even ashamed to appear before my eyes! Well, I'm going to send you to a third master, but if you don't learn anything this time, I'm no longer going to be your father."

The son spent a whole year with the third master too, and when he returned home, the father asked, "My son, what have you learned?"

"Dear Father," he responded, "I've learned to understand the croaking of frogs."

Now the father was so infuriated that he jumped up, summoned his men, and said, "This creature is no longer my son. I'm expelling him and want you to take him out into the forest and kill him."

The count's men took him into the forest, but they felt so sorry for the son that they could not bring themselves to kill him and let him go. Then they cut out the eyes and tongue of a deer to provide the old man with proof of their deed.

Meanwhile, the young man wandered about, and after some time he came to a castle, where he asked for a night's lodging.

"All right," said the lord of the castle, "—if you're prepared to spend the night in the old tower. You may go there, but let me warn you that you'll be risking your life. The tower is full of wild dogs that bark and howl continually, and at certain times they must be given a human being, whom they devour right away."

The entire region had been enduring great sorrow and suffering because of this, and yet, nobody could do anything about it. However, the young man was fearless and said, "I shall go down and face the barking dogs. Just give me something that I can throw to them. They won't harm me."

Since he insisted, they gave him some food for the wild beasts and brought him down to the tower. When he entered, the dogs did not bark but wagged their tails in a friendly way and gathered around him. They ate what he set before them and did not touch a hair of his head. The next morning, to everyone's astonishment, he reappeared alive and well and said to the lord of the castle, "The dogs have spoken to me in their language and revealed to me why they've been dwelling here and causing terror in your country. They're under a curse and are compelled to protect a great treasure lying under the tower. They'll never find peace until the treasure is dug up, and they've told me how this can be done."

All those who heard this rejoiced, and the lord of the castle said he would adopt him as his son if he could accomplish this task successfully. The young count went back down to the tower, and since he knew what was to be done, he completed it and brought up a chest filled with gold. From then on the wild dogs no longer howled, nor were they ever seen again, and the land was freed of this plague.

After a while the young man decided to go to Rome, and along the way he passed a swamp where some frogs were sitting and croaking. He stopped and listened, and when he heard what they were saying, he grew very pensive and sad. At last, when he arrived in Rome, he learned that the pope had just died, and the cardinals could not agree on a successor. Eventually, they resolved to wait for a divine miracle to reveal the person they should elect. At the very moment that they came to this decision the young count happened to enter the church, and two white doves swooped down to his shoulders and rested on them. The cardinals recognized this as a sign from God and asked him on the spot whether he wanted to be pope. At first he was undecided and did not know if he was worthy enough, but the doves persuaded him to do it, and finally he consented. He was annointed and consecrated, and thus the prophecy that he had heard from the frogs along the way was fulfilled. Indeed, it had been this very prophecy that had upset him, for he had not expected to become the holy pope. After that he had to sing mass and did not know a single word of it, but the two doves were still sitting on his shoulders and whispered the words in his ear.

◈ 34 ◈

Clever Else

THERE ONCE WAS A MAN who had a daughter called Clever Else. When she had grown up, her father said, "It's time for her to get married."

"I agree," said her mother. "If only someone would come along and take her."

At last someone named Hans came from far away, and he began courting her. However, he set one condition: Clever Else had to prove she was really smart.

"Oh," said her father, "she's as bright as the newborn day."

"Oh," said her mother, "she can see the wind coming down the road and hear flies cough."

"Fine and good," said Hans. "But if she isn't really smart, I'm not going to take her."

When they were sitting at the table and had finished their meal, the mother said, "Else, go down to the cellar and fetch some beer."

Clever Else took the pitcher from the wall, went down to the cellar, and along the way played with the lid by flapping it to pass the time. When she got down there, she took a stool and put it in front of the keg so she would not have to stoop, for she was afraid of hurting her back or causing herself some unexpected injury. Then she set the pitcher in front of her and turned the tap. While the beer was running, she kept her eyes busy by looking up at the wall, where she gazed around for some time. At last she caught sight of a pickax hanging directly above her. The masons had left it hanging there by mistake. Suddenly Clever Else began to weep, and she said, "If I get Hans and we have a child and he grows up and we send him to the cellar to draw some beer, the pickax will fall on his head and kill him."

Then she just sat there and wept and bawled with all her might on account of the impending disaster. Upstairs the others waited for the beer, but Clever Else did not return. Then the mother said to the maid, "You'd better go down to the cellar and see what's keeping Else."

The maid went and found her sitting in front of the keg and bawling with all her might.

"Else, why are you crying?" asked the maid.

"Why shouldn't I cry? If I get Hans and we have a child and he grows up and we send him to draw some beer, there's a good chance that the pickax will fall on his head and kill him."

"What a clever Else we've got!" said the maid, who sat down next to her and also began to weep about the disaster.

After a while, when the maid did not return and the others upstairs were getting thirsty for the beer, the father said to the servant, "You'd better go down to the cellar and see what's keeping Else and the maid."

The servant went downstairs and found Else and the maid sitting together and weeping.

"Why are you crying?" he asked.

"Oh," said Else, "why shouldn't I cry? If I get Hans and we have a child and he grows up and we send him to draw beer, the pickax will fall on his head and kill him."

"What a clever Else we've got!" said the servant, who sat down next to her and also began to howl loudly.

Upstairs the others waited for the servant, but when he did not appear, the husband said to his wife, "You'd better go down to the cellar and see what's keeping Else."

The wife went down and found all three wailing and wanted to know the reason. So Else told her that her future child would probably be killed by the pickax when he grew up and was sent to draw some beer, for the pickax would fall down.

"What a clever Else we've got!" her mother said, and she sat down next to her and began weeping.

Now, the husband waited upstairs awhile longer, but when his wife did not return and he grew thirstier and thirstier, he said, "I'd better go down to the cellar myself and see what's keeping Else."

When he reached the cellar and saw them all sitting together and weeping, he learned that Else's future child was the cause of it, for he might be killed by the pickax if he were under it drawing beer at the exact same time that the ax fell. Then he exclaimed, "What a clever Else we've got!" And he sat down and wept too.

The bridegroom continued to sit alone upstairs for a long time. But when it seemed that nobody would return, he thought, They're probably waiting for me to come downstairs. I'd better go down and see what they're up to.

When he got there and saw the five of them screaming and moaning quite pitifully, he asked, "Has there been an accident of some kind?"

"Oh, dear Hans," Else said, "if we get married and have a child, and he grows up and we happen to send him here to draw beer, then the pickax that's been left behind up there could fall on his head and split his skull in two! Don't you think that's reason enough to cry?"

"Well," said Hans, "I certainly don't need more brains than that for my household. Since you're such a clever Else, I'll have you for my wife." So he took her by the hand, led her upstairs, and married her.

One day, after Hans had been living with Else for some time, he said, "Wife, I'm going to go to work and earn some money, and I want you to go into the field and cut the wheat so we can have some bread."

"Yes, my dear Hans, I'll do that."

When Hans had gone away, she cooked some good porridge and took it with her into the field. When she got there, she said to herself,

"What should I do first, cut the wheat or sleep? I think I'll sleep first." So she lay down in the wheatfield and fell asleep.

Meanwhile, Hans had been back at home for some time, and when Else did not appear, he said, "What a clever Else I've got! She's so industrious that she doesn't even come home to eat."

But when evening came and she still did not appear, Hans went out to see what she had cut. However, nothing was cut, and she was lying asleep in the wheatfield. Hans hurried back home and fetched a net with bells used for catching birds. He hung it over Else while she continued sleeping. After that he ran home, locked the front door, and sat down on a chair to work.

Finally, when it was already quite dark, Clever Else awoke. As she stood up she heard jingling all around her, and the little bells rang at each step she took. Then she became frightened and so confused that she did not know whether she was really Clever Else.

"Is it me, or isn't it me?" she asked.

Since she did not know what to answer, she just stood there in doubt for a while. Finally, she thought, I'll go home and ask whether it's me or not. They'll surely know.

She ran to the front door, but it was locked. Then she knocked at the window and called out, "Hans, is Else inside?"

"Yes," answered Hans. "She's here."

That made her frightened, and she said, "Oh, God, then I'm not me," and she went to another house, but when the people heard the bells, they did not want to open the door. Since there was no place for her to go, Clever Else ran out of the village, and nobody has ever seen her again.

◈ 35 ◈

The Tailor in Heaven

ONE FINE DAY it happened that the good Lord decided to go for a walk in the heavenly garden. He took all the apostles and saints with him, and nobody was left in heaven except Saint Peter. The Lord ordered him not to let a soul enter during his absence. So Saint Peter stood at the gate and kept watch. Soon someone knocked, and Saint Peter asked who was there and what he wanted.

"I'm a poor honest tailor," a slick voice answered, "and I'd like to come in."

"Sure, you're honest!" said Saint Peter. "About as honest as a thief on the gallows. Your light fingers have stolen many pieces of cloth from people, and I'm certainly not going to let you enter heaven. The Lord has forbidden me to let anyone in while he's out."

"Have mercy," the tailor cried out. "They were just scraps of cloth that fell from the tables by themselves. They weren't stolen, and they're not even worth talking about. Look, I'm limping. I've got blisters all over my feet from walking here, and I can't possibly turn back. Let me in, and I'll do all the dirty work. I'll carry the babies, wash their diapers, clean the benches they play on, and mend their tattered clothes."

Saint Peter let himself be moved by pity and opened heaven's gate just wide enough for the lame tailor to slip his lean body through. He was ordered to sit down in a corner behind the door and to keep absolutely still so the Lord would not notice him upon his return and get angry. The tailor obeyed, but once when Saint Peter stepped out the door, the tailor got up, full of curiosity, and explored all the nooks and crannies of heaven, inspecting everything he saw. Finally, he came to a place where there were many beautiful and exquisite chairs, and in the middle was an armchair made of solid gold and studded with glistening jewels. It was much taller than the other chairs, and a golden footstool stood in front of it. This was the Lord's armchair, and he sat in it when he was at home. It was from this seat that he could see everything that happened on earth. The tailor stood still and looked at the chair for a good long time, for it appealed to him more than anything else he had seen. Finally, his curiosity got the better of him, and he climbed up and sat down in the chair. Then he could see everything that was happening on earth, and he noticed an ugly woman washing some clothes at a brook. When she secretly put two veils aside, the tailor became so infuriated by the sight that he grabbed the golden footstool and hurled it down from heaven at the old thief on earth. Upon realizing that he could not retrieve the footstool, the tailor slipped quietly out of the armchair, took his place behind the door again, and pretended he had not been stirring up trouble.

When the Lord and Master returned with his heavenly retinue, he did not notice the tailor behind the door. But when he sat down in his armchair, he did indeed remark that his footstool was missing. He asked Saint Peter what had happened to it, but Saint Peter did not know. Then the Lord asked him whether he had let anyone in.

"I don't know of anyone who's been here," Saint Peter replied, "except a lame tailor who's still sitting behind the door."

Then the Lord had the tailor appear before him and asked him whether he had taken the footstool and what he had done with it.

"Oh, Lord," the tailor answered joyfully. "I threw it in anger at an old woman on earth because she was stealing two veils while washing clothes."

"How ridiculous you are!" exclaimed the Lord. "If I were to judge as you do, what do you think would have happened to you by now? I would no longer have any chairs, benches, armchairs, or even fire tongs, because I'd have thrown them all at sinners. It's clear that you can't stay here any longer. I want you to leave through heaven's gate. Then you may go wherever you will. Nobody shall dole out punishment but me, the Lord your God."

Saint Peter had to lead the tailor through heaven's gate, and since the tailor's shoes were torn and his feet were covered with blisters, the tailor took a stick in his hand for a cane and walked to Waitawhile, where the good soldiers sit and make merry.

❖ 36 ❖

The Magic Table, the Golden Donkey, and the Club in the Sack

IN DAYS OF OLD there was a tailor who had three sons and only one goat. Since they all lived on the goat's milk, she had to be fed well and be taken out each day to graze somewhere. The sons took turns doing this, and one day the oldest son led her to the churchyard, where the finest grass was growing. He let her graze there and run about. In the evening, when it was time to go home, he asked her, "Goat, have you had enough?"

The goat answered:

"Oh, my, I'm stuffed!
Enough's enough.
Meh! Meh!"

"Then let's head for home," said the boy. He took her by the rope, led her back to the barn, and tied her up.

"Well," said the old tailor, "did the goat have a proper feeding?"

"Oh," answered the son, "she's really stuffed. I can tell she's had more than enough."

But the father wanted to make sure of everything himself. So he went down to the barn, patted the precious creature, and asked, "Goat, have you had enough?"

The goat replied:

"How can I have eaten enough
when the ground was dry and horribly rough
and the leaves and grass were much too tough?
Meh! Meh!"

"What's this I hear!" the tailor exclaimed, and he ran upstairs to his
son. "You liar!" he yelled. "You said the goat had enough to eat, and
yet you let her starve!" And in his rage he grabbed his yardstick from
the wall, gave his son a good beating, and drove him out of the house.

The next day it was the second son's turn, and he chose a place near
the garden hedge where only the very best grass was growing, and the
goat combed it clean. In the evening, when the son wanted to go
home, he asked, "Goat, have you had enough?"
The goat answered:

"Oh, my, I'm stuffed!
Enough's enough.
Meh! Meh!"

"Then let's head for home," said the boy, and he pulled her home
and tied her up in the barn.

"Well," said the old tailor, "did the goat have a proper feeding?"

"Oh," answered the son, "she's really stuffed. I can tell she's had
more than enough."

Since the tailor did not trust his son, he went down to the barn and
asked, "Goat, have you had enough?"
The goat replied:

"How can I have eaten enough
when the ground was dry and horribly rough
and the leaves and grass were much too tough?
Meh! Meh!"

"The godless scoundrel!" the tailor screamed. "How could he let
such a good creature starve?" And he ran out, grabbed his yardstick,
and beat his second son out of the house.

Now it was the third son's turn, and he wanted to do a good job.
He looked for bushes with the finest leaves and let the goat eat them.
In the evening, when he wanted to go home, he asked, "Goat, have
you had enough?"
The goat answered:

"Oh, my, I'm stuffed!
Enough's enough.
Meh! Meh!"

"Then let's head for home," said the boy. He led her into the barn and tied her up.

"Well," said the old tailor, "did the goat have a proper feeding?"

"Oh," answered the son, "she's really stuffed. I can tell she's had more than enough."

Since the tailor did not trust him, he went downstairs and asked, "Goat, have you had enough?"

The wicked animal replied:

"How can I have eaten enough
when the ground was dry and horribly rough
and the leaves and grass were much too tough?
Meh! Meh!"

"Oh, you pack of liars!" the tailor exclaimed. "One as devious and unreliable as the next! You're not going to make a fool of me anymore!" And in his rage he lost control of himself, ran upstairs, and gave his third son such a terrible beating with his yardstick that the boy ran out of the house.

Now the old tailor was alone with his goat. The next morning he went down into the barn, petted the goat, and said, "Come, my dear little goat, I myself shall take you out to graze."

He took her by the rope and led her to green hedges, clusters of yarrow, and to other things that goats like to eat.

"This time you can eat to your heart's content," he said to her, and let her graze until evening. Then he said, "Goat, have you had enough?"

The goat answered:

"Oh, my, I'm stuffed!
Enough's enough.
Meh! Meh!"

"Then let's head for home," said the tailor, and he led her into the barn and tied her up. Just as he was about to leave, he turned around once more and said, "Now you've really had enough for once!"

But the goat was just as ornery to him as usual and cried out:

"How can I have eaten enough
when the ground was dry and horribly rough
and the leaves and grass were much too tough?
Meh! Meh!"

When the tailor heard that, he was stunned, and he realized he had driven his sons away without cause.

"Just you wait!" he exclaimed. "You ungrateful creature! Sending you away would be much too mild a punishment for you. I'm going to brand you so you'll never be able to show your face among honest tailors anymore."

He ran upstairs in great haste, fetched his razor, lathered the goat's head, and shaved it as smooth as the palm of his hand. And, since he thought the yardstick would be too good for her, he got out his whip and gave her such a thrashing that she leapt high in the air and dashed away.

When the tailor was all alone in his house, he fell into a great depression and wished his sons were there again. But no one knew where they had gone. Meanwhile, his oldest son had been taken on as an apprentice with a carpenter. He worked hard and learned diligently, and when the time came for him to depart and begin his travels as a journeyman, the master gave him a little table that did not appear to be anything special and was made out of ordinary wood. However, it had one good quality. Whenever one put it down and said, "Table, be covered," it would immediately be covered by a clean tablecloth, and on it would be a plate with a fork and a knife, and dishes with roasted and stewed meat, as much as there was room for on the table, and a large glass of sparkling red wine to tickle one's throat. The young journeyman thought, That's enough to keep you going for the rest of your life! Naturally, his spirits were high as he set out on his travels in the world. He did not care whether an inn was good or bad or whether he would find something to eat there or not. If he had no desire to stop at an inn, he just went into a field, a forest, or a meadow, wherever he liked. Then he took the little table off his back, set it down before him, and said, "Be covered!" In seconds everything his heart desired was there.

At length he decided to return to his father in the hope that his father's anger might have subsided and that he might be glad to see him with the magic table. Now, it happened that on his way home he stopped at an inn, which was filled with guests. They greeted him warmly and invited him to sit down and eat with them; otherwise, he would have trouble getting something to eat so late.

"No," the carpenter said, "I don't want to take away your last few morsels. Instead, I'd prefer you to be my guests."

They all laughed and thought he was joking with them, but he set up his little table in the middle of the room and said, "Table, be covered!"

Within seconds the table was covered with much better food than the innkeeper could have produced, and the guests inhaled the lovely aroma with their nostrils.

"Help yourselves, dear friends," said the carpenter, and when the guests realized he meant it, they did not have to be asked twice. They drew up their seats, pulled out their knives, and plunged in bravely.

What astonished them was that a new dish appeared by itself as soon as one dish became empty. The innkeeper stood in a corner and watched everything without knowing what to say, but he thought, I could certainly use a cook like that in my business.

The carpenter and his companions enjoyed themselves until late into the night. Finally, they went to sleep, and the young journeyman put his magic table against the wall and went to bed too. The innkeeper's thoughts, however, left him no peace, and he recalled that there was an old table in the storage room that looked just like the magic one. He went and got it and then switched it quietly with the magic table. The next morning the carpenter paid for the lodging and packed the table on his back without realizing that he had the wrong one. He set out on his way and at noon came to his father, who welcomed him with great joy.

"Well, my dear son, what have you learned?" he asked him.

"Father, I've become a carpenter."

"That's a good trade," replied the old man, "but what have you brought back with you from your travels?"

"Father, the best thing I've brought back is this table."

The tailor examined it from all sides and said, "I can't say that you've made a masterpiece. It's just a shabby old table."

"But it's a magic table," answered his son. "When I put it down and tell it to be covered, the most delicious dishes appear at once, and wine as well. It will warm your heart with joy. Just invite all our relatives and friends. I'll provide them with good refreshments and a fine meal. My table will give them more than enough to eat."

When the company was assembled, he set the table in the middle of the parlor and said, "Table, be covered!" But the table did not move an inch. It remained just as bare as any ordinary table that cannot understand speech. The poor journeyman now realized that his table had been switched, and he was ashamed at having to appear like a liar. His relatives laughed at him, but they were forced to return home without having anything to eat or drink. His father got out his sewing material again and resumed working, while the son found a job with a master.

The second son had gone to a miller to serve an apprenticeship. When his years were up, the master said, "Since you've done such a good job, I'm going to give you a special kind of donkey. He doesn't draw carts, nor does he carry sacks."

"Well, what's he good for?" asked the young journeyman.

"He spits gold," the miller replied. "If you set him on a piece of cloth and say 'Bricklebrit,' the good animal will spit out gold pieces from the front and behind."

"That's a wonderful thing," said the journeyman, who thanked his master and went out into the world. Whenever he needed money, he only had to say "Bricklebrit" to his donkey, and it would rain gold pieces, which he picked off the ground. Wherever he went, only the best was good enough for him, and the more expensive the better, for his purse was always full. After he had traveled about in the world for some time, he thought, You really ought to seek out your father. If you return to him with the gold donkey, he's bound to forget his anger and give you a nice welcome.

It so happened that he stopped at the same inn in which his brother's magic table had been switched. He led his donkey by the bridle, and the innkeeper wanted to take the animal from him and tie it up, but the young journeyman said, "Don't bother yourself. I'll lead my gray steed into the stable myself and tie him up because I must know where he is."

The innkeeper found this strange and thought that whoever had to take care of his donkey himself did not have much money to spend. But when the stranger reached into his pocket, took out two gold coins, and told him to buy something very good for him, the innkeeper's eyes opened wide. He promptly ran and brought out the best food he could find. After the meal the guest asked the innkeeper what he owed him, and the innkeeper, who had no scruples about chalking up double the amount, charged him another couple of gold pieces. The journeyman reached into his pocket, but his gold had just run out.

"Wait a minute, innkeeper," he said. "I just want to go and fetch some gold."

As he left he took the tablecloth with him, and the innkeeper did not know what to make of that. Since he was curious, he sneaked after him, and when the guest bolted the stable door, the innkeeper peeped through a knothole. The stranger spread the tablecloth out under the donkey and said "Bricklebrit," and instantly the animal began to spit so much gold from the front and the rear that it was like a good rainfall.

"The devil take me!" said the innkeeper. "What a way to mint ducats! I wouldn't mind having a money purse like that!"

The guest paid his bill and went to sleep, but the innkeeper crept into the stable, led the money-maker away, and tied up another donkey in its place. Early the next morning the journeyman departed with a donkey that he thought was his gold donkey. At noon he arrived at his father's house, and the father was delighted to see his son again and gave him a nice welcome.

"What have you made of yourself, my son?" asked the old man.

"A miller, dear Father," he replied.

"What have you brought back with you from your travels?"

"Nothing but a donkey."

"There are plenty of donkeys here," the father said. "I really would have preferred a good goat."

"Yes," responded the son, "but this is not an ordinary donkey. It's a gold donkey. If I say 'Bricklebrit,' the good animal spits out enough gold to cover a piece of cloth. Just call our relatives together, and I'll make them all rich people."

"I like that idea," said the tailor. "Then I won't have to torture myself anymore with this sewing."

He himself ran off to gather the relatives together. As soon as they were all assembled, the miller told them to make room. Then he spread his piece of cloth on the floor and brought the donkey into the parlor.

"Now, pay attention," he said, and cried out "Bricklebrit!" But what fell were not gold pieces, and it was quite clear that the animal knew nothing about the art of making gold, for there are very few donkeys who become so accomplished. The poor miller made a long face. He realized that he had been cheated and apologized to his relatives, who went home as poor as they had come. As for the old man, there was nothing left to do but resume tailoring, and the son hired himself out to a miller.

The third brother had become an apprentice to a turner, and since this is a craft that demands great skill, his apprenticeship had lasted the longest. During this time he had received a letter from his brothers in which they told him about their terrible experiences with the inn-keeper who had stolen their magical gifts on the last night before they were to arrive home. When he finished his apprenticeship as turner and was about to set out on his travels, his master gave him a sack because he had done such a good job.

"There's a club in the sack," said the master.

"I can carry the sack on my back, and it may come in handy, but what can I do with the club? It will only make the sack heavy."

"I'll tell you," responded the master. "If someone threatens to harm you, you just have to say, 'Club, come out of the sack,' and the club will jump out at the people and dance on their backs so spiritedly that they won't be able to move a bone in their body for a week. And the club won't let up until you say 'Club, get back in the sack.'"

The journeyman thanked him, swung the sack over his shoulder, and if anyone came too close to him and threatened him, he would say, "Club, come out of the sack," and the club would immediately jump out and dust off the fellow's coat or jacket without waiting for him to take it off, and then it would finish off all the others, one by one. And that would all happen so quickly that it would be over before one had any time to think.

It was evening when the young turner arrived at the inn where his two brothers had been cheated. He put his knapsack down on the table in front of him and began to tell stories about the remarkable things he had seen in the world.

"Yes," he said, "some people come across such things as a magic table, a gold donkey, and the like. These are wonderful things and not to be laughed at, but they're nothing compared to the treasure I've acquired. And I've got it right here in my sack."

The innkeeper pricked up his ears. What in the world could that be? he thought. Perhaps the sack is filled with jewels. There's no reason why they shouldn't be mine as well, for all good things come in threes.

When it was bedtime, the guest stretched himself out on the bench and put his sack underneath his head as a pillow. When the innkeeper thought the guest was sound asleep, he went over to him and cautiously tugged and pulled at the sack to see if he could quietly replace it with another. But the turner had been waiting for this moment, and just as the innkeeper was about to make a final hearty tug, he cried out, "Club, come out of the sack!"

Immediately the club jumped out of the sack and beat the innkeeper all over his body until the seams of his clothes burst. The innkeeper screamed for mercy, but the louder he screamed the harder the club beat in rhythm on his back until the innkeeper eventually fell to the ground exhausted. Then the turner said, "If you don't give me the magic table and the gold donkey, the dance will soon begin again."

"Oh, no!" the innkeeper exclaimed. "I'll gladly return everything to you. Just have that cursed hobgoblin crawl back into the sack!"

"Mercy shall prevail over justice this time," said the journeyman, "but you'd better watch your step in the future." Then he cried out, "Club, get back in the sack!"

The next morning the turner took the magic table and the gold donkey and continued his journey home to his father. The tailor was delighted to see him again and asked him what he had learned in foreign countries.

"Dear Father," he replied, "I've become a turner."

"That's a craft that demands a lot of skill," said the father. "What have you brought back with you from your travels?"

"A precious thing, dear Father," he replied. "A club in a sack."

"What!" exclaimed the father. "A club! That's not worth the trouble! You can chop off a club from any old tree."

"But not this kind, dear Father. If I say, 'Club, come out of the sack,' the club will come out and start dancing vigorously on anyone who threatens me, and the club won't stop until the person is lying on the ground and begging for mercy. You see, this club helped me get back the magic table and the gold donkey that the thieving innkeeper stole from my brothers. Now, I want you to invite both of them and all our relatives, for I'm going to provide them with food and drink and fill their pockets with gold as well."

Although the old tailor did not entirely believe him, he gathered all the relatives together. The turner spread out a piece of cloth in the parlor, led the gold donkey inside, and said to his brother, "Now, dear brother, speak to him."

The miller said "Bricklebrit," and within seconds there were gold pieces pouring onto the cloth as though there had been a sudden thunderstorm. Moreover, the donkey did not stop until they all had more than they could carry. (I can tell from the look on your face that you would have liked to have been there too.) Then the turner fetched the table and said, "Now, dear brother, speak to it."

No sooner did the carpenter say "Table, be covered," than it was covered and offered an abundance of the finest dishes. Never in his life had the old tailor enjoyed such a meal as the one held in his house that day. All the relatives stayed late into the night, and they were merry and happy. The tailor locked up his needle and thread and his yardstick and flat iron in a cupboard and lived with his sons in joy and splendor.

But what ever happened to the goat that was to blame for the tailor's driving out his three sons? Let me tell you.

She was so ashamed of her bald head that she ran to a foxhole and crawled inside. When the fox came home, a pair of eyes glared at him out of the darkness. He became so frightened that he ran away. When he encountered the bear, he looked so upset that the bear said, "What's the matter, brother fox? Why are you making such a face?"

"Oh," answered Red Fox, "a gruesome beast is sitting in my cave, and he glared at me with fiery eyes!"

"Well, we'll soon get rid of him," said the bear, and he went to the cave and looked inside. But when he saw the fiery eyes, he too was struck by fear. He wanted nothing to do with the gruesome beast and took off. Soon he met the bee, and when the bee noticed that the bear was looking very pale, she said, "Bear, you look so miserable. What's happened to your good spirits?"

"It's easy for you to talk," the bear responded, "but there's a gruesome beast with glaring eyes in Red Fox's house, and we can't drive him out."

"I feel sorry for you, bear," said the bee. "You and the fox barely acknowledge me when you see me because I'm such a poor weak creature. Still, I think I can help you."

She flew into the foxhole, landed on the goat's smooth-shaven head, and stung her so hard that the goat jumped up screaming *"Meh! Meh!"* and ran like mad out into the world. And to this day nobody knows what has become of her.

Thumbling

THERE WAS ONCE A POOR FARMER who was sitting by the hearth one evening and poking the fire, while his wife was spinning nearby.

"How sad that we have no children!" he said. "It's so quiet here, and other homes are full of noise and life."

"Yes," his wife responded with a sigh. "If only we had a child, just one, even if it were tiny and no bigger than my thumb, I'd be quite satisfied. We'd surely love him with all our hearts."

Now it happened that the wife fell sick, and after seven months she gave birth to a child that was indeed perfect in every way but no bigger than a thumb.

"It's just as we wished," they said, "and he shall be dear to our hearts."

Because of his size they named him Thumbling. Although they fed him a great deal, the child did not grow any bigger but stayed exactly as he was at birth. Still, he had an intelligent look and soon revealed himself to be a clever and nimble fellow who succeeded in all his endeavors.

One day the farmer was getting ready to chop wood in the forest, and he said to himself, "If only there were someone who could drive the wagon into the forest after me."

"Oh, Father," cried Thumbling, "I'll take care of the wagon. You can count on me. It'll be in the forest whenever you want it."

The man laughed and said, "How're you going to manage that? You're much too small to handle the reins."

"That's not important," Thumbling said. "I just need Mother to hitch the horse, and I'll sit down in his ear and tell him which way to go."

"Well," answered the father. "Let's try it once."

When the time came, the mother hitched up the horse and put Thumbling in his ear. Then the little fellow shouted commands. "Giddyap! Whoa! Giddyap!" Everything went quite well, as if a master were at the reins, and the wagon drove the right way toward the forest. As it took a turn and the little fellow cried out "Giddyap! Giddyap!" two strangers happened to come along.

"My word!" said one of them. "What's that? There goes a wagon without a driver, and yet, I hear a voice calling to the horse."

"There's something strange going on here," said the other. "Let's follow the wagon and see where it stops."

The wagon drove right into the forest up to the spot where the wood was being chopped. When Thumbling saw his father, he called out to him, "You see, Father, here I am with the wagon! Now just get me down."

The father grabbed the horse with his left hand, and with his right he took his little son out of its ear. Then Thumbling plopped himself sprightly on a piece of straw. When the two men caught sight of him, they were so amazed that they could not open their mouths. One of the men took the other aside and said, "Listen, that little fellow could make our fortune if we exhibit him in the big city for money. Let's buy him."

They went to the farmer and said, "Sell us the little man, and we'll see to it that he's treated well."

"No," answered the father, "he's the apple of my eye, and I wouldn't sell him for all the gold in the world."

But when Thumbling heard the offer, he crawled up the pleat of his father's coat, stood up on his shoulder, and whispered into his ear, "Father, don't you worry. Just give me away. I'll manage to get back soon."

So the father gave him to the two men for a tidy sum of money.

"Where do you want to sit?" they asked Thumbling.

"Oh, set me on the brim of your hat. Then I'll be able to walk back and forth and look at the countryside without any danger of falling off."

They did as he requested, and after Thumbling took leave of his father, they set out on their way. They walked until dusk, and just then the little fellow said, "Put me down. It's urgent."

"Just stay up there," said the man on whose head he was sitting. "I don't mind. I'm used to the birds dropping something on me every now and then."

"No," said Thumbling. "I know what's proper. Hurry up and put me down!"

The man took off his hat and set the little fellow on a field by the wayside. Then Thumbling jumped and crawled among the clods scattered here and there on the ground. Suddenly he slipped into a mousehole, which was what he had been looking for.

"Good-bye, gentlemen!" he cried out, laughing at them. "Just go home without me."

They ran over to the spot and stuck sticks into the mousehole, but their efforts were in vain. Thumbling kept retreating farther and farther into the hole. When it became pitch dark outside, the two men had to head back home, full of rage but with empty purses.

When Thumbling saw they were gone, he crawled out of the

underground passage and said, "It's so dangerous walking in the field after dark. You can easily break a neck or a leg." Fortunately, he stumbled upon an empty snail shell. "Thank goodness," he said. "I can spend the night here in safety." After he got inside and was about to go to sleep, he heard two men walking by and talking.

"How are we going to manage to get the rich pastor's money and silver?" one of them asked.

"I can tell you how," said Thumbling, interrupting them.

"What was that?" the other thief said in horror. "I heard a voice!"

The two men remained standing there and listened. Then Thumbling spoke again. "Take me with you, and I'll help you."

"Where are you, then?"

"Just look on the ground and pay attention to where the voice is coming from," he answered.

After a while the thieves found him and lifted him up in the air.

"You little tyke," they said. "How are you going to help us?"

"Look," he answered, "I'll crawl between the iron bars into the pastor's room, and I'll hand you whatever you want."

"All right," they said. "Let's see what you can do."

When they got to the pastor's house, Thumbling crawled into the room and immediately cried out with all his might, "Do you want to have everything that's here?"

The thieves were alarmed and said, "Speak softly so nobody wakes up."

But Thumbling pretended not to understand and screamed once more, "What do you want? Do you want everything that's here?"

The maid, who was sleeping in the room next-door, heard the voices. She sat up in bed and listened. But the thieves had retreated some distance out of fright. Gradually they regained their courage and thought, The little fellow is just teasing us. So they came back and whispered to him, "Now, be serious and hand us something."

Once again Thumbling screamed as loud as he could, "Sure, I'll give you all you want! Just reach in here with your hands!"

The maid was still listening and heard everything quite clearly. She jumped out of bed and stumbled into the room through the door. The thieves rushed away and ran as if a wild huntsman were after them. Since the maid could not see a thing, she went to light a candle. When she returned with it, Thumbling had left without being seen and headed into the barn. The maid searched the entire place, but after finding nothing, she went back to bed and thought she had only been seeing and hearing things in her dreams.

In the meantime, Thumbling climbed about in the hay and found himself a nice place to sleep. He intended to rest there until daybreak and then return home to his parents. However, life did not turn out the way he expected! Indeed, there is a great deal of sorrow and misery in this world! When the day dawned, the maid got out of bed to feed the cows. Her first round was in the barn where she picked up an armful of hay, and it was that very hay in which Thumbling was lying asleep. Indeed, he was sleeping so soundly that he did not notice a thing, nor did he wake up until he was in the jaws of a cow that picked him up with the hay.

"Oh, God!" he exclaimed. "How did I get into this churning mill?"

But soon he realized where he was, and he had to be careful not to get caught between the cow's teeth or else he would be crushed. Soon he slipped down into the cow's stomach with the hay.

"Hey, they forgot to put windows in this room!" he said. "No sunshine possible here, and it seems they won't be bringing candles."

He was not very pleased with the accommodations, and the worst of it was that the fresh hay kept coming through the door, and the space became cramped. At last his fright became so great that he cried out as loud as he could, "No more fodder! No more fodder!"

The maid was milking the cow when she heard the voice without seeing anybody. She recognized it as the same voice she had heard during the night and became so frightened that she slipped off her stool and spilled the milk. She ran in haste to her master and exclaimed, "Oh, God, Pastor! The cow just talked!"

"You're crazy," responded the parson, but he decided to go into the barn himself to check on the matter. No sooner did he set foot in the barn than Thumbling cried out once again, "No more fodder! No more fodder!"

Now even the parson became frightened, and he concluded that an evil spirit had got into the cow and ordered it to be killed. So the cow was slaughtered, and the stomach where Thumbling was stuck was thrown on the dung heap. Thumbling had great difficulty working his way through, but he managed to find a way out for himself. However, just as he was about to stick out his head, another misfortune occurred: a hungry wolf came running by and swallowed the whole stomach with one gulp. Yet, Thumbling did not lose courage. Perhaps, he thought, the wolf will listen to reason. So he called to him from his belly, "Dear wolf, I happen to know where you can find a wonderful meal."

"Tell me where," said the wolf.

"It's in such and such a house. You have to crawl through the drain, and then you'll find all the cake, bacon, and sausages you want to eat."

Thumbling gave him an exact description of his father's house, and the wolf did not have to be told twice. When night came, he squeezed his way through the drain into the pantry and ate to his heart's content. When he had eaten his fill, he wanted to go back outside. However, he had become so fat that he could not return the same way. Thumbling had counted on this and began making a racket in the wolf's belly. Indeed, he threw a fit and yelled as loud as he could. "Will you be quiet!" said the wolf. "You're waking everyone up." "So what!" said the little fellow. "You've had your fill. Now I want to have some fun too." And he kept screaming with all his might.

At last his father and mother woke up, ran to the pantry, and looked through a crack in the door. When they saw the wolf in there, they ran back. The man fetched an ax, and the woman, a scythe.

"Stay behind me," said the man as they approached the pantry. "If my blow doesn't kill him right away, then swing your scythe and cut his body to pieces."

When Thumbling heard his father's voice, he cried out, "Dear Father, I'm in here! I'm stuck in the wolf's body."

"Thank God!" said his father, full of joy. "Our dear son has come back to us." And he told his wife to put down the scythe so Thumbling would not be hurt. Then he lifted his arm and gave the wolf such a blow on his head that he fell down dead. He and his wife fetched a pair of scissors and a knife, cut the wolf's body open, and pulled the little fellow out.

"Oh," said the father, "we've been worried to death about you!"

"Yes, Father, I've traveled about the world a great deal. Thank God that I can breathe fresh air again!"

"Where in heaven's name have you been?"

"Oh, Father, I was in a mousehole, a cow's stomach, and a wolf's belly. Now I'm going to stay with you."

"And we shall never sell you again for all the riches in the world," said his parents. They hugged and kissed their dear Thumbling. Then they gave him something to eat and drink and had some new clothes made for him because his old ones had been spoiled during his journey.

◈ 38 ◈

The Wedding of Mrs. Fox

FIRST TALE

ONCE UPON A TIME there was an old fox with nine tails who believed his wife was unfaithful to him and wanted to put her to the test. So he stretched himself out under the bench, kept perfectly still, and pretended to be dead as a doornail. Mrs. Fox went up to her room and shut herself in, while her maid, Miss Cat, went to the hearth and started cooking. When it became known that the old fox had died, suitors began to present themselves. Now, the maid heard someone outside knocking at the door, and when she went and opened it, there was a young fox, who said:

"What are you doing now, Miss Cat?
Are you wide awake or asleep on the mat?"

She answered:

"I'm not asleep. I'm wide awake.
What do you think, for goodness sake!
I'm using butter to brew warm beer.
You can be my guest if you stay right here."

"No, thank you, Miss Cat," said the fox. "But tell me, what's Mrs. Fox doing?"

"She's sitting in her room
and weeping in her gloom.
Her eyes are now quite red,
for old Mr. Fox is dead."

"Be so kind as to tell her, Miss Cat, that a young fox is here who would very much like to court her."
"Very well, my young man."

The cat went up the stairs, *trip-trap,*
and knocked upon the door, *tap-tap.*
"Mrs. Fox, are you in there?"
"Oh, yes, Kitty Cat, yes, my dear."
"Well, a suitor's here to see you."
"What's he like? I want a clue.

Does he have nine beautiful tails like my late Mr. Fox?"
"Oh, no," answered Miss Cat. "He has only one."
"Then he's not for me."
Miss Cat went downstairs and sent the suitor away. Soon there again was a knock at the door, and there was another fox outside who wanted to court Mrs. Fox. Since he had only two tails, he fared no better than the first one. After that, others came, each with one tail more than the previous one, and they were all rejected. At last a fox

came who had nine tails like old Mr. Fox. When the widow heard that, she spoke joyfully to the maid:

"It's time to open the gate and the door,
and sweep Mr. Fox out over the floor."

However, just as the wedding was being held, old Mr. Fox stirred from under the bench, rose up, and gave the whole crowd a good beating. Then he drove everyone, including Mrs. Fox, out of the house.

SECOND TALE

AFTER OLD MR. FOX HAD DIED, the wolf came courting. When he knocked at the door, the cat who was Mrs. Fox's maid opened it, and she was greeted by the wolf, who said:

"Good day, Mrs. Cat of Sweeping-Pit.
Are you all alone with your bright wit?
I'm sure you're making something tasty right now."

The cat answered:

"I'm crumbling bread into my milk right here.
Be my guest and pull up a chair."

"No, thank you, Mrs. Cat," the wolf replied. "Is Mrs. Fox at home?"
The cat said:

"She's sitting in her room
and is weeping in her gloom.
Many are the tears she's shed,
for old Mr. Fox is dead."

The wolf answered:

"If she wants another husband who's very fair,
tell her that I'm right down here."
The cat ran up without a sound
and let her tail just swish around
until she reached the parlor door,
where with five golden rings she knocked.
"Mrs. Fox, are you there?" she called and knocked once more.

"If you want another husband who's very fair,
I can tell you that he's right down there."

Mrs. Fox asked, "Is the gentleman wearing red trousers, and does he have a pointed mouth?"

"No," said the cat.

"Then he's not for me."

After the wolf was turned down, he was followed by a dog, a stag, a hare, a bear, a lion, and all the animals of the forest, one after the other. However, they all lacked one of the distinguished qualities of old Mr. Fox, and each time, the cat had to send the suitor away. Finally, a young fox appeared, and Mrs. Fox asked, "Is the gentleman wearing red trousers, and does he have a pointed mouth?"

"Yes," said the cat. "That he does."

"Then let him come up," said Mrs. Fox, and she ordered the maid to prepare the wedding feast.

"It's time to open the windows
and make sure that old Mr. Fox now goes.
Indeed, he brought back many mice,
but he ate them all alone
and never did he offer me one."

Then young Mr. Fox was married to Mrs. Fox. Afterward there was dancing and rejoicing, and if they have not stopped dancing, then they are still at it even now.

◈ 39 ◈

The Elves

FIRST TALE

THERE WAS ONCE A SHOEMAKER who, through no fault of his own, had become so poor that he had only enough leather left for a single pair of shoes. That evening he cut out the shoes, which he planned to work on the next morning, and since he had a clear conscience, he lay down quietly in his bed, commended himself to God, and fell asleep. In the morning, after he had said his prayers and was about to sit down to do his work, he saw the two shoes standing all finished on his workbench. He was so astounded by this that he did not know what to say. He took the shoes in his hand to examine them more closely and saw that the shoes were perfect. Not a single bad stitch could be found, and it was as if the shoes were intended to be masterpieces.

Shortly after, a customer entered the shop, and he liked the shoes so much he paid more than the usual price for them. The money enabled the shoemaker to purchase leather for two pairs of shoes. In the evening he cut them out and planned to begin work on them with renewed vigor the next morning. However, it was not necessary, for the shoes were already finished by the time he awoke. Once again he found customers for them, and they gave him enough money to purchase leather for four pairs of shoes. The following morning he found the four pairs of shoes already made, and so it went: whatever he cut out in the evening was finished by morning, and soon he had a decent income again and eventually became a well-to-do man.

Now one evening, not long before Christmas, it happened that the man had been cutting leather, and just before he went to bed, he said to his wife, "What would you think about staying up tonight? If we do that, we might be able to see who's been lending us such a helping hand."

His wife agreed and lit a candle. Then they hid themselves behind some clothes that were hanging in the corner of the room and watched closely. When it was midnight, two cute little naked elves scampered into the room, sat down at the shoemaker's workbench, took all the work that had been cut out, and began to stitch, sew, and hammer so skillfully and nimbly with their little fingers that the amazed shoemaker could not take his eyes off them. Indeed, they did not stop until everything was done and the shoes were left standing on the workbench. Then they quickly ran away.

The next morning the wife said, "The little men have made us rich. We ought to show them that we're grateful for their help. Do you know what? Since they run around without any clothes on and must be freezing, I'm going to sew some shirts, coats, jackets, and trousers for them. I'll also knit a pair of stockings for each, and you can make them both a pair of shoes."

"That's fine with me," the husband said.

In the evening, after they had finished everything, they put the gifts on the workbench, instead of the cut-out leather, and hid themselves in order to see how the elves would react. At midnight the elves came scampering into the room and wanted to get right down to work, but they found the nice little clothes instead of the cut-out leather. At first they were puzzled, but then they were tremendously pleased. They put the clothes on quickly, smoothed them down, and said:

"Now we look so fine and dandy,
no more need to work and be so handy!"

Then they skipped, danced, and jumped over chairs and benches. Finally, they danced right out the door and were never seen again. But the shoemaker continued to be prosperous until the end of his life and succeeded in all his endeavors.

SECOND TALE

ONCE UPON A TIME there was a poor servant girl who was industrious and neat. She swept the house every day and dumped the dirt on a large pile outside the door. One morning, when she was about to start work again, she found a letter on the pile, and since she could not read, she put the broom in the corner and took the letter to her employers. It was an invitation from the elves, who asked the girl to be godmother for one of their children at a christening. The maiden did not know what to do, but her employers finally persuaded her that it would not be wise to refuse the invitation, and she accepted.

Three elves came and led her to a hollow mountain where the little folk lived. Everything there was tiny and indescribably dainty and splendid. The mother was lying on a black ebony bed with pearl knobs. The covers were embroidered with gold. The cradle was ivory. The bathtub was made of gold. After the maiden performed her duties as godmother, she wanted to go back home, but the elves implored her earnestly to spend three days with them. She remained and had a pleasant and joyful time. The little folk did all they could to please her. Finally, when she insisted it was time for her to leave, they filled her pockets with gold and led her back out the mountain.

When she arrived home, she wanted to resume her work, so she took the broom that was standing in the corner and began sweeping. At that moment some strange people came out of the house and asked her who she was and what she was doing there. Indeed, she had not been gone for three days, as she had thought, but she had spent seven years in the mountains with the little folk. In the meantime, her former employers had died.

THIRD TALE

THE ELVES HAD STOLEN a mother's child from the cradle and had replaced the baby with a changeling who had a fat head and glaring eyes and would do nothing but eat and drink. In her distress the mother went to her neighbor and asked for advice. The neighbor told her to carry the changeling into the kitchen, put him down on the hearth, start a fire, and boil water in two eggshells. That would make the changeling laugh, and when he laughed, he would lose his power.

• 152 •

The woman did everything the neighbor said, and when she put the eggshells filled with water on the fire, the blockhead said:

"Now I'm as old
as the Westerwald,
and in all my life I've never seen
eggshells cooked as these have been."

And the changeling began to laugh. As soon as he laughed, a bunch of elves appeared. They had brought the right child with them and put him down on the hearth and took the changeling away.

◈ 40 ◈

The Robber Bridegroom

ONCE UPON A TIME there was a miller who had a beautiful daughter, and when she was grown-up, he wanted to see her well provided for and well married. If the right suitor comes along and asks to marry her, he thought, I shall give her to him.

It was not long before a suitor appeared who seemed to be very rich, and since the miller found nothing wrong with him, he promised him his daughter. The maiden, however, did not love him the way a bride-to-be should love her bridegroom, nor did she trust him. Whenever she looked at him or thought about him, her heart shuddered with dread.

One day he said to her, "You're my bride-to-be, and yet, you've never visited me."

"I don't know where your house is," the maiden replied.

"My house is out in the dark forest," said the bridegroom.

She tried to make excuses and told him she would not be able to find the way. But the bridegroom said, "Next Sunday I want you to come out and visit me. I've already invited the guests, and I shall spread ashes on the ground so you can find the way."

When Sunday arrived and the maiden was supposed to set out on her way, she became very anxious but could not explain to herself why she felt so. She filled both her pockets with peas and lentils to mark the path. At the entrance to the forest, she found that ashes had been spread, and she followed them while throwing peas right and left on the ground with each step she took. She walked nearly the whole day until she came to the middle of the forest. There she saw a solitary house, but she did not like the look of it because it was so dark and dreary. She went inside and found nobody at home. The place was deadly silent. Then suddenly a voice cried out:

"Turn back, turn back, young bride.
The den belongs to murderers,
Who'll soon be at your side!"

The maiden looked up and saw that the voice came from a bird in a cage hanging on the wall. Once again it cried out:

"Turn back, turn back, young bride.
The den belongs to murderers,
Who'll soon be at your side!"

The beautiful bride moved from one room to the next and explored the entire house, but it was completely empty. Not a soul could be found. Finally, she went down into the cellar, where she encountered a very, very old woman, whose head was constantly bobbing.

"Could you tell me whether my bridegroom lives here?" asked the bride.

"Oh, you poor child," the old woman answered. "Do you realize where you are? This is a murderer's den! You think you're a bride soon to be celebrating your wedding, but the only marriage you'll celebrate will be with death. Just look! They ordered me to put this big kettle of water on the fire to boil. When they have you in their power, they'll chop you to pieces without mercy. Then they'll cook you and eat you, because they're cannibals. If I don't take pity on you and save you, you'll be lost forever."

The old woman then led her behind a large barrel, where nobody could see her.

"Be still as a mouse," she said. "Don't budge or move! Otherwise, it will be all over for you. Tonight when the robbers are asleep, we'll escape. I've been waiting a long time for this chance."

No sooner was the maiden hidden than the godless crew came home, dragging another maiden with them. They were drunk and paid no attention to her screams and pleas. They gave her wine to drink, three full glasses, one white, one red, and one yellow, and soon her heart burst in two. Then they tore off her fine clothes, put her on a table, chopped her beautiful body to pieces, and sprinkled the pieces with salt. Behind the barrel, the poor bride shook and trembled, for she now realized what kind of fate the robbers had been planning for her. One of them noticed a ring on the murdered maiden's little finger, and since he could not slip it off easily, he took a hatchet and chopped the finger off. But the finger sprang into the air and over the barrel and fell right into the bride's lap. The robber took a candle and went looking for it, but he could not find it. Then another robber said, "Have you already looked behind the barrel?"

Now the old woman called out, "Come and eat! You can look for it tomorrow. The finger's not going to run away from you."

"The old woman's right," the robbers said, and they stopped looking and sat down to eat. The old woman put a sleeping potion into their wine, and soon they lay down in the cellar, fell asleep, and began snoring. When the bride heard that, she came out from behind the barrel and had to step over the sleeping bodies lying in rows on the ground. She feared she might wake them up, but she got safely through with the help of God. The old woman went upstairs with her and opened the door, and the two of them scampered out of the murderers' den as fast as they could. The wind had blown away the ashes, but the peas and lentils had sprouted and unfurled, pointing the way in the moonlight. They walked the whole night, and by morning they had reached the mill. Then the maiden told her father everything that had happened.

When the day of the wedding celebration came, the bridegroom appeared, as did all the relatives and friends that the miller had invited. As they were all sitting at the table, each person was asked to tell a story. The bride, though, remained still and did not utter a word. Finally, the bridegroom said, "Well, my dear, can't you think of anything? Tell us a good story."

"All right," she said. "I'll tell you a dream: I was walking alone through the forest and finally came to a house. There wasn't a soul to be found in the place except for a bird in a cage on the wall that cried out:

'Turn back, turn back, young bride.
The den belongs to murderers,
Who'll soon be at your side!'

Then the bird repeated the warning.

(My dear, it was only a dream.)

"After that I went through all the rooms, and they were empty, but there was something about them that gave me an erie feeling. Finally, I went downstairs into the cellar, where I found a very, very old woman, who was bobbing her head. I asked her, 'Does my bridegroom live in this house?' 'Oh, you poor child,' she responded, 'you've stumbled on a murderers' den. Your bridegroom lives here, but he wants to chop you up and kill you, and then he wants to cook you and eat you.'

(My dear, it was only a dream.)

"The old woman hid me behind a large barrel, and no sooner was I hidden than the robbers returned home, dragging a maiden with them. They gave her all sorts of wine to drink, white, red, and yellow, and her heart burst in two.

(My dear, it was only a dream.)

"One of the robbers saw that a gold ring was still on her finger, and since he had trouble pulling it off, he took a hatchet and chopped it off. The finger sprang into the air, over the barrel, and right into my lap. And here's the finger with the ring!"

With these words she produced the finger and showed it to all those present.

The robber, who had turned white as a ghost while hearing her story, jumped up and attempted to flee. However, the guests seized

him and turned him over to the magistrate. Then he and his whole
band were executed for their shameful crimes.

◈ 41 ◈

Herr Korbes

ONCE UPON A TIME there were a hen and a rooster who wanted to
take a trip together. The rooster built a beautiful carriage that had four
red wheels, and then he hitched four mice to it. The hen climbed into
the carriage along with the rooster, and they drove off together. Soon
they came across a cat who asked, "Where are you going?"

"We're going to see Herr Korbes today.
We're off without delay."

"Take me with you," said the cat.
"Gladly," answered the rooster. "Sit in the back so you won't fall
off in front.

Be sure you take good care,
for I've got clean red wheels down there.
Roll on, you wheels, high ho!
Squeak, squeak, you mice, high ho!
We're going to see Herr Korbes today.
We're off without delay."

Soon a millstone came, then an egg, a duck, a pin, and finally a
sewing needle, who all got into the carriage and rode along. However, when they arrived at Herr Korbes's house, he was not there.
The mice pulled the carriage into the barn. The hen and the rooster
flew up on a perch. The cat settled down by the hearth. The duck
took a place by the well sweep. The egg wrapped itself in a towel.
The pin stuck itself in a chair cushion. The sewing needle jumped on
the bed right into the pillow. And the millstone set itself down above
the door.

When Herr Korbes came home, he went to the hearth to make a
fire, but the cat threw ashes right into his face. He ran quickly into the
kitchen to wash the ashes off, but the duck splashed water in his face.
As he tried to dry himself with the towel the egg rolled toward him

and broke open, so his eyes became glued shut. Now he wanted to rest and sit down in the chair, but the pin stuck him. In his rage he ran and threw himself down on his bed, but the sewing needle stuck him as his head hit the pillow. He let out a scream and was so furious that he decided to run out into the wide world. However, just as he got through the front door, the millstone jumped down and killed him.

Herr Korbes must have been a very wicked man.

◆ 42 ◆

The Godfather

A POOR MAN HAD SO MANY CHILDREN that he had already asked everyone in the world to be godfather, and when he had yet another child, there was nobody left to ask. He did not know what to do, and in his distress he lay down, fell asleep, and had a dream showing him that he should go outside the town gate and ask the first person he met to be godfather. When he awoke, he decided to undertake what the dream had shown. He went out in front of the gate and asked the first man he met to be godfather. The stranger gave him a little bottle of water and said, "This water has miraculous powers. You can cure the sick with it, but you must keep your eye on Death. If he's standing at the head of the sick person, then give the patient some of the water, and he'll get well. However, if Death is standing at the patient's feet, there is nothing that can be done, and the patient must die."

From then on the man could always predict whether a sick person could be saved or not. He became famous because of his skill and earned a great deal of money. One day he was summoned to the king's child, and when he entered the room, he saw Death standing by the child's head and cured him with the water. The same thing happened a second time. But the third time, Death was standing at the foot of the bed, and the child had to die.

Once, the man decided to visit the godfather and tell him how well he had been doing with the water. When he entered the house, though, he noticed there were some very strange things happening. On the first landing he encountered a shovel and a broom having a terrible argument that led to blows.

"Where does the godfather live?" he asked them.

"One flight up," answered the broom.

When he came to the second landing, he saw a bunch of dead fingers lying there.

"Where does the godfather live?" he asked.

"One flight up," replied one of the fingers.

On the third landing there was a pile of skulls who told him to go up one flight. On the fourth landing he saw some fish sizzling in a pan over a fire. They were frying themselves and also told him, "One flight up." After he had climbed to the fifth floor, he came to a door of a room and looked through the keyhole. There he saw the godfather, who had a pair of long horns. When he opened the door and went inside, the godfather quickly jumped into bed and covered himself.

"Godfather, you certainly have a strange household!" the man said. "When I came to the first landing, a broom and shovel were quarreling so violently that they gave each other terrible blows."

"How can you be so simpleminded!" said the godfather. "That was the kitchen boy and the maid just talking to each other."

"On the second landing I saw dead fingers lying about."

"My goodness, how foolish you are! Those were salsify roots."

"On the third landing there were skulls lying about."

"You stupid man, those were cabbage heads."

"On the fourth landing I saw fish frying themselves."

Just as he said that, the fish came in and served themselves on a platter.

"And when I came to the fifth landing, I looked through the keyhole, and I saw you, godfather, and you had such long, long horns."

"Now, that's just not true!"

The man became frightened and ran away.

Indeed, there is no telling what the godfather might have done to him if he had stayed.

◆ 43 ◆

Mother Trudy

ONCE UPON A TIME there was a little girl who was stubborn and curious, and whenever her parents told her to do something, she would not obey them. Well, how could things possibly go well for her?

One day she said to her parents, "I've heard so much about Mother Trudy that I'd like to see her someday. People say that there are unusual things about her house, and there are also strange things inside. All that's made me very curious."

However, her parents gave her strict instructions not to go near the house.

"Mother Trudy is an evil woman," they said. "She does wicked things, and if you go to her, you'll no longer be our child."

But the girl did not pay any attention to her parents' instructions and went to Mother Trudy's house all the same. When she got there, Mother Trudy asked, "Why are you so pale?"

"Oh," she answered, trembling all over, "I'm so terrified by what I've just seen."

"What have you seen?"

"I saw a black man on your stairs."

"That was a charcoal burner."

"Then I saw a green man."

"That was a huntsman."

"After that I saw a bloodred man."

"That was a butcher."

"Oh, Mother Trudy, I was so petrified. I looked through the window and didn't see you, but I saw the devil with a fiery head."

"Oho!" she said. "Then you've seen the witch in her proper dress. I've been wanting you here and waiting for a long time. Now you shall provide me with light!"

Then she changed the girl into a block of wood and threw it into the fire. And when the wood was blazing, she sat down next to it, warmed herself, and said, "That really does give off a bright light."

◈ 44 ◈

Godfather Death

A POOR MAN HAD TWELVE CHILDREN and had to work day and night just to feed them. When the thirteenth was born, the man was in such great distress that he did not know what to do. So he just ran out onto the large highway, having decided to ask the first man he met to be godfather. The first man he encountered was the good Lord, who already knew what was on his mind, and he said to him, "Poor man, I feel sorry for you. I shall hold your child at the christening, and I shall take care of him and see that he's happy on earth."

"Who are you?" asked the man.

"I am your dear Lord."

"Then I don't want you to be godfather," said the man. "You give to the rich and let the poor go hungry."

The man said that because he did not know how wisely God distributes wealth and poverty. Thus he turned away from God and moved on. Then the devil came up to him and said, "What are you looking for? If you make me your child's godfather, I'll give him plenty of gold and all the pleasures of the world as well."

"Who are you?" asked the man.

"I'm the devil."

"Then I don't want you to be godfather," the man said. "You deceive people and lead them astray."

He continued on his way, and soon spindle-legged Death came toward him and said, "Take me as godfather."

"Who are you?" the man asked.

"I'm Death, and I make all people equal."

"You're just the right one," said the man. "You take the rich and poor alike without making distinctions. I want you to be my child's godfather."

"I shall make your child rich and famous," Death answered. "Indeed, whoever has me for a friend shall never know need."

"Next Sunday is the christening," said the man. "Make sure you're there on time."

Death appeared as he had promised, and he made for a very proper godfather.

When the boy was old enough, his godfather appeared one day and told him to come along with him. He led him into the forest, showed him an herb that grew there, and said, "Now you shall receive your christening gift. I'm going to make you into a famous doctor. Whenever you are summoned to a sick person, I shall appear on each occasion. If I stand at the head of the patient, you can firmly declare that you'll make him well again. Then give him some of the herb, and he'll recover. However, if I stand at the feet of the patient, he's mine, and you must say there's nothing you can do, and no doctor in the world can save him. But beware that you don't use the herb against my will or you shall be in for trouble!"

It did not take long for the young man to become the most famous doctor in the whole world. His reputation was such that people said, "He only has to look at a sick person, and he can tell the condition and whether the person will get well or must die." People came from far and wide to seek his help in curing the sick, and they gave him so much money that he was soon a rich man.

Now it happened that the king fell ill. The doctor was summoned and was supposed to determine whether recovery was possible. When he approached the bed, Death was standing at the feet of the king. So he knew no cure was possible.

If only I could outwit Death just once! thought the doctor. Of course, he'll hold it against me, but since I'm his godson, perhaps he'll let it pass. It's worth a try. So he took the sick man and turned him the other way around so that Death stood at his head. Then he gave him some of the herb, and the king began recovering and became well again. But Death went to the doctor, pointed his finger at him, and threatened him with angry and sinister looks.

"Well, you've pulled the wool over my eyes. I'll forgive you this once because you're my godson. But if you try it again, you'll be risking your own neck. I myself shall come and take you away!"

Soon thereafter, the king's daughter fell seriously ill. She was his only child, and he wept day and night until he could no longer see out of his eyes. Then he issued a proclamation that whoever saved his daughter from death would become her husband and inherit the crown. When the doctor approached her bed, he saw Death at her feet. He should have recalled his godfather's warning, but he was swayed by the great beauty of the princess and the happiness he envisioned having as her husband, so he threw caution to the winds. Death gave him angry looks, raised his hand, and threatened him with his withered fist, but the doctor refused to take notice. Instead he lifted the sick maiden, put her head where the feet had been, and gave her the herb. Immediately her cheeks flushed red, and life could be seen stirring in her once more.

When Death found himself cheated out of his claim a second time, he strode up to the doctor and said, "It's all over for you! Now it's your turn to die."

He grabbed the doctor so hard with his icy hand that the young man could not resist. Then he led him down into an underground cave. There the doctor saw thousands and thousands of candles burning in countless rows, some large, some medium, others small. With every moment some went out and others flared up again, so that the little flames seemed to be constantly changing and popping up and down.

"You see," said Death, "these candles are the lights of people's lives. The large ones belong to the children, the medium ones to married couples in their best years, the small ones to old people. But often children and young people can have small candles too."

"Show me my life candle," the doctor said, for he thought it would still be quite large.

Death pointed to a tiny stub that was just about to go out and said, "There it is. You see it?"

"Oh, dear godfather," the doctor was struck by horror, "light a new one for me! Please do me this favor so I can enjoy my life and become king and marry the beautiful princess."

"I can't," replied Death. "First one candle must go out before a new one can be lit."

"Then put the old one on top of a new candle so it will continue to burn after it goes out," the doctor pleaded.

Death pretended that he wanted to fulfill his wish. He reached for a large new candle, but since he really wanted revenge, he purposely made a mistake in transferring the stub, and it went out. All at once the doctor fell to the ground and had indeed fallen into the hands of Death.

❖ 45 ❖

Thumbling's Travels

A TAILOR HAD A SON who turned out to be small, not much bigger than a thumb. He was, therefore, called Thumbling. However, he had plenty of courage and said to his father, "I intend to go out into the world, and I shall do it."

"That's right, my son," said the old man, who took a long darning needle, held it over a candle, and made a knob of sealing wax on it. "Now you've got a sword to take with you on the way."

The little tailor wanted to eat one more meal with his family and hopped into the kitchen to see what his mother was cooking for the last time. She had just finished, and the dish stood on the hearth.

"Mother," he said, "what's there to eat today?"

"See for yourself," said his mother. So Thumbling jumped onto the hearth and looked inside the dish. However, he stuck his neck out too far, and the steam from the food caught hold of him and carried him up and out the chimney. For a while he rode around in the air on the steam, until he finally sank to the ground. Now the little tailor was out in the wide world. He traveled about and began working for a master tailor as an apprentice, but the food was not good enough for him.

"Mistress," he said to the master's wife, "if you don't give us something better to eat, I'm going to leave tomorrow morning, and I'll write with chalk on your door, 'Too much potatoes, too little meat! Bye, bye, potato king!' "

"What more do you want, grasshopper?" the master's wife asked, and she grew so angry that she grabbed a rag and tried to hit him. However, my little tailor crawled nimbly under the thimble, peeped out from under, and stuck his tongue out at her. She lifted the thimble and was about to grab him when Thumbling hopped into the rag. As the master's wife tried to untangle the rag and find him, he disappeared into a crack in the table.

"Ho, ho, mistress!" he called out and raised his head. When she went to hit him, he jumped down into the drawer. At length she caught him and kicked him out of the house.

The little tailor traveled on and came to a forest. There he met a band of robbers who planned to steal the king's treasure. When they saw the little tailor, they thought, A little fellow like that can crawl through a keyhole and serve us as a picklock.

"Hey, you!" one of the robbers called. "Yes, you giant Goliath! Do you want to come with us to the treasure chamber? We want you to crawl in and throw out the money."

Thumbling thought about it awhile, and at last he said yes and went with them to the treasure chamber. He examined the door from top to bottom to see if there was a crack. It did not take long for him to discover one wide enough to slip through. He wanted to go through right then and there, but one of the guards standing before the door noticed him and said to the other, "Just look at that ugly spider crawling there! I'm going to stamp it to death."

"Leave the poor creature alone," said the other. "It's never done a thing to harm you."

So Thumbling made it safely through the crack into the treasure chamber, opened the window under which the robbers were standing, and threw down to them one taler after another. Just as the little tailor was right in the middle of his work, he heard the king coming to inspect the treasure chamber. Hastily Thumbling crawled into a hiding place. When the king noticed that many hard coins were missing, he could not figure out how they might have been stolen, since the locks and bolts were in good condition and everything seemed to be well-protected. As he left the chamber, he said to the two guards, "Be on the alert! Somebody's after the money."

When Thumbling resumed his work, the guards heard the money inside moving and jingling, *clink-clank, clink-clank*. They quickly ran inside and tried to grab the thief. However, the little tailor had heard them coming and was much swifter than they were. He jumped into a corner and covered himself with a taler so that nothing could be seen of him. Then he began to tease the guards.

"Here I am!"

The guards ran over, but when they got to the spot, he was already in another place beneath a taler and called out, "Hey, here I am!"

The guards rushed quickly to the next spot, but Thumbling was long since in a third corner and called out, "Hey, here I am!"

So he made fools of them and drove them all around the treasure chamber until they were exhausted and went away. Then, little by little, he proceeded to toss all the talers out the window. As he threw the last one with all his might, he nimbly hopped on it himself and flew with it out the window. The robbers congratulated him with great words of praise.

"You're a tremendous hero!" they said. "Do you want to be our captain?"

Thumbling thanked them but said that he wanted to see the world first. Then they divided the loot, and the little tailor asked for only a kreuzer because he could not carry any more than that.

Once again he buckled his sword around his waist; he said farewell to the robbers and began traveling. He worked as an apprentice for several masters, but he did not find the work to his taste. Finally, he hired himself out as a servant in an inn. However, the maids could not stand him because he saw everything they did on the sly without their being able to see him. Moreover, he told the innkeeper what they stole off the plates and took from the cellar to fill their own pockets.

"Just wait!" the maids said. "We'll pay you back!"

Indeed, they arranged to play a mean trick on him. Sometime later, when one of the maids was mowing in the garden and saw Thumbling running around in the grass and climbing up and down the plants, she quickly mowed him up with the grass, wrapped everything in a large cloth, and secretly threw it to the cows. Among the cows was a big black one that swallowed Thumbling down without hurting him. Yet, he did not like it down there, for it was very dark, and there was no light. When the cow was being milked, he cried out:

"Strip, strap, strull,
how soon will the bucket be full?"

But because of the noise from the milking, no one could understand what he said. Afterward the master of the house entered the barn and said, "Tomorrow that cow shall be slaughtered."

Thumbling became frightened, and he shouted loud and clear, "Let me out first! I'm sitting inside!"

The master heard the voice quite well, but he did not know where it came from.

"Where are you?" he asked.

"In the black one," Thumbling answered, but the master did not realize what that was supposed to mean and went away.

The next morning the cow was slaughtered, and fortunately Thumbling was not struck by anything during the chopping and slicing. However, he got mixed in with the sausage meat. When the butcher arrived and began his work, he cried out with all his might, "Don't chop too deep! Don't chop too deep! I'm stuck down here!"

Not a soul heard his voice because the noise of the chopping knives was too great. Now poor Thumbling was really in trouble, but where there's a will there's a way. Indeed, he jumped so nimbly between the chopping knives that none touched him, and he got away with his skin intact. Still, he could not find his way out of the meat entirely and was stuffed into a blood sausage with bits of bacon. The space there was rather cramped. Besides that he was hung up in a chimney to be smoked, and time hung very heavy on his hands. Finally, during winter he was taken down because the sausage was to be served to a guest. When the innkeeper's wife began cutting the sausage into slices, he took care not to stick his head too far out, otherwise it would have been cut off. At last he saw a chance to escape, cleared a way for himself, and jumped out.

Since things had gone so badly for him at that house, the little tailor did not want to stay any longer and resumed his travels. But his freedom did not last long. He crossed paths with a fox in an open field, and because the fox was lost in thought, he just snapped Thumbling up.

"Hey, Mr. Fox!" the little tailor exclaimed. "It's me you've got stuck in your throat! Let me go!"

"You're right," the fox replied. "There's practically nothing to eat on you, and I should let you go, but only if you promise me all the chickens in your father's barnyard."

"With all my heart!" said Thumbling. "You shall have every single chicken. I swear it!"

The fox let him go and even carried him back home. When the father saw his dear son again, he gladly gave the fox all the chickens he had.

"To make up for it, I've brought you a tidy sum of money," said Thumbling, and he handed his father the kreuzer that he had earned during his travels.

"But why did the fox get all those poor little chickens to eat?"

"Oh, you fool, don't you think that your father would care more for his child than for all the chickens in his barnyard?"

◈ 46 ◈

Fitcher's Bird

ONCE UPON A TIME there was a sorcerer who used to assume the guise of a poor man and go begging from house to house to catch beautiful girls. No one knew where he took them, since none of the girls ever returned.

One day he appeared at the door of a man who had three beautiful daughters. He looked like a poor, weak beggar and carried a basket on his back as though to collect handouts in it. He begged for some food, and when the oldest daughter came out to hand him a piece of bread, he had only to touch her, and that compelled her to jump into his basket. Then he rushed away with great strides and carried her to his house in the middle of a dark forest. Everything was splendid inside the house, and he gave her whatever she desired.

"My darling," he said, "I'm sure you'll like it here, for there's everything your heart desires."

After a few days had gone by, he said, "I must go on a journey and leave you alone for a short time. Here are the keys to the house. You may go wherever you want and look at everything except one room, which this small key here opens. If you disobey me, you shall be punished by death." He also gave her an egg and said, "I'm giving you this egg for safekeeping. You're to carry it wherever you go. If you lose it, then something awful will happen."

She took the keys and the egg and promised to take care of everything. When he was gone, she went all around the house and explored it from top to bottom. The rooms glistened with silver and gold, and she was convinced that she had never seen such great splendor. Finally, she came to the forbidden door. She wanted to walk past it, but curiosity got the better of her. She examined the key, which looked like all the others, stuck it into the lock, turned it a little, and the door sprang open. But, what did she see when she entered? There was a large bloody basin in the middle of the room, and it was filled with dead people who had been chopped to pieces. Next to the basin was a block of wood with a glistening ax on top of it. She was so horrified by this that she dropped the egg she had been holding in her hand, and it plopped into the basin. She took it out and wiped the blood off, but to no avail: the blood reappeared instantly. She wiped and scraped, but she could not get rid of the spot.

Not long after this, the sorcerer came back from his journey, and the first things he demanded from her were the keys and the egg. When she handed them to him, she was trembling, and he perceived right away, by the red spots on the egg, that she had been in the bloody chamber.

"Since you went into that chamber against my will," he said, "you shall go back in, against your will. This is the end of your life."

He threw her down, dragged her along by her hair, cut her head off on the block, and chopped her into pieces, so that her blood flowed on the floor. Then he tossed her into the basin with the others.

"Now I shall fetch the second daughter," said the sorcerer.

Once again he went to the house in the guise of a poor man and begged. When the second daughter brought him a piece of bread, he caught her as he had the first, just by touching her. Then he carried her away, and she fared no better than her sister, for she succumbed to her own curiosity. She opened the door to the bloody chamber, looked inside, and had to pay for this with her life when the sorcerer returned from his journey.

Now he went and fetched the third daughter, but she was smart and cunning. After he had given her the keys and the egg and had departed, she put the egg away in a safe place. Then she explored the house and eventually came to the forbidden chamber. But, oh, what did she see? Her two dear sisters lay there in the basin cruelly murdered and chopped to pieces. However, she set to work right away, gathered the pieces together, and arranged them in their proper order: head, body, arms, and legs. When nothing more was missing, the pieces began to move and join together. Both the maidens opened their eyes and were alive again. Then they all rejoiced, kissed, and hugged each other.

When the sorcerer returned, he demanded his keys and egg right away, and when he could not discover the least trace of blood, he said, "You've passed the test, and you shall be my bride."

But, he no longer had any power over her and had to do what she requested.

"All right," she answered. "But first I want you to carry a basket full of gold to my father and mother, and you're to carry it on your back by yourself. In the meantime I shall prepare for the wedding."

Then she ran to her sisters, whom she had hidden in a little chamber.

"The time has come when I can save you," she said. "The villain himself shall carry you back home. But as soon as you get there, you must send me help."

She put her two sisters into a basket and covered them completely with gold until nothing could be seen of them at all. Then she called the sorcerer to her and said, "Now take the basket away. But don't you dare stop and rest along the way! I'll be keeping an eye on you from my window."

The sorcerer lifted the basket onto his back and went on his way. The basket, however, was so heavy that sweat ran down his face. At one point he sat down and wanted to rest for a while, but one of the sisters called from the basket, "I can see through my window that you're resting. Get a move on at once!"

Whenever he stopped along the way, he heard a voice and had to keep moving. Although he had run out of breath and was groaning, he finally managed to bring the basket with the gold and the two maidens to their parents' house.

Back at his place, the bride was preparing the wedding feast and sent invitations to all the sorcerer's friends. Then she took a skull with grinning teeth, decorated it with jewels and a wreath of flowers, carried it up to the attic window, and set it down so it faced outward. When everything was ready, she dipped herself into a barrel of honey, cut open a bed, and rolled around in the feathers so she looked like a strange bird, and it was impossible to recognize her. Afterward she went out of the house, and on the way she met some of the wedding guests, who asked:

"Where are you coming from, oh, Fitcher's bird?"
"From Fitze Fitcher's house, haven't you heard?"
"And what may the young bride be doing there?"
"She's swept the whole house from top to bottom.
Just now she's looking out the attic window."

Finally, she met the bridegroom who was walking back slowly. He also asked:

"Where are you coming from, oh, Fitcher's bird?"
"From Fitze Fitcher's house, haven't you heard?"
"And what may the young bride be doing there?"
"She's swept the whole house from top to bottom.
Just now she's looking out the attic window."

The bridegroom looked up and saw the decorated skull. He thought it was his bride and nodded and greeted her in a friendly way. However, once he and his guests were all gathered inside the house, the bride's brother and relatives arrived. They had been sent to rescue her, and they locked all the doors of the house to prevent anyone from escaping. Then they set fire to the house, and the sorcerer and all his cronies were burned to death.

◈ 47 ◈

The Juniper Tree

ALL THIS TOOK PLACE A LONG TIME AGO, most likely some two thousand years ago. There was a rich man who had a beautiful and pious wife, and they loved each other very much. Though they did not have any children, they longed to have some. Day and night the wife prayed for a child, but still none came, and everything remained the same.

Now, in the front of the house there was a yard, and in the yard stood a juniper tree. One day during winter the wife was under the tree peeling an apple, and as she was peeling it, she cut her finger, and her blood dripped on the snow.

"Oh," said the wife, and she heaved a great sigh. While she looked at the blood before her, she became quite sad. "If only I had a child as red as blood and as white as snow!" Upon saying that, her mood changed, and she became very cheerful, for she felt something might come of it. Then she went home.

After a month the snow vanished. After two months everything turned green. After three months the flowers sprouted from the ground. After four months all the trees in the woods grew more solid, and the green branches became intertwined. The birds began to sing, and their song resounded throughout the forest as the blossoms fell from the trees. Soon the fifth month passed, and when the wife stood under the juniper tree, it smelled so sweetly that her heart leapt for

• 171 •

joy. Indeed, she was so overcome by joy that she fell down on her knees. When the sixth month had passed, the fruit was large and firm, and she was quite still. In the seventh month she picked the juniper berries and ate them so avidly that she became sad and sick. After the eighth month passed, she called her husband to her and wept.

"If I die," she said, "bury me under the juniper tree."

After that she was quite content and relieved until the ninth month had passed. Then she had a child as white as snow and as red as blood. When she saw the baby, she was so delighted that she died.

Her husband buried her under the juniper tree, and he began weeping a great deal. After some time he felt much better, but he still wept every now and then. Eventually, he stopped, and after more time passed, he took another wife. With his second wife he had a daughter, while the child from the first wife was a little boy, who was as red as blood and as white as snow. Whenever the woman looked at her daughter, she felt great love for her, but whenever she looked at the little boy, her heart was cut to the quick. She could not forget that he would always stand in her way and prevent her daughter from inheriting everything, which was what the woman had in mind. Thus the devil took hold of her and influenced her feelings toward the boy until she became quite cruel toward him: she pushed him from one place to the next, slapped him here and cuffed him there, so that the poor child lived in constant fear. When he came home from school, he found no peace at all.

One time the woman went up to her room, and her little daughter followed her and said, "Mother, give me an apple."

"Yes, my child," said the woman, and she gave her a beautiful apple from the chest that had a large heavy lid with a big, sharp iron lock.

"Mother," said the little daughter, "shouldn't brother get one too?"

The woman was irritated by that remark, but she said, "Yes, as soon as he comes home from school." And, when she looked out of the window and saw he was coming, the devil seemed to take possession of her, and she snatched the apple away from her daughter.

"You shan't have one before your brother," she said and threw the apple into the chest and shut it.

The little boy came through the door, and the devil compelled her to be friendly to him and say, "Would you like to have an apple, my son?" Yet, she gave him a fierce look.

"Mother," said the little boy, "how ferocious you look! Yes, give me an apple."

Then she felt compelled to coax him.

"Come over here," she said as she lifted the lid. "Take out an apple for yourself."

And as the little boy leaned over the chest, the devil prompted her, and *crash!* She slammed the lid so hard that his head flew off and fell among the apples. Then she was struck by fear and thought, How am I going to get out of this? She went up to her room and straight to her dresser, where she took out a white kerchief from a drawer. She put the boy's head back on his neck and tied the neckerchief around it so nothing could be seen. Then she set him on a chair in front of the door and put the apple in his hand.

Some time later little Marlene came into the kitchen and went up to her mother, who was standing by the fire in front of a pot of hot water, which she was constantly stirring.

"Mother," said Marlene, "brother's sitting by the door and looks very pale. He's got an apple in his hand, and I asked him to give me the apple, but he didn't answer, and I became very scared."

"Go back to him," said the mother, "and if he doesn't answer you, give him a box on the ear."

Little Marlene returned to him and said, "Brother, give me the apple."

But he would not respond. So she gave him a box on the ear, and his head fell off. The little girl was so frightened that she began to cry and howl. Then she ran to her mother and said, "Oh, Mother, I've knocked my brother's head off!" And she wept and wept and could not be comforted.

"Marlene," said the mother. "What have you done! You're not to open your mouth about this. We don't want anyone to know, and besides there's nothing we can do about it now. So we'll make a stew out of him."

The mother took the little boy and chopped him into pieces. Next she put them into a pot and let them stew. But Marlene stood nearby and wept until all her tears fell into the pot, so it did not need any salt.

When the father came home, he sat down at the table and asked, "Where's my son?"

The mother served a huge portion of the stewed meat, and Marlene wept and could not stop.

"Where's my son?" the father asked again.

"Oh," said the mother, "he's gone off into the country to visit his mother's great uncle. He intends to stay there awhile."

"What's he going to do there? He didn't even say good-bye to me."

"Well, he wanted to go very badly and asked me if he could stay there six weeks. They'll take good care of him."

"Oh, that makes me sad," said the man. "It's not right. He should have said good-bye to me." Then he began to eat and said, "Marlene, what are you crying for? Your brother will come back soon." Without pausing he said, "Oh, wife, the food tastes great! Give me some more!" The more he ate, the more he wanted. "Give me some more," he said. "I'm not going to share this with you. Somehow I feel as if it were all mine."

As he ate and ate he threw the bones under the table until he was all done. Meanwhile, Marlene went to her dresser and took out her best silk neckerchief from the bottom drawer, gathered all the bones from beneath the table, tied them up in her silk kerchief, and carried them outside the door. There she wept

bitter tears and laid the bones beneath the juniper tree. As she put them there, she suddenly felt relieved and stopped crying. Now the juniper tree began to move. The branches separated and came together again as though they were clapping their hands in joy. At the same time smoke came out of the tree, and in the middle of the smoke there was a flame that seemed to be burning. Then a beautiful bird flew out of the fire and began singing magnificently. He soared high in the air, and after he vanished, the juniper tree was as it was before. Yet, the silk kerchief was gone. Marlene was very happy and gay. It was as if her brother were still alive, and she went merrily back into the house, sat down at the table, and ate.

Meanwhile, the bird flew away, landed on a goldsmith's house, and began to sing:

"My mother, she killed me.
My father, he ate me.
My sister, Marlene, she made sure to see
my bones were all gathered together,
bound nicely in silk, as neat as can be,
and laid beneath the juniper tree.
Tweet, tweet! What a lovely bird I am!"

The goldsmith was sitting in his workshop making a golden chain. When he heard the bird singing on his roof, he thought it was very beautiful. Then he stood up, and as he walked across the threshold, he lost a slipper. Still, he kept on going, right into the middle of the street with only one sock and a slipper on. He was also wearing his apron, and in one of his hands he held the golden chain, in the other his tongs. The sun was shining brightly on the street as he walked, and then he stopped to get a look at the bird.

"Bird," he said, "how beautifully you sing! Sing me that song again."

"No," said the bird, "I never sing twice for nothing. Give me the golden chain, and I'll sing it for you again."

"All right," said the goldsmith. "Here's the golden chain. Now sing the song again."

The bird swooped down, took the golden chain in his right claw, went up to the goldsmith, and began singing:

"My mother, she killed me.
My father, he ate me.
My sister, Marlene, she made sure to see
my bones were all gathered together,
bound nicely in silk, as neat as can be,
and laid beneath the juniper tree.
Tweet, tweet! What a lovely bird I am!"

Then the bird flew off to a shoemaker, landed on his roof, and sang:

"My mother, she killed me.
My father, he ate me.
My sister, Marlene, she made sure to see
my bones were gathered together,
bound nicely in silk, as neat as can be,
and laid beneath the juniper tree.
Tweet, tweet! What a lovely bird I am!"

When the shoemaker heard the song, he ran to the door in his shirt
sleeves and looked up at the roof, keeping his hand over his eyes to
protect them from the bright sun.

"Bird," he said. "How beautifully you sing!" Then he called into
the house, "Wife, come out here for a second! There's a bird up there.
Just look. How beautifully he sings!" Then he called his daughter and
her children, and the journeyman, apprentices, and maid. They all came
running out into the street and looked at the bird and saw how beautiful
he was. He had bright red and green feathers, and his neck appeared
to glisten like pure gold, while his eyes sparkled in his head like stars.

"Bird," said the shoemaker, "now sing me that song again."

"No," said the bird. "I never sing twice for nothing. You'll have to
give me a present."

"Wife," said the man, "go into the shop. There's a pair of red shoes
on the top shelf. Get them for me."

His wife went and fetched the shoes.

"There," said the man. "Now sing the song again."

The bird swooped down, took the shoes in his left claw, flew back
up on the roof, and sang:

"My mother, she killed me.
My father, he ate me.
My sister, Marlene, she made sure to see
my bones were all gathered together,
bound nicely in silk, as neat as can be,
and laid beneath the juniper tree.
Tweet, tweet! What a lovely bird I am!"

When the bird finished the song, he flew away. He had the chain in
his right claw and the shoes in his left, and he flew far away to a mill.
The mill went *clickety-clack, clickety-clack, clickety-clack.* The miller had
twenty men sitting in the mill, and they were hewing a stone. Their
chisels went *click-clack, click-clack, click-clack.* And the mill kept going
clickety-clack, clickety-clack, clickety-clack. The bird swooped down and
landed on a linden tree outside the mill and sang:

"My mother, she killed me."

Then one of the men stopped working.

"My father, he ate me."

Then two more stopped and listened.

"My sister, Marlene, she made sure to see."

Then four more stopped.

"My bones were all gathered together,
bound nicely in silk, as neat as can be."

Now only eight kept chiseling.

"And laid beneath . . ."

Now only five.

". . . the juniper tree."

Now only one.

"*Tweet, tweet!* What a lovely bird I am!"

Then the last one also stopped and listened to the final words.
"Bird, how beautifully you sing! Let me hear that too. Sing your
song again for me."
"No," said the bird. "I never sing twice for nothing. Give me the
millstone, and I'll sing the song again."
"I would if I could," he said. "But the millstone doesn't belong to
me alone."
"If he sings again," said the others, "he can have it."
Then the bird swooped down, and all twenty of the miller's men
took beams to lift the stone. "Heave-ho! Heave-ho! Heave-ho!" Then
the bird stuck his neck through the hole, put the stone on like a collar,
flew back to the tree, and sang:

"My mother, she killed me.
My father, he ate me.
My sister, Marlene, she made sure to see
my bones were all gathered together,
bound nicely in silk, as neat as can be,
and laid beneath the juniper tree.
Tweet, tweet! What a lovely bird I am!"

When the bird finished his song, he spread his wings, and in his right claw he had the chain, in his left the shoes, and around his neck the millstone. Then he flew away to his father's house.

The father, mother, and Marlene were sitting at the table in the parlor, and the father said, "Oh, how happy I am! I just feel so wonderful!"

"Not me," said the mother. "I feel scared as if a storm were about to erupt."

Meanwhile, Marlene just sat there and kept weeping. Then the bird flew up, and when he landed on the roof, the father said, "Oh, I'm in such good spirits. The sun's shining so brightly outside, and I feel as though I were going to see an old friend again."

"Not me," said his wife. "I'm so frightened that my teeth are chattering. I feel as if fire were running through my veins."

She tore open her bodice, while Marlene sat in a corner and kept weeping. She had her handkerchief in front of her eyes and wept until it was completely soaked with her tears. The bird swooped down on the juniper tree, where he perched on a branch and began singing:

"My mother, she killed me."

The mother stopped her ears, shut her eyes, and tried not to see or hear anything, but there was a roaring in her ears like a turbulent storm, and her eyes burned and flashed like lightning.

"My father, he ate me."

"Oh, Mother," said the man, "listen to that beautiful bird singing so gloriously! The sun's so warm, and it smells like cinnamon."

"My sister, Marlene, made sure to see."

Then Marlene laid her head on her knees and wept and wept, but the man said, "I'm going outside. I must see the bird close up."

"Oh, don't go!" said the wife. "I feel as if the whole house were shaking and about to go up in flames!"

Nevertheless, the man went out and looked at the bird.

"My bones were all gathered together,
bound nicely in silk, as neat as can be,
and laid beneath the juniper tree.
Tweet, tweet! What a lovely bird I am!"

After ending his song, the bird dropped the golden chain, and it fell around the man's neck just right, so that it fit him perfectly. Then he went inside and said, "Just look how lovely that bird is! He gave me this beautiful golden chain, and he's as beautiful as well!"

But the woman was petrified and fell to the floor. Her cap slipped off her head, and the bird sang again:

"My mother, she killed me."

"Oh, I wish I were a thousand feet beneath the earth so I wouldn't have to hear this!"

"My father, he ate me."

Then the woman fell down again as if she were dead.

"My sister, Marlene, she made sure to see."

"Oh," said Marlene, "I want to go outside too and see if the bird will give me something." Then she went out.

"My bones were all gathered together,
bound nicely in silk, as neat as can be."

Then the bird threw her the shoes.

"And laid them beneath the juniper tree.
Tweet, tweet! What a lovely bird I am!"

Marlene felt gay and happy. She put on the new red shoes and danced and skipped back into the house.

"Oh," she said, "I was so sad when I went out, and now I feel so cheerful. That certainly is a splendid bird. He gave me a pair of red shoes as a gift."

"Not me," said the wife, who jumped up, and her hair flared up like red-hot flames. "I feel as if the world were coming to an end. Maybe I'd feel better if I went outside."

As she went out the door, *crash!* the bird threw the millstone down on her head, and she was crushed to death. The father and Marlene heard the crash and went outside. Smoke, flames, and fire were rising from the spot, and when it was over, the little brother was standing there. He took his father and Marlene by the hand, and all three were very happy. Then they went into the house, sat down at the table, and ate.

❖ 48 ❖

Old Sultan

A FARMER HAD A FAITHFUL DOG NAMED SULTAN, and when the dog had grown old and lost all his teeth, he could no longer grip things tightly. One day, as the farmer was standing by the front door with his wife, he said, "I'm going to shoot old Sultan tomorrow. He's no longer of any use to us."

His wife felt sorry for the faithful creature, and she replied, "Couldn't we just keep him on and feed him? After all, he's served us so many years and has been loyal to us."

"My God!" the husband exclaimed. "Don't you have any sense? He doesn't have a tooth left in his head, and there's not a thief who'd be afraid of him. It's time for him to go. He served us well, but he was also fed well in return."

The poor dog was basking nearby in the sun and overheard everything that was said. He was sad that the next day was to be his last. But he had a good friend, the wolf, and in the evening he sneaked out into the forest to see him and whine about his impending fate.

"Listen, cousin," said the wolf. "Keep your spirits up. You can depend on me to help you out of your dilemma. In fact, I've already thought of something. Early tomorrow morning your master will be going out with his wife to make hay, and they'll take their little child with them because nobody will be staying at home. They generally lay the child behind the hedge in the shade while they work. Now, I want you to lie down next to the child as if you wanted to guard him. I'll come out of the forest and steal the child. Then you've got to take to your heels as if you wanted to get the child away from me. I'll let him drop, and you bring him back to his parents, who'll believe that you rescued him. Then they'll be too grateful to think of harming you. On the contrary, they'll be completely indebted to you and give you anything you want."

The dog liked the scheme, and he carried it out just as planned. When the wolf stole the child and began carrying him through the fields, the father screamed, and when old Sultan brought the child back, he was happy and patted the dog.

"Nobody's going to touch a hair on your head," he said. "You can stay here and eat your fill for as long as you live." Then he turned to his wife and said, "Go home right away and cook some bread mush.

He won't need to chew that. Also, bring the pillow from my bed. I want to give him that as a gift to lie on."

From then on old Sultan had it good, and he could not have wished for a better life. Soon after, the wolf visited him and was glad to learn that everything succeeded so well.

"Now, cousin," he said, "I hope you'll wink an eye when I steal a fat sheep from your master every now and then. Times are getting hard for all of us."

"Don't count on that," the dog answered. "I intend to stay faithful to my master, and I can't let you do it."

The wolf did not believe that the dog meant what he said. So during the night he crept into the yard to steal a sheep. However, the farmer, who had learned about the wolf's plan from the faithful Sultan, was waiting for him and gave him a good thrashing with a flail. The wolf was forced to scamper away, but he cried out at the dog, "Just wait, you traitor! You'll pay for this!"

The next morning the wolf sent the boar as his second to challenge the dog to meet him out in the forest and settle their affair. Old Sultan could find no one who would be his second except for a three-legged cat. And, when they went out together, the poor cat limped and had to hold his tail erect because of the pain he was suffering. The wolf and his second were already at the spot. When they saw the opponent coming, they thought he was carrying a saber with him because they mistook the cat's erect tail for a saber. Moreover, on seeing the cat limping on three legs, they thought he was picking up stones to throw at them. The wolf and the boar became so frightened that the boar crept into some bushes and the wolf jumped up a tree. When the dog and cat arrived at the spot, they were puzzled to find no one there. However, the wild boar had not been able to conceal himself completely in the bushes. One of his ears was showing, and as the cat was looking cautiously about, the boar twitched his ear. The cat thought a mouse might be stirring in the bushes and jumped on it. She took a good hard bite, and the boar leapt with a loud cry and ran away.

"The guilty one's sitting up there in the tree!" he screamed.

The dog and the cat looked up and saw the wolf, who was so ashamed he had shown such cowardice that he accepted the dog's offer of peace.

◈ 49 ◈

The Six Swans

ONCE THERE WAS A KING who was hunting in a vast forest, and he began chasing a deer so intensely that none of his men could follow him. When evening drew near, he stopped, looked around him, and realized he was lost. He searched for a way out of the forest but was unable to find one. Then he caught sight of an old woman, nodding her head back and forth and heading toward him. She was, however, a witch.

"Dear woman," he said to her, "can you show me the way out of the forest?"

"Oh, yes, Your Majesty," she answered. "I certainly can, but on one condition, and if you don't fulfill it, you'll never find your way out of the forest, and you will starve to death."

"What kind of condition?" asked the king.

"I have a daughter," said the old woman, "who is as beautiful as any maiden in the world. Indeed, she is worthy to be your wife, and if you make her your queen, I'll show you the way out of the forest."

The king was so tremendously frightened that he consented, and the old woman led him to her little hut, where her daughter was sitting by the fire. The maiden greeted the king as though she had been expecting him, and he observed that she was very beautiful. Nevertheless, he did not like her, and he could not look at her without secretly shuddering. After he had lifted the maiden onto his horse, the old woman showed him the way, and once the king reached the royal palace again, the wedding was celebrated.

The king had already been married before this, and he had seven children by his first wife, six boys and a girl, whom he loved more than anything in the world. Since he now feared that the stepmother might not treat them well and might even harm them, he brought them to a solitary castle in the middle of a forest. It lay so well concealed and the way to it was so hard to find that he himself would not have found it if a wise woman had not given him a ball of yarn with magic powers. When he threw the ball before him, the yarn unwound itself and showed him the way.

Now, the king went out to visit his dear children so often that the queen began to notice his absences. Since she was curious and wanted to know what he was doing out in the forest all alone, she gave his servants a great deal of money, and they revealed the secret. They also told her about the ball of yarn that alone could show the way. For a while she had no peace of mind, but she finally discovered where the king kept the ball. Then she made small white silk shirts, and she used the witchcraft that she had learned from her mother to sew a magic spell into them.

One day when the king had gone hunting, she took the little shirts, went out into the forest, and let the ball of yarn show her the way. When the children saw someone coming in the distance, they thought their dear father was coming to see them and ran joyfully out to greet him. But she threw a shirt over each one of them, and as soon as they were touched by the shirts, they were turned into swans and flew away over the forest. The queen went home delighted with herself, thinking that she was rid of her stepchildren. However, the girl had not run outside with her brothers, and the queen knew nothing about the girl.

The following day the king went to visit his children, but he found only the girl.

"Where are your brothers?" the king asked.

"Oh, dear Father," she answered, "they've gone away and left me alone." And she told him how, from her window, she had seen her brothers turn into swans, and how they had flown away over the forest. Then she showed him the feathers that they had dropped in the yard and left for her to gather.

The king mourned for his sons but had no idea that the queen had done this evil deed. Yet, he did fear that his daughter might also be stolen from him, and he wanted to take her with him. However, she was afraid of the stepmother and begged the king to allow her to spend one last night in the forest castle. I can't stay here any longer, the poor girl thought. I shall go and search for my brothers.

When night came, she fled the castle and went straight into the forest. She walked the whole night long and the entire next day without stopping, until she became so exhausted that she could go no farther. Then she saw a hut, and after entering it, she found a room with six small beds. Since she was afraid to lie down in any of the beds, she crawled underneath one and lay down on the hard floor, intending to spend the night there. However, just when the sun was about to set, she heard a rustling sound and saw six swans come flying through the window. They landed on the floor and blew at each other until all their feathers were blown off. After that their swan skins slipped off like shirts. The maiden observed all this, and when she recognized her brothers, she rejoiced and crawled out from under the bed. Her brothers were delighted to see their little sister, but their joy was short-lived.

"You can't stay here," they said to her. "This is a robbers' den. When they come home and find you here, they'll kill you."

"Can't you protect me?" asked their sister.

"No," they replied. "You see, we can take off our swan skins for only a quarter of an hour every evening. During this time we assume our human form, but after that we're changed back into swans."

Their sister wept and asked, "Can't you be set free?"

"We don't think so," they said. "The conditions are too hard. You'd have to go six years without speaking to anyone or laughing, and during this time you'd have to sew six little shirts for us made of asters. If just one single word were to fall from your lips, then all your work would be for naught."

Nevertheless, the maiden decided to set her brothers free, even if it might cost her her life. She left the hut, went into the middle of the forest, climbed a tree, and spent the night there. The next morning she got down, gathered asters, and began to sew. She could not talk to anyone, nor did she have a desire to laugh: she just sat there and concentrated on her work.

After she had spent a long time there, the king of the country happened to go hunting in the forest, and his huntsmen came to the tree where the maiden was perched. They called to her and said, "Who are you?"

She did not answer.

"Come down to us," they said. "We won't harm you."

She merely shook her head. When they continued to bother her with questions, she threw them her golden necklace and thought that would satisfy them. Yet, they persisted. Then she threw them her girdle, and when this did not work either, she threw down her garters and little by little everything that she had on and could do without until she had nothing left but her little shift. Still the huntsmen did not let themselves be deterred by all this. They climbed the tree, carried her down, and led her to the king, who asked, "Who are you, and what were you doing in that tree?"

She did not answer. He tried questioning her in all the languages he knew, but she remained as silent as a fish. Eventually, her beauty moved the king's heart, and he fell deeply in love with her. He covered her with his cloak, lifted her onto his horse, and brought her to his castle. There he had her dressed in rich garments, and her beautiful features were as radiant as the day is bright. Still, it was impossible to get her to utter a single word. He had her sit next to him at the table, and her modest ways and her polite manners pleased him so much that he said, "This maiden is the one I shall marry and no other woman in the world except her."

Within a few days he married her, but the king had an evil mother, who was dissatisfied with this marriage and spoke ill of the young queen.

"That wench! Why won't she speak?" she said. "Where does she come from? She's not worthy of a king."

A year later, when the queen gave birth to her first child, the old woman took the child away from her and smeared the queen's mouth with blood while she was asleep. Then the old woman went to the king and accused the young queen of being a cannibal. The king refused to believe this and would not tolerate anyone harming his wife. Meanwhile, the queen continued to sit and sew the shirts, and did not pay attention to anything else.

The next time, she gave birth to another handsome boy, and her wicked mother-in-law tried the same deception, but the king could not bring himself to believe the charges brought against his wife.

"She's too pious and good," he said. "She'd never do anything like that. If she could talk, she could defend herself, and her innocence would come to light."

However, when the old woman stole the third newborn baby and accused the queen, who did not say one word in her own defense, the king could do nothing but hand her over to a court, which condemned her to death by fire.

The day came for the sentence to be carried out, but it was also the last day of the six years during which she had not been allowed to speak or laugh. Indeed, this meant that she had set her brothers free from the power of the magic spell. The six shirts were finished except for the left sleeve of the last shirt. When the queen was led to the stake, she carried the shirts over her arm, and as she stood on the stack of wood and the fire was about to be lit, she looked up and saw the six swans come flying through the air. Now she knew that her rescue was near at hand, and her heart jumped for joy. The swans swooped down and landed close by so that she could throw the shirts over them. As soon as the shirts touched them, the swan skins fell off, and her brothers stood before her in the flesh. They looked handsome and vigorous. Only the youngest was missing his left arm, and he had a swan's wing on his shoulder instead. They embraced and kissed each other, and the queen went up to the king, who was quite stunned by all this.

"Dearest husband," she said. "Now I may speak and tell you that I'm innocent and was unjustly accused."

She told him how the old woman had been deceiving him and had taken away her three children and hidden them. Then, to the king's great joy, the children were brought to him, and as a punishment the wicked mother-in-law was tied to the stake and burned to ashes. Thereafter, the king and queen, along with her six brothers, lived for many years in peace and happiness.

◈ 50 ◈

Brier Rose

IN TIMES OF OLD there lived a king and queen, and every day they said, "Oh, if only we had a child!" Yet, they never had one.

Then one day, as the queen went out bathing, a frog happened to crawl ashore and say to her, "Your wish shall be fulfilled. Before the year is out, you shall give birth to a daughter."

The frog's prediction came true, and the queen gave birth to a girl who was so beautiful that the king was overjoyed and decided to hold a great feast. Not only did he invite his relatives, friends, and acquaintances, but also the wise women, in the hope that they would be generous and kind to his daughter. There were thirteen wise women in his kingdom, but he had only twelve golden plates from which they could eat. Therefore, one of them had to remain home.

The feast was celebrated with tremendous splendor, and when it drew to a close, the wise women bestowed their miraculous gifts upon the child. One gave her virtue, another beauty, the third wealth, and so on, until they had given her nearly everything one could possibly wish for in the world. When eleven of them had offered their gifts, the thirteenth suddenly entered the hall. She wanted to get revenge for not having been invited, and without greeting anyone or looking around, she cried out with a loud voice, "In her fifteenth year the princess shall prick herself with a spindle and fall down dead!"

That was all she said. Then she turned around and left the hall. Everyone was horrified, but the twelfth wise woman stepped forward. She still had her wish to make, and although she could not undo the evil spell, she could nevertheless soften it.

"The princess shall not die," she said. "Instead, she shall fall into a deep sleep for one hundred years."

Since the king wanted to guard his dear child against such a catastrophe, he issued an order that all spindles in his kingdom were to be burned. Meanwhile, the gifts of the wise women fulfilled their promise in every way: the girl was so beautiful, polite, kind, and sensible that whoever encountered her could not help but adore her.

Now, on the day she turned fifteen, it happened that the king and queen were not at home, and she was left completely alone in the palace. So she wandered all over the place and explored as many rooms and chambers as she pleased. She eventually came to an old tower, climbed its narrow winding staircase, and came to a small door. A rusty key was stuck in the lock, and when she turned it, the door sprang open, and she saw an old woman in a little room sitting with a spindle and busily spinning flax.

"Good day, old granny," said the princess. "What are you doing there?"

"I'm spinning," said the old woman, and she nodded her head.

"What's the thing that's bobbing about in such a funny way?" asked the maiden, who took the spindle and wanted to spin too, but just as she touched the spindle, the magic spell began working, and she pricked her finger with it.

The very moment she felt the prick, she fell down on the bed that was standing there, and she was overcome by a deep sleep. This sleep soon spread throughout the entire palace. The king and queen had just returned home, and when they entered the hall, they fell asleep, as did all the people of their court. They were followed by the horses in the stable, the dogs in the courtyard, the pigeons on the roof, and the flies on the wall. Even the fire flickering in the hearth became quiet and fell asleep. The roast stopped sizzling, and the cook, who was just about to pull the kitchen boy's hair because he had done something wrong, let him go and fell asleep. Finally, the wind died down so that not a single leaf stirred on the trees outside the castle.

Soon a brier hedge began to grow all around the castle, and it grew higher each year. Eventually, it surrounded and covered the entire castle, so that it was no longer visible. Not even the flag on the roof could be seen. The princess became known by the name Beautiful Sleeping Brier Rose, and a tale about her began circulating throughout the country. From time to time princes came and tried to break through the hedge and get to the castle. However, this was impossible because the thorns clung together tightly as though they had hands, and the young men got stuck there. Indeed, they could not pry themselves loose and died miserable deaths.

After many, many years had gone by, a prince came to this country once more and heard an old man talking about the brier hedge. Supposedly there was a castle standing behind the hedge, and in the castle was a remarkably beautiful princess named Brier Rose, who had been sleeping for a hundred years, along with the king and queen and their entire court. The old man also knew from his grandfather that many princes had come and had tried to break through the brier hedge, but they had got stuck and had died wretched deaths.

"I am not afraid," said the young prince. "I intend to go and see the beautiful Brier Rose."

The good old man tried as best he could to dissuade him, but the prince would not heed his words.

Now the hundred years had just ended, and the day on which Brier

Rose was to wake up again had arrived. When the prince approached the brier hedge, he found nothing but beautiful flowers that opened of their own accord, let him through, and then closed again like a hedge. In the castle courtyard he saw the horses and the spotted hunting dogs lying asleep. The pigeons were perched on the roof and had tucked their heads beneath their wings. When he entered the palace, the flies were sleeping on the wall, the cook in the kitchen was still holding his hand as if he wanted to grab the kitchen boy, and the maid was sitting in front of the black chicken that she was about to pluck. As the prince continued walking, he saw the entire court lying asleep in the hall with the king and queen by the throne. Then he moved on, and everything was so quiet that he could hear himself breathe.

Finally, he came to the tower and opened the door to the small room in which Brier Rose was asleep. There she lay, and her beauty was so marvelous that he could not take his eyes off her. Then he leaned over and gave her a kiss, and when his lips touched hers, Brier Rose opened her eyes, woke up, and looked at him fondly. After that they went downstairs together, and the king and queen woke up along with the entire court, and they all looked at each other in amazement. Soon the horses in the courtyard stood up and shook themselves. The hunting dogs jumped around and wagged their tails. The pigeons on the roof lifted their heads from under their wings, looked around, and flew off into the fields. The flies on the wall continued crawling. The fire in the kitchen flared up, flickered, and cooked the meat. The roast began to sizzle again, and the cook gave the kitchen boy such a box on the ear that he let out a cry, while the maid finished plucking the chicken.

The wedding of the prince with Brier Rose was celebrated in great splendor, and they lived happily to the end of their days.

◈ 51 ◈

Foundling

ONCE UPON A TIME a forester went out hunting in the forest, and as he entered it, he heard some cries like those of a small child. He followed the sounds and eventually came to a big tree where he saw a little child sitting on the top. The child's mother had fallen asleep with him under the tree, and a hawk had seen the child in her lap. So it had swooped down, carried the child away with its beak, and set him down on top of the tree. The forester climbed the tree and brought the child down, and he thought, You ought to take him home with you and raise him with your little Lena.

So he took the boy home, and the two children grew up together. However, the boy who had been found on top of the tree was called Foundling because he had been carried off by a bird. Foundling and Lena were very fond of each other. In fact, they loved each other so much that they became sad if they were not constantly within sight of each other.

Now the forester had an old cook, and one evening she took two buckets and began fetching water. But she did not go to the well simply one time but many times. When Lena saw this, she asked, "Tell me, old Sanna, why are you fetching so much water?"

"If you promise to keep quiet, I'll let you in on my secret."

Lena of course replied that she would not tell a soul. Then the cook said, "Early tomorrow morning, when the forester goes out hunting, I'm going to heat some water over the fire, and when it's boiling, I'm going to throw Foundling in and cook him."

Early the next morning the forester got up to go out hunting, and when he had gone, the children were still in bed. Then Lena said to Foundling, "If you won't forsake me, I won't forsake you."

"Never ever," said Foundling.

"Well then, I'm going to tell you something," said Lena. "Last night old Sanna was fetching many buckets of water into the house, and I asked her why she was doing that. She said that if I wouldn't tell a soul, she'd let me in on her secret. I promised her not to tell a living soul. Then she said that early this morning, when my father goes out hunting, she would boil a kettle full of water, throw you in, and cook you. So let's get up quickly, dress ourselves, and go away together."

Then the two children got up, dressed themselves quickly, and went away. When the water in the kettle began to boil, the cook went into the bedroom to get Foundling and throw him into the kettle. But as she entered the room and went over to the beds, she saw that the two children were gone and became greatly alarmed.

"What shall I say when the forester comes home and sees that the children are gone?" she said. "I'd better send some people after them to get them back."

The cook sent three servants to run after them and bring them back. But the children were sitting at the edge of the forest and saw the three servants coming from afar.

"If you won't forsake me, I won't forsake you," said Lena.

"Never ever," said Foundling.

"Then change yourself into a rosebush, and I'll be the rose on it," said Lena.

When the three servants reached the edge of the forest, they saw nothing but a rosebush with a little rose on it. The children were nowhere to be seen.

"There's nothing doing here," they said, and they went home, where they told the cook they had seen nothing but a rosebush with a rose on it. Then the cook scolded them. "You blockheads! You should have cut the rosebush in two, plucked the rose, and brought it back with you. Now go quickly and do it!"

So they had to set out once more and look for the children. But when the children saw them coming from afar, Lena said, "If you won't forsake me, I won't forsake you."

"Never ever," said Foundling.

"Then change yourself into a church, and I'll be the chandelier hanging in it," Lena said.

When the three servants arrived at the spot, there was nothing but a church and a chandelier inside it.

"What's there to do here? Let's go home."

When they got home, the cook asked whether they had found anything. They said no. They had found nothing but a church with a chandelier inside.

"You fools!" the cook scolded. "Why didn't you destroy the church and bring back the chandelier?"

This time the old cook herself set out on foot and pursued the children with the three servants. But the children saw the three servants coming from afar and also the cook, who was waddling behind them.

"Foundling," said Lena. "If you won't forsake me, I won't forsake you."

"Never ever," said Foundling.

"Then change yourself into a pond," said Lena, "and I'll be the duck swimming on it."

When the cook arrived and saw the pond, she lay down beside it and began to drink it up. However, the duck quickly swam over, grabbed her head in its beak, and dragged her into the water. The old witch was thus drowned, and the children went home together. They were very happy, and if they have not died, they are still alive.

◈ 52 ◈

King Thrushbeard

A KING HAD A DAUGHTER whose beauty was beyond comparison, but she was so proud and haughty that no suitor was good enough for her. Indeed, she rejected one after the other and ridiculed them as well. Once her father held a great feast and invited all the marriageable young men from far and wide to attend. They were all lined up according to their rank and class: first came the kings, then the dukes, princes, counts, and barons, and finally the gentry. The king's daughter was conducted down the line, and she found fault with each one of the suitors there. One was too fat for her. "That wine barrel!" she said. Another was too tall. "Tall and thin, he looks like a pin!" The third was too short. "Short and fat, he's built like a vat!" The fourth was too pale. "He resembles death!" The fifth was too red. "What a rooster!" The sixth did not stand straight enough. "Green wood, dried behind the stove!"

There was not a single man whom she did not criticize, but she made the most fun of a good king who stood at the head of the line and had a chin that was a bit crooked.

"My goodness!" she exclaimed, and laughed. "He's got a chin like a thrush's beak!" From then on, everyone called him Thrushbeard.

When her father saw that she did nothing but ridicule people, and that she scorned all the suitors who were gathered there, he was furious and swore that she would have to marry the very first beggar who came to his door. A few days later a minstrel came and began singing beneath the windows to earn some money. When the king heard him, he said, "Have him come up here."

The minstrel, who was dressed in dirty, tattered clothes, entered the hall and sang in front of the king and his daughter. When he was finished, he asked for a modest reward.

"Your singing has pleased me so much," the king said, "that I shall give you my daughter for your wife."

The king's daughter was horrified, but the king said, "I swore I'd give you to the very first beggar who came along, and I intend to keep my word."

All her objections were to no avail. The minister was fetched, and she was compelled to wed the minstrel. When that was done, the king said, "It's not fitting for you to stay in my palace any longer since you're now a beggar woman. I want you to depart with your husband."

The beggar took her by the hand, and she had to go with him on foot. When they came to a huge forest, she asked:

"Tell me, who might the owner of this forest be?"
"King Thrushbeard owns the forest and all you can see.
If you had taken him, it would belong to you."
"Alas, poor me! What can I do?
I should have wed King Thrushbeard. If only I knew!"

Soon they crossed a meadow, and she asked again:

"Tell me, who might the owner of this meadow be?"
"King Thrushbeard owns the meadow and all you can see.
If you had taken him, it would belong to you."
"Alas, poor me! What can I do?
I should have wed King Thrushbeard. If only I knew!"

Then they came to a large city, and she asked once more:

"Tell me, who might the owner of this city be?"
"King Thrushbeard owns the city and all you can see.
If you had taken him, it would belong to you."
"Alas, poor me! What can I do?
I should have wed King Thrushbeard. If only I knew!"

"I'm not at all pleased by this," said the minstrel. "Why are you always wishing for another husband? Do you think I'm not good enough for you?"

Finally, they came to a tiny cottage, and she said:

"Oh, Lord! What a wretched tiny house!
It's not even fit for a mouse."

The minstrel answered, "This house is mine and yours, and we shall live here together."

She had to stoop to get through the low doorway.

"Where are the servants?" the king's daughter asked.

"What servants?" answered the beggar. "You must do everything yourself if you want something done. Now, make a fire at once and put the water on so you can cook me my meal. I'm very tired."

However, the king's daughter knew nothing about making a fire or cooking, and the beggar had to lend a hand himself if he wanted anything done in a tolerable fashion. After they had eaten their meager meal, they went to bed. But the next morning he got her up very early because she had to take care of the house. For a few days they lived like this and managed as best they could. When they had consumed all their provisions, the man said, "Wife, we can't go on this way any longer. We've used everything up, and we're not earning a thing. You've got to weave baskets."

He went out to cut some willows and brought them home, but the rough willows bruised her tender hands.

"I see that won't work," said the man. "Let's try spinning. Perhaps you'll be better at that."

She sat down at the spinning wheel and tried to spin, but the hard thread soon cut her soft fingers, and blood began to flow.

"See now," said the man. "You're not fit for any kind of work. I made a bad bargain when I got you. But let's see how things go if I start a business with pots and earthenware. You're to sit in the marketplace and sell the wares."

Oh, she thought, if some people from my father's kingdom come to the marketplace and see me selling wares, they'll surely make fun of me!

But there was no way to avoid it. She had to obey her husband if she did not want to die of hunger. The first time everything went well. People gladly bought her wares because she was beautiful, and they paid what she asked. Indeed, many gave her money and did not even bother to take the pots with them. So the couple lived off their earnings as long as they lasted. Then her husband bought a lot of new earthenware. His wife sat down with it at a corner in the marketplace, set her wares around her, and offered them for sale. Suddenly, a drunken hussar came galloping along and rode right over the pots so that they were all smashed to pieces. She began to weep and was paralyzed with fear.

"Oh, what's going to happen to me!" she exclaimed. "What will my husband say?"

She ran home and told him about the accident, and he responded by saying, "In heaven's name, who would ever sit down at a corner in the marketplace with earthenware? Now stop your weeping. I see full well that you're not fit for proper work. I've already been to the king's castle and have asked whether they could use a kitchen maid, and they've promised me to take you on. In return you'll get free meals."

Now the king's daughter became a kitchen maid and had to assist the cook and do the lowest kind of work. She sewed two little jars inside her pockets and carried home the leftovers so they could have some food to live on. One day it happened that the king's oldest son was celebrating his wedding, and the poor woman went upstairs, stood outside the door of the large hall, and wanted to look inside. When the candles were lit, each guest entered, one more exquisitely dressed than the next, and everything was full of splendor. With a sad heart she thought about her fate and cursed her pride and arrogance for bringing about her humiliation and great poverty. Sometimes the servants threw her pieces of the delicious dishes they were carrying in and out of the hall, and she could also smell the aroma of the food. She put the pieces into her pockets and intended to carry them home.

Suddenly the king's son entered. He was dressed in velvet and silk and had a golden chain around his neck. And, when he saw the beautiful woman standing in the doorway, he grabbed her by the hand and wanted to dance with her, but she refused. Indeed, she was horrified because she saw it was King Thrushbeard, who had courted her and whom she had rejected with scorn. Although she struggled, it was to no avail, for he pulled her into the hall. Then the string that held her pockets together broke, and the jars fell out, causing the soup to spill and the scraps of food to scatter on the floor. When the people saw that, they laughed a good deal and poked fun at her. She was so ashamed that she wished she were a thousand fathoms under the earth. She ran out the door and tried to escape, but a man caught up with her on the stairs and brought her back. When she looked at him, she saw it was King Thrushbeard again, and he said to her in a friendly way, "Don't be afraid. I and the minstrel who lived with you in the wretched cottage are one and the same person. I disguised myself out of love for you, and I was also the hussar who rode over your pots and smashed them to pieces. I did all that to humble your proud spirit and to punish you for the insolent way you behaved toward me."

Then she shed bitter tears and said, "I've done a great wrong and don't deserve to be your wife."

However, he said, "Console yourself. The bad days are over. Now we shall celebrate our wedding."

The chambermaids came and dressed her in splendid clothes, and her father came along with his entire court, and they wished her happiness in her marriage with King Thrushbeard. Then the real rejoicing began, and I wish that you and I had been there too.

❖ 53 ❖

Snow White

ONCE UPON A TIME, in the middle of winter, when snowflakes were falling like feathers from the sky, a queen was sitting and sewing at a window with a black ebony frame. And as she was sewing and looking out the window, she pricked her finger with the needle, and three drops of blood fell on the snow. The red looked so beautiful on the white snow that she thought to herself, If only I had a child as white as snow, as red as blood, and as black as the wood of the window frame!

Soon after she gave birth to a little daughter who was as white as snow, as red as blood, and her hair as black as ebony. Accordingly, the child was called Snow White, and right after she was born, the queen died. When a year had passed, the king married another woman, who was beautiful but proud and haughty, and she could not tolerate anyone else who might rival her beauty. She had a magic mirror and often she stood in front of it, looked at herself, and said:

"Mirror, mirror, on the wall,
who in this realm is the fairest of all?"

Then the mirror would answer:

"You, my queen, are the fairest of all."

That reply would make her content, for she knew the mirror always told the truth.

In the meantime, Snow White grew up and became more and more beautiful. By the time she was seven years old, she was as beautiful as the day is clear and more beautiful than the queen herself. One day when the queen asked her mirror:

"Mirror, mirror, on the wall,
who in this realm is the fairest of all?"

The mirror answered:

"You, my queen, may have a beauty quite rare,
but Snow White is a thousand times more fair."

The queen shuddered and became yellow and green with envy. From that hour on, her hate for the girl was so great that her heart throbbed and turned in her breast each time she saw Snow White. Like weeds, the envy and arrogance grew so dense in her heart that she no longer had any peace, day or night. Finally, she summoned a huntsman and said, "Take the child out into the forest. I never want to lay eyes on her again. You are to kill her and to bring me back her lungs and liver as proof of your deed."

The huntsman obeyed and led Snow White out into the forest, but when he drew his hunting knife and was about to stab Snow White's innocent heart, she began to weep and said, "Oh, dear huntsman, spare my life, and I'll run into the wild forest and never come home again."

Since she was so beautiful, the huntsman took pity on her and said, "You're free to go, my poor child!" Then he thought, The wild beasts will soon eat you up. Nevertheless, he felt as if a great weight had been lifted off his mind, because he did not have to kill her. Just then a young boar came dashing by, and the huntsman stabbed it to death. He took out the lungs and liver and brought them to the queen as proof that the child was dead. The cook was ordered to boil them in salt, and the wicked woman ate them and thought that she had eaten Snow White's lungs and liver.

Meanwhile, the poor child was all alone in the huge forest. When she looked at all the leaves on the trees, she was petrified and did not know what to do. Then she began to run, and she ran over sharp stones and through thornbushes. Wild beasts darted by her at times, but they did not harm her. She ran as long as her legs could carry her, and it was almost evening when she saw a little cottage and went inside to rest. Everything was tiny in the cottage and indescribably dainty and neat. There was a little table with a white tablecloth, and on it were seven little plates. Each plate had a tiny spoon next to it, and there were also seven tiny knives and forks and seven tiny cups. In a row against the wall stood seven little beds covered with sheets as white as snow. Since she was so hungry and thirsty, Snow White ate some vegetables and bread from each of the little plates and had a drop of wine to drink out of each of the tiny cups, for she did not want to take everything from just one place. After that she was tired and began trying out the beds, but none of them suited her at first: one was too long, another too short, but at last, she found that the seventh one was just right. So she stayed in that bed, said her prayers, and fell asleep.

When it was completely dark outside, the owners of the cottage returned. They were seven dwarfs who searched in the mountains for minerals with their picks and shovels. They lit their seven little candles, and when it became light in the house, they saw that someone had been there, for none of their things was in the exact same spot in which it had been left.

"Who's been sitting in my chair?" said the first dwarf.

"Who's been eating off my plate?" said the second.

"Who's been eating my bread?" said the third.

"Who's been eating my vegetables?" said the fourth.

"Who's been using my fork?" said the fifth.

"Who's been cutting with my knife?" said the sixth.

"Who's been drinking from my cup?" said the seventh.

Then the first dwarf looked around and noticed that his bed had been wrinkled and said, "Who's been sleeping in my bed?"

The others ran over to their beds and cried out, "Someone's been sleeping in my bed too!"

But when the seventh dwarf looked at his bed, he saw Snow White lying there asleep. So he called the others over to him, and when they came, they were so astounded that they fetched their seven little candles to allow more light to shine on Snow White.

"Oh, my Lord! Oh, my Lord!" they exclaimed. "What a beautiful child!"

They were so delirious with joy that they did not wake her up. Instead, they let her sleep in the bed, while the seventh dwarf spent an hour in each one of his companions' beds until the night had passed. In the morning Snow White awoke, and when she saw the seven dwarfs, she was frightened. But they were friendly and asked, "What's your name?"

"My name's Snow White," she replied.

"What's brought you to our house?" the dwarfs continued.

She told them how her stepmother had ordered her to be killed, how the huntsman had spared her life, and how she had run all day until she had eventually discovered their cottage.

Then the dwarfs said, "If you'll keep house for us, cook, make the beds, wash, sew, and knit, and if you'll keep everything neat and orderly, you can stay with us, and we'll provide you with everything you need."

"Yes," agreed Snow White, "with all my heart."

So she stayed with them and kept their house in order. In the morning they went to the mountains to search for minerals and gold. In the evening they returned, and their dinner had to be ready. During the day Snow White was alone, and the good dwarfs made sure to caution her.

"Beware of your stepmother," they said. "She'll soon know that you're here. Don't let anybody in!"

Since the queen believed she had eaten Snow White's liver and lungs, she was totally convinced that she was again the most beautiful woman in the realm. And when she went to her mirror, she said:

"Mirror, mirror, on the wall,
who in this realm is the fairest of all?"

The mirror answered:

"You, my queen, may have a beauty quite rare,
but beyond the mountains, where the seven dwarfs dwell,
Snow White is thriving, and this I must tell:
Within this realm she's still a thousand times more fair."

The queen was horrified, for she knew that the mirror never lied, which meant that the huntsman had deceived her and Snow White was still alive. Once more she began plotting ways to kill her. As long as Snow White was the fairest in the realm, the queen's envy would leave her no peace. Finally, she thought up a plan. She painted her face and dressed as an old peddler woman so that nobody could recognize her. Then she crossed the seven mountains in this disguise and arrived at the cottage of the seven dwarfs, where she knocked at the door and cried out, "Pretty wares for sale! Pretty wares!"

Snow White looked out of the window and called out, "Good day, dear woman, what do you have for sale?"

"Nice and pretty things! Staylaces in all kinds of colors!" she replied and took out a lace woven from silk of many different colors.

I can certainly let this honest woman inside, Snow White thought. She unbolted the door and bought the pretty lace.

"My goodness, child! What a sight you are!" said the old woman. "Come, I'll lace you up properly for once."

Snow White did not suspect anything, so she stood in front of the old woman and let herself be laced with the new staylace. However, the old woman laced her so quickly and so tightly that Snow White lost her breath and fell down as if dead.

"Well, you used to be the fairest in the realm, but not now!" the old woman said and rushed off.

Not long after, at dinnertime, the dwarfs came home, and when they saw their dear Snow White lying on the ground, they were horrified. She neither stirred nor moved and seemed to be dead. They lifted her up, and when they saw that she was laced too tightly, they cut the staylace in two. At once she began to breathe a little, and after a while she had fully revived. When the dwarfs heard what had happened, they said, "The old peddler woman was none other than the wicked queen! Beware, don't let anyone in when we're not with you!"

When the evil woman returned home, she went to her mirror and asked:

"Mirror, mirror, on the wall,
who in this realm is the fairest of all?"

Then the mirror answered as usual:

"You, my queen, may have a beauty quite rare,
but beyond the mountains, where the seven dwarfs dwell,
Snow White is thriving, and this I must tell:
Within this realm she's still a thousand times more fair."

When the queen heard that, she was so upset that all her blood rushed to her heart, for she realized that Snow White had recovered.

"This time I'm going to think of something that will destroy her," she said, and by using all the witchcraft at her command, she made a poison comb. Then she again disguised herself as an old woman and crossed the seven mountains to the cottage of the seven dwarfs, where she knocked at the door and cried out, "Pretty wares for sale! Pretty wares!"

Snow White looked out the window and said, "Go away! I'm not allowed to let anyone in."

"But surely you're allowed to look," said the old woman, and she took out the poison comb and held it up in the air. The comb pleased the girl so much that she let herself be carried away and opened the door. After they agreed on the price, the old woman said, "Now I'll give your hair a proper combing for once."

Poor Snow White did not give this a second thought and let the old woman do as she wished. But no sooner did the comb touch her hair than the poison began to take effect, and the maiden fell to the ground and lay there unconscious.

"You paragon of beauty!" said the wicked woman. "Now you're finished!" And she went away.

Fortunately, it was nearly evening, the time when the seven dwarfs began heading home. And, when they arrived and saw Snow White lying on the ground as if she were dead, they immediately suspected the stepmother and began looking around. As soon as they found the poison comb, they took it out, and Snow White instantly regained consciousness. She told them what had happened, and they warned her again to be on her guard and not to open the door for anyone.

In the meantime, the queen returned home, went to the mirror, and said:

"Mirror, mirror, on the wall,
who in this realm is the fairest of all?"

Then the mirror answered as before:

"You, my queen, may have a beauty quite rare,
but beyond the mountains, where the seven dwarfs dwell,
Snow White is thriving, and this I must tell:
Within this realm she's still a thousand times more fair."

When she heard the mirror's words, she trembled and shook with rage.

"Snow White shall die!" she exclaimed. "Even if it costs me my own life!"

Then she went into a secret and solitary chamber where no one else ever went. Once inside she made a deadly poisonous apple. On the outside it looked beautiful—white with red cheeks. Anyone who saw it would be enticed, but whoever took a bite was bound to die. When the apple was ready, the queen painted her face and dressed herself up as a peasant woman and crossed the seven mountains to the cottage of the seven dwarfs. When she knocked at the door, Snow White stuck her head out of the window and said, "I'm not allowed to let anyone inside. The seven dwarfs have forbidden me."

"That's all right with me," answered the peasant woman. "I'll surely get rid of my apples in time. But let me give you one as a gift."

"No," said Snow White. "I'm not allowed to take anything."

"Are you afraid that it might be poisoned?" said the old woman. "Look, I'll cut the apple in two. You eat the red part, and I'll eat the white."

However, the apple had been made with such cunning that only the red part was poisoned. Snow White was eager to eat the beautiful apple, and when she saw the peasant woman eating her half, she could no longer resist, stretched out her hand, and took the poisoned half. No sooner did she take a bite than she fell to the ground dead. The queen stared at her with a cruel look, then burst out laughing and said, "White as snow, red as blood, black as ebony! This time the dwarfs won't be able to bring you back to life!"

When she got home, she asked the mirror:

"Mirror, mirror, on the wall,
who in this realm is the fairest of all?"

Then the mirror finally answered, "You, my queen, are now the fairest of all." So her jealous heart was satisfied as much as a jealous heart can be satisfied.

When the dwarfs came home that evening, they found Snow White lying on the ground. There was no breath coming from her lips, and she was dead. They lifted her up and looked to see if they could find something poisonous. They unlaced her, combed her hair, washed her with water and wine, but it was to no avail. The dear child was dead and remained dead. They laid her on a bier, and all seven of them sat down beside it and mourned over her. They wept for three whole days, and then they intended to bury her, but she looked so alive and still had such pretty red cheeks that they said, "We can't possibly bury her in the dingy ground."

Instead, they made a transparent glass coffin so that she could be seen from all sides. Then they put her in it, wrote her name on it in gold letters, and added that she was a princess. They carried the coffin to the top of the mountain, and from then on one of them always stayed beside it and guarded it. Some animals came also and wept for Snow White. There was an owl, then a raven, and finally a dove. Snow White lay in the coffin for many, many years and did not decay. Indeed, she seemed to be sleeping, for she was still as white as snow, as red as blood, and her hair as black as ebony.

Now it happened that a prince came to the forest one day, and

when he arrived at the dwarfs' cottage, he decided to spend the night. Then he went to the mountain and saw the coffin with beautiful Snow White inside. After he read what was written on the coffin in gold letters, he said to the dwarfs, "Let me have the coffin, and I'll pay you whatever you want."

But the dwarfs answered, "We won't give it up for all the gold in the world."

"Then give it to me as a gift," he said, "for I can't go on living without being able to see Snow White. I'll honor her and cherish her as my dearly beloved."

Since he spoke with such fervor, the good dwarfs took pity on him and gave him the coffin. The prince ordered his servants to carry the coffin on their shoulders, but they stumbled over some shrubs, and the jolt caused the poisoned piece of apple that Snow White had bitten off to be released from her throat. It was not long before she opened her eyes, lifted up the lid of the coffin, sat up, and was alive again.

"Oh, Lord! Where am I?" she exclaimed.

The prince rejoiced and said, "You're with me," and he told her what had happened. Then he added, "I love you more than anything else in the world. Come with me to my father's castle. I want you to be my wife."

Snow White felt that he was sincere, so she went with him, and their wedding was celebrated with great pomp and splendor.

Now, Snow White's stepmother had also been invited to the wedding celebration, and after she had dressed herself in beautiful clothes, she went to the mirror and said:

"Mirror, mirror, on the wall,
who in this realm is the fairest of all?"

The mirror answered:

"You, my queen, may have a beauty quite rare,
but Snow White is a thousand times more fair."

The evil woman uttered a loud curse and became so terribly afraid that she did not know what to do. At first she did not want to go to the wedding celebration. But, she could not calm herself until she saw the young queen. When she entered the hall, she recognized Snow White. The evil queen was so petrified with fright that she could not budge. Iron slippers had already been heated over a fire, and they were brought over to her with tongs. Finally, she had to put on the red-hot slippers and dance until she fell down dead.

◈ 54 ◈

The Knapsack, the Hat, and the Horn

ONCE UPON A TIME there were three brothers who found themselves getting poorer and poorer. Eventually their plight became so great that they had nothing to eat and were starving.

"We can't go on like this," they said. "We'd better go out into the world and see if we can change our luck."

So they set out and traveled quite some distance. Their way took them over fields of green grass, but they did not encounter much luck. Then one day they reached a large forest, and in the middle of the forest there was a mountain. When they came closer, they saw that the mountain was all silver.

"Now that I've found the good luck that I was searching for," said the oldest, "I don't want anything more."

He took as much of the silver as he could carry, turned around, and went back home. But the others said, "We expect much more from our luck than mere silver."

Indeed, they did not touch any of the silver and continued on their way. After they had traveled a few more days, they came to a mountain that was all gold. The second brother stopped, pondered the situation, and was undecided.

"What should I do?" he asked. "Should I take enough gold to last me the rest of my life, or should I continue on my way?"

Finally, he decided to fill his pockets with as much gold as they could hold, said farewell to his brother, and went home. But the third brother said, "Silver and gold mean nothing to me. I won't give up on my luck. Maybe I'll come across something better."

He went on, and after three days he came to a forest that was so much greater than the others that it appeared to be endless. Since he had found nothing to eat or drink, he was at the point of collapsing and decided to climb a tree to find out whether he could see the end of the forest. However, there were nothing but treetops as far as his eyes could see. Tormented by hunger, he climbed down the tree and said to himself, "If only I could get something to fill my stomach once more!" When he reached the bottom of the tree, he was amazed to find a table spread with food, and his nose picked up the aroma.

"This time," he said, "my wish has been granted in the nick of time!"

Without asking who had brought the food and who had cooked it, he approached the table and ate heartily until he had satisfied his hunger. When he was finished, he thought, It would be a shame to leave this fine tablecloth out here in the forest where it might be ruined. So he folded it neatly and put it into his knapsack. Then he moved on, and in the evening when he grew hungry again, he decided to test his little tablecloth. After spreading it out on the ground, he said, "I wish you were covered again with good food." No sooner did he utter his wish than the tablecloth was covered with the most delicious kinds of food. "Now I realize in what kitchen the cooking's been done for me," he said. "You're more precious to me than mountains of silver and gold."

Indeed, he knew that he had a magic tablecloth. But the tablecloth was not enough to get him to return home and settle down. On the contrary, he wanted to continue traveling about the world and to keep trying his luck. One evening, as he was going through a lonely forest, he met a charcoal burner covered with black soot. The charcoal burner was preparing a meal of baked potatoes on a fire.

"Good evening, blackbird," said the traveler. "How are things in this lonely place?"

"One day's just like the next," responded the charcoal burner, "and every night, potatoes. Would you like to have some? You can be my guest."

"No thanks," answered the traveler. "I don't want to take away your meal. You weren't counting on a guest, but if you'll put up with me, I'd like to invite you to a meal."

"Who's going to prepare it for you?" said the charcoal burner. "You apparently don't have anything with you, and there's nobody within miles of here who could bring you something."

"Despite that, you shall have the most delicious meal you've ever tasted," he answered. Then the traveler took the tablecloth from his knapsack, spread it on the ground, and said, "Table, be covered!"

All at once there were boiled and roasted meats, and they were as hot as if they had just come out of the kitchen. The charcoal burner gaped, but he did not have to be asked twice to help himself to the food. Indeed, he shoveled bigger and bigger pieces of meat into his black mouth. When they had eaten their fill, the charcoal burner grinned and said, "Listen, your tablecloth has won my approval. Something like that would be perfect for me in this forest, where nobody ever cooks anything for me. Let me propose an exchange: there's an old soldier's knapsack hanging in the corner. It's clearly a plain old thing, but it has miraculous powers. Since I no longer need it, I'll let you have it in exchange for the tablecloth."

"First I must know what kind of miraculous powers they are," responded the traveler.

"Let me tell you," answered the charcoal burner. "If you tap it with your hand, a corporal will appear with six men armed from head to foot, and whatever you command, they will carry it out."

"As far as I'm concerned, it's a deal," said the traveler. "Let's exchange."

He gave the charcoal burner the tablecloth, took the knapsack off the hook, slung it over his shoulder, and said good-bye. When he had gone a short distance, he decided to test the knapsack's miraculous powers and tapped it. All at once seven stalwart soldiers appeared, and the corporal said, "What does my lord and master desire?"

"I want you to march back to the charcoal burner on the double and demand my magic tablecloth from him."

They did an about-face to the left, and before he knew it, they were back with the tablecloth, which they had taken from the charcoal burner without much trouble. Now the traveler ordered them to retire, and he continued his journey hoping that his luck would shine even brighter. At sundown he came across another charcoal burner who was preparing dinner by a fire.

"Would you care to join me?" asked the sooty fellow. "Potatoes with salt, but no grease. If you want some, just sit down by my side."

"No thanks," he said. "This time you shall be my guest." And he spread his tablecloth on the ground. A moment later it was covered with the most delicious dishes. They ate and drank together and were in good spirits. After the meal the charcoal burner said, "Up there on the shelf there's an old worn-out hat that has strange powers. As soon as someone puts it on and turns it around on his head, cannons will begin firing just as if twelve in a row went off at the same time. There's nothing that can withstand them, for they can demolish anything in sight. The hat is of no use to me, and I'd gladly exchange it for your tablecloth."

"It's a deal," the traveler answered. He took the hat, put it on, and left the tablecloth behind. Yet, no sooner had he gone a short distance than he tapped his knapsack, and his soldiers fetched the tablecloth for him once again. "One thing follows the next," he thought. "I feel as if my luck hasn't run out yet." And his intuition did not deceive him.

After he had traveled another day, he came across a third charcoal burner who invited him to eat a meal of potatoes without grease, just like the others. Once more the traveler invited the charcoal burner to join him in a meal set by his magic tablecloth, and the charcoal burner enjoyed the food so much that he offered him a horn in exchange for the tablecloth. This horn had very different powers from those of the hat. As soon as it was blown, first the walls and fortifications would be turned to rubble, and then cities and villages would be leveled. Of course, the traveler did not hesitate to give up the magic tablecloth for the horn, but later on he sent his team of soldiers to demand it back. At length he had accumulated all three things, the knapsack, the hat, and the horn.

"Now, I'm a made man," he said, "and it's time to return home and see how my brothers are doing."

By the time he returned home, his brothers had built a beautiful house with their silver and gold and were leading a carefree life. Yet, when he entered their house, his brothers refused to recognize him as their brother because he was wearing a tattered coat, a shabby hat on his head, and a battered knapsack on his back. Instead, they ridiculed him and said, "You're an impostor! Our brother scorned silver and gold to follow his lucky star. When he returns here, it won't be as a beggar but as a mighty king in full splendor and riding in a carriage."

Upon saying that, they drove him out of the house, but he became so enraged that he tapped his knapsack and kept tapping it until one hundred and fifty men stood before him in a row. He ordered them to surround his brothers' house, and two of them were to take hazel switches and whip his insolent brothers until they knew who he was. There was a tremendous uproar, and people ran to help the two brothers in their predicament, but they could do nothing against the soldiers. Eventually, the king got wind of this, and in his anger he ordered a captain to take a company of soldiers and to drive the troublemaker from the city. But the man with the knapsack responded by assembling a huge troop of soldiers who forced the captain and his men to retreat with bloody noses.

"I'll bring this vagabond under control yet!" the king said.

The following day the king sent an even larger company against him, but it managed to accomplish even less than the other one. The man with the knapsack called up even more soldiers to oppose the king's men, and since he wanted to end everything quickly, he turned his hat around on his head a few times. Then the heavy artillery came into play, and the king's men were devastated and forced to flee.

"I'm not going to make peace," he said, "until the king gives me his daughter for my wife and I rule the entire kingdom in his name."

The king was informed of this declaration, and he said to his daughter, "Necessity is a tough nut to crack. There's nothing I can do but give in to his demand. If I am to have peace and keep the crown on my head, I must give you away."

So the marriage was celebrated, but the king's daughter was disturbed because her husband was a commoner who wore a shabby hat and an old knapsack on his back. She wanted very much to get rid of him and was constantly thinking of ways to do it. Then the thought occurred to her, Could it be that his miraculous powers are in the knapsack? So she feigned affection for him and caressed him, and when his heart softened, she said, "If only you would take off that wretched knapsack! It's so unbecoming that it makes me ashamed of you."

"My dear girl," he answered, "this knapsack is my greatest treasure. As long as I have it, I don't have to fear anything in the world." And he revealed to her the miraculous powers with which the knapsack was endowed. Then she embraced him as if she wanted to kiss him, but she nimbly lifted the knapsack from his shoulders and ran away with it. As soon as she was alone, she tapped it and commanded the soldiers to seize their former master and escort him out of the royal palace. They obeyed her, and the devious woman ordered more men to follow him and chase him right out of the country. He would certainly have been lost had he not been wearing his hat, and no sooner were his hands free than he turned the hat a few times. Within seconds cannons began to thunder and demolish everything in sight. The king's daughter herself had to go and beg for mercy. Since she pleaded so passionately and promised to change her ways for the better, he let himself be persuaded and granted her peace.

After that she pretended to be friendly and behaved as if she loved him. It did not take long before she succeeded in deceiving him, so he confided to her that, even if someone got hold of his knapsack, that person could do nothing against him as long as he had the old hat. Once she knew that secret, she waited until he fell asleep. Then she took the hat away from him and had him thrown out on the street.

He still had the horn, however, and his rage was so great that he blew it with all his might. All at once everything collapsed—the walls, the fortifications, the cities, and the villages—and the king and his daughter were crushed to death. If he had not stopped blowing at that point, everything would have been devastated, and not a single stone would have remained standing on top of another.

After that nobody dared to oppose him, and he made himself king of the entire country.

◈ 55 ◈

Rumpelstiltskin

ONCE UPON A TIME there was a miller who was poor, but he had a beautiful daughter. Now it happened that he was talking with the king one time, and in order to make himself seem important, he said to the king, "I have a daughter who can spin straw into gold."

"That is an art that pleases me!" the king replied. "If your daughter is as talented as you say, then bring her to my castle tomorrow, and I'll put her to a test."

When the maiden was brought to him, he led her into a room that was filled with straw. There he gave her a spinning wheel and spindle and said, "Now get to work! If you don't spin this straw into gold by morning, then you must die." Then he locked the door himself, and she remained inside all alone.

The miller's poor daughter sat there feeling close to her wits' end, for she knew nothing about spinning straw into gold, and her fear grew greater and greater. When she began to weep, the door suddenly opened, and a little man entered.

"Good evening, mistress miller, why are you weeping so?"

"Oh," answered the maiden, "I'm supposed to spin straw into gold, and I don't know how."

The little man then asked, "What will you give me if I spin it for you?"

"My necklace," the maiden said.

The little man took the necklace and sat down at the wheel, and *whizz, whizz, whizz,* three times round, the spool was full. Then he inserted another one, and *whizz, whizz, whizz,* the second was full. And so it went until morning, when all the straw was spun, and all

the spools were filled with gold. The king appeared right at sunrise, and when he saw the gold, he was surprised and pleased, but his heart grew even greedier. He locked the miller's daughter in another room that was even larger than the first and ordered her to spin all the straw into gold if she valued her life. The maiden did not know what to do and began to weep. Once again the door opened, and the little man appeared and asked, "What will you give me if I spin the straw into gold for you?"

"The ring from my finger," answered the maiden.

The little man took the ring, began to work away at the wheel again, and by morning he had spun all the straw into shining gold. The king was extremely pleased by the sight, but his lust for gold was still not satisfied. So he had the miller's daughter brought into an even larger room filled with straw and said to her, "You must spin all this into gold tonight. If you succeed, you shall become my wife." To himself he thought, Even though she's just a miller's daughter, I'll never find a richer woman anywhere in the world.

When the maiden was alone, the little man came again for a third time and asked, "What will you give me if I spin the straw into gold once more?"

"I have nothing left to give," answered the maiden.

"Then promise me your first child when you become queen."

Who knows whether it will ever come to that? thought the miller's daughter. And since she knew of no other way out of her predicament, she promised the little man what he had demanded. In return the little man spun the straw into gold once again. When the king came in the morning and found everything as he had wished, he married her, and the beautiful miller's daughter became a queen.

After a year she gave birth to a beautiful child. The little man had disappeared from her mind, but now he suddenly appeared in her room and said, "Now give me what you promised."

The queen was horrified and offered the little man all the treasures of the kingdom if he would let her keep her child, but the little man replied, "No, something living is more important to me than all the treasures in the world."

Then the queen began to grieve and weep so much that the little man felt sorry for her. "I'll give you three days' time," he said. "If you can guess my name by the third day, you shall keep your child."

The queen spent the entire night trying to recall all the names she had ever heard. She also sent a messenger out into the country to inquire high and low what other names there were. On the following day, when the little man appeared, she began with Kaspar, Melchior, Balzer, and then repeated all the names she knew, one after the other. But to all of them, the little man said, "That's not my name."

The second day she had her servants ask around in the neighboring area what names people used, and she came up with the most unusual and strangest names when the little man appeared.

"Is your name Ribsofbeef or Muttonchops or Lacedleg?"

But he always replied, "That's not my name."

On the third day the messenger returned and reported, "I couldn't find a single new name, but as I was climbing a high mountain at the edge of the forest, where the fox and the hare say good night to each other, I saw a small cottage, and in front of the cottage was a fire, and around the fire danced a ridiculous little man who was hopping on one leg and screeching:

'Today I'll brew, tomorrow I'll bake.
Soon I'll have the queen's namesake.
Oh, how hard it is to play my game,
for Rumpelstiltskin is my name!' "

You can imagine how happy the queen was when she heard the name. And as soon as the little man entered and asked "What's my name, Your Highness?" she responded first by guessing.

"Is your name Kunz?"

"No."

"Is your name Heinz?"

"No."

"Can your name be Rumpelstiltskin?"

"The devil told you! The devil told you!" the little man screamed, and he stamped so ferociously with his right foot that his leg went deep into the ground up to his waist. Then he grabbed the other foot angrily with both hands and ripped himself in two.

◆ 56 ◆

Sweetheart Roland

ONCE UPON A TIME there was a woman who was a real witch, and she had two daughters, one ugly and evil, whom she loved because she was her own daughter, and the other beautiful and good, whom she hated because she was her stepdaughter. At one time the stepdaughter had a beautiful apron that the other daughter liked and coveted so much out of envy that she told her mother she wanted the apron and had to have it.

"Be quiet, my child," said the old woman. "You shall have it soon. Your stepsister has long since deserved to die, and tonight, when she's asleep, I'll come and chop off her head. Just make sure that you lie on the far side of the bed, and push her toward the front."

That would have been the end of the poor maiden had she not been standing in a corner and listening to everything. That day she was not allowed to go outside at all, and when bedtime came, the witch's daughter climbed into bed first so she could lie down on the far side. But after she fell asleep, the other sister pushed her gently toward the front and took her place on the far side, next to the wall. During the night the old woman crept into the room. She held an ax in her right hand and with her left hand felt around to see if someone was actually lying up front. Then she gripped the ax with both hands and began chopping until she chopped off her own child's head.

When she left the room, the maiden stood up and went to her sweetheart, whose name was Roland, and knocked at his door. When he came outside, she said to him, "Listen, dearest Roland, we must flee in haste. My stepmother tried to kill me, but she killed her own daughter instead. When the sun rises and she sees what she's done, we'll be lost."

"Before we go, you'd better take her magic wand first," said Roland. "Otherwise, we won't be able to escape if she comes after us."

The maiden fetched the magic wand, and she also took her dead sister's head and let three drops of blood drip on the floor, one in front of the bed, one in the kitchen, and one on the stairs. Then she hurried away with her sweetheart.

Now, when the witch got up the next morning, she called her daughter and wanted to give her the apron, but she did not come.

"Where are you?" she cried out.

"Here I am! On the stairs sweeping," answered one of the drops of blood.

The old woman went out but saw no one on the stairs and called out once again.

"Where are you?"

"Here I am! In the kitchen warming myself," the second drop of blood replied.

The old woman went into the kitchen, but she found no one there and called once again.

"Where are you?"

"Here I am! In bed sleeping," the third drop of blood cried.

The old woman went into the room and approached the bed. Yet, what did she see but her own daughter swimming in blood! And it was the witch herself who had chopped off her head.

The old woman became furious and rushed to the window. Since she could see quite far into the world, she spotted her stepdaughter fleeing with her sweetheart Roland.

"That won't help you!" she exclaimed. "Even though you've had a head start, you'll never escape me!" She put on her seven-league boots, in which she covered an hour's walk in one step, and it did not take her long before she had overtaken them. However, when the maiden saw the old woman coming, she used the magic wand to turn her sweetheart Roland into a lake and herself into a duck that swam in the middle of the lake. The witch stood on the shore, threw bread crumbs into the water, and tried her best to lure the duck to shore. But the duck would not let itself be enticed, and by nightfall the old woman had to turn back without having accomplished anything.

Meanwhile, the maiden and her sweetheart resumed their natural forms and continued walking the whole night through until daybreak. Then the maiden changed herself into a beautiful flower growing in the middle of a brier hedge, and her sweetheart was changed into a fiddler. Shortly after, the witch came striding along and said to the fiddler, "Dear fiddler, may I pluck the beautiful flower?"

"Of course," he answered, "and I'll play a tune while you're doing it."

Since she knew who the flower was, she quickly crawled into the hedge to pluck it. However, he began to play a tune, and willy-nilly she was compelled to dance because it was a magic melody. The faster he played, the more violent were the jumps she was forced to make, and the thorns tore the clothes from her body and scratched her so that blood flowed from her wounds. Since the fiddler did not let up, she had to keep dancing until she fell to the ground dead.

Once they were free, Roland said, "Now I'll go to my father and arrange for the wedding."

"In the meantime, I'll stay here and wait for you," said the maiden. "Just to make sure that nobody recognizes me, I'll turn myself into a red stone."

Roland departed, and the maiden lay in the field as a red stone and waited for her sweetheart. However, when Roland returned home, he was ensnared by another woman, who made him forget the maiden. Meanwhile, the poor maiden stayed in the field a long time, but when he failed to come back, she grew sad, turned herself into a flower, and thought, Someone will surely come along and trample me.

It so happened that a shepherd was tending his sheep on the field and saw the flower. Since it was so beautiful, he plucked the flower, took it with him, and tucked it away in a chest. From that time on, amazing things began to happen in the shepherd's cottage. When he got up in the morning, all the work would already be done: the room would be swept clean, the table and benches would be dusted, the fire in the hearth would be made, and water would be inside. At noon when he came home, the table would be set and a good meal would be served. He could not figure out how all this was happening, for he never saw a living soul, and his cottage was too small for anyone to hide in. Of course, he liked the good service, but eventually he became frightened and went to a wise woman to ask for her advice.

"There's magic behind all this," the wise woman said. "You must get up very early some morning and keep a lookout for anything that moves in the room. Then, if you see something, no matter what it is, quickly throw a white cloth over it. That will hold the magic in check."

The shepherd did as she told him, and on the following morning, right at daybreak, he saw the chest open and the flower come out. In the wink of an eye he ran over and threw the white cloth over the flower, and suddenly the transformation came to an end: a beautiful maiden stood before him, and she confessed that she had been the flower and had kept house for him. Then she told him about her adventures, and since he took a liking to her, he asked her to marry him. However, she answered no, because she wanted to remain true to her sweetheart Roland, even though he had forsaken her. Still, she promised the shepherd that she would remain there and continue to keep house for him.

Now the time had come for Roland to celebrate his wedding. According to the old custom of that country, a proclamation was issued, and all the girls were to gather together at the wedding and sing in honor of the bridal pair. When the faithful maiden heard about this, she grew so sad that she thought her heart would burst. She did not want to go to the wedding, but the other girls came and took her with them. Whenever her turn came to sing, she would step back, but finally she was the only one left and was obliged to sing a song. As she began to sing and her voice reached Roland's ears, he jumped up and exclaimed, "I know that voice! That's my true bride. I don't want anyone else."

Everything that he had forgotten and everything that had vanished from his mind suddenly filled his heart again. So the faithful maiden married her sweetheart Roland. Her sorrows came to an end just as her joy began to flourish.

◈ 57 ◈

The Golden Bird

IN DAYS OF OLD there was a king who had a beautiful pleasure garden behind his castle, and in this garden there was a tree that bore golden apples. After the apples became ripe, they were counted, but on the very next morning one was missing. This was reported to the king, and he ordered the tree to be guarded every night.

Now, the king had three sons, and at nightfall he sent the oldest to the garden. When midnight came, however, he could not prevent himself from sleeping, and the next morning another apple was missing. The following night the second son had to keep watch, but he did not fare any better. When the clock struck twelve, he fell asleep, and in the morning another apple was missing. Then it was the third son's turn to keep watch. He was also ready, but the king did not trust him and thought he would do even worse than his brothers. Finally, he gave him permission, and the young prince lay down under the tree, kept watch, and fought off sleep. When the clock struck twelve, there was a rustling above him, and in the moonlight he saw a bird flying through the air. The bird's feathers were made of pure gold and glistened as it descended onto the tree. When the bird pecked off an apple, the young prince shot an arrow at it. The bird flew off, but the arrow clipped one of the golden feathers, and it dropped to the ground. The young prince picked up the feather, brought it to the king the next morning, and told him what had happened during the night. The king assembled his councillors and everyone declared that a feather like this was worth more than the entire kingdom.

"If the feather is so precious," the king announced, "then one alone won't do for me. I must have, and intend to have, the whole bird."

So the oldest son set out; he believed he would certainly find the bird because he was so clever. After he had gone a short way, he saw a fox sitting at the edge of a forest, took aim with his gun, and was about to fire when the fox cried out, "Don't shoot! I'll give you some good advice if you hold your fire. You're on the right way to the golden bird, and tonight you'll come to a village where you'll see two inns facing each other. One will be brightly lit with a great deal of merrymaking inside. Be sure you keep away from that place. Instead, you should go into the other inn, even though it looks dismal."

How can such a foolish beast give sensible advice? thought the prince, and he pulled the trigger. However, his shot missed the fox, who stretched out his tail and dashed quickly into the forest. Then the prince continued his journey, and by evening he arrived at the village where the two inns were standing: in one of them there was singing and dancing, while the other appeared rather dismal and shabby.

I'd certainly be a fool, he thought, if I were to stay at that dismal-looking inn instead of staying at this fine one here. So he went into the cheerful inn, lived to the hilt like a king, and forgot the bird, his father, and all the good lessons he had ever learned.

After some time had passed, it became clear that the oldest son would not return. Therefore, the second son set out to look for the golden bird. Like the oldest son, he too met the fox, who gave him good advice that he did not heed. He came to the two inns and saw his brother at the window of the inn in which there were sounds of carousing. When his brother called out to him, he could not resist; he went inside and began living only to satisfy his lust.

Some more time passed, and now the youngest prince wanted to set out and try his luck. But his father would not let him.

"It's no use," the king said. "He'll have less of a chance of finding the golden bird than his brothers. And, if he has a mishap, he won't know how to fend for himself. He's not the smartest person in the world."

However, the prince kept insisting, and the king finally gave him permission to set out. Once again the fox was sitting at the edge of the forest, pleaded for his life, and gave good advice. Since the young prince was good-natured, he said, "Don't worry, little fox, I won't harm you."

"You won't regret it," answered the fox. "Now climb on my tail, and I'll help you get there more quickly."

No sooner did the prince sit down on the fox's tail than the fox began to run. And he went up hill and down dale so swiftly that the wind whistled through the prince's hair. When they came to the village, the prince got off the tail, followed the fox's good advice, and, without looking around, entered the shabbier inn. After spending a pleasant night there, he went out to the field the next morning and found the fox already sitting on the ground.

"I'm going to tell you what else you've got to do," said the fox. "If you go straight ahead, you'll eventually come to a castle. In front of this castle there's a whole troop of soldiers lying on the ground, but don't pay any attention to them, for they'll all be snoring and sleeping. Go right through the middle of their ranks and straight into the castle. Next, you're to go through all the rooms until you come to a chamber where the golden bird is hanging in a wooden cage. Nearby you'll also find a golden cage hanging just for decoration. But be careful not to take the bird out of its plain cage and put it into the splendid one. Otherwise, you'll be in for trouble."

Upon saying these words, the fox stretched out his tail again, and the prince sat down on it. The fox raced up hill and down dale so swiftly that the wind whistled through the prince's hair. When the prince arrived at the castle, he found everything just as the fox had said it would be. Upon entering the last room, he saw the golden bird sitting in its wooden cage and also a golden cage beside it. The three golden apples were lying about the room as well. The prince thought it would be ridiculous to leave the beautiful bird in the plain, ugly cage. So he opened the door, grabbed hold of the bird, and put it into the golden cage. At that very moment the bird uttered a piercing cry that caused the soldiers to wake up; they rushed inside and took him off to prison. The next morning he was brought before the court, and after he confessed to everything, he was sentenced to death. However, the king said he would spare his life under one condition: the prince had to promise to bring him the golden horse that ran faster than the wind; if he did, he would receive the golden bird as his reward.

The prince set out, but he sighed and grew sad, for he did not know where to find the golden horse. Suddenly, he saw his old friend the fox again, sitting by the roadside.

"You see," said the fox, "all this happened because you didn't listen to me. However, keep your spirits up. I'm here to assist you, and I'll tell you how to get the golden horse. First, you must go straight ahead until you come to a castle where the horse is standing in the stable. There will be grooms lying on the ground in front of the stable, but they'll be snoring and sleeping, and you'll be able to lead the golden horse out of its stall with ease. But make sure you put the plain wooden and leather saddle on the horse and not the golden one that's hanging nearby. Otherwise, you'll be in for trouble."

Then the fox stretched out its tail, and the prince sat down on it. The fox raced up hill and down dale so swiftly that the wind whistled through the prince's hair. Shortly after, everything happened as the fox said it would. The prince entered the stable where the golden horse was standing. However, when he was about to put the saddle on the horse, he thought, I'd be putting this beautiful horse to shame if I didn't give it the fine saddle that it deserves! Yet, no sooner did the golden saddle touch the horse than it began to neigh loudly, which caused the grooms to wake up; they seized the prince and threw him into prison. The next morning he was sentenced to death by the court. However, the king promised to spare his life and grant him the golden horse, as well, if the prince would fetch him the beautiful princess from the golden castle.

Now, the prince set out with a heavy heart, but fortunately for him he soon encountered the faithful fox.

"I really should leave you to your bad luck," said the fox, "but I feel sorry for you and want to help you out of your difficulty. This path leads directly to the golden castle. You'll arrive there in the evening, and at night, when everything's quiet, the beautiful princess will go to the bathhouse to bathe herself. When she goes there, you're to run up to her and give her a kiss. Then she'll follow you, and you can take her with you. But don't allow her to take leave of her parents. Otherwise, you'll be in for trouble."

The fox stretched out his tail, and the prince sat down on it. The fox raced up hill and down dale so swiftly that the wind whistled through the prince's hair. When he arrived at the golden castle, it was just as the fox had said it would be. The prince waited until midnight, when everyone lay in a deep sleep and the beautiful maiden went to the bathhouse. Then he ran up to her and gave her a kiss. She said she would gladly go with him, but she implored him with tears to let her say farewell to her parents. At first he resisted her pleas, but when she kept on weeping and fell at his feet, he finally gave in. But no sooner did the maiden approach her father's bed than he and everyone else in the castle woke up, and the prince was seized and put in prison. The next morning the king said to him, "Your life is worth nothing, and you'll be pardoned only if you take away the mountain that's lying in front of my window and blocking my view. If you successfully perform this task within eight days, you shall have my daughter as reward."

The prince began to dig and shovel without stopping, but when he saw how little he had accomplished after seven days, that all his work amounted to nothing, he gave up all hope and became very depressed. However, on the evening of the seventh day, the fox appeared and said, "You don't deserve my assistance, but just go and get some sleep. I'll do the job for you."

The next morning, when the prince awoke and looked out the window, the mountain had vanished. His heart filled with joy, and he rushed to the king and reported that he had completed his task. Whether the king liked it or not, he had to keep his word and give him his daughter.

The prince and the king's daughter now set out together, and it did not take long before the faithful fox joined them.

"Nothing could be better than what you have now," said the fox, "but the golden horse goes along with the princess from the golden castle."

"How am I to get it?" asked the prince.

"I'll tell you," answered the fox. "First you must bring the beautiful maiden to the king who sent you to the golden castle. There will be enormous rejoicing, and they'll gladly give you the golden horse. When they lead it out, mount it right away and shake hands with everyone and say good-bye. Make sure that the beautiful maiden is the last person, and when you have clasped her hand, swing her up to you in one motion and gallop away. Nobody can possibly catch you, for the horse runs faster than the wind."

Everything went as planned, and the prince carried off the beautiful maiden on the golden horse. The fox followed them, and then he said to the prince, "Now I'll help you get the golden bird. As you begin approaching the castle where the golden bird's being kept, let the maiden get down from the horse, and I'll look after her. Then ride the golden horse into the castle courtyard. There will be great rejoicing at the sight of the golden horse, and they'll carry out the golden bird. As soon as you have the cage in your hand, race away and fetch the princess."

After this plan had also been successfully carried out and the prince was about to ride home with his treasures, the fox said, "Now I want you to reward me for my help."

"What would you like?" asked the prince.

"When we come to the forest, I want you to shoot me dead and cut off my head and paws."

"What kind of gratitude is that?" said the prince. "I can't possibly do what you wish."

"If you won't do it, I'll have to leave you. But before I depart, I want to give you one last piece of advice. Beware of two things: don't buy flesh that's bound for the gallows, and don't sit on the edge of a well." Upon saying that, the fox ran into the forest.

What a strange animal! the prince thought. He's got all kinds of weird notions. Who would want to buy flesh bound for the gallows? And I've never had any desire to sit on the edge of a well.

He continued his journey with the beautiful maiden, and his way led again through the village where his two brothers had remained. Upon noticing that there was a great commotion and uproar, he asked what was going on and was told that two men were about to be hanged. When he came closer to the scene, he saw that the men were his brothers, who had committed all sorts of terrible acts and had squandered all their possessions. He asked whether they could be pardoned in some way.

"If you're willing to buy their freedom," the people answered. "But why would you want to waste your money on such evil criminals and set them free?"

However, he did not think twice about it and purchased their freedom. When they were released, he continued the journey in the company of his brothers. After some time they came to the forest where they had first met the fox, and since it was cool and lovely there and the sun was very hot, the two brothers said, "Let's go over to the well and rest awhile. We could also eat and drink."

He agreed, and during their conversation he forgot the fox's warning and sat down on the edge of the well, not suspecting anything evil. But the two brothers pushed him backward into the well, took the maiden, the horse, and the bird, and went home to their father.

"Not only have we brought you the golden bird," they said to the king, "but we've also got the golden horse and the maiden from the golden castle."

There was a great celebration, but the horse refused to eat, the bird did not sing, and the maiden sat and wept.

Meanwhile, the youngest brother managed to survive. Fortunately, the well had been dry, and he fell on soft moss without harming himself. For a while he could not get out, but his faithful fox stood by his side even then and helped him out of his dilemma. He jumped down the well and scolded the prince for not listening to his advice.

"But I won't abandon you," the fox said. "You'll soon see the light of day."

The fox told him to grab his tail and hold it tightly. Then he pulled him up to the top.

"You're still not completely out of danger," the fox said. "Your brothers were not positive that you had died. So they've ordered that the forest be surrounded by guards who are to shoot you on sight."

Along the way the prince came across a poor man, with whom he exchanged clothes. That was how the prince succeeded in reaching the king's court without being recognized. However, the bird began to sing, the horse began to eat, and the beautiful maiden stopped weeping. The king was astonished and asked, "What does all this mean?"

"I don't know," said the beautiful maiden, "but I was sad, and now I'm very cheerful. I feel as if my true bridegroom had come."

She told the king what had happened, even though the two older brothers had threatened to kill her if she revealed anything. The king ordered everyone in the castle to gather around him, and the young prince appeared also, as a poor man in rags. But the princess recognized him at once and embraced him. The godless brothers were seized and executed, while the youngest married the beautiful princess and was designated heir to the king.

But what happened to the poor fox? Well, many years later the prince went walking through the forest again and encountered the fox, who said, "Now you have everything you desired, but there's been no end to my misfortune, even though it's been within your power to free me."

Once again the fox implored him to shoot him dead and cut off his head and paws. This time the prince did it, and no sooner was it done than the fox turned into none other than the brother of the beautiful princess, who was finally released from a magic spell that had been cast over him. Now nothing more was missing from their happiness as long as they lived.

◈ 58 ◈

The Dog and the Sparrow

THERE ONCE WAS A SHEEPDOG whose master was cruel and let him starve. When he could no longer stand it, he departed sadly. Along the road he met a sparrow who said, "Brother dog, why are you so sad?"

"I'm hungry and have nothing to eat," the dog answered.

"Dear brother," responded the sparrow, "come with me to the city, and I'll see that you get plenty to eat."

So they went into the city together, and when they came to a butcher shop, the sparrow said to the dog, "Stay here. I'm going to peck off a piece of meat, and it will drop down for you."

The bird flew to a counter and looked around to make sure that nobody had noticed him. Then he pecked, pulled, and tugged until a piece of meat lying near the edge of the counter slipped down to the ground. The dog grabbed it at once, ran into a corner, and devoured it.

"Now come with me to another shop," said the sparrow. "I'll get you one more piece so you'll be full."

When the dog had eaten the second piece, the sparrow asked, "Brother dog, have you had enough?"

"Yes, I've had enough meat," he answered. "But I still haven't had any bread."

"You'll get that too," said the sparrow. "Just come along with me."

So he led him to a baker's shop and pecked at some rolls until they tumbled down, and when the dog desired even more, the sparrow led him to another shop and fetched more bread for him. After that had been consumed, the sparrow said, "Brother dog, have you had enough now?"

"Yes," he answered. "Let's take a little walk outside the city."

Then the two of them went strolling down the highway, but the weather was so warm that, after they had gone a little way, the dog said, "I'm tired and would very much like to sleep."

"All right, just go to sleep," answered the sparrow. "In the meantime I'll sit down on a branch."

The dog lay down on the road and fell soundly asleep. While he lay there and slept, a wagoner came along with his wagon loaded with two barrels of wine and drawn by three horses. The sparrow realized that the wagon was heading straight down the lane in which the dog was lying and that it was not going to swerve.

"Wagoner, don't do that, or I'll make you a poor man!" the sparrow cried out.

"You won't make me poor!" the wagoner bellowed as he whipped the horses and drove the wagon over the dog, killing him with the wheels.

"You've run over my brother dog and killed him! That will cost you your wagon and horses!" exclaimed the sparrow.

"Don't make me laugh! My horses and wagon!" said the wagoner. "You can't do anything to harm me."

He drove on, but the sparrow crawled under the canvas and pecked at one of the bungholes of a barrel until a bung came out. Then all the wine ran out without the wagoner noticing it. Only after he turned around at one point did he realize that the wagon was dripping. So he examined the barrels and found that one was empty.

"Oh, poor me!" the wagoner cried out.

"Not poor enough yet," said the sparrow, and he flew down onto the head of one of the horses and pecked its eyes out. When the wagoner saw that, he pulled out his ax and tried to hit the sparrow with it. But the bird flew into the air, and the wagoner instead struck his horse on the head and it fell down dead.

"Oh, poor me!" the wagoner cried out.

"Not poor enough yet," said the sparrow, and when the wagoner drove away with two horses, the sparrow crawled under the canvas again and pecked out the bung of the second barrel so that all the wine flowed out. When the wagoner became aware of that, he cried out once more, "Oh, poor me!"

But the sparrow answered, "Not poor enough yet." He flew down and landed on the head of the second horse and pecked its eyes out. The wagoner ran over and took out his ax, but the sparrow flew up into the air and thus caused the wagoner to strike his second horse dead.

"Oh, poor me!"

"Not poor enough yet," said the sparrow, who landed on the head of the third horse and pecked its eyes out. The wagoner swung his ax at the sparrow in rage without bothering to look around. However, he missed the bird and struck his third horse dead.

"Oh, poor me!" he cried out.

"Not poor enough yet," answered the sparrow. "Now I'm going to make you poor at your own home." And he flew off.

The wagoner had to leave the wagon standing there and walked home highly annoyed and furious. "Oh," he said to his wife, "you can't imagine the bad luck I've had! The wine ran out, and all three horses are dead."

"Oh, husband!" she answered. "A wicked bird has flown into our house! It's brought all the birds in the whole world together, and they've descended on our wheat in the loft and are eating it up."

The wagoner climbed up to the loft, and there he saw thousands of birds on the floor eating the wheat, and the sparrow was sitting in the middle.

"Oh, poor me!" the wagoner cried out.

"Not poor enough yet," answered the sparrow. "Wagoner, it's going to cost you your life!" And the sparrow flew off.

With all his property gone, the wagoner now went downstairs and sat by the stove, feeling angry and bitter. Then the sparrow landed outside his window and called out, "Wagoner, it's going to cost you your life."

The wagoner grabbed his ax and threw it at the sparrow. But it missed the bird and merely broke the windowpane in two. The sparrow hopped inside the house, sat down on the stove, and called out, "Wagoner, it's going to cost you your life!"

Now the wagoner was furious and blind with rage. He chopped the stove in two and continued to chop all the furniture—the mirror, the benches, the table—and finally the walls of the house, all in an effort to hit the sparrow, who flew from spot to spot. At last the wagoner caught the bird with his hand.

"Do you want me to kill it?" his wife asked.

"No!" he yelled. "That would be too merciful. I want it to die a more cruel death. I'm going to swallow it."

Then he took the bird and swallowed him whole. However, the sparrow began to flutter inside his body and fluttered back up again into the man's mouth. Once there he stuck out his head and cried, "Wagoner, it's going to cost you your life!"

The wagoner handed the ax to his wife and said, "Wife, kill the bird in my mouth!"

His wife swung the ax, but she missed and hit the wagoner right on the head, and he fell down dead. But the sparrow flew up and away.

◈ 59 ◈

Freddy and Katy

ONCE THERE WAS A MAN NAMED FREDDY and a woman named Katy
who got married and began living together in wedlock. One day
Freddy said, "I'm going to the field, Katy. When I return, I want
some roast meat on the table to take care of my hunger and a cool
drink for my thirst."

"Just run along, Freddy," Katy answered. "Just go. I'll have everything ready the way you want it."

When noontime drew near, she got a sausage from the chimney,
put it in a frying pan, added butter, and set it on the fire. The sausage
began to fry and sizzle, and while Katy was standing there and
holding the handle of the pan, she began thinking, and it occurred to
her, You could go down into the cellar and draw the beer before the
sausage is done. She fixed the pan so it would not tip, took a tankard,
and went down into the cellar, where she began to draw the beer. As
the beer was flowing into the tankard and Katy was gazing at it, she
suddenly recalled, Hey, the dog's upstairs, and since he's not tied up,
he could get the sausage from the pan. Oh, it's a lucky thing I thought
of that!

She ran up the cellar stairs in a jiffy, but her spitz had already
grabbed the sausage with his jaws and was dragging it along the
ground. Still, Katy was quick to act: she ran after him and chased him
a long way over the fields, but the dog was faster and clasped the
sausage tightly as he dashed off with it beyond her reach.

"What's gone is gone," said Katy, who turned back home. Since
she was tired from running, she walked very slowly and cooled
herself off. In the meantime, the beer continued to flow from the keg,
for Katy had forgotten to shut the tap. When the tankard became full
and there was no more room in it, the beer flowed over onto the cellar
floor until the whole keg was empty. As soon as Katy reached the top
of the stairs, she saw the accident and cried out, "Heavens! How are
you going to keep Freddy from noticing it?"

She thought for a while until she finally remembered a sack with
fine wheat flour that was still up in the loft. It had been bought at
the last fair, and she thought it would be a good idea to fetch it and
sprinkle it over the beer. "Yes," she said, "a stitch in time saves
nine." She climbed up to the loft, brought down the sack and threw it

right on the tankard full of beer, causing it to topple. Now even Freddy's drink swam about in the cellar. "That's quite all right," said Katy. "They all belong in the same boat together." Then she scattered the flour all over the cellar. When she was finished, she was tremendously pleased with her work and said, "How clean and neat everything looks here!"

At noon Freddy came home and said, "Well, wife, what have you made for me?"

"Oh, Freddy," she answered, "I wanted to fry a sausage for you, but while I was drawing the beer in the cellar, the dog came and made off with the pan. Then, while I was chasing the dog, the beer ran over, and as I went to dry up the beer with the wheat flour, I knocked over the tankard. But don't get upset, the cellar is all dry again."

"Katy, Katy!" he said. "You shouldn't have done that! Just think! You let the sausage be carried off, you let the beer run out of the keg, and on top of it, you squandered our fine flour!"

"Well, Freddy, I didn't know that. You should have told me."

If that's the way your wife is, Freddy thought, then you'd better take precautions. Now, Freddy had saved up a nice sum in talers that he finally changed into gold, and he went to Katy and said, "Look, these here are yellow chips, and I'm going to put them into a pot and bury them in the stable under the cow's manger. Make sure you keep away from them, or I'll teach you a lesson!"

"Don't worry, Freddy," she said. "I promise not to touch them."

Soon after, while Freddy was away, some peddlers came to the village selling clay pots and bowls, and they asked the young woman whether she wanted to trade with them.

"Oh, you're so kind," she said. "I don't have any money and can't buy anything. But if you can use yellow chips, I'll make a trade with you."

"Yellow chips? Why not? But we'd like to have a look first."

"Well, just go into the barn and dig under the cow's manger and you'll find the yellow chips. I'm not allowed to go there."

The scoundrels went there, dug up the ground, and found pure gold. Then they put it into their pack and ran off, leaving the pots and bowls behind in the house. Katy thought she should make use of her new kitchenware, but since there was already so much of it in the kitchen, she knocked the bottoms out of all the new pots and hung them as ornaments on the fence poles all around the house. When Freddy came and saw the new ornaments, he asked, "Katy, what have you done?"

"Well, Freddy, I bought them with the yellow chips that were buried under the cow's manger. I didn't go near them myself. I made the peddlers dig them up."

"Oh, wife!" said Freddy. "What have you done? They weren't yellow chips. They were pure gold, our entire fortune! You shouldn't have done that."

"Well, Freddy," she said. "I didn't know that. You should have told me before."

Katy stood there awhile and tried to think of something. Finally, she said, "Listen, Freddy, we can get the gold back. Let's run after the thieves."

"All right," said Freddy. "Let's try it, but take some butter and cheese so that we have something to eat along the way."

"Yes, Freddy, I'll take some along."

They set out on foot, and since Freddy was faster, Katy trailed after him. It's to my advantage, she thought. If we turn back, then I'll have a head start. Now she came to a hill where there were deep wagon ruts on both sides of the road. "Just look!" said Katy. "They've trampled and torn apart the poor earth, so that it's all beaten up! It will never get well again as long as it lives." Out of the kindness of her heart, she took out the butter and smeared the ruts on the right and left so they would not be hurt so much by the wheels. While she was performing this charitable work and was bending over, a cheese rolled out of her pocket and down the hill.

"I've already climbed up the hill once," said Katy, "and I'm not going down again. Let some other cheese run down and fetch it back."

So she took another cheese and rolled it down the hill. However, this cheese did not come back either, so she sent a third one after it and thought, Perhaps they don't like to walk alone and are waiting for company. When all three of them failed to return, she said, "I'm not sure what all this means, but it's possible that the third one didn't find the way and has gone astray. I'll just send a fourth to call them all back."

The fourth did not do the job any better than the third. Then Katy became so annoyed that she threw the fifth and sixth down the hill too, and they were the last she had. For a while she stood and waited for them to come back, but when they did not return, she said, "Oh, you're just the right ones to send in search of death because you really drag your feet. Do you think I'm going to wait for you any longer? I'm moving on, and you can catch up with me. You've got younger legs than mine."

Katy went on and found Freddy, who had stopped to wait for her because he wanted something to eat.

"Now let's have some of the food you brought along."

She handed him the dry bread.

"Where's the butter and cheese?" her husband asked.

"Oh, Freddy," said Katy, "I smeared the ruts with the butter, and the cheese will soon be here. One got away from me, and so I sent the others after it."

"You shouldn't have done that, Katy," said Freddy. "Just think! You smeared the butter on the road, and you let the cheese roll down the hill!"

"Well, Freddy, you should have told me."

They ate the dry bread together, and Freddy said, "Katy, did you lock up the house before you left?"

"No, Freddy, you should have told me before."

"Well, then go home and lock it up before we continue on our way. Also, bring something else to eat with you. I'll wait for you here."

As Katy began walking back, she began thinking, Freddy obviously wants something else to eat. Since he doesn't like butter and cheese, I'll bring him some dried pears in a handkerchief and a jug full of vinegar to drink.

When she was about to leave the house again, she bolted the upper half of the door and took the lower half off the hinges. Then she carried it on her back because she thought the house would be safer if she kept the door with her. Then she took her time walking back since she thought to herself, Freddy will have all the more time to rest himself.

Once she reached her husband again, Katy said, "There, Freddy, now you have the house door, and you'll be able to keep the house safe yourself."

"Oh, God!" he said. "What a clever wife I've got! She takes off the lower half of the door so that anyone can walk in, and she bolts the upper half. Now it's too late to go home again, but since you brought the door here, you'll carry it the rest of the way yourself."

"I don't mind carrying the door, Freddy, but the dried pears and the jug of vinegar are too heavy for me. I'll hang them on the door and let the door carry them."

Now they went into the forest to look for the thieves, but they did not find them. When it finally became dark, they climbed up into a tree to spend the night. No sooner were they sitting up high than some men came along who tend to carry off things that do not want to be carried away and who tend to find things before they are lost. They camped out right beneath the tree in which Freddy and Katy were sitting. They made a fire and began to divide their loot. Freddy climbed down the other side of the tree and gathered some stones, after which he climbed back. He wanted to throw the stones at the thieves to kill them. However, he missed, and the thieves cried out, "Soon it will be morning, and the wind's knocking down the pinecones."

Katy was still carrying the door on her back, and since it was so heavy and weighing her down, she thought the dried pears were to blame and said, "Freddy, I've got to throw the dried pears down."

"No, Katy, not now," he answered. "They could give us away."

"Oh, Freddy, I've got to! They're too heavy for me."

"Well then, do it, for all I care!"

She rolled the pears down between the branches, and the thieves said, "Here come some bird droppings."

Shortly afterward, since the door was still very heavy on her back, Katy said, "Oh, Freddy, I've got to pour out the vinegar."

"No, Katy, you mustn't do that. It could give us away."

"Oh, Freddy, I've got to! It's too heavy for me."

"Well then, do it, for all I care!"

So she poured out the vinegar, and it splattered all over the thieves.

"The dew's already falling," the men said to one another.

Finally, Katy thought, Could it be the door that's been weighing me down? And she said, "Freddy, I've got to throw the door down."

"No, Katy, that could give us away."

"Oh, Freddy, I've got to. It's too heavy for me."

"No, Katy, hold on to it tight."

"Oh, Freddy, I'm going to let it drop."

"All right!" Freddy answered irritably. "Let it drop for all I care!"

Then the door fell down with a great crash, and the thieves below cried out, "The devil's coming down the tree!"

They cleared out and left everything behind. Early the next morning, when Freddy and Katy came down the tree, they found all their gold again and carried it home.

When they were home once more, Freddy said, "Katy, you've got to be industrious and work hard now."

"Yes, Freddy, of course I will. I'll go into the field and cut down the fruit."

When Katy went into the field, she said to herself, "Should I eat before I cut, or should I sleep before I cut. I think I'll eat!" So Katy ate and became tired from eating. When she started to cut some fruit, she began daydreaming and cut all her clothes to pieces—her apron, her dress, and her blouse. Upon snapping out of her dream, she stood there half naked and said to herself, "Is that me, or is it someone else? Oh, that's not me!"

Meanwhile, it was already night, and Katy ran into the village and knocked on her husband's window.

"Freddy!" she called out.

"What is it?"

"I'd like to know if Katy's inside."

"Yes, yes," answered Freddy. "She's probably lying down asleep."

"Good," she said. "Then I'm clearly at home already," and she ran off.

Outside the village Katy came across some thieves who were planning a theft. She went up to them and said, "I want to help you steal."

The thieves thought she knew her way around the region and agreed to let her join them. Then Katy went in front of the houses and called out, "Folks, do you have anything you want stolen?"

This won't do! thought the thieves, and they wished they could get rid of Katy.

"There's a turnip patch owned by the parson outside the village," they said to her. "We want you to go there and pull up some of the turnips for us."

Katy went to the patch and began to pull up some turnips, but she was so lazy that she remained in a crouched position. Soon a man came by, stopped, watched her, and thought the devil was tearing up all the turnips in the patch. So he ran to the parson in the village and said, "Parson, the devil's in your turnip patch, and he's tearing up all your turnips."

"Oh, God!" exclaimed the parson. "I've got a lame foot and can't run out to banish him."

"I'll carry you on my back," said the man, and he carried him out to the field. When they got to the turnip patch, Katy straightened herself up.

"Oh, it's really the devil!" the parson cried, and they both rushed off. Indeed, since his fright was so great, the parson was able to run faster with his lame foot than the man who had carried him with his two sound legs.

◆ 60 ◆

The Two Brothers

ONCE UPON A TIME there were two brothers, one rich and the other poor. The rich brother was a goldsmith and evil-hearted. The poor brother earned a living by making brooms and was kind and honest. He had two sons who were twins, and they looked so much alike that they seemed like two peas in a pod. Every now and then the twins went to their rich uncle's house and were given the leftovers to eat.

One day the poor man happened to be in the forest gathering brushwood when he saw a bird pure as gold and more beautiful than any bird he had ever seen. So he picked up a little stone, threw it at the bird, and was lucky enough to hit it. However, only a single golden feather dropped to the ground, and the bird flew off. The man took the feather and brought it to his brother, who examined it and said, "It's pure gold," and he gave him a lot of money for it.

The next day the poor man climbed a birch tree to cut a few branches. Just then the same bird flew out, and after the man searched awhile, he found a nest with an egg in it. The egg was made of gold, and he took it home with him. Afterward he showed it to his brother, who once again said, "It's pure gold," and he gave him what it was worth. Finally, the goldsmith said, "I'd like to have the bird itself."

The poor man went into the forest for a third time and saw the golden bird perched on a tree. He took a stone, knocked the bird down, and brought it to his brother, who gave him a huge amount of gold for it.

Now I'll be able to take care of things, the poor man thought, and went home with a happy feeling.

The goldsmith was clever and cunning and knew exactly what kind of bird it was. He called his wife and said, "Roast this golden bird for me, and make sure that none of it gets lost! I want to eat it all by myself."

Indeed, the bird was not an ordinary creature. It possessed a miraculous power, and whoever ate its heart and liver would find a gold piece under his pillow every morning. The goldsmith's wife prepared the bird, put it on a spit, and let it roast. Now it happened that, while the bird was roasting over the fire, the wife had to leave the kitchen to take care of something else. Just then the two sons of the poor broom-maker ran in, stopped in front of the spit, and turned it a few times. When two little pieces dropped from the bird into the pan, one of the boys said, "Let's eat the two little pieces. I'm so hungry, and nobody's bound to notice it."

So they ate the two pieces, but the wife returned and saw that they had eaten something.

"What did you eat?" she asked.

"A couple of pieces that fell out of the bird," they answered.

"That must have been the heart and liver," the wife said, and she was horrified. She quickly slaughtered a cock, took out its heart and liver, and put them in the golden bird so her husband would not miss them and get angry. When the golden bird was done, she carried it to the goldsmith, who consumed it all by himself and left nothing over. However, when he reached under his pillow the next morning expecting to find a gold piece, there was nothing there out of the ordinary.

In the meantime, the two boys did not realize how fortunate they had been. When they got up the next morning, something fell on the floor making a tingling sound. Upon looking to see what made the sound, they found two gold pieces, which they brought to their father. He was amazed and said, "How can that have happened?"

When they found another two the following morning and continued to find two every morning thereafter, the father went to his
brother and told him the strange story. The goldsmith knew immediately how everything had happened and that the children had eaten the
heart and liver of the golden bird. Since he was envious and hard-
hearted, he sought revenge and said to the father, "Your children are
in league with the devil. Don't take the gold, and don't let them stay
in your house any longer. The devil's got them in his power and can
also bring about your own ruin."

The father was afraid of the devil, and even though it was painful
for him, he led the twins out into the forest and with a sad heart left
them there. The two boys wandered around the forest and searched
for the way back home, but they repeatedly lost their way and could
not find it. Finally, they encountered a huntsman, who asked, "Where
do you come from?"

"We're the poor broom-maker's sons," they answered and then
told him that their father no longer wanted them in his house because
every morning there was a gold piece under each one of their pillows.

"Well," said the huntsman, "that's really nothing terrible as long as
you remain good and upright and don't become lazy."

The kind man took a liking to the boys, and since he did not have
any sons himself, he took them home with him and said, "I shall be
your father and bring you up."

So they learned all about hunting from him, and he saved the gold
pieces that they found every morning when they got up, in case they
might need them in the future. One day, when they were finally
grown-up, their foster father took them into the forest and said,
"Today you're to be tested in shooting to determine whether I can
release you from your apprenticeship and pronounce you full-fledged
huntsmen."

They went with him to the raised blind and waited for a long time,
but no game appeared. Then the huntsman looked above him, and
when he saw some wild geese flying by in a triangle formation, he
said to one of the brothers, "Now shoot one from each corner."

He did it and passed the test. Soon after, more geese came flying by
in the number two formation. The huntsman told the other brother
likewise to shoot one goose from each corner, and he also passed the
test. Now the foster father said, "You have completed your apprenticeship, and I pronounce you both full-fledged huntsmen."

At that point the two brothers went into the forest together, took
counsel with each other, and decided on a plan of action. When they
sat down in the evening to eat, they said to their foster father, "We're
not going to touch the food or take a single bite until you grant us one
request."

"What is your request?" he asked.

"Since we're now full-fledged huntsmen," they replied, "we must also prove ourselves. So we want your permission to leave and travel about the world."

"You speak like real huntsmen," said the old man joyfully. "Your desire is my very own wish. Set out on your journey; everything will go well for you."

In a merry mood, they then ate and drank together. When the appointed day for their departure arrived, their foster father gave each of them a good gun and a dog and had each of them take as many of the saved-up gold pieces as he desired. Then the old man accompanied them part of the way, and when they were about to take their leave, he gave them a shiny knife and said, "If ever you should separate, stick this knife into a tree at the crossroad. Then if one of you comes back, he can see how his absent brother is doing, for the side of the blade facing the direction he took will rust if he's dying but will stay bright as long as he's alive."

The two brothers continued on their way and came to a huge forest that was impossible to cross in one day. So they spent the night there and ate what they had in their hunting pouches. On the second day they went onward but still did not reach the end. Now they had nothing more to eat, and one of them said, "We must shoot something, or we'll starve."

He loaded his gun and looked around. When he saw an old hare running by, he took aim, but the hare cried out:

"Dear huntsman, if you let me live,
two of my young to you I'll give."

Then the hare jumped into the bushes and brought back two young ones. The little creatures were so frisky and charming that the huntsmen did not have the heart to kill them. So they kept them, and the little hares followed at their heels. Soon after, a fox came slinking by, and they were about to shoot it when the fox cried out:

"Dear huntsman, if you let me live,
two of my young to you I'll give."

He also brought two young ones, and the huntsmen had no desire to kill the little foxes. They gave them to the hares for company, and the animals continued to follow the huntsmen. Soon a wolf came out of the thicket, and just as the huntsmen took aim at him, he cried out:

"Dear huntsman, if you let me live,
two of my young to you I'll give."

The huntsmen added the two young wolves to the other animals, and they all followed the two young men. Then a bear came, and he had no desire to have his days of wandering ended, so he cried out:

"Dear huntsman, if you let me live,
two of my young to you I'll give."

Two young bears joined the other animals, and now there were eight of them. Finally, who should come along shaking his mane but the lion! And he also cried out:

"Dear huntsman, if you let me live,
two of my young to you I'll give."

He too fetched two of his young ones, and now the huntsmen had two lions, two bears, two wolves, two foxes, and two hares who followed and served them. Meanwhile, however, the brothers were still starving, and they said to the foxes, "Listen, you tricky creatures, get us something to eat. After all, we know you're crafty and cunning."

"There's a village not far from here," they answered. "In the past we were able to get many a chicken there. We'll show you the way."

The brothers went to the village, bought themselves something to eat, and had their animals fed. Then they continued on their way. But the foxes were very familiar with the region and knew exactly where the chicken yards were, so they could guide the huntsmen to the right spots. For a while they traveled about, but they could not find employment that would allow them all to remain together. Eventually, the brothers said, "There's no other way. We'll have to separate."

They divided the animals so that each had a lion, a bear, a wolf, a fox, and a hare. Then they said farewell, took a vow of brotherly love unto death, and stuck the knife that their foster father had given them into a tree. Then one went to the east, the other to the west.

Soon the younger brother arrived with his animals in a city that was completely draped in black crepe. He went into an inn and asked the innkeeper whether he could put up his animals there. The innkeeper gave him a stable that had a hole in the wall. The hare crawled through it and fetched himself a head of cabbage; the fox fetched a hen, and after he had eaten the hen, he went and got a cock as well. However, the wolf, the bear, and the lion were too big to slip through the hole. So the innkeeper took them to a meadow where a cow was grazing, and there they could eat their fill. After the huntsman had taken care of his animals, he asked the innkeeper why the city was draped in black crepe.

"Because our king's only daughter shall perish tomorrow," said the innkeeper.

"Is she that sick?" asked the huntsman.

"No," the innkeeper replied. "She's hale and hearty, but she must die nonetheless."

"But why?" asked the huntsman.

"Outside the city there's a dragon living on a high mountain," said the innkeeper. "Every year he demands that he be given a pure virgin or he'll lay waste to the entire country. Now all the maidens have been given to him, and there's no one left but the king's daughter. Despite that, the dragon shows no mercy. She must be delivered to him, and that's to be done tomorrow."

"Why doesn't someone slay the dragon?" asked the huntsman.

"Ah," responded the innkeeper. "Many, many knights have tried, but they've all forfeited their lives. The king's promised to give his daughter's hand in marriage to the man who slays the dragon, and this man would also inherit the kingdom after the king's death."

The huntsman said nothing more, but the next morning he took his animals and climbed the dragon's mountain with them. At the top was a small church, and there were three full goblets on the altar with a piece of paper next to them that said, "Whoever drinks these goblets shall become the strongest man on earth and shall be able to wield the sword that lies buried at the threshold of the door." The huntsman did not drink the goblets but went outside and searched for the sword in the ground, which he was not able to move. Then he went back inside, drank the goblets, and was now strong enough to pull out the sword and wield it with ease. When the hour came for the maiden to be delivered to the dragon, the king, the marshal, and the entire court accompanied her. From afar she could see the huntsman standing on top of the dragon's mountain. She thought it was the dragon standing there and waiting for her, and she did not want to go. But finally she had to begin the painful journey; the whole kingdom would have been lost otherwise. The king and his court returned home in full mourning, but the king's marshal was assigned to stay there and watch everything from a distance.

When the king's daughter reached the top of the mountain, it was not the dragon standing there but the young huntsman, who comforted her and told her he wanted to save her. He led her into the church and locked her inside. Shortly after, with a great roar the seven-headed dragon descended on the spot. When he caught sight of the huntsman, he was astounded, and he said, "What do you think you're doing on this mountain?"

"I've come to fight you," replied the huntsman.

"Many a knight has lost his life here," declared the dragon. "I'll soon finish you off as well!" Then flames shot from his seven jaws.

The flames were intended to set fire to the dry grass, and the dragon hoped to smother the huntsman with the fire and smoke, but the huntsman's animals came running to his aid and stamped the fire out. The dragon then attacked the huntsman, but the man swung his sword so swiftly that it sang in the air and cut off three of the dragon's heads. Now the dragon was really furious: he rose up, began shooting flames directly at the huntsman, and got set to dive down at him. However, the huntsman once again lashed out with his sword and cut off three more heads. The monster sank to the ground and was exhausted. Nevertheless, he tried to charge the huntsman again, but the young man used his last bit of strength to cut off the dragon's tail. Then, since the huntsman could not continue fighting, he called his animals, who tore the dragon to pieces. When the battle was over, the huntsman opened the church and found the princess lying on the ground. She had fainted from fear and fright during the combat. So he carried her outside, where she regained consciousness and opened her eyes. When he showed her the dragon's devastated body and told her she was now free, the princess was overjoyed and said, "Now you shall be my very dear husband, for my father promised my hand in marriage to the man who could slay the dragon."

The princess then took off her coral necklace and divided it among the animals as little collars to reward them, and the lion received the golden clasp to the necklace. However, her handkerchief with her name embroidered on it went to the huntsman, who proceeded to cut out the tongues of the seven dragon's heads, wrap them in the handkerchief, and put them away carefully.

When that was done, he felt so tired and exhausted from the fire and battle that he said to the maiden, "We're both so tired and exhausted, perhaps it would be best if we slept awhile."

The princess agreed, and they lay down on the ground. Then the huntsman said to the lion, "I want you to keep watch so that no one surprises us in our sleep."

When the huntsman and the princess fell asleep, the lion lay down beside them to keep watch, but he too was tired from the battle. So he called the bear and said, "Lie down beside me. I've got to sleep a little. If anything happens, wake me up."

The bear lay down next to the lion, but he too was tired. So he called the wolf and said, "Lie down beside me. I've got to sleep a little. If anything happens, wake me up."

The wolf lay down next to the bear, but he too was tired. So he called the fox and said, "Lie down beside me. I've got to sleep a little. If anything happens, wake me up."

The fox lay down beside the wolf, but he too was tired. So he called the hare and said, "Lie down beside me. I've got to sleep a little. If anything happens, wake me up."

The hare lay down next to the wolf, but he too was tired. However, there was no one left whom he could call on to help him, and soon he fell asleep. Once that happened, they were all asleep and sleeping soundly, the princess, the huntsman, the lion, the bear, the wolf, the fox, and the hare.

Meanwhile, the marshal, who had been assigned the task of watching everything from a distance, did not see the dragon fly off. So, when everything was calm on the mountain, he summoned his courage and climbed the mountain, where he found the dragon lying on the ground and torn to pieces. Not far from there were the king's daughter and the huntsman with his animals. They were all sound asleep, and since the marshal was a wicked and godless man, he took his sword and cut off the huntsman's head. Next he lifted the maiden in his arms and carried her down the mountain. When she awoke, she was petrified, but the marshal said, "I've got you in my power, so you'd better say that it was I who slew the dragon."

"I can't do that," she replied. "It was a huntsman with his animals. They were the ones who did it."

Then the marshal drew out his sword and threatened to kill her if she did not obey him. Thus he forced her to promise that she would do as he commanded. Afterward he brought her to the king, who was overcome by joy upon seeing his dear daughter alive again when he had thought she had already been torn to pieces by the dragon.

"I've slain the dragon and saved the maiden and the whole kingdom," said the marshal. "Therefore I claim your daughter for my wife as you promised."

"Is what he says true?" the king asked the maiden.

"Oh, yes," she answered. "It must probably be true, but I insist that the wedding be held in a year and a day and not before." Indeed, she hoped to hear from her dear huntsman by then.

Meanwhile, the animals were still lying asleep beside their dead master on the dragon's mountain. Then a bumble bee came and landed on the hare's nose, but the hare brushed it aside with his paw. The bumble bee came a second time, but the hare brushed it aside again and continued to sleep. Finally, it came a third time and stung him on the nose, so that he woke up. As soon as the hare was awake, he woke the fox, and the fox woke the wolf, who woke the bear, and the bear woke the lion. And when the lion saw that the maiden was gone and his master was dead, he began roaring dreadfully loud and cried out, "Who did that? Bear, why didn't you wake me?"

The bear asked the wolf, "Why didn't you wake me?"

And the wolf asked the fox, "Why didn't you wake me?"

The fox asked the hare, "Why didn't you wake me?"

The poor hare was the only one who did not know what to answer, and the guilt fell on his shoulders. They wanted to pounce on him, but he pleaded with them and said, "Don't kill me! I'll bring our master back to life. I know a mountain where a root grows that cures and heals all kinds of sicknesses and wounds. You only have to stick the root in the sick person's mouth. But it takes two hundred hours to get to the mountain."

"Well, you've got to dash there and back and fetch the root within twenty-four hours," declared the lion.

The hare raced away, and within twenty-four hours he was back with the root. The lion put the huntsman's head back in position, and the hare stuck the root in his mouth. All at once, everything functioned together again: his heart beat, and life returned to him. When the huntsman awoke, he was distressed not to find the maiden by his side. She must have gone away while I was asleep to get rid of me, he thought.

In his great haste the lion had put his master's head on backward. However, the huntsman was so preoccupied by his sad thoughts about the king's daughter that he did not notice it. Only at noon, when he wanted to eat something, did he realize that his head was on backward. He was at a loss to understand how that had happened, and he asked the animals. The lion told him that they had all been so tired that they had fallen asleep and that upon awakening they had found him dead with his head cut off. The hare had then fetched the root of life, but the lion in his haste had held his head the wrong way. After saying all that, the lion wanted to correct his mistake. So he tore off the head of the huntsman, turned it around, and the hare healed him again with the root.

The huntsman nevertheless remained in a gloomy mood. He traveled about the world and made his animals dance before crowds of people. After a year had passed, he happened to return to the same city where he had rescued the king's daughter from the dragon, and this time the city was draped completely in crimson.

"What does all that mean?" he asked the innkeeper. "A year ago the city was draped in black. What's the meaning of the crimson?"

"A year ago the princess was supposed to have been delivered to the dragon," answered the innkeeper. "But the marshal fought and slew the dragon. Tomorrow his wedding with the princess will be celebrated. That's why the city, in its mourning, was draped in black then, and that's why the city, in its joy, is draped in crimson today."

At noon on the next day, when the wedding was to take place, the huntsman said to the innkeeper, "Do you think, innkeeper, that it might be possible for me to eat bread from the king's table right here at your place?"

"Well," said the innkeeper, "I'd be willing to bet a hundred gold pieces that you can't possibly do that."

The huntsman accepted the wager and put up a pouch with one hundred gold pieces to match the innkeeper's money. Then he called the hare and said, "Go there, my speedster, and fetch me some of the bread fit for a king."

Now, the little hare was the weakest of the animals, and it was impossible for him to pass his task on to any of the others: he had to perform it by himself. My God, he thought, if I amble down the street by myself, the butchers' dogs will soon be after me! And it happened just as he thought it would. The dogs chased after him and wanted to tear his good fur to shreds. However, you should have seen the hare run! He sped to the castle and took refuge in the sentry box without the guard noticing him. When the dogs came and tried to get him out, the soldier would take no nonsense from them and hit them with the butt of his rifle, so they ran away yelping and howling. When the hare saw the coast was clear, he ran into the palace and straight to the king's daughter. Then he sat down under her chair and scratched her foot.

"Get out of here!" she said, for she thought it was her dog. The hare scratched her foot a second time, and she repeated "Get out of here!" for she thought it was her dog. But the hare did not let himself be deterred and scratched a third time. Then she looked down and recognized the hare by his coral collar. So she picked him up, carried him into her chamber, and said, "My dear hare, what do you want?"

"My master, the dragon-slayer, is here," he answered, "and he's sent me to fetch some bread fit for a king."

The princess was filled with joy. She summoned the baker and ordered him to bring her a loaf of bread fit for a king.

"But the baker must also carry it for me," said the hare. "Otherwise, the butchers' dogs will hurt me."

The baker carried the bread up to the door of the inn for the hare. Then the hare stood up on his hind legs, took the loaf of bread in his front paws, and brought it to his master.

"You see, innkeeper," the huntsman said, "the hundred gold pieces are mine."

The innkeeper was astonished, but the huntsman continued to speak. "Well, innkeeper, I've got the bread, but now I want some of the king's roast as well."

"I'd like to see that," said the innkeeper, but he did not want to bet anymore.

The huntsman called the fox and said, "Little fox, go there and fetch me a roast fit for a king."

The red fox knew the shortcuts better than the hare, and he went through holes and around corners without the dogs catching sight of him. Once at the castle he sat under the chair of the princess and scratched her foot. When she looked down, she recognized the fox by his coral collar, carried him into her chamber, and said, "My dear fox, what do you want?"

"My master, the dragon-slayer, is here," he answered, "and he's sent me to ask for a roast fit for a king."

She summoned the cook and ordered him to prepare a roast fit for a king and to carry it for the fox up to the door of the inn. There the fox took the dish from him, wagged his tail to brush off the flies that had settled on the roast, and brought it to his master.

"You see, innkeeper," said the huntsman, "bread and meat are here, but now I want to have some vegetables fit for a king." So he called the wolf and said, "Dear wolf, go straight to the castle and fetch me some vegetables fit for a king."

So the wolf went straight to the castle, for he was afraid of no one, and when he reached the princess, he tugged at her dress from behind so that she had to turn around. She recognized him by his coral collar, took him into her chamber, and said, "My dear wolf, what do you want?"

"My master, the dragon-slayer, is here," he answered, "and he's sent me to ask for some vegetables fit for a king."

She summoned the cook, who had to prepare some vegetables fit for a king, and she ordered him to carry them for the wolf to the door of the inn. There the wolf took the dish and brought it to his master.

"You see, innkeeper, now I've got bread, meat, and vegetables, but I also want some sweets fit for a king." So he called the bear and said, "Dear bear, since you're fond of licking sweet things, go and fetch me sweets fit for a king."

So the bear trotted off to the castle, and everyone cleared out of his way. When he reached the sentry box, the guards barred his way with their guns and did not want to let him enter the royal castle. But he stood up on his hind legs and slapped the guards left and right, forcing them to fall apart. Then he went straight to the king's daughter, stood behind her, and growled softly. She looked behind her, recognized the bear, and told him to go with her into her chamber.

"My dear bear," she said, "what do you want?"

"My master, the dragon-slayer, is here," he answered, "and I'm to ask for some sweets fit for a king."

She summoned the confectioner and ordered him to make sweets fit for a king and to carry them up to the door for the bear. There the bear licked the sugarplums that had rolled off, stood on his hind legs, and brought them to his master.

"You see, innkeeper," said the huntsman, "now I've got bread, meat, vegetables, and sweets, but I also want to drink wine fit for a king." So he called his lion and said, "Dear lion, since you like to indulge yourself and get tipsy, go and fetch me some wine fit for a king."

When the lion strode down the street, the people fled from him, and when he came to the guards, they wanted to bar his way, but he only had to let out a roar, and they all dashed away. The lion then went to the royal chamber and knocked on the door with his tail. The king's daughter came out and would have been petrified had she not recognized him by the golden clasp of her necklace. She invited him inside and said, "My dear lion, what do you want?"

"My master, the dragon-slayer, is here, and I'm to ask for some wine fit for a king."

She summoned the cupbearer and ordered him to give the lion some wine fit for a king.

"I want to go with him to make sure that I get the right kind," said the lion.

He went downstairs with the cupbearer, and when they were below, the cupbearer was about to draw some ordinary wine that the king's servants usually drank when the lion said, "Stop! I want to taste the wine first." He drew half a measure for himself and drank it down. "No," he said, "that's not the right kind."

The cupbearer glared at him and was cross. Then he went on and was about to offer him wine from another barrel reserved for the king's marshal.

"Stop!" said the lion. "I want to taste the wine first." He drew half a measure for himself and drank it down. "It's better than the first, but it's still not the right kind."

Now the cupbearer got angry and said, "How can a stupid beast understand anything about wine?"

But the lion gave him such a blow behind the ears that he fell hard on the ground. When he got up, he did not utter a word but led the lion into a special small cellar where the king's wine was kept solely for his private use. The lion drew half a measure for himself, tasted the wine, and said, "That's the right kind," and he ordered the cupbearer to fill six bottles with the wine. Then they climbed back upstairs, and when the lion left the cellar and stepped outside, he began to stagger back and forth. Since he was a bit drunk, the cupbearer had to carry the wine up to the door for him. There the lion took the basket in his mouth and carried it to his master.

"You see, innkeeper," the huntsman said, "I've got bread, meat, vegetables, sweets, and wine fit for a king, and now I want to dine with my animals."

He sat down at the table, ate and drank, and shared his meal with the hare, the fox, the wolf, the bear, and the lion. The huntsman was in good spirits, for he realized that the king's daughter was fond of him. After the meal was over, he said, "Innkeeper, now that I've eaten and drunk just like a king, I'm going to the king's palace, where I shall marry his daughter."

"How are you going to do that?" asked the innkeeper. "She already has a bridegroom, and the wedding's to be celebrated today."

The huntsman took out the handkerchief that the king's daughter had given him on the dragon's mountain, and it still contained the seven tongues of the monster.

"All I need," he said, "is what I'm holding here in my hand."

The innkeeper looked at the handkerchief and said, "Even if I believe everything else, I can't believe this, and I'm willing to stake my house and everything I own on it."

Then the huntsman took out a pouch with a thousand gold pieces in it, put the pouch on the table, and said, "I'll match your house and property with this."

Meanwhile, the king and his daughter were sitting at the royal table, and the king asked her, "What did all those wild animals want who came to you and kept running in and out of my castle?"

"I'm not allowed to say," she answered. "But you'd do well to send for the master of those animals."

The king sent a servant to the inn and had the stranger invited to the palace. The servant arrived just as the huntsman concluded the bet with the innkeeper.

"You see, innkeeper," said the huntsman, "the king's sent a servant to invite me to the palace, but I refuse to go the way I am." Then he turned to the servant and said, "Please be so kind as to tell the king to send me royal garments, a coach with six horses, and servants to attend me."

When the king heard the answer, he said to his daughter, "What should I do?"

"You'd do well to honor his request and send for him," she said.

So the king sent royal garments, a coach with six horses, and servants to attend him. When the huntsman saw them coming, he said, "You see, innkeeper, my request has been honored," and he dressed himself in the royal garments, took the handkerchief with the seven tongues of the dragon, and drove to the palace. When the king saw him coming, he said to his daughter, "How shall I receive him?"

"You'd do well to go and meet him," she answered.

The king went to meet him and led him up to the palace, while the animals followed behind. The king showed the young huntsman to a place next to him and his daughter. The seat on the other side was taken by the marshal, who did not recognize the huntsman. Just then the seven heads of the dragon were carried out for display, and the king said, "Since the marshal cut off the seven heads of the dragon, I shall give him my daughter to be his wife today."

Then the huntsman stood up, opened the seven jaws, and said, "Where are the seven tongues of the dragon?"

Upon hearing that, the marshal was so frightened that he turned pale and did not know what to reply. Finally, he said, "Dragons have no tongues."

"Liars should have no tongues," said the huntsman. "But the dragon's tongues can prove who the real dragon-slayer is."

Then he unwrapped the handkerchief to reveal the seven tongues. When he stuck each tongue back into the mouth where it belonged, each fit perfectly. Next he took the handkerchief, on which the name of the king's daughter had been embroidered, showed it to the maiden and asked her to point out which man she had given it to.

"To the man who slew the dragon," she replied.

Then he called his animals, took off their coral collars and the golden clasp from the lion, and asked the maiden to tell to whom they belonged.

"The necklace and the golden clasp were mine," she answered, "but I divided the necklace among the animals who had helped in slaying the dragon."

Then the huntsman said, "After I was weary from the fight, I lay down to rest and sleep, and the marshal came and cut off my head. Then he carried off the king's daughter and pretended it was he who had slain the dragon. To prove that he's been lying, I have brought the tongues, the handkerchief, and the necklace." And then he told how his animals had healed him through a miraculous root and how he had traveled around for a year and had finally come back to the spot where he learned about the treachery of the marshal, thanks to the innkeeper's story.

"Is it true that this man slew the dragon?" the king asked his daughter.

"Yes," she replied, "it's true. Now I may reveal the marshal's shameful crime, for it has been exposed without my speaking about it. You see, the marshal made me take a vow of silence, and that's why I had insisted upon waiting a year and a day before celebrating the wedding."

The king summoned twelve councillors and ordered them to pronounce judgment on the marshal, and they sentenced him to be torn apart by four oxen. Thus the marshal was executed and the king gave his daughter to the huntsman and named him viceroy over the entire kingdom. The wedding was celebrated with great rejoicing, and the young king sent for his father and foster father and overwhelmed them with fine gifts. Nor did he forget the innkeeper. He too was sent for, and the young king said, "You see, innkeeper, I've married the king's daughter, and your house and property are mine."

"Yes," he said, "by right everything is yours."

But the young king said, "No, it is by mercy that I shall act. You shall keep your house and property. Moreover, I want you to retain the one thousand gold pieces as a gift."

Now, the young king and young queen were in good spirits and had a happy life together. He often went out hunting, since that gave him pleasure, and his faithful animals always accompanied him. Nearby was a forest, however, that was said to be enchanted. Whoever entered did not return very easily. But the young king had a great desire to go hunting in it, and he kept bothering the old king until he obtained permission to go there. So he rode out with a large retinue, and when he came to the forest, he saw a doe as white as snow and said to his men, "Wait here until I return. I want to hunt that beautiful doe."

He rode into the forest in pursuit of the doe, and only his animals followed him. His men stopped and waited until evening, but he did not come back. So they rode home and said to the young queen, "The young king went hunting after a beautiful white doe in the enchanted forest and did not return."

Upon hearing this she became very worried about him. Meanwhile, he had kept riding after the beautiful doe, never managing to overtake it. Each time he thought he had the doe within his aim, the animal would dart away and run off into the distance, until finally it vanished altogether. When the huntsman realized that he had gone deep into the forest, he took out his horn and blew it. There was no response, however, for his men could not hear it. After night began to fall, he saw that he could not get home that day. So, intending to spend the night there, he dismounted and built a fire near a tree. While he was sitting by the fire and his animals were lying beside him, he thought he heard a human voice. He looked around but did not see anyone. Soon after, he heard a groan that sounded as though it were coming from above. When he looked up, he saw an old woman sitting in the tree moaning and groaning.

"*Oooh! Oooh!* I'm freezing," she cried.

"Climb down," he said, "and warm yourself if you're freezing."

"No, your animals will bite me," she replied.

"They won't harm you, granny," he answered. "Just come down."

However, she was a witch and said, "I'm going to throw down a switch from the tree. If you hit them on their backs with it, they won't hurt me."

Then she threw the switch to him, and when he hit them with it, they immediately lay still and were turned to stone. When the witch was safe from the animals, she jumped down, touched him with a switch, and he was turned to stone. Whereupon she laughed and then dragged him and the animals to a pit where there were already many more such stones.

When the young king did not come back at all, the young queen's worries and fears increased. Now, it happened that just at this time the other brother, who had gone to the east when the twins had separated, came to this kingdom. He had been looking for employment and had found none. Therefore, he had been traveling about and having his animals dance in front of crowds of people. Eventually, it occurred to him to take a look at the knife they had stuck into the tree upon their separation to see how his brother was doing. When he got there, his brother's side of the knife was half rusty and half bright. At once he became alarmed and thought, My brother must have met with a great misfortune. But perhaps I can still save him, for half the knife is bright.

He went off to the west with his animals, and when he arrived at the city gate, the guards approached him and asked whether they should announce his arrival to his wife, for the young queen had been upset for several days about his absence and had been afraid that he had been killed in the enchanted forest. The guards, of course, believed that he was none other than the young king himself because he resembled him so much and also had the wild animals following him. The brother realized that they had mistaken him for his brother and thought, It's perhaps best that I pretend to be him. Then I'll be able to rescue him more easily.

So he let himself be conducted by the guards into the palace and was jubilantly received. The young queen thought for sure he was her husband and asked him why he had stayed away so long.

"I lost my way in the forest and could not find the way back any sooner," he said.

In the evening he was taken to the royal bed, but he placed a double-edged sword between himself and the young queen. She did not know what to make of it, but she did not dare to ask.

He remained there a few days and inquired into everything concerning the enchanted forest. Finally, he said, "I must go hunting there once more."

The king and the young queen tried to talk him out of it, but he insisted and set out with a large retinue. When he reached the forest, he went through everything his brother had. He saw a white doe and said to his men, "Stay here and wait until I return." He rode into the forest, and his animals followed after him. But he could not overtake the doe and went so deep into the forest that he had to spend the night there. After he had built a fire, he heard a groan above him.

"*Oooh! Oooh!* I'm freezing!"

He looked up and saw the same witch sitting in the tree.

"If you're freezing, climb down, granny," he said, "and warm yourself."

"No, your animals will bite me," she replied.

"They won't harm you," he said.

"I'm going to throw down a switch from the tree to you," she said. "If you hit them with it, they won't hurt me."

When the huntsman heard that, he did not trust the old woman and said, "I won't hit my animals. Either you come down, or I'll come get you!"

"Do you really think you can do something?" she cried. "There's no way you can harm me!"

But he answered, "If you don't come down, I'll shoot you down."

"Go ahead and shoot," she said. "I'm not afraid of your bullets."

So he took aim and fired at her, but the witch was protected against lead bullets, and she let out a shrill laugh. "You'll never hit me!" she exclaimed.

But the huntsman knew just what to do: he took off three silver buttons from his jacket and loaded his gun with them, for her witchcraft was powerless against them. When he now pulled the trigger, she fell from the tree with a scream. Then he put his foot on her and said, "You old witch, if you don't tell me right away where my brother is, I'll pick you up with both my hands and throw you into the fire."

Since she was terribly frightened, she begged for mercy and said, "He's been turned to stone along with his animals, and they're lying in a pit."

He forced her to go with him, and there he threatened her by saying, "You old monkey, now you'd better restore life to my brother and all the other creatures that are lying there, or I'll throw you into the fire!"

She took a switch and touched the stones, and his brother and the animals came back to life again, and many others as well, such as merchants, artisans, and shepherds, who arose, thanked the huntsman for their release, and went home. Meanwhile, when the twin brothers saw each other again, they kissed each other, and their hearts were full of joy. Then they grabbed the witch, tied her up, and put her into the fire. After she had been burned, the forest opened up all by itself and became bright and clear, so that one could see the royal castle, which was about a three-hour walk from there.

Now the two brothers headed toward home together and along the way told each other about their adventures. When the younger one said that he was viceroy for the whole kingdom, the other said, "I realized that right away. When I came into the city, I was mistaken for you and shown every royal honor. The young queen thought I was her husband, and I had to sleep in your bed."

When the other heard that, he became so jealous that he drew his sword and cut off his brother's head. However, when he saw his brother lying there dead and his red blood flowing, he was overcome by remorse.

"My brother rescued me!" he exclaimed. "And in return I've killed him!"

He uttered cries of grief, and then his hare came and offered to fetch the root of life. The hare dashed off and returned at just the right time. The dead brother was brought back to life and did not even notice his wound. When they continued on their journey, the younger brother said, "You look like me. You're dressed in royal garments like me, and your animals are like mine. Let's enter from opposite gates and go to the king's chamber at the same time from opposite directions."

So they took separate paths, and simultaneously the guards came from opposite gates to the old king and announced that the young king had returned with his animals from the hunt.

"It's not possible," the king said. "The gates are an hour's walk apart."

Just then, however, the two brothers arrived at the palace courtyard from two sides and came upstairs.

"Tell me," the king said to his daughter, "which one is your husband. They look exactly alike, and I can't tell them apart."

The young queen was very upset and could not tell them apart either. Finally, she remembered the necklace that she had given the animals. She searched and found the golden clasp on the lion, and then she exclaimed happily, "The man whom this lion follows is my husband!"

Then the young king laughed and said, "Yes, you've found the right one."

Now they all sat down at the table and ate and drank, and they were in a merry mood. That night, when the young king went to bed, his wife asked him, "Why did you always place a double-edged sword in our bed these last few nights? I thought you might want to slay me."

Then he realized how faithful his brother had been.

◈ 61 ◈

Little Farmer

THERE ONCE WAS A VILLAGE where all the farmers were rich except one who was poor, and he was called Little Farmer. He did not even have a cow, much less the money to buy one. Since he and his wife wanted to own one, he said to her one day, "Listen, I have a good idea. We'll ask our cousin the carpenter to make us a calf out of wood and then paint it brown so that it will look like all the other cows. In time it's bound to get big and become a cow."

His wife liked the idea, and their cousin the carpenter took his plane and saw and built a perfect-looking calf. Then he painted it brown and lowered its head to make it seem that the calf was eating. When the cows were driven out to pasture the next morning, Little Farmer called the cowherd to him and said, "Look, I've got a little calf here, but it's still quite small and needs to be carried."

"All right," said the cowherd, and he lifted it in his arms and carried it to the pasture. There he put it down on the grass, and the little calf just stayed at the same spot as if it were eating.

"It'll soon be running around by itself," the cowherd said. "Just look at how it won't stop eating!"

In the evening, when he wanted to drive the herd back home, he said to the calf, "If you can stand there and eat your fill, then you can also walk back on your own four legs. I don't feel like carrying you in my arms again."

Meanwhile, Little Farmer stood in front of his door waiting for his little calf. When the cowherd drove the cows through the village and the little calf was missing, he asked where it was.

"It's still standing and eating in the pasture," said the cowherd. "It didn't want to stop and come with me."

"My God!" said Little Farmer. "I've got to have my calf back."

Then they went back to the meadow together, but someone had stolen the calf, and it was gone.

"It must have gone astray," said the cowherd.

"Don't give me that story!" said Little Farmer, and he took the cowherd to the mayor, who decided that the cowherd was negligent and ordered him to give Little Farmer a cow to replace the missing calf.

Now Little Farmer and his wife had the cow that they had longed for in the past. They were exceedingly happy, but they had no fodder and could not give it anything to eat. They soon had to slaughter it and salted the meat so it would keep. Then Little Farmer took the cowhide to the city, where he intended to sell it and buy a new calf with the profit. On the way he passed a mill where a raven was sitting with broken wings. Out of pity for the bird, he picked it up and wrapped it in the hide. Just then the weather became bad, and a storm arose with wind and rain. Since he could not continue on his way, he stopped at the mill where he requested lodging. The miller's wife was alone at the house and said to Little Farmer, "Lie down on the straw over there," and she gave him bread and cheese. Little Farmer ate the food and lay down with the cowhide next to him. Now the miller's wife thought, I'm sure he's asleep since he was so tired.

Soon the priest arrived, and the miller's wife welcomed him warmly. "My husband's away," she said. "So let's treat ourselves to a feast!"

Little Farmer's ears perked when he heard her talking about a feast. He was very disturbed that she had made him put up with bread and cheese. Then the miller's wife brought out four different things: a roast, a salad, a cake, and some wine. As they were about to sit down and eat there was a knock at the door.

"Oh, God! It's my husband," said the wife. She quickly hid the roast in the tile stove, the wine under the pillow, the salad on the bed, the cake under the bed, and the priest in the hallway cupboard. Then she let her husband in and said, "Thank God you're here again! That's some weather outside. You'd think that the world were coming to an end!"

The miller saw Little Farmer lying on the straw and asked, "What's that fellow doing there?"

"Ah," said his wife, "the poor fellow came here in the storm and rain and asked for shelter. So I gave him some bread and cheese and showed him to that place on the straw."

"Well, I've got no objections," said the husband, "but get me something to eat and be quick about it."

"There's nothing but bread and cheese," the wife said.

"I'll eat anything," answered her husband, "even if it's just bread and cheese." Then he glanced over at Little Farmer and called, "Come over here and eat a little more with me!"

Little Farmer did not have to be asked twice but got up and joined the miller in his meal. Afterward the miller noticed the cowhide wrapped around the raven lying on the floor, and he asked, "What have you got there?"

"I've got a fortune-teller that's wrapped up inside," answered Little Farmer.

"Can he predict my future?" asked the miller.

"Why not?" responded Little Farmer. "However, he only predicts four things, and the fifth he keeps to himself."

The miller was curious and said, "Let him predict my future."

So Little Farmer pressed the raven's head so that it cawed *"Krr! Krr!"*

"What did he say?" asked the miller.

"His first prediction is that there's wine under the pillow," Little Farmer answered.

"Good heavens!" exclaimed the miller, who went over and found the wine. "Go on," he said.

Little Farmer made the raven caw again and said, "His second prediction is that there's a roast in the tile stove."

"Good heavens!" exclaimed the miller, who went over and found the roast.

Little Farmer made the raven caw once more and said, "His third prediction is that there's salad on the bed."

"Good heavens!" exclaimed the miller, who went over and found the salad.

Finally, Little Farmer pressed the raven's head one more time so that it cawed, and he said, "His fourth prediction is that there's cake under the bed."

"Good heavens!" exclaimed the miller, who went over and found the cake.

Now the two of them sat down at the table, but the miller's wife was frightened to death. So she went to bed and took all the keys with her. The miller wanted to know the fifth prediction, but Little Farmer said, "First let's eat these four things in peace, for the fifth is something awful."

So they ate, and afterward they bargained over how much money the miller should pay Little Farmer for the fifth prediction. Finally, they agreed on three hundred talers, and Little Farmer pressed the raven's head one more time so that it cawed loudly.

"What did he say?" asked the miller.

"He said the devil's hiding in the hallway cupboard outside," replied Little Farmer.

"I want the devil out of there at once!" said the miller, and he unlocked the front door. The wife was forced to turn over the keys, and Little Farmer opened the cupboard. Then the priest ran out as fast he could, and the miller exclaimed, "It's true! I saw the black scoundrel with my own eyes!"

At dawn the next morning Little Farmer made off with his three hundred talers. When he returned home, his affairs began to show gradual improvement. He built himself a charming house, and the farmers said, "Little Farmer's surely been to that land where golden snow falls and where people take home money by the shovelful."

So Little Farmer was summoned by the mayor and ordered to reveal where he had gotten his wealth.

"I sold my cowhide in the city for three hundred talers," he said.

When the farmers heard that, they all wanted to take advantage of the opportunity. They ran home, slaughtered all their cows, and then skinned them in order to sell them in the city at a great profit.

"My maid must go first," the mayor declared.

However, when she got to the city, the merchant gave her only three talers for a cowhide, and when the rest of them came, he did not give them even that much.

"What am I supposed to do with all these cowhides?" he asked.

Now, the farmers were furious that Little Farmer had pulled the wool over their eyes, and they wanted revenge. So they went to the mayor and accused the farmer of fraud. The innocent Little Farmer was unanimously sentenced to death by a jury and was to be rolled into the water in a barrel full of holes. Little Farmer was led out to the water, and a priest was brought to read him the last rites. All the others had to leave, and when Little Farmer looked at the priest, he recognized the man who had been with the miller's wife.

"Since I set you free from the cupboard," he said, "you can set me free from the barrel."

Just at that moment the shepherd came by with his flock of sheep, and Little Farmer happened to know that for a long time this man had wanted to become mayor. Therefore, Little Farmer screamed with all his might, "No, I won't do it! Even if the whole world wants it, I won't do it!"

When the shepherd heard the screams, he went over and asked, "What's going on? What won't you do?"

"They want to make me mayor," said Little Farmer, "providing that I get into this barrel, but I won't do it."

"If that's all that it takes to become mayor," said the shepherd, "I'll get in right away."

"If you get in," said Little Farmer, "they'll make you mayor for sure."

The shepherd was happy to comply and got inside. Then Little Farmer slammed the lid down, took the shepherd's flock, and drove it away. Meanwhile, the priest went to the villagers and said he had read the last rites. They then went and rolled the barrel toward the water. When the barrel began to roll, the shepherd cried out, "I'll gladly be mayor!"

They believed it was no one else but Little Farmer screaming and said, "We believe you, but first we want you to look around down there." And they rolled the barrel into the water.

Then the farmers went home, and when they returned to the village, Little Farmer came along in good spirits, calmly driving a flock of sheep. The farmers were astonished and said, "Little Farmer, where are you coming from? Are you coming from the water?"

"Of course," he answered. "I sank deep down into the water until I reached the bottom. Then I kicked the lid off the barrel and crawled out. There were beautiful meadows with lots of sheep grazing on them. So I brought back a flock of them with me."

"Are there any more left?" the farmers asked.

"Oh, yes," said Little Farmer, "more than you could possibly use."

So the farmers decided to fetch some sheep too, each one a flock, and the mayor declared, "I'm going first!"

They all went down to the water together, and just then there happened to be in the sky the small flocks of clouds that are called little fleece. They were reflected in the water, and the farmers exclaimed, "We can already see the fleece of the sheep down below!"

The mayor pushed to the front and announced, "I'll dive down first and look around. If everything looks all right, I'll call you."

So he jumped into the water, and there was a big *splash!* It sounded as if he had yelled "Rush!" and the whole group of farmers plunged into the water after him. Thus the entire village was wiped out, and since Little Farmer was the sole survivor and heir, he became a rich man.

❖ 62 ❖

The Queen Bee

ONCE TWO PRINCES WENT FORTH in search of adventure, and after they fell into a wild, decadent way of life, they never returned home again. Their youngest brother, who was called Simpleton, went out to look for them, but when he finally found them, they ridiculed him for thinking that he, as naive as he was, could make his way in the world when they, who were much more clever, had not been able to succeed.

At length the three of them traveled together and came to an anthill. The two oldest wanted to smash it and watch the small ants crawl around in fright and carry away their eggs, but Simpleton said, "Leave the little creatures in peace. I won't let you disturb them."

They continued on their way and came to a lake where a great many ducks were swimming. The two brothers wanted to catch a few and roast them, but Simpleton would not let them.

"Leave the creatures in peace," he said. "I won't let you kill them."

Next they came to a beehive, and there was so much honey in the hive that it had dripped down the tree trunk. The two older brothers wanted to build a fire underneath it and suffocate the bees to get at the honey. However, Simpleton prevented them again and said, "Leave the creatures in peace. I won't let you burn them."

Finally, the three brothers came to a castle, and they saw nothing but stone horses standing in the stables. Not a living soul could be seen. They went through all the halls until they reached the end, where there was a door with three locks hanging on it. In the middle of the door there was a peephole through which one could look into the room. In there they saw a gray dwarf sitting at a table. They called to him once, then twice, but he did not hear them. Finally, they called a third time, and he got up, opened the locks, and came out. However, he did not say a word. Instead, he just led them to a richly spread table, and after they had something to eat and drink, he brought each one to his own bedroom.

The next morning the gray dwarf went to the oldest brother, beckoned to him, and conducted him to a stone tablet on which were inscribed three tasks that had to be performed if the castle was to be disenchanted. The first task involved gathering one thousand pearls that were lying in the moss of the forest. They belonged to the king's daughter and had to be collected from the moss before sundown. If one single pearl was missing, the seeker would be turned to stone.

The oldest brother went to the moss and searched the entire day, but when the day drew to a close, he had found only one hundred. Consequently, he was turned into stone as was ordained by the tablet. The next day the second brother undertook the adventure, but he did not fare much better than the oldest: he found only two hundred pearls and was turned into stone. Finally, it was Simpleton's turn to search for the pearls in the moss. However, because it was so difficult to find them and everything went so slowly, he sat down on a stone and began to weep. While he was sitting on the stone and weeping, the king of the ants whose life he had once saved came along with five thousand ants, and it did not take long before the little creatures had gathered the pearls together and stacked them in a pile.

Now, the second task was to fetch the key to the bedroom of the king's daughter from the lake. When Simpleton came to the lake, the ducks whose lives he had once saved came swimming toward him and then dived down to fetch the key from the depths.

Next came the third task, which was the hardest. The king had three daughters who lay asleep, and Simpleton had to pick out the youngest and the loveliest. However, they all looked exactly alike, and the only difference between them was that they each had eaten a different kind of sweet before falling asleep: the oldest had eaten a piece of sugar, the second a little syrup, the youngest a spoonful of honey. Just then the queen bee whom Simpleton had protected from the fire came along and tested the lips of all three princesses. At last she settled on the mouth of the princess who had eaten honey, and thus the prince was able to recognize the right daughter. Now the magic spell was broken, and everyone was set free from the deep sleep. All those who had been turned into stone regained their human form. Simpleton married the youngest and loveliest daughter and became king after her father's death, while his two brothers were married to the other two sisters.

◈ 63 ◈

The Three Feathers

ONCE UPON A TIME there was a king who had three sons. Two of them were bright and clever, but the third was just called Simpleton because he did not speak much and was naive. When the king became old and weak and began thinking about his end, he was uncertain about which of his sons should inherit his kingdom.

"I want you to go forth," he said to them, "and whoever brings me the finest carpet shall be king after my death."

To make sure that they would not quarrel among themselves, he led them outside the castle, blew three feathers into the air, and said, "You're to follow the flight of the feathers."

One feather flew to the east, the next to the west, and the third flew straight ahead but not very far, and soon it fell to the ground. So one brother went to the right, the other to the left, and the two of them made fun of Simpleton because he had to stay where the third feather had fallen.

Now Simpleton sat down and was sad. However, all at once he noticed there was a trapdoor next to the feather. He lifted it up, discovered some stairs, and went down. Then he came to another door, knocked, and heard a voice calling from inside:

"Maiden, maiden, green and small,
hop to it, hoptoad, and don't you fall.
Hoptoad's dog, hop back and forth,
and quickly see who's at the door."

The door opened, and there he saw a large fat toad surrounded by lots of little toads. The large toad asked him what he desired, and he answered, "I'd like to have the most beautiful and finest carpet."

Then the toad called one of the young ones and said:

"Maiden, maiden, green and small,
hop to it, hoptoad, and don't you fall.
Hoptoad's dog, hop lively, hop sprightly,
Fetch me the box as quick as can be."

The young toad fetched the box, and the fat toad opened it and gave Simpleton a carpet so beautiful and fine that nobody on earth could possibly have woven it. So he thanked her and climbed back up the stairs.

In the meantime, the two others, who considered their brother so stupid, did not think that he would find anything, let alone bring it back. "Why should we exert ourselves by searching?" they said, and they snatched some material from the first shepherd's wife they met and brought it home to the king. At the same time Simpleton also returned and brought his beautiful carpet. When the king saw it, he was astonished and said, "According to my decree the kingdom belongs to the youngest."

However, the two oldest would not leave their father in peace and declared it was impossible for Simpleton to become king since he had no understanding of anything. Therefore, they begged the king to set a new condition, and the father said, "Whoever brings me the most beautiful ring shall inherit the kingdom."

He led the three brothers outside, blew three feathers into the air, and beckoned them to follow the feathers. Once again the two oldest went to the east and the west, and Simpleton went straight ahead, where the feather flew and fell next to the trapdoor. He climbed down again to the fat toad and said to her that he needed the most beautiful ring in the world. The toad had the large box brought to her immediately, took out a ring, and gave it to him. The ring sparkled with precious gems and was so beautiful that no goldsmith on earth could possibly have made it.

In the meantime, the two oldest made fun of Simpleton for wanting to search for a golden ring. Again they did not exert themselves but just knocked the nails out of an old wagon ring and brought it to the king. However, when Simpleton displayed his golden ring, the father declared once more, "The kingdom belongs to him."

Nevertheless, the two oldest sons kept pestering the king until he set a third condition and proclaimed that whoever brought home the most beautiful woman would inherit the kingdom. He blew the three feathers into the air again, and they flew just as they had before.

Simpleton did not waste any time and went directly to the toad and said, "I'm to bring home the most beautiful woman in the world."

"My goodness!" answered the toad. "The most beautiful woman! I don't happen to have her right on hand, but you shall still get her nonetheless." Then the toad gave him a yellow turnip that had been hollowed out and had six little mice harnessed to it.

"What am I to do with that?" asked Simpleton quite sadly.

"Just put one of my little toads inside," answered the toad.

Then he chose one of the toads from the group at random and put her into the yellow shell. No sooner was the little toad inside than she turned into a remarkably beautiful maiden, the turnip into a coach, and the six mice into horses. Then he kissed her, drove off with the horses at a rapid pace, and brought her to the king. His brothers also returned, but they had not exerted themselves. Instead, they had taken the first good-looking peasant women they could find. When the king saw them, he said, "The kingdom belongs to my youngest son after my death."

Once again the two oldest sons made such a racket that it was deafening to the king's ears. "We'll never accept Simpleton as king!" They demanded that preference be shown to the one whose woman could jump through a hoop hanging in the middle of the hall, for they thought, Peasant women can do that easily. They're very strong, but the delicate maiden will jump to her death.

The old king relented on this occasion as well, and the two peasant women jumped through the hoop. However, they were so clumsy that they fell and broke their chubby arms and legs. Then Simpleton's beautiful maiden jumped through the hoop as gracefully as a deer, and all objections by the two oldest sons had to stop. So Simpleton received the crown and reigned wisely for a long time thereafter.

◆ 64 ◆

The Golden Goose

THERE WAS ONCE A MAN WHO HAD THREE SONS, and the youngest, who was called Simpleton, was constantly mocked, disdained, and slighted. Now, one day it happened that the oldest brother decided to go into the forest to chop wood, and before he went, his mother gave him a nice, fine pancake and a bottle of wine so that he would not have to suffer from hunger or thirst. When he reached the forest, he met a gray old dwarf, who wished him good day and said, "Give me a piece of the pancake from your pocket, and let me have a drink of wine. I'm very hungry and thirsty."

However, the clever son answered, "If I give you my pancake and my wine, then I won't have anything for myself. So get out of my way," and he left the dwarf standing there and went farther into the forest. When he began chopping down a tree, it did not take long for him to make a slip and cut himself in the arm. So he had to return home and have his arm bandaged. All this happened because of the gray dwarf.

Shortly thereafter, the second son went into the forest, and the mother gave him a pancake and a bottle of wine, just as she had given the oldest. The second son too met the gray old dwarf, who asked him for a piece of the pancake and a drink of wine. But the second son also spoke quite sensibly. "Whatever I give you, I'll be taking from myself. So get out of my way." Then he left the dwarf standing there and went farther into the forest. Soon his punishment came as well. After he had whacked a tree a few times, he struck himself in the leg. Consequently, he had to be carried home.

Then Simpleton said, "Father, let me go now and chop some wood."

"Your brothers hurt themselves doing that," said the father. "So I want you to steer clear of the woods, especially since you know nothing about chopping down trees."

However, Simpleton kept insisting until his father finally said, "Go ahead. Perhaps you'll learn something after you've hurt yourself."

The mother gave him a pancake made out of water and ashes along with a bottle of sour beer. When he went into the forest, he too met the gray old dwarf, who greeted him and said, "Give me a piece of your pancake and a drink out of your bottle. I'm very hungry and thirsty."

"I have only a pancake made of ashes and some sour beer," answered Simpleton. "If that's all right with you, let's sit down and eat."

So they sat down, and when Simpleton took out his cake made of ashes, it turned out to be a fine pancake, and the sour beer was good wine. After they had eaten and drunk, the dwarf said, "Since you have such a good heart and gladly share what you have, I'm going to grant you some good luck. There's an old tree over there. Just go and chop it down, and you'll find something among the roots." Then the dwarf took leave of him.

Simpleton went over and chopped down the tree. When it fell, he saw a goose with feathers of pure gold lying among the roots. He lifted the goose up and carried it with him to an inn, where he intended to spend the night. Now, the innkeeper had three daughters, and when they saw the goose, they were curious to know what kind of strange bird it was. Moreover, they each wanted to have one of its golden feathers. The oldest thought, I'll surely find an opportunity to pluck one of its feathers.

At one point Simpleton went out, and she seized the goose by its wing, but her hand and fingers remained stuck to it. Soon afterward the second sister came and also intended to pluck a golden feather. However, no sooner did she touch her sister than she became stuck to her. Finally, the third sister came with the same intention, but the other two screamed, "Keep away! For heaven's sake, keep away!"

But she did not comprehend why she should keep away and thought, If they're there, I see no reason why I can't be. So she ran over, and when she touched her sister, she became stuck to her, and all three had to spend the night with the goose.

The next morning Simpleton took the goose in his arm, set out, and did not bother himself about the three sisters who were stuck to the goose. They were compelled to run after him constantly, left and right, wherever his legs took him. In the middle of a field they came across the parson, and when he saw the procession, he said, "Shame on you, you naughty girls! Is that the right way to behave?"

Upon saying that, he grabbed the youngest sister by the hand and attempted to pull her away, but when he touched her, he also got stuck and had to run along behind them. Shortly afterward the sexton came by and saw the parson trailing the three girls on their heels. In his amazement he called out, "Hey, Parson, where are you off to in such a hurry? Don't forget that we have a christening today!"

The sexton ran up to the parson, and as soon as he touched his sleeve, he became stuck like the others. Now the five of them had to trot after Simpleton, one stuck to the other, and they approached two farmers who were coming from the fields with their hoes. The parson called out to them to set them loose. However, as soon as they touched the sexton, they got stuck, and now there were seven of them trailing Simpleton and his goose.

After some time Simpleton came to a city ruled by a king who had a daughter that was so serious, she never laughed. Consequently, the king issued a decree that whoever could make her laugh would have her for his wife. When Simpleton heard that, he went before the king's daughter with his goose and its followers, and when she saw the seven people all attached to one another and running along, she burst out laughing, and it appeared as if she would never stop. So Simpleton demanded the princess as his bride, but the king had no desire to have him for a son-in-law and raised all kinds of objections. Eventually, he said that first Simpleton would have to produce a man capable of drinking the contents of a cellar full of wine before he could wed his daughter.

Now, Simpleton quickly remembered the gray dwarf, for he thought that he might help him. Therefore, he went out into the forest, right to the spot where he had chopped down the tree. There he saw a man with a sad face sitting and moping. Simpleton asked what was bothering him so much, and he answered, "I'm terribly thirsty and don't seem to be able to quench my thirst. I can't stand cold water, and just now I emptied a barrel of wine, but that was like a drop on a hot stone."

"Well, I can help you," said Simpleton. "Just come with me, and you'll be able to drink your fill."

He led him to the king's cellar, and the man rushed over to the large barrels and set to work: he drank so much that his sides began to hurt, but before the day was over, he had emptied the entire cellar. So once again Simpleton demanded his bride, but the king was perturbed that such a common fellow, whom everyone called Simpleton, was to have his daughter. Therefore, he set a new condition: now Simpleton had to produce a man who could eat a mountain of bread.

Simpleton immediately reacted by going directly into the forest. There, on the same spot as before, he saw a man sitting who was pulling in a belt around his waist. The man made an awful face and said, "I've eaten an oven full of coarse bread, but what good is that when I'm as hungry as a lion. My stomach's still empty, and I have to pull in my belt if I don't want to die of hunger."

Simpleton was glad to hear that and said, "Get up and come with me. You shall eat your fill."

He led him to the king's courtyard, where the king had gathered all the flour of the entire kingdom and had had it baked into a tremendous mountain. However, the man from the forest stepped up to it, began eating, and consumed the whole mountain in one day. Now for the third time, Simpleton claimed his bride, but the king found another way out and demanded a ship that could sail on land and water.

"As soon as you come sailing back in it," he said, "you shall have my daughter for your wife."

Simpleton went straight into the forest and encountered the gray old dwarf to whom he had given his cake.

"I've drunk and eaten for you," said the dwarf. "Now I'll also give you the ship. I'm doing all this because you treated me so kindly."

Then he gave him the ship, and when the king saw it, he could no longer prevent him from marrying his daughter. The wedding was celebrated, and after the king's death, Simpleton inherited the kingdom and lived happily ever after with his wife.

◆ 65 ◆

All Fur

ONCE UPON A TIME there was a king whose wife had golden hair and was so beautiful that her equal could not be found anywhere on earth. Now, it happened that she became sick, and when she felt she was about to die, she called the king to her and said, "If you desire to marry again after my death, I'd like you to take someone who is as beautiful as I am and who has golden hair like mine. Promise me that you will do this."

After the king had promised her that, she closed her eyes and died. For a long time the king could not be consoled and did not think about remarrying. Finally, his councillors said, "This cannot continue. The king must marry again so that we may have a queen."

Messengers were sent far and wide to search for a bride who might equal the beauty of the dead queen. Yet, they could not find anyone like her in the world, and even had they found such a woman, she certainly would not have had such golden hair. So the messengers returned with their mission unaccomplished.

Now, the king had a daughter who was just as beautiful as her dead mother, and she also had the same golden hair. When she was grown-up, the king looked at her one day and realized that her features were exactly the same as those of his dead wife. Suddenly he fell passionately in love with her and said to his councillors, "I'm going to marry my daughter, for she is the living image of my dead wife."

When the councillors heard that, they were horrified and said, "God has forbidden a father to marry his daughter. Nothing good can come from such a sin, and the kingdom will be brought to ruin."

When she heard of her father's decision, the daughter was even more horrified, but she still hoped to dissuade him from carrying out his plan. Therefore, she said to him, "Before I fulfill your wish, I must have three dresses, one as golden as the sun, one as silvery as the moon, and one as bright as the stars. Furthermore, I want a cloak made up of a thousand kinds of pelts and furs, and each animal in your kingdom must contribute a piece of its skin to it." She thought, He'll never be able to obtain all those furs, and by demanding this, I shall divert my father from his evil intentions.

The king, however, persisted, and the most skillful women in his realm were assembled to weave the three dresses, one as golden as the sun, one as silvery as the moon, and one as bright as the stars. His huntsmen had to catch all the animals in his entire kingdom and take a piece of their skin. Thus a cloak was made from a thousand kinds of fur. At last, when everything was finished, the king ordered the cloak to be brought and spread out before her. Then he announced, "The wedding will be tomorrow."

When the king's daughter saw that there was no hope whatsoever of changing her father's inclinations, she decided to run away. That night, while everyone was asleep, she got up and took three of her precious possessions: a golden ring, a tiny golden spinning wheel, and a little golden reel. She packed the dresses of the sun, the moon, and the stars into a nutshell, put on the cloak of all kinds of fur, and blackened her face and hands with soot. Then she commended herself to God and departed. She walked the whole night until she reached a great forest, and since she was tired, she climbed into a hollow tree and fell asleep.

When the sun rose, she continued to sleep and sleep until it became broad daylight. Meanwhile, it happened that the king who was the lord of this forest was out hunting in it, and when his dogs came to the tree, they started to sniff and run around it and bark.

"Go see what kind of beast has hidden itself there," the king said to his huntsmen.

The huntsmen obeyed the king's command, and when they returned to him, they said, "There's a strange animal lying in the hollow tree. We've never seen anything like it. Its skin is made up of a thousand different kinds of fur, and it's lying there asleep."

"See if you can catch it alive," said the king. "Then tie it to the wagon, and we'll take it with us."

When the huntsmen seized the maiden, she woke up in a fright and cried to them, "I'm just a poor girl, forsaken by my father and mother! Please have pity on me and take me with you."

"You'll be perfect for the kitchen, *All Fur,*" they said. "Come with us, and you can sweep up the ashes there."

So they put her into the wagon and drove back to the royal castle. There they showed her to a little closet beneath the stairs that was never exposed to daylight.

"Well, you furry creature," they said, "you can live and sleep here."

Then she was sent to the kitchen, where she carried wood and water, kept the fires going, plucked the fowls, sorted the vegetables, swept up the ashes, and did all the dirty work. All Fur lived there for a long time in dire poverty. Ah, my beautiful princess, what shall become of you?

At one time a ball was being held in the castle, and All Fur asked the cook, "May I go upstairs and watch for a while? I'll just stand outside the door."

"Yes," said the cook. "Go ahead, but be back in half an hour. You've got to sweep up the ashes."

All Fur took her little oil lamp, went to her closet, took off her fur cloak, and washed the soot from her face and hands so that her full beauty came to light again. Then she opened the nut and took out the dress that shone like the sun. When that was done, she went upstairs to the ball, and everyone made way for her, for they had no idea who she was and believed that she was nothing less than a royal princess. The king approached her, offered her his hand, and led her forth to dance. In his heart he thought, Never in my life have my eyes beheld anyone so beautiful! When the dance was over, she curtsied, and as the king was looking around she disappeared, and nobody knew where she had gone. The guards who were standing in front of the castle were summoned and questioned, but no one had seen her.

In the meantime, the princess had run back to her closet and had undressed quickly. Then she blackened her face and hands, put on the fur cloak, and became All Fur once more. When she went back to the kitchen, she resumed her work and began sweeping up the ashes.

"Let that be until tomorrow," said the cook. "I want you to make a soup for the king. While you're doing that, I'm going upstairs to watch a little. You'd better not let a single hair drop into the soup or else you'll get nothing more to eat in the future!"

The cook went away, and All Fur made the soup for the king by brewing a bread soup as best she could. When she was finished, she fetched her golden ring from the closet and put it into the bowl in which she had prepared the soup. When the ball was over, the king ordered the soup to be brought to him, and as he ate it, he was convinced that he had never eaten a soup that had tasted as good. However, he found a ring lying at the bottom of the bowl when he had finished eating, and he could not imagine how it could have got there. He ordered the cook to appear before him, and the cook became terrified on learning that the king wanted to see him.

"You must have let a hair drop into the soup," he said to All Fur. "If that's true, you can expect a good beating!"

When he went before the king, he was asked who had made the soup.

"I did," answered the cook.

However, the king said, "That's not true, for it was much different from your usual soup and much better cooked."

"I must confess," responded the cook. "I didn't cook it. The furry creature did."

"Go and fetch her here," said the king.

When All Fur appeared, the king asked, "Who are you?"

"I'm just a poor girl that no longer has a mother or father."

"Why are you in my castle?" the king continued.

"I'm good for nothing but to have boots thrown at my head," she replied.

"Where did you get the ring that was in the soup?" he asked again.

"I don't know anything about the ring," she answered. So the king could not find out anything and had to send her away.

Some months later there was another ball, and like the previous time, All Fur asked the cook's permission to go and watch.

"Yes," he answered. "But come back in half an hour and cook the king the bread soup that he likes so much."

She ran to the little closet, washed herself quickly, took the dress as silvery as the moon out of the nut, and put it on. When she appeared upstairs, she looked like a royal princess. The king approached her again and was delighted to see her. Since the dance had just begun, they danced together, and when the dance was over, she again disappeared so quickly that the king was unable to see where she went. In the meantime, she returned to the little closet, made herself into the furry creature again, and returned to the kitchen to make the bread soup. While the cook was still upstairs, she fetched the tiny golden spinning wheel, put it into the bowl, and covered it with the soup. Then the soup was brought to the king, and he ate it and enjoyed it as much as he had the previous time. Afterward he summoned the cook, who again had to admit that All Fur had made the soup. Now All Fur had to appear before the king once more, but she merely repeated that she was good for nothing but to have boots thrown at her and that she knew nothing about the tiny golden spinning wheel.

When the king held a ball for the third time, everything happened just as it had before. To be sure, the cook now asserted, "Furry creature, I know you're a witch. You always put something in the soup to make it taste good and to make the king like it better than anything I can cook."

However, since she pleaded so intensely, he let her go upstairs at a given time. Thereupon she put on the dress as bright as the stars and entered the ballroom wearing it. Once again the king danced with the beautiful maiden and thought that she had never been more beautiful. While he danced with her, he put a golden ring on her finger without her noticing it. He had also ordered the dance to last a very long time, and when it was over, he tried to hold on to her hands, but she tore herself away and quickly ran into the crowd, vanishing from his sight. However, she had stayed upstairs too long, more than half an hour, and she could not take off her beautiful dress but had to throw her fur cloak over it. Moreover, she was in such a hurry, she could not make herself completely black, and one of her fingers was left white. Then All Fur ran into the kitchen and cooked the soup for the king. While the cook was away, she put the golden reel into the bowl. So, when the king found the reel at the bottom of the bowl, he summoned All Fur and saw the ring that he had put on her finger during the dance. Then he seized her hand and held it tight, and when she tried to free herself and run away, the fur cloak opened a bit, and the dress of bright stars was unveiled. The king grabbed the cloak and tore it off her. Suddenly her golden hair toppled down, and she stood there in all her splendor unable to conceal herself any longer. After she had wiped the soot and ashes from her face, she was more beautiful than anyone who had ever been glimpsed on earth.

"You shall be my dear bride," the king said, "and we shall never part from each other!"

Thereupon the wedding was celebrated, and they lived happily together until their death.

The Hare's Bride

THERE ONCE WAS A WOMAN who lived with her daughter, and near their dwelling they had a beautiful cabbage garden. During the winter, however, a little hare got into the garden and began eating up the cabbage. So the woman said to her daughter, "Go out into the garden and chase the hare away."

"*Shoo! Shoo!*" cried the maiden to the hare. "Stop eating all our cabbage!"

"Come here, maiden," said the hare. "Sit down on my tail and come with me to my little hut."

The maiden was unwilling, and the next day the hare again came and ate the cabbage.

"Go out into the garden," said the mother, "and chase the hare away."

"*Shoo! Shoo!*" cried the maiden. "Stop eating all our cabbage!"

"Come here, maiden," said the hare. "Sit down on my tail and come with me to my little hut."

The maiden was unwilling. On the third day the hare again came and ate the cabbage. The woman then said to her daughter, "Go out into the garden and chase the hare away."

"*Shoo! Shoo!* Stop eating all our cabbage!" cried the maiden.

"Come here, maiden," said the hare. "Sit down on my tail and come with me to my little hut."

The maiden sat down on the hare's tail, and the hare carried her far away to his hut and said, "Now, cook some green cabbage and millet. I'm going out to invite the wedding guests."

Then all the wedding guests gathered together. (Who were the wedding guests? Well, I can tell you what someone else told me: all the hares were there, the crow as parson to marry the couple, the fox as sexton, and the altar was under the rainbow.) However, the maiden was sad because she was so alone. Then the hare came back and said, "Open the door! Open the door! The wedding guests are all nice and merry."

The bride said nothing but wept. The hare went away and then came back again.

"Open the door! Open the door! The wedding guests are hungry."

Again the bride said nothing but wept, and the hare went away.

Then he came and said, "Open the door! Open the door! The wedding guests are waiting."

The bride said nothing, and the hare went away. However, this time the maiden made a straw doll, dressed it in her clothes, gave it a big spoon, stood it in front of the kettle with the millet, and then went home to her mother.

Again the hare came and said, "Open the door! Open the door!"

Finally, he opened the door and smashed the doll on its head so that the cap fell off. When he realized that it was not his bride, the hare went off and was sad.

◆ 67 ◆

The Twelve Huntsmen

ONCE UPON A TIME there was a prince who was betrothed to a maiden and loved her very much. One day, as he was sitting with her and feeling very happy, he received news that his father was seriously ill and wanted to see him one more time before he died.

"I must go away now and leave you," he said to his beloved. "Please take this ring to remember me by. When I become king, I shall come back for you."

Then he rode away, and when he got home, he saw that his father was very sick and on the verge of death.

"Dearest son," the king said to him, "I wanted to see you one more time before my end. Promise me that you shall marry according to my will," and he named a certain king's daughter who was to become his wife.

So distressed was the son that he did not even stop to think about what he was doing and said, "Yes, dear Father, your will shall be done."

The king then closed his eyes and died. Some time later, when the son had been proclaimed king and the period of mourning had passed, he had to keep the promise that he had given his father. So he made it known that he wanted to wed the king's daughter, and soon she was promised to him. When his first bride heard about that, she grieved so much about his infidelity that she almost died. Then her father said to her, "My dear child, why are you so sad? Name your wish, and I shall grant it."

She thought for a moment and then said, "Dear Father, I would like to have eleven young women who all look like me in face, form, and stature."

"If it's possible," said the king, "your wish shall be fulfilled." And he ordered his men to search all over his whole kingdom for as long as was necessary until they found eleven young women who looked exactly like his daughter in face, form, and stature.

When the young women appeared before the princess, she ordered twelve hunting outfits made, one just like the next, and the eleven young women had to put on the outfits, while she herself put on the twelfth. She then took leave of her father and rode away with the eleven young women until they came to the court of her former bridegroom, whom she loved so dearly. There she asked whether he needed any huntsmen and whether he would like to take all twelve of them into his service. The king looked at her and did not recognize her. But since they were fine-looking fellows, he said, yes, he would gladly employ them. And so they became the king's twelve huntsmen.

Now, the king had a lion that was a remarkable animal, for he could detect anything hidden and secret. One evening he happened to come to the king and said, "You think you've got twelve huntsmen?"

"Yes," said the king. "Twelve huntsmen they are."

"You're wrong," said the lion. "They're twelve women."

"That's not true at all," answered the king. "How are you going to prove that?"

"Oh, just have some peas scattered in your antechamber," responded the lion. "You'll be able to tell right away. Men walk firmly when they walk over peas. Not a pea will move. But women trip and skid and glide their feet, and the peas will roll."

The king liked his advice very much and ordered peas to be scattered over the floor. However, one of the king's servants was kindly disposed to the huntsmen, and when he heard that they were going to be put to a test, he went to them and told them everything. "The lion wants to prove to the king that you're women," he said.

The king's daughter thanked him and afterward spoke to her young women. "Control yourselves when you walk over the peas. Just step on them firmly."

The next morning, when the king summoned the twelve huntsmen to him and they entered the antechamber where the peas were lying, they stepped so firmly on them and had such a strong and steady gait that not a single pea moved or rolled. After they departed, the king said to the lion, "You lied to me. They walk like men."

"They knew they were being put to a test," answered the lion. "So they controlled themselves when they walked. Now, if you have twelve spinning wheels brought into the antechamber, they'll go over to them and be delighted. No man would ever do that."

The king liked the advice, and he ordered that twelve spinning wheels be brought into the antechamber. However, the servant who sided with the huntsmen went to them and revealed the lion's plan.

When they were alone, the princess said to the eleven young women, "Control yourselves and do not look at the spinning wheels when you enter the room."

The next morning, when the king summoned his twelve huntsmen, they came through the antechamber and did not even so much as glance at the spinning wheels. Once again the king said to the lion, "You lied to me. It's clear that they're men, for they didn't even glance at the spinning wheels."

"They knew they were being put to a test and thus controlled themselves," answered the lion.

However, the king did not believe him anymore. The twelve huntsmen became his steady companions whenever he went out hunting, and the longer they were with him, the fonder he grew of them. Now, it happened one day that news came of the king's betrothed, who was bound to arrive soon. When the true bride heard that, it was almost like a stab in her heart, and she was so hurt that she fell to the ground unconscious. The king, who thought that something had happened to his dear huntsman, ran over to help him and pulled off his glove. However, when he saw the ring that he had given to his first bride and looked at her face, he recognized her. His heart was moved so much that he gave her a kiss, and when she opened her eyes, he said, "You are mine, and I am yours. No one in the world can ever change that."

So the king sent a message to the other bride telling her to return to her own kingdom, for he already had a wife, and whoever finds his old key does not need a new one. Thereupon the wedding was celebrated, and the lion regained favor with the king, for he had really been telling the truth all along.

◆ 68 ◆

The Thief and His Master

JAN WANTED HIS SON TO LEARN A TRADE. Therefore, he went to church and prayed to the Lord to tell him what would be best for his son. The sexton was standing behind the altar and said, "Thieving, thieving."

So Jan went to his son and told him he had to learn how to be a thief because the Lord wanted it that way. He then set out with his son to look for a man who knew something about thieving. After they had traveled for a long time, they finally reached a great forest, where they found a little cottage with an old woman sitting inside.

"Do you happen to know a man who's good at thieving?" Jan asked.

"You can learn what you want here," said the woman. "My son's a master thief."

Then Jan talked with her son and asked him whether he was really good at thieving.

"Your son will be taught well," said the master thief. "Come back in a year, and if you can still recognize him, I won't take any money for my services. However, if you don't recognize him, you must give me two hundred talers."

The father went home again, and the son learned all kinds of witchcraft and thieving. When the year was over, the father set out by himself and began fretting because he did not know how he would be able to recognize his son. As he was walking along and fretting he encountered a little dwarf, who said, "Man, what are you worrying about? You look quite gloomy."

"Oh," Jan said, "I hired my son out as an apprentice to a master thief a year ago. He told me to return about now, and if I can't recognize my son, I must pay him two hundred talers. But if I recognize my son, I won't have to give him anything. Now I fear I won't be able to recognize him, and I don't know where I'll get the money to pay him."

Then the dwarf told him to take a crust of bread with him and stand beneath the chimney once he got there. "You'll see a basket up on the crossbeam, and a bird will peep out of it. That will be your son."

So Jan went there and threw a crust of black bread in front of the basket, and a bird came out and looked at it.

"Hello there, son, is that you?" said the father.

The son was glad to see his father, but the master thief said, "The devil must have given you the clue! How else could you have recognized your son?"

"Let's go, Father," said the boy.

Then the father and son set out for home. On the way a coach came driving by, and the son said, "I'm going to turn myself into a big greyhound. Then you can earn a lot of money by selling me."

A nobleman called from the coach, "Hey, my good fellow, do you want to sell your dog?"

"Yes," said the father.

"How much do you want for it?"

"Thirty talers."

"Well, man, that's certainly a lot, but since it's such a fine-looking dog, I'll pay."

The nobleman took the dog into his coach, but after they had driven along for a while, the dog jumped out of the coach window. Now he was no longer a greyhound and went back to his father.

They made their way home together, and on the following day there was a fair in the neighboring village. So the boy said to his father, "Now I'm going to turn myself into a fine-looking horse, and you'll sell me at the fair. But when you sell me, make sure that you take off the bridle so I can become a human being again."

The father took the horse to the fair, and the master thief came and bought the horse for a hundred talers. However, the father forgot to take off the bridle, and the master thief went home with the horse and put him in the stable. When the maid crossed the entrance to the stable, the horse cried out, "Take my bridle off! Take my bridle off!"

The maid stopped and listened. "My goodness! You can talk!"

She went and took the bridle off, and the horse became a sparrow and flew out the door. Then the master thief also became a sparrow and flew after him. They met and held a contest in midair, but the master lost and fell into the water, where he turned himself into a fish. The boy also turned himself into a fish, and they held another contest. Once again the master lost, and he turned himself into a rooster, while the boy changed himself into a fox and bit the master's head off. So the master died, and he has remained dead up to this very day.

◈ 69 ◈

Jorinda and Joringel

ONCE UPON A TIME there was an old castle in the middle of a great, dense forest. An old woman lived there all by herself, and she was a powerful sorceress. During the day she turned herself into a cat or a night owl, but in the evening she would return to her normal human form. She had the ability to lure game and birds, which she would slaughter and then cook or roast. If any man came within a hundred steps of the castle, she would cast a spell over him, so that he would not be able to move from the spot until she broke the spell. If an innocent maiden came within her magic circle, she would change her into a bird and stuff her into a wicker basket. Then she would carry the basket up to a room in her castle where she had well over seven thousand baskets with rare birds of this kind.

Now, once there was a maiden named Jorinda, who was more beautiful than any other maiden in the kingdom. She was betrothed to a handsome youth named Joringel. During the time before their marriage, they took great pleasure in being in each other's company. One day they went for a walk in the forest so they could be alone and talk intimately with one another.

"Be careful," Joringel said, "that you don't go too close to the castle."

At dusk the sun shone brightly through the tree trunks and cast its light on the dark green of the forest. The turtledoves were singing mournfully in the old beech trees, and at times Jorinda wept. Then she sat down in the sunshine and sighed, and Joringel sighed too. They became very sad as if they were doomed to die, and when they looked around them, they became confused and did not know how to get home. The sun was still shining half above and half behind the mountains. When Joringel looked through the bushes and saw the wall of the old castle not very far away, he became so alarmed that he was nearly frightened to death, while Jorinda sang:

"Oh, my bird, with your ring of red,
sitting and singing your tale of woe!
You tell us now that the poor dove is dead.
You sing your tale of woe—*oh-oh, oh-oh!*"

Just then, as Joringel looked at Jorinda, she was turned into a nightingale singing *"oh-oh, oh-oh!"* A night owl with glowing eyes flew around her three times, and each time it cried, *"To-whoo! To-whoo! To-whoo!"*

Joringel could not budge. He stood there like a stone, unable to weep, to talk, or to move hand or foot. When the sun was about to set, the owl flew into a bush and then immediately returned as a haggard old woman, yellow and scrawny, with large red eyes and a crooked nose that almost touched her chin with its tip. She muttered something to herself, caught the nightingale, and carried it away in her hand. Joringel was still unable to speak, nor could he move from the spot. The nightingale was gone. Soon the woman came back and said with a muffled voice, "Greetings, Zachiel. When the moon shines into the basket, let him loose, Zachiel, just at the right moment."

Then Joringel was set free, and he fell on his knees before the woman and begged her to give Jorinda back to him, but she said he would never get her back again and went away. He shouted, he wept, he moaned, but it was all in vain. "Oh, no, what's to become of me?"

Joringel went off and eventually came to an unfamiliar village, where he tended sheep for a long time. He often went round and round the castle and always kept his distance. Finally, he dreamed one night that he had found a flower as red as blood, and in the middle of it was a pearl. He plucked the flower and went with it to the castle: everything that he touched with the flower was set free from the magic spell. He also dreamed that he managed to regain his Jorinda with the flower.

When he awoke the next morning, he began searching all over the mountains and valleys for the flower of his dream. He searched for nine days, and early on the ninth day he found a flower as red as blood. In its middle was a large dewdrop as big as the finest pearl. He carried this flower day and night until he reached the castle. When he came to within a hundred steps of the castle, he was not spellbound but was able to get to the gate. Overjoyed by that, Joringel touched the gate with the flower, and it sprang open. So he entered, crossed the courtyard, and listened for the sound of birds. Finally, he heard them and went toward the room where the sorceress was feeding the birds in their seven thousand baskets. When she saw Joringel, she became angry, very angry. She began berating him and spitting poison and gall at him, but she could only come within two feet of him, and he paid no attention to her. Instead, he went and examined the baskets with the birds. Since there were hundreds of nightingales, he did not know how he would be able to find his Jorinda again. While he was examining the baskets, he noticed that the old woman had stealthily picked up one of the baskets and was heading toward the door. Quick as a flash he ran over and touched the basket with the flower and the old woman as well. Now she could no longer use her magic, and thus Jorinda appeared before him. She threw her arms around his neck and was just as beautiful as before. After Joringel had turned all the other birds into young women, he went home with his Jorinda, and they lived happily together for a long time.

◈ 70 ◈

The Three Sons of Fortune

A FATHER ONCE CALLED HIS THREE SONS to him and gave the first a rooster, the second a scythe, and the third a cat.

"I'm already quite old," he said, "and my death is near. So I want to provide for you before my end. I have no money, and what I'm giving you now does not seem to be worth much. But everything depends on whether you use these gifts intelligently. Just search for a country where such things are still unknown, and your fortune will be made."

After the father's death, the oldest son set out with his rooster, but wherever he went, the people already knew about roosters. As he approached the cities he saw roosters from afar perched on towers and turning with the wind. As he approached villages he heard several roosters crowing, and nobody found anything remarkable about his bird. It seemed as if the oldest son would not make his fortune with the rooster, but finally he landed on an island where the people knew nothing about roosters and did not even know how to regulate the time of their days. To be sure, they knew when it was morning and evening, but if they happened to wake during the night, then nobody knew how to determine what time it was.

"Just look at this noble creature!" he said. "It's got a ruby red crown on its head and wears spurs like a knight. It will crow three times during the night at set hours, and when it crows the last time, you'll know that the sun is about to rise. But, if it crows during broad daylight, you'd better prepare yourself for a certain change in the weather."

The people were extremely pleased by the rooster, and they did not sleep a wink the next night so that they could listen and enjoy the rooster, which crowed loudly and clearly at two, four, and six in the morning to announce the time. Then they asked him whether the rooster was for sale and how much he wanted for it.

"I want about as much gold as a donkey can carry," he answered.

"So little for such a precious bird!" they all exclaimed as if in a chorus, and they gladly gave him what he demanded.

When he returned home with his wealth, his brothers were astounded, and the second said, "Well, it's time for me to set out and see whether I can make as much of a profit with my scythe as you did with your rooster."

At first it did not seem he would, for everywhere he went he met farmers with scythes on their shoulders just as good as his. However, he eventually reached an island where the people knew nothing about scythes. When the grain was ripe there, they brought cannons to the fields and shot down the grain. That was a very uncertain way of doing things: some of the cannons would hit targets beyond the grain, while others would shoot off the ears instead of the stems. A great deal was destroyed in the process, and over and beyond that, the noise was unbearable. So the man went out to the fields and began to mow the grain so quietly and quickly that the people gaped in amazement. They were willing to give him anything he wanted for the scythe, and he received a horse loaded with as much gold as it could carry.

Now the third brother wanted to see if he could make something out of his cat, and he had the exact same experiences as his brothers. As long as he stayed on the mainland, he accomplished nothing: there were cats everywhere. Indeed, there were so many that the newborn kittens were generally thrown into the water to drown. Therefore, he sailed to an island, and fortunately for him, it happened that nobody there had ever seen a cat before. In fact, the mice had multiplied so much that they had gained the upper hand. They could dance all over the tables and benches whether the master was home or not. The people complained a great deal about this plague, and even the king in his castle did not know what to do about it: there were mice squeaking in every corner and gnawing whatever they could lay hold of with their teeth.

Once the cat began to hunt them, she was soon able to clear out several rooms in the castle. So the people begged the king to buy this miraculous creature for the kingdom. The king gladly gave the third brother what he demanded, and that was a mule loaded with gold, and he returned home with the greatest treasure of all.

The cat continued to have a great time hunting mice in the royal castle, and she killed so many that it was impossible to count them. Finally, she became hot from all that work and got thirsty. So she stopped in her tracks, turned her head, and cried out, *"Meow! Meow!"*

Upon hearing these strange cries, the king and his entire court became so terrified that they all ran out of the castle in dread. When they were outside the castle, the king held a council meeting to determine what measures should be taken. At last it was decided to send a page to the cat to demand that she leave the castle or be removed by force. The councillors said, "Since we're accustomed to the mice, it would be better to be plagued by them than to surrender our lives to such a monster."

So the page went to the castle to ask the cat whether she would voluntarily evacuate the castle. But the cat, whose thirst had become even greater in the meantime, merely answered with *"Meow! Meow!"*

The page understood that to mean "Not at all! Not at all!" and he brought the reply to the king.

"Well," said the councillors. "She shall have to yield to force."

Cannons were brought before the castle, which was soon set on fire by a barrage of shots. When the fire reached the room where the cat was sitting, she jumped safely out of the window. However, the besiegers did not stop until the whole castle was leveled to the ground.

◈ 71 ◈

How Six Made Their Way in the World

ONCE UPON A TIME there was a man who had mastered all kinds of skills. He had fought in the war and had conducted himself correctly and courageously, but when the war was over, he was discharged and received three pennies for traveling expenses.

"Just you wait!" he said. "I won't put up with that. If I find the right people, I'll force the king to turn over all the treasures of his kingdom to me."

Full of rage, he went into the forest, and there he saw a man tearing up six trees as if they were blades of wheat. "Will you be my servant and travel with me?" he asked.

"Yes," the man answered. "But first I want to bring this little bundle of firewood home to my mother." He took one of the trees and wrapped it around the others, lifted the bundle onto his shoulders, and carried it away. Then he returned and went off with his master, who said, "We two shall certainly make our way anywhere in the world."

After they had walked for a while, they found a huntsman who was kneeling down and taking aim at something with his gun.

"Huntsman, what are you going to shoot?" the master asked him.

"There's a fly sitting on the branch of an oak tree two miles from here. I want to shoot out its left eye," he answered.

"Oh, come with me," said the man. "If we three stick together, we'll certainly make our way anywhere in the world."

The huntsman was willing and went with him. As they approached seven windmills they saw the sails rotating swiftly, even though there was no wind coming from any direction, nor was there a leaf stirring.

"What in the world can be driving those windmills? There's not a breeze around," the man said. He continued on with his servants for about two miles, and then they saw a man sitting on a tree. He was holding one nostril closed while blowing through the other.

"My goodness! What are you doing up there?" the man asked.

"Two miles from here are seven windmills," he said. "I'm blowing them so that they'll turn."

"Oh, come with me," said the man. "If we four stick together, we'll certainly make our way anywhere in the world."

So the blower got down from the tree and went along with them. After some time they saw a man standing on one leg, while the other was lying unbuckled on the ground next to him.

"You've made things comfortable for yourself," said the man. "Time for a rest, I suppose?"

"I'm a runner," he answered, "and I've unbuckled my leg so that I don't run too fast. When I run with two legs, I go faster than any bird can fly."

"Oh, come with me. If we five stick together, we certainly shall make our way anywhere in the world."

So he went along with them, and shortly thereafter they met a man who was wearing a cap that completely covered one of his ears.

"Where are your manners?" the master asked him. "You shouldn't drape your cap over one ear like that. You look like a dunce."

"It's got to be this way," said the man. "If I put on my cap straight, then a tremendous frost will come, and all the birds in the air will freeze and drop down dead to the ground."

"Oh, come with me," said the master. "If we six stick together, we'll certainly make our way anywhere in the world."

Now the six came to a city where the king had proclaimed that whoever ran a race against his daughter and won would become her husband. But whoever lost would have to pay for it with his head. Then the man appeared before the king and said, "I want to race but under the condition that one of my servants runs for me."

The king answered, "Then his life must also be placed at stake, and you and he will forfeit your lives if you lose."

When they agreed on the terms and everything was set, the master buckled on the runner's other leg and said to him, "Now show us how quick you are and help us win."

The runner and the king's daughter were both given jugs and set off running at the same time. Yet, within seconds after the king's daughter had run but a short stretch, the spectators could no longer see the runner, for he soared by them just like the wind. In a short time he arrived at the spring, filled the jug with water, and turned around. Halfway back, however, he was overcome by fatigue, put the jug on the ground, lay down, and fell asleep. For his pillow he had taken a dead horse's skull that had been lying on the ground so that he would not be too comfortable and would wake up in time to continue the race. In the meantime, the king's daughter, who was much better at running than ordinary people, had reached the spring and was hurrying back with her jug full of water. When she saw the runner lying asleep on the ground, she was delighted and said, "Now the enemy's been delivered into my hands." She emptied his jug and continued running. Everything would have been lost for the runner if the huntsman had not by chance been standing on the top of the castle and if he had not seen everything with his sharp eyes.

"I'll make sure that the king's daughter does not defeat us!" he said, and he loaded his gun and aimed so carefully that he shot the horse's skull out from under the runner's head without hurting him. The runner awoke, jumped up, and saw that his jug was empty and that the king's daughter was way ahead of him. However, he did not lose heart, but ran back to the spring with the jug, filled it anew with water, and managed to beat the king's daughter home with ten minutes to spare.

"You see," he said, "it was about time that I really started using my legs. I wouldn't exactly call that *running*, what I was doing before."

However, the king was vexed—and his daughter, even more so— that a common discharged soldier should win the race. Therefore, they consulted with each other, seeking a way to get rid of him and all his companions as well. Finally, the king said to her, "I've got an idea. Don't fret. They'll never show their faces around here again." Then he went to the six and said, "I want you to eat, drink, and be merry," and he led them to a room that had an iron floor. The doors were also made of iron, and the windows were lined with iron bars. In the room there was a table covered with delicious food, and the king said to them, "Go inside and enjoy yourselves."

When they were inside, the king had the door locked and bolted. Then he summoned the cook and commanded him to make a fire and keep it going under the room until the iron became burning hot. The cook did that, and it began to get hot in the room. The six, who were sitting at the table, felt very warm, but they thought this was due to the food. However, when the heat became greater and greater and they wanted to leave the room, they found the doors and windows locked. Now they realized that the king had devised something evil and meant to suffocate them.

"He won't succeed!" said the man with the cap. "I'm going to let a frost come that will put the fire to shame and send it crawling away."

So he put his cap on straight, and immediately there was a frost, causing all the heat to disappear and the food on the table to freeze. After two hours had passed and the king thought they had all perished in the heat, he had the door opened and looked in himself to see how they were. Yet, when the door was opened, all six of them were well and vigorous. Indeed, they declared that it would be nice to get outside and warm themselves, for the food had frozen to the dishes because of the cold conditions in the room. The king stormed furiously down the stairs, scolded the cook, and asked him why he had not done what he had ordered. But the cook answered, "There's more than enough heat. Just look for yourself."

The king saw a tremendous fire blazing under the iron room and realized that he could not get the better of the six by doing something like that. So he tried to think of something new to get rid of the unwelcome guests. He summoned the master and said, "If you will accept gold and give up your claim to my daughter, you can take away as much gold as you like."

"That's fine with me, Your Majesty," he answered. "If you give me as much as my servant can carry, I won't claim your daughter."

The king was satisfied with that, and the master added, "In two weeks I shall return here to fetch the gold." Then he summoned all the tailors in the entire kingdom, and for two weeks they had to sit and sew a sack. When it was finished, the strong man, who could tear up trees, swung the sack over his shoulder and went to the king, who said, "Who's that powerful fellow carrying such a bundle of canvas on his shoulder? Why, it's as big as a house!" Suddenly he became horrified and thought, What a lot of gold he'll carry away! So the king ordered that a ton of gold be brought, and all of that took sixteen of his strongest men to carry, but the strong man grabbed it with one hand, put it into the sack and said, "Why don't you bring more right away? This will barely cover the bottom."

Gradually, the king had his whole treasure brought, and the strong man tossed it all into the sack, but it only became half full.

"Bring some more!" the strong man cried. "These few crumbs aren't enough to fill it."

So seventeen thousand wagons of gold from all over the kingdom had to be driven to the spot, and the strong man stuffed them all into the sack along with the oxen that were harnessed to the wagons.

"Since I don't have the time to inspect everything," he said, "I'll just take what comes until the sack's completely full."

When everything was in the sack, there was still room for a lot more, but the strong man said, "I think it's time to put an end to this. Sometimes one has to tie up a sack even if it's not quite full." Then he hoisted it onto this back and went away with his companions.

When the king saw one single man carrying away all the treasures of his kingdom, he was furious and ordered his cavalry to pursue the six and take the sack away from the strong man. Two of the king's regiments soon caught up with the six and called to them:

"You're our prisoners! Put down the sack with the gold, or else you'll be cut to pieces!"

"What did you say?" asked the blower. "We're your prisoners? Before that ever happens, all of you will soon be dancing around in the air." With that he held one nostril and blew through the other at the two regiments, sending them flying in every which direction, up into the blue and over hill and dale. Some were scattered this way, others that way, while a sergeant begged for mercy. Since he was a brave fellow, who had nine wounds and did not deserve to be humiliated, the blower let up a bit, and the sergeant came out of it without being harmed. Then the blower said to him, "Now go home to the king and tell him, all he has to do is send a few more regiments, and I'll blow them all sky high!"

When the king received the message, he said, "Let those fellows go. There's something extraordinary about them."

So the six brought their wealth back home, divided it among themselves, and lived happily until their death.

❖ 72 ❖

The Wolf and the Man

ONCE THE FOX WAS TELLING THE WOLF about the strength of human beings, and he maintained that no animal could defeat a man. Therefore, animals had to use cunning if they were to protect themselves against him.

"If only I could have a chance to see a man just once, then I'd go after him just the same!" answered the wolf.

"I can help you do that," said the fox. "Just come to me early tomorrow morning, and I'll show you one."

The wolf was right on time early the next day, and the fox brought him to the path that the huntsman took every day. First came an old discharged soldier.

"Is that a man?" asked the wolf.

"No," answered the fox. "That used to be one."

Next came a little boy who was on his way to school.

"Is that a man?"

"No, but he'll become one someday."

Finally, the huntsman came with a double-barreled gun on his back and a hunting knife at his side. Then the fox said to the wolf, "Look, here comes a man. You can go after him, but as for me, I'm going back to my den."

So the wolf went after the man, and when the huntsman saw him coming, he said, "It's a shame that I didn't load my gun with bullets." Still, he took aim and let the wolf have a load of buckshot in his face.

The wolf winced but did not let himself be frightened. Indeed, he kept charging so that the huntsman let him have a second load of buckshot. Yet, the wolf was able to bear the pain and sprang at the huntsman, who now drew out his shiny knife and gave him a few gashes left and right, causing the wolf to bleed all over and return howling to the fox.

"Well, brother wolf," said the fox, "did you manage to finish off the man?"

"Ah," answered the wolf. "I had no idea that the man was so strong. First he took a stick from his shoulder and blew into it. Then something flew into my face that tickled me in the most terrible way. After that he blew into the stick again, and something flew into my nose like lightning and hail. When I got very close, he drew a shiny rib from his body and began beating me so badly that I almost lost my life."

"You see what a braggart you are!" said the fox. "You always talk so big that your deeds can never match your words."

◈ 73 ◈

The Wolf and the Fox

THE WOLF HAD THE FOX LIVING WITH HIM, and since the wolf was stronger, the fox had to do whatever the wolf wanted. So the fox's greatest desire was to get rid of his master.

One day they both happened to be walking through the forest, and the wolf said, "Red Fox, get me something to eat, or else I'll eat you instead!"

"I know of a farmyard where there are two young lambs," the fox responded. "If you want, we can go and fetch one."

That was fine with the wolf, and off they went. The fox stole a little lamb, brought it to the wolf, and departed. Meanwhile, the wolf ate the lamb but was not satisfied. He wanted to have the other as well and went to fetch it. However, he was so clumsy while trying to get it that the lamb's mother heard him and made such a terrible noise by bleating and whining that the farmers came running. Upon discovering the wolf, they beat him mercilessly until he retreated, limping and howling, back home to the fox.

"That was some trap you led me into!" he said. "I wanted to get the other lamb, but the farmers caught me and beat me to a pulp."

"Why are you such a glutton?" replied the fox.

The following day they went out into the fields again, and once more the greedy wolf said, "Red Fox, get me something to eat, or else I'll eat you instead!"

"I know of a farmhouse where the wife will be baking pancakes tonight. Let's go there and get some."

They went to the farm, and the fox sneaked around the house, looking and sniffing about until he discovered where the dish was. Then he snatched six pancakes and brought them to the wolf.

"Now you've got plenty to eat," he said and went his way.

The wolf gulped down the pancakes in a jiffy and said, "They've only increased my appetite." So he went to the farmhouse and reached for the dish. However, it fell to the ground and made such a tremendous crash that the farmer's wife came out. When she saw the wolf, she called some people, who rushed to her side and beat the wolf so badly that he ran back to the fox in the forest with two lame legs and howled like mad. "That was some nasty trap you led me into!" he exclaimed. "The farmers caught me and tanned my hide."

However, the fox answered, "Why are you such a glutton?"

On the third day they were out in the fields again, and although the wolf could only limp with great difficulty, he said:

"Red Fox, get me something to eat, or else I'll eat you instead!"

"I know of a man who's been doing some slaughtering, and the salted meat is in a barrel in his cellar. Let's go and get it."

"This time I'm going to tag along with you," said the wolf. "Then you can help me if I can't get away."

"That's all right with me," said the fox, and he showed him all the shortcuts and ways that enabled them finally to get into the cellar. There they found plenty of meat, and immediately the wolf began gobbling it down. I've got some time before I have to stop, he thought.

The fox also enjoyed the meat, but he kept looking around, and he often ran to the hole through which they had come, to make sure that his body was still thin enough to slip through.

"My dear fox," said the wolf, "could you tell me why you're continuously running back and forth and jumping in and out of the cellar?"

"I just want to see if anybody's coming," the sly fox answered. "Just don't eat too much."

Right at that moment the farmer came. He had heard the fox jumping in and out of the cellar. When the fox saw him coming, he went right through the hole in one jump and landed outside. The wolf wanted to follow him, but he had eaten too much and was so fat that he could not get through. Consequently, he got stuck in the hole. Then the farmer came with a club and beat him to death, while the fox ran into the forest, glad to be rid of the old glutton.

◆ 74 ◆

The Fox and His Cousin

THE SHE-WOLF GAVE BIRTH TO A CUB and invited the fox to be godfather. "In truth, he is a close relative of ours," she said. "He's got a good head on his shoulders and is very clever. He can instruct my son and help him get by in the world."

The fox appeared, made an honorable impression, and said, "My dear cousin, whom I hold in such great esteem, thank you for the honor that you have bestowed on me. You can rest assured that I shall conduct myself in a way that will make you happy."

The fox enjoyed the meal during the christening feast, and he was very merry. Afterward he said, "My dear cousin, it is our duty to look after the child. You must have good food so that he'll grow big and strong. I know a barn full of sheep where we can easily fetch a good piece of meat."

The wolf liked the suggestion, and she went out with the fox toward the barnyard. He pointed out the barn to her from the distance and said, "You'll be able to creep in there unnoticed. In the meantime, I'll look around on the other side to see whether I can catch a chicken."

He did not move, however, but lay down, stretched out his legs, and rested at the edge of the forest. The wolf crept into the barn but came across a dog that made such a racket that the farmers came running. They caught the wolf and poured burning lye over her coat. Nevertheless, she managed to escape and dragged herself into the forest. The fox was lying there and made sounds as if he were moaning. "Ah!" he said, "dear wolf, I've had a terrible time of it! The farmers attacked me and broke every limb of my body! If you don't want me to waste away here and perish, you must carry me away."

Although the wolf herself could barely move, she was greatly worried about the fox. Therefore, she lifted him onto her back and slowly carried the fox, who was perfectly sound and fit, toward her house. When they arrived, he cried out, "Farewell, dear cousin, I hope the roasting you got has done you some good!"

The fox laughed in her face and then ran off.

◆ 75 ◆

The Fox and the Cat

ONE DAY THE CAT HAPPENED TO MEET MR. FOX in the forest, and because she thought to herself, He is so clever, experienced, and greatly respected in the world, she spoke to him in a friendly way. "Good day, my dear Mr. Fox. How are things going with you? What's up? How are you managing in these hard times?"

The fox, consumed by his own arrogance, examined the cat from head to toe and pondered for some time whether he should deign to answer or not. Finally, he said, "Oh, you miserable whisker-licker, you spotted fool, you meager mouse-hunter, what nerve you have! How dare you ask how things are going with me? What have you ever learned? How many skills have you acquired?"

"I can do only one thing," responded the cat modestly.

"What's that?" asked the fox.

"When the dogs are chasing after me, I can save myself by scrambling up a tree."

"Is that all?" said the fox. "I've acquired over a hundred skills and have a bagful of tricks besides. You're so pitiful that you make me want to cry. But I'll take you with me and teach you how to get away from dogs."

Just at that moment a huntsman approached with four dogs. The cat sprang nimbly up a tree and sat down at the top, where the branches and leaves completely concealed her.

"Open your bag, Mr. Fox! Open your bag!" the cat called out to him, but the dogs had already pounced on him and held him tight.

"Oh, Mr. Fox," cried the cat, "you and your hundred skills don't seem to be working right now. If you had been able to climb up here like me, you wouldn't be doomed to die!"

◆ 76 ◆

The Pink Flower

THERE ONCE WAS A QUEEN whom the Lord had prevented from having children. Every morning she went into the garden and begged God in heaven to bestow a son or daughter on her. Eventually, an angel came down from heaven and said, "You may now rest content. You shall have a son who will have the power to wish for anything he wants in the world and have all his wishes granted."

The queen went to the king and told him the good news, and when the time came, she gave birth to a son, and the king's joy was great. Soon she began taking walks every day with her child in the animal park, and it was there that she bathed herself in a clear spring. Once, when the child was already somewhat older, she happened to fall asleep holding him on her lap. Then the old cook, who knew the child possessed magic wishing powers, came by and stole the boy away from her. Next the cook took a chicken, tore it apart, and let the blood drip on her apron and dress. Then he carried the child to a secret place, where a wet nurse was compelled to suckle him. Finally, he ran to the king and accused the queen of allowing her child to be stolen by wild animals. When the king saw the blood on her apron, he believed the cook and became so furious that he had a tall tower built that neither the rays of the sun nor the rays of the moon could penetrate. Then he ordered his wife to be walled up and imprisoned in this tower, where she was to sit for seven years without food or drink so she would perish. However, God sent her two angels. They came to her from heaven in the form of white doves and were commanded to fly to her twice a day and to bring her food until the seven years were over.

Meanwhile, the cook kept thinking, If the child has the power of wishing and I'm here, then he could easily bring about my end. So he left the castle and went to the boy, who was already big enough to talk.

"Wish yourself a beautiful castle with a garden and everything else that goes along with it," he said.

No sooner did the boy complete the wish than everything that he had wished for stood before him. After some time had passed, the cook said, "It's not good for you to be so alone, wish yourself a beautiful maiden to keep you company."

So the prince wished for a maiden, and all at once she stood before him and was more beautiful than any painter could have portrayed her. Now, the two of them played together and loved each other with all their hearts, and the old cook went hunting like a nobleman. However, it occurred to him that the prince might one day wish to be with his father, and this thought disturbed the cook a great deal. So he went out, took the maiden aside, and said, "Tonight, when the boy's asleep, go to his bed and plunge this knife into his heart and bring me his heart and tongue. If you refuse to do this, you will lose your own life."

Thereupon he went away, and when he returned the next day, she had not done it and said, "Why should I shed innocent blood when the boy has never harmed a living soul."

"If you continue to refuse, then it will cost you your own life," the cook declared again.

When he had gone away, she had a little fawn fetched and slaughtered. Then she took out its heart and tongue and put them on a plate. When she saw the old cook coming, she said to the boy, "Lie down in bed and pull the covers over you."

Then the villain entered and said, "Where's the boy's heart and tongue?"

The maiden handed him the plate, but the prince threw the covers off him and said, "You old sinner! Why did you want to kill me? Now I shall pronounce your sentence: You shall become a black poodle and wear a golden chain around your neck, and you shall eat burning coals until the flames come spewing from your throat."

Immediately after these words were said, the old man was turned into a poodle and had a golden chain around his neck. All the cooks of the castle were ordered to bring him live coals, which he ate until he spewed flames from his throat. The prince remained in the castle a little longer, but he continued to think about his mother and wonder whether she was still alive. Finally, he said to the maiden, "I want to return to my homeland. If you'll come with me, then I'll take good care of you."

"Ah," she answered. "It's a long way off, and what shall I do in a foreign country where nobody knows me?"

Since she did not really want to go and they did not want to be separated from each other, he made a wish that turned her into a beautiful pink flower and then he put her into his pocket. Then he went back to his homeland, and the poodle had to tag along after him. His first stop was the tower in which his mother was imprisoned. Since the tower was so high, he wished for a ladder that would reach the top. Thereupon he climbed the ladder, looked inside, and called out, "Dearest Mother, Your Royal Highness, are you still alive, or are you dead?"

"I've just eaten, and I'm content," she answered, for she thought that the angels had come.

"I'm your dear son that the wild animals supposedly stole from your lap," he said. "But I'm still alive and shall rescue you soon."

Now he climbed down, went to his father, and had himself announced as a huntsman from a foreign land seeking employment. The king answered that he was willing to employ him if he was a skillful huntsman and could procure game for him. However, there had never been deer or any other game in the entire region or even on its borders. Still, the huntsman promised to provide him with as much venison as he needed for the royal table. Then he ordered all the huntsmen to assemble and ride out into the forest with him. After they went outside, he ordered them to form a circle that was to remain open at one end, and he stepped stepped into the middle of the circle and began wishing. Suddenly some two hundred or more deer came running into the circle, and the huntsmen shot them dead. Afterward the dead animals were loaded onto sixty farm wagons and driven back home to the king. After having gone many years without it, the king, for once, was able to deck his table with venison.

So delighted was the king by the game that he ordered the entire court to dine with him the following day, and he made a great banquet. When they were all gathered together, the king said to the huntsman, "Because you were so skillful, you shall sit next to me."

"My Lord and Majesty, I beg your pardon. I'm nothing but a common huntsman."

However, the king said, "You shall sit next to me," and insisted until the huntsman did as he was told.

While the huntsman was sitting there, he thought about his mother and wished that one of the king's high officials would ask after the queen, how she was doing in the tower and whether she was still alive or had perished. No sooner had he wished it than the marshal began to speak: "Your Majesty, we're sitting here and celebrating in joy, but how is the queen doing in the tower? Is she still alive or has she perished?"

"She let my dear son be torn to pieces by wild beasts," the king answered. "So I don't want to hear anything about her."

Then the huntsman stood up and said, "Most gracious Father, she's still alive, and I am her son. The wild beasts did not steal me. Rather it was the evil old cook who took me from her arms after she had fallen asleep. And it was he who sprinkled the blood of a chicken on her apron." He then took the dog with the golden chain and said, "This is the villain," and he ordered burning coals brought, which the dog was forced to eat in the presence of the entire court, so that flames spewed from his throat. After that the huntsman asked the king if he wanted to see the cook in his true form and then wished the dog back into the cook, who suddenly stood there in a white apron with a knife at his side. When the king saw him, he became furious and ordered him to be thrown into the deepest dungeon.

The huntsman resumed talking and said, "Father, do you also want to see the maiden who looked after me so tenderly and was supposed to murder me but refused, even though her own life was at stake?"

"Yes," the king answered. "I'd like to see her very much."

"Most gracious Father," said the son. "I'm going to show her to you in the form of a beautiful flower." And he reached into his pocket, pulled out the pink flower, and placed it on the royal table. The king had never seen a flower as beautiful as that. His son then said to him, "Now I'll show her to you in her true form," and he wished the flower to become a maiden. All at once she was there and was so beautiful that no painter could ever have made her look more beautiful.

Now the king sent two chambermaids and two servants to the tower to fetch the queen to the royal table. But, when she was led into the hall, she refused to eat anything at all and said, "Our most gracious and merciful Lord, who kept me alive in the tower, shall soon grant me salvation."

She lived three days more and then died in bliss. After she was buried, the two white doves that had brought her the food in the tower and who were really angels from heaven, followed her and perched on her grave. The old king had the cook torn into four parts, but his grief gnawed at his heart, and he died soon after. His son married the beautiful maiden whom he had brought home in his pocket in the form of a flower, and only God knows whether they are still living today.

◈ 77 ◈

Clever Gretel

THERE WAS ONCE A COOK NAMED GRETEL, who wore shoes with red heels, and when she went out in them, she whirled this way and that way and was as happy as a lark. "You really are quite pretty!" she would say to herself. And when she returned home, she would drink some wine out of sheer delight. Since the wine would whet her appetite, she would take the best things she was cooking and taste them until she was content. Then she would say, "The cook must know what the food tastes like!"

One day her master happened to say to her, "Gretel, tonight I'm having a guest for dinner. Prepare two chickens for me and make them as tasty as possible."

"I'll take care of it, sir," Gretel responded. So she killed two chickens, scalded them, plucked them, stuck them on a spit, and toward evening placed them over a fire to roast. The chickens began to turn brown and were almost ready, but the guest did not make his appearance. So Gretel called to her master, "If the guest doesn't come soon, I'll have to take the chickens off the fire. It would be a great shame if they weren't eaten now, while they're still at their juiciest."

"Then I'll run and fetch the guest myself," said the master.

When the master had left the house, Gretel laid the spit with the chickens to one side and thought, If I keep standing by the fire, I'll just sweat and get thirsty. Who knows when they'll come? Meanwhile, I'll hop down into the cellar and take a drink.

She ran downstairs, filled a jug with wine, and said, "May God bless it for you, Gretel!" and she took a healthy swig. "The wine flows nicely," she continued talking, "and it's not good to interrupt the flow." So she took another long swig. Then she went upstairs and placed the chickens back over the fire, basted them with butter, and merrily turned the spit. Since the roast chickens smelled so good, Gretel thought, Perhaps something's missing. I'd better taste them to see how they are. She touched one of them with her finger and said, "Goodness! The chickens are really good! It's a crying shame not to eat them all at once!" She ran to the window to see if her master was on his way with the guest, but when she saw no one coming, she returned to the chickens and thought, That one wing is burning. I'd better eat it up.

So she cut it off, ate it, and enjoyed it. When she had finished, she thought, I'd better eat the other wing or else my master will notice that something's missing. After she had consumed the two wings, she returned to the window, looked for her master, but was unable to see him. Who knows, it suddenly occurred to her, Perhaps they've decided not to come and have stopped somewhere along the way. Then she said to herself, "Hey, Gretel, cheer up! You've already taken a nice chunk. Have another drink and eat it all up! When it's gone, there'll be no reason for you to feel guilty. Why should God's good gifts go to waste?"

Once again she ran down into the cellar, took a good honest drink, and then went back to eat up the chicken with relish. When the one chicken had been eaten and her master still had not returned, Gretel looked at the other bird and said, "Where one is, the other should be too. The two of them belong together: whatever's right for one is right for the other. I think if I have another drink, it won't do me any harm." Therefore she took another healthy swig and let the second chicken run to join the other.

Just as she was in the midst of enjoying her meal, her master came back and called, "Hurry, Gretel, the guest will soon be here!"

"Yes, sir, I'll get everything ready," answered Gretel.

Meanwhile, the master checked to see if the table was properly set and took out the large knife with which he wanted to carve the chickens and began sharpening it on the steps in the hallway. As he was doing that the guest came and knocked nicely and politely at the door. Gretel ran and looked to see who was there, and when she saw the guest, she put her finger to her lips and whispered, "Shhh, be quiet! Get out of here as quick as you can! If my master catches you, you'll be done for. It's true he invited you to dinner, but he really wants to cut off both your ears. Listen to him sharpening his knife!"

The guest heard the sharpening and hurried back down the steps as fast as he could. Gretel wasted no time and ran screaming to her master. "What kind of guest did you invite!" she cried.

"Goodness gracious, Gretel! Why do you ask? What do you mean?"

"Well," she said, "he snatched both chickens just as I was about to bring them to the table, and he's run away with them!"

"That's not at all a nice way to behave!" said her master, and he was disappointed by the loss of the fine chickens. "At least he could have left me one of them so I'd have something to eat."

He then shouted after the guest to stop running, but the guest pretended not to hear. So the master ran after him, with the knife still in his hand, and screamed, "Just one, just one!" merely meaning that the guest should at least leave him one of the chickens and not take both. But the guest thought that his host was after just one of his ears, and to make sure that he would reach home safely with both his ears, he ran as if someone had lit a fire under his feet.

◈ 78 ◈

The Old Man and His Grandson

ONCE UPON A TIME there was a very old man, so old that his eyes had grown dim, his ears were hard of hearing, and his knees trembled. When he sat at the table, he could barely hold his spoon, and often he spilled soup on the tablecloth, while some of it would also drip from his mouth. His son and daughter-in-law found this disgusting and eventually forced the old grandfather to sit in a corner behind the stove. They gave him his food in a clay bowl and very little at that. Whenever he would glance sadly in the direction of the table, tears would well up in his eyes.

One day his hands trembled so much that he could not even hold on to the bowl, and it fell to the ground and broke. The young woman scolded him, but he only sighed and did not respond. So for a few pennies she bought him a wooden bowl, and from then on he had to eat out of that. Some time later, as they were sitting there again, the small four-year-old grandson was piecing together some wooden planks on the ground.

"What are you doing?" asked the father.

"I'm making a little trough," answered the child. "My mother and father shall eat out of it when I grow up."

Then husband and wife looked at each other for a while and soon began to weep. Within seconds they brought the old grandfather back to the table, and from then on they always let him eat with them. Nor did they ever say anything again if he happened to spill a little something here and there.

◈ 79 ◈

The Water Nixie

A LITTLE BROTHER AND SISTER were playing by a well, and while they were playing, they both fell into the water. Down at the bottom of the well was a nixie, who said, "Now I've got you, and now you shall work hard for me." And she took them away with her.

She gave the girl dirty, tangled flax to spin and a bottomless bucket to carry water in. The boy was forced to chop down a tree with a blunt ax, and all they got to eat were dumplings that were as hard as rocks. Eventually, the children lost their patience, and one Sunday they waited until the nixie was in church and then ran away.

When church was over, the nixie found that the chickens had flown the coop, and she pursued them by taking leaps and bounds. However, the children saw her coming from afar, and the girl threw behind her a brush, which formed a huge mountain with thousands and thousands of bristles, and the nixie had great difficulty climbing over them. At last she made it over, and when the children saw that, the boy threw behind him a comb, which formed a huge mountain with thousands and thousands of teeth, but the nixie managed to grab hold of them and eventually climbed over. Then the girl threw behind her a mirror, which formed a glass mountain. It was so very, very slippery that it was impossible to cross, and the nixie thought, I'd better run home and fetch my ax. Then I'll cut the glass mountain in two. But by the time she had returned and had chopped up the glass, the children had long since made their escape, and the water nixie had to trudge back home.

◆ 80 ◆

The Death of the Hen

ONCE A HEN WENT WITH A ROOSTER TO THE NUT HILL, and they agreed that whoever found a kernel would share it with the other. Soon the hen found a very big nut, but she kept quiet about it because she wanted to eat the kernel all by herself. However, the kernel was so large that she could not swallow it, and it got stuck in her throat. Fearing that she might choke to death, she screamed, "Rooster, please run as fast as you can and fetch me some water or else I'll choke to death!"

The rooster ran as fast as he could to the well and said, "Well, you must give me some water. The hen's lying on the nut hill, and she's about to choke to death."

"First run to the bride," the well answered, "and get some red silk for me."

The rooster ran to the bride and said, "Bride, I need some red silk from you. The silk is for the well, who'll give me some water to take to the hen, who's lying on the nut hill, where she's swallowed a large kernel and is about to choke to death."

The bride answered, "First run and fetch me my wreath that got caught on the branch of a willow."

So the rooster ran to the willow, pulled the wreath from the branch, and brought it back to the bride. In return the bride gave him some red silk, and the rooster brought it to the well, who gave him water in exchange. Then the rooster brought the water to the hen, but by the time he reached her, she had choked to death and lay there motionless and dead. The rooster became so sad that he uttered a loud cry, and all the animals came and mourned for her. Six mice built a little wagon that was to carry the hen to her grave. When the wagon was finished, the mice harnessed themselves to it, and the rooster was to drive the wagon. Along the way they encountered the fox, who asked, "Where are you going, rooster?"

"I'm off to bury the hen."

"May I ride with you?"

"Yes, but since you're heavy, take a seat in the back. If you sat up front, my horses would fall, and the wagon would crack!"

The fox sat down in the back. Then the wolf, the bear, the stag, the lion, and all the animals in the forest took a seat in the back. Thus they continued their journey until they came to a brook.

"How shall we get across?" asked the rooster.

A straw was lying near the brook and said, "I'll lay myself across. Then you can drive over me."

However, as soon as the six mice touched the bridge, the straw slipped and fell into the water, and the six mice went tumbling after and drowned. So the situation was just as bad as it had been before, but a hot piece of coal came along and said, "I'm large enough. I'll lay myself across, and you can drive over me."

Then the coal also laid itself across the water, but unfortunately it grazed the surface a little. Soon it started hissing, and before long it was extinguished and died. When a stone saw that, it took pity on the rooster and offered its help. It lay down across the water, and now the rooster himself pulled the wagon across. When he reached the other side and was already on land with the dead hen, he wanted to help the others in the back out of the wagon, but there were too many of them, and the wagon slipped backward causing everyone to fall into the water and drown. So the rooster was all alone with the dead hen, and he dug a grave for her. He laid her in it and made a mound on top. Afterward he sat down on the mound and grieved until he too died. And then everyone was dead.

◆ 81 ◆

Brother Lustig

ONCE UPON A TIME there was a great war, and when the war was over, many soldiers were discharged. So it was that Brother Lustig too received his walking papers and nothing else but a small loaf of ration bread and four kreuzers in money. With that he set out on his way.

In the meantime, Saint Peter had disguised himself as a poor beggar and taken a place by the roadside, so when Brother Lustig passed by, he begged for alms.

"My dear beggar," Brother Lustig said, "I don't think I have much to offer. You see, I was once a soldier, and now I've been discharged and have nothing but this small loaf of ration bread and four kreuzers in cash. When that's all gone, I'll have to go begging just like you. Still, I want to give you something."

Thereupon he divided the loaf into four parts and gave the apostle one part along with one kreuzer. Saint Peter thanked him and then went farther along the road, where he sat down again, disguised as another beggar, and waited for the soldier to come along. When Brother Lustig approached, Saint Peter begged for alms once again. The soldier responded as he had before and gave him a quarter of the bread and a kreuzer. Saint Peter thanked him and went farther along the road, only to sit down a third time in the disguise of yet another beggar. When he addressed Brother Lustig, the soldier gave him the third part of his bread and a third kreuzer. Saint Peter thanked him, and Brother Lustig continued on his way with nothing more than a fourth of the bread and a kreuzer. Then he went into a tavern, where he ate the bread and ordered a beer for a kreuzer. After he had finished eating and drinking, he moved on, and Saint Peter came toward him once more, now in the guise of a discharged soldier.

"Good day, comrade," spoke Saint Peter. "Could you give me a piece of bread and a kreuzer for a drink?"

"Where shall I get it from?" answered Brother Lustig. "I've been discharged from the army, and they gave me nothing but a loaf of ration bread and four kreuzers in money. Then I met three beggars along the road and gave each one of them a fourth of my bread and a kreuzer. I ate the last piece of bread in a tavern and spent my last kreuzer on a drink. Now my pockets are empty, and if you're broke as well, we can go begging together."

"No," replied Saint Peter. "That won't be necessary. I know something about doctoring, and I'll be able to earn as much as I need by doing that."

"I see," said Brother Lustig. "Well, I don't know the first thing about doctoring, so I'll have to go begging alone."

"Why don't you come along with me?" said Saint Peter. "If I earn something, I'll give you half."

"That's fine with me," said Brother Lustig, and they went away together.

Shortly after, they came to a farmhouse and heard a tremendous crying and groaning from inside. When they entered, they found a sick man lying in bed on the verge of death with his wife weeping and wailing very loudly.

"Stop your weeping and wailing," Saint Peter said. "I'll make your husband well again." He took a salve from his pocket, and in the very next moment he healed the sick man so that he could get up, and he appeared to be quite healthy.

The husband and wife were ecstatic and asked, "How can we reward you? What can we give you?"

Saint Peter did not want to take anything, and the more the farmer and his wife insisted, the more Saint Peter refused. But Brother Lustig nudged Saint Peter and said, "You've got to take something. We need it."

Finally, the farmer's wife brought in a lamb and told Saint Peter that he had to accept it. Yet, he still refused. Then Brother Lustig poked him in the side and said, "Take it, you stupid fool. We need it."

At last Saint Peter said, "All right, I'll take the lamb, but I'm not going to carry it. If you want it, then you must carry it."

"No need to worry," said Brother Lustig. "I'll manage with ease," and he picked it up and carried it away on his shoulder.

After they departed, they came to a forest. In the meantime, Brother Lustig had begun feeling the weight of the lamb, and since he was also hungry, he said to Saint Peter, "Look, that's a nice spot. We could cook and eat the lamb over there."

"That's fine with me," answered Saint Peter. "But I don't know how to cook. If you want to cook, here's a kettle. In the meanwhile, I'll take a look around until the meal's ready. But don't start eating till I get back. I'll return on time."

"Go ahead," said Brother Lustig. "I know a thing or two about cooking, and I'll take care of everything."

So Saint Peter went off, and Brother Lustig slaughtered the lamb, started a fire, threw the meat into the kettle, and cooked it. When the lamb was done and the apostle had still not returned, Brother Lustig took the lamb out of the kettle, cut it up, and found the heart. "That's supposed to be the best part," he said. First he just tasted it, but then he succumbed and ate it up.

At last Saint Peter came back and said, "You can eat the whole lamb yourself. Just give me the heart. It's the only thing I want."

Brother Lustig took the knife and fork and pretended to be busily looking for the heart, but he could not find it. After a while he declared, "There's none here."

"Where do you suppose it is?" asked the apostle.

"I don't know," answered Brother Lustig, "but just think how foolish both of us are! Here we're looking for the lamb's heart, and we've both forgotten that a lamb doesn't have a heart."

"My word!" said Saint Peter. "That's something quite new to me! Every animal has a heart. Why shouldn't a lamb have one?"

"That's not so, brother. A lamb doesn't have a heart. If you really think about it, you'll see I'm right. It truly doesn't have one."

"Very well," said Saint Peter. "If there's no heart, then I don't need any of the lamb. You can eat it up yourself."

"Whatever I can't eat, I'll take with me in my knapsack," said Brother Lustig, and he ate half the lamb and stuck the rest in his knapsack.

After they set out again, Saint Peter made a large stream of water rise up and flow directly across their path, forcing them to wade through it.

"You go first," said Saint Peter.

"No," answered Brother Lustig. "You go first," and he thought, If the water's too deep, I'll stay behind.

So Saint Peter waded through, and the water barely touched his knees. But when Brother Lustig began to walk through, the water grew deeper and rose to his neck. Then he called out, "Brother, help me!"

But Saint Peter asked, "Will you confess that you ate the lamb's heart?"

"No," he replied. "I didn't eat it." Then the water grew deeper until it reached his mouth. "Help me, brother!" cried the soldier.

Then Saint Peter asked one more time, "Will you confess that you ate the lamb's heart?"

"No," he answered. "I didn't eat it."

Since Saint Peter did not want to let him drown, he had the water sink and helped him across. So they continued traveling and came to a kingdom, where they heard that a king's daughter was sick and on the brink of death.

"Hey now, brother," said the soldier to Saint Peter, "this is our chance. If we make her well, we'll be set for the rest of our lives." But Saint Peter did not quicken his pace, and Brother Lustig cried, "Pick up your feet, dear brother! We've got to make it there before it's too late."

However, the more Brother Lustig pushed and shoved, the slower Saint Peter went, and at last they heard that the king's daughter had died.

"You see," said Brother Lustig. "That's what we get when you drag your feet."

"Just be quiet," answered Saint Peter. "I can do more than just heal the sick. I can bring the dead back to life."

"Well, if that's the case," said Brother Lustig, "I'm glad, but I expect you to earn half the kingdom for us at the very least."

Then they went to the royal palace, where everyone was in deep mourning. However, Saint Peter told the king he would restore his daughter to life, and when he was taken to her, he said, "Bring me a kettle of water." After it was brought, he ordered everyone to go outside except Brother Lustig. Then he cut off all the limbs of the dead maiden, threw them into the water, made a fire under the kettle, and let everything boil. After all the flesh had fallen off, he took out the beautiful white bones and placed them on a table, where he arranged them according to their natural order. When that had been done, he stepped up to the table and said three times, "In the name of the most holy Trinity, I call upon you to arise, dead woman!"

At the third time, the king's daughter stood up, and she was alive, well, and beautiful. The king was overjoyed by this and said to Saint Peter, "Name your reward, and even if it's half my kingdom, I shall give it to you."

But Saint Peter replied, "I don't want anything in return."

Oh, you dumb fool! thought Brother Lustig to himself, and he poked his comrade in the side and said, "Don't be an idiot. Even if you don't want anything, think of me."

Although Saint Peter still refused to accept anything, the king noticed that the other wanted something, and he ordered his treasurer to fill his knapsack with gold. Thereupon they continued on their way, and when they reached a forest, Saint Peter said to Brother Lustig, "Now let's divide the gold."

"That's all right with me," he answered. "Let's get to it."

So Saint Peter divided the gold into three piles, and Brother Lustig thought, He's off his rocker with his ridiculous ideas. Why is he making three piles when there are only two of us?

"I've divided everything just right," said Saint Peter. "One pile for me, one for you, and one for the person who ate the lamb's heart."

"Oh, that was me," answered Brother Lustig, who snatched up the gold as quickly as he could. "Believe me, I ate it."

"How can that be?" asked Saint Peter. "A lamb doesn't have a heart."

"Hey, where'd you get that idea, brother? Of course a lamb has a heart, just like all the animals. Why should the lamb be different?"

"Very well, I understand now," said Saint Peter. "Keep the gold for yourself, but I'm not staying with you any longer. I'm going my own way."

"As you wish, dear brother," answered the soldier. "Farewell."

Then Saint Peter turned down a different road, while Brother Lustig thought, Well, I'm glad to see him go. He's certainly a strange sort of a saint!

Now the soldier had plenty of money, but he did not know how to handle it: in the course of time he squandered it and gave it away so that his pockets soon became empty again. Then he came to a country where he heard that the king's daughter had just died.

Hey now, he thought to himself, that can turn out to be a good thing for you. You'll bring her back to life and have them reward you the way one ought to be rewarded. So he went to the king and offered to restore his dead daughter to life. Since the king had heard that a discharged soldier was traveling about and bringing dead people back to life, he thought Brother Lustig was this man. But he did not trust him and asked his councillors for advice. They told him to take a chance because his daughter was dead anyway.

So Brother Lustig had a kettle of water brought to him and ordered everyone to leave the room, whereupon he cut off the limbs, threw them into the water, and made a fire underneath, just as he had seen Saint Peter do. When the water began to boil, the flesh fell off the bones, and he took them out and put them on the table, but he did not know how to arrange them and proceeded to mix them all up. Then he stood in front of the table and said, "In the name of the most holy Trinity, I call upon you to arise, dead woman!" He said that three times, but the bones did not stir. He said it again three times, but it was all in vain. "You stupid woman, get up!" he cried. "Get up, or you'll regret it!"

Just as he was uttering those words, Saint Peter suddenly came through the window in his former guise as a discharged soldier and said, "You godless man, what do you think you're doing? How can this dead maiden get up when you've mixed up all her bones?"

"Brother dear, I've done the best I could," he answered.

"Well, this time I'll help you out of your mess, but I warn you, if you ever try something like this again, you'll suffer the consequences. What's more, I don't want you to ask for or to accept the least little thing from the king." Thereupon Saint Peter arranged the bones in their right order and said to the maiden three times, "In the name of the most holy Trinity, I call upon you to arise, dead woman!"

And the king's daughter stood up, and she was as fit and as beautiful as she was before. So Saint Peter went back out the window, and Brother Lustig was glad that everything had turned out so well. However, he was annoyed that he was not permitted to accept anything. I'd like to know, he thought, what's going on in that crazy head of his. Whatever he gives with the one hand, he takes away with the other. That makes no sense!

Now the king offered Brother Lustig whatever he wanted, but he was forbidden to take anything. Nevertheless, he managed by hints and cunning to get the king to order his knapsack to be filled with gold. Thereafter he left the castle. However, as he was passing through the gate, Saint Peter was waiting for him outside and said, "What kind of a man are you anyway! Didn't I forbid you to take anything? But now your knapsack's filled with gold."

"What could I do?" answered Brother Lustig. "They just stuffed it right in."

"I'm warning you, you'd better not try anything like that a second time, or else you'll pay for it."

"My word, brother! Don't worry. Now that I've got some gold, what would I want with bone-washing?"

"Indeed!" said Saint Peter. "A long time that gold will last! But just so you don't go astray again, I'm going to give your knapsack the power to obtain anything you wish. Farewell now, you won't be seeing me again."

"May God be with you," said Brother Lustig, who thought, I'm glad to see you go, you queer bird. You can be sure that I won't tag along after you. And he did not give even a second thought to the magic power that his knapsack now possessed.

Brother Lustig resumed his wandering, and he also squandered and wasted his gold just as he had done the first time. When he had nothing left but four kreuzers, he stopped at an inn and thought, The money's got to go sometime, and he ordered wine and bread for the four kreuzers. As he was sitting there and drinking his wine the smell of roast goose reached his nostrils. Brother Lustig looked around a bit until he discovered that the innkeeper was keeping two geese warm in the oven. Then he remembered that his comrade had said that he could obtain whatever he wished to be in his knapsack. I might as well try it out with the geese, he thought. So he went outside, stood in front of the door, and said, "I wish the two roast geese would move from the oven into my knapsack." Right after he said that, he unbuckled his knapsack and looked inside, and there they were. "Ah, that's the way," he said. "Now I'm a made man!"

He went to a meadow and set about eating the geese. When he was in the middle of his meal, two journeymen came along and looked hungrily at the goose that had not been touched yet. One's enough for me, thought Brother Lustig, and he called the two journeymen to come over and said, "Here, take the goose and eat it in honor of my good health."

They thanked him and took the goose to the inn, where they ordered half a bottle of wine and a loaf of bread. When they unpacked the goose that they had received as a gift and began to eat it, the innkeeper's wife observed them and said to her husband, "Those two are eating a goose. Why don't you take a look to see if one of ours is missing from the oven?"

The innkeeper went over and found the oven empty. "What! You thieving rascals! So you think you can get a cheap meal off us? You'd better pay at once, or else I'll beat your hides with a green hazel stick."

"But we're not thieves," the two said. "A discharged soldier gave us the goose out there on the meadow."

"Don't try to fool me! The soldier was here, but he went out the door like an honest fellow. I watched him closely. You're the thieves, and you're going to pay!"

However, since they could not pay, he took the stick and beat them out the door. Meanwhile, Brother Lustig went his way and came to a place where there was a magnificent castle with a shabby inn nearby. He went to the inn and asked for a night's lodging, but the innkeeper turned him away and said, "There's no more room here. The place is full of noble guests."

"I'm surprised that noblemen would come to you and not go to that magnificent castle," said Brother Lustig.

"Well," answered the innkeeper, "it's quite difficult to spend the night there. Anyone who's ever tried has not come out alive."

"If others have tried it," said Brother Lustig, "then I'm going to try too."

"You'd better leave it alone," said the innkeeper. "It will cost you your neck."

"I'm not worried about my neck right now," said Brother Lustig. "Just give me the keys and some good food and drink."

So the innkeeper gave him the keys and food and drink. Brother Lustig took everything with him into the castle and enjoyed the meal. Eventually, he became sleepy and lay down on the ground because there was no bed. Soon he fell asleep, but he was awakened in the night by a loud noise. When he opened his eyes, he saw nine ugly devils dancing in a circle around him. "Just dance as long as you want," said Brother Lustig, "but don't any of you come too close to me." Yet, the devils kept pressing toward him and almost stepped on his face with their hideous feet. "Quiet down, you ghastly devils!" he cried. But they got worse and worse. Then Brother Lustig became angry and shouted, "All right! I'll quiet you down soon enough!" So he took the leg of a chair and started swinging at them. However, nine devils against one soldier was too much, and when he hit those in front of him, the others behind him grabbed him by the hair and pulled unmercifully.

"You nasty pack of devils!" he exclaimed. "I've just about had enough of this. Just wait. Into my knapsack, all nine of you!"

Before they knew it, they were inside, and he buckled the knapsack and threw it into a corner. Then all was suddenly quiet, and Brother Lustig lay down again and slept until daylight. Now the innkeeper came with the nobleman who owned the castle to see how things had gone with him. When they saw that he was well and cheerful, they were astonished and asked, "Didn't the ghosts do anything to you?"

"They tried their best," he answered, "but I stuck nine of them into my knapsack. Now you can move back into your castle and live in peace and quiet. Nobody will ever haunt it again."

The nobleman thanked him, rewarded him generously, and asked him to remain in his employ, where he would be taken care of for the rest of his life.

"No," he answered. "I'm used to traveling about, and I want to move on."

So Brother Lustig set out again, and when he got to a smithy, he put the knapsack that contained the nine devils on the anvil and asked the blacksmith and his helpers to flatten it out. They then pounded with their large hammers with all their might, and the devils let loose terrible howls. When he opened the knapsack afterward, eight of the devils were dead, but one of them, who had sat in a crease, was still alive, and he slipped out and went back to hell.

Now, Brother Lustig traveled about the world for a long time, and anyone who knows about his adventures has a good deal to tell. However, he eventually grew old and thought about his end. So he went to a hermit who was known to be a pious man. "I'm tired of wandering, and I want to try now to get into the kingdom of heaven," he said.

"There are two paths," the hermit responded. "One is wide and pleasant and leads to hell. The other is narrow and rough and leads to heaven."

Well, I'd have to be a fool, he thought, if I took the narrow and rough one. So he set out and took the wide and pleasant path and eventually came to a large black gate, which was the gate of hell. Brother Lustig knocked, and the gatekeeper looked out to see who was there. However, when he saw Brother Lustig, he was terrified, for he was the very same ninth devil who had been in the knapsack and who had escaped with a black eye. Therefore, he quickly bolted the gate, ran to the head of the devils, and said, "There's a fellow with a knapsack outside who wants to come in, but whatever you do, don't let him in, or he'll wish the whole of hell into his knapsack. The one time he got me in it, he gave me a nasty beating."

So Brother Lustig was told to move on, for he would not be admitted into hell. Well, if they don't want me there, he thought, I'll go and see if I can find a place to stay in heaven, for I've got to stay somewhere. He turned around and continued on his way until he got to the gate of heaven and knocked. Saint Peter happened to be sitting right there as gatekeeper, and Brother Lustig recognized him right away. Here's an old friend, he thought. Things will go better here.

But Saint Peter said, "Do you think you can make me believe that you really want to get into heaven?"

"Come, let me in, brother. I've got to find a place somewhere. If they had let me into hell, I wouldn't have come here."

"No," said Saint Peter. "I won't let you in."

"Well, if you don't want to let me in, then take back your knapsack, because I don't want to keep anything that belongs to you," said Brother Lustig.

"All right, give it to me," answered Saint Peter.

So Brother Lustig handed him the knapsack through the bars of the gate, and Saint Peter hung it up beside his chair.

Suddenly Brother Lustig said, "Now I wish myself into my knapsack."

Within seconds he was inside the knapsack and inside heaven as well. So Saint Peter was obliged to let him stay there.

Gambling Hans

ONCE UPON A TIME there was a man who did nothing but gamble, so people called him Gambling Hans. Since he gambled all the time, he eventually lost his house and everything else he owned. Now, on the day before his creditors were to take possession of his house, the Lord and Saint Peter appeared and requested a night's lodging. So Gambling Hans said, "As far as I'm concerned, you can spend the night, but I can't give you a bed or anything to eat."

The Lord said that he had only to provide lodgings and that they would buy themselves something to eat. All that was acceptable to Gambling Hans, whereupon Saint Peter gave him three groschen and told him to go to the baker and fetch some bread. So Gambling Hans departed, but as he passed the house where the other gamblers lived, the same men who had won everything from him, they called out to him, "Hans, come on in!"

"Not on your life," he said. "You just want to win the three groschen from me too."

However, the others did not let up, and they got him to come in and gamble away the three groschen. In the meantime, Saint Peter and the Lord were waiting, and when Hans did not come back after a while, they went out to see what was keeping him. When he saw them coming, he pretended to have dropped the money in a puddle of water and crawled around as if he were looking for it. But the Lord knew quite well that he had gambled the money away. Now Saint Peter gave him another three groschen, and this time he did not let himself be tempted and brought back the bread. After that the Lord asked him whether he had any wine, and he replied, "I'm sorry, sir. The barrels in the cellar are all empty."

Then the Lord told him to go down into the cellar. "The best wine is still down there."

At first Gambling Hans did not want to believe him, but finally he said, "I'll go down, but I know there isn't any."

Yet, when he tapped the barrel, the very best wine came out, and he brought them the wine. The two spent the night there, and early the next morning the Lord told Gambling Hans he would grant him three favors, thinking that he would want to go to heaven, but Gambling Hans asked for a deck of cards that would enable him to always win, dice that would enable him to always win, and a tree that not only had all sorts of fruits, but if anyone ever climbed the tree, he would not be able to get down unless Hans gave the order. The Lord granted him everything he wanted and went on his way with Saint Peter.

Now Gambling Hans began gambling in earnest, and soon he was on the verge of winning half the world. At this point Saint Peter said to God, "Lord, this won't do. Soon he'll win the whole world. We must send Death after him."

So they sent Death after him, and when Death arrived, Gambling Hans was at the gambling table.

"Hans, come outside for a moment," Death said.

"Just wait a little while until the game is over," Hans responded. "In the meantime, why don't you climb the tree outside and pick a few things for us to nibble on along the way."

Death climbed the tree, but when he wanted to get down, he was unable to, and Gambling Hans let him stay up there for seven years, during which time nobody died.

Again Saint Peter said to God, "Lord, this won't do. No one is dying anymore. We shall have to go ourselves."

So they went themselves, and the Lord ordered Gambling Hans to release Death. Hans then went straight up to Death and said, "Get down." And Death seized him and strangled him on the spot. Then they went together to the otherworld, and Gambling Hans went straight to the gate of heaven, where he knocked.

"Who's there?"

"Gambling Hans."

"Oh, we don't need you here. Go away."

Then he went to the gate of purgatory and knocked again.

"Who's there?"

"Gambling Hans."

"Oh, we've got enough misery and trouble here, and we don't want to gamble. Go away."

Then he went to the gate of hell, where they let him right in. There was nobody at home except Lucifer and the hunchback devils (for the straight-back devils were taking care of business on earth). So he sat down right away and began gambling again. Now, Lucifer had nothing to lose but his hunchback devils, and Gambling Hans won them from him because of his deck of cards that helped him always win. After that, he took off with the hunchback devils, and they went to Hohenfurt together and pulled out some hop poles. Next they went up to heaven and attacked the heavenly kingdom with the poles. Soon heaven was about to collapse, and Saint Peter said, "Lord, this won't do. We must let him in, or else he'll overthrow all of heaven."

They let him in, but Gambling Hans instantly began gambling again, and there was such a noise and racket that nobody could hear himself speak. Once again Saint Peter said, "Lord, this won't do. We must throw him out or else he'll cause all sorts of chaos in heaven."

So they seized him and threw him out. His soul was smashed to pieces as a result, and some of the flying fragments worked their way into many gamblers who are still alive this very day.

◆ 83 ◆

Lucky Hans

AFTER HANS HAD SERVED HIS MASTER for seven years, he said to him, "Master, my time is up, and since I want to go back home to my mother now, I'd like to have my wages."

"You've served me faithfully and honestly," said the master, "and I shall reward you in kind."

So he gave Hans a gold nugget as big as his head, whereupon Hans pulled a kerchief out of his pocket, wrapped it around the nugget, lifted it to his shoulder, and set out for home. As he was meandering along, one foot following the other, he caught a glimpse of a rider trotting toward him on a lively horse. The man appeared to be very cheerful and vigorous.

"Ah!" said Hans very loudly. "Riding is such a wonderful thing! All you have to do is sit there as if you were in a chair. You never have to worry about stumbling on stones. You can save on shoes and get wherever you want in a jiffy."

Upon hearing Hans speak this way, the rider stopped his horse and cried out, "If that's so, why in the world are you walking, Hans?"

"I have to," he answered. "I've got to carry this large nugget. Sure, it's gold, but it's so heavy that I can't keep my head straight, and my shoulder's been feeling the weight."

"I'll tell you what," said the horseman. "Let's exchange. I'll give you my horse, and you give me your gold nugget."

"Gladly," said Hans. "But let me warn you, it's a terribly heavy load to carry."

The horseman dismounted, took the gold, and helped Hans get on the horse. The horseman put the reins firmly into his hands and said,

"If you want to go at a quick pace, you've got to click your tongue and shout 'Giddyap! Giddyap!' "

Hans was in seventh heaven as he sat on the horse, and he began riding free and easy. After a while he thought he ought to be going faster. So he clicked his tongue and shouted, "Giddyap! Giddyap!" whereupon the horse broke out into such a fast trot that Hans was thrown off and was soon lying in a ditch between the road and the fields. The horse would have run away too if it had not been stopped by a farmer who happened to be coming that way and driving a cow before him. Hans pulled himself together and got up on his feet, but he was very irritated and said to the farmer, "Riding's no fun at all, especially when you wind up with a mare like this one that bucks and throws you off. I'm never getting on that horse again. Now, your cow's a different story. You can walk behind it at your ease. Not only that, you're sure of having milk, butter, and cheese every day. I'd give anything to have a cow like that!"

"Well," said the farmer, "if you really like my cow so much, then I'd be glad to trade the cow for the horse."

Hans agreed with utmost joy. So the farmer swung himself onto the horse and rode off in a hurry. Now Hans drove the cow before him in a leisurely way and thought about his lucky deal. All I need now is a piece of bread—and I'm sure to get some bread—then I'll be able to eat my butter and cheese with it as often as I like. If I get thirsty, I'll just milk my cow and drink the milk. What more could my heart possibly ask for? When he reached a tavern, he stopped and ate up everything he had with great relish, both his lunch and supper, and he ordered a glass of beer with his last few hellers. Then he continued to drive his cow onward toward his mother's village. As midday approached and Hans was traipsing over a heath that would take at least another hour to cross, the heat became unbearable. Indeed, it became so hot that his tongue stuck to the roof of his mouth with thirst. There's a way to remedy this situation, thought Hans. I'll just milk my cow and refresh myself with the milk.

He tied the cow to a withered tree, and since he did not have a bucket, he put his leather cap underneath. However, no matter how much he tried, not one drop of milk came out. And since he was so clumsy in the attempt, the cow finally lost her patience and gave him such a kick in the head with one of her hind legs that he fell down. It took a long time for him to recover and regain a sense of where he was. Fortunately, a butcher happened to come his way at that moment. He was pushing a young pig in a wheelbarrow and called out to Hans, "Somebody's been playing tricks on you!" He helped good old Hans to his feet, and then Hans proceeded to tell him what had happened. The butcher handed him his flask and said, "Just take a drink, and you'll feel better. That cow of yours probably won't give you milk because it's too old. At best it's fit only for the plow or for the slaughterhouse."

"No fooling," said Hans, who stroked his hair. "Who would ever have thought that? Naturally it's a good thing to have a beast around your home that you can slaughter. It'll sure make for a lot of meat! But I don't care for beef that much. It's not juicy enough for me. On the other hand, a young pig like yours has quite a different taste. And, just think of the sausages!"

"Listen, Hans," said the butcher. "I'd like to do you a personal favor, as a friend, and trade the pig for your cow."

"May God reward your kindness!" said Hans, and he handed over the cow to the butcher, who, in turn, got the pig out of the wheelbarrow and gave Hans the rope to which the pig was tied so he could lead it away.

As Hans resumed his journey he thought to himself how everything was going just as he wished. Whenever anything disturbing happened, it was always set right immediately. Soon he met up with a boy carrying a white goose under his arm. They said good day to each other, and Hans began to tell him about his luck and how he always managed to make such advantageous trades. The boy responded and said he was carrying the goose to a christening feast. "Just lift her," he continued, and he grabbed the goose by her wings. "See how heavy she is? They've been fattening her up for the last eight weeks. Anyone who takes a bite of her after she's been roasted will have to wipe the fat from both sides of his mouth."

"I agree," said Hans as he weighed the goose with one hand. "She certainly is heavy enough, but my pig is no lightweight either."

Meanwhile, the boy began looking around suspiciously in all directions and shaking his head. "Listen," he spoke again, "there's something the matter here, and it concerns your pig. Somebody stole a pig from the mayor's sty in the village I just passed through. I fear, yes, I really fear that you've got the pig in your hands. They've sent some people out, and it would be terrible if they caught you with the pig. The very least they'd do to you would be to throw you into a dark dungeon."

Good old Hans was horrified. "Oh, God!" he said. "Couldn't you help me out of this mess? You know your way around these parts better than I do. Take my pig there and give me your goose."

"This means my taking a risk too," responded the boy. "But I don't want to be at fault for your getting into trouble." So he took the rope in his hand and quickly moved off with the pig down a side road.

Now good old Hans felt free of his worries and continued his journey homeward with the goose under his arm. "When I really think about it," he said, "I got the better of him in the deal. First there's the fine roast meat, then the large amount of fat that will drip out and supply me with enough goose fat for my bread for the next three months, and finally there are the beautiful white feathers. I'll have my pillow stuffed with them, and nobody will ever have to rock me to sleep again. I'm sure my mother will be delighted about that!"

As he was passing through the last village he came upon a scissors grinder standing next to his cart. His wheel was humming, and he was singing along:

"I sharpen scissors and grind away,
and let the wind guide me from day to day."

Hans stopped and watched him. Finally, he went over to the man and said, "You feel so well because you like what you're doing, don't you?"

"Yes," said the scissors grinder. "This business has got a solid foundation. A good scissors grinder is someone who always finds money whenever he digs into his pocket. But, tell me, where did you buy that beautiful goose?"

"I didn't buy it, I traded my pig for it."

"And the pig?"

"That I got for a cow."

"And the cow?"

"That I received for a horse."

"And the horse?"

"That I got for a gold nugget that was as big as my head."

"And the gold?"

"Oh, that made up my wages for seven years' service."

"Say, you really know how to look out for your interests. Now, if only you could manage it so that you would hear money jingling in your pocket whenever you stood up, your luck would be made!"

"How can I manage that?" Hans asked.

"You've got to become a scissors grinder like me. All you really need for that is a grindstone. The rest takes care of itself. Now, I happen to have one here for you. It's a little damaged, but you won't have to give me anything for it except your goose. What about it?"

"How can you even ask?" Hans answered. "You'll make me the luckiest man on earth. If I have money whenever I put my hand in my pocket, I won't have to worry about a thing anymore." So he handed him the goose and took the grindstone in return.

"Now," said the scissors grinder, as he picked up a plain, ordinary stone that was lying near him on the ground, "I'm going to give you this solid stone as part of the bargain. You can hit as hard as you want on it and straighten out all your old nails. Just make sure that you take good care of it."

Hans lifted the stones, put them on his back, and continued happily on his way. His eyes sparkled for joy. "I must have been born under a lucky star!" he exclaimed. "Everything I wish for comes true. It's as though the gods were looking after me."

In the meantime, since he had been walking all day, he had become tired. In addition he was suffering from hunger because he had eaten up all his provisions to celebrate the great cow trade he had made. It was only with great difficulty that he managed to continue, and even then, he had to stop every other minute. The stones were weighing him down unmercifully, and he could not help thinking how nice it would be if he could get rid of them at that moment. Finally, he saw a well in a field, and as he crawled toward it he resembled a snail. He was hoping to rest and refresh himself with a cool drink of water, and he laid the rocks carefully on the edge of the well, right next to him, to avoid damaging them. After that he sat down and leaned over to drink. But he made a false move and nudged the stones just enough that they fell into the water. As Hans saw the stones sink to the bottom he jumped up for joy. He then knelt down and thanked God with tears in his eyes for showing him such mercy and for relieving him of the stones in such a gracious way. Indeed, those stones had become a great burden for him.

"Nobody under the sun is as lucky as I am!" exclaimed Hans, and with a light heart and free from all his burdens, he now ran all the way home until he reached his mother.

◈ 84 ◈

Hans Gets Married

ONCE UPON A TIME there was a young farmer whose name was Hans. His cousin wanted very much to arrange a marriage for him with a rich wife. So he had Hans sit down behind the stove and then heated it. After that he gave Hans a bowl of milk and a large chunk of white bread and a freshly minted coin that sparkled.

"Hans," he said, "hold on tight to the coin. Take the white bread and crumble it into the milk and stay seated. I don't want you to move from the spot till I get back."

"All right," said Hans. "You can depend on me."

The matchmaker put on an old pair of patched pants and went to the next village, where he called on a rich farmer's daughter.

"Wouldn't you like to marry my cousin Hans?" he asked. "You'll get a forthright, sensible man who's sure to please you."

"How solid is he?" asked the greedy father. "Does he have plenty of bread to break?"

"My dear friend," responded the matchmaker. "My cousin's sitting solidly with both feet on the ground. He's got a pretty penny in his hand and plenty of bread to break. Besides, he's got just as many patches [for that was what they called the pieces of land in that region] as I've got patches on my pants." And he slapped his patches as he said this. "If you want to take the trouble to come along with me right now, I'll show you everything's just as I say."

Since the greedy man did not want to pass up such a good opportunity for his daughter, he said, "If what you say is true, I have no further objections to the marriage."

So the wedding was celebrated on the appointed day, and when the young wife expressed a desire to go out into the fields to see her husband's property, Hans quickly took off his Sunday suit and put on his patched overalls. "I might spoil my good clothes," he said.

They went together into the field, and wherever there was a vineyard, field, or meadow along the way, Hans pointed with his finger and slapped a large or small patch of his overalls and said, "That patch is mine, and that one, too, my dear. Just take a look." By that he meant that his wife was not to gaze at the fields but at his overalls, which did indeed belong to him.

"Were you also at the wedding?"

"Of course, I was there in my finest attire. I had my hair powdered with snow, but the sun came out and melted it. My dress was made from a spider's web, but when I passed through some bushes, the thorns tore it apart. My shoes were made of glass, but then I tripped over a stone, and they went 'clink!' and broke in two."

❖ 85 ❖

The Golden Children

THERE ONCE WAS A POOR MAN and a poor woman who had nothing but a little hut and supported themselves by fishing and were living hand-to-mouth. One day, however, as the husband was sitting by the water's edge and casting out his net, he happened to pull in a fish made entirely of gold. His astonishment was great, and while he was examining the fish, it began to speak and said, "Listen to me, fisherman. If you throw me back into the water, I'll turn your little hut into a splendid castle."

"What's the use of a castle," responded the fisherman, "if I don't have anything to eat?"

"I'll take care of that too," continued the golden fish. "There'll be a cupboard in the castle. When you open it, there'll be dishes with the very best food on them and as much as you desire."

"If that's the case," said the man, "I can certainly do you a favor."

"Indeed," said the fish. "But there is a condition attached to this: You're not allowed to tell anyone in the world, no matter who it may be, how you came by your good fortune. If you so much as breathe a single word, all of it will be over."

The man threw the miraculous fish back into the water and went home. However, instead of finding his hut in its usual place, he discovered a great castle and stood gaping at it in amazement. Then he went inside and saw his wife dressed in beautiful clothes and sitting in a splendid room. She was extremely happy and asked, "Husband, how did all this happen so suddenly? I'm really pleased."

"Yes," said the man, "it pleases me too, but I'm also tremendously hungry. Give me something to eat."

"I haven't got a thing," his wife said. "And I don't know where to find anything in the new house."

"No need to worry," said the husband. "Over there's a cupboard. Just go and open it."

When she opened the cupboard, she found cake, meat, fruit, and wine. Everything looked at her enticingly. "What more could my heart desire?" she exclaimed with joy.

They sat down at the table and ate and drank together. After they had finished eating, the wife asked, "Where in the world did all this come from, husband?"

"Ah," said the husband. "Don't ask me about it. I'm not allowed to reveal a thing. If I tell you, then our good fortune will vanish."

"Very well," she said. "If I'm not supposed to know, then I don't want to know." However, she was not being sincere, and she kept thinking about the matter day and night. In addition, she kept tormenting and pestering her husband until he lost his patience and declared that everything had come from a miraculous golden fish, which he had caught, and that he had given the fish back its freedom for the castle. As soon as he said that, the beautiful castle vanished instantly, cupboard and all, and once again they found themselves sitting in the old fishing hut.

Now the man had to start his work all over again, and he went fishing. As luck would have it, however, he caught the golden fish once more.

"Listen," said the fish, "if you throw me back into the water, I'll give you the castle again, and this time the cupboard will be filled with boiled and roast meats. Just be firm, and whatever you do, don't reveal who gave you all this, otherwise you'll lose everything again."

"I'll certainly be on my guard," answered the fisherman, and he threw the fish back into the water. When he returned home, everything had been restored to its former splendor, and his wife was ecstatic about their good fortune. Yet, curiosity got the better of her, and in a few days she began asking questions again about how it all had happened and how he had managed everything. Her husband kept silent for a long time, but eventually she annoyed him so much that he exploded and revealed the secret. In an instant the castle vanished, and they found themselves sitting in the hut once again.

"See what you've done!" said the husband. "Now we'll have to live in poverty again."

"Ah," said his wife. "I'd rather live in poverty than not know who's giving us all that wealth. After all, I want to keep my peace of mind."

The man went fishing again, and after a while the same thing occurred: He pulled in the golden fish for the third time.

"Listen," said the fish. "It's clear to me that I'm bound to keep falling into your hands. So take me home with you and cut me into six pieces. Give your wife two of these to eat and two to your horse.

Then bury two in the ground, and you'll reap blessings from them all."

The man took the fish home with him and did as he had been told. Then it came to pass that the two pieces he had buried in the ground grew into two golden lilies, his horse had two golden foals, and his wife gave birth to two children who were all gold. The children grew up and became tall and handsome while the lilies and horses grew along with them. One day the boys said, "Father, we want to mount our golden steeds and go out into the world."

That made the old man very sad, and he replied, "How shall I bear your absence when I won't know what's happening to you?"

"The two golden lilies will stay here," they said. "So you'll be able to tell from them how we are. If they are fresh, then we're doing well. If they wilt, then we're sick. If they perish, then we shall be dead."

They rode away and came to an inn, where many people were seated inside. When the people caught sight of the two golden boys, they began to laugh at them and mock them. Hearing their mockery, one of the brothers felt ashamed and decided that he did not want to see the world anymore. So he turned around and went back to his father. However, the other brother continued his journey and came to a great forest. Just as he was about to ride into it, some people told him, "Don't ride through the forest. It's full of robbers. They'll be rough with you, especially when they see that you're made of gold, and your horse as well. They'll kill you for sure."

But he would not let himself be scared by that and said, "I've got to get through, and get through I shall." Then he took a bearskin and covered himself and his horse with it so that nothing more of their gold could be seen. He then rode calmly into the forest. When he had gone a little way, he heard a rustling sound in the bushes and voices talking together.

"There's one," a voice cried out from one side.

"Let him go. He's just one of those lazy vagabonds, poor as a church mouse. We won't get a thing from him," a voice said from the other side.

So the golden youth rode safely through the forest, and no harm befell him.

One day he came riding into a village and saw a maiden who was so beautiful that he could not imagine any maiden more beautiful than her in the whole world. His love for her was so overwhelming that he went straight up to her and said, "I love you with all my heart. Will you be my wife?"

The maiden took such an immediate liking to him that she, in turn, gave her consent. "Yes, I'll be your wife," she said, "and remain true to you for the rest of my life."

So they held the wedding, and just as the celebration was in full swing, the bride's father came home and was very much surprised indeed to find his daughter married.

"Where's the bridegroom," he asked.

They pointed to the golden youth, who was still wearing the bearskin, and the father was furious and said, "Never shall a daughter of mine marry a lazy vagabond!" And he wanted to murder him.

Then his daughter pleaded as hard as she could. "But, Father," she said, "he's my husband, and I love him with all my heart."

Eventually, the father calmed down, but he could not get over the idea that his daughter might have married a common, wretched beggar, and he woke up early the next morning to see for himself. When he looked into their room, he saw a dazzling golden man in bed, and the discarded bearskin was lying on the floor. Then he went back to his room and thought, It's a good thing that I kept my temper, otherwise I might have committed an awful crime.

In the meantime, the golden youth dreamed that he was out hunting a splendid stag, and when he awoke in the morning, he said to his wife, "I want to go out hunting."

She was anxious and begged him to stay at home. "You could easily have an accident," she said.

But he answered, "I must go hunting, and hunting I shall go." He got up and went into the forest, and before long, a proud stag stopped in front of him, just as in his dream. He took aim and was about to shoot, but the stag ran off. He chased the animal over ditches and through bushes and did not get tired all day. But in the evening the stag disappeared before his eyes, and the youth now looked around him. He saw he was standing before a small cottage, and inside was a witch. When he knocked, the old woman came out and asked, "What are you doing in the middle of the great forest so late?"

"Have you seen a stag?" he asked.

"Yes," she replied. "I know the stag quite well." Now a little dog that had come outside with her began to bark viciously at the man.

"If you don't shut up, you nasty cur," he said, "I'll shoot you dead!"

"What will you do?" the witch cried angrily. "You'd shoot my little dog dead?" Immediately she turned him into a stone, and he lay flat on the ground.

Meanwhile, his bride waited for him in vain and thought, I'm sure that my fears have come true as well as everything else that was weighing so heavily on my heart.

However, the other brother, who was standing near the golden lilies at home, saw one of the lilies suddenly droop. "Oh, God!" he said. "My brother's had a great accident. I've got to go and see if I can save him."

"Stay here," said the father. "What shall I do if I lose you as well?"

"I must go," he replied. "And go I will."

He mounted his golden steed, rode off, and came to the forest where his brother was lying on the ground as a stone. The old witch came out of her house and called out to him. She wanted to trap him too, but he kept his distance from her and said, "If you don't bring my brother back to life, I'm going to shoot you."

Unwillingly, she touched the stone with her finger, and the brother regained his human form at once. There was great rejoicing when the two brothers saw each other again: they embraced, kissed each other, and rode out of the forest together, the one to his bride, the other home to his father.

"I was positive that you had rescued your brother," said the father. "I knew when the other golden lily suddenly straightened up and began to bloom again."

From then on they lived happily, and everything went well for them until they died.

◈ 86 ◈

The Fox and the Geese

ONCE THE FOX CAME TO A MEADOW where there was a flock of nice, plump geese. Then he laughed and said, "I've come just at the right moment. You're sitting there together so perfectly that all I have to do is eat you up one by one."

The geese jumped up and began cackling in fright. They screamed for mercy and begged piteously for their lives. However, the fox closed his ears to their pleas. "No mercy!" he said. "You've got to die."

Finally, one of the geese plucked up her courage and said, "Well, if we poor geese must surrender our innocent young lives, then show us some mercy by allowing us one last prayer so that we won't have to die in sin. After that we'll line up in a row, so that you'll be able to pick yourself out the fattest at your convenience."

"All right," said the fox. "That's a fair and pious request. Go ahead and pray, and I'll wait until you're done."

So the first goose began a good long prayer and kept saying *"Ga!Ga!"* Since she ran on and on, the second decided not to wait for her turn and began repeating *"Ga!Ga!"* Then the third and fourth followed, and soon they were all cackling together.

After they have finished praying, the tale shall be continued, but at the moment they are still cackling away.

◆ 87 ◆

The Poor Man and the Rich Man

IN OLDEN TIMES, when the Lord was still walking upon the earth among mortals, he happened to grow tired, and night descended before he could reach an inn. Two houses were standing in front of him, just opposite one another. The large and beautiful one belonged to a rich man, while the small and shabby one belonged to a poor man. I'm sure I won't be a burden to the rich man, thought the Lord, so I'll spend the night at his place.

When the rich man heard someone knocking at his door, he opened the window and asked the stranger who he was and what he wanted.

"I'd like to have a night's lodging," answered the Lord.

The rich man examined the traveler from head to toe, and since the Lord was dressed very simply and did not look like he had much money in his pockets, he shook his head and said, "I can't put you up. My rooms are full of herbs and seeds. If I were to put up everyone who knocked at my door, then I'd soon have to go out begging for myself. Look for a place somewhere else."

With that he slammed the window shut and left the Lord standing there. So the Lord turned around and went across the street to the small house. No sooner had he knocked than the poor man already had the door open and asked the traveler to enter.

"Stay the night with me," he said. "It's already dark, and you won't be able to go much farther tonight."

The Lord was pleased to hear that, and he entered the house. The poor man's wife welcomed him by shaking his hand. She told him to make himself feel at home and to feel free to use anything they had, even though they did not have much. Whatever they had, he could gladly have. Then she put potatoes on the fire, and while they were cooking, she milked the goat so that they would at least have a little milk with the meal. When the table had been set, the Lord sat down and ate with them, and he enjoyed the meager repast because there were grateful faces around him. When they had eaten and it was time to go to bed, the wife whispered to her husband, "Listen, dear husband, let's make up a bed of straw for ourselves tonight so that the poor traveler can sleep in our bed and rest. He's been traveling the whole day and is probably very tired."

"Good idea," he answered. "I'll go and offer it to him." And he went to the Lord and told him that, if he did not mind, he could sleep in their bed and give his limbs a proper rest.

The Lord did not want to take the old couple's bed, but they insisted until he finally took their bed and lay down in it. Meanwhile, they made a bed of straw for themselves and lay on the ground. The next morning they were up before daybreak and cooked breakfast for their guest as well as they could manage. When the sun began to shine through the little window and the Lord stood up, he ate with them again and got set to continue his journey. As he was standing in the doorway he turned around and said, "Because you are so kind and good, I'm going to grant you three wishes, and they shall indeed be fulfilled."

"There's nothing I want more than eternal salvation," said the man, "and also that we stay healthy and get our daily bread as long as we wish. As for the third thing, I don't know what to wish."

"Don't you want to wish for a new house in place of this old one?" asked the Lord.

"Oh, yes," said the man. "I'd certainly be pleased if I could have that as well."

Right before his departure the Lord gave them his blessings once more, fulfilled their wishes, and turned the old house into a new one. When the rich man got up, it was broad daylight. As he looked out his window toward the other side of the road, he saw a new clean house with a red tiled roof instead of the old shack that used to be there. His eyes popped wide open, and he called his wife. "Can you tell me what's going on?" he asked. "Just yesterday there was a dumpy house standing there, and today there's this new beautiful one. Run over and find out what happened."

His wife went over and asked the poor man, who told her, "Last night a traveler came by looking for a night's lodging, and right before his departure this morning he granted us three wishes, eternal salvation, good health and our daily bread for the rest of our lives, and lastly a beautiful new house in place of our old shack."

The rich man's wife hurried back and told her husband what had happened. Then the man said, "I'd like to beat myself to a pulp. If I had only known! The stranger came to our house first and wanted to spend the night with us, but I turned him away."

"Hurry," said his wife, "and get on your horse. Perhaps you can still catch up to the man and get him to grant you three wishes too."

The rich man followed her good advice, galloped off on his horse, and managed to catch up with the Lord. He used sweet talk with the Lord and begged him not to take it amiss that he had not let him into

his house right away; he had gone to look for the door key, but the stranger had disappeared in the meantime. The rich man assured him that, if he passed by again, he would find a place to stay at his house.

"Very well," said the Lord. "If I come back again, I shall stay with you."

Then the rich man asked him whether he also could have three wishes, like his neighbor.

The Lord said yes, but that they would not turn out well for him, and it might be best if he refrained from wishing for anything. The rich man disagreed and asserted that he would be able to choose something to make himself happy if he knew for certain that the wishes would be fulfilled.

"Ride home," said the Lord. "The three wishes you make shall be fulfilled."

Now the rich man had what he wanted. So he rode home and began to contemplate what he should wish for. As he was thus steeped in thought he let the reins drop, and the horse began jumping so much that his thoughts were continually disturbed and he could not collect them. He patted the horse on its neck and said, "Calm down, Lizzy," but the horse kept on bouncing up and down. Finally, he got so annoyed that he lost his patience. "I wish you'd break your neck!" he exclaimed.

As soon as he had said that, he was thrown to the ground, and the horse lay dead as a doornail. Thus the first wish was fulfilled. Since the rich man was greedy by nature, he did not want to leave the saddle behind. So he cut it off, swung it over his back, and proceeded on foot. You've got two wishes left, he thought, and consoled himself with that. As he went walking through the sand under the blazing noonday sun, he got hot and surly. The saddle rested heavily on his back, and he was having a great deal of trouble thinking of a wish. "If I wished for all the riches and treasures of the world," he said to himself, "I'm sure that I'd think of all sorts of other things later on. There'll be this and that, but I'm going to fix things so that I'll cover every wish that one could possibly make."

Then he sighed and said, "If only I were that Bavarian farmer who also had three wishes. He'd know what to do: First he'd wish for a lot of beer, then as much beer as he could drink, and finally a whole barrel of beer." Sometimes he thought he had finally come upon a good wish, but afterward it always seemed to be too little. Along the way he began thinking about how easy his wife had it at home, where she was probably in a cool room and enjoying a fine meal. Just the thought of that annoyed him so much that, before he knew it, he blurted out, "I wish she were sitting on this saddle at home and couldn't get off, instead of my carrying it on my back!" And, just as the last word left his lips, the saddle vanished from his back, and he realized that his second wish had been fulfilled. He became so hot now that he began to run. He was looking forward to sitting down alone in his room, where he would think of something great for his last wish. However, when he arrived home and opened the door to the living room, his wife was sitting on the saddle in the middle of the room. Since she could not get off, she was screaming and complaining.

"Bear with it," he said. "I'm going to get you all the riches in the world with my wish. Just stay where you are."

However, she yelled at him, "What good are all the riches in the world to me if I have to sit on this saddle. You wished me up here, and now you'd better get me off!"

Whether he liked it or not, he had to use the third wish to get her off the saddle and rid of it. His wish was fulfilled at once, and so he got nothing but irritation, trouble, and abuse from the wishes and lost a horse in the bargain. On the other hand, the poor people spent their lives happily, peacefully, and devoutly until they reached their blissful end.

◈ 88 ◈

The Singing, Springing Lark

ONCE UPON A TIME there was a man who was about to go on a long journey, and right before his departure he asked his three daughters what he should bring back to them. The oldest wanted pearls, the second, diamonds, but the third said, "Dear Father, I'd like to have a singing, springing lark."

"All right," said the father. "If I can get one, you shall have it."

So he kissed all three daughters good-bye and went on his way. When the time came for his return journey, he had purchased pearls and diamonds for the two oldest, but even though he had looked all over, he had not been able to find the singing, springing lark for his youngest daughter. He was particularly sorry about that because she was his favorite. In the meantime, his way took him through a forest, in the middle of which he discovered a magnificent castle. Near the castle was a tree, and way on top of this tree he saw a lark singing and springing about.

"Well, you've come just at the right time," he said, quite pleased, and he ordered his servant to climb the tree and catch the little bird. But when the servant went over to the tree, a lion jumped out from under it, shook himself, and roared so ferociously that the leaves on the trees trembled.

"If anyone tries to steal my singing, springing lark," he cried, "I'll eat him up."

"I didn't know that the bird belonged to you," said the man. "I'll make up for my trespassing and give you a great deal of gold if only you'll spare my life."

"Nothing can save you," said the lion, "unless you promise to give me the first thing you meet when you get home. If you agree, then I'll not only grant you your life, but I'll also give you the bird for your daughter."

At first the man refused and said, "That could be my youngest daughter. She loves me most of all and always runs to meet me when I return home."

But the servant was very scared of the lion and said, "It doesn't always have to be your daughter. Maybe it'll be a cat or dog."

The man let himself be persuaded and took the singing, springing lark. Then he promised the lion he would give him the first thing that met him when he got home.

Upon reaching his house, he walked inside, and the first thing that met him was none other than his youngest and dearest daughter: she came running up to him, threw her arms around him, and kissed him. When she saw that he had brought her a singing, springing lark, she was overcome with joy. But her father could not rejoice and began to cry.

"My dearest child," he said. "I've had to pay a high price for this bird. In exchange I was compelled to promise you to a wild lion, and when he gets you, he'll tear you to pieces and eat you up." Then he went on to tell her exactly how everything had happened and begged her not to go there, no matter what the consequences might be. Yet, she consoled him and said, "Dearest Father, if you've made a promise, you must keep it. I'll go there, and once I've made the lion nice and tame, I'll be back here safe and sound."

The next morning she had her father show her the way. Then she took leave of him and walked calmly into the forest. Now, it turned out that the lion was actually an enchanted prince. During the day he and his men were lions, and during the night they assumed their true human form. When she arrived there, she was welcomed in a friendly way, and they conducted her to the castle. When night came, the lion became a handsome man, and the wedding was celebrated in splendor. They lived happily together by remaining awake at night and asleep during the day. One day he came to her and said, "Tomorrow there will be a celebration at your father's house since your oldest sister is to be married. If you wish to attend, my lions will escort you there."

She replied that, yes, she would very much like to see her father again, and she went there accompanied by the lions. There was great rejoicing when she arrived, for they all had believed that she had been torn to pieces by the lions and had long been dead. But she told them what a handsome husband she had and how well off she was. She stayed with them just as long as the wedding celebration lasted. Then she went back to the forest.

When the second daughter was about to be married, she was again invited to the wedding, but this time she said to the lion, "I don't want to go without you."

However, the lion said it would be too dangerous for him because he would be changed into a dove and have to fly about with the doves for seven years if the ray of a burning candle were to fall upon him.

"Please, come with me," she said. "I'll be sure to take good care of you and protect you from the light."

So they went off together and took their small child with them. Once there she had a hall built for him, so strong and thick that not a single ray of light could penetrate it. That was the place where he was to sit when the wedding candles were lit. However, its door was made out of green wood, and it split and developed a crack that nobody saw. The wedding was celebrated in splendor, but when the wedding procession with all the candles and torches came back from church and passed by the hall, a ray about the width of a hair fell upon the prince, and he was instantly transformed. When his wife entered the hall to look for him, she could find only a white dove sitting there, and he said to her, "For seven years I shall have to fly about the world, but for every seven steps you take I shall leave a drop of red blood and a little white feather to show you the way. And, if you follow the traces, you'll be able to set me free."

Then the dove flew out the door, and she followed him. At every seventh step she took, a drop of blood and a little white feather would fall and show her the way. Thus she went farther and farther into the wide world and never looked about or stopped until the seven years were almost up. She was looking forward to that and thought they would soon be free. But, they were still quite far from their goal.

Once, as she was moving along, she failed to find any more feathers or drops of blood, and when she raised her head, the dove had also vanished. I won't be able to get help from a mortal, she thought, and so she climbed up to the sun and said to her, "You shine into every nook and cranny. Is there any chance that you've seen a white dove flying around?"

"No," said the sun, "I haven't, but I'll give you a little casket. Just open it when your need is greatest."

She thanked the sun and continued on her way until the moon came out to shine in the evening. "You shine the whole night through and on all the fields and meadows. Is there any chance that you've seen a white dove flying around?"

"No," said the moon, "I haven't, but I'll give you an egg. Just crack it open when your need is greatest."

She thanked the moon and went farther until the Night Wind stirred and started to blow at her. "You blow over every tree and under every leaf. Is there any chance that you've seen a white dove flying around?"

"No," said the Night Wind, "I haven't, but I'll ask the three other winds. Perhaps they've seen one."

The East Wind and the West Wind came and reported they had not seen a thing, but the South Wind said, "I've seen the white dove. It's flown to the Red Sea and has become a lion again, for the seven years are over. The lion's now in the midst of a fight with a dragon that's really an enchanted princess."

Then the Night Wind said to her, "Here's what I would advise you to do: Go to the Red Sea, where you'll find some tall reeds growing along the shore. Then count them until you come to the eleventh one, which you're to cut off and use to strike the dragon. That done, the lion will be able to conquer the dragon, and both will regain their human form. After that, look around, and you'll see the griffin sitting by the Red Sea. Get on his back with your beloved, and the griffin will carry you home across the sea. Now, here's a nut for you. When you cross over the middle of the sea, let it drop. A nut tree will instantly sprout up out of the water, and the griffin will be able to rest on it. If he can't rest there, he won't be strong enough to carry you both across the sea. So if you forget to drop the nut into the sea, he'll let you fall into the water."

She went there and found everything as the Night Wind had said. She counted the reeds by the sea, cut off the eleventh, and struck the dragon with it. Whereupon the lion conquered the dragon, and both immediately regained their human form. But when the princess, who had previously been a dragon, was set free from the magic spell, she picked the prince up in her arms, got on the griffin, and carried him off with her. So the poor maiden, who had journeyed so far, stood alone and forsaken again, and sat down to cry. Eventually, she took heart and said, "I'll keep going as far as the wind blows and so long as the cock crows until I find him." And off she went and wandered a long, long way until she came to the castle where the two were living together. Then she heard that their wedding celebration was soon to take place. "God will still come to my aid," she remarked as she opened the little casket that the sun had given her. There she found a dress as radiant as the sun itself. She took it out, put it on, and went up to the castle. Everyone at the court and the bride herself could not believe their eyes. The bride liked the dress so much she thought it would be nice to have for her wedding and asked if she could buy it.

"Not for money or property," she answered, "but for flesh and blood."

The bride asked her what she meant by that, and she responded, "Let me sleep one night in the bridegroom's room."

The bride did not want to let her, but she also wanted the dress very much. Finally, she agreed, but the bridegroom's servant was obliged to give him a sleeping potion. That night when the prince was asleep, she was led into his room, sat down on his bed, and said, "I've followed you for seven years. I went to the sun, the moon, and the four winds to find out where you were. I helped you conquer the dragon. Are you going to forget me forever?"

But the prince slept so soundly that it merely seemed to him as if the wind were whispering in the firs. When morning came, she was led out again and had to give up her golden dress.

Since her ploy had not been of much use, she was quite sad and went out to a meadow, where she sat down and wept. But as she was sitting there, she remembered the egg that the moon had given her. She cracked it open, and a hen with twelve chicks came out, all in gold. The peeping chicks scampered about and then crawled under the mother hen's wings. There was not a lovelier sight to see in the world. Shortly after that she stood up and drove them ahead of her over the meadow until they came within sight of the bride, who saw them from her window. She liked the little chicks so much that she came right down and asked if she could buy them.

"Not with money or possessions, but for flesh and blood. Let me sleep another night in the bridegroom's room."

The bride agreed and wanted to trick her as she had done the night before. But when the prince went to bed, he asked his servant what had caused all the murmuring and rustling during the night, and the servant told him everything: that he had been compelled to give him a sleeping potion because a poor girl had secretly slept in his room, and that he was supposed to give him another one that night.

"Dump the drink by the side of my bed," said the prince.

At night the maiden was led in again, and when she began to talk about her sad plight, he immediately recognized his dear wife by her voice, jumped up, and exclaimed, "Now I'm really free from the spell! It was all like a dream. The strange princess had cast a spell over me and made me forget you, but God has delivered me from the spell just in time."

That night they left the castle in secret, for they were afraid of the princess's father, who was a sorcerer. They got on the griffin, who carried them over the Red Sea, and when they were in the middle, she let the nut drop. Immediately a big nut tree sprouted, and the griffin was able to rest there. Then he carried them home, where they found their child, who had grown tall and handsome. From then on they lived happily until their death.

❖ 89 ❖

The Goose Girl

THERE ONCE WAS AN OLD QUEEN whose husband had been dead for many years, and she had a beautiful daughter. When the daughter grew up, she was betrothed to a prince who lived far away. Soon the time came for her to be married, and the princess got ready to depart for the distant kingdom. So the old queen packed up a great many precious items and ornaments and goblets and jewels, all made with silver and gold. Indeed, she gave her everything that suited a royal dowry, for she loved her child with all her heart. She also gave her a chambermaid, who was to accompany her and deliver her safely into the hands of her bridegroom. Each received a horse for the journey, but the princess's horse was named Falada and could speak. When the hour of departure arrived, the old mother went into her bedroom, took a small knife, and cut her finger to make it bleed. Then she placed a white handkerchief underneath her finger, let three drops of blood fall on it, and gave it to her daughter.

"My dear child," she said, "take good care of these three drops, for they will help you on your journey when you're in need."

After they had bid each other a sad farewell, the princess stuck the handkerchief into her bosom, mounted her horse, and began her journey to her bridegroom. After riding an hour, she felt very thirsty and said to her chambermaid, "Get down and fetch some water from the brook with the golden cup you brought along for me. I'd like to have something to drink."

"If you're thirsty," said the chambermaid, "get down yourself. Just lie down by the water and drink. I'm not going to be your servant."

Since the princess was very thirsty, she dismounted, bent over the brook, and drank some water, but she was not allowed to drink out of the golden cup.

"Dear Lord!" she said.

Then the three drops of blood responded, "Ah, if your mother knew, her heart would break in two!"

But the princess was humble. She said nothing and got back on her horse. They continued riding a few miles, but the day was warm, the sun was scorching hot, and soon she got thirsty again. When they came to a stream, she called to her chambermaid once more. "Get down and bring me something to drink from my golden cup," for she had long since forgotten her nasty words.

"If you want to drink," the chambermaid said even more haughtily than before, "drink by yourself. I'm not going to be your servant."

Since she was very thirsty, the princess dismounted, lay down next to the running water, and wept.

"Dear Lord!" she said.

Once again the drops of blood responded, "Ah, if your mother knew, her heart would break in two!"

As she was leaning over the bank and drinking the water, her handkerchief with the three drops of blood fell out of her bosom and floated downstream without her ever noticing it, so great was her fear. But the chambermaid had seen it and was pleased because she knew that now she could have power over the princess. Without the three drops of blood, the princess was weak and helpless. So, as she was about to get back on the horse named Falada, the chambermaid said, "That's my horse. Yours is the nag!"

The princess had to put up with all that. Moreover, the chambermaid spoke rudely to her and ordered her to take off her royal garments and to put on the maid's shabby clothes. Finally, she had to swear under open skies that she would never tell a soul at the royal court what the chambermaid had done. If the princess had not given her word, she would have been killed on the spot. But Falada saw all this and took good note of it.

Now the chambermaid mounted Falada, and the true bride had to get on the wretched nag. Thus they continued their journey until they finally arrived at the royal castle. There was great rejoicing when they entered the courtyard, and the prince ran to meet them. He lifted the chambermaid from her horse, thinking that she was his bride. Then he led her up the stairs, while the princess was left standing below. Meanwhile, the old king peered out a window, and when he saw her standing in the courtyard, he was struck by her fine, delicate, and beautiful features. He went straight to the royal suite and asked the bride about the girl she had brought with her, the one standing below in the courtyard, and who she was.

"I picked her up along the way to keep me company. Just give her something to keep her busy."

But the old king had no work for her and could only respond, "I have a little boy who tends the geese. Perhaps she could help him."

The boy's name was Conrad, and the true bride had to help him tend the geese.

Shortly after, the false bride said to the young king, "Dearest husband, I'd like you to do me a favor."

"I'd be glad to," he answered.

"Well then, summon the knacker and have him cut off the head of the horse that carried me here. It gave me nothing but trouble along the way."

However, the truth was that she was afraid the horse would reveal what she had done to the princess. When all the preparations had been made and faithful Falada was about to die, word reached the ears of the true princess, and she secretly promised the knacker a gold coin if he would render her a small service. There was a big dark gateway through which she had to pass every morning and evening with the geese, and she wanted him to nail Falada's head on the wall under the dark gateway, where she could always see it. The knacker promised to do it, and when he cut off the horse's head, he nailed it on hard to the wall under the dark gateway.

Early the next morning, when she and Conrad drove the geese out through the gateway, she said in passing:

"Oh, poor Falada, I see you hanging there."

Then the head answered:

"Dear Queen, is that you really there?
Oh, if your mother knew,
her heart would break in two!"

She walked out of the city in silence, and they drove the geese into the fields. When she reached the meadow, she sat down and undid her hair, which was as pure as gold. Conrad liked the way her hair glistened so much that he tried to pull out a few strands. Then she said:

"Blow, wind, oh, blow with all your might!
Blow Conrad's cap right out of sight,
and make him chase it everywhere
until I've braided all my hair
and put it up all right."

Then a gust of wind came and blew off Conrad's cap into the fields, and he had to run after it. By the time he returned with it, she had finished combing and putting her hair up, and he could not get a single strand of it. Conrad became so angry that he would not speak to her after that. Thus they tended the geese until evening, when they set out on their way home.

The next morning, when they drove the geese through the dark gateway, the maiden said:

"Oh, poor Falada, I see you hanging there."

Then Falada responded:

"Dear Queen, is that you really there?
Oh, if your mother knew,
her heart would break in two!"

Once she and Conrad were out in the fields again, she sat down in the meadow and began to comb out her hair. Conrad ran up and tried to grab it, but she quickly said:

"Blow, wind, oh, blow with all your might!
Blow Conrad's cap right out of sight,
and make him chase it everywhere
until I've braided all my hair
and put it up all right."

The wind blew and whisked the cap off his head and drove it far off so that Conrad had to run after it. When he came back, she had long since put up her hair, and he could not get a single strand. Thus they tended the geese until evening. However, upon returning that evening, Conrad went to the old king and said, "I don't want to tend the geese with that girl anymore."

"Why not?" asked the old king.

"Well, she tortures me the whole day long."

The old king ordered him to tell him what she did, and Conrad said, "In the morning, when we pass through the dark gateway, there's a horse's head on the wall, and she always says:

'Oh, poor Falada, I see you hanging there.'

"And the head answers:

'Dear Queen, is that you really there?
Oh, if your mother knew,
her heart would break in two!' "

And thus Conrad went on to tell the king what had happened out on the meadow, and how he had had to chase after his cap.

The old king ordered him to drive the geese out again the next day, and when morning came, the old king himself sneaked behind the dark gateway and heard her speak to Falada's head. Then he followed her into the fields and hid behind some bushes in the meadow. Soon he saw with his own eyes how the goose girl and the goose boy brought the geese to the meadow, and how she sat down after a while and undid her hair that glistened radiantly. Before long, she said:

"Blow, wind, oh, blow with all your might!
Blow Conrad's cap right out of sight,
and make him chase it everywhere
until I've braided all my hair
and put it up all right."

Then a gust of wind came and carried Conrad's cap away, so that he had to run far, and the maiden calmly combed and braided her hair. All this was observed by the old king. He then went home unnoticed, and when the goose girl came back that evening, he called her aside and asked her why she did all those things.

"I'm not allowed to tell you, nor am I allowed to bemoan my plight to anyone. Such is the oath I swore under the open skies. Otherwise, I would have been killed."

Although he kept on insisting and would give her no peace, she would not talk. Then he said, "If you don't want to tell me anything, then let the iron stove over there listen to your sorrows."

After the king departed, she crawled into the iron stove and began to lament and weep and pour her heart out.

"Here I sit now," she said. "Forsaken by the world, and yet I'm a king's daughter. A wicked chambermaid forced me to give her my royal garments, and then she took my place with my bridegroom. Now I must do menial work as a goose girl. Oh, if my mother knew, her heart would break in two!"

Meanwhile, the old king stood next to the stovepipe outside and listened to what she said. Afterward he went back into the room and ordered her to come out of the stove. He had her dressed in royal garments, and it was like a miracle to see how beautiful she really was. The old king called his son and revealed to him that he had the wrong bride, who was nothing but a chambermaid. The true bride, however, was standing there before him, the former goose girl. The young king was extremely pleased, for he saw how beautiful and virtuous she was.

Now a great feast was prepared, and all their friends and the entire court were invited to attend. At the head of the table sat the bridegroom, with the princess at one side and the chambermaid at the other, but the chambermaid was so distracted that she could no longer recognize the princess, who was dressed in such a dazzling manner. After they finished eating and drinking and were all in high spirits, the old king gave the chambermaid a riddle to solve: what punishment did a woman deserve who deceived her lord in such and such a way? Whereupon he told her the whole story and concluded by asking, "How would you sentence her?"

"She deserves nothing better," said the false bride, "than to be stripped completely naked and put inside a barrel studded with sharp nails. Then two white horses should be harnessed to the barrel and made to drag her through the streets until she's dead."

"You're the woman," said the king, "and you've pronounced your own sentence. All this shall happen to you."

When the sentence had been carried out, the young king married his true bride, and they both reigned over their kingdom in peace and bliss.

◈ 90 ◈

The Young Giant

A FARMER HAD A SON no bigger than the size of a thumb. After some years had passed, his son did not show the least sign of getting any bigger or even growing so much as a hair's breadth. One day, when the farmer was preparing to go out to the field to do some plowing, the little fellow said, "Father, I want to go with you."

"You want to go with me?" asked the farmer. "Well, I think you'd better stay here. You're of no use to me out there, and you could get lost."

When he heard that, Thumbling began to cry, so his father stuck him in his pocket and took him along in order to have some peace and quiet. Once he was out in the field, he pulled his son out again and set him down in a freshly plowed furrow. As the boy was sitting there a big giant came over the hill.

"Do you see the big bogeyman over there?" said the father, who just wanted to scare the little fellow so he would behave. "He's coming to get you."

It took the giant only a few steps with his long legs before he reached the furrow. Then he lifted Thumbling up carefully with two fingers, examined him, and carried him away without saying a word. The father stood there so petrified with fright that he could not utter a sound. He was certain his child was now lost to him and he would never set eyes on him again.

In the meantime, the giant took the boy home and let him suckle at his breast, and Thumbling grew and became big and strong like most giants. When two years had passed, the old giant took him into the woods to test him.

"Pull up a stick for yourself," he said.

By now the boy had become so strong that he tore up a young tree right out of the ground, roots and all. But the giant thought, We must do better than that. So he took him home again and nursed him for two more years. When he tested him once more, the boy's strength had increased so much that he could tear an old tree out of the ground. Yet, it still was not enough for the giant, who nursed him another two years, and when he then took him into the woods, he said, "Now, make sure you tear up a stick of decent size!"

The boy tore up the thickest possible oak tree right out of the ground so that it cracked in two, and this was mere child's play for him.

"That's enough now," said the giant. "You've learned all you need to know," and he took him back to the field where he had found him. His father was plowing there as the young giant came over to him and said, "Look, Father, look what a fine man your son has grown up to be!"

The farmer was frightened and said, "No, you're not my son. I don't want you. Go away!"

"Of course I'm your son! Let me do your work. I can plow just as well as you can, or even better."

"No, no, you're not my son. I don't want you, and I don't want you to plow either. Go away!"

However, since the farmer was afraid of the big man, he let go of the plow, stepped aside, and sat down at the edge of the field. Then the young man grabbed the plow and merely pressed his hand on it, but his grip was so powerful that the plow sank deep into the earth. The farmer could not bear to watch all that, and so he called over to him. "If you're so set on plowing, then you've got to learn not to press down so hard. Otherwise, you'll ruin the field."

Then the young man unharnessed the horses and began pulling the plow himself. "Just go home, Father," he said, "and have Mother cook me a large dish of food. In the meantime, I'll plow the field for you."

The farmer went home and told his wife to cook the food, and the young man plowed the field, two whole acres, all by himself. After that he harnessed himself to the harrow and harrowed the field with two harrows at the same time. When he was finished, he went into the woods and pulled up two oak trees, put them on his shoulders, and attached a harrow at each end of a tree and a horse at each end of the other tree. Then he carried everything to his parents' house as if it were a bundle of straw. When he reached the barnyard, his mother did not recognize him and asked, "Who's that horrible big man?"

"That's our son," the farmer said.

"No," she said, "that can't be our son. We never had one that large. Our son was a tiny thing." Then she yelled at him, "Go away! We don't want you!"

The young man did not respond but led the horses into the stable and gave them oats and hay and whatever else they normally had. When he was finished, he went into the kitchen, sat down at a bench, and said, "Mother, I'd like to eat now. Is supper almost ready?"

"Yes," she replied, and brought him two tremendous bowls of food that would have lasted her and her husband a week. However, the young man finished everything by himself and then asked whether she could give him something more.

"No," she said, "that's all we have."

"That was really just a nibble. I've got to have more."

She did not dare contradict him. So she went out and put a large pig's trough full of food on the fire. When it was ready, she carried it in.

"At last, a few more crumbs of food to eat," he said and gobbled up everything that was in it. But that was not enough to satisfy his hunger.

"Father," he said, "I can tell I'll never get enough to eat here. So, if you'll get me an iron staff strong enough that I won't break it across my knees, I'll make my way out into the world."

The farmer was happy to hear that. He hitched two horses to his wagon and went to the blacksmith, who gave him a staff so big and thick that the two horses could barely pull it. The young man laid it across his knees, and *crack!* he broke it in two, as if it were a beanstalk, and threw it away. His father hitched four horses to his wagon and fetched another staff, one so large and thick that the four horses could barely pull it. Once again his son snapped it across his knees and threw it away. "Father," he said, "this one's no use to me. You've got to harness some more horses and fetch a stronger staff."

Then his father hitched up eight horses to his wagon and brought back a staff so large and thick that the eight horses could barely pull it. When his son took it in his hand, he immediately broke off a piece from the top and said, "Father, I see that you can't get the kind of staff I need. So I won't stay around here any longer."

The young man went away, and he began passing himself off as a journeyman blacksmith. Soon he came to a village that had a black-smith among its inhabitants. He was a greedy man who never gave anyone a thing and kept everything for himself. The young man went to the smithy and asked him whether he could use a journeyman.

"Yes," said the blacksmith, who looked him over and thought, That's a sturdy fellow. He'll certainly be good at hammering, and he's sure to earn his keep. Then he asked, "How much wages do you want?"

"None at all," he answered. "But every two weeks when the other journeymen receive their wages, I shall give you two blows that you must be able to withstand."

The miser voiced great satisfaction with the terms, because he thought he could save money this way. The next morning the strange journeyman was supposed to hammer first, and when the master brought out the red-hot bar and the journeyman dealt the blow, the iron flew all over in pieces, and the anvil sank so deep into the ground that they could not get it out again. The miser became furious and said, "That's all! I can't use you anymore. You hammer much too roughly. What do I owe you for the one blow?"

"I'll give you just a tiny tap, that's all," said the journeyman, and he lifted his foot and gave him such a kick that he flew over four stacks of hay. Then the journeyman picked out the thickest iron staff he could find in the smithy, used it as a walking stick, and went on his way. After he had been traveling for a while, he came to a large farming estate and asked the bailiff if he needed a foreman.

"Yes," said the bailiff, "I can use one. You look like a sturdy and able fellow. What would you like your wages to be for the year?"

Again he answered that he did not want to be paid, but that the bailiff would have to withstand three blows that he would give him at the end of every year. The bailiff was satisfied with that, for he too was a miser. The next morning the hired workers got up early because they were supposed to drive to the forest and cut wood, but the young man was still in bed. One of the workers called to him, "Hey, it's time to get up! We're going to the forest, and you've got to come with us."

"Not yet," he replied in a rude and surly voice. "You all go. I'll get there and back before the rest of you anyway."

Then the workers went to the bailiff and told him that the foreman was still in bed and would not drive to the forest with them. The bailiff told them to wake him again and order him to hitch up the horses. But the foreman answered just as he had before, "You all go. I'll get there and back before the rest of you anyway."

So he remained in bed another two hours, and when he finally managed to get up, he fetched two bushels of peas from the loft, cooked himself a porridge, and took his own sweet time in eating it. After that was done, he went out and hitched up the horses and drove to the forest. Near the forest was a ravine through which he had to drive. When he drove through it, he stopped the horses, got out, walked behind the wagon, and took some trees and bushes to build a large barricade that would prevent horses from getting through the ravine. When he arrived at the forest, the others were just leaving with their loaded wagons and heading home.

"Drive on," he said to them. "I'll still get home before you."

He did not drive very far into the forest, for as soon as he saw two of the biggest oak trees, he ripped them out of the ground, threw them into his wagon, and turned back. When he reached the barricade, the others were still standing around, since they had been prevented from getting through.

"You see," he said. "If you had stayed with me, you'd have made it home just as quickly, and you'd have had another hour's sleep."

He wanted to drive on, but his horses could not work their way through the barricade. So he unharnessed them, set them on top of the

• 331 •

wagon, took hold of the shafts, and whisked everything through as easily as if the wagon were loaded with feathers. Once he was on the other side, he said to the workers, "You see, I got through faster than you." And he drove on, while the others had to stay where they were. At the barnyard he grabbed hold of one of the trees, lifted it by his hand, showed it to the bailiff, and said, "How do you like this nice cord of wood?"

The bailiff said to his wife, "He's a good man, our foreman. Even if he does sleep long, he still makes it home sooner than the others."

So the young man served the bailiff for a year, and when it was over and the other workers received their wages, it was time for him to collect his pay as well. However, the bailiff was afraid of the blows he had coming to him. He begged the foreman to forgo everything and said that, in return, he would make him bailiff and take over the job as foreman himself.

"No," said the young man. "I don't want to be bailiff. I'm foreman and want to stay foreman. And I intend to dole out what we agreed upon."

The bailiff offered to give him whatever he wanted, but it did no good. The foreman rejected everything he proposed, and the bailiff did not know what to do except to ask him for a two-week period of grace. He needed time to think of a way out of his situation. The foreman granted him an extension, and now the bailiff summoned all his clerks together. He asked them to think up a way to help him and to advise him. After they had deliberated a long time, they finally said that nobody's life was safe from the foreman: he could kill a man as easily as he could a gnat. They advised the bailiff, therefore, to order the foreman to climb down into the well and clean it out; when he was down below, they would roll one of the millstones that were lying around there over to the well and heave it on his head. Then he would never see the light of day again.

The bailiff liked the idea, and the foreman was willing to climb down into the well. Once he was standing below, they rolled down the largest millstone they could find and were convinced they broke his skull with it. However, he called up to them, "Chase the chickens away from the well! They're scratching around in the sand and throwing grains into my eyes so that I can't see."

So the bailiff yelled, *"Shoo! Shoo!"* as if he were scaring the chickens away. When the foreman had finished his work, he climbed up and said, "Just look at what a fine necklace I've got on now!" but he meant the millstone that he was wearing around his neck.

Now the foreman wanted to receive his pay, but the bailiff requested another two weeks' grace to think up a new plan. The clerks met again and advised him to send the foreman to the haunted mill to grind grain at night since nobody had ever emerged alive from it the next morning. The bailiff liked the proposal and called the foreman to him that very same evening. He ordered him to carry eight bushels of grain to the mill and grind it that night because they needed it right away. So the foreman went to the loft and put two bushels in his right pocket and two in his left. He carried the other four in a sack that he slung over his shoulder so that half was on his back and half on his chest. And off he went to the haunted mill.

The miller told him he could easily grind the grain during the day, but not at night, because the mill was haunted, and anyone who had gone in there at night had not been alive in the morning to return.

"Don't worry, I'll manage," said the foreman. "Why don't you go and get some sleep." Then he went into the mill and poured the grain into the hopper. Toward eleven o'clock he went into the miller's room and sat down on a bench. After he had been sitting there awhile, the door suddenly opened, and an enormous table came in. Next he saw wine, roast meat, and all sorts of good food appear on the table by themselves, but nobody carried these things in. After that the chairs slid to the table, but nobody came. All at once he saw fingers handling knives and forks and putting food on the plates. Aside from that, he could not see a thing. Since he was hungry and saw all this food, he too sat down at the table, ate along with all those present, and enjoyed the meal. When he had eaten his fill and the others had also emptied their plates, he distinctly heard all the lights being suddenly snuffed out, and when it was pitch dark, he felt something like a smack in the face. Then he said, "If anything like that happens again, I'm going to strike back."

When he received a second smack in the face, he struck back, and so it went the whole night. He took nothing without paying it back generously, with interest, and kept himself busy by smacking anything that came near him. At daybreak, however, everything stopped. When the miller got up, he went by to see how the foreman was, and he was amazed to find him alive.

"I had a very fine meal," said the foreman. "Then I got some smacks in the face, but I also gave some in return."

The miller was happy and said that the mill was now released from its curse, and he wanted to pay the foreman a reward.

"I don't want money," said the foreman, "I already have enough." Then he took the flour on his back, went home, and told the bailiff he had done his job and now wanted to be paid the wages they had agreed upon.

When the bailiff heard that, he really became alarmed and upset. He paced up and down the room, and beads of sweat ran down his forehead. So he opened the window to get some fresh air, but before he knew it, the foreman had given him such a kick that he went flying through the window out into the sky. He flew and flew until he was completely out of sight.

Then the foreman said to the bailiff's wife, "If he doesn't return, you'll have to take the other blow."

"No, no!" she exclaimed. "I won't be able to withstand it," and she opened the other window because beads of sweat were running down her face also. Then he gave her a kick too, and she went flying out the window. Since she was lighter than her husband, she soared much higher.

Her husband called out to her, "Come over here!"

But she replied, "No, you come over here to me! I can't make it there."

So they soared through the sky, and neither could get to the other. Whether they are still soaring, I don't know, but I do know that the young giant took his iron staff and continued on his way.

◆ 91 ◆

The Gnome

ONCE UPON A TIME there was a rich king who had three daughters. Every day they went walking in the palace garden, where the king, who loved trees, had planted many different kinds, but he was most fond of one particular tree, which he protected by placing it under a spell: Whosoever picked one of its apples would be sent a hundred fathoms underground. When harvest time came, the apples on that tree were as red as blood. Every day the three daughters looked under the tree to see if the wind had blown an apple to the ground, but they never found one. Gradually the tree became so full and its branches so heavy that it seemed the tree would collapse.

By then the youngest sister had such a craving for an apple from this tree that she said to her sisters, "Our father loves us far too much to put a curse on us. I think he cast the spell mainly with strangers in mind." So she plucked a nice plump apple, ran to her sisters, and said, "Just taste it, dear sisters! I've never tasted anything so delicious in all my life."

Then the two other princesses also took a bite of the apple, and suddenly all three sank deep down into the earth, leaving no trace whatsoever behind them. At noon the king wanted to call them to the dining table, but they were nowhere to be found. He looked all around the castle and garden but could not find them. Finally, he became so distressed that he made it known throughout the country that whoever brought his daughters back could have one of them for his wife. As a result, more men than you can imagine went out searching for them all over the kingdom, for the princesses were known to be beautiful and kind to all. Indeed, they were loved by everyone in the country.

Among the searchers were three huntsmen who had spent a week looking for them and had eventually come to a great castle. When they went inside it, they found beautiful rooms, and in one of the rooms the table was set with delicious dishes that were still steaming hot, but there was not a living soul to be seen or heard in the whole castle. They waited half a day more, and the food remained steaming hot. At last they were so hungry that they sat down and ate up all the food. Then they agreed to stay in the castle and drew lots to see which one would remain at home there while the other two continued to look for the princesses. The lot fell to the oldest, and the next day he stayed at home while the two youngest went out searching. At noon a tiny little gnome came and asked for a piece of bread. The huntsman took a loaf of bread that he found there and cut off a slice. As he was handing it to the little man the gnome let it drop and asked him to kindly pick up the piece for him. As the huntsman was bending over, the gnome took a stick, grabbed him by his hair, and gave him a good beating. The next day the second huntsman stayed home, and he fared no better. When the other two returned in the evening, the oldest asked him, "Well, how did things go?"

"Very badly."

So the two oldest confided in each other about their plight and did not tell the youngest anything about it, because they did not like him. They always called him Stupid Hans, because he was not particularly worldly-wise.

On the third day the youngest stayed home, and again the gnome came to fetch a piece of bread. When the huntsman handed him a piece, the gnome let it drop again and asked him to kindly pick it up for him.

"What?" cried the huntsman. "Can't you pick the bread up yourself? If you won't make the effort to take better care of your daily bread, then you really don't deserve to eat it."

Then the gnome got very angry and ordered him to do it. But the young huntsman acted swiftly: he grabbed the gnome and thrashed him soundly. The gnome shrieked loudly and said, "Stop! Stop! Let me go, and I'll tell you where the king's daughters are."

When he heard that, he stopped thrashing him. The gnome told the huntsman that he came from beneath the earth, where there were more than a dozen other gnomes like him, and if the huntsman would

• 335 •

go with him, he would show him where the king's daughters were. Then the gnome pointed to a deep well without any water in it and told him to beware of his companions, for they were not to be trusted, and that he would have to save the king's daughters by himself. To be sure, his brothers wanted to rescue the king's daughters too, but they did not want to exert themselves or take any risks. The best way would be to take a large basket, get into it with his hunting knife and a bell, and then have himself lowered down into the well. There he would find three rooms, and in each one he would see a princess picking out the lice from a many-headed dragon. In each room he would have to cut the dragon's heads off.

After the gnome had told him all that, he disappeared, and toward evening the other two huntsmen returned and asked him how his day went.

"So far, so good," he said, and he told them that he had not seen anyone until noon, when a tiny gnome had come and asked for a piece of bread. After he had handed it to him, the gnome had dropped it and asked him to pick it up. When he refused, the dwarf began to spit at him. They had a quarrel, and he gave the gnome a beating. Afterward the little fellow told him where the king's daughters were.

Upon hearing that, the two brothers became so livid that they turned green with envy. The next morning they went to the well together and drew lots to see who would be the first to get into the basket. The lot fell to the oldest again, and he had to get into the basket and take the bell with him.

"If I ring," he said, "you must pull me up quickly."

When he was just a little way down, he rang the bell, and they pulled him up again. Then the second brother got in and did the very same thing. Finally, it was the youngest brother's turn, and he let himself be lowered all the way to the bottom. After he got out of the basket, he took his hunting knife, went to the first door, and listened. When he heard the dragon snoring loudly, he opened the door slowly and saw one of the king's daughters picking lice from the nine dragon's heads in her lap. So he took his hunting knife and cut off all nine heads. The princess jumped up, threw her arms around him, and kissed him many times. Then she took her necklace of pure gold and hung it around his neck. After that he went to the second princess, who was picking lice from seven dragon's heads, and he rescued her as well. Finally, he went to the youngest, who had a four-headed dragon to louse, and he set her free too. Now they were all enormously happy and could not stop hugging and kissing him. Soon he rang the bell very loudly so those above could hear. One after the other, he put the princesses into the basket and had them pulled up. When his turn came, he remembered the gnome saying that his brothers were not to be trusted. So he took a big stone that was lying there and put it into the basket. When the basket was about midway up, the wicked brothers cut the rope so that the basket with the stone inside fell to the ground. Since they thought that he was now dead, they ran away with the king's three daughters and made them promise to tell their father that they were the ones who had rescued them. Afterward the two of them went to the king and asked to marry his daughters.

In the meantime, the youngest huntsman walked around the three rooms morosely, for he thought he was doomed to die. Then he saw a flute hanging on the wall and said, "Why are you hanging there? This is no place for merrymaking!" He looked at the dragon's heads too and said, "You can't help me either." He paced up and down the floor so much that he wore the ground smooth. At last he had an idea: he took the flute from the wall and played a tune on it. Suddenly many gnomes appeared, and with each note he played, another would emerge, and he kept on playing until the room was full of them. They asked him what he desired, and he said that he would like to return to the top of the earth again and see the light of day. Then they each grabbed a strand of his hair and flew up to earth with him. When he was above, he went straight to the king's castle, where one of the princesses was soon to be married. Next he found the room in which the king was sitting with his three daughters. When the princesses saw him, they fainted. The king got very angry and immediately had him put in prison. He thought the huntsman had harmed his daughters, but when the princesses regained consciousness, they begged the king to release him. When the king asked them why, they said they were not allowed to tell him the reason. However, their father said they should tell it to the stove. Meanwhile, he left the room, listened at the door, and heard everything. Shortly after, he had the two older brothers hanged on the gallows and gave the youngest daughter to the young huntsman for his wife.

When the wedding took place, I was wearing a pair of glass shoes and bumped into a stone. The stone said, "Clink!" and my slippers broke in two.

◈ 92 ◈

The King of the Golden Mountain

A MERCHANT HAD TWO CHILDREN, a boy and a girl, who were still infants and could not walk. About this time the merchant had invested his entire fortune in richly laden ships that had gone out to sea. Just when he was about to make a lot of money through this venture, he received news that the ships had sunk. So now, instead of being a rich man, he was a poor one and had nothing left but a field outside the city. In order to take his mind off his troubles somewhat, he went out to his field, and as he was pacing back and forth a little black dwarf suddenly stood beside him and asked him why he was so sad and what was gnawing at his heart.

"If you could help me," said the merchant, "I'd certainly tell you."

"Who knows," answered the black dwarf, "maybe I can help you."

Then the merchant told him that he had lost his whole fortune at sea and had nothing left but the field.

"Don't worry," said the dwarf. "You shall have as much money as you want if you promise to bring me in twelve years the first thing that brushes against your leg when you return home. And you must bring it to this spot."

The merchant thought, What else can that be but my dog? Of course, he did not think of his little boy and so said yes. Then he gave the black dwarf a signed and sealed agreement and went home.

When he returned to his house, his little boy was so happy to see him that he held himself up by some benches, toddled over to his father, and grabbed him around the legs. The father was horrified, for he remembered the agreement, and he knew now what he had signed away. Still, he thought the dwarf might have been playing a joke on him since he did not find any money in his chests and boxes. One month later, however, when he went up into his attic to gather some old tinware to sell, he saw a huge pile of money lying on the floor. Soon he was in good spirits again and bought new provisions, with the result that he became an even greater merchant than before and trusted in God to guide his destiny. In the meantime, his son grew and learned how to use his brains wisely. As he neared his twelfth birthday, however, the merchant became so worried that one could see the anxiety written on his face. His son asked him what was bothering him, and the father did not want to tell him. But the son persisted until he finally revealed everything to him: how without thinking he had promised him to a black dwarf and received a lot of money in return, and how he had given the dwarf a signed and sealed agreement to deliver him to the dwarf on his twelfth birthday.

"Oh, Father," said the son. "Don't be discouraged. Everything will turn out all right. The black dwarf has no power over me."

The son had himself blessed by the priest, and when the hour arrived, he went out to the field with his father. There he drew a circle and stepped inside it with his father. The black dwarf came then and said to the old man, "Have you brought what you promised me?"

The father kept quiet, but the son said, "What do you want here?"

"I've come to discuss matters with your father, not with you."

"You deceived my father and led him astray," replied the son. "Give me back the agreement."

"No," said the black dwarf. "I won't give up my rights."

They bickered for a long time until it was finally agreed that, since the son no longer belonged to his father, nor did he belong to his archenemy, he was to get into a little boat and drift downstream on the river. His father was to shove the boat off with his foot, and the son's fate was to be decided by the river. The boy said farewell to his father, got into the little boat, and the father had to shove it off with his own foot. The little boat soon capsized with the bottom up and the top facedown. The father thought his son was lost, and he went home and mourned for him.

However, the boat did not sink but continued to drift calmly downstream with the boy safely inside. Finally, it touched down upon an unknown shore and stood still. The boy went ashore, saw a beautiful castle lying before him, and went toward it. When he entered, he realized it was enchanted. He went through all the rooms, but they were empty except for the last chamber, where he found a snake all coiled up. The snake was an enchanted princess, who was glad to see him and said, "Have you come at last, my savior? I've been waiting now twelve years for you. This kingdom is enchanted, and you must release it from the magic spell."

"How can I do that?" he asked.

"Tonight twelve black men wearing chains will come and ask you what you're doing here. You must keep quiet and refuse to answer them. Let them do whatever they want with you: they will torture you, beat you, and stab you. Let them do that, just don't talk. At midnight they must go away. The second night twelve other men will come, and the third night there will be twenty-four, who will chop off your head. But at midnight their power will be gone, and if you have held out until then and have not uttered a single word, I shall be saved and shall come to you carrying the Water of Life. I shall rub you with it, and you shall be alive again and as healthy as you were before."

Now, everything happened just as she had said: the black men could not force a word out of him, and on the third night the snake turned into a beautiful princess who came with the Water of Life and brought him back to life. Then she embraced him and kissed him, and there was joy and jubilation throughout the castle. Soon thereafter they celebrated their wedding, and he was king of the Golden Mountain.

Thus they lived happily together, and the queen gave birth to a handsome boy. After eight years had passed, the king's thoughts turned to his father. His heart went out to him, and he wished he could see him again. But the queen did not want to let him go and said, "I can tell that this will bring me bad luck."

Still, he gave her no peace until she consented to let him go. Upon his departure she gave him a wishing ring and said, "Take this ring and put it on your finger; with it you can transport yourself immediately to wherever you want to go. But you must promise me never to use it to wish me away from here to your father's place."

He promised her, put the ring on his finger, and wished that he was home, outside the city where his father lived. Before he knew it, he actually found himself there and started to walk toward the city. However, when he reached the city gate, the sentries would not let him enter because he was wearing such strange clothes, even though they were rich and splendid. So he climbed a hill where a shepherd was tending his flock, changed clothes with him, and put on the shepherd's old coat. This time when he went into the city, the sentries did not challenge him. After he got to his father's house, he revealed his identity, but his father would not believe he was his son and said that, to be sure, he had had a son, but he was long since dead. Nevertheless, the father offered the man a plate of food since he saw he was a poor, needy shepherd.

"I'm really your son," said the shepherd to his parents. "Don't you remember any birthmarks you'd recognize me by?"

"Yes," said his mother, "our son had a raspberry mark under his right arm."

He pulled up his shirt, and when they saw the raspberry mark, they no longer doubted that he was their son. Then he told them that he was king of the Golden Mountain and that he had a princess as his wife and a handsome seven-year-old son.

"Now that can't possibly be true," said his father. "What kind of a king would run around in a tattered shepherd's coat?"

Immediately the son got angry, and not thinking of his promise, he turned his ring and wished both his wife and son there, and within seconds they were with him. But the queen wept and accused him of breaking his promise and making her unhappy.

"I did it without thinking. There was nothing underhanded about my actions," he kept saying, and he eventually convinced her. Indeed, she appeared to be satisfied, but there was evil on her mind.

Shortly thereafter he led her outside the city to the field and showed her the spot on the riverbank where the little boat had been shoved off. While they were there, he said, "I'm tired now. Sit down next to me. I'd like to sleep a little on your lap."

He laid his head on her lap, and she loused him a bit until he fell asleep. While he was sleeping, she took the ring off his finger and drew her foot out from under him, leaving only her slipper behind. Finally, she took her child in her arms and wished herself back in her kingdom. When he awoke, he was lying there all alone. His wife and child were gone, and the ring as well. Only the slipper, as a token, had been left behind. "You can't go back home again to your parents," he said to himself. "They'd only say you were a sorcerer. You'd better pack up and get back to your kingdom."

So he went on his way and finally came to a mountain where three giants were standing and quarreling because they could not decide how best to divide their father's inheritance. When they saw him riding by, they called to him and said that since little people were shrewd, they wanted him to divide the inheritance among them. This inheritance consisted of three things: First, a sword that chopped off everyone's head except that of the person who held it and said, "All heads off except mine!" Second, a cloak that made one invisible if one put it on. Third, a pair of boots that carried the person who wore them to any spot he wished in a matter of seconds.

"Give me the three objects," said the king, "so I can see if they're in good condition."

They handed him the cloak, and when he had put it on his shoulders, he was invisible and then turned into a fly. After that he resumed his true form and said, "The cloak is good. Now give me the sword."

"No," they said. "We won't give it to you. If you say, 'All heads off except mine!' we'd lose our heads, and you alone would keep yours."

Nevertheless, they gave it to him on condition that he try it out on a tree. He did that, and the sword cut the trunk of a tree in half as if it were made of straw. Now he wanted to have the boots, but they said, "No, we won't give them away. If you put them on and wish yourself on top of the mountain, then we would stand here below with nothing."

"Oh, no," he said, "I would never do anything like that."

So they gave him the boots as well. But, when he had all three objects, he could think of nothing but his wife and child and sighed to himself, "Oh, if only I were on top of the Golden Mountain!" And he vanished right before the eyes of the giants. Thus their inheritance was divided.

When he drew near the castle, he heard cries of joy and the sounds of fiddles and flutes. The people at the court told him that his wife was celebrating her wedding with another man. So he got angry and said, "That faithless woman! It was she who duped me and then left me while I slept!" He hung his cloak around his shoulders and went unseen into the castle. When he entered the hall, there was a large table covered with delicious food, and the guests were eating and drinking, laughing and joking. The queen was sitting in a royal chair at the center of the table. She was wearing magnificent clothes and had her crown on her head. He went over to her, took a place right behind her, and nobody was aware of his presence. When they put a piece of meat on her plate, he snatched it and ate it. And, when they gave her a glass of wine, he snatched it and drank it. They kept giving her food and wine, but she would always end up with nothing because her plate and glass would vanish immediately. She became so upset and distraught that she left the table, went into her chamber, and began weeping, while he stayed behind her all the time.

"Has the devil got me in his power?" she asked. "I thought my savior had come."

Then he smacked her in the face and said, "Your savior came! Now he's got you in his power, you faithless thing! Did I deserve to be treated the way you treated me?"

He made himself visible, went into the hall, and announced, "The wedding is over! The true king has arrived!"

The kings, princes, and ministers who were assembled there began jeering and mocking him, but he wanted to make short work of them and said, "Will you leave or not?"

At that they charged and tried to capture him, but he took out his sword and said, "All heads off except mine!"

Then their heads rolled to the ground, and he alone was master and king of the Golden Mountain.

◆ 93 ◆

The Raven

ONCE UPON A TIME there was a queen who had a daughter that was still so little she had to be carried in her mother's arms. One day the child was very naughty, and no matter what the mother said, she would not keep quiet. The mother became impatient, and as she looked at the ravens flying around outside the castle, she opened the window and said, "I wish you were a raven and would fly away! Then I'd have my peace and quiet."

No sooner had she said those words than the child was changed into a raven and flew from her arms out through the window. She headed for a dark forest, where she stayed for a long time, and her parents heard nothing more from her.

Some time later, a man was making his way into this forest and heard the raven call. He went toward the voice, and as he came closer the raven said, "I am a king's daughter by birth and have been cursed by a spell. However, you can set me free."

"What am I to do?" he asked.

"Go deeper into the forest," she said, "and you'll see a house. There's an old woman sitting inside. She'll offer you something to eat and drink, but you must not touch a thing. If you eat or drink anything, you'll fall into a sleep and won't be able to release me from the spell. In the garden behind the house there's a big pile of tanbark. You're to stand on it and wait for me. I shall come three days in a row at two o'clock in the afternoon with a carriage. The first time my carriage will be drawn by four white stallions, the second time by four bay stallions, and the last time by four black ones. But if you fail to stay awake, I won't be set free."

The man promised to do everything she had demanded, but the raven said, "Oh, I can already tell you won't set me free. You'll take something from the old woman."

Again the man assured her he would touch neither food nor drink. However, once he was inside the house, the old woman went over to him and said, "Poor man, you're all worn out. Come and refresh yourself. Have something to eat and drink."

"No," said the man. "I don't want to eat or drink."

But she would not leave him in peace and kept saying, "Well, if you don't want to eat, just take a sip from the glass. One little sip won't count."

Finally, he let himself be persuaded and drank. Toward two in the afternoon he went outside into the garden and climbed onto the pile of tanbark to wait for the raven. As he stood there he suddenly felt so tired that he could not help himself and had to lie down and rest a little. He did not want to fall asleep, but no sooner had he stretched himself out than his eyes closed by themselves, and he fell asleep. He slept so soundly that nothing in the world could have wakened him. At two o'clock the raven came driving up in a carriage with four white horses, but she was already in full mourning and said, "I know he's asleep." When she drove into the garden, he was indeed fast asleep. She climbed out of the carriage, went over to him, and shook him and called him, but he did not awake.

At noon the next day the old woman came to him again and brought him food and drink, but he did not want to take anything. However, she refused to leave him in peace and kept talking to him until he took another drink from the glass. Toward two o'clock he went into the garden and climbed onto the pile of tanbark to wait for the raven. Then he suddenly felt so tired that his limbs could no longer support him. Since he could not help himself, he lay down and fell into a deep sleep. When the raven drove up in her carriage drawn by four bay stallions, she was already in full mourning and said, "I know he's asleep." She went over to him, but he lay asleep and could not be wakened.

The next day the old woman asked him what the matter was and why he was not eating or drinking. Did he want to die?

"I don't want to eat or drink," he replied. "Nor am I allowed to."

In spite of this, she set a bowl of food and a glass of wine in front of him, and as the smell reached his nostrils, he could not resist and took a deep draft. When the time came, he went outside into the garden and climbed onto the pile of tanbark to wait for the princess. Yet, he was even more tired than he had been on the previous days. So he lay down and slept like a log. At two o'clock the raven came, and her carriage was drawn by four black horses. The carriage and everything else were also black, and she was already in full mourning. "I know he's asleep," she said, "and he won't be able to set me free." When she went over to him, he was lying there sound asleep. She shook him and called him, but she could not wake him up. So she put a loaf of bread beside him, then a piece of meat, and lastly a bottle of wine. No matter how much he took from any of them, they would always replenish themselves. After that she drew a gold ring from her finger and placed it on his finger. Her name was engraved on it. Finally, she left him a letter on the ground in which she explained that the things she had given him would never run out, and she concluded her letter by saying, "I clearly see that you can't set me free in a place like this. But if you still want to save me, then come to the golden castle of Mount Stromberg. It's within your power. That I know for sure." And after she had given him all those things, she climbed back into her carriage and drove off to the golden castle of Mount Stromberg.

When the man woke and saw that he had slept through everything, he was terribly sad and said, "I'm sure she's been here, and I haven't set her free." Then he noticed the things lying beside him, and he read the letter that explained everything that had happened. So he stood up and set out for the golden castle of Mount Stromberg, even though he did not know where it was. After he had wandered about the world for a long time, he finally came to a dark forest and continued wandering for fourteen days. When he realized that he could not find his way out, he lay down exhausted on the fourteenth evening and fell asleep under a bush. The next day he moved on, and in the evening, as he was about to lie down under another bush, he heard such a moaning and groaning that he was unable to sleep. When the hour came for people to light their lamps, he saw a light glimmering in the distance, got up, and went toward it. Shortly after, he came to a house that appeared to be very small because a big giant was standing in front of it. If you try to go inside, he thought to himself, and the giant catches sight of you, he'll put an end to your life. Finally, he decided to risk it and stepped toward the door. When the giant saw him, he said, "It's good that you've come. I haven't had a thing to eat for a long time. So I'm going to gobble you up for supper."

"You'd better not," said the man. "I don't like to be gobbled up. If you want something to eat, I have enough here to fill your stomach."

"If that's true," said the giant, "you can rest easy. I wanted to eat you only because I had nothing else."

They went in and sat down at the dinner table, and the man took out the bread, wine, and meat that never ran out.

"I like this very much," said the giant, and he ate to his heart's content.

After supper the man asked him, "Can you tell me the location of the golden castle of Mount Stromberg?"

The giant said, "I'll look it up on my map. It shows all the cities, villages, and houses." He got out a map that he kept in the room and looked for the castle, but it was not on it. "Don't worry," he said. "I've got even larger maps in the closet upstairs. We can look for it on them." Yet, it was all in vain.

Now, the man wanted to move on, but the giant begged him to stay a few more days until his brother returned. He had merely gone out to fetch some provisions. When the brother came back, they asked him about the golden castle of Mount Stromberg.

"When I'm finished eating," he answered, "I'll look it up on the map."

A little later he climbed upstairs with them to his room, and they looked for it on his map but could not find it. Then he got out other maps that were even older, and they kept on looking until they finally located the castle. However, it was thousands of miles away.

"How will I ever get there?" asked the man.

"I've got two hours to spare," said the giant. "I'll carry you as far as I can, but then I must return home and nurse our child." So he carried the man until he was about a hundred hours' walk from the castle and said, "You can go the rest of the way by yourself."

Then the giant turned back, while the man went on day and night until he finally came to the golden castle of Mount Stromberg. But the castle was up on a glass mountain, and he saw the enchanted maiden drive around the castle in her carriage and go inside. He was happy to have caught a glimpse of her and wanted to climb up to her. Yet, whenever he tried, he slipped down again on the glass. Once he realized that he could not reach her, he was very distressed and said to himself, "I'll stay down here and wait for her." So he built a little hut for himself and stayed there for one year. Every day he watched the princess drive around on top of the mountain, but he could not climb up to her.

One day he peered out of his hut and saw three robbers fighting. When he called out to them "God be with you!" they stopped fighting, listened to see where the cry came from, and then resumed fighting when they could not see anyone. It was dangerous just to be near them, but again the man called out "God be with you!" Again they stopped, looked around, and resumed their fighting when they could not see anyone. Finally, he called out for a third time "God be with you!" and this time he thought to himself, You'd better go see what these three are up to. So he went out to them and asked them why they were fighting. One of them said he had found a stick and that whenever he struck a door with it, the door would spring open. The second said he had a cloak and that whenever he hung it over his shoulders, he would be invisible. The third said he had caught a horse and that one could ride it everywhere, even up the glass mountain. However, they did not know whether to share these things or to part ways. Then the man said, "I'll make an exchange with you. I'll take those three things, and to be honest, I don't have any money, but I do have other things that are worth more than money. First, however, I must test your things to see whether you've told me the truth."

They let him sit on the horse, put the cloak over his shoulders, and handed him the stick. As soon as he had all three objects, they could no longer see him. So he gave them all a good beating and cried out, "Now, you lazy scoundrels, you've got what you've deserved. Are you satisfied?"

The man rode up the glass mountain, and when he got to the top, he found the castle door was closed. So he struck the gate with the stick, and it immediately sprang open. He entered and went up the stairs until he came to a hall. There sat the maiden, and she had a goblet filled with wine in front of her. However, she could not see him because he was wearing the cloak. When he went over to her, he pulled off the ring that she had given him and dropped it into the goblet so that it rang out.

"That's my ring!" she exclaimed. "Then the man who's going to set me free must be here somewhere."

They searched all over the castle, but they could not find him. Indeed, he had gone outside, mounted the horse, and thrown off the cloak. When they finally saw him out by the gate, they rejoiced. So he dismounted and took the princess in his arms. She kissed him and said, "Now that you've set me free, we shall celebrate our wedding tomorrow."

❖ 94 ❖

The Clever Farmer's Daughter

ONCE UPON A TIME there was a poor farmer who had only a small house and one daughter but no land. One day the daughter said, "I think we should ask the king for a little piece of farming land."

When the king learned about their poverty, he gave them a small field, which the farmer and his daughter cleared so they could sow a little wheat and plant some kind of fruit. When they had almost finished their work, they found a mortar of pure gold on the ground.

"Listen," said the farmer to his daughter, "since the king was so gracious as to give us this field, we ought to give him this mortar in return."

But the daughter did not agree and said, "Father, if we give the mortar without the pestle, then we'll have to find the pestle as well. I think we'd be better off if we kept quiet about the whole thing."

However, the farmer did not listen to her. He took the mortar, carried it to the king, and said that he had found it on the heath. Now he wanted to offer it to the king in his honor. The king took the mortar and asked the farmer if he had found anything else.

"No," replied the farmer.

Then the king asked him about the pestle and told him to bring it to him. The farmer replied that there was no pestle, but that was like talking to the wind. He was thrown into prison, where he was to stay until he produced the pestle. The servants brought him bread and water every day, the usual fare in prison, and every day they heard the farmer sighing "Oh, if only I had listened to my daughter! Oh, if only I had listened to my daughter!" Finally, the servants went to the king and told him how the prisoner kept crying "Oh, if only I had listened to my daughter!" and how he refused to eat and drink. The king ordered the servants to bring the prisoner before him, and he asked the farmer to tell him why he kept sighing "Oh, if only I had listened to my daughter!"

"What did your daughter tell you?"

"She told me not to bring you the mortar; otherwise, you'd want to have the pestle as well."

"If you have such a clever daughter, I want to see her."

So she had to appear before the king, who asked her if she really was so clever and said that he wanted to give her a riddle to solve, and that if she solved it, he would marry her. She replied right away that she would solve it. Then the king said, "Come to me, not dressed, not naked, not on horse, not by carriage, not on the road, not off the road, and if you do, I'll marry you."

The farmer's daughter went home and got undressed until she was completely naked, so that she was not dressed. Next she took a large fishnet and wrapped it completely around her so that she was not naked. Then she took some money, leased a donkey, and tied the fish net to its tail. The donkey had to drag her along so that she neither rode nor drove. And, since the donkey had to drag her along the wagon tracks, only her big toes could touch the ground so that she was neither on the road nor off it. Thus, when she appeared before the king this way, he said she had solved the riddle and had fulfilled all the conditions. He released her father from the prison, took her as his wife, and ordered her to look after all the royal possessions.

Now, some years went by, and one day, when the king was out reviewing his troops, a group of farmers happened to stop in front of his castle. They had been selling wood, and some of the wagons were drawn by horses, others by oxen. One of the farmers had three horses, and his mare gave birth to a foal that ran away and lay down between two oxen hitched to another farmer's wagon. When the two farmers came together, they started bickering, throwing things at each other, and making a lot of noise. The farmer with the oxen wanted to keep the foal and claimed that the oxen had given birth to it. The other said no, his horse had given birth to it, and the foal was his. The quarrel was taken before the king, and he declared that wherever the foal had laid itself down, there it should stay. So the farmer with the oxen got the foal, even though it did not belong to him. The other farmer went away, wept, and grieved over his foal. However, since he had heard that the queen came from a farmer's family and was compassionate, he went to her and asked whether she could help him get his foal back.

"Yes," she said. "But you must promise not to tell that I've helped you. Now, here's what you have to do: Early tomorrow morning when the king goes out to review his guard, you're to place yourself in the middle of the road where he has to pass. Bring a large fishnet with you and pretend to fish with it. You're to keep fishing and shaking the net out as though it were full." Then the queen also told him what to answer the king when he questioned him.

The next day the farmer got up and went fishing on dry land. When the king rode by and saw that, he sent his messenger to ask the foolish man what he was doing.

"I'm fishing," he replied.

When the messenger asked how he could fish without water, the farmer answered, "If two oxen can manage to give birth to a foal, then I can manage to catch a fish on dry land."

The messenger brought the farmer's answer back to the king, who summoned the farmer and said he knew that the farmer had not thought up the answer himself. The king wanted to know, on the spot, who had helped him with the answer. But the farmer refused to talk and kept repeating, may God help him if he did not think up the answer himself. So they laid him down on a bundle of straw, beat and tortured him until he confessed that he had got the idea from the queen.

When the king returned home, he said to his wife, "Why did you dupe me? I no longer want you for my wife. Your time is up! Go back to the farmhouse where you belong." However, he granted her one last request: she could take the dearest and best thing that she could think of with her, and that was to be her parting gift.

"Very well, dear husband," she said. "Your wish is my command." Then she embraced him, kissed him, and asked him to drink to her parting. He agreed, and she ordered a strong sleeping potion. The king took a big swig, but she only drank a little. Soon he fell into a deep sleep, and when she saw that, she called a servant, took a beautiful white linen sheet, and wrapped him in it. The servant had to carry him outside and put him into a carriage. Then she drove him to her house and put him to bed. He slept a whole day and night, and when he woke up, he looked around him and said, "My God! Where am I?" He called his servants, but nobody came.

Finally, his wife came to the bed and said, "Dear King, you ordered me to take the dearest and best thing with me from the castle. Since you are the dearest and best thing I know, I took you with me."

Tears began to well up in the king's eyes, and he said, "Dear wife, you shall be mine, and I shall be yours forever." Then he took her back with him to the royal castle and married her again. And I am sure that they are still living together even today.

◈ 95 ◈

Old Hildebrand

ONCE UPON A TIME there was a farmer and his wife. The village priest had taken a liking to the farmer's wife and kept wishing he could spend one whole day alone with her in pleasure. The woman would have liked that too.

One day he came to her and said, "Listen, my dear, I've figured out a way we can spend a whole day together in pleasure. Here's the plan: On Wednesday you must take to your bed and tell your husband you're sick. You'd best moan and groan as much as possible and keep it up until Sunday, when I'm to hold my sermon. Then I'll preach that if anybody has a sick child at home, a sick husband, a sick wife, a sick father, a sick mother, a sick sister or brother, or whoever else might be sick at home, he should make a pilgrimage to Mount Cuckold in Italy. There one can purchase a peck of bay leaves for a kreuzer. Then the sick child, the sick husband, the sick wife, the sick father, the sick mother, the sick sister, or whoever else might be sick will get well at once."

"That's fine with me," replied the farmer's wife.

On Wednesday, as was agreed, the farmer's wife lay down in bed and moaned and groaned as if the world were coming to an end. Her husband brought her everything he could think of, but nothing helped. When Sunday came, the farmer's wife said, "I feel just miserable, as if I were going to die any minute. But before my end comes, I'd like to do just one more thing: I'd like to hear the priest hold his sermon today."

"Oh, no, my sweet," answered the farmer. "Don't do that. If you get up, you could make things worse. Look, I'll go to church, listen to the sermon carefully, and then I'll return home and tell you everything he's said."

"Well, all right," said the farmer's wife. "Go and pay close attention and tell me everything he says."

So the farmer went to church, and the priest began to preach the sermon and said, if anyone had a sick child at home, a sick husband, a sick wife, a sick father, a sick mother, a sick sister or brother, or whoever else might be sick, he should make a pilgrimage to Mount Cuckold in Italy, where a peck of bay leaves costs a kreuzer, then the sick child, the sick husband, the sick wife, the sick father, the sick mother, the sick sister or brother, and whoever else might be sick would get well at once. Any person wanting to make the journey was to come to the priest after mass, and he would give them the sack for the bay leaves and the kreuzer. Nobody was happier than the farmer when he heard that, and after the mass he went straight to the priest, who gave him the sack and the kreuzer. Then the farmer went home, and before he even got through the door of his house, he shouted, "Hurray, my dear wife, now you're as good as cured! The priest preached that if anyone with a sick child at home, a sick husband, a sick wife, a sick father, a sick mother, a sick sister or brother, or whoever else might be sick makes a pilgrimage to Mount

Cuckold in Italy, where a peck of bay leaves costs a kreuzer, then the sick child, the sick husband, the sick wife, the sick father, the sick mother, the sick sister or brother, or whoever else might be sick would get well at once. I've already got the kreuzer and the sack for the bay leaves from the priest, and I'm going to start out on my journey right away so you can get well that much sooner."

He then departed. However, he had hardly left when his wife got up, and the priest lost no time in getting there. Now, let us leave the two of them alone for a while and go on with the farmer.

Once the farmer was on his way, he walked at a rapid pace so he could reach Mount Cuckold all the sooner. Along the way he met his neighbor, an egg dealer, who was returning from the market, where he had sold all his eggs.

"Praise the Lord!" said the egg dealer. "Where are you off to in such a rush, neighbor?"

"To all eternity, neighbor," said the farmer. "My wife's sick, and I heard our priest preach today that if anyone had a sick child at home, a sick husband, a sick wife, a sick father, a sick mother, a sick sister or brother, or whoever else might be sick and that person makes a pilgrimage to Mount Cuckold in Italy, where a peck of bay leaves costs a kreuzer, then the sick child, the sick husband, the sick wife, the sick father, the sick mother, the sick sister or brother, or whoever else might be sick will get well at once. Then I got the kreuzer and the sack for the bay leaves from the priest, and now I'm off on my pilgrimage."

"Hold on, neighbor!" said the egg dealer to the farmer. "Are you so simpleminded that you believed him? Don't you know what's happening? The priest wants to spend a pleasant day alone with your wife. That's why they cooked up a plan to get rid of you."

"Goodness gracious!" said the farmer. "I'd surely like to know if that's true."

"Well," said the neighbor. "I'll tell you what: You just get into my egg basket, and I'll carry you home. Then you can see for yourself."

So that is what they did. The neighbor put the farmer in his egg basket and carried him home on his back. When they got there, believe you me, there was a lot going on! The farmer's wife had already slaughtered whatever she could find in the barnyard and had also baked a lot of pancakes. The priest had also arrived and was strumming on his fiddle. When the neighbor knocked, the farmer's wife asked who was outside.

"It's me, neighbor," the egg dealer said. "I need a place for the night. I wasn't able to sell my eggs at the market, and now I've got to carry them home. But they're much too heavy for me, and I won't be able to make it home before darkness."

"Well, neighbor," said the farmer's wife, "you've come at a very bad time, but since there's nothing we can do about it, come in and sit down on the bench by the stove."

So the neighbor took a seat on the bench by the stove and set the basket down. In the meantime, the priest and the farmer's wife continued having a merry old time. Finally, the priest said, "Listen, my dear, since you have such a fine voice, I want you to sing me a song."

"Oh, I can't," said the farmer's wife. "I used to be able to sing all day long in my youth. But those days are gone forever."

"Oh, c'mon," said the priest again. "Just a little song for me."

Then the farmer's wife began to sing:

"I sent my husband far away
to cuckold's mountain for the day."

The priest joined in:

"I wish he'd spend the whole year there
and keep the sack for all I care.
                    Hallelujah!"

Now the neighbor, who was sitting back by the stove, began to sing (but I must tell you first that the farmer's name was Hildebrand):

"Hey, Hildebrand, your wife's a wench!
How can you watch this from the bench!?
                    Hallelujah!"

And now the farmer inside the basket started singing:

"Oh, I can't stand this anymore!
I'm getting out, for I'm quite sore!
                    Hallelujah!"

So he jumped out of the basket, gave the priest a good beating, and drove him out of the house.

◈ 96 ◈

The Three Little Birds

MORE THAN A THOUSAND YEARS AGO there were many petty kings in this country, and one of them lived on the mountain called Köterberg. He was very fond of hunting, and one day, when he left his castle and went down the mountain with his huntsmen, he came upon three maidens tending their cows. When they saw the king with his men, the oldest pointed at the king and called to the other two, "Hallo, hallo! If I can't have that man over there, I don't want any at all."

Then the second responded from the other side of the mountain and pointed at the fellow walking on the king's right. "Hallo, hallo! If I can't have that man over there, I don't want any at all."

Finally, the youngest pointed at the fellow on the king's left and called out, "Hallo! hallo! If I can't have that man over there, I don't want any at all."

The two men were the king's ministers, and the king had heard what the maidens had said. After he returned from the hunt, he summoned the three maidens and asked them what they had said the day before on the mountain. They refused to answer, but the king asked the oldest if she would take him for her husband. She said yes, and her two sisters also married the two ministers, for the maidens were all beautiful and had fine features, especially the queen, who had hair like flax.

The two sisters did not bear any children, and once when the king had to take a trip, he asked them to stay with the queen and cheer her up, for she was with child. While he was away, she gave birth to a little boy who had a bright red star as a birthmark. But the two sisters decided to throw the pretty baby boy into the river. After they had thrown him in (I think it was the Weser), a little bird flew up in the air and sang:

"Get ready for your death.
I'll see what I can do.
Get ready for the wreath.
Brave boy, can that be you?"

When the two sisters heard that, they feared for their lives and ran off. Later the king returned home, and they told him the queen had given birth to a dog, and the king responded, "Whatever God does is always for the best."

However, a fisherman lived by the river, and he fished the little boy out of the water while he was still alive. Since his wife had not given birth to any children, they fed and cared for him.

After a year had passed, the king went on another journey, and the queen gave birth to a second boy during his absence. The two wicked sisters again took the baby away and threw him into the river. Then the little bird flew up into the air once more and sang:

"Get ready for your death.
I'll see what I can do.
Get ready for the wreath.
Brave boy, can that be you?"

When the king came home, the sisters told him the queen had again given birth to a dog, and he responded as before, "Whatever God does is always for the best."

However, the fisherman fetched this baby out of the water too, and he fed and cared for him.

Once again the king went on a journey, and the queen gave birth to a little girl, whom the wicked sisters also threw into the river. Then the little bird flew up into the air once more and sang:

"Get ready for your death.
I'll see what I can do.
Get ready for the wreath.
Brave girl, can that be you?"

When the king came back home, the sisters told him the queen had given birth to a cat. This time the king became so angry that he had his wife thrown into prison, where she was forced to stay for many years.

In the meantime, the children grew up, and one day the oldest went out fishing with some other boys, but they did not want him around and said, "You foundling, go your own way!"

The boy was very upset by that and asked the old fisherman whether it was true. Then the fisherman told him how he had been out fishing one day and had found him in the water. The boy then said he wanted to go out and search for his father. The fisherman begged him to remain, but there was no holding him back. At last the fisherman gave in, and the boy went forth. He walked for many days until he came to a large and mighty river, where he found an old woman standing and fishing.

"Good day, grandma," said the boy.

"Why, thank you kindly."

"You'll be fishing there a long time before you catch any fish."

"And you'll be searching a long time before you find your father. How are you going to get across the river?" asked the old woman.

"God only knows."

Then the old woman picked him up and carried him across on her back. Once he was on the other side, he continued his search for his father a long time, but he could not find him.

When a year had gone by, the second boy went out looking for his brother. He too came to the river, and the same thing happened to him as with his brother. Now only the daughter was left alone at home, and she grieved so much for her brothers that finally the fisherman had to let her go too. Soon she came to the large river also and said to the old woman, "Good day, grandma."

"Why, thank you kindly."

"May God help you with your fishing."

When the old woman heard that, she treated the girl in a friendly way. She carried her across the river, gave her a stick, and said, "Now, my daughter, just keep going straight ahead, and when you come to a big black dog, you must be quiet. Don't be afraid or laugh or stop to look at it. Then you'll come to a large open castle. You must drop the stick on the threshold and go right through the castle and out the other side, where you'll see an old well. A big tree will be growing from the well, and on the tree a cage with a bird inside will be hanging. Take the cage down and get a glass of water from the well. Then carry both things back the same way you came. When you come to the threshold, pick up the stick, and when you come to the dog again, hit it in the face with the stick, but see to it that you don't miss. Then come back here to me."

The girl found everything just as the woman had said, and on her way back from the castle she met her two brothers, who had been searching half the world for each other. They went on together to the spot where the black dog was lying. Then she hit it on the face, and it turned into a handsome prince who accompanied them to the river. The old woman was still standing there and was happy to see them. She carried all four of them across the river, and then she departed, because she had now been released from the magic spell.

The others traveled back to the old fisherman, and they were all glad to have found each other again. Once inside the house, they hung the birdcage on the wall. But the second son was still restless. So he took a bow and went hunting. When he became tired, he took out his flute and began playing a little tune. The king, who was out hunting too, heard the music and went toward it. When he saw the boy, he said, "Who's given you permission to hunt here?"

"Nobody."

"Who're your parents?"

"I'm the fisherman's son."

"But he doesn't have any children."

"If you think I'm lying, come along with me."

The king did so and asked the fisherman, who told him all that had happened. Suddenly, the little bird in the cage began to sing:

"Oh, King of noble blood,
your children are back for good.
But their mother sits in prison
with nothing much to live on.
Her sisters are the wicked ones,
who took away your daughter and sons
and left them to the river's fate,
but the fisherman came 'ere it was too late."

When they heard the song, they were all astounded. The king took the little bird, the fisherman, and the three children with him to his castle, where he had the prison opened and his wife released. However, she had become very sick and was haggard. So her daughter gave her a drink of water from the well, and she regained her health. But the two wicked sisters were burned to death, and the daughter married the prince.

◆ 97 ◆

The Water of Life

ONCE UPON A TIME there was a king who was sick, and nobody thought he would live. His three sons were very saddened by this and went down into the palace garden, where they wept. There they met an old man who asked them why they were so distressed, and they told him that their father was so sick that he would probably die. Nothing seemed to help.

"I know of a remedy," the old man said. "It's the Water of Life. If he drinks it, he'll regain his health. But it's difficult to find."

"Well, I'll find it," said the oldest, and he went to the sick king and requested permission to leave and search for the Water of Life, for that was the only cure for his illness.

"No," said the king. "The danger is much too great. I'd rather die instead."

But the son pleaded so long that finally the king had to give his consent. Deep down the prince felt, If I bring him the water, I'll be my father's favorite and shall inherit the kingdom.

So he set out and, after he had been riding for some time, he came across a dwarf, who called to him and said, "Where are you going in such haste?"

"You meddling twirp," the prince said contemptuously, "that's none of your affair!" And he rode on.

But the little dwarf became furious and put a curse on him. Meanwhile, the prince found himself traveling through a mountain gorge, and the further he rode, the more the mountains closed together until the way became so narrow that he could not proceed. Nor could he turn his horse or get out of his saddle. He sat there as if he were in a prison.

The sick king waited a long time for the prince, but he did not come back. Then the second son said, "Father, let me go and search for the Water of Life," and he thought to himself, If my brother's dead, then the kingdom will fall to me.

At first the king did not want to let him go either, but finally he gave in. So the prince set out on the same road that his brother had taken and met the dwarf, who stopped him and asked where he was going in such haste.

"You meddling twirp," said the prince, "that's none of your affair!" And he rode off without turning around.

But the dwarf put a curse on him, and he ended up in a mountain gorge, where he became trapped like his brother. Indeed, that is what happens to arrogant people.

Now, when the second son also failed to return, the youngest offered to set forth and fetch the water, and eventually the king had to let him go too. When he met the dwarf and was asked where he was going in such haste, he stopped and answered, "I'm looking for the Water of Life because my sick father is on the brink of death."

"Do you know where to find it?"

"No," said the prince.

"Well, since you've behaved yourself in a proper manner and are not arrogant like your faithless brothers, I'll tell you how to get to the Water of Life: you'll find it gushing from a fountain in the courtyard of an enchanted castle, but you'll never make your way inside unless I give you an iron wand and two loaves of bread. You're to knock three times on the castle gate with the iron wand, then it will spring open. Inside are two lions lying on the ground. They will open their jaws, but if you throw a loaf of bread to each of them, they will be quiet. Then you must hurry and fetch some of the Water of Life before the clock strikes twelve. Otherwise, the gate will slam shut, and you will be locked in."

The prince thanked him, took the wand and the bread, and went on his way. When he arrived there, everything was just as the dwarf had said. After the third knock the gate sprang open, and when he had calmed the lions with the bread, he entered the castle and went into a big beautiful hall, where he found enchanted princes sitting all around. He took the rings from their fingers and also grabbed a sword and loaf of bread that were lying on the floor. Then he moved on to the next room, where he encountered a beautiful maiden, who was delighted to see him. She kissed him and said that he had set her free and could have her entire kingdom as reward. If he would return in a year's time, their wedding would be celebrated. Then she also told him where to find the fountain with the Water of Life, but that he had to hurry and draw the water before the clock struck twelve. So he went on and finally came to a room with a beautiful, freshly made bed, and since he was tired, he wanted to rest a little. Once he lay down, however, he fell asleep. When he awoke, the clock was striking a quarter to twelve, and he jumped up in a fright, ran to the fountain, and drew some water in a cup that happened to be lying on the ledge. Then he rushed outside, and just as he was running through the iron gate, the clock struck twelve, and the gate slammed so hard that it took off a piece of his heel.

Nevertheless, he was happy that he had found the Water of Life, and on his way home he passed the dwarf again. When the little man saw the sword and the bread, he said, "You've managed to obtain some valuable things. With the sword you'll be able to defeat whole armies, and the bread will always replenish itself."

But the prince did not want to return home to his father without his brothers, and so he asked, "Dear dwarf, could you tell me where my two brothers are? They went out looking for the Water of Life before me and never came back."

"They're trapped in between two mountains," said the dwarf. "I put them there with a magic spell because they were so arrogant."

Then the prince pleaded until finally the dwarf decided to release them but not without a warning. "Beware of them," he said. "They have evil hearts."

When he was reunited with his brothers, he was happy and told them all that had happened: how he found the Water of Life and was now bringing back a cupful to their father, how he had rescued the beautiful princess and was going to marry her after waiting a year, and how he would receive a vast kingdom after their marriage. Once his story was told, he rode on with his brothers, and they came to a country plagued by war and famine. The king was already convinced that he would soon perish because the situation was so desperate. But the prince went to him and gave him the bread, which he used to feed his people and satisfy their hunger. After that the prince also gave him the sword, which he used to defeat the enemy armies, and he was then able to live in peace and quiet. So the prince took back the loaf of bread and the sword, and the brothers rode on. However, they passed through two other countries plagued by famine and war, and on each occasion the prince gave the king his bread and sword. In this way he was able to help save three kingdoms.

Later on they boarded a ship and sailed across the sea. During the trip the two older brothers plotted together against their brother. "The youngest found the Water of Life, and we are empty-handed. So our father will give him the kingdom that is ours by right, and our brother will deprive us of our happiness."

Overcome by a desire for revenge, they planned to put an end to their brother. They waited until he was sound asleep. Then they poured the Water of Life from his cup into their own and replaced it with bitter salt water. When they arrived home, the youngest brought the cup to the sick king and told him to drink it and he would get well. No sooner did the king drink the bitter salt water than he became sicker than ever. And as he began to moan the two oldest brothers came and accused the youngest of wanting to poison the king, while they, on the other hand, had brought the true Water of Life, and they handed it to their father. As soon as he drank some, he felt his sickness on the wane and became as strong and healthy as in the days of his youth. After that the two older brothers went to the youngest and belittled him. "Oh, we know you found the Water of Life," they said, "but we're the ones who've received the reward for all your trouble. You should have been smarter and kept your eyes open. We took the water from you when you fell asleep at sea, and in a year's time one of us will fetch the beautiful princess. Still, you had better not expose us. Father will not believe you anyway, and if you breathe a single word about it, your life will be worth nothing. If you keep quiet, we'll let you live."

The old king was angry at his youngest son because he believed that his son had wanted to take his life. So he summoned his ministers and ordered them to sentence his son to be shot in secret. So, one day, as the prince went out hunting, suspecting no danger, one of the king's huntsmen had to accompany him. When they were all alone out in the forest, the huntsman looked so sad that the prince asked him, "Dear hunter, what's the matter?"

"I can't say," answered the huntsman, "and yet I should."

"Tell me," said the prince. "Whatever it is, I'll forgive you."

"Ah," said the huntsman. "The king has ordered me to kill you."

The prince was taken aback by this news and said, "Dear huntsman, let me live. I'll give you my royal garments, and you give me your common ones in exchange."

"I'll gladly do that," said the huntsman. "I couldn't have shot you anyway."

They exchanged clothes, and the huntsman went home, while the prince went deeper into the forest.

After a while three wagons loaded with gold and jewels arrived at the king's castle for his youngest son. They had been sent by the three kings who had defeated their enemies with the prince's sword and who had nourished their people with his bread. The wagons were an expression of their gratitude, and when the old king saw that, he began to think, Perhaps my son was innocent? And he said to the people at his court, "If only he were still alive! Now I regret that I ordered him to be killed."

"He's still alive," said the huntsman. "I didn't have the heart to carry out your order," and he told the king what had happened.

The king felt greatly relieved, and he had it proclaimed in all the surrounding kingdoms that his son was free to return and was back in favor with the king.

In the meantime, the princess had decided to build a glittering gold road that would lead up to her castle. She told her guards that whoever came riding to her straight up the middle of the road would be the right man and they should let him enter. However, whoever rode up on the side of the road would not be the right man, and they were not to let him enter.

When the year of waiting was almost up, the oldest son thought he would get an early start and pass himself off as her savior. Then he would get her for his wife and the kingdom as well. So he rode forth, and when he came to the castle and saw the beautiful road, he thought, It would be a terrible shame if you rode on it. So he turned off to the right and rode along the side. But when he got to the castle gate, the guards told him that he was not the right man and he had better go away. Soon thereafter the second prince set out, and when he came to the gold road and his horse set its hoof down on it, he thought, It would be a terrible shame if you damaged the road. He turned to the left and rode along the side. However, when he reached the gate, the guards told him he had better go away, for he was not the right man.

When the year was completely over, the third son prepared to ride out of the forest and hoped to forget his sorrows in the company of his beloved. As he set out he kept thinking about her and wishing he were already with her. When he arrived at the gold road, he did not even notice it, and his horse rode right down the middle of it. Once he reached the gate, it opened, and the princess welcomed him with joy. She pronounced him her savior and lord of the realm, and they were blissful as they celebrated their wedding. When it was over, she told him his father had sent for him and had pardoned him. So he rode home and explained to his father how his brothers had deceived him and why he had kept quiet about it. The old king wanted to punish them, but they had taken flight on a ship, sailed away, and never returned as long as they lived.

◆ 98 ◆

Doctor Know-It-All

ONCE UPON A TIME there was a poor farmer named Crab, who drove a cord of wood into town with his two oxen and sold the wood to a doctor for two talers. When the farmer went inside to get his money, the doctor was just about to sit down to dinner, and the farmer admired the fine food and drink at the doctor's table. His heart yearned for something like that, and he thought how nice it would be if he were a doctor. He lingered there awhile and finally asked if it was possible for someone like him to become a doctor.

"Of course," said the doctor. "There's not much to it."

"What do I have to do?" asked the farmer.

"First, you must buy yourself an ABC book, the kind with the picture of a rooster in it. Second, you must get cash for your wagon and two oxen and purchase some clothes and other things that doctors tend to need. Third, you must have a sign painted with the words 'I am Doctor Know-It-All' and nail it above your front door."

The farmer did everything he was told, and when he had doctored for some time but not very long, a rich and mighty nobleman was robbed of some money, and he heard about Doctor Know-It-All, who was living in such and such a village and would probably know what had become of the money. So the nobleman had his carriage hitched up, drove out to the village, and inquired at the farmer's house whether he was Doctor Know-It-All.

Yes, that was he, the farmer responded. Then the nobleman requested that he return with him and help him get back his stolen money. The farmer agreed, but added that Greta, his wife, had to come along too. The nobleman gave his approval, offered them both a seat in his carriage, and they drove off together. When they came to the nobleman's mansion, the table was already set, and Doctor Know-It-All was to eat with the lord, but he wanted his wife, Greta, to eat with them too. So they all sat down together at the table.

Now, when the first servant arrived with a dish of delicious food, the farmer nudged his wife and said, "Greta, that was the first," and he meant that that was the man with the first course. But the servant thought he meant "that's the first thief," and since he really was the thief, he got scared and went out to tell his accomplices, "The doctor knows everything. There's trouble ahead. He said I was the first."

The second servant did not even want to go in, but he had no choice. When he entered with his dish, the farmer nudged his wife and said, "Greta, that's the second." This servant too got scared and hurried out. The third fared no better. Again the farmer said, "Greta, that's the third." The fourth had to carry in a covered dish, and the nobleman asked the doctor to demonstrate his skill and guess what lay under the cover. Crabs were being served, and when the farmer looked at the dish, he was at a loss for words. "Poor Crab!" he finally cried.

When the nobleman heard that, he exclaimed, "There, he knows! I'm sure he must also know who has the money."

The servant was frightened to death and winked at the doctor to step outside for a moment. When he got outside, all four servants confessed to him that they had stolen the money. They proposed that he take charge of it and offered a large sum in addition if he would not expose them. Otherwise, they would soon be dangling from the gallows. Then they led him to the place where they had hidden the money. The doctor was satisfied, went back inside, sat down at the table, and said, "Sir, now I intend to look in my book to see where the money's been hidden."

In the meantime, the fifth servant had crawled into the stove to see if he could hear what else the doctor knew. As the doctor sat there at the table, he opened his ABC book and turned the pages back and forth looking for the rooster. Since he could not find it right away, he said, "I know you're there. I'm bound to find you."

The servant in the stove thought that the doctor was talking about him, and he jumped out of the stove in fright and said, "That man knows everything!"

Then Doctor Know-It-All showed the nobleman where the money was, but he did not reveal who had stolen it. As a reward he received money from both sides and became a famous man.

◈ 99 ◈

The Spirit in the Glass Bottle

ONCE UPON A TIME there was a poor woodcutter who worked from morning until late into the night. When he had finally saved up some money, he said to his son, "You're my only child, and I want you to have an education. So I'm going to give you the money that I've earned by the bitter sweat of my brow. If you learn something honest and decent, then you can support me in my old age, when my bones are stiff and I must sit at home."

The boy went off to a university and studied so hard that his teachers praised him, and he stayed there for some time. After he had studied at a few universities and was still trying to master everything he could, his father's small earnings ran out, and he had to return home.

"Ah," said the father sadly. "I have no more to give you. In these hard times I can just about earn enough for our keep and not a farthing more."

"Dear Father," answered the son, "don't even think about it. If this is God's will, then it will all turn out for the best. I know I can adjust."

As the father was getting ready to go out into the forest and earn something by chopping and piling up cordwood, his son said, "I want to go and help you."

"But that will be too difficult for you, my son," said the father. "You're not used to the hard work, and you won't be able to take it. Besides, I have only one ax and no money to buy another one."

"Just go to our neighbor," answered the son. "He'll lend you an ax until I've earned enough money to buy one myself."

So the father borrowed an ax from the neighbor, and the next morning at daybreak they went out together into the forest. The son helped his father and was quite cheerful and alert. When the sun was overhead, the father said, "Let's rest and eat our lunch. After that the work will go twice as fast."

The son took his bread and said, "Why don't you rest, Father? I'm not tired. I want to take a walk and look around the forest a little to see if I can find birds' nests."

"Don't be so foolish," said the father. "What do you want to run around for? Later on you'll be tired and won't be able to lift an arm. Stay here and sit down with me."

But the son went out into the forest and ate his bread. He was happy and gay and gazed up at the green branches to see if he could discover a nest. He searched all over the forest until he came to a huge dangerous-looking oak. It must have been hundreds of years old at the very least, and it would have taken more than five men to span it. He stood still, looked at the tree, and said, "I'm sure that many birds have built their nests here." Suddenly he seemed to hear a voice. He listened and heard a muffled voice calling, "Let me out, let me out!" He looked around him but could not detect a thing. It appeared as if the voice were coming out of the ground. So he called out, "Where are you?"

"I'm stuck down here in the roots of the oak," the voice answered. "Let me out, let me out!"

The student began to clear away the brushwood and search among the roots until he finally found a glass bottle in a little niche. Then he lifted it in the air against the light and saw something jumping up and down inside that resembled a frog.

"Let me out, let me out!" it kept crying, and since the student suspected no harm, he pulled the cork out of the bottle. Immediately, a spirit rose out of the bottle and began to expand itself. It grew so fast that in a few moments a horrible fellow, half as big as the tree, stood before the student.

"Do you know what your reward will be for letting me out?" the spirit asked in a frightening voice.

"No," the student answered fearlessly. "How should I know?"

"Well, I'll tell you," cried the spirit. "You're going to get a broken neck."

"You should have told me that in the first place," responded the student, "then I would never have let you out. But my head's going to stay right where it is until we consult a few more people."

"I don't care about more people!" exclaimed the spirit. "You're going to get your just reward. Do you think that I was being held prisoner in there for such a long time because people felt pity for me? No, I was being punished, for I'm the almighty Mercurius, and I must break the neck of anyone who lets me out of the bottle."

"Take it easy," said the student. "Not so fast! First you must prove that you were really in that little bottle and that you're not a fake. If you can really get back inside, then I'll believe you, and you can do whatever you like with me."

"That's as simple as pie," said the spirit contemptuously, whereupon he proceeded to shrink himself and make himself as thin and as small as he was before. Then he went back through the opening and down the neck of the bottle. No sooner was he inside than the student took the cork he had pulled off and shoved it back on the bottle. After that he tossed the bottle into its old place among the roots, and the spirit saw that he had been outwitted.

Now the student started back to his father, but the spirit cried out pitifully, "Oh, let me out! Let me out!"

"No," answered the student. "Not a second time. I'm not about to let anyone free who's already tried to take my life once, especially after I've got him where I want him."

"If you let me go," called the spirit, "I'll give you enough money to last you as long as you live."

"No," responded the student. "You'd only trick me just as you did the first time."

"You're throwing away a golden opportunity," said the spirit. "I won't harm you. On the contrary, I'm offering you a generous reward."

I'll risk it, thought the student. Maybe he'll keep his word. Besides, he can't harm me. So he pulled out the cork, and the spirit rose up as high as he had the previous time and expanded himself until he became as big as a giant.

"Now you'll receive your reward," he said, and handed the student a little patch of cloth that resembled a bandage and said, "If you rub a wound with one end, the wound will heal. And if you rub steel or iron with the other end, it will turn into silver."

"I must try it first," said the student. He went over to a tree, sliced the bark with his ax, and rubbed the slit with one end of the patch. The bark closed immediately, and the wound healed.

"Now everything's settled," the student said to the spirit, "and we can part company."

The spirit thanked him for setting him free, and the student thanked the spirit for his gift and went back to his father.

"Where have you been keeping yourself? Did you forget that we've got work to do? I told you you'd never be able to finish the job."

"Don't worry, Father. I'll catch up."

"Catch up!" said the father angrily. "That's no way."

"Watch me, Father! I'm going to chop that tree right down, and it's going to make a big crash." He took his patch, rubbed his ax with it, and gave the tree a tremendous blow. However, since the ax had turned to silver, the blade bent. "Father, just look at the bad ax you gave me! It's all bent."

The father was taken aback and said, "Oh, look what you've done now! I'll have to pay for the ax, and I don't know where I'll get the money. You're useless!"

"Don't be angry," answered the son. "I'll pay for the ax all right."

"You dumbhead," cried the father. "What are you going to pay with? You've got nothing except what I give you. Your head's full of ideas from studying, but you don't understand the first thing about wood chopping."

After a while the student said, "Father, I can't work anymore. Let's call it a day."

"What's this now?" he answered. "Do you think that I want to sit with my hands in my lap like you? I've still got work to do, but you can head home if you want."

"Father, this is the first time I've been in this forest. I don't know the way home. Please come with me."

Once the father's anger had subsided, he let himself be persuaded to go home with his son. Then he said, "Go and sell that damaged ax and see what you can get for it. I'll have to earn the rest to pay back our neighbor."

The son took the ax and brought it to a goldsmith in the city, who tested it, put it on the scales, and said, "It's worth four hundred talers, but I don't have that much in cash."

"Give me what you have," said the student, "and you can owe me the rest."

The goldsmith gave him three hundred talers and owed him a hundred. After that the student went home and said, "Father, I have the money. Go and ask our neighbor how much he wants for the ax."

"I already know that," answered the old man. "One taler and six groschen."

"Then give him two talers and twelve groschen. That's double the amount and should more than do. See, Father, I have money to spare," and he gave his father a hundred talers and said, "You'll never want for money, and now you can live in comfort."

"My God!" said the old man. "How did you ever come by this fortune?"

Then the student told his father how everything had happened and how he had struck gold by trusting in his luck. Now he took the rest of the money and went back to the university, where he continued studying. And since he was able to heal any kind of wound with his patch, he became the most famous doctor in the world.

◈ 100 ◈

The Devil's Sooty Brother

A DISCHARGED SOLDIER had nothing to live on and no longer knew what to do with his life. So he went out into the forest, and after walking for a while, he met a little man who was actually the devil himself.

"What's the matter?" the little man said to him. "You look so gloomy."

"I'm hungry and have no money," said the soldier.

"If you hire yourself out to me and will be my servant," the devil said, "you'll have enough for the rest of your life. But you've got to serve me seven years, and after that you'll be free. There's just one other thing I've got to tell you: you're not allowed to wash yourself, comb your hair, trim your beard, cut your nails or hair, or wipe your eyes."

"If that's the way it must be, let's get on with it," the soldier said, and he went away with the little man, who led him straight to hell and told him what his chores were: he was to tend the fires under the kettles in which the damned souls were sitting, sweep the house clean and carry the dirt out the door, and keep everything in order. However, he was never to peek into the kettles, or things would go badly for him.

"I understand," said the soldier. "I'll take good care of everything."

So the old devil set out again on his travels, and the soldier began his duty. He put fuel on the fires, swept and carried the dirt out the door, and did everything just as he was ordered. When the old devil returned, he checked to see if everything had been done according to his instructions, nodded his approval, and went off again. Now, for the first time, the soldier took a good look around hell. There were kettles all about, and they were boiling and bubbling with tremendous fires under each one of them. He would have given his life to know what was in them if the devil had not strictly forbidden it. Finally, he could no longer restrain himself: he lifted the lid of the first kettle a little and looked inside, only to see his old sergeant sitting there.

"Aha, you crumb!" he said. "Fancy meeting you here! You used to step on me, but now I've got you under my foot." He let the lid drop quickly, stirred the fire, and added fresh wood. After that he moved to the second kettle, lifted the lid a little, and peeked inside. There sat his lieutenant. "Aha, you crumb!" he said. "Fancy meeting you here! You used to step on me, but now I've got you under my foot." He shut the lid again and added a log to the fire to make it really good and hot for him. Now he wanted to see who was sitting in the third kettle, and it turned out to be his general. "Aha, you crumb! Fancy meeting you here! You used to step on me, but now I've got you under my foot." He got out a bellows and pumped it until the fire of hell was blazing hot under him.

And so it was that he served out his seven years in hell. He never washed, combed himself, trimmed his beard, cut his nails, or wiped his eyes. The seven years passed so quickly that he was convinced that only six months had gone by. When his time was completely up, the devil came and said, "Well, Hans, what've you been doing all this time?"

"I've tended the fires under the kettles, and I've swept and carried the dirt out the door."

"But you also peeked into the kettles. Well, you're just lucky that you added more wood to the fire; otherwise, you would have forfeited your life. Now your time is up. Do you want to go back home?"

"Yes," said the soldier. "I'd like to see how my father's doing at home."

"All right, if you want to get your proper reward, you must go and fill your knapsack with the dirt you've swept up and take it home with you. And you must also go unwashed and uncombed, with long hair on your head and a long beard, with uncut nails, and with bleary eyes. And if anyone asks you where you're coming from, you've got to say 'From hell.' And if anyone asks you who you are, you're to say 'I'm the devil's sooty brother and my king as well.' "

The soldier said nothing. Indeed, he carried out the devil's instructions, but he was not at all satisfied with the reward. As soon as he was out in the forest again, he took the knapsack and wanted to shake it out. But when he opened it, he discovered that the dirt had turned into pure gold. "Never in my life would I have imagined that," said the soldier, who was delighted and went into the city. An innkeeper was standing in front of his inn as Hans approached, and when he caught sight of Hans, the innkeeper was terrified because the soldier looked so dreadful, even more frightening than a scarecrow. He called out to him and asked, "Where are you coming from?"

"From hell."

"Who are you?"

"The devil's sooty brother and my king as well."

The innkeeper did not want to let him inside, but when Hans showed him the gold, he went and unlatched the door himself. Then Hans ordered the best room and insisted on the finest service. He ate and drank his fill but did not wash or comb himself as the devil had instructed. Finally, he lay down to sleep, but the innkeeper could not get the knapsack of gold out of his mind. Just the thought of it left him no peace. So he crept into the room during the night and stole it.

When Hans got up the next morning and went to pay the innkeeper before leaving, his knapsack was gone. However, he wasted no words and thought, It's not your fault that this happened, and he turned around and went straight back to hell, where he complained about his misfortune to the devil and asked for help.

"Sit down," said the devil. "I'm going to wash and comb you, trim your beard, cut your hair and nails, and wash out your eyes."

When he was finished with the soldier, he gave him a knapsack full of dirt again and said, "Go there and tell the innkeeper to give you back your gold; otherwise, I'll come and fetch him, and he'll have to tend the fires in your place."

Hans went back up and said to the innkeeper, "You stole my money, and if you don't give it back, you'll go to hell in my place and you'll look just as awful as I did."

The innkeeper gave him back the money and even more besides. Then he begged him to be quiet about what had happened.

Now Hans was a rich man and set out on his way home. He bought himself a pair of rough linen overalls and wandered here and there playing music, for he had learned that from the devil in hell. Once he happened to play before an old king in a certain country, and the king was so pleased that he promised Hans his oldest daughter in marriage. However, when she heard that she was supposed to marry a commoner in white overalls, she said, "I'll go drown myself in the deepest lake before I do that." So the king gave Hans his youngest daughter, who was willing to marry him out of love for her father. So the devil's sooty brother got the king's daughter, and when the old king died, he got the whole kingdom as well.

◆ 101 ◆

Bearskin

ONCE UPON A TIME there was a young fellow who enlisted as a soldier, fought bravely, and was always in the thick of things when the bullets were whistling about. As long as the war lasted, things went well for him, but when peace was announced, he was discharged, and the captain told him to go wherever he wanted. Since his parents were dead, he no longer had a home. Therefore, he went to his brothers and asked them to put him up until war broke out again. But the brothers were hard-hearted and said, "What's to be done with you? We certainly can't use you. You've got to make it on your own."

The soldier had nothing left except his gun, which he swung over his shoulder, and he then set out into the world. Eventually he came to a large heath, where nothing but a circle of trees could be seen. He sat down beneath them and was overcome with sadness as he pondered his fate. I have no money, he thought. I've learned nothing but how to use weapons, and now I'm not needed because peace has been announced. I already see that I'm bound to starve.

Suddenly he heard a rustling noise, turned around, and came face-to-face with a stranger wearing a green jacket. The man looked quite stately, but he had an awful cloven foot. "I already know what you need," said the man. "Money and property shall be yours, as much as you can stand, but first I must know whether you're a fearful type because I don't want to spend my money for nothing."

"A soldier and fear don't mix," the young man answered. "Just put me to the test."

"I certainly will," responded the man. "Look behind you!"

The soldier turned around and saw a huge, growling bear coming at him. "Oho!" exclaimed the soldier. "When I get done tickling your nose, you won't want to growl anymore." He took aim and shot the bear in the muzzle so that the beast collapsed on the spot and did not move a limb.

"I clearly see," said the stranger, "that you don't lack courage, but there's one more condition you must meet."

"Just as long as it won't cost me my soul," answered the soldier, who knew quite well with whom he was dealing. "If it doesn't, then I'm prepared to do anything."

"You'll have to judge for yourself," answered the man in the green jacket. "For the next seven years you're not to wash, or comb your hair and beard, or cut your nails, or say the Lord's Prayer. Then I'll give you a jacket and cloak that you must wear all the time. If you die during these seven years, you're mine. If you stay alive, you're free for the rest of your life, and you'll be rich besides."

The soldier thought about his desperate situation, and since he had often risked his life in the past, he was now willing to risk it again and agreed to the terms. The devil took off his green jacket, handed it to the soldier, and said, "Whenever you wear this jacket and reach into the pocket, you'll always come up with a handful of money." Then the devil skinned the bear and said, "This shall be your cloak and your bed as well, for you're to sleep in it and are not allowed to use any other bed. And your name shall be Bearskin because of your outfit." The devil then disappeared.

The soldier put on the jacket, reached into the pocket right away, and found it was just as the devil had said. Then he threw the bearskin over his shoulders, went into the world, and was in good spirits. He began doing whatever gave him pleasure and whatever made it hard on his pocket. In the first year things were still tolerable, but by the second he already looked like a monster. His face was almost entirely covered by hair. His beard resembled a piece of coarse felt. His fingers turned into claws, and his face was so dirty that cress could have sprouted there if one had sown the seeds. Everyone who crossed his path ran away in fright. Nevertheless, wherever he went, he gave money to the poor to pray that he survive the seven years, and he paid so well for everything, he was always able to obtain lodgings.

In the fourth year he came to an inn, and the innkeeper did not want to let him stay or even give him a place in the stable because he feared his horses might bolt when they saw him. Yet, when Bearskin reached into his pocket and pulled out a handful of ducats, the innkeeper softened and gave him a room in the rear building. Still, he had to promise not to show himself lest the inn get a bad name.

One evening, as Bearskin was sitting alone and wishing with all his heart that the seven years were over, he heard someone moaning loudly in the next room. Since he was a compassionate person, he opened the door of the room and saw an old man weeping uncontrollably and wringing his hands above his head. Bearskin stepped closer, but the man jumped up and wanted to run away. Yet, when he heard a human voice, he was persuaded to stay, and Bearskin used kind words to get him to reveal the cause of all his troubles. The old man told him that his fortune had declined little by little until he had become so poor that he and his daughters had reached the brink of starvation. Now he could not even pay the innkeeper and was to be put in prison.

"If that's all there is to your troubles," said Bearskin, "I've got plenty of money to help." He summoned the innkeeper, paid him, and put a pouch full of gold into the pocket of the unfortunate man.

When the old man saw that all his worries were gone, he did not know how to express his gratitude. "Come with me," he said to Bearskin. "My daughters are remarkably beautiful. I want you to choose one of them for your wife. When she hears what you've done for me, she won't refuse. Of course, you look a bit strange, but she'll get you back into shape before you know it."

Bearskin was delighted by the thought of this, and he went along. When the oldest daughter caught sight of him, she was so terribly frightened that she let out a shriek and ran away. Although the second remained there and examined him from head to foot, she said, "How can I marry a man who no longer resembles a human being? I'd rather have the shaved bear that passed through here on show and was taught to act like a man. At least it was wearing a hussar's uniform and white gloves. If it were just a question of ugliness, I could get used to him."

But the youngest daughter said, "He must be a good man to have helped you out of your trouble. If you've promised him a bride in return, then your word must be kept."

It was a shame that Bearskin's face was covered with dirt and hair. Otherwise, one could have seen how his heart leapt for joy when he heard those words. He took a ring from his finger, broke it in two, and gave her one half, while he kept the other half for himself. In her half he wrote his name, and in his half, her name, and he asked her to take good care of it. He then took his leave and said, "I must wander for another three years. If I don't return, then you are free because I'll be dead. But pray to God to keep me alive."

The poor bride dressed herself all in black, and when she thought about her betrothed, tears would come to her eyes. Meanwhile, her sisters showed her nothing but scorn and contempt.

"Take care," said the oldest, "if you hold out your hand to him, he'll smash it with his paw."

"Watch out," said the second, "bears love sweets, and if he likes you, he'll eat you up."

"You must always do what he wants," resumed the oldest; "otherwise, he'll start to growl."

And the second added, "The wedding will certainly be a merry one, since bears dance so well."

The bride kept silent and did not let herself be discouraged. In the meantime, Bearskin traveled about the world from place to place, did good wherever he could, and gave generously to the poor so they would pray for him. Finally, when the last day of the seven years arrived, he went out to the heath again and sat down inside the circle of trees. It was not long before the wind started to howl and the devil stood before him with a look of displeasure. Then he tossed Bearskin his old jacket and demanded the green one back.

"You're not done yet," said Bearskin. "You've still got to clean me."

Whether he liked it or not, the devil had to fetch water, wash Bearskin off, comb his hair, and cut his nails. When the devil finished, Bearskin looked like a stalwart soldier and was much more handsome than he had ever been before.

As soon as the devil was safely out of the way, Bearskin felt very much relieved. He went into the city, purchased a splendid velvet jacket, took a seat in a carriage drawn by four white horses, and drove to the house of his bride. Nobody recognized him. The father thought he was a distinguished army colonel and led him into the room where his daughters were sitting. Bearskin had to take a seat between the two oldest, and they gave him wine, brought him the finest delicacies, and thought he was the handsomest man they had ever seen. On the other hand, the bride sat in her black dress across from him and did not raise her eyes or say one word. When he finally asked the father whether he could have one of his daughters for his wife, the two oldest jumped up and ran to their rooms to put on their best clothes, for each one imagined that she would be the one chosen. As soon as he was left alone with his bride, the stranger took out his half of the ring and dropped it into a cup of wine that he handed her across the table. She took it, but when she had drunk the wine and found the ring lying at the bottom of the cup, her heart began to pound. She took out the other half of the ring that she had been wearing on a ribbon around her neck and matched it with his: it was clear that both parts fit perfectly together. Then he said, "I'm your betrothed, whom you last saw as Bearskin. Through the grace of God I've regained my human form and have become clean again."

He went toward her, embraced her, and gave her a kiss. Just then the two sisters came in all dressed up in their best gowns, and when they saw that the handsome young man had chosen the youngest sister and had turned out to be Bearskin, they ran outside in rage and anger. One drowned herself in a well, the other hanged herself from a tree.

In the evening someone knocked on the door, and when the bridegroom opened it, there stood the devil in his green jacket.

"I just want you to know," he said, "that I got two souls in exchange for your one."

❖ 102 ❖

The Wren and the Bear

ONCE, DURING THE SUMMERTIME, as the bear and the wolf were walking through the forest, the bear heard a bird singing a beautiful song and said, "Brother wolf, what kind of bird can sing as beautifully as that?"

"That's the king of the birds," said the wolf. "We must bow down before him."

However, it was nothing but the wren, popularly known as the fence king.

"If that's the case," said the bear, "I'd like very much to see his royal palace. Please take me there."

"You can't go there just like that," said the wolf. "You'll have to wait until the queen comes."

Soon thereafter the queen arrived carrying some food in her bill, and the king as well, and they began feeding their young ones. The bear wanted to run in right after them, but the wolf held him by his sleeve and said, "No, you've got to wait until His Majesty and Her Highness have gone away again."

So they took note of the place where the nest was and trotted off. However, the bear could not rest until he saw the royal palace, and after a short while, he went back to it. The king and queen had already flown away, and he looked inside and saw five or six young birds lying there.

"Is that the royal palace?" exclaimed the bear. "It's a miserable palace. And you're not royal children in the least. You're a disgrace!"

When the young wrens heard that, they were tremendously angry and cried out, "No, we're not! Our parents are honorable people. Bear, you're going to pay for your remarks!"

The bear and the wolf became frightened. They turned around, went back to their dens, and sat. But the young wrens kept crying and shrieking, and when their parents returned with food, they said, "We're not going to touch so much as a fly's leg until you establish whether we're a disgrace or not. The bear was just here, and he insulted us."

"Calm down," said the old king. "I'll settle this matter."

He flew away with the queen to the bear's den and called inside,

"Hey, you grumbly old bear, why did you insult my children? You'll pay for this. We'll have to settle this matter in a bloody war!"

So war was declared against the bear, who summoned all the four-legged animals: the ox, donkey, steer, stag, deer, and all those beasts that walk upon the earth. To counter this, the wren summoned everything that flies: not only the big and small birds, but also the gnats, hornets, bees, and flies had to come too.

When the time came for the war to begin, the wren sent out scouts to discover who the commanding general of the enemy forces was. The gnat was the wiliest of them all and roamed out into the forest, where the enemy had assembled. Then he hid under a leaf on the tree where the password was to be given out. The bear was standing right there, and he called the fox to him and said, "Fox, you're the sliest of all the animals. I want you to be our general and to lead us."

"Fine," said the fox. "But what shall we use as signals?"

Since nobody had any ideas, the fox said, "I've got a nice long bushy tail that looks almost like a red plume. If I lift up my tail, that will mean everything's all right, and you should charge. But, if I let it droop, then run for your lives."

Once the gnat heard that, he flew back to the wren and reported everything down to the last detail. At daybreak, when the battle was to commence, the four-legged animals came thundering with such a clatter that the earth began to tremble. The wren and his army also came flying through the air. They buzzed, shrieked, and swarmed so much that everyone in the surrounding area was frightened to death. As both sides attacked, the wren sent the hornet out with instructions to dive under the fox's tail and to sting him with all his might. Now, when the fox felt the first sting, he twitched and lifted a leg, but he stood his ground and kept holding up his tail. With the second sting, he had to lower his tail momentarily. But by the third sting he could no longer stand the pain and had to howl and tuck his tail between his legs. When the other animals saw that, they thought all was lost and began to run, each to his own den. And so the birds won the battle.

The king and queen flew home to their children and called, "Children, rejoice! Eat and drink to your heart's content. We've won the war."

But the young wrens said, "We're not going to eat a thing until the bear comes to our nest to beg our pardon and say that we're a credit to the family."

Then the wren flew to the bear's den and cried out, "Hey, you grumbly bear, I want you to go to my nest and ask my children for pardon. You'd better tell them they're a credit to the family; otherwise, your ribs will be broken to pieces."

On hearing this, the bear became extremely frightened, and he crawled to the nest, where he apologized. Now the young wrens were finally satisfied, so they sat down together and ate, drank, and made merry till late in the night.

◈ 103 ◈

The Sweet Porridge

ONCE UPON A TIME there was a poor but pious girl who lived alone with her mother. When they had nothing left to eat, the girl went out into the forest, where she met an old woman who already knew about her troubles and gave her a small pot. She instructed the girl to say to it "Little pot, cook," for it would then make a good, sweet millet porridge. And the girl was to say "Little pot, stop!" to make it stop cooking.

The girl brought the pot home to her mother, and it put an end to their poverty and hunger. From then on they ate sweet porridge as often as they liked. One day, when the girl had gone out, the mother said, "Little pot, cook," and it began cooking. After she had eaten her fill, she wanted the pot to stop, but she had forgotten the right words. So the pot continued to cook, and the porridge ran over the rim and proceeded to fill the kitchen and the whole house, then the next house and the street, as if it wanted to feed the entire world. The situation was desperate, and nobody knew what to do. Finally, when only one house was left standing without any porridge in it, the girl returned home and merely said, "Little pot, stop!" It stopped cooking, and whoever sought to go back into the town had to eat his way through.

◈ 104 ◈

The Clever People

ONE DAY A FARMER got his hornbeam stick from the corner and said to his wife, "Trina, I'm going for a trip into the country, and I'll be gone three days. If the cattle dealer comes by while I'm away and wants to buy our three cows, you can let them go for two hundred talers, but nothing less than that. Nothing less, do you hear?"

"In God's name, why don't you just leave," she answered. "I can take care of everything."

"Yes, that's what you say!" responded her husband. "But you're still suffering from that fall you took on your head when you were young. So I'm telling you, don't do anything stupid. Otherwise, I'll color your back black and blue, and I won't need paint for that, just this stick in my hand. And you'll wear those colors for a good year at least. You can depend on that!" Upon saying this, the farmer went his way.

The next morning the cattle dealer showed up, and the woman did not have to exchange many words with him. After he had inspected the cows and heard the price, he said, "I'll gladly pay that amount, because that's what I call a fair price among friends. So I'll just take the cows with me right now."

He took off their chains, drove them out of the stable, and just as he was about to head through the farmyard gate, the woman grabbed him by the arm and said, "First you must give me the two hundred talers; otherwise, I can't let you go."

"Right," answered the man, "but to tell you the truth, I forgot to take my money belt with me. However, you don't have to worry. I'll leave you a deposit for sure. I'll just take two of the cows with me and leave the third here. That way you'll have good security."

That made sense to the woman, so she let the man go off with the two cows and thought, Hans will certainly be happy when he sees how clever I was.

The farmer returned home on the third day, as he said he would, and asked right away whether the cows had been sold.

"Certainly, my dear Hans," answered his wife, "and just like you said, for two hundred talers. They're not even worth that amount, but the man took them without putting up an argument."

"Where's the money?" asked the farmer.

"I don't have the money," replied the wife. "He forgot to bring his money belt, but he'll return with the money soon. He left behind a good deposit."

"What kind of a deposit?" asked the man.

"One of the cows. He won't get it until he's paid for the others. I was clever about it. I kept the smallest because it eats the least."

The farmer was furious. He raised his stick in the air and was about to paint her black and blue, as he had promised, when suddenly he lowered his hand and said, "You're the silliest goose that ever waddled the face of God's earth, but I feel sorry for you. I'm going out on the highway, and I'll wait for three days to see whether I can find anyone more stupid than you are. If I come across one, then you're free. If I don't, you'll get what's coming to you, but with no deduction!"

He went out to the large highway, sat down on a rock, and waited to see what would happen. Soon a hay cart came along, and a woman was standing in the middle of it, instead of sitting up front on the stack of hay, or walking beside the oxen and guiding them.

That seems to be just the type you're looking for, he thought. So the farmer jumped up and ran like someone out of his mind back and forth in front of the cart.

"What is it you want, friend?" she said. "I don't know you. Where do you come from?"

"I fell out of heaven," answered the man, "and I don't know how to get back. Do you think you can drive me there?"

"No," said the woman. "I don't know the way. But since you're from heaven, perhaps you can tell me how my husband is. He's been up there for three years, and I'm sure you must have seen him."

"Of course, I've seen him, but things don't always go well for everyone up there. He tends the sheep, but those dear animals make life hard for him. They jump around in the mountains and get lost in the woods. Then he has to chase after them and drive them back home. Most of his clothes are tattered, and they'll fall off his back soon. There aren't any tailors there to mend things because Saint Peter won't let them in, as you probably know from that old fairy tale."

"Who would have thought of that?" the woman exclaimed. "Do you know what? I'm going to get his Sunday coat that's still hanging in the closet at home. I'm sure it'll be respectable enough to wear up there. You'll be so kind as to take it with you, won't you?"

"It won't work," answered the farmer. "Nobody's allowed to bring clothes into heaven. They take them away from you at the gate."

"Listen to me," said the woman. "I sold all my best wheat yesterday and received a tidy sum for it. I want to send him the money. If you put the purse in your pocket, nobody will notice it."

"If you think that's the only way," replied the farmer, "then I'll gladly do you the favor."

"Just stay right here," she said. "I'll drive home right away and fetch the purse. I may as well keep standing. It's better than sitting up front because this way I make the cart lighter for the oxen."

She spurred the oxen on and drove off, while the farmer thought, She's got all it takes to become a lunatic. If she really brings the money back, my wife can thank her lucky star that she won't get a beating.

It did not take the woman long to return with the money, and she herself put it into his pocket. Before she went away, she thanked the farmer a thousand times for his kindness. Back at home she found her son, who had just returned from the fields. She told him all about the day's extraordinary event and added, "I'm really happy that I got this opportunity to send something to my poor husband. Who would have ever thought that he'd be short of anything in heaven?"

Her son was totally amazed. "Mother," he said, "it's not every day that someone appears from heaven. I'm going right out to see if I can still find him. I want to know what it's like there and how the work's going."

He saddled the horse and rode away in great haste. Soon he found the farmer sitting under a willow tree and counting the money that was in the purse. "Have you seen the man who fell out of heaven?" the young man called to him.

"Yes," answered the farmer, "he's already started on his way back and has climbed the mountain over there, where it'll be closer for him. If you ride hard, you might be able to overtake him."

"Oh," said the young man, "I've been working the whole day, and the ride here has completely knocked me out. Since you know the man, you could do me a favor: get on my horse, and when you catch up to him, persuade him to return."

Aha, thought the farmer, he's also one of those people not destined to become a beacon of light. Then he said, "I'll be glad to do you the favor." Then he mounted the horse and galloped off.

The young man sat there until midnight, but the farmer did not return. Well, he thought, I'm sure the man from heaven was in a great hurry and didn't want to turn back. So the farmer probably gave him the horse to bring to Father. He went home and told his mother what had happened and said he had sent the horse to his father so that he would not always have to walk around on foot.

"You did the right thing," his mother said. "You're still young, and your legs are strong."

When the farmer arrived home, he put the horse in the stable next to the cow held in deposit. Then he went to his wife and said, "Trina, it's your lucky day. I found two people who're even simpler than you. This time you'll get off without a beating. I'll save it up for another time."

Then he lit his pipe, sat down in his grandfather chair, and said, "That wasn't a bad deal. Two lean cows for a sleek horse and a large purse of money to boot. If stupidity were always to turn in such a profit, I'd gladly give it my due respect."

So thought the farmer, but I'm sure you like the simple people better.

❖ 105 ❖

Tales About Toads

I

ONCE UPON A TIME there was a little girl whose mother gave her a bowl of milk and bread every afternoon. The child sat down with it outside in the yard, and when she began to eat, a toad would hop out of a crack in the wall, dip its head into the milk, and eat along with her. The girl took delight in this, and if the toad did not appear on time, she would sit down with her bowl and cry out:

"Toad, toad, it's time to come,
be so good, and we'll have some fun.
I've brought you bread and milk to eat.
Toad, toad, come take your seat."

Upon hearing this, the toad would come hopping and enjoy the meal. Moreover, it would show its gratitude by bringing her all kinds of beautiful things from its secret treasure—sparkling stones, pearls, and gold trinkets. But the toad would only drink the milk and leave the bread lying there.

One day the girl took her little spoon, hit the toad gently on its head, and said, "Toad, you must eat the bread."

Her mother, who was standing in the kitchen, heard her daughter talking to someone, and when she saw that she was hitting a toad with her little spoon, she ran outside with a log and killed the good creature.

From then on a change came over the child. As long as the toad had eaten with her, she had grown big and strong. Now she lost her beautiful rosy cheeks and became thinner by the day. It was not long before the owl, the bird of ill omen, began to screech in the night, and the robin gathered twigs and leaves for a funeral wreath. Soon thereafter the child lay in her coffin.

II

A little orphan girl was sitting on the city wall and spinning when she suddenly saw a toad come hopping out of a crack. So she quickly spread her blue silk neckerchief beside her, because she knew that toads like to walk on neckerchiefs more than anything else. As soon as the toad caught sight of that, it turned back, but it soon returned carrying a tiny golden crown. It laid the crown on the kerchief and went away again.

The crown was made out of delicately spun gold and glittered, and the girl picked it up in her hands. The toad soon came back a second time, but when it didn't see the crown, it hopped to the wall and began hitting its head against it out of grief. The toad continued doing this until its strength gave out, and it finally lay there dead. If the little girl had left the crown lying on the kerchief, the toad would probably have brought even more of its treasures out of the hole.

III

"Hoo-hoo, hoo-hoo," called the toad.

"Come out," said the child.

The toad came out, and the child asked it about his little sister. "Have you seen Little Red Stocking by any chance?"

"No," the toad said. "I haven't seen her either. How about you? Hoo-hoo, hoo-hoo, hoo-hoo."

❖ 106 ❖

The Poor Miller's Apprentice and the Cat

THERE ONCE WAS A MILLER who lived in a mill. He had neither wife nor children, but three hired men. One day, after the men had been with him for some years, he said to them, "I'm getting old, and soon I'll retire and just sit by the stove. So I want you to go out and see who can bring back the best horse. The winner will get my mill. In return he'll have to take care of me until I die."

Now, the youngest of the hired hands was the apprentice, and the other two thought he was a simpleton and did not deserve the mill. He, in fact, did not even want it, but he set out with the other two, and when they came to a village, the two men said to simple Hans, "Why don't you stop here? You'll never get a horse as long as you live."

But Hans went on with them, and when night came, they arrived at a cave and lay down to sleep inside. The two clever ones waited until Hans fell asleep. Then they got up and made off, while Hans continued sleeping. They thought that they had made a smart move, but we shall see what happens to men like that.

When the sun rose and Hans woke up, he was lying in the deep cave; he looked all around and cried, "Oh, God, where am I?" Then he got up and crawled out of the cave. He went into the forest and began thinking, they've abandoned me and left me here all alone. How shall I ever get a horse? While he was walking along and pondering his situation, he met a little cat covered with many different spots, and she spoke to him in a friendly way.

"Where are you going, Hans?"

"Why? You can't help me."

"I know quite well what you're looking for," said the cat. "You want a fine horse. Come with me and be my faithful servant for seven years. Then I'll give you the finest horse you'll ever see in your life."

This is really a strange cat, Hans thought, but I might as well see if she's telling the truth.

So she took him with her to her enchanted castle, where there were nothing but kittens for servants. They were cheerful and good-natured creatures and ran nimbly up and down the stairs. In the evening, when Hans and the cat sat down at the dinner table, three of the kittens had to play music: one played the double bass, the second the fiddle, and the third took a trumpet and blew until its cheeks were all puffed out. After they had finished their meal, the table was carried away, and the cat said, "Now, Hans, come and dance with me."

"No," he answered. "I don't dance with pussycats. I've never done anything like that."

"Then bring him to bed," she said to the kittens.

One kitten lit the way to the bedroom, another took off his shoes, a third his stockings, and a fourth blew the light out. The next morning they returned and helped him out of bed: one put on his stockings, the second got his shoes, the third washed him, and the fourth dried his face with its tail.

"That feels very soft," said Hans.

Now, he also had to serve the cat, and he was supposed to chop firewood every day. She gave him a silver ax, silver wedges, a silver saw, and a copper mallet for this chore. Well, he chopped the wood into small pieces and stayed at the castle for some time. He had plenty to eat and drink but saw nobody except the cat with many different spots and her servants.

One day she said to him, "Go and mow my meadow and get the hay ready." She gave him a silver scythe and a golden whetstone and told him to return everything to her in proper condition when he was finished. Hans did as he was told, and when he was finished with the work, he brought in the hay and returned the scythe and whetstone. Then he asked whether he could have his payment.

"No," said the cat. "First you must do one more thing for me. Here: You have wood made of silver, an ax, a square, and everything you need, all in silver. I want you to build me a small cottage."

Now, Hans built the cottage, and when it was finished, he pointed out that he had completed his task and still did not have a horse. Indeed, even though it felt like only six months, the seven years had passed. So the cat asked whether he would like to see her horses.

"Yes," said Hans.

Then she went to her cottage and opened the door: twelve proud horses were standing there, and their coats were so sparkling bright and shiny that his heart jumped with joy. The cat gave Hans something to eat and drink and said, "It's time for you to go home, but I'm not going to give you your horse now. I'll bring it with me in three days' time."

The cat showed Hans the way to the mill, and he set out. However, she had not given him any new clothes, so he had to keep wearing the old tattered overalls he had been wearing all these years, and they had become much too short all over for him. When he reached home, the two other hired men were there already. Of course, each of them had brought a horse with him, but one horse was blind, and the other lame.

"Well, Hans," they asked, "where's your horse?"

"I'm expecting it in three days."

They laughed and said, "Where in the world could you ever get a horse? We can't wait to see your fine creature!"

Hans went into the miller's house, but the miller told him he was too ragged and disheveled to sit at the table. If anyone happened by, he would disgrace them. So Hans had to remain outside, and they gave him some food. When they went to sleep in the evening, the other two hired men refused to give him a bed. Finally, he had to crawl into the goose house and lie down on some hard straw. When he awoke the next morning, the three days were already up, and a coach drawn by six horses arrived at the mill. My, how the horses glistened in the sunlight! It was a beautiful sight, and a servant had brought a seventh horse, which was intended for the poor miller's apprentice. A dazzling princess then stepped out of the coach and went into the mill. This princess was none other than the cat with many different spots whom Hans had served for seven years. She asked the miller where the apprentice was.

"We couldn't let him sleep in the mill," said the miller. "He was too ragged and dirty. So he's lying in the goose house."

The princess had him fetched immediately, and when they got him out, he had to hold his overalls together in order not to expose himself. The servant unpacked a bundle of splendid clothes and then washed him and dressed him. When Hans was ready, no king could have looked more handsome. After this the maiden demanded to see the horses that the other hired men had brought: one was blind and the other lame. Then she ordered her servant to bring the seventh horse. When the miller saw it, he said he had never seen a horse like it in his yard.

"It's for the apprentice," she said.

"Now the mill is his," said the miller.

But the princess said that he could keep his mill, and he could have the horse too. She took her faithful Hans by the hand, led him into the coach, and drove off with him. First they went to the small cottage that he had built for her with the silver tools, but it had become a huge castle, and everything in it was made of silver and gold. Afterward she married him, and he was rich, so rich that he had more than enough money for the rest of his life.

So, remember, don't ever let anyone tell you that simpletons can never amount to anything.

◆ 107 ◆

The Two Travelers

MOUNTAINS AND VALLEYS NEVER MEET, but people often do, especially the good and the bad. So it was that the paths of a shoemaker and a tailor crossed during their travels. The tailor was a handsome, little fellow, always merry and in good spirits. When he saw the shoemaker coming from the other direction, he recognized his trade by his knapsack and decided to sing a little ditty just to tease him:

"First sew the seam;
now pull the thread;
rub it right, rub it left, and use the wax;
now hit the nail on the head."

However, the shoemaker could not take a joke and made a sour face as if he had just drunk some vinegar. Indeed, he looked as if he would grab the little tailor by the scruff of his neck. Yet, the little fellow began to laugh, handed the shoemaker his bottle, and said, "No harm meant. Just drink and swallow down your anger."

The shoemaker took a tremendous swig, and the storm brewing on his face began to blow over. He gave the bottle back to the tailor and said, "I've done ample justice to your bottle. They say that drinking helps, and thirst can mean your end. Say, how would you like to be my traveling companion?"

"That's fine with me," answered the tailor, "just as long as you intend to head for the big cities, where there's plenty of work."

"That's exactly where I'm going," said the shoemaker. "You can't make a living in a small nest, and the people in the country still prefer to run around barefoot."

So they walked on together, putting one foot in front of the other like weasels in the snow. Both had plenty of time but very little money. When they came to a city, they went around asking for work. Since the little tailor looked so bright and cheerful with his rosy red cheeks, everyone was glad to give him some work to do, and if he was really lucky, he would also get a kiss from the master's daughter on his way out the front door. Whenever he rejoined the shoemaker, he always had more in his knapsack than his companion, and the sullen shoemaker would look peevish and remark, "The bigger the fool, the greater his luck." But the tailor would only burst out laughing and start singing. Whatever he earned, he would share with his companion. Whenever he had but a few pennies in his pocket, he would order something good and pound the table in pure delight until the glasses began to dance. His motto was "Easy come, easy go."

After they had been traveling for some time, they came to a great forest, which they had to cross to get to the capital city. However, there were two footpaths through it, one that took seven days, and the other, only two. Neither of the travelers knew which path was shorter. So they sat down under an oak tree to discuss what supplies they would need and how much bread they should take. The shoemaker said, "One should always plan in advance. I'm going to take enough bread for seven days."

"What!" said the tailor. "You think I want to carry bread for seven days on my back like a pack animal and not be able to enjoy the scenery? I'm going to trust in God and not worry about the future. The money in my pocket is as good in summer as in winter, but bread gets dry and moldy in hot weather. My coat always stops at my ankles. There's no reason why we won't be able to find the right path. I'm taking bread enough for two days, and that's it for me."

So each one bought his own supply of bread, and they went into the forest trusting in chance.

The forest was as quiet as a church. There was no wind, and the brook had stopped murmuring, just as the birds had stopped singing. Not one ray of sun pierced the dense foliage of the trees. The load on the shoemaker's back was so heavy that he did not say a word, and sweat was pouring down his churlish and moody face. On the other hand, the tailor was as cheerful as could be. He skipped along, whistling with a leaf between his lips or singing a song. God in heaven must be pleased that I'm so merry, he thought.

So it went for two days, but on the third day, when there was still no end to the forest in sight and the tailor had eaten all his bread, his spirits fell a bit, but he did not lose heart. He kept on trusting in God and in chance. By the end of the third day, however, he lay down under a tree hungry and got up hungry the next morning. The same thing happened on the fourth day, and when the shoemaker sat down on a fallen tree and began eating his meal, the tailor could do nothing but look on. When he asked for a little piece of bread, his companion laughed scornfully and said, "You've always been so merry. Now you can see what it feels like to be in a bad way. Birds who sing too early in the morning wind up in the claws of a hawk by evening."

In short, the shoemaker showed the tailor no mercy. On the fifth morning the poor tailor was so exhausted that he could no longer get up, nor could he utter a word. His cheeks were white, and his eyes were red. Then the shoemaker said to him, "I'll give you a piece of bread today, but in return I'm going to cut out your right eye."

The unfortunate tailor wanted desperately to stay alive and had no choice: he wept one last time with both his eyes and then extended his head to the shoemaker, who had a heart of stone and cut out the right eye with a sharp knife. Now the tailor recalled the words of his mother, who used to say whenever she caught him nibbling in the pantry "Eat as much as you want, suffer as much as you must." After he had eaten the bread that cost him dearly, he got up on his legs, forgot his misfortune, and consoled himself with the thought that he could still see well enough with one eye. But on the sixth day his hunger began getting the better of him and almost demolished his heart. In the evening he collapsed under a tree, and on the seventh morning he was so worn out that he could not get up, and death peered over his shoulder.

"Well, I'll be merciful and give you another piece of bread," said the shoemaker, "but it won't be for nothing. In return I'm going to cut out your other eye."

These words made the tailor realize just how frivolous he had been with his life. He begged the dear Lord for forgiveness and said, "Do what you must. I'll suffer what I must. But just remember, our Lord Almighty will determine the proper time to judge you, and one day you will have to pay for your evil deed, for I've given you no cause to act like this. Part of my craft demands that I make even stitches, but if I no longer have eyes, I can no longer sew, and I'll have to go begging. So, when you've finished blinding me, don't leave me lying here alone; otherwise, I'll surely perish."

The shoemaker, who had banished God from his heart, took his knife and cut out the left eye. Then he gave the tailor a piece of bread to eat, handed him a stick, and pulled him along behind him. As the sun was just about to set, they came out of the forest, and at the edge of the forest there was a gallows standing in the field. The shoemaker led the blind man over to the gallows, then left him lying there, and went his way. The unfortunate tailor was worn out from pain and hunger and fell asleep. When dawn came, he awoke but had no idea where he was. Two poor sinners were hanging on the gallows, and a crow sat on the head of each one.

"Brother," said one of the dead men, "are you awake?"

"Yes, I'm awake," answered the other.

"Well, let me tell you something," the first one said again. "Anyone who washes himself in the dew that fell on us last night can regain his sight. If the blind knew that, many of them who have given up hope could have their sight restored."

When the tailor heard that, he took his handkerchief and pressed it in the grass. When it was moistened, he washed his eye sockets with it. Suddenly, the words of the hanged man came true, and a pair of fresh, sound eyes filled his sockets. It was not long before the tailor saw the sun rise over the mountains. The large capital city, with its magnificent gates and turrets, lay before him on a plain. The golden domes and the crosses on the steeples began to glisten. He could distinguish each and every leaf on the trees and watched the birds as they flew overhead and the gnats as they danced in the air. He took a sewing needle out of his pocket, and when he succeeded in threading the needle as well as he had ever done before, his heart leapt for joy. Then he threw himself down on his knees, thanked God for the mercy the Lord had shown him, and said his morning prayers. Nor did he forget to pray for the poor sinners who were hanging there like bell clappers banging against one another in the wind. After that he put on his knapsack, and the pain he had been suffering began to vanish as he went his way singing and whistling.

The first thing he encountered was a brown foal running freely in a field. He caught the foal by his mane and intended to swing himself on his back and ride into the city. However, the foal pleaded for his freedom. "I'm still much too young," he said. "Even a tailor as light as you are would break my back in two. Let me go free and grow strong. Perhaps there'll be a time when I can repay you."

"Run off," said the tailor. "I see that you're a frisky fellow like me!" He smacked the foal on his back with a switch so that he kicked up his hind legs in joy and galloped into the field jumping over hedges and ditches.

The tailor had not eaten a thing since the day before. "Indeed, the sun is filling my eyes," he said, "but it's not filling me with bread. I just want to get my hands on something halfway edible, and the first thing to cross my path will have to suffer the consequences." Meanwhile, a stork came striding toward him very solemnly across the meadow.

"Stop, stop," called the tailor, and grabbed him by his hind leg. "I don't know whether you taste good, but my hunger leaves me no other choice. I'm going to cut off your head and roast you."

"Don't do that," replied the stork. "I'm a sacred bird, and you're not supposed to harm me because I benefit all humankind. If you spare my life, I'll make it up to you some other time."

"Well then, take off, Friend Longlegs," said the tailor.

The stork flapped its wings and flew off gracefully with his long legs dangling in the air.

"What's going to come of all this?" said the tailor to himself. "My hunger's getting greater and greater, and my stomach emptier and emptier. Whatever crosses my path now is done for."

Just as he said that, he saw two ducks swimming toward him on a pond. "You've come just in the nick of time," he said. After he had caught one of them and was about to wring its neck, an old mother duck, which had been hiding in the reeds, suddenly began quacking loudly. She swam up to him with her beak wide open and implored him to have mercy on her children. "Just think," she said, "how your mother would grieve if someone were to catch you and put an end to your life!"

"Calm yourself," said the kindhearted tailor. "Your children are safe," and he put the captured duck back into the water.

When he turned around, he stood facing a half-hollow tree and glimpsed wild bees flying in and out. "Now I'll get a quick reward for my good deed," said the tailor. "The honey will refresh me."

Just then the queen bee came flying out, threatening him, and said, "If you harm my people and destroy my nest, then our stings will plunge into your skin like ten thousand burning needles. But, if you leave us in peace and go your way, we'll do you a service in return some other day."

Here again the little tailor saw that there was nothing doing. "Three dishes empty," he said, "and nothing on the fourth. That's what I call a bad meal." So he dragged himself with his starving stomach into the city, where, since the church bells were ringing in the noon hour, there was food already cooked and ready for him at the inn. He sat down to eat right away, and after he was finished, he said, "Now I feel like working."

He went around the city looking for a master tailor and soon found someone willing to house him. Since he knew all the essentials of his craft from top to bottom, it was not long before he became famous, and everyone wanted to have his new coat made by the little tailor. His reputation grew with each day. "I can't improve on my craft any more than I have," he said, "and yet things keep getting better every day." At last the king appointed him court tailor.

But the world is full of surprises. That very same day his former companion, the shoemaker, became court shoemaker. When he caught sight of the tailor and noticed that he had two sound eyes again, his conscience began bothering him, and he thought, Before he takes revenge on me, I'd better dig his grave. However, he who digs a grave for others shall more than likely fall in himself.

In the evening, when it had turned dusk and the shoemaker had finished his work, he sneaked off to the king and said, "Sire, the tailor's an arrogant man. He's been boasting that he can recover the golden crown that was lost hundreds of years ago."

"I'd certainly appreciate having it back," said the king, and he summoned the tailor the next day and ordered him to bring back the crown or to leave the city forever.

Oho, thought the tailor, only a fool promises the impossible. If that grumpy king expects me to do something that nobody in the world can do, why should I wait until tomorrow? I might as well get out of town today.

So he packed his knapsack, but when he was outside the city gates, he began to regret his having to abandon his good fortune and turn his back on the city where he had been doing so well. He made his way to the pond where he had met the ducks. There on the bank was the old mother duck whose little ones he had spared, preening herself with her bill. She recognized him immediately and asked him why he was so gloomy.

"You won't be surprised once I tell you what's happened to me," responded the tailor, and he told her what had befallen him.

"If that's all there's to it," said the duck, "then we can help you. The crown fell into the water, and it's lying on the bottom of the pond. We'll get it out for you in a second. Just spread out your handkerchief on the bank."

She dived down into the water with her twelve ducklings, and within five minutes she came up again, swimming in the middle of the crown, which was resting on her wings. Her twelve ducklings surrounded her and helped her carry the crown by supporting it with their bills. Then they swam ashore and deposited the crown on the handkerchief. You cannot imagine how magnificent the crown was. When the sun's rays struck it, it sparkled like a hundred thousand garnets. The tailor tied the four corners of his handkerchief together and carried the crown to the king, who was overjoyed and hung a golden chain around the tailor's neck.

When the shoemaker saw that his trick had failed, he thought up something new and went to the king and said, "Sire, the tailor's been boasting again. Now he claims that he can make a wax model of the entire royal palace, with all the trimmings and furnishings."

The king summoned the tailor and ordered him to make a wax model of the entire royal palace with all the trimmings and furnishings. And, if he did not succeed in building one, or if a single nail were missing on a wall, he would have to spend the rest of his life underground in a dungeon.

It's getting worse and worse, the tailor thought. It's more than anyone can bear. He swung his knapsack over his back and left again. When he got to the hollow tree, he sat down and slumped over. The bees came flying out of the tree, and the queen bee asked him whether he had a stiff neck, since he was holding his head in such a strange way.

"Oh, no," answered the tailor. "Something else is bothering me," and he told her what the king had demanded of him. The bees began to buzz and hum among themselves, and the queen bee said, "Just go home for now, and come back tomorrow about this time and bring a large cloth with you. Everything will be all right."

So he turned around, while the bees flew straight to the royal palace and right through the open windows. They crawled around in every nook and cranny and inspected everything very carefully. Then they zoomed back and built a wax model of the palace so quickly that you would have thought it was actually growing before your eyes. It was finished that very evening, and when the tailor came the next morning, he found the whole building standing there in all its splendor, and not a nail was missing in the walls, nor a tile on the roof. Moreover, it was snow white and very delicate and smelled as sweet as honey. The tailor wrapped it carefully in his cloth and brought it to the king, who could not get over his surprise. He put the model in his largest hall and rewarded the tailor with a big stone house.

The shoemaker, however, was persistent. He went to the king a third time and said, "Sire, it's come to the tailor's attention that there's no water in the castle courtyard. So now he's been boasting that he can make crystal clear water gush as high as a man right in the middle of the yard."

The king had the tailor fetched and said, "By tomorrow I shall expect water to rise in my courtyard just as you have promised. If it doesn't, my executioner will make you a head shorter in the very same yard."

The poor tailor did not stop to think twice but rushed out through the city gates since his life was at stake this time. Tears rolled down his cheeks, and as he walked along in this gloomy state the foal, whose freedom he had granted some time ago, came galloping up to him. The foal had, in the meantime, grown up to be a fine bay horse.

"Now the hour has arrived," the horse said to him, "for me to repay you for your good deed. I know already what you need, and help is near at hand. Just climb up on my back, for now I can carry two like you."

The tailor took heart again and mounted the horse with one jump. Into the city the horse galloped and then straight into the courtyard. Quick as lightning, he sped around the yard three times, and the third time he fell to the ground. There was a dreadful crash, and suddenly a piece of earth in the middle of the courtyard shot up into the air like a bullet and flew out over the castle. Immediately a stream of water gushed forth as high as a man on horseback. The water was as clear as crystal, and the sunbeams began to dance on it. When the king saw that, he jumped up in amazement and went to embrace the little tailor in the presence of his entire court.

The tailor's good fortune did not last long, however. The king had more than enough daughters, one more beautiful than the next, but no sons. The wicked shoemaker now went to the king a fourth time and said, "Sire, the tailor's arrogance has not subsided. Now he's boasting that, if he wanted to, he could have a son brought to Your Majesty through the air."

The king had the tailor summoned and said, "If you can have a son brought to me within nine days, you shall have my oldest daughter for your wife."

This reward is certainly great, the tailor thought to himself. Normally I'd do anything to get it. But the cherries are hanging too high for me. If I were to climb after them, the branch would break, and I'd fall to the ground. He went home, sat down at his worktable, crossed his legs, and pondered what he should do. At last he exclaimed, "It won't work! I can't live here in peace anymore. I've got to get away!"

The tailor packed his knapsack and rushed out through the city gate. When he came to the meadows, he spotted his old friend the stork, who was pacing back and forth like a worldly philosopher. From time to time he stopped to inspect a frog up close until he finally swallowed it in one gulp. Then the stork came over and greeted him. "I see you've got your knapsack on your back. Why do you want to leave the city?"

The tailor told him that the king had demanded something impossible of him and bemoaned his bad luck.

"Don't grow any gray hairs over this," said the stork. "I'll help you out of this predicament. I've been bringing babies to this city for a long time now. For once I can also make it my business to fetch a little prince out of the well. Go home and calm yourself. Just be at the palace nine days from today, and I'll be there too."

The little tailor went home and made sure to be on time at the palace. Soon after, the stork came flying and knocked on the window. The tailor opened it for him, and Daddy Longlegs climbed cautiously inside and strode solemnly across the smooth marble floor. In his beak he was carrying a baby who was as lovely as an angel, and who stretched out his arms toward the queen. The stork set the baby down in her lap, and she hugged and kissed him and was overcome with joy. Before the stork flew away, he took his traveling sack from his shoulder and handed it to the queen, who found bags of assorted sugar candy inside. She divided the bags among the little princesses, but the oldest received nothing. Instead, she got the merry tailor for her husband.

"I feel as though I've just won the grand lottery," said the tailor. "My mother was right. She always used to say 'Trust in God, and with a little bit of luck you're bound to find happiness.' "

The shoemaker had to make the shoes in which the tailor danced at his wedding. Then the king banished the shoemaker from the city forever. On his way to the forest he came to the gallows in the field.

Since he was exhausted from his anger and rage and the heat of the day, he threw himself down on the ground. When he closed his eyes and was about to sleep, the two crows cawed loudly, swooped down from the heads of the hanged men, and pecked his eyes out. Half-crazed, he ran into the forest and must have perished there, for nobody has ever seen him or heard anything about him since.

◈ 108 ◈

Hans My Hedgehog

ONCE UPON A TIME there was a farmer who had plenty of money and property, but rich as he was, his happiness was not complete: he had no children with his wife. When he went into town with the other farmers, they often made fun of him and asked why he had no children. One day he finally got angry, and when he went home, he said, "I want to have a child, even if it's a hedgehog."

Then his wife gave birth to a child whose upper half was hedgehog and bottom half, human. When she saw the child, she was horrified and said, "You see how you cursed us!"

"There's nothing we can do about it now," said her husband. "The boy must be christened, but we'll never find a godfather for him."

"There's only one name I can think of for him," said the wife, "and that's Hans My Hedgehog."

After he was christened, the pastor said, "He won't be able to sleep in a regular bed because of his quills."

Therefore, they gathered together some straw, spread it on the floor behind the stove, and laid Hans My Hedgehog on it. His mother could not nurse him because he might have stuck her with his quills. So he lay behind the stove for eight years, and eventually his father got tired of him and wished he might die, but he did not die. He just kept lying there.

One day there was a fair in town, and the farmer decided to go to it and asked his wife if she would like anything.

"Some meat and a few rolls," she said. "That's all we need for the house."

Then he asked the maid, and she wanted a pair of slippers and stockings with clocks. Finally, he went and asked his son, "Hans My Hedgehog, what would you like to have?"

"Father," he said, "just bring me back some bagpipes."

When the farmer returned home, he gave his wife the meat and rolls he had bought. Then he handed the maid the slippers and stockings with clocks. Finally, he went behind the stove and gave Hans My Hedgehog his bagpipes. Upon receiving the bagpipes, he said, "Father, please go to the blacksmith and have him shoe my rooster; then I'll ride away and never come back."

The father was happy at the idea of getting rid of him and had his rooster shod. When the rooster was ready, Hans My Hedgehog mounted it and rode away, taking some donkeys and pigs with him, which he wanted to tend out in the forest. Once he reached the forest, he had the rooster fly him up into a tall tree, where he sat and tended the donkeys and pigs. He sat there for many years until the herd was very large, and he never sent word to his father of his whereabouts.

As he sat in the tree he played his bagpipes and made beautiful music. One day a king, who had lost his way in the forest, came riding by. When he heard the music, he was so surprised that he sent his servant to look around and see where the music was coming from. The servant looked around, but all he could see was a small animal, sitting up in a tree, that seemed to be a rooster with a hedgehog sitting on top of it playing music. The king told the servant to ask the creature why he was sitting there and whether he knew the way back to the king's kingdom. Hans My Hedgehog climbed down from the tree and said he would show him the way if the king would promise in writing to give him the first thing he met at the castle courtyard when he returned home.

No danger in that, thought the king. Hans My Hedgehog can't understand writing, so I can write whatever I want. The king took pen and ink and wrote something down, and after he had done this, Hans My Hedgehog showed him the way, and the king arrived home safely. When his daughter saw him coming from afar, she was so overcome with joy that she ran out to meet him and kissed him. Then he thought of Hans My Hedgehog and explained to her what had happened: he had been forced to make a promise in writing to a strange creature who had demanded to have the first thing the king met upon returning home. This creature had been sitting on a rooster as though it were a horse and had been playing beautiful music. The king told his daughter that he had, however, written down that Hans My Hedgehog was not to get what he demanded. Anyway, it made no difference, since he could not read. The princess was happy to hear that and said it was a good thing since she would never have gone with him anyway.

Hans My Hedgehog continued tending his donkeys and pigs. He was always cheerful sitting there perched in his tree, playing his bagpipes. Now it happened that another king came driving by with his servants and couriers. He too had lost his way, and the forest was so large that he did not know how to get back home. He too heard the beautiful music from afar and told a courier to go and see what it was. So the courier went to the tree and saw the rooster sitting there with Hans My Hedgehog on its back, and the courier asked him what he was doing up there.

"I'm tending my donkeys and pigs, but what can I do for you?"

The courier asked him whether he could show them the way out of the forest since they were lost and could not make it back to their kingdom. Hans My Hedgehog climbed down from the tree with his rooster and told the old king that he would show him the way if the king would give him the first thing that met him when he returned home to his royal castle. The king agreed and put it in writing that Hans My Hedgehog was to have what he demanded. When that was done, Hans My Hedgehog rode ahead of him on the rooster and showed the way. The king reached his kingdom safely, and as he entered the castle courtyard there was great rejoicing. His only daughter, who was very beautiful, ran toward him and embraced him. She was very happy to see her old father again and asked him what in the world had kept him so long. He told her he had lost his way and would not have made it back at all had it not been for a strange creature, half human, half hedgehog, who had helped him find his way out of the forest. The creature had been sitting astride a rooster up in a tall tree and had been playing beautiful music. In return for his aid the king had promised to give him the first thing that met him at the castle courtyard. Now he was very sorry that it had happened to be her. However, out of love for her old father, the princess promised him that she would go with Hans My Hedgehog whenever he came.

In the meantime, Hans My Hedgehog kept tending his pigs, and the pigs had more pigs, and eventually there were so many that the entire forest was full of them. Then Hans My Hedgehog decided that he no longer wanted to live in the forest, and he sent word to his father to clear out all the pigsties in the village, for he was coming with such a huge herd of pigs that anyone who wanted to slaughter one could have his pick. On hearing this, his father was distressed for he had believed that Hans My Hedgehog had long been dead. Nevertheless, Hans My Hedgehog mounted his rooster, drove his pigs ahead of him into the village, and ordered the slaughtering to begin. Whew! There was such chopping and butchering that the noise could be heard for miles around. Afterward Hans My Hedgehog said, "Father, have the blacksmith shoe my rooster one more time. Then I'll ride away and never return as long as I live."

His father, glad that Hans My Hedgehog would never return again, had the rooster shod. When Hans My Hedgehog departed, he set out for the first kingdom, but the king had given his men orders to stop anyone who was riding on a rooster and playing bagpipes from entering the castle. If necessary, they were to use their guns, spears, or swords. So, when Hans My Hedgehog came riding, they attacked him with their bayonets, but he put spurs to his rooster, and the bird rose in the air, flew over the gate, and landed on the ledge of the king's window. He called to the king to keep his promise and give him the princess; otherwise, he would take his life and his daughter's as well. Then the king implored his daughter to go with Hans My Hedgehog to save their lives. So she dressed herself all in white, and her father gave her a coach with six horses, splendid servants, money, and property. She got into the coach and was followed by Hans My Hedgehog, with his bagpipes and his rooster by his side. They then said good-bye and drove away, and the king thought that was the last he would ever see of his daughter, but things happened much differently. When they had gone a little way, Hans My Hedgehog took off her beautiful clothes and stuck her with his quills until she was covered with blood.

"This is what you get for being so deceitful!" he said. "Go back home. I don't want you."

Then he sent her away, and she lived in disgrace for the rest of her life. Meanwhile, Hans My Hedgehog, carrying his bagpipes, continued his journey on his rooster. Eventually, he came to the second kingdom, which belonged to the other king he had led out of the forest. However, this king had ordered his men to present arms and greet him by shouting "Long may he live!" After that they were to escort him into the royal palace. When the king's daughter saw him, she was startled and frightened because he looked so strange. Yet, there was nothing she could do, so she thought, for she had promised her father to go with him. Therefore, she welcomed Hans My Hedgehog, and then they were married. After the wedding ceremony he led her to the royal table, where they sat down together and ate and drank. When evening came and it was time to go to bed, she was quite afraid of his quills, but he said not to be scared because he had no intention of harming her. Then he told the old king to have four men stand watch in front of the bedroom door and to make a big fire, for when he got inside and was prepared to go to bed, he would slip out of his hedgehog's skin. The men were then to rush in quickly, throw the skin on the fire, and stand there until it was completely consumed.

When the clock struck eleven, he went into the room, stripped off the hedgehog's skin, and left it on the floor. Right after this the men came, picked up the skin, and threw it into the fire. When the fire had consumed it, he was set free and lay in bed just like a human being, but he was pitch black, as if he had been burned. The king sent for his doctor, who rubbed him with special ointments and balms, and gradually, he became white and turned into a handsome young man. When the princess saw that, she was very happy. The next morning they got up in a joyful mood and had a fine meal. Then the marriage was performed again properly with Hans as a human, and the old king bequeathed his kingdom to Hans My Hedgehog.

After some years had passed, Hans, with his wife, drove to visit his father, and he told the old man that he was his son. The father, however, said he had no son, though he once had one, but he had been born with quills, like a hedgehog, and had gone out into the world. Hans My Hedgehog revealed himself to his father then, and the old man rejoiced and went back with him to his kingdom.

My tale is done,
and now, it's on the run.

❖ 109 ❖

The Little Shroud

A MOTHER HAD A LITTLE BOY of seven who was so fair and lovely that no one could look at him without treating him kindly. His mother loved him more than anything else in the world, but he suddenly fell ill, and the dear Lord took him away. The mother could not stop grieving and wept day and night. Soon after the boy was buried, he began to appear at night in places where he had formerly sat and played when he had been alive. Then, whenever his mother wept, he would weep too, and when morning came, he would disappear. Finally, since his mother would not stop her weeping, he came one night clad in the little white shroud that he had worn in his coffin and with a wreath on his head. He sat down at her feet and said, "Oh, Mother, please stop weeping. Otherwise, I won't be able to get to sleep in my coffin. My little shroud is all wet from the tears you've been shedding on it."

Upon hearing this, his mother became frightened and stopped weeping. The next night, the child came again with a light in his hand and said, "You see, now my shroud is almost dry, and I can rest in my grave."

Then his mother commended her grief to the dear Lord and bore it silently and patiently. The child never returned after that but slept in his little bed beneath the ground.

◈ 110 ◈

The Jew in the Thornbush

ONCE UPON A TIME there was a rich man, and he had a servant who was a hard and honest worker. He was the first one out of bed each morning, and the last into bed each night. And, if there was some unpleasant task to do that nobody else would touch, he was always the first to take it on, and he never complained. He was always content and had a cheerful disposition. After he had served one year, his master refused to pay him any wages, for he thought, That's the smartest thing to do. I can save money this way, and he won't be in a position to leave me and will have to continue working for me, nicely and obediently.

Indeed, the servant said nothing and continued working the second year as he had the first. When he received nothing at the end of the second year as well, he let it go by and stayed on. After the third year was over, his master reflected momentarily, reached into his pocket but came out with nothing. Finally, the servant spoke up. "Master, I've served you honestly for three years. Now, be so kind as to give me my due, for I would like to go and have a look about the world."

"All right, my good man," answered the miser. "You've served me diligently, and you shall be paid generously for your work." He reached into his pocket again and counted out three farthings, one by one. "Here's a farthing for each year you've served me. That's an ample amount and more money than you'd ever get from any other master."

The good servant, who understood very little about money, put his capital into his pocket and thought, Now you've got your pocket full, and you won't have to worry anymore or put up with drudgery.

So he set out, traveling over hill and dale, skipping and singing to his heart's content. On one occasion he happened to pass by some bushes, and out came a little dwarf, who called to him, "Where are you going, my merry fellow? I can see you don't have a worry in the world."

"Why should I be gloomy," answered the servant. "I've got all I need with three years' pay jingling in my pocket."

"How much is your treasure?" the dwarf asked.

"How much? Three solid farthings and not a cent less."

"Listen," said the dwarf, "I'm a poor needy man. Give me your

three farthings, for I can't
work anymore. You're still young
and can easily earn a living."

Since the servant had a kind heart and felt
sorry for the dwarf, he handed him the three farthings
and said, "In God's name, I won't miss them at all."

"I see you have a kind heart," said the dwarf. "So, I'm going to
grant you three wishes, one for each farthing, and they shall all be
fulfilled."

"Aha," said the servant. "You're one of those people who can do
incredible things. If that's the way it is, my first wish is for a fowling
gun that hits everything that I aim it at. The second is for a fiddle that
will make everyone dance when I play it. The third is for the power to
make people grant me anything I request."

"All your wishes shall come true," said the dwarf. Then he reached into the bush, and, just think, he pulled out a fiddle and a gun made to order. He gave them to the servant and said, "After this, nobody will refuse any request you make."

The servant said to himself, "Nothing could be better than this, dear fellow," and he moved merrily on his way. Soon thereafter he met a Jew with a long goatee, who was standing and listening to the song of a bird perched high on top of a tree.

"It's miraculous!" the Jew exclaimed. "Such a small creature with such an awfully powerful voice! If only it were mine! If only someone could sprinkle salt on its tail!"

"If that's all there is to it," said the servant, "I'll have the bird down in a jiffy." He took aim with his gun, hit the bird between the eyes, and it fell down into a thornbush.

"All right, you lousy swindler," he said to the Jew, "go and get the bird."

"My!" said the Jew. "I wish you wouldn't call me lousy, but even if you think I'm a swindler, I'll do as you command, since you're the one who shot the bird." He got down on the ground and worked his way into the bush. Just as he was right in the middle, the servant was overcome by a mischievous spirit, and he took out his fiddle and began to play. All at once the Jew began to lift his legs high and leap in the air. The more the servant played, the better the Jew danced. But the thorns ripped the Jew's coat to shreds, combed his goatee, and scratched and pricked his entire body.

"My!" exclaimed the Jew. "What's the sense of all this fiddling? Please stop all this fiddling, sir. I have no desire to dance."

The servant kept playing nevertheless, for he thought, You've skinned plenty of people, so now the thorns will give you some of your own treatment in return. He continued fiddling so that the Jew had to leap higher and higher, and parts of his coat remained hanging on the thorns.

"Woe is me!" cried the Jew. "I'll give the gentleman whatever he demands if only he'll stop fiddling! You can have a whole bag of gold."

"Well, if you're going to be that generous," said the servant, "then I'll gladly stop my music. But I must hand it to you, your dancing is something special." Upon saying this, he took the bag of gold and went his way.

The Jew remained standing there and kept glaring at the servant until he was far away and out of sight. Then he yelled with all his might, "You miserable musician, you're nothing but a common, beer-hall fiddler! Wait till I catch you alone! I'll chase you until the soles fall right off your feet. You tramp, all one has to do is put a coin in your mouth, and you'll be worth six farthings," and he continued cursing the servant with whatever came into his head. After he had vented his anger and was feeling somewhat relieved, he ran into the city to see the judge.

"Woe is me, Your Honor! See how a crook robbed me on the highway! Just look at what he did to me! A stone would be moved to pity. My clothes have been torn to shreds! My body's been scratched and pricked! My life's meager fortune along with a bag of gold was taken! My precious ducats, each piece finer than the next. For God's sake, have the man thrown in prison!"

"Was it one of those soldiers who cut you with his saber?" asked the judge.

"God forbid!" said the Jew. "He didn't have a saber but a gun that was hanging over his shoulder and a fiddle around his neck. It's easy to recognize the villain."

The judge sent his men in search of the servant, and they found him trudging along the road very slowly. They also found the gold on him, and when they brought him back to the court, he said, "I didn't touch the Jew, and I didn't take his money. He gave it to me of his own free will so that I'd stop fiddling since he couldn't stand my music."

"God forbid!" screamed the Jew. "He's lying like a rug."

The judge did not believe the servant either and said, "That's a poor excuse. No Jew would ever do what you said," and he sentenced the good servant to hang on the gallows, because he had committed highway robbery. As the servant was being led away, the Jew yelled after him, "You slouch, you miserable musician, now you'll get what you deserve!"

The servant climbed calmly up the ladder with the hangman, but on the last rung he turned around and said to the judge, "Grant me one last request before I die."

"All right," said the judge, "as long as you don't ask me to spare your life."

"It's not about my life," answered the servant. "I'd like to play my fiddle just one last time."

The Jew began raising a great commotion. "For God's sake, don't allow it! Don't allow it!"

But the judge said, "Why shouldn't I grant him such brief pleasure? I said I'd grant him a request, and I'm going to keep my word." In any case, it was impossible for the judge to deny the request, because of the power given to the servant by the dwarf.

The Jew cried out, "Woe is me! Woe is me! Tie me up, tie me up tight!"

The good servant then took the fiddle from his neck, got it ready, and as he stroked the fiddle with the bow everyone started to shake and sway—the judge, the clerk, and the officers. The rope fell out of the hand of the person who was supposed to tie up the Jew, and with the second stroke of the bow, they all raised their legs. Even the hangman let go of the good servant and got ready to dance. With the third stroke of the bow, everyone leapt up high and began to dance, and the judge and the Jew led the way, jumping highest of all. Soon everyone joined in the dancing, all the people who had come to the marketplace out of curiosity, old and young, fat and skinny, they all mixed together. Even the dogs that came running stood on their hind legs and hopped about. And the longer the servant played, the higher the dancers leapt so that they bumped their heads against each other and began screaming in a dreadful way. Finally, the judge was out of breath and cried out, "I'll spare your life if you'll only stop fiddling!"

The good servant was moved by this plea, put down his fiddle, hung it around his neck again, and climbed down the ladder. Then he went over to the Jew, who was lying on the ground and gasping for breath, and said, "You lousy swindler, confess and tell us where you got the money from, or I'll take the fiddle from my neck and begin playing again."

"I stole it, I stole it!" he screamed, "but you earned it honestly."

Then the judge had the Jew led up to the gallows, and he was hanged as a thief.

◈ 111 ◈

The Expert Huntsman

ONCE UPON A TIME there was a young fellow who had learned the locksmith's trade, and he told his father that he wanted to go out into the world and try his luck.

"All right," said his father. "That's fine with me," and he gave him some money for his journey.

So the young man wandered about looking for work. After some time he found that he was not very successful as a locksmith. Moreover, the trade no longer suited his temperament, for he had developed a desire to become a huntsman. Then one day as he was traveling along, he met a huntsman clad in green, who asked him where he came from and where he was going. The young man told him he was a locksmith but no longer liked the trade and wanted to become a huntsman, and he asked whether the man could take him on as an apprentice.

"Yes, I can if you want to come along with me."

The young fellow went with him, hired himself out for several years, and learned the craft of hunting. After his apprenticeship had ended, he wanted to try his luck elsewhere. The only wage he received from the huntsman was an air gun, but it was made in such a special way that it never missed when fired.

The young huntsman set off and soon came to a very large forest that was impossible to cross in one day. When evening came, he climbed a high tree to keep away from wild animals. Toward midnight he thought he saw the glimmer of a small light in the distance. He looked through the branches at the spot and took note of where the light was coming from. Then he removed his hat and threw it toward the light so that he would have a marker to point him in the direction he wanted to go. After he climbed down, he went after his hat, put it on again, and proceeded straight ahead. The farther he went, the bigger the light grew, and when he got up close to it, he saw a tremendous fire with three giants around it roasting an ox on a spit.

"I want to take a taste," said one of them, "to see if the meat is ready to eat." He ripped off a piece of the meat and was about to put it in his mouth when the huntsman shot it out of his hand. "Well, what do you know about that," said the giant. "The wind just blew that piece right out of my hand." So he took another piece, but just as he was about to bite into it, the huntsman again shot it away. The giant slapped the companion sitting next to him in the face and yelled at him furiously. "Why do you keep tearing the meat out of my hand?"

"I didn't take it from you," the other said. "A sharpshooter probably shot it away."

The giant took a third piece, but he had barely touched it when the huntsman shot it out of his hand. Then the giants said, "Anyone who can shoot a tiny piece of meat from one's mouth must be a fine marksman. We could use someone like that." So they shouted as loud as they could, "Hey, sharpshooter, come over here! Sit down at our fire, and eat your fill. We won't hurt you, but if you don't come, and make us use force to get you, then you're lost."

Now, the young fellow joined the giants and told them he was an expert huntsman, that whatever he took aim at with his gun he was sure to hit. After hearing this, the giants told him things would go well for him if he came along with them. There was a large river at the other end of the forest, they explained, and on the other side of the river was a tower, and in the tower there was a beautiful princess, whom they intended to carry away.

"All right," said the huntsman. "I'll get her for you soon enough."

"Wait, there's something else," the giants continued. "There's a little dog that starts barking as soon as anyone approaches, and when it barks, everyone at the royal court wakes up. That's why we can't get in. Do you think you can shoot the little dog?"

"Certainly," he said. "That's just trifling sport for me."

Upon reaching the river, the huntsman got into a boat and sailed across. When he landed, the little dog came running and was about to bark when the huntsman took out his air gun and shot it dead. When the giants saw that, they rejoiced, thinking that they had the princess for sure, but the huntsman wanted first to check on things at the castle and told them to stay outside until he called them. So he went into the castle, where everyone was asleep, and it was as quiet as a church. When he opened the first room, he saw a saber of pure silver hanging on the wall. It had a gold star on it, and the king's name was inscribed on the handle. Nearby on a table lay a sealed letter, which he opened, and it said that whoever had possession of the saber could kill anything he encountered. So he took the saber from the wall, put it on his belt, and moved on. Next he came to the room where the princess was lying asleep. She was so beautiful that he stopped in his tracks, gazed at her, and held his breath. He thought to himself, How can I put an innocent maiden like this in the hands of those wild giants? They have nothing but evil on their minds. He looked around some more and saw a pair of slippers underneath her bed. Her father's name and a star were on the right slipper, and on the left, her own name and a star. She was also wearing a large, silk neckerchief embroidered with gold. Her father's name was on the right side, and her own name on the left, all in gold letters. The huntsman took a pair of scissors, cut off the right corner of the neckerchief, and slipped it into his knapsack. He also put in the right slipper with the king's name on it. The maiden kept sleeping, all wrapped up in her nightgown. Then he cut off a piece of the gown as well, without touching her, and put it into his knapsack with the rest of the articles. After that he went away and let her sleep undisturbed. When he returned to the castle gate, the giants were still standing there and waiting for him. They thought he was going to bring the princess with him. Instead, he called to them to come in, that the maiden was already in his power, but he could not open the door for them; they would have to crawl through a hole that he had found in the wall. When the first giant began to crawl through, the huntsman wound the giant's hair around his hand, yanked the head in, and cut it off with one stroke of the saber. Then he pulled the body all the way in. Next he called the second giant and then cut off his head, and finally, the third one. The huntsman was glad to have saved the beautiful maiden from her enemies. He cut their tongues out, put them into his knapsack, and thought to himself, Now I'll go home to my father and show him what I've already achieved. After that I'll travel about the world. Whatever good fortune God intends to bestow upon me will be enough for me.

When the king woke up in the castle, he saw the three giants lying there dead. Then he went into his daughter's bedchamber, woke her up, and asked her who could have possibly come and killed the giants.

"Dear Father," she said, "I don't know. I was asleep."

When she got up and wanted to put on her slippers, the right one was missing, and when she looked at her neckerchief, the right corner had been cut off and was missing. Then she glanced down at her nightgown and saw that a piece had been taken out of it. The king ordered the entire court to assemble, all the soldiers and everyone who was there, and he asked who had killed the giants and saved his daughter.

Now, the king had an ugly, one-eyed captain, who claimed that he had done it. Thereupon the old king announced that he should have his daughter to wed since he had saved her. But the maiden said, "Dear Father, I'd rather leave home and go as far away from here as my legs will carry me than marry him."

Since she refused to marry the captain, the king commanded her to take off her royal garments, put on peasant clothes, and leave the court. He ordered her, furthermore, to go to a potter and start selling his wares. So she took off her royal garments, went to a potter, and borrowed a stock of his earthenware. She promised to pay him back if she sold everything by evening. Then the king told her to go sit by the roadside and sell the earthenware. In the meantime, he ordered some farmers to drive their wagons over her wares and crush everything into a thousand pieces. When the princess set out her wares along the road, the wagons came and smashed everything to pieces. She burst into tears and said, "Oh, Lord, how am I going to pay the potter now?"

In this way the king wanted to force her to marry the captain. However, she went back to the potter and asked him if he would lend her some more earthenware. He told her no, not until she paid for the stock that he had already given her. She went to her father then and screamed and moaned and told him she wanted to go far away from there.

"I'll have a cottage built for you out in the forest," he said. "You shall stay there for the rest of your life and cook for anyone who comes along. But you're not allowed to accept money for this."

When the cottage was finished, a sign was hung outside the door, and on it was written "Today for nothing, tomorrow for money." She lived there a long time, and news spread throughout the world that a maiden was living there who cooked for nothing, just as the sign said on the door.

Word of this also reached the huntsman, and he thought, That's something for you. After all, you're poor and have no money. So he took his air gun and knapsack, in which he had put all the tokens he had taken from the castle, went into the forest, and found the cottage with the sign, "Today for nothing, tomorrow for money." Now, he was still wearing the saber with which he had cut off the heads of the giants, and he carried it into the cottage with him. He asked to have something to eat and was delighted to see the beautiful maiden, who was as pretty as a picture. She asked him where he had come from and where he was going, and he replied, "I'm just traveling about the world."

Then she asked him where he had got the saber, for her father's name was on it. In response, he inquired whether she was the king's daughter.

"Yes," she answered.

"With this saber," he said, "I cut off the heads of three giants," and as proof he took the tongues out of his knapsack. Then he also showed her the slipper, the corner of her neckerchief, and the piece of nightgown. She was overcome with joy, for she realized that he was the one who had saved her. Then they went to the king together and brought him back to the cottage. She led her father into her room and told him that the huntsman was really the one who had saved her. When the old king saw the proof, all his doubts vanished, and he said he was glad to finally know how everything had happened. Now the huntsman was entitled to marry the princess, and the princess was very happy indeed.

They dressed up the huntsman as a foreign lord, and the king had a banquet prepared. When they went to the table, the captain came and sat on the left side of the princess and the huntsman, on the right. The captain thought that the huntsman was a foreign lord who had come for a visit. When they had finished eating and drinking, the old king said to the captain that he wanted him to solve a riddle: if someone said he had killed three giants but could not find their tongues when asked to look for them, how would that be possible?

"They probably didn't have any tongues," said the captain.

"Not so," replied the king. "Every creature has a tongue," and he asked the captain what such a boaster deserved to have done to him.

"He should be torn to pieces," the captain replied.

The king told him he had pronounced his own sentence. The captain was thrown into prison and subsequently torn into four pieces. The princess, though, was wed to the huntsman, and he returned home to fetch his father and mother, who came to live happily with their son, and after the old king's death he inherited the kingdom.

◆ 112 ◆

The Fleshing Flail From Heaven

A FARMER ONCE SET OUT to plow with a pair of oxen. When he got to his field, the horns of both oxen began to grow. They grew and grew, and by the time he was ready to go home, the horns were so big that the oxen would not fit through the farm gate. Fortunately, a butcher happened to come along at that moment and was willing to take them over. They agreed that the farmer would bring a measure of turnip seeds to the butcher, and the butcher was to pay one Brabant taler for each seed. That's what I call a good bargain!

Now, the farmer went home, got the measure of turnip seeds, and carried them in a sack on his back. However, along the way one little seed fell out of the sack. The butcher paid him the price agreed upon, but if the farmer had not lost the little seed, he would have received one more Brabant taler. While the farmer was in town, the seed had grown into a tree that reached all the way to heaven, and when the farmer saw this on his way back, he thought to himself, You can't let an opportunity like this pass you by. You've got to go up and see for yourself what the angels are doing there. So he climbed up and saw the angels threshing oats. He watched them doing this, and while he was watching, he noticed that the tree he was standing on had begun to wobble. He looked down and saw that somebody was chopping it down. It'd be terrible, he thought, if you were to fall all the way down. Given his desperate situation, he could think of nothing better to do than to twist a rope out of the oat chaff that lay there in heaps. After that he grabbed a hoe and a fleshing flail that were lying around there in heaven, and he let himself down by the rope. However, when he landed on earth, he landed in a deep, deep hole, so he was lucky to have taken the hoe, because he was able to hack out steps for himself. He climbed the steps and took the flail with him because he wanted to have proof whenever anyone doubted his story.

◈ 113 ◈

The Two Kings' Children

ONCE UPON A TIME there was a king who had a little boy, and according to the constellation of the stars, it was predicted that he would be killed by a stag when he turned sixteen. One day, when he had reached that age, the huntsmen went out hunting with him in the forest, but the prince got separated from them. Suddenly he saw a big stag and kept trying to shoot it without much success. Finally, the stag ran away and led him on a chase until they were out of the forest. All at once a big, lanky man was standing there instead of the stag and said, "Well, it's a good thing I've got you now. I wore out six pair of glass skates chasing after you and could never catch you."

He took the prince with him and dragged him across a large lake toward a big royal castle. Once there the prince had to sit down at a table and eat something with the man. After they had eaten together, the king said, "I've got three daughters, and I want you to watch over the oldest one for me from nine in the evening until six in the morning. Each time the clock strikes the hour, I shall come and call you. If you don't answer me, you'll be put to death in the morning. However, if you answer me, you shall have my daughter for your wife."

When the young people went up to the bedchamber, there was a stone statue of Saint Christopher standing there, and the king's daughter said to him, "My father will come at nine o'clock and every hour until the clock strikes six. If he asks anything, I want you to answer him in place of the prince."

The stone Saint Christopher nodded his head very fast, then more and more slowly until he finally came to a stop.

The next morning the king said to the young prince, "You've done well, but I can't give you my daughter. Now, I want you to watch over my second daughter. Then I'll consider giving you my oldest daughter for your wife. I shall come every hour on the hour, and when I call, you must answer me. If you don't answer, your blood will flow."

The prince went with the second daughter up to the bedchamber, where there was a stone statue of Saint Christopher, much larger than the first, and the king's daughter said to him, "If my father asks a question, I want you to answer."

The big stone Saint Christopher nodded his head very fast, then more and more slowly until he came to a stop. The prince lay down on the threshold, put his hand under his head, and went to sleep.

The next morning the king said to him, "You've done well, but I can't give you my daughter. Now, I want you to watch over my youngest daughter. Then I'll consider giving you the second for your wife. I shall come every hour, and when I call, answer me. If you don't answer me when I call, your blood will flow."

Again the prince went with the youngest daughter up to the bedchamber, and there stood a Saint Christopher, much bigger and taller than the other two. The king's daughter said to him, "If my father calls, I want you to answer."

The big, tall Saint Christopher nodded his head for a good half hour before he came to a stop, and the prince lay down on the threshold and fell asleep.

The next morning the king said, "Indeed, you kept watch very well, but I can't give you my daughter yet. Now, I've got a very large forest, and if you cut it down for me between six this morning and six this evening, I'll consider giving her to you."

The king gave him a glass ax, a glass wedge, and a glass mattock. When the prince reached the forest, he began chopping right away, and the ax broke in two. Then he took the wedge and began hitting it with the mattock, but it splintered into tiny pieces the size of grains of sand. This made the prince very downcast, for he thought he would now have to die. So he sat down and wept.

At noon the king said, "One of you girls must bring him something to eat."

"No," said the oldest, "we won't bring him anything. Let the one he watched over last take him something."

So the youngest daughter had to go and bring him something to eat. When she reached the forest, she asked him how everything was going.

"Oh," he said, "things are going very badly."

She told him to come over to her and have a little something to eat.

"No," he responded. "I can't, for I've got to die, and I don't want to eat anymore."

She spoke kindly to him and implored him to try, so he went over to her and ate something. After he had eaten, she said, "Now I'll louse you a little, and then you'll feel much better."

When she loused him, he became so tired that he fell asleep. Then she took her kerchief, made a knot in it, and struck the ground three times with it.

"Workers, come out!" she cried.

Suddenly numerous gnomes appeared from beneath the earth and asked the princess what her command was.

"In three hours' time," she said, "this great forest must be cut down, and the wood stacked in piles."

The gnomes went and called all their relatives to come out and help them with the work. Then they started, and within three hours everything was finished, and they went and reported to the king's daughter. Once again she took out her white kerchief and said, "Workers, go home!" And they all vanished on the spot.

When the prince woke up, he was very happy, and she said, "When the clock strikes six, you're to go home."

He did as she had said, and the king asked him, "Have you cut down the whole forest?"

"Yes," said the prince.

When they were sitting at the table, the king said, "I can't give you my daughter for your wife yet. You must first do something else."

The prince asked what he had to do.

"I have a very large pond," said the king. "You must go there tomorrow morning and clean it out so that it glistens like a mirror, and there must be all kinds of fish in it."

The next morning the king gave him a glass scoop and said, "You must be finished with the pond by six o'clock."

The prince departed, and when he reached the pond, he stuck the scoop into the muck, and the end broke off. Then he tried a pickax, but it broke as well, and he became discouraged. At noon the youngest daughter brought him something to eat and asked him how everything was going. The prince said that things were going very badly, and he was bound to lose his head. "All the tools broke apart on me again."

"Oh," she said, "you should come and eat something first, then you'll feel much better."

"No," he said, "I can't eat. I feel too sad."

But she spoke so kindly to him that he finally had to come and eat something. Once again she loused him, and he fell asleep. She took her kerchief once more, tied a knot in it, and struck the ground three times with it. "Workers, come out!" she cried.

Suddenly numerous gnomes appeared and asked her what she desired.

"In three hours' time the pond must be all cleaned up and must shine so brightly that you can see your own reflection in it. Then you must fill it with all kinds of fish."

The gnomes went off and called all their relatives to come and help them. They finished everything in two hours, returned to the king's daughter, and reported, "We've done what you commanded."

Once again she took her kerchief and struck the ground three times. "Workers, go home!" And they all vanished on the spot.

When the prince woke up, the pond was finished, and just as the king's daughter was about to leave him, she told him to go home at six o'clock. When he got there, the king asked, "Have you finished the pond?"

"Yes," said the prince. "Everything's fine."

When they were sitting at the table again, the king said, "Indeed, you finished the pond, but I can't give you my daughter yet. You must first do one more thing."

"What's that?" asked the prince.

"I've got a big mountain with nothing on it but thornbushes. I want them all cut down, and then you must build the most magnificent castle imaginable, and all the proper furnishings must be in it."

When the prince got up the next morning, the king gave him a glass ax and glass drill to take with him and told him that he had to be finished by six o'clock. As the prince began to chop the first thornbush with the ax, it broke into little pieces that flew all around him, and the drill also turned out to be useless. Then he became very dejected and waited to see if his beloved would come again and help him out of this desperate situation.

At noon she came and brought him something to eat. He went to meet her and told her everything that had happened. Then he ate something, let her louse him, and fell asleep. Once again she took her kerchief and struck the ground with it three times. "Workers, come out!" she cried.

Numerous gnomes again appeared and asked her what she desired.

"In three hours' time," she said, "you must cut down all the thornbushes and build the most magnificent castle imaginable on the mountain, and all the proper furnishings must be in it."

They went off and called all their relatives to come and help them, and when the time was up, everything was finished. Then they went and reported to the king's daughter, whereupon she took the kerchief and struck the ground three times with it. "Workers, go home!" she said, and they all vanished on the spot.

When the prince woke up and saw everything, he was as happy as a bird in the air. Since the clock had just struck six, they went home together, and the king asked, "Is the castle finished now?"

"Yes," said the prince.

When they were sitting at the table, the king said, "I can't give you my youngest daughter until the two oldest are married."

The prince and the king's daughter were very sad, and the prince did not know what to do. Then one night he went to the king's daughter, and they ran away together. After they had gone a short distance, the daughter looked around and saw her father pursuing them. "Oh," she said, "what shall we do? My father's after us, and he'll soon catch up. Wait, I'll turn you into a rosebush and myself into a rose, and I'll protect myself by hiding in the middle of the bush."

When the father reached the spot, there was a rosebush with a rose standing there. When he tried to pluck the rose, the thorns pricked his fingers, so he had to return home. His wife asked him why he had not brought back the couple. He told her that he had almost caught them, but then had lost sight of them and had found only a rosebush and a rose where he had thought they were.

"If you had only plucked the rose," the queen said, "the bush would have come along."

So he went away again to fetch the rose. In the meantime, the two had made their way far over some fields, and the king had to run after them. Once again the daughter looked around and saw her father coming after them. "Oh," she said, "what shall we do now? Wait, I'll turn you into a church and myself into a pastor. Then I'll stand in the pulpit and preach."

When the king reached the spot, a church was standing there, and a pastor was preaching in the pulpit. So he listened to the sermon and returned home. The queen asked him why he had failed to bring back the couple with him, and he replied, "I ran after them a long time, and just as I thought I had caught up with them, I came upon a church with a pastor preaching in the pulpit."

"You should have taken the pastor with you," said his wife. "The church would have come along. It's no use sending you anymore. I'll have to go myself."

After she had gone a long way and saw the two from afar, the king's daughter looked around and saw her mother coming. "We've run out of luck now," she said. "My mother herself is coming. Wait, I'll turn you into a pond and myself into a fish."

When the mother reached the spot, there was a large pond, and a fish was leaping about in the middle of it. The fish stuck its head out of the water, looked around, and was as merry as could be. The mother tried very hard to catch the fish, but she was unable to land it. Then she got so angry that she drank the entire pond dry just to catch the fish. However, she became so sick that she had to spit out the water, and she vomited the entire pond out again. "It's plain to me that I'm helpless against you." So she made her peace and asked them to return with her, which they did. Now, the queen gave her daughter three walnuts and said, "These will help you in your greatest need."

Then the young couple set off again. After they had walked for ten hours, they had approached the castle where the prince came from, and nearby was a village. When they arrived in the village, the prince said, "Stay here, my dearest. I'll go up to the castle first and then come back to fetch you with a carriage and servants."

When he got to the castle, everyone was happy to see him again. He told them he had a bride, who was now in the village, and he wanted to go fetch her in a carriage. They harnessed the carriage right away, and several servants climbed on back. Just as the prince was about to get in, his mother gave him a kiss, and he forgot everything that had happened and everything he wanted to do. His mother then ordered them to unharness the carriage, and they all went back into the castle. Meanwhile, the king's daughter sat in the village and waited and waited. She thought the prince would come and fetch her, but no one came. Finally, she hired herself out at the mill that belonged to the castle. She had to sit by the river every afternoon and wash the pots and jars. Once the queen came out of the castle and took a walk along the river. When she saw the beautiful maiden, she said, "What a lovely girl! She's quite appealing!" Then everyone around her took a look, but nobody recognized her.

The king's daughter served the miller as maid honestly and faithfully for a long time. Meanwhile, the queen had found a wife for her son, and she came from a country far away. When the bride arrived, they were to be married right away, and crowds of people gathered to see the event, and the maid asked the miller if she might go and watch too.

"Go right along," said the miller.

Before she left, she cracked open one of the three walnuts and found a beautiful dress inside. She put it on, wore it to the church, and stood near the altar. All at once the bride and bridegroom arrived and sat down in front of the altar. When the pastor was about to bless them, the bride looked to one side and saw the maid dressed as a lady standing there. Then she stood up and said that she would not marry until she had a dress as beautiful as the lady's. So they returned home and sent servants to ask the lady if she would sell the dress. No, she told them, she would not sell it, but they might be able to earn it. They asked her what they would have to do, and she said that they could have the dress if she could sleep outside the prince's door that night. They said yes, she could do that, but the servants were ordered to give the prince a sleeping potion.

The king's daughter lay down on the threshold and whimpered all night: she had had the forest cut down for him, she had had the pond cleaned up for him, she had had the castle built for him, she had turned him into a rosebush, then a church, and finally a pond, and yet, he had forgotten her so quickly. The prince did not hear a thing, but her cries woke the servants, who listened but did not know what to make of it all.

When they got up the next morning, the bride put on the dress and went to the church with the bridegroom. Meanwhile, the beautiful maid opened the second walnut, and she found a dress more splendid than the first, put it on, and wore it to the church, where she stood near the altar. Then everything happened as on the previous day. Once again the maid lay down in front of the prince's door, but this time the servants did not give the prince a sleeping potion but something to keep him awake, and he went to bed. The miller's maid whimpered once more, as she had before, and told him about all the things she had done for him. The prince heard it all and became very sad, for he remembered everything that had happened. He wanted to go to her right then and there, but his mother had locked the door. However, the next morning he went straight to his beloved and told her what had happened and begged her not to be angry with him for having forgotten her for so long. Then the king's daughter opened the third walnut and found a dress that was even more beautiful than the other two. She put it on and went to the church with her bridegroom. Groups of children gathered around them and gave them flowers and placed colored ribbons at their feet. After they were blessed at the wedding, they had a merry celebration, but the false mother and false bride were sent away.

And the lips are still warm on the last person who told this tale.

◈ 114 ◈

The Clever Little Tailor

ONCE UPON A TIME there was a princess who was extremely proud. Whenever a suitor appeared before her, she gave him a riddle to solve, and if he could not guess it, she would ridicule him and send him away. She let it be proclaimed that whoever could solve her riddle would be allowed to marry her, no matter who the person might be.

In time three tailors happened to meet. The two oldest thought that, because they had sewn many a fine stitch and had got them all right, they could not miss with the princess and would hit upon the right answer. The third tailor was a young blunderhead who had tramped about and knew next to nothing about his trade, but he thought that here he might find some luck. Otherwise, where else would he find it? The other two tailors said to him, "You'd be better off staying at home. You won't get very far with your hollow head."

The little tailor would not let himself be disheartened and said that he had his mind set on it and knew how to take care of himself. So he sallied forth as if he owned the world.

Together the three of them announced themselves to the princess and asked her to give them the riddle. They told her that finally the right people had come, for they all had such fine minds that one could thread a needle with each one of them.

So the princess said, "I have two kinds of hair on my head. What are the colors?"

"If that's all there's to it," said the first tailor, "one's black, and the other's white, just like the cloth they call pepper and salt."

"Wrong," said the princess. "Let the second try."

"Well, if it's not black and white," said the second tailor, "then it's got to be brown and red, like my father's frock coat."

"Wrong," said the princess. "Let the third try. I can tell by his face that he thinks he knows the answer."

The little tailor stepped forward boldly and said, "The princess has silver and golden hair on her head, and those are the two colors."

When the princess heard that, she turned pale and nearly fainted from fright, for the little tailor had guessed right, and she had been firmly convinced that nobody in the world would ever solve the riddle. When her heart began to beat again, she said, "You haven't won me yet, for you must do one more thing. Down in the stable there's a bear, and you must spend the night with him. If you're still alive when I get up in the morning, then I'll marry you."

She thought that she would get rid of the tailor this way since the bear had never let anyone that he had got his paws on survive. But the little tailor would not let himself be frightened by this. Indeed, he was delighted and said, "Nothing ventured, nothing gained."

When evening came, the little tailor was taken down to the bear, who headed right for the little fellow to give him a big welcome with his paws.

"Easy does it," said the little tailor. "I'll calm you down quick enough."

Then, as though he had nothing in the world to worry about, he casually took some walnuts out of his pocket and began cracking them open with his teeth and eating the kernels. When the bear saw this, he felt like having some nuts too. So the little tailor reached into his pocket and gave him a handful. However, these were not nuts but small stones. The bear put them into his mouth and could not crack open any of them, no matter how much he tried.

Good gracious, thought the bear. What a stupid oaf you are! You can't even crack open nuts. And he said to the little tailor, "Will you crack open some nuts for me?"

"What kind of a fellow are you anyway?" asked the little tailor. "You have such a big mouth, and yet, you can't even crack open little nuts." Then he took the stones and stealthily substituted a nut for them and cracked it in two in his mouth.

"I've got to try this thing once more," said the bear. "When I see you do it, I can't imagine why I can't do it too."

Once again the little tailor gave him plain stones, and the bear worked at it and bit with all his might, but you don't think he succeeded, do you?

After that was over, the little tailor took a fiddle from under his coat and played a little tune. When the bear heard the music, he could not help but dance, and after he had danced for a while, he was so delighted that he said to the little tailor, "Is it hard to play the fiddle?"

"It's child's play. Watch me. I place the fingers of my left hand down here and move the bow with my right. Then you can have a merry old time—whoop-de-doo and away we go!"

"I'd like to learn how to play the fiddle," said the bear. "Then I could dance as much as I liked. What do you think about that? Will you give me lessons?"

"Gladly," said the little tailor, "if you have talent for it. But show me your paws. They're tremendously long. I'll have to cut your nails a bit."

He fetched a vice, and the bear put his paws into it. Then the tailor tightened the vice and said, "Now wait until I return with the scissors," and he let the bear growl as long as he liked, while the tailor lay down on a bundle of straw in the corner and fell asleep.

That night, when the princess heard the bear's tremendous growling, she thought that he had made an end of the tailor and was growling out of joy. The next morning she got up feeling quite at ease and happy, but when she glanced out the window toward the stable, she saw the little tailor standing outside, looking as cheerful and fresh as a fish in water. After this she could not break her agreement because she had given her promise in public. The king summoned a coach, and she had to drive to church with the little tailor to get married. When the couple climbed into the coach, the other two tailors, who were false-hearted and begrudged the little tailor his luck, went to the stable and set the bear free. Now, the bear ran after the coach in a great rage, and the princess heard him panting and growling. In her fright she cried out, "Ah, the bear's after us and wants to get you!"

The little tailor, alert as ever, immediately stood on his head, stuck his feet out the window, and shouted, "You see the vice? If you don't go away, then you'll soon be back in it!"

When the bear saw that, he turned and ran away. Our little tailor drove calmly to the church and was married to the princess. Thereafter, he lived as happily as a lark with her, and whoever does not believe me must pay me a taler.

◆ 115 ◆

The Bright Sun Will Bring It to Light

A JOURNEYMAN TAILOR was traveling around and practicing his trade. However, at one time he could not find any work and became so poverty-stricken that he did not have a single farthing for food. Just at this point in his travels he met a Jew, who he thought probably had a lot of money with him. So he dismissed God from his heart, went straight toward the Jew, and said, "Give me your money, or I'll strike you dead."

"Spare my life!" said the Jew. "I don't have much money, just eight farthings."

"You've got more money than that! Out with it!" the tailor responded.

Then he used force and beat the Jew until he was nearly dead. Just as the Jew was on the point of death, he uttered his last words, "The bright sun will bring it to light!" Upon saying this, he died.

The tailor searched the man's pockets for money but could not find anything more than the eight farthings that the Jew had told him about. So he picked him up, carried him behind a bush, and continued on his travels, practicing his trade along the way.

After he had been traveling a long time, he came to a city where he worked for a master tailor who had a beautiful daughter. He fell in love with her, married her, and they had a good and happy marriage. Some time later, after they had already had two children, the father-in-law and the mother-in-law died, and the young couple had the house to themselves.

One morning, as the man sat at the table in front of the window his wife brought him some coffee. He poured it into a cup and was about to drink it when the sun shone upon the coffee and cast a reflection on the wall so that little rings flickered here and there. The tailor looked up and said, "Ah, yes, the sun wants very much to bring it to light, but it can't."

"Good gracious, my dear husband!" said his wife. "What's that? What do you mean by that?"

"I can't tell you," he answered.

But she said, "If you really love me, you must tell me." She spoke very sweetly, swore she would never tell a soul about it, and gave him no peace.

So he told her how, many years ago, he had been traveling around in rags and without money, when he met a Jew and killed him. Then the Jew had said in his death throes, "The bright sun will bring it to light!" Now the sun wanted to bring it to light and had cast its reflection on the wall, where it made rings. But it was not able to bring it to light.

After telling her this, he implored her not to tell anyone; otherwise, he would lose his life. She promised him not to tell, but after he sat down to work, she went to her neighbor and told her the story in confidence, making her promise not to tell a soul about it. Yet, after three days had passed, the whole city knew the story, and the tailor was brought before the court and convicted.

So, after all, the bright sun did manage to bring it to light.

❖ 116 ❖

The Blue Light

ONCE UPON A TIME there was a soldier who had served the king faithfully for many years, but when the war was over and he could no longer do his job because of the many wounds he had received, the king said to him, "You can go home. I don't need you anymore, and you won't get any more money because I pay wages only to those who can serve me."

The soldier became very depressed because he could not see how he would be able to keep himself alive. After his departure he walked the entire day until evening, when he reached a forest. In the distance he saw a light, and as he went toward it, he came upon a house that belonged to a witch.

"Give me a night's lodging and a little food and drink," he said to her. "Otherwise, I shall perish."

"Oho!" she replied. "Who'd ever give a forlorn soldier anything? But I'll be merciful and take you in if you do what I demand."

"What is it you demand?" asked the soldier.

"That you spade up my garden tomorrow morning."

The soldier agreed, and the next day he worked with all his might but could not finish the work until evening.

"Well, it's obvious," said the witch, "that you can't move on today. I'll let you stay another night if you chop a cord of wood for me and split it into small pieces tomorrow."

The soldier needed an entire day for this job too, and in the evening the witch suggested that he spend another night in her house.

"Tomorrow I'll give you something easy to do. There's an old dry well behind my house. My light has fallen into it, and it's got a blue flame that hasn't burned out yet. I want you to bring it back to me."

The next day the old woman led him to the well and let him down in a basket. He found the blue light and gave the signal for her to pull him up. She pulled him up, but just as he got near the edge of the well, she reached down with her hand and wanted to take the blue light from him.

"No, you don't," he said, for he sensed her evil intentions. "I won't give you the light until both my feet are firmly on the ground."

The witch became furious, let him drop to the bottom of the well, and went away. The poor soldier fell on the damp ground without hurting himself, and the blue light continued to burn. But what good could that do him? It was clear to him that his fate was sealed. For a while he sat there very sadly. Then he reached into his pocket without thinking and found his pipe, half filled with tobacco. This will be your last pleasure, he thought to himself, and pulled out the pipe, lit it with the blue light, and began to smoke. As the smoke floated in circles around the bottom of the well, a little black dwarf suddenly appeared before him and asked, "Master, what do you command?"

"What am I supposed to command?" replied the soldier, completely amazed.

"I must do everything you demand," said the dwarf.

"Good," responded the soldier. "Then first help me out of this well."

The dwarf took him by the hand and led him through an underground passage, and the soldier did not forget to take the blue light with him. Along the way the dwarf showed him the treasures that the witch had gathered and hidden there, and the soldier took as much gold as he could carry. When he was back above ground, he said to the dwarf, "Now go and tie up the old witch and bring her to the court."

It was not long before she came riding by quick as the wind. She was tied to the back of a wildcat and screaming in a frightful manner. Soon after that the dwarf returned alone.

"It's all as you wished," he said. "The witch is already hanging on the gallows. What more do you command, master?" asked the dwarf.

"Nothing right now," replied the soldier. "You can go home, but be on hand whenever I call you."

"All you have to do," said the dwarf, "is light your pipe with the blue light, then I'll be at your side immediately." Then he vanished before the soldier's eyes.

The soldier returned to the city from which he had come. He stopped at the best inn and had fine clothes made for himself. Then he ordered a room and told the innkeeper to furnish it as splendidly as possible. When it was ready and the soldier had moved in, he called the black dwarf and said, "I served the king faithfully, but he sent me away and let me starve. Now I want to get my revenge for that."

"What shall I do?" asked the dwarf.

"Late tonight, when the king's daughter is in bed, I want you to bring her here in her sleep. I shall make her work like a maid for me."

"This will be an easy thing for me to do," said the dwarf, "but it's a dangerous thing for you to do. If anyone finds out about this, you'll pay for it dearly."

When the clock struck twelve, the door burst open, and the dwarf entered carrying the king's daughter.

"Aha, you're here at last!" cried the soldier. "Well, get to work. Go fetch the broom and sweep the floor."

When she was finished, he ordered her to come over to his easy chair, where he stretched out his feet and said, "Pull my boots off!" Then he threw them in her face, and she had to pick them up, clean them, and polish them until they sparkled. There was no resistance on her part, and she did everything he commanded in silence and with her eyes half closed. At the first crow of the cock, the dwarf carried her back to the royal palace and put her into her bed.

The next morning, when the king's daughter got up, she went to her father and told him she had had a strange dream. "I was carried through the streets as fast as lightning and brought into the room of a soldier. Then I had to serve him, wait on him like a maid, and do all the menial tasks, such as sweeping the floor and polishing his boots. It was only a dream, and yet, I'm as tired as if I'd really done it all."

"The dream could have been true," said the king. "Take my advice and fill your pocket with peas. Then make a little hole in the pocket. If you're carried off again, the peas will fall out and leave a trail on the street."

Unknown to the king, while he was talking, the dwarf was standing there invisible and overheard everything. That night, when he carried the sleeping princess through the streets once more, some peas did indeed fall out of her pocket, but they could not leave a trail because the cunning dwarf had already strewn peas on all the streets. So the king's daughter again had to perform the services of a maid until the crow of the cock. The next morning the king sent his servants out to search for the trail, but in vain. All they could find were poor children sitting on every street, picking up peas, and saying, "It rained peas last night."

"We've got to think up something else," said the king. "Keep your shoes on when you go to bed, and before you return this time, hide one of them. I'll find it for sure."

The black dwarf heard the plan, and that night, when the soldier demanded that he bring him the king's daughter, the dwarf tried to dissuade him, telling him that he did not know how to stop this scheme and that if the shoe was found in his room, the soldier would have to pay dearly for it.

"Do what I tell you," responded the soldier. And the king's daughter had to work like a maid again on the third night. However, before she was carried back to the palace, she hid a shoe underneath his bed.

The next morning the king had the entire city searched for the shoe. It was found in the soldier's room, but the soldier himself had already left the city at the behest of the little dwarf. He was soon overtaken, however, and thrown into prison. In his hurry to escape he had forgotten to take the best things he possessed, the blue light and the gold, and now he had only one ducat left in his pocket. As he was standing in chains at the window of his prison cell, he saw one of his old comrades passing by, and he knocked on the windowpane. When his comrade approached, the soldier said, "Do me a favor, and get me the little bundle that I left in my room at the inn. I'll give you a ducat for your trouble."

His comrade ran there and brought back the bundle. As soon as the soldier was alone, he lit his pipe and called the black dwarf.

"Have no fear," the dwarf said to his master. "Go wherever they take you, and let them do what they want. Just remember to take the blue light with you."

The next day the soldier was brought to trial, and although he had done no evil, the judge sentenced him to death. As he was being led out to be executed he asked the king to grant him one last favor.

"What kind of a favor?" asked the king.

"I'd like to smoke my pipe along the way."

"You can smoke three pipes," answered the king, "but don't think that I'll spare your life."

Then the soldier took out his pipe and lit it with the blue light. By the time a few rings of smoke had risen, the dwarf was already standing there. He held a little cudgel in his hand and said, "What does my master command?"

"Beat those false judges and their assistants to the ground, and don't spare the king either, for he has treated me poorly!"

Then the dwarf struck like lightning and zigzagged here and there. He just had to touch someone with his cudgel, and the person immediately collapsed to the ground and did not dare to budge again. In his fright the king asked for mercy, and in order to save his life, he gave the soldier his kingdom and his daughter for a wife.

❖ 117 ❖

The Stubborn Child

ONCE UPON A TIME there was a stubborn child who never did what his mother told him to do. The dear Lord, therefore, did not look kindly upon him and let him become sick. No doctor could cure him, and in a short time he lay on his deathbed. After he was lowered into his grave and was covered over with earth, one of his little arms suddenly emerged and reached up into the air. They pushed it back down and covered the earth with fresh earth, but that did not help. The little arm kept popping out. So the child's mother had to go to the grave herself and smack the little arm with a switch. After she had done that, the arm withdrew, and then, for the first time, the child had peace beneath the earth.

❖ 118 ❖

The Three Army Surgeons

THREE ARMY SURGEONS who were traveling around the world thought that they had learned all there was to know about their profession. One day they came to an inn, where they wanted to spend the night, and the innkeeper asked them where they were coming from and where they were heading.

"We're traveling about the world and practicing our profession."

"Well, show me what you can do," said the innkeeper.

Then the first surgeon said he would cut off his own hand and put it back on again in the morning. The second said he would tear out his heart and put it back in place in the morning. The third said he would poke out his eyes and put them back in their sockets in the morning.

"If you can do that," said the innkeeper, "then you certainly know all there is to know about your profession."

But the truth of the matter was, they had a salve that immediately healed any wound when they rubbed it on, and they carried the salve in a little flask that they kept with them all the time. So, just as they told the innkeeper they would, each one cut a different organ from his body: the hand, the heart, and the eyes. Then they put them on a plate and gave them to the innkeeper, who handed the plate to the maid, who was to put it in the cupboard for safekeeping.

Unknown to everyone, however, the maid had a sweetheart, who was a soldier, and when the innkeeper, the three surgeons, and everyone in the house was asleep, the soldier came and wanted something to eat. The maid opened the cupboard and brought him some food, but she was so enraptured that she forgot to shut the cupboard door. She sat down at the table next to her sweetheart and began chatting away. In her bliss she could not imagine anything going wrong, but the cat came creeping inside, found the cupboard open, and carried off the hand, heart, and eyes of the three surgeons. After the soldier had eaten and the maid was about to clear away the dishes and shut the cupboard, she noticed that the plate given to her by the innkeeper was empty. Filled with dread, she said to her sweetheart, "I'm lost! What am I to do! The hand's gone. The heart and eyes are also gone. They'll make me pay for this tomorrow!"

"Calm down," he said. "I'll help you out of this mess. There's a thief hanging on the gallows outside. I'll go and cut off his hand. Which hand was it?"

"The right one."

The maid gave him a sharp knife, and he went to the gallows, cut off the right hand from the poor sinner, and brought it to the maid. Then he grabbed a cat and poked its eyes out. Now only the heart was missing.

"Haven't you just slaughtered a pig? Isn't the meat in the cellar?"

"Yes," said the maid.

"Well, that's perfect," said the soldier, who went and brought back the pig's heart.

The maid put everything together on the plate and placed it back in the cupboard. After her lover departed, she calmly went to bed.

In the morning, when the surgeons got up, they told the maid to fetch the plate with the hand, heart, and eyes. She brought it to them from the cupboard, and the first surgeon took the thief's hand and rubbed salve on it. Immediately the hand grew back on him. The second took the cat's eyes and put them into his sockets. The third put the pig's heart back into place. As the innkeeper stood and watched all this he marveled at their skill and said that he had never seen anything like it before. Indeed, he was going to praise and recommend them to everyone he met. Then they paid the bill and continued on their journey.

As they walked along, the surgeon with the pig's heart kept leaving the other two to sniff around in corners the way pigs do. The others tried to hold him back by his coattails, but that did not help. He broke loose and ran to all those spots that were most infested with garbage. The second surgeon also began acting in a strange way. He kept rubbing his eyes and said to the third one, "Comrade, what's going on? These aren't my eyes. I can't see a thing. Please lead me; otherwise, I'll fall."

So they proceeded with difficulty till evening, when they came to another inn. They entered the main room, where a rich man was sitting at a table and counting his money. The surgeon with the thief's hand walked around him, and his hand began twitching. Finally, when the gentleman turned his head, the surgeon reached into the pile and took a handful of money. One of his companions saw him do this and said, "Friend, what are you doing? You know it's not proper to steal. Shame on you!"

"Oh, no!" he exclaimed. "I can't stop myself. My hand keeps twitching, and I've got to grab things whether I like it or not."

Afterward they went to bed, and their room was so dark that it was impossible to see one's hand before one's face. Suddenly the surgeon with the cat's eyes woke up, then roused the others, and said, "Brothers, look! Do you see the little white mice running around?"

The other two sat up in their beds, but they could not see a thing. So he said, "Something's wrong with us. We didn't get our own organs back. The innkeeper cheated us, and we've got to return."

The next morning the three surgeons made their way back to the inn and told the innkeeper that they had not received their right organs. One had got a thief's hand; the second, cat's eyes; and the third, a pig's heart. The innkeeper said that it must have been the maid's fault and wanted to call her. However, she had seen the three surgeons coming and had run out the back door and never returned. The three surgeons told the innkeeper then that he had better give them lots of money; otherwise, they would burn his house down. So he gave them what he had on hand and whatever else he could raise, and the three departed. The money lasted them the rest of their lives, but they would have preferred to have had their own organs restored to them.

◈ 119 ◈

The Seven Swabians

ONCE SEVEN SWABIANS GOT TOGETHER. The first was Herr Schulz, the second Jackli, the third Marli, the fourth Jergli, the fifth Michal, the sixth Hans, and the seventh Veitli. They had all made up their minds to travel about the world in search of adventure and to perform great deeds. To be on the safe side they decided it would be best to arm themselves. So they had a single spear made for them that was quite long and strong. All seven were needed to carry it. The bravest and manliest was first, and this had to be Herr Schulz. The rest followed in order, with Veitli bringing up the rear.

One day in July they had managed to walk a great distance but still had far to go before they would reach the next village, where they planned to spend the night. It was already dusk, and all of a sudden a beetle or hornet flew right past them from behind a bush on the meadow and buzzed in a hostile manner. Herr Schulz became so scared that he almost dropped the spear, and in his fright his whole body broke out in sweat.

"Listen! Listen!" he called to his companions. "My God, I hear a drum!"

Jackli, who was carrying the spear right behind Herr Schulz, smelled some kind of an odor and said, "Something's going on here, for sure. I can smell the powder and the fuse."

These words were enough for Herr Schulz to take flight, and he jumped like lightning over a fence. However, he landed on the prongs of a rake that had been left there from haying, and the handle went right into his face and gave him a nasty blow. "Ow! Ow!" yelled Herr Schulz. "Take me prisoner. I surrender! I surrender!"

The other six leapt after him, one on top of the other, and they also shouted, "If you surrender, then I surrender! If you surrender, then I surrender!"

Finally, when no enemy came to tie them up and lead them away, they realized they had been misled. Since they did not want the story to be spread, which would have made them into the fools and the laughingstock of the entire region, they swore to each other that they would keep quiet about this until one of them opened his mouth by mistake. Then they continued on their way.

The second danger they experienced cannot be compared with the first. After they had traveled some days, their way took them through a fallow field, where a hare was basking in the sun sound asleep. Its ears were pointing straight up, and its big glassy eyes were wide open. At the sight of this ferocious, wild animal the Seven Swabians became frightened and held a council on what would be the least dangerous thing to do. Although they all wanted to flee, they were also worried that the monster would pursue them and swallow them all, skin and bones. So they said, "We'll just have to fight a great and perilous battle. Nothing ventured, nothing gained!"

All seven took hold of the spear, with Herr Schulz in front and Veitli in the rear. Herr Schulz wanted to go easy and hold back with the spear, while Veitli, quite courageous in the rear, wanted to attack and yelled,

"Charge and uphold the Swabian name,
Or else I wish you'd all get lame!"

But Hans knew how to counter that and said:

"For heaven's sake, you can certainly talk,
but when a dragon's around, you're the first to balk."

Michal exclaimed:

"Well, I'm sure as sure as I can be,
the devil's up there in front of me!"

Then it was Jergli's turn to speak:

"If not the devil, it'll be his mother,
or maybe even the devil's stepbrother."

Marli had a good idea and said to Veitli:

"Go, Veitli, you march ahead,
while I stand behind you instead."

But Veitli was not listening, and Jackli said:

"Herr Schulz must be the first to fight.
It's both his honor and his right."

Then Herr Schulz took heart and said solemnly:

"Well, men, off we go now into the fray.
We'll soon learn who's brave enough to win the day."

Then they all advanced toward the dragon. Herr Schulz crossed himself and called upon God to grant them aid, but this was to no avail. As he came closer and closer to the enemy he became terribly afraid and cried out, "Strike with all your might! Strike! Might! Strike!"

All this commotion woke the hare, who was frightened and ran away as quickly as it could. When Herr Schulz saw the hare in full retreat, he rejoiced and cried out:

"My God, Veitli, take a gander over there!
Our monster was nothing but a hare!"

After that the Swabian League kept looking for further adventures
and eventually arrived at the banks of the Moselle, a calm, deep, and
murky river. Very few bridges are built over it, but it can be crossed
at various points by boat. Since the seven Swabians were unaware of
this, they called out to a man who was finishing some work on the
other side of the river and asked how they could get across. Due to
the distance and their accent, the man could not understand what they
had said and called back to them in his Trier dialect, "Wat? Wat?"
Herr Schulz thought he meant "Wade, wade through the water,"
and since he was the first, he plunged into the Moselle. It was not
long before he sank into the mud and was covered by the large rolling
waves. However, the wind blew his hat to the opposite bank, and a
frog sat down next to it and croaked "Wat, wat, wat."
The other six Swabians heard the cries from the other side and said,
"Our companion, Herr Schulz, is calling us. If he can wade across,
why can't we?"
Therefore, they all plunged into the river and were drowned.
Thus it was that a frog was the death of six men, and no one from
the Swabian League ever returned home.

◈ 120 ◈

The Three Journeymen

THERE WERE THREE JOURNEYMEN who had agreed to stay together
during their travels and to always work in the same city. Yet, after a
while their masters could not pay them, and eventually they had
nothing to live on and were reduced to rags.
"What shall we do?" one of them said. "We can't stay here any
longer. Let's set out on our travels again. Then, if we don't find any
work in the next city we come to, we'll part ways. But, before we do
that, let's arrange with the innkeeper to keep him posted about our
whereabouts so that each of us can get news of the others through
him."
His companions thought that this was the best solution, and they
set out on their journey. Along the way they met a richly clad
gentleman, who asked them who they were.
"We're journeymen and are looking for work. We've been together

until now, but if we don't find any work, then we're going to part ways."

"There's no need for that," said the man. "If you'll do what I tell you, you'll have more than enough money and work. In fact, you'll be respected gentlemen and will be able to drive around in carriages."

"Just as long as we won't be endangering our souls and salvation, we'll do whatever you want," said one of them.

"There's no danger," responded the man. "I won't make any claims on your souls."

However, one of the other journeymen had been looking at the man's feet, and when he caught sight of a horse's hoof and a human foot, he did not want to have anything to do with the man. But the devil said, "You have nothing to fear. I'm not interested in your souls but in someone else's, and he's already half mine and his time is about to run out."

Since they now felt safe, they agreed to the devil's proposal, and he told them what he wanted them to do. The first journeyman was to answer every question with "All three of us." The second, with "For money." The third, with "That's all right." These answers were to be given one after the other, but the men were not allowed to say anything else. If they did not follow the devil's instructions, then all their money would disappear immediately, but as long as they followed them, their pockets would always be full. At the outset the devil gave them as much money as they could carry and told them to stop at such and such an inn in the next city. When they got there, the innkeeper went over to them and asked, "What do you want to eat?"

The first one answered, "All three of us."

"Yes," said the innkeeper. "That's what I assume."

"For money," said the second.

"Obviously," said the innkeeper.

"And that's all right," said the third.

"Of course it's all right," said the innkeeper.

They received something fine to eat and drink, and the service was good. After the meal they had to pay, and the innkeeper brought the bill to one of them.

"All three of us," said the first.

"For money," said the second.

"And that's all right," said the third.

"Of course it's right," said the innkeeper. "All three of you must pay. I can't serve anyone without money."

Then they paid him but gave him much more money than he had charged. The other guests at the inn observed this and said, "Those fellows must be crazy."

"That's exactly what they are," said the innkeeper. "They're not particularly smart in the head."

The journeymen stayed at the inn for some time, and they said nothing but "All three of us," "For money," and "That's all right." However, they watched and knew everything that happened there.

One day a great merchant happened to enter the inn. He was carrying a lot of money with him and said, "Innkeeper, I want you to keep my money for me. Those three crazy journeymen are here, and they might steal it from me."

The innkeeper took the money bag, and as he carried it up to the room he felt it was heavy with gold. So he gave the three journeymen a room downstairs, while the merchant was to have a special room upstairs. At midnight, when the innkeeper thought they were all sleeping, he and his wife went with an ax and beat the merchant to death. After the murder they went back to bed. The next morning there was a great commotion: the merchant lay dead in bed, swimming in blood. All the guests gathered together quickly, and the innkeeper said, "The three crazy journeymen did this."

The guests agreed and said, "It couldn't have been anyone else."

The innkeeper summoned the journeymen and said to them, "Did you kill the merchant?"

"All three of us," said the first one.

"For money," said the second.

"And that's all right," said the third.

"You've all heard it now," said the innkeeper. "They themselves have confessed."

The journeymen were taken to the prison and were to be put on trial. When they saw that things were getting serious, they became afraid, but the devil came that night and said, "Just hold out one more day and don't throw away your good luck. Not a hair on your heads will be touched."

The next morning they were brought before the court, and the judge asked, "Are you the murderers?"

"All three of us."

"Why did you kill him?"

"For money."

"You villains!" said the judge. "Didn't you dread committing such a sin?"

"That's all right."

"They've confessed and are still unrepentant as well," said the judge. "Take them out and execute them forthwith."

So they were conducted outside, and the innkeeper was obliged to join the group of witnesses. The executioner's assistants took hold of the journeymen and led them up onto the scaffold, where the executioner was waiting for them with a bare sword. Just then a coach drawn by four bloodred chestnut horses suddenly appeared, and it was moving so rapidly that sparks flew from the pavement. Someone was waving a white cloth from the window, and the executioner said, "Pardon is coming."

"Pardon! Pardon!" was also the cry from the coach. Then the devil, dressed in splendid fashion as a distinguished gentleman, stepped out of the coach and said, "You three are innocent, and you may now tell us what you saw and heard."

Then the oldest said, "We didn't kill the merchant. The murderer is standing among us," and he pointed to the innkeeper. "If you want proof, go into his cellar, where you'll find other bodies hanging. He's killed those people as well."

So the judge sent the executioner's assistants to the cellar, and they found everything exactly as the journeyman had said. When they reported this to the judge, he ordered the executioner to cut off the innkeeper's head on the scaffold. Then the devil said to the three journeymen, "Now I have the soul that I wanted. You're all free and shall have money for the rest of your lives."

◆ 121 ◆

The Prince Who Feared Nothing

ONCE UPON A TIME there was a prince who was tired of living at home in his father's house, and since he feared nothing, he thought, I'll go out into the wide world, where I won't be bored. There are plenty of marvelous things to see there. So he took leave of his parents and set out on his journey. He was on the move from morning till evening, and he followed the road no matter where it led him.

One day he happened to come to a giant's house, and since he was tired, he sat down in front of the door to rest. As he began examining his surroundings he noticed some playthings lying in the giant's yard: several huge bowling balls, along with ninepins as big as a man. After a while he felt like playing. So he set up the ninepins and began to bowl. Whenever the pins fell, he yelled and shouted and was in good spirits. The giant heard the noise, stuck his head out of a window, and spotted a human being who was no bigger than other humans and yet was playing with his ninepins.

"Hey, you little worm!" the giant yelled. "How can you bowl with my ninepins? Where did you get the strength to do that?"

The prince looked up, saw the giant, and said, "You clumsy oaf, you think you're the only one with strong arms? I can do whatever I feel like doing."

The giant came down, watched with great amazement as he bowled, and said, "Remarkable! If that's the kind of human you are, go and fetch me an apple from the Tree of Life."

"What do you want with it?" asked the prince.

"I don't want it for myself," replied the giant, "but for my bride, who's been wanting it for some time. I traveled all around the world but couldn't find the tree."

"I'll find it for sure," said the prince. "I can't imagine that anything would prevent me from picking the apple."

"Don't think it will be easy," said the giant. "The garden where the tree's located is surrounded by an iron fence, and there are wild animals side-by-side in front of the fence. They keep guard and won't let anyone inside."

"But they'll let me in," said the prince.

"Well, if you manage to get into the garden and see the apple hanging on the tree, it won't be yours yet. There's a ring hanging in front of it, and you've got to put your hand through it if you want to get the apple and break it off. Nobody has ever succeeded in doing that."

"I'll succeed," said the prince.

He took leave of the giant, went over hill and dale, through fields and forests, until he finally found the miraculous garden. The animals were lying around it, but they had lowered their heads and were sleeping. Nor did they awake when he approached them. So he stepped over them, climbed the fence, and reached the garden safely. Right in the middle stood the Tree of Life, and the red apples glistened on the branches. He climbed up the trunk, and as he was about to reach for an apple, he saw a ring hanging in front of it. Yet, he had no difficulty sticking his hand through the ring and picking the apple. The ring closed tightly around his arm, and suddenly he felt tremendous power surging through his veins. After climbing down the tree with the apple, he did not want to climb back over the fence. Instead, he grabbed hold of the large gate and needed to shake the gate only once before it burst open with a loud noise. Then he went out, and the lion that had been lying in front of the gate woke up and sprang after him, but the lion was neither furious nor ferocious. Rather, he followed the prince meekly, as if the prince were his master.

The prince brought the promised apple to the giant and said, "You see, I had no difficulty getting it."

The giant was happy that his wish had been fulfilled so quickly. He rushed to his bride and gave her the apple that she had desired for such a long time. She was a beautiful and smart maiden, and when she noticed that the giant was not wearing the ring on his arm, she said, "I won't believe that you were the one who fetched the apple until I see the ring on your arm."

"I just need to go home and get it," said the giant, who thought it would be easy to take it from the human by force if he would not give it up of his own free will. So the giant demanded the ring from the prince, who refused to give it to him.

"The ring must be wherever the apple is," said the giant. "If you won't give it to me of your own free will, you'll have to fight me for it."

They wrestled with one another for a long time, but the giant could not get the better of the prince, who had been strengthened by the magic power of the ring. Then the giant thought of a trick and said, "All this fighting has made me hot, and you too. Let's go for a swim in the river and cool ourselves off before we begin again."

Since the prince did not suspect anything devious, he went with him to the river, took off his clothes and the ring as well, and jumped into the river. The giant immediately grabbed the ring and ran away with it, but the lion, who had seen him steal it, set out after the giant, ripped the ring out of his hand, and brought it back to his master. Then the giant hid behind an oak tree, and when the prince was busy dressing himself again, the giant attacked him and poked out both his eyes.

Now the poor prince stood there blind and helpless. The giant came back again, seized his hand like someone who wanted to guide him, and led him to the edge of a high cliff. Then he left the prince standing there and thought, Just a few more steps and he'll fall to his death. Then I'll be able to take the ring off.

But the faithful lion had not abandoned his master. He held on tightly to the prince's clothes and gradually pulled him back. When the giant came to rob the dead man, he saw that his trick had been in vain. "There must be a way to get rid of such a weak human like that!" he said to himself angrily. Then he took the prince's arm and led him by a different path to the edge of the cliff again. But the lion, who had sensed the giant's evil intention, helped the prince out of danger here too. When they came to the precipice, the giant let go of the blind man's hand and intended to leave him alone, but right then the lion shoved the giant over the cliff, and he was smashed to pieces on the bottom.

The faithful animal pulled his master back from the edge of the cliff once again and led him to a tree beside a clear, flowing brook. There the prince sat down, while the lion crouched over and sprayed water in the prince's face with his paw. No sooner did a few drops wet the sockets of his eyes than he could see something again, and he noticed a little bird that flew right past him and bumped into a tree trunk. Immediately the bird fluttered down into the water and bathed itself in the brook. Then it flew away quickly and made its way through the trees without bumping into them, as if it had regained its sight. The prince realized that this was a sign from God, bent over the water, and washed and bathed his face in it. When he straightened up, his eyes were brighter and purer than they had ever been.

The prince thanked God for his great mercy and went on into the wide world with his lion. One day he happened to come upon a castle that was enchanted. A maiden with a beautiful figure and fine appearance stood at the gate, but she was quite black. She addressed him and said, "Oh, if only you could release me from the evil spell that has been cast over me!"

"What must I do?" asked the prince.

"You must spend three nights in the great hall of the enchanted castle," she replied. "But you must not show the least sign of fear in your heart. They will torture you terribly, but if you can bear it without uttering a sound, then I'll be released from the spell, and they won't be allowed to take your life."

"I'm not afraid," said the prince. "With God's help I'll try."

So he went cheerfully into the castle, and when it became dark, he sat down in the great hall and waited. It was quiet until midnight, but then he heard a loud noise, and little devils began coming out from all corners. They pretended not to see him, sat down in the middle of the hall, started a fire, and began to play a game. When one of them lost, he said, "Something's wrong. There's someone here who doesn't belong to us, and it's his fault that I'm losing."

"Hey, you behind the stove!" called another. "Just wait! I'm coming to get you."

The shrieking became louder and louder. Anyone else who had heard it would have become horrified, but the prince sat there very calmly and was not afraid. Eventually, however, the devils jumped up from the floor and attacked him. There were so many of them that he could not protect himself. They dragged him around the floor, pinched him, stabbed him, beat him, and tormented him, but he did not utter a sound. Toward morning they disappeared, and he was so worn out that he could barely move his limbs. At daybreak the black maiden came into the hall carrying a small bottle with the Water of Life in it. She washed him with the water, and soon he felt all his pain disappear, and new vigor flowed through his veins.

"You've made it through one night safely," she said. "But there are two more to go."

She went away again, and as she left he noticed that her feet had turned white. That night the devils came again and began their game anew: they attacked the prince and beat him much harder than the night before so that his body was covered with wounds. Yet, he endured it all, and they had to leave him after a while. When the sun began to rise, the maiden appeared and healed him with the Water of Life. Afterward, as she was leaving, he saw with joy that she had already become white to the tips of her fingers.

Now, he had only one more night to endure, but it was the worst. The devil's pack came again. "Are you still here?" they exclaimed. "We're going to torture you until you can no longer breathe."

They stabbed and beat him, tossed him back and forth, and tugged at his arms and legs as if they wanted to pull him apart. Despite it all, he survived and did not utter a sound. Finally, the devils disappeared,

but he lay there unconscious and could not move, nor could he raise his eyes when the maiden came in and poured the Water of Life all over him. Suddenly all the pain was gone, and he felt reinvigorated, as if he had just woken up from a good night's sleep. When he opened his eyes, he saw the maiden standing beside him. She was white as snow and as beautiful as the day is bright.

"Get up," she said, "and swing your sword three times over the stairs. Then the spell will be broken."

After he had done that, the entire castle was released from the magic spell, and the maiden turned into a rich princess. The servants came and announced that the table was already set in the great hall and dinner was to be served. Then the couple sat down together, ate and drank, and in the evening their wedding was celebrated midst great rejoicing.

◈ 122 ◈

The Lettuce Donkey

ONCE UPON A TIME there was a young huntsman who went out into the forest to shoot some game. He was merry and lighthearted and whistled on a leaf as he marched along. Then he encountered an ugly old hag, who said, "Good day, my dear huntsman, you're certainly cheerful and content, but I'm suffering from hunger and thirst. Would you give me some alms?"

The huntsman felt sorry for the poor woman, so he reached into his pocket and gave her whatever he could afford. As he was about to continue on his way, the old woman held him back and said, "Listen to what I have to say, my dear huntsman. Since you've been so kind, I'm going to give you a gift. Just keep going straight ahead, and after a while you'll come to a tree. Nine birds will be sitting on it. They'll have a cloak in their claws and will be fighting over it. Take aim with your gun and shoot into the middle of them. They'll let go of the cloak for sure, and one of the birds will also be hit and drop dead at your feet. Take the cloak with you. It's a wishing cloak, and if you throw it around your shoulders, you need only wish yourself somewhere, and you'll be there in a split second. Take the heart out of the dead bird and swallow it whole. Then each and every morning, when you get up, you'll find a gold coin underneath your pillow."

The huntsman thanked the wise woman and thought to himself, Those are great things she's promised me. If only they would come true! When he had gone about a hundred paces, he heard a great deal of screaming and squawking in the branches above him. As he looked up he saw a bunch of birds tearing at a piece of cloth with their beaks and claws. They screeched, tugged, and scuffled as if each wanted it for itself alone. "Well," said the huntsman, "this is extraordinary. Everything's happening just as the old hag said it would." He took the gun from his shoulder, aimed, and fired right into the middle of the birds so that their feathers fluttered about. Immediately the birds, with loud cries, took flight, but one fell to the ground dead along with the cloak. The huntsman then did what the old woman had told him to do: he cut the bird open, found the heart, swallowed it, and took the cloak home with him.

The next morning, when he woke up, he remembered the woman's promise and wanted to see if it had actually come to pass. As he lifted his pillow in the air the gold coin glimmered before his eyes. The following day he found another one, and so forth each time he got up. He collected a heap of gold but eventually began thinking, What's the use of all my gold if I stay at home? It's time I set out and see the world.

He took leave of his parents, swung his knapsack and gun over his shoulders, and went out into the world. One day he happened to pass through a dense forest, and when he reached the end of it, a stately castle stood on the plain before him. In one of its windows an old woman and a marvelously beautiful maiden were standing and looking down at him. The old woman, however, was a witch and said to the maiden, "Someone's coming from the forest with a wonderful treasure in his body. We've got to get it out of him, my darling daughter, for it's really much more suited for us. You see, he's got a bird's heart in him, and every morning there's a gold coin under his pillow." She told the maiden the whole story about the huntsman and what role she was to play. Finally, she threatened her and, with fury in her eyes, said, "If you don't obey me, you'll regret it!"

As the huntsman came closer he spied the maiden and said to himself, "I've been wandering around for so long that it's time to take a rest. I'll stop at this beautiful castle, for I've got plenty of money to pay." But his real reason was that he had caught sight of the beautiful maiden.

He went into the castle and was received in a hospitable way and entertained courteously. It was not long before he fell in love with the witch's daughter. He thought of nothing else but her, had eyes only for her, and gladly did whatever she demanded. At that point the old woman said to her, "Now we've got to get the bird's heart. He won't even notice it's missing." She prepared a potion, and when it was ready, she poured it into a cup and gave it to the maiden, who had to hand it to the huntsman.

"Now, my dearest," she said, "drink to my health."

So he took the cup, and after he had swallowed the drink, he vomited up the bird's heart. The maiden had to carry it off secretly and then swallow it herself, for that was what the old woman wanted. From then on the huntsman no longer found gold under his pillow, rather it lay under the maiden's pillow, and the old woman fetched it from there every morning. However, he was so much in love with the maiden and so infatuated that he had no other thought in his head than to spend time with her. Now the old witch said, "We've got the bird's heart, but we must also take the wishing cloak from him."

"Why not let him keep that?" answered the maiden. "After all, he's already lost his wealth."

The old woman became angry and said, "Such a cloak is a wonderful thing. You won't find many like it in the world. I must have it, and I will have it."

She gave the maiden instructions and told her that if she did not obey them, things would go badly for her. So the maiden did what the old woman told her to do; she stood at the window and gazed into the wide blue sky as if she were very sad.

"Why are you standing there so sadly?" asked the huntsman.

"Ah, my darling," she replied, "the Garnet Mountain lies over there, where precious jewels grow. Whenever I think about them, I get such a great longing for them that I become sad. But who can fetch them? Only the birds with their wings can fly there. A human being, never!"

"If that's all that's bothering you," said the huntsman, "I'll soon ease your woes." Upon saying this, he spread his cloak over her and wished to be on top of the Garnet Mountain. Within a split second they were both sitting on top of it. The elegant jewels glimmered from all sides, and it was a joy just to look at them. Together they selected the most precious of the jewels. However, the old woman had used her witchcraft to make the huntsman's eyelids heavy, and he said to the maiden, "Let's sit down and rest a bit. I'm so tired that I can't stand on my feet anymore."

They sat down, and he laid his head in her lap and went to sleep. When he was sound asleep, she took the cloak from his shoulders and hung it around herself. She gathered the garnets and jewels together and wished herself back home.

After the huntsman had finished sleeping and awoke, he saw that his beloved had deceived him and had left him alone on top of the wild mountain. "Oh," he said, "the world is full of treachery!" He sat there, overcome with sorrow and pain, and did not know what to do. The mountain, however, belonged to the wild and monstrous giants who dwelt there and who were always up to mischief. He had not been sitting there long before three of them came strolling toward him. He lay down as if he had fallen into a deep sleep. As the giants came by, the first one poked him in the foot and said, "Who's this earthworm lying here and contemplating his navel?"

"Trample him to death!" said the second.

But the third one said contemptuously, "He's not worth the trouble. Let him live. He can't survive here, and if he climbs higher, to the peak, the clouds will snatch him and carry him away."

As they moved on they continued talking, but the huntsman had heard their words, and when they were out of sight, he got up and climbed to the peak. He sat there awhile until a cloud drifted by, grabbed him, and carried him away. For a long time it floated about in the sky. Then it began sinking and settled down on a large vegetable garden surrounded by walls, where the huntsman landed softly between the cabbages and vegetables. He looked around him and said, "If I only had something to eat! I'm so hungry that it'll be hard to go anywhere from here, and there's nothing but vegetables. No apples or pears or any kind of fruit." Finally, he thought, If need be, I can eat some of the lettuce. It doesn't taste very good, but it will refresh me.

So he picked out a fine head of lettuce and ate some of the leaves. No sooner had he taken a few bites than he had a strange sensation and felt completely changed: he sprouted four legs, a thick neck, and two long ears, and to his horror he saw that he had been transformed into a donkey. Nevertheless, since he still felt very hungry, and the juicy lettuce appealed to his present nature, he kept eating it with great zest. Eventually, he came to another kind of lettuce, and after he had swallowed a few leaves, he felt a new kind of sensation and returned to his human form.

Now the huntsman lay down and slept off his fatigue. When he awoke the next morning, he broke off a head of the bad lettuce and one of the good and thought, This ought to help me regain what belongs to me, and I'll be able to punish the treacherous women as well. He put the lettuce in his knapsack, climbed over the mountain, and set out to find the castle of his beloved. When he had wandered about several days, he was fortunate enough to find it again. Then he colored his face brown so that his own mother would not have recognized him, went into the castle, and asked for lodgings. "I'm so tired," he said, "that I can't go any farther."

"Countryman, who are you, and what's your business?" asked the witch.

"I'm a royal messenger and was sent out to search for the most delicious lettuce under the sun. I was lucky enough to have found it, and I'm carrying it with me, but the heat of the sun has been so strong that the tender leaves are beginning to wilt, and I don't know whether I'll be able to carry it any farther."

When the old woman heard of the delicious lettuce, she had a great yearning for it and said, "My dear countryman, let me taste the wonderful lettuce."

"Why not?" he answered. "I've brought two heads with me, and I'll give you one."

He opened the sack and handed her the bad one. The witch did not suspect anything, and her mouth watered so much for the new meal that she herself went into the kitchen to prepare it. When the lettuce was ready, she could not wait until it was on the table. She immediately took a few leaves and put them in her mouth. No sooner had she swallowed them than she too lost her human form and ran around in the courtyard as a donkey. Now the servant girl came into the kitchen, saw the lettuce all ready and wanted to serve it, but on the way she succumbed to her old habit of trying things and ate a couple of leaves. The magic power took effect immediately, and she too was changed into a donkey. She ran outside to the old woman, and the bowl with the lettuce fell to the ground. Meanwhile, the messenger sat with the beautiful maiden, and when nobody came with the lettuce and her longing for it also grew greater, she said, "I don't know what's keeping the lettuce."

The huntsman thought, The lettuce has probably worked, and so he said, "I'll go to the kitchen and see what's happening."

When he got there, he saw two donkeys running around the courtyard and the lettuce on the ground. "Very good," he said. "The two have gotten their due," and he picked up the remaining leaves, put them into the bowl, and brought them to the maiden.

"I've brought you the delicious food myself so that you won't have to wait any longer," he said.

Then she ate some of the lettuce and was instantly robbed of her human form. Like the others, she ran out to the courtyard as a donkey. Next the huntsman washed his face so that the women as donkeys could recognize him, and he went down to the courtyard and said, "Now you're going to get what you deserve for your treachery." He tied all three to a rope and drove them ahead until they came to a mill, where he knocked on the window. The miller stuck his head out and asked what he wanted.

"I've got three bad animals, and I don't want to keep them anymore," he responded. "If you take them, feed them, and treat them as I tell you to, then I'll pay you whatever you want."

"Why not?" said the miller. "How do you want me to treat them?"

The huntsman told the miller to give the old donkey, actually the witch, three beatings a day and one feeding; the younger, actually the servant, one beating a day and three feedings; and the youngest, actually the maiden, no beatings and three feedings. He could not bring himself to have the maiden beaten. He then went back to the castle, where he found everything he needed.

After a few days the miller came and said he had to report the death of the old donkey that was supposed to receive three beatings and one feeding a day. "The other two," he continued, "are not dead yet, to be sure, but they are so sad that they'll be dead before long."

Then the huntsman took pity on them, forgot his anger, and told the miller to drive them back to the castle. When they arrived, he gave them some of the good lettuce to eat so that they became human beings again. The beautiful maiden fell upon her knees in front of him and said, "Ah, my dearest, forgive me for the evil I've done you. My mother forced me to do it. Everything happened against my will, for I love you with all my heart. Your wishing cloak is hanging in a closet, and I'll drink something to make me throw up the bird's heart."

But he had a change of heart and said, "Just keep it. It doesn't make any difference now because I want to take you for my faithful wife."

Then the wedding was held, and they lived happily together until they died.

◆ 123 ◆

The Old Woman in the Forest

THERE WAS ONCE A POOR SERVANT GIRL who went traveling with her masters through a large forest, and as they were passing through the middle of it, some robbers came out of a thicket and murdered all the people they could find. Everyone was killed except the maiden, who had jumped from the carriage in her fright and hidden behind a tree. After the robbers departed with their booty, she came out, looked at the terrible disaster, and burst into tears. "What am I to do?" she said. "Oh, poor me, I'll never find my way out of the forest. There's not a single soul living here, and I'll probably starve to death."

She walked about searching for a way out but could find none. When evening came, she sat down under a tree, commended herself to God, and planned to remain there no matter what might happen. But after she had been sitting there awhile, a white dove came flying to her with a little golden key in its beak. It put the key in her hand and said, "Do you see that large tree over there? You'll find a little lock on it, and if you open it with this key, you'll find plenty of food in it and won't have to go hungry anymore."

She went to the tree, opened it, and found milk in a small bowl and white bread to dip into it, so she could eat to her heart's content. When she was full, she said, "Now's the time when the chickens at home usually go to roost. I'm so tired I wish I could lie down in my bed also."

Then the dove flew by again, carrying another little golden key in its beak, and said, "Open the tree over there, and you'll find a bed."

She opened it and found a lovely soft bed. Then she prayed to the dear Lord to protect her during the night, lay down, and fell asleep. In the morning the dove came a third time with another little key and said, "Open that tree over there, and you'll find some clothes." When she opened it, she found clothes lined with jewels and gold, more splendid than those of a princess.

Thus she lived for some time, and the dove came every day and

took care of everything she needed, and it was a good, quiet life. However, one day the dove came and said, "Would you do a favor for me?"

"Gladly," said the maiden.

"I'm going to lead you to a small cottage," said the dove. "You are to go inside, where you'll find an old woman seated right next to the hearth. She'll say good day to you, but you're not to answer her, no matter what she does. Go past her to the right, where you'll come upon a door. Open it, and you'll find a room where there'll be a lot of different kinds of rings lying on a table. You'll see magnificent ones with glistening stones, but you're to leave them alone. Pick out a simple one that will be lying among them and bring it to me as fast as you can."

The maiden went to the cottage and through the door. There sat the old woman who glared at her and said, "Good day, my child." But the maiden did not answer her and proceeded toward the door.

"Where are you going?" cried the old woman, who grabbed her skirt and tried to hold onto her. "This is my house. Nobody's allowed to go in there if I don't want them to."

But the maiden said nothing, broke away from the woman, and went straight into the room. There she saw a large number of rings lying on a table, glistening and glimmering before her eyes. She tossed them about and looked for the simple one but could not find it. While she was looking for the ring, she noticed the old woman slinking by with a birdcage in her hand. The woman was about to make off with it, but the maiden went up to her and took the cage out of her hand. When she lifted it up and looked inside, she saw a bird with a simple ring in its beak. She took the ring and ran happily out of the house with it. She thought the white dove would come and fetch the ring now, but it did not appear. So she leaned against a tree, intending to wait for the dove. As she was standing there the tree seemed to become soft and flexible, and it lowered its branches. Suddenly the branches wrapped themselves around her and were two arms. When she looked around her, she saw that the tree had turned into a handsome man, who embraced her and kissed her affectionately.

"You've saved me and set me free from the power of the old woman," he said. "She's a wicked witch, and she had turned me into a tree. For a few hours every day I was a white dove. As long as she possessed the ring, I couldn't regain my human form."

His servants and horses had also been released from the magic spell that had changed them too into trees, and they were now standing beside him. They all then traveled to his kingdom, for he was a prince, and the couple got married and lived happily until their death.

◈ 124 ◈

The Three Brothers

THERE WAS ONCE A MAN who had three sons, and he owned nothing but the house in which he lived. Now each of his sons hoped very much to inherit the house after his death. Since the father cared for them equally, he did not want to hurt their feelings, nor did he want to sell the house, because it had belonged to generations of his ancestors. Otherwise, he would have divided the money from a sale among his sons. Finally, he had an idea and said to his sons, "Go out into the world, and see what you can make of yourselves. Learn a trade, and when you return, whichever one of you puts on the best performance of his skills shall get the house."

The sons were satisfied with this proposal. The oldest decided he wanted to become a blacksmith; the second, a barber; and the third, a fencing master. They agreed on a time when they would all return home and then set upon their way. It so happened that each of them found a good master, and each learned something decent and useful. The blacksmith had to shoe the king's horses and thought, Now you'll get the house for sure. The barber shaved only distinguished gentlemen and believed that the house was already his. The fencing master received many cuts but gritted his teeth and did not let himself get discouraged, for he thought to himself, If you're afraid of a cut, you'll never get the house.

When the appointed time arrived, they went back to their father, but they did not know what would be the best way to show off their talents. So they sat down together and discussed the matter, and while they were sitting there, a hare came running across the field in their direction. "Oh," said the barber, "that's just what I needed." He took a bowl and soap and worked up a lather until the hare was close by. Then he lathered it on the run and shaved a little beard for the hare, also on the run. In the process he neither cut the hare nor hurt it in any way.

"I like that," said the father. "Unless your brothers do something extraordinary, the house is yours."

Before long a man came riding by in a carriage at full speed. "Now you'll see what I can do, Father," said the blacksmith, who rushed after the carriage, ripped the four shoes from the horse, which continued to gallop, and put on four new ones, also at full speed.

"Remarkable!" said the father. "You do your stuff just as well as your brother. Now I don't know who should get the house."

Then the third son said, "Father, let me show you what I can do." And since it had begun to rain, he took his sword, swung it over his head, and made crosscuts, so that not a drop of rain fell on him. When it began to rain harder and then finally so hard that it was pouring cats and dogs, he swung the sword faster and faster and remained as dry as if he were sitting safely under cover. When the father saw that, he was astonished and said, "That's truly the best performance. The house is yours."

The other two brothers accepted the decision, as they had promised to do, and since they cared for each other so much, all three of them stayed in the house together and practiced their trades. Indeed, they had learned their crafts so well and were so skillful that they earned a great deal of money. They lived happily together in this way until their old age, and when one of them fell sick and died, the other two grieved so much that they too soon fell sick and died. Since they had all been so skillful and had cared so much for each other, they were all buried in the same grave.

◆ 125 ◆

The Devil and His Grandmother

THERE ONCE WAS A GREAT WAR, and the king, who had many soldiers, paid his men so poorly that they could not live on their wages. Three of his soldiers got together, therefore, and planned to desert. Two began talking, and one said to the other, "If we're caught, they'll hang us on the gallows. So what do you think we should do?"

"Do you see the large wheatfield over there?" the other said. "Well, if we hide in it, nobody will ever find us. The army's not allowed to set foot in there and will be moving on tomorrow."

So they crept into the wheatfield, but the army did not move on; it remained right where it was. The three soldiers had to sit for two nights and two days in the wheatfield and were practically dying of hunger. Yet, if they had gone out into the open, it would have meant certain death for them. Finally, they said, "What's the sense of deserting if we have to die a miserable death?"

Just then a fiery dragon came flying through the air, dived down toward the field, and asked them why they were hiding there.

"We're three soldiers," they said, "and we've deserted because our pay was so poor. Now we'll die of hunger if we stay here, or we'll swing from the gallows if we leave."

"Well, if you'll serve me for seven years," said the dragon, "I'll take you right through the middle of the army, and you won't be caught."

"Since we have no other choice, we'll accept your offer," they responded.

Then the dragon grabbed them with his claws, carried them away through the sky over the army, and set them down on the ground again far away from the wheatfield.

The dragon, however, was none other than the devil, and he gave them a little whip and said, "All you have to do is crack and snap this whip in the air, and you'll have all the money you'll ever need dancing about you. Indeed, you'll be able to live like great lords, keep horses, and drive around in carriages. But at the end of seven years, you'll be mine." Upon saying this, he took out a book and placed it in front of them: they all had to sign their names in agreement. "But," he added, "before you're finally mine, I'll give you a riddle; if you solve it, you'll be free, and I'll have no power over you."

Then the dragon flew away, and the three soldiers began their journey with their little whip. They always had money, ordered the finest clothes to be made for them, and traveled about the world. Wherever they were, they lived joyously and splendidly. They drove around with horses and a carriage, ate and drank, but did no evil. The time went by quickly for them. When the seven years were drawing to an end, two of them became extremely anxious, but the third took it lightly and said, "Brothers, don't worry. I'm nobody's fool; I'll guess the riddle."

They all went out into the fields, where they sat down, two of them with gloomy faces. Then an old woman came along and asked them why they were so sad.

"Oh, what's it to you? You can't help us."

"Who knows," she answered. "Just tell me your troubles."

So they told her that they had been the devil's servants for almost seven years, and he had supplied them with money as though it were water. However, they had signed their lives over to him and would become his if they could not solve a riddle after the seven years were up.

"If you want some help," the old woman said, "then one of you must go into the forest, where he'll find a cliff that's caved in and looks like a hut. He must enter the hut, and there he'll find help."

That won't save us, thought the two sad ones, and they remained seated, while the cheerful one set out on his way and went deep into the forest until he found the rock hut. Inside it he found a very old woman sitting there who was the devil's grandmother. She asked him where he had come from and what he wanted. He told her everything that had happened, and since she found him very pleasing, she took pity on him and said she would help him. She lifted a large stone that concealed the entrance to a cellar and said, "Hide down there, and you'll be able to hear everything that's said here. Sit still and don't move. When the dragon comes, I'll ask him about the riddle. He tells me everything. So pay attention to what he says."

At midnight the dragon came flying home and demanded his dinner. The grandmother set the table and brought food and drink. This made him happy, and they ate and drank together. During their conversation she asked him how his day had been and how many souls he had captured.

"I wasn't particularly lucky today," he answered, "but I've got three soldiers lined up for sure."

"Oh, three soldiers," she said. "They're tough individuals. They might still get away from you."

"They're mine," responded the devil scornfully. "I'm going to ask them a riddle they'll never be able to solve."

"What kind of a riddle?" she asked.

"Let me tell you: There's a dead monkey lying in the great North Sea. That will be their roast. A whale's rib will be their silver spoon, and an old hollow horse's hoof will be their wineglass."

When the devil had gone to bed, the old grandmother lifted up the stone and let the soldier out.

"Did you pay close attention to everything?"

"Yes," he said. "I know enough now to take care of things."

After saying this, he had to leave by a different way: he went stealthily through a window and rushed back to his companions. He told them how the devil had been tricked by his old grandmother and he had overheard the solution to the riddle. Now they were all so cheerful and in such good spirits that they took the whip and snapped it in a lively fashion until a great deal of money danced about the ground.

When the seven years were completely up, the devil came with the book, showed them their signatures, and said, "I'm going to take you with me to hell, where you'll be given a meal. If you can guess what kind of a roast you're going to have, you'll be free and may keep the little whip."

The first soldier then began to talk. "In the great North Sea there's a dead monkey. That will probably be the roast."

The devil was annoyed and went "Hm! Hm! Hm!" and asked the second soldier, "What will be your spoon?"

"The rib of a whale will be our silver spoon."

The devil made a face, muttered "Hm! Hm! Hm!" again, and asked the third soldier, "Do you know what your wineglass will be?"

"An old horse's hoof will be our wineglass."

At that the devil flew away with a loud cry and no longer had power over them. As for the three soldiers, they kept the little whip and whipped up as much money as they wanted, and they lived happily until the day of their death.

❖ 126 ❖
Faithful Ferdinand and Unfaithful Ferdinand

ONCE UPON A TIME there was a man and a woman who did not have any children while they were rich, but when they became poor, they had a little boy. Since nobody was willing to stand as godfather for their child, the father said that he would go to the next village to see if he could find one. Along the way he met a beggar, who asked him where he was going. The father told him that he was going to see if he could find a godfather for his son, as nobody was willing to act as godfather in his village because he was so poor.

"Oh," said the beggar. "You're poor, and I'm poor. So I might as well be your godfather. But I'm so poor that I won't be able to give your child anything. Go home and tell the midwife to bring the child to the church."

When they all arrived at the church, the beggar was already inside, and he named the child Faithful Ferdinand. As he was about to leave the church the beggar said, "Go home now. I can't give you anything, and I don't want you to give me anything either."

However, he gave the midwife a key and told her to give it to the father when she reached the house. He was to keep it until the boy became fourteen. At that time the boy was to go out to the heath, where he would find a castle. The key would fit the castle door, and everything inside would belong to him.

When the boy was seven, and had grown nice and strong, he went to play with some other boys. Their godfathers had given them all presents, one more wonderful than the next, but Faithful Ferdinand had nothing to talk about. He burst into tears and ran home to his father. "Didn't I get anything at all from my godfather?" he asked.

"Oh, yes," said the father. "You received a key. If there's a castle on the heath, you're to go there and open it."

So he went to the heath, but there was no sign of a castle. When seven more years passed and he was fourteen, he went to the heath again, and this time a castle was standing there. When he opened it, there was only a horse inside, a white horse, and the boy was so excited to have a horse that he mounted it and galloped home to his father. "Now that I've got a white horse," he said, "I'm going to travel about."

So he set out, and as he was riding along he found a pen along the way. At first he wanted to pick it up, but then he thought to himself, Oh, you'd better leave it there. You're bound to find a pen where you're going if you need one.

But just as he was about to ride away, a voice called out from behind him, "Faithful Ferdinand, take it with you."

He looked around but could not see anyone. Then he went back and picked it up. After he rode on for a while, he came to a sea, where he discovered a fish lying on the shore and gasping for air. "Wait, my little fish," he said, "and I'll help you back into the water."

He grabbed the fish by the tail and threw it back into the water. Then the fish stuck its head out of the sea and said, "Since you helped me out of the mud, I'm going to give you a flute. Whenever you're in trouble, just play it, and I'll come to your aid. And if you ever drop something into the water, just play it, and I'll get it out for you."

Now Faithful Ferdinand continued on his way, and he came across a man, who asked him where he was going.

"Just to the next town."

"What's your name?"

"Faithful Ferdinand."

"What do you know about that? We have almost the same name. I'm called Unfaithful Ferdinand."

The two of them traveled to the next town together, but there was trouble ahead: Unfaithful Ferdinand knew everything that anyone thought and wanted to do. He knew all this because he practiced all kinds of black magic. Now, at the inn where they decided to stay, there was a fine maiden who had an honest face and nice manners. She fell in love with Faithful Ferdinand, for he was very handsome, and she asked him where he was going. He told her that he was just traveling about, and she said that he really should stay right there because the king of that country wanted to hire a servant or an outrider, and he could work in the king's employ. He responded that he could not just go to someone out of the blue and offer his services. Then the maiden said, "Oh, I'll take care of that." She went straight to the king and told him that she knew of a fine servant for him. The king was glad to hear this and had Faithful Ferdinand summoned. When the king wanted to make him a servant, Faithful Ferdinand asked to be an outrider because he wanted to be with his horse. So the king made him an outrider.

When Unfaithful Ferdinand learned about this, he said to the maiden, "What's going on? You can't just help him and forget about me!"

"Oh," said the maiden. "I'll help you too," and she thought, You'd better keep on his good side, for he's not to be trusted. So she went to the king again and said that she had a servant for him, and the king was pleased.

Now, whenever Unfaithful Ferdinand dressed the king in the morning, His Majesty would always complain, "Oh, if only my beloved could be here with me!" Since Unfaithful Ferdinand kept a grudge against Faithful Ferdinand, and since he also kept hearing the king lament, he finally said, "You have the outrider, don't you? Well, why don't you send him to find her, and if he doesn't bring her back, have him beheaded."

So the king summoned Faithful Ferdinand and told him that his beloved was in such and such a place, and Faithful Ferdinand was to bring her to him, and if he did not succeed, he would have to die. Faithful Ferdinand went straight to his white horse, who was kept in the stable, and began to sigh and moan, "Oh, what an unlucky person I am!"

Then he heard a voice behind him. "Faithful Ferdinand, why are you crying?"

He turned around, saw nobody near him, and continued to moan. "Oh, my dear little white horse, I must leave you now. I'm going to my doom."

Then he heard the voice again. "Faithful Ferdinand, why are you crying?"

Suddenly he realized for the first time that it was his horse asking the question. "Is it you, my little white horse? Can you talk?" And he continued, "I've got to go to such and such a place and fetch the king's bride. Can you tell me how to do it?"

"Go to the king," the white horse replied, "and tell him that if he'll give you what you need, you'll get her, and you'll need a shipload of meat and a shipload of bread to succeed. There are huge giants in the sea, and if you don't bring them meat, they'll tear you to pieces, and there are huge birds who'll peck your eyes out if you don't bring them bread."

So the king ordered all the butchers in the land to slaughter animals and all the bakers to bake bread until the ships were loaded. When they were full, the white horse said to Faithful Ferdinand, "Now, I want you to climb up on my back and go aboard the ship with me. When the giants come, you're to say:

'Easy does it, my dear giants,
don't think that I've forgotten you,
for I've brought you meat to chew.'

"And when the birds come, you're to say:

'Easy does it, my nice dear birds,
don't think that I've forgotten you,
for I've brought you bread to chew.'

"Then they won't do anything to you, and when you come to the castle, the giants will help you. Just take a few of them with you and go up into the castle, where you'll find the princess lying asleep, but you mustn't wake her. Have the giants pick her up with the bed and carry her to the ship."

Then everything happened the way the little white horse said it would. Faithful Ferdinand gave the giants and birds the meat and bread he had brought with him. In return, the giants willingly carried the princess in her bed to the king. When she arrived at the king's palace, she told him that she could not live without her private papers that were still in her castle. So Faithful Ferdinand was summoned again, at the instigation of Unfaithful Ferdinand, and the king commanded him to fetch the papers from the castle; otherwise, he would have to die.

Faithful Ferdinand went out into the stable, where he began moaning and said, "Oh, my dear little white horse, I must go away again. What shall we do?"

The white horse told him to have the ships fully loaded as before, and everything happened as it had the first time: the giants and birds ate their fill of the meat and bread and were appeased. When they reached the castle, the horse told Faithful Ferdinand to go into the princess's bedroom, where he would find the papers lying on the table. So he went in and got them. When they were on the sea again, he let his pen drop into the water, and at that the horse said, "Now I can't help you."

But Faithful Ferdinand remembered the flute, and he began to play. Soon the fish came with the pen in its mouth and gave it to him. Afterward Faithful Ferdinand brought the papers to the palace, where the wedding was then held.

The queen, however, was unable to love the king because he did not have a nose. On the other hand, she loved Faithful Ferdinand very much. One day, when all the noblemen of the court were gathered together, the queen said she knew some tricks. She said, in fact, that she could cut off a head and put it back on, and she wanted a volunteer to demonstrate her skill. Nobody wanted to be first, but upon Unfaithful Ferdinand's prompting, Faithful Ferdinand felt obliged to volunteer. The queen cut off his head and put it back on again, and it healed immediately. Only a red thread appeared around his neck, where she cut him.

"My dear," the king said to her, "where did you learn that?"

"Oh," she replied, "I know many more tricks like that. Shall I try it out on you too?"

"Oh, yes," he said.

Then the queen cut off his head, but she did not put it back on again. Rather, she pretended she could not get it on because it would not stick properly. So the king was buried, and she married Faithful Ferdinand.

Faithful Ferdinand continued to ride his white horse nevertheless, and once when he got on it, the horse told him to head for another heath he knew and to gallop around it three times. When Faithful Ferdinand did this, the white horse stood up on its hind legs and turned into a prince.

❖ 127 ❖

The Iron Stove

IN THE DAYS WHEN WISHING STILL HELPED, an old witch cast a spell over a prince, so that he had to sit in a big iron stove in the forest. He spent many years there, and nobody was able to rescue him. One day a princess got lost in that forest and could not find the way back to her father's kingdom. She wandered about for nine days and finally came to the iron stove. As she stood in front of it she heard a voice from inside, which asked, "Where do you come from and where are you going?"

"I've lost the way to my father's kingdom," she answered, "and I can't get back home."

Then the voice from the iron stove said, "I'll help you get home again quickly if you'll promise to do what I ask. My father is a greater king than yours, and I want to marry you."

She was frightened by this and thought, Dear Lord, what shall I do with an iron stove! But, she wanted so very much to return home to her father that she promised to do what he asked. Then he said, "I want you to come back with a knife and scrape a hole in the iron," and he gave her an escort, who walked beside her without saying a word and brought her home in two hours.

Now, there was great rejoicing in the castle when the princess returned, and the old king embraced and kissed her. Yet, she was very sad and said, "Dear Father, you can't imagine what happened to me! I'd never have been able to escape from the big, wild forest if I hadn't come across an iron stove, but I had to promise it that I'd return there to rescue and marry it."

The old king was so horrified by this that he almost fainted, for she was his only daughter. After some deliberation, they decided to send the miller's beautiful daughter in her place. They led the maiden into the forest, gave her a knife, and told her to scrape away at the iron stove. She scraped for twenty-four hours but could not make the slightest dent. At daybreak a voice called out from the iron stove, "It seems to me that it's dawn outside."

"It seems so to me too," she answered. "I think I hear the clattering of my father's mill."

"So, you're a miller's daughter! Then get out of here at once, and tell them to send the king's daughter."

She returned to the castle and told the old king that the man in the stove did not want her, he wanted his daughter. The old king was horrified, and his daughter began to weep. However, they still had the swineherd's daughter, who was even more beautiful than the miller's daughter. They agreed to give her a nice sum of money to go to the iron stove in place of the king's daughter. So she was taken into the forest, and she too had to scrape for twenty-four hours, but she could not get anything off. At daybreak a voice cried out from the stove, "It seems to me that it's dawn outside."

"It seems so to me too," she answered. "I think I hear my father blowing his horn."

"So, you're a swineherd's daughter! Get out of here at once, and have them send the king's daughter. Tell her that everything will happen to her the way I promised, and if she doesn't come, the whole kingdom will collapse and be demolished, and not one stone will be left standing."

When the king's daughter heard that, she began to cry. But there was nothing she could do: she had to keep her promise. So she took leave of her father, put a knife in her pocket, and went to the iron stove in the forest. When she got there, she started scraping, and the iron gave way. After two hours she had managed to scrape a small hole. She looked inside and saw such a handsome youth glimmering in gold and jewels that her heart was swept away. She continued her scraping until she had made a hole large enough for him to crawl out through.

"You are mine," he said, "and I am yours, for you have set me free."

He wanted to take her with him to his kingdom, but she requested permission to see her father once more. The prince granted it, but she was not to say more than three words to her father, and then she was to return to the prince. So she went home, but she spoke more than three words, whereupon the iron stove vanished immediately and was carried far away over glass mountains and sharp swords. Yet, the prince had been released and was no longer locked up in the stove.

After this happened, the princess said good-bye to her father and took some money with her, though not much, and went back into the big forest to look for the iron stove, which was not to be found. For nine days she searched until her hunger became so great that she did not know what to do since she had nothing more to live on. When evening came, she climbed a small tree and sat down. She planned to spend the night there because she was afraid of the wild animals. Then, at midnight, she saw a little light in the distance and thought, Oh, I think I might be safe there. She climbed down the tree and went toward the light, praying along the way. Finally, she came to an old cottage with a great deal of grass growing around it and a small pile of wood in front. Lord, what kind of a place is this! she thought. She looked through the window and saw nothing but small fat toads, and yet, there was also a nicely covered table with wine and a roast, and the plates and cups were made of silver. So she summoned her courage and knocked on the door. The fat toad replied at once:

"Maiden, maiden, green and small,
    hop to it, hoptoad, and don't you fall.
Hoptoad's dog,
    hop back and forth,
    and quickly see who's at the door."

Then a small toad went to the door and opened it. When the princess entered, they all welcomed her and made her sit down while they asked, "Where have you come from? Where are you going?"

She told them everything that had happened to her and how she had disobeyed the prince's command not to say more than three words, which had caused the stove along with the prince to disappear, and now she intended to search over hill and valley until she found him. Then the fat old toad said:

"Maiden, maiden, green and small,
    hop to it, hoptoad, and don't you fall.
Hoptoad's dog,
    hop back and forth and do it sprightly.
Fetch me the box as quick as can be."

After the small toad left and then came back with the box, they gave her food and drink and took her to a nicely made bed that was like silk and velvet. She lay down on it and slept with God's blessing. When morning came, she got up, and the old toad gave her three needles from the box, which she was to take with her. She would need them because she had to cross over a high glass mountain, three sharp swords, and a great lake. If she could manage to do all that, then she would regain her beloved. The toad also gave her three objects that she was to guard very carefully, namely three big needles, a plow wheel, and three nuts. Upon receiving them, she departed, and when she came to the glass mountain, which was very slick, she stuck the three needles first beneath her feet and then ahead of them, and this was the way she managed to get over it. When she was on the other side, she hid them in a place that she marked carefully. Next she came to the three sharp swords, and she seated herself on the plow wheel and rolled over them. Finally, she came to the great lake, and after crossing it, she arrived at a large, beautiful castle. She went inside and sought work as if she were a poor maiden who wanted to hire herself out. She knew, in fact, that the prince whom she had rescued from the iron stove in the big forest was in this castle. So the princess was taken on as a kitchen maid at low wages. The prince, in the meantime, had already found another maiden whom he wanted to marry, for he thought that the princess had long since died.

That evening, after she had finished washing up and was through with her work, the kitchen maid searched in her pocket and found the three nuts the old toad had given her. She bit one open and was going to eat the kernel when—lo and behold!—she discovered a splendid royal dress inside. When the bride heard about it, she came and asked if she could buy the dress, for she said that it was not fit for a servant girl. But the kitchen maid replied that she would not sell it, rather the bride could have it if she would allow the maid to sleep one night in the bridegroom's chamber. The bride consented because she did not have a dress as beautiful. When evening came, she said to her bridegroom, "That silly kitchen maid wants to sleep in your room."

"If you don't mind," he said, "neither do I."

Nonetheless, the bride gave him a glass of wine with a sleeping potion in it. Then the bridegroom and the kitchen maid went into the chamber to sleep, but he slept so soundly that she could not wake him, which made her weep the entire night, lamenting, "I rescued you from the wild forest and the iron stove. I searched for you and went across a glass mountain, three sharp swords, and a great lake until I found you. And now you won't listen to me."

The servants outside the bedroom door heard her weeping the entire night and told their master the next day. When the kitchen maid had finished washing up that evening, she bit open the second nut, and there was another dress, even more beautiful than the first one. The bride saw it and wanted to buy this one too, but the kitchen maid did not want money. She requested instead to sleep in the bridegroom's chamber again. However, the bride gave him another sleeping potion, and he slept so soundly that he could not hear a thing. The kitchen maid wept the entire night, lamenting, "I rescued you from the forest and the iron stove. I searched for you and went across a glass mountain, three sharp swords, and a great lake until I found you. And now you won't listen to me."

The servants outside the bedroom door heard her weeping the entire night and told their master about this in the morning. When the kitchen maid had finished washing up the third night and bit open the third nut, she found a dress lined with pure gold that was even more beautiful than the other two. When the bride saw it, she wanted to have it, but the kitchen maid would give it to her only if she was granted permission to sleep in the bridegroom's chamber a third night. This time, however, the bridegroom was alert and did not drink the sleeping potion. When the kitchen maid began to weep and lament, "Dearest love, I rescued you from the cruel wild forest and the iron stove," the prince jumped up and said, "You are the true bride! You are mine, and I am yours."

That very night he got into a carriage with her, and they took away the false bride's dresses so that she could not get up. When they came to the great lake, they sailed across it, and when they came to the three sharp swords, they sat down on the plow wheel, and when they came to the glass mountain, they stuck the three needles into it. At last they arrived at the old cottage, but when they entered, it became a large castle. The toads were released from a magic spell and turned out to be princes and princesses, and they were all very happy. Then the wedding was celebrated, and the prince and the princess remained in the castle, which was larger than the castle of the king's daughter. However, since the king complained of being left alone, they traveled to him and brought him back to their castle. Now they had two kingdoms and lived a happily married life.

There once was a mouse, but he's gone,
and now my tale is done.

◈ 128 ◈

The Lazy Spinner

A MAN AND HIS WIFE lived in a village, and the wife was so lazy that she never wanted to do any work. Whenever her husband gave her something to spin, she never finished it, and whatever she did spin, she did not wind but left it tangled on the bobbin. If her husband scolded her, she used her quick tongue and said, "How can I wind the yarn if I don't have a reel? You go into the forest first and fetch me one."

"If that's what's the matter, then I'll go into the forest and get some wood for a reel."

Upon hearing this, his wife became anxious, because she would have to wind the yarn and start spinning again if he found the wood to make a reel. So she gave the matter some thought and came up with a good idea. She secretly followed her husband into the forest, and just as he climbed up a tree to select and cut the wood, she crawled into some bushes below him, where he could not see her, and called up:

"He who chops wood for reels shall die.
She who winds yarn shall be ruined all her life."

The husband listened, laid down his ax for a moment, and wondered what all this could possibly mean. "Oh, well," he said, "you must have been hearing things. No need to frighten yourself about nothing." So he took his ax again and was about to begin chopping when he heard the voice from below once more:

"He who chops wood for reels shall die.
She who winds yarn shall be ruined all her life."

He stopped again, and in his fear and terror, he tried to grasp what was happening. After some time had passed, his courage returned. He reached for his ax a third time and was about to chop when he heard the voice cry out loudly for a third time:

"He who chops wood for reels shall die.
She who winds yarn shall be ruined all her life."

This was too much for him, and he lost all desire to chop the wood. He quickly climbed down the tree and made his way home. His wife ran as fast as she could via the byways to get home before he did. When he entered the living room, she acted innocent, as if nothing had happened, and said, "Well, did you bring me a nice piece of wood for a reel?"

"No," he said, "I've realized that it makes no sense to wind," and he told her what he had encountered in the forest, and from then on he left her in peace.

Yet, some time later the husband began complaining again about the messy condition of the house. "Wife," he said, "it's a disgrace the way you just leave your spun wool on the bobbin."

"You know what?" she said. "Since we haven't managed to get a reel, you go up to the loft, and I'll stand here below. Then I'll throw the yarn up to you, and you throw it back down to me. That way we'll have a skein."

"Yes, that'll work," said her husband. So they did this, and when they were finished, he said, "We've got the yarn skeined, and now it needs to be boiled as well."

His wife became uneasy again and said, "Yes, indeed, we'll boil it first thing tomorrow morning," but she was really thinking up a new trick. Early the next morning she got up, made the fire, and set the kettle on it, but instead of putting the yarn in the kettle, she put in a clump of tow and let it boil. After this she went to her husband, who was still lying in bed, and said to him, "I've got to go out awhile. So I want you to get up and look after the yarn that's in the kettle on the fire. Make sure you do this right away, and watch things closely, for if the cock crows and you're not taking care, the yarn will become tow."

The husband agreed since he certainly did not want anything to go wrong. He got up as fast as he could and went into the kitchen. But when he reached the kettle and looked inside, he was horrified to discover nothing but a clump of tow. Then the husband was as quiet as a mouse, for he thought that he had done something wrong and was to blame. In the future he no longer mentioned yarn and spinning. But you yourself must admit that his wife was a nasty woman.

◆ 129 ◆

The Four Skillful Brothers

THERE ONCE WAS A POOR MAN who had four sons. When they had grown up, he said to them, "My dear children, you must now go out into the world, for I have nothing to give you. Make your way to foreign countries. Learn a trade and try to succeed as best you can."

So the four brothers got ready for their journey, took leave of their father, and went out of the town gate together. After they had traveled for some time, they came to a crossroads that led in four different directions. Then the oldest son said, "We must separate here, but let us meet again at this spot four years from today. In the meantime, we shall try our luck."

So each one went his way, and the oldest met a man, who asked him where he was going and what his plans were.

"I want to learn a trade," he answered.

"Then come with me," the man said, "and become a thief."

"No," the oldest son responded. "That's no longer considered an honest trade, and one generally ends up dangling from the gallows."

"Oh," said the man, "you needn't be afraid of the gallows. I'll just teach you how to get what nobody else can otherwise fetch, and I'll show you how to do this without ever being caught."

So the oldest son let himself be persuaded, and the man taught him how to become a skillful thief. The young man became so adroit that nothing was safe from him once he wanted to have it.

The second brother met a man who asked him the same question about what he wanted to learn in the world.

"I don't know yet," he answered.

"Then come with me and become a stargazer. You won't find anything better than this, for nothing will ever remain hidden from you."

The second son liked the idea and became such a skillful stargazer that when he had finished studying and was about to depart, his master gave him a telescope and said, "With this you'll be able to see everything that happens on the earth and in the sky, and nothing can remain hidden from you."

The third brother served an apprenticeship under a huntsman and learned all there was to know about hunting, so that he became a full-fledged huntsman. His master gave him a gun as a gift upon his departure and said, "You won't miss whatever you aim at with this gun. You'll hit it for sure."

The youngest brother also met a man who spoke to him and asked him about his plans.

"Do you have any desire to become a tailor?"

"Not that I know of," said the young man. "I've never had the least desire to sit bent over from morning till night and to swing the needle or iron back and forth."

"Oh, come now!" answered the man. "You really don't know what you're talking about. With me you'll learn a totally different kind of tailoring that's respectable and decent and may even bring you great honor."

The young man let himself be persuaded. He went with him and learned all the basics of the trade from the man, and upon his departure the master gave him a needle and said, "With this you'll be able to sew together anything you find, whether it be as soft as an egg or as hard as steel. And you'll be able to make anything into one complete piece so that not a single seam will show."

When the designated four years were over, the four brothers met together at the crossroads at the same time. They embraced, kissed each other, and returned home to their father.

"Well," said the father delightedly, "look what the wind has blown back to me again!"

They told him what had happened to them and how each had learned a particular trade. As they sat in front of the house under a big tree, the father then said, "Well, I'm going to put you to the test to see what you can do." After this he looked up and said to the second son, "There's a chaffinch's nest up there in the top of this tree between two branches. Tell me how many eggs are in it."

The stargazer took his telescope, looked up, and said, "Five."

Then the father said to the oldest son, "Fetch the eggs without disturbing the bird that's sitting on them."

The skillful thief climbed up the tree and took the five eggs from under the bird, who sat there quietly without noticing a thing. Then he brought the eggs down to his father, who took them and placed one on each corner of the table and the fifth in the middle and said to the huntsman, "I want you to shoot the five eggs in two with one shot."

The huntsman took aim with his gun and shot the eggs just as his father had demanded. Indeed, he hit all five of them with one shot, and he certainly must have had some of that powder that shoots around corners.

"Now it's your turn," said the father to the fourth son. "I want you to sew the eggs together again and also the young birds that are in them, and I want you to repair any damage that the shot has done to them."

The tailor got his needle and sewed just as his father had demanded. When he was finished, the thief had to carry the eggs up to the nest again and put them back under the bird without it noticing anything. The bird sat on them until they hatched, and after a few days the young chicks crawled out of the eggs and had little red stripes around their necks where the tailor had sewn them together.

"Yes," said the old man to his sons. "I must praise you to the skies. You've made good use of your time and have learned something beneficial. I can't say which of you deserves the most praise, but if you soon have an opportunity to apply your skills, we'll find out who's the best."

Not long after this there was a great uproar in the country: the king's daughter had been carried off by a dragon. Day and night the king worried over this, and he let it be proclaimed that whoever brought her back could have her for his wife. The four brothers discussed the situation together. "This could be our chance to show what we can do," and they decided to set out together to free the king's daughter.

"I'll soon find out where she is," said the stargazer, and he looked through his telescope and said, "I already see her. She's sitting on a rock in the sea very far away from here, and next to her is the dragon, who's guarding her."

Then the stargazer went to the king and requested a ship for himself and his brothers. Together they sailed across the sea until they came to the rock. The king's daughter was sitting there, but the dragon was lying asleep with his head in her lap.

"I can't take a risk and shoot," said the huntsman. "I might hit the beautiful maiden at the same time."

"Well, then I'll try out my skill," said the thief, who crawled to the maiden and stole her from under the dragon so quietly and nimbly that the monster did not notice a thing and kept on snoring. The brothers joyfully hurried off with her, boarded the ship, and sailed away on the open sea. Upon awakening, however, the dragon discovered that the king's daughter was gone, and snorting furiously, it flew after them through the sky. Just as it was hovering above the ship, about to dive down upon the vessel, the huntsman took aim with his gun and shot it through the heart. The monster fell down dead, but it was so large and powerful that it smashed the entire ship to pieces in its fall. Fortunately those on board were able to grab hold of some planks and swim about on the open sea. Once again they were in terrible danger, but the tailor, who was always alert, took his marvelous needle and hastily sewed together the planks with a few big stitches. Then he sat down on the planks and collected all the parts of the ship, which he then sewed together in such a skillful way that in a short time the ship was seaworthy once again and they could sail home safely.

When the king saw his daughter once more, there was great rejoicing, and he said to the four brothers, "One of you shall have the princess for your wife, but you must decide among yourselves which one it's to be."

A violent quarrel broke out among the brothers then, for each one had a claim. The stargazer said, "If I hadn't seen the king's daughter, all your skills would have been in vain. That's why she should be mine."

The thief said, "Your seeing her would not have helped much if I hadn't fetched her out from under the dragon. That's why she should be mine."

The huntsman said, "The monster would have torn all of you apart along with the king's daughter if my bullet hadn't hit the beast. That's why she should be mine."

The tailor said, "And if I hadn't patched the ship together for you with my skill, you'd all have drowned miserably. That's why she should be mine."

Then the king made his decision known. "Each of you has a just claim, and since it would be impossible to give the maiden to each of you, no one shall have her. Nevertheless, I shall reward each of you with half a kingdom."

The brothers were satisfied with this decision and said, "It's better this way than to be at odds with each other." So each of them received half a kingdom, and they lived happily with their father as long as it pleased God.

◈ 130 ◈

One-Eye, Two-Eyes, and Three-Eyes

THERE WAS A WOMAN who had three daughters. The oldest was called One-Eye because she had only a single eye in the middle of her forehead. The second was called Two-Eyes because she had two eyes like all other human beings. The youngest was called Three-Eyes because she had three eyes, with her third eye located in the middle of her forehead like her oldest sister's. However, since Two-Eyes did not look any different from other people, her mother and sisters could not stand her. "You with your two eyes," they would say to her, "you're no better than the ordinary folk! You don't belong to us." They pushed her around and gave her shabby hand-me-down clothes to wear and leftover food to eat. Whenever they could, they caused her as much grief as possible.

One day it happened that Two-Eyes had to go out to the fields and tend the goat. She was still very hungry because her sisters had given her so little to eat. So she sat down on the ridge of a hill and began to weep, and she wept so much that two little brooks flowed from her eyes. When she paused and looked up in her misery, a woman was standing there.

"Two-Eyes, why are you crying?" she asked.

"Because I have two eyes like other people," she answered. "That's why my mother and sisters can't stand me. They push me from one corner to the next and give me shabby hand-me-down clothes to wear and only leftovers to eat. Today they gave me so little that I'm still very hungry."

"Two-Eyes," said the wise woman, "dry your face. I'm going to tell you something that will keep you from going hungry anymore. Just say to your goat:

'Little goat, bleat,
and bring me things to eat.'

"Then a nicely set table with the most wonderful food will appear before you, and you'll be able to eat to your heart's content. When you've had enough and no longer need the table, just say:

'Little goat, bleat,
I've had enough to eat.'

"Then it will disappear before your eyes."

Upon saying this, the wise woman went away, and Two-Eyes thought, I must try it right away to see if she was telling the truth, for I'm much too hungry to wait. Then she said:

"Little goat, bleat,
and bring me things to eat.'

No sooner had she uttered the words than a table stood there covered with a white cloth, and on top of it was a plate with a knife, a fork, and a silver spoon. The most wonderful dishes were laid out on the table, all steaming hot, as if they had just been brought from the kitchen. Then Two-Eyes said the shortest prayer she knew, "Lord God, be our guest at all times. Amen," and reached for the food. She enjoyed everything, and when she was full, she said the words the wise woman had taught her:

"Little goat, bleat,
I've had enough to eat.'

Immediately the table and everything on it vanished. That's a great way to keep house, thought Two-Eyes, who was very happy and in good spirits.

In the evening when she came home with her goat, she found a clay bowl with food that her sisters had set out for her, but she did not touch a thing. The next day she went out again with her goat and left the few crumbs that had been set out for her as they were. Her sisters did not see this at all the first couple of times, but when it kept happening they could not help but notice and said, "Something's wrong with Two-Eyes. She's stopped eating the food we give her, and she used to eat it all up. She must have found another recourse." Since they wanted to get to the bottom of this, they decided that, when Two-Eyes drove the goat out to pasture, One-Eye should go along. Then she would be able to see what their sister was up to and whether anyone was bringing her food and drink.

The next time Two-Eyes was about to set out, One-Eye came to her and said, "I want to go into the fields with you to see whether the goat is being tended properly and getting enough to eat."

But Two-Eyes realized what One-Eye had in mind. She drove the goat out to the tall grass and said, "Come, One-Eye, let's sit down here, and I'll sing you something."

One-Eye sat down, and since she was tired from the unaccustomed walk and the heat of the sun, Two-Eyes kept singing:

"One-Eye, are you awake?
One-Eye are you asleep?"

One-Eye closed her one eye and fell asleep. When Two-Eyes saw that One-Eye was sound asleep and would not be able to reveal anything later on, she said:

"Little goat, bleat,
and bring me things to eat."

And she sat down at the table and ate and drank until she was full. Then she called out:

"Little goat, bleat,
I've had enough to eat."

And everything disappeared in a second. Then Two-Eyes woke One-Eye and said, "One-Eye, you wanted to tend the goat and yet you fell asleep! The goat could have run all over the place in the meantime. Come, let's go home."

They returned to the house, and Two-Eyes left her bowl untouched again, and One-Eye could not tell their mother why her sister did not eat. As an excuse she said, "I fell asleep out there."

The next day the mother said to Three-Eyes, "This time I want you to go along and find out whether Two-Eyes eats out there or whether someone brings her food and drink, for she must be eating and drinking in secret."

Now, Three-Eyes went to Two-Eyes and said, "I want to go to the fields with you to see whether the goat is being tended properly and getting enough to eat."

But Two-Eyes realized what Three-Eyes had in mind and drove the goat out to the tall grass and said, "Come, Three-Eyes, let's sit down here, and I'll sing you something."

Three-Eyes sat down and was tired from the walk and the heat of the sun, and Two-Eyes sang her little ditty again:

"Three-Eyes, are you awake?"

But instead of singing, as she should have done:

"Three-Eyes, are you asleep?"

she sang:

"*Two-Eyes,* are you asleep?"

and she kept singing:

"Three-Eyes, are you awake?
Two-Eyes, are you asleep?"

Then two of Three-Eyes's eyes closed and went to sleep, but the third did not fall alseep because it had not been addressed by the ditty. To be sure, Three-Eyes closed it, but only as a trick, pretending that it had fallen asleep along with the others. Yet, it blinked and could still see everything all right.

When Two-Eyes thought that Three-Eyes was sleeping soundly, she uttered her little rhyme:

"Little goat, bleat,
and bring me things to eat."

And she ate and drank to her heart's content. Then she ordered the table to be gone by saying:

"Little goat, bleat,
I've had enough to eat."

All the while Three-Eyes was watching everything. Then Two-Eyes went over to her, woke her, and said, "Hey, Three-Eyes, you fell asleep! Is that the way to tend a goat? Come, let's go home."

When they returned to the house, Two-Eyes refused to eat again, and Three-Eyes said to their mother, "Now I know why that haughty thing doesn't eat. When she's out there, she says to the goat:

'Little goat, bleat,
and bring me things to eat.'

"And then a table appears covered with the finest food, much better than what we have here. And when she's full, she says:

'Little goat, bleat,
I've had enough to eat.'

"And everything vanishes. I saw it all quite clearly. She put two of my eyes to sleep with a little rhyme, but fortunately the one in my forehead stayed awake."

Then the jealous mother yelled at Two-Eyes, "Do you think you can live better than we do? Well, I'll soon put an end to your taste for the good life." She fetched a butcher knife and stabbed the goat in the heart so that it fell down dead.

When Two-Eyes saw this, she went outside full of grief, sat down on the ridge of the hill, and wept bitter tears. Suddenly the wise woman stood before her again and said, "Two-Eyes, why are you crying?"

"Why shouldn't I cry?" she answered. "My mother stabbed to death the goat that set the table so nicely for me every day when I recited your rhyme. Now I'll have to put up with hunger and distress again."

"Two-Eyes," said the wise woman. "I want to give you some good advice. Ask your sisters to let you have the entrails of the slaughtered goat and bury them in the ground outside the entrance to the house. This will bring you good luck."

Then she disappeared, and Two-Eyes went home and said to her sisters, "Dear sisters, I'd like to have something from the goat, and I'm not asking much. Just give me the entrails."

The sisters laughed and said, "If that's all you want, you can surely have them."

Two-Eyes took the entrails, and in the evening she quietly buried them outside the entrance to the house, just as the wise woman had advised her. The next morning, when they all awoke and stepped outside the front door, there was a magnificent and splendid tree standing there. Its leaves were made of silver and its fruits were made of gold; it was more beautiful and delicious than anything in the whole wide world. Of course, they did not know how the tree had got there in the night. Only Two-Eyes knew that it had grown from the entrails of the goat, for it stood on the exact same spot where she had buried them in the ground. Then the mother said to One-Eye, "Climb up, my child, and pick some fruit for us."

One-Eye climbed up the tree, but each time she wanted to grab one of the golden apples, the branch slipped out of her hands, and that happened every time so that she could not pick a single apple no matter what she did. Then the mother said, "Three-Eyes, now you climb up. With your three eyes you can look around better than One-Eye."

One-Eye slid down the tree, and Three-Eyes climbed up, but she was no more agile than her sister, and despite her sharp sight, the golden apples evaded her grasp. Finally, the mother became impatient and climbed up herself, but she had as much difficulty as One-Eye and Three-Eyes, and her hands came up with nothing but thin air.

Then Two-Eyes said, "I'd like to go up once. Maybe I'll have better luck."

"You with your two eyes!" her sisters exclaimed. "What do you think you can do?"

But Two-Eyes climbed up, and the golden apples did not retreat from her grasp. Instead they dropped by themselves into her hand, so that she was able to pick one after the other and brought down a whole apron full of apples. Her mother took them from her, and rather than treating her better, she and One-Eye and Three-Eyes grew envious, because she was the only one who could fetch the fruit, and thus they became even more harsh with her.

It happened that one day, as they were all standing together at the tree, a young knight came riding toward them.

"Quick, Two-Eyes," the two sisters cried, "crawl under there so that you won't disgrace us," and they hurriedly took a barrel standing near the tree and placed it over poor Two-Eyes, and they also shoved under it the golden apples that she had just picked. As the knight came closer they could see that he was a handsome nobleman. He stopped and admired the splendid gold and silver tree and said to the two sisters, "Whose tree is this? Whoever gets one of its branches for me can have anything she wants from me."

Then One-Eye and Three-Eyes told him that the tree belonged to them and that they would certainly break off a branch for him. They both made a great effort yet were unable to do it, for the branches and fruit drew back from them each time they tried to grab hold of them.

"It's certainly strange," the knight said. "You said the tree belongs to you, and yet, you don't have the power to break anything off it."

They insisted that the tree was theirs. But as they were talking Two-Eyes rolled a few golden apples from under the barrel toward the knight's feet, for she was angry that One-Eye and Three-Eyes had not told the truth. When the knight saw the apples, he was astonished and asked where they had come from. One-Eye and Three-Eyes answered that they had another sister, who was not allowed to show herself because she had only two eyes like other ordinary people. But the knight demanded to see her and shouted, "Two-Eyes, come out!"

Two-Eyes came out from under the barrel feeling consoled, and the knight was surprised by her great beauty and said, "You, Two-Eyes, you can certainly break off a branch of the tree for me."

"Yes," answered Two-Eyes. "Of course I can, for the tree belongs to me." And she climbed up with ease and broke off a branch with fine silver leaves and golden fruit and handed it to the knight.

"What am I to give you in return for this, Two-Eyes?" asked the knight.

"Ah," answered Two-Eyes. "I must put up with hunger and thirst, worry and distress from early morning until late at night. If you would take me with you and free me from all of this, I'd be happy."

So the knight lifted Two-Eyes onto his horse and brought her to his father's castle. There he gave her beautiful clothes and food and drink to her heart's content, and since he loved her so much, he married her, and the wedding was celebrated with great rejoicing.

After Two-Eyes had been taken away by the handsome knight, the two sisters were extremely jealous of her good fortune. Still, the wonderful tree will remain with us, they thought. Even if we can't pick off any fruit from it, people will still come and stop in front of it and praise it. Who knows what good luck may be in store for us? But the tree disappeared by the next morning, along with their hopes. And when Two-Eyes looked out her bedroom window, she was delighted to see it standing there, for it had followed her to her new home.

Two-Eyes lived happily for a long time, and one day when two poor women came to the castle and begged for alms, Two-Eyes looked into their faces and recognized her sisters. One-Eye and Three-Eyes had become so poor that they had to wander about and beg for bread from door to door. Two-Eyes, however, bade them welcome and treated them with such kindness and care that they both deeply regretted the evil they had done to their sister in their youth.

❖ 131 ❖

Pretty Katrinelya and Pif Paf Poltree

"GOOD DAY, Father Berry-Tea."

"Why, thank you indeed, Pif Paf Poltree."

"Could I have your daughter for my wife?"

"Oh, yes, if Mother Milk-Cow, Brother High-and-Mighty, Sister Dear-Cheese, and Pretty Katrinelya are willing, then you can have her."

"Then where can I find Mother Milk-Cow?"

"In the barn milking the cow."

"Good day, Mother Milk-Cow."

"Why, thank you indeed, Pif Paf Poltree."

"Could I have your daughter for my wife?"

"Oh, yes, if Father Berry-Tea, Brother High-and-Mighty, Sister Dear-Cheese, and Pretty Katrinelya are willing, then you can have her."

"Then where can I find Brother High-and-Mighty?"

"In the shed chopping up all the wood he can see."

"Good day, Brother High-and-Mighty."

"Why, thank you indeed, Pif Paf Poltree."

"Could I have your sister for my wife?"

"Oh, yes, if Father Berry-Tea, Mother Milk-Cow, Sister Dear-Cheese, and Pretty Katrinelya are willing, then you can have her."

"Then where can I find Sister Dear-Cheese?"

"Weeding in the garden, if you please."

"Good day, Sister Dear-Cheese."

"Why, thank you indeed, Pif Paf Poltree."

"Could I have your sister for my wife?"

"Oh, yes, if Father Berry-Tea, Mother Milk-Cow, Brother High-and-Mighty, and Pretty Katrinelya are willing, then you can have her."

"Then where can I find Pretty Katrinelya?"

"Counting out her pennies in the parlor."

"Good day, Pretty Katrinelya."

"Why, thank you indeed, Pif Paf Poltree."

"Do you want to be my bride?"

"Oh, yes, if Father Berry-Tea, Mother Milk-Cow, Brother High-and-Mighty, and Sister Dear-Cheese are willing, then I'll be your bride."

"Pretty Katrinelya, how much dowry do you have?"

"Fourteen pennies in cash, three and a half groschen that are owed to me, half a pound of dried fruits, a handful of pretzels, and a handful of roots. As you can surely see, that makes for a fine dowry.

"Now, Pif Paf Poltree, what do you do? Are you a tailor?"

"Much better than that."

"A shoemaker?"

"Much better than that."

"A farmer?"

"Much better than that."

"A carpenter?"

"Much better than that."

"A blacksmith?"

"Much better than that."

"A miller?"

"Much better than that."

"Perhaps you're a broom-maker?"

"Yes, that's what I am. Isn't that a wonderful way to earn a living?"

◈ 132 ◈

The Fox and the Horse

A FARMER HAD A FAITHFUL HORSE that had grown old and could no longer do his work. So his master did not want to feed it anymore and said, "You're of no more use to me now, but I won't abandon you entirely: show me that you're still strong enough to bring me a lion, then I'll keep you. But for now, get out of my stable!" And he chased the horse out into the open field.

The horse was sad about this and went into the forest to seek a little shelter from the weather. There he met the fox, who asked, "Why are you hanging your head and moping about all by yourself?"

"Ah," answered the horse, "greed and loyalty can't live side by side in the same house. My master has forgotten how much work I've done for him over the years, and since I can no longer plow properly, he won't feed me and has chased me away."

"Without a word of consolation?" asked the fox.

"The consolation was meager. He told me that, if I was still strong enough to bring him a lion, he would keep me, but he knows full well that I can't do that."

"Well, I'm going to help you," said the fox. "Just lie down, stretch yourself out, and don't move. Pretend you're dead."

The horse did what the fox commanded, while the fox went to the lion, whose den was not far away, and said, "There's a dead horse lying out there. If you want a great meal, come along with me."

The lion went with him, and when they were at the horse's side, the fox said, "It's not so comfortable for you here. You know what I'll do? I'll tie the horse to you by his tail so you can drag him and eat him in peace and quiet."

The lion liked the idea, assumed a position for the fox to attach the horse to him, and kept still. However, the fox bound the lion's legs together with the horse's tail, and he tied and twisted it so tightly and firmly that the lion would not have been able to tear himself loose even if he used all his might. When the fox finally finished his work, he tapped the horse on his shoulder and said, "Pull, horse, pull!"

All at once the horse jumped up and dragged the lion with him. The lion began to roar so loudly that all the birds in the forest flew away out of fright, but the horse let him roar and pulled and dragged him over the fields to his master's door. When his master saw that, he reconsidered everything in a better light and said to the horse, "You shall stay here with me and shall be treated well."

And he gave him all he wanted to eat until the day of the horse's death.

◈ 133 ◈

The Worn-out Dancing Shoes

ONCE UPON A TIME there was a king who had twelve daughters, one more beautiful than the next. They slept together in a large room, where their beds stood side by side, and in the evening, when they went to sleep, the king shut and locked the door. However, when he opened it in the morning, he would see that their shoes were worn out from dancing, and nobody could discover how this kept happening. Finally, the king had it proclaimed that whoever could find out where his daughters danced during the night could choose one of them for his wife and be king after his death. But anyone who came and failed to uncover everything after three days and nights would lose his life.

Not long after this proclamation a prince came and offered to undertake the venture. He was well received, and in the evening he was conducted to a room adjoining the bedchamber of the king's daughters. His bed was set up there, and he was told to watch and find out where they went dancing. And, just to make sure they could not do anything in secret or go out anywhere else, the door of their room that led to his was kept open. Still, the prince's eyes became as heavy as lead, and he fell asleep. When he awoke the next morning, all twelve of them had been to a dance, for their shoes were standing there with holes in their soles. The same thing happened the second and third night, and his head was cut off without mercy. After that there were many who came to try their luck, but they were all destined to leave their lives behind them.

Now, it happened that a poor soldier, who had been wounded and could no longer serve in the army, headed toward the city where the king lived. Along the way he met an old woman, who asked him where he was going.

"I really don't know myself," he said, and added jokingly, "but I'd certainly like to find out where the king's daughters go dancing and where they wear out their shoes so I could become king."

"That's not so difficult," said the old woman. "Just don't drink the wine that's brought to you in the evening, and then pretend that you've fallen asleep." Then she gave him a little cloak and said, "When you put this cloak on, you'll be invisible, and you'll be able to follow all twelve of them."

After receiving such good advice, the soldier now became serious about the entire matter and plucked up his courage to present himself in front of the king as a suitor. He was welcomed just as cordially as the others had been and was given royal garments to put on. In the evening, at bedtime, he was led to the antechamber, and as he was preparing to go to bed the oldest daughter brought him a beaker of wine, but he had tied a sponge underneath his chin and let the wine run into it and did not drink a single drop. Then he lay down, and after lying there a little while, he began to snore as if in a very deep sleep.

When the princesses heard his snoring, they laughed, and the oldest said, "He too could have done better things with his life." After this they stood up, opened the closets, chests, and boxes, and took out splendid clothes. They groomed themselves in front of their mirrors and hurried about, eager to attend the dance. But the youngest said, "I don't know. You're all happy, yet I have a strange feeling. I'm sure that something bad is going to happen to us."

"You're a silly goose," said the oldest. "You're always afraid. Have you forgotten how many princes have already tried in vain? I didn't really need to give the soldier a sleeping potion. The lout would never have awakened even without it."

When they were all ready, they first took a look at the soldier, but he had shut his eyes tight, and since he neither moved nor stirred, they thought they were definitely safe. So the oldest went to her bed and knocked on it. Immediately it sank into the ground, and they climbed down through the opening, one after another, with the oldest in the lead. The soldier, who had seen everything, did not hesitate long. He put on his little cloak and climbed down after the youngest. Halfway down the stairs he stepped on her dress slightly, causing her to become terrified and cry out, "What's that? Who's holding my dress?"

"Don't be so stupid," said the oldest. "You've just caught it on a hook."

They went all the way down, and when they were at the bottom, they stood in the middle of a marvelous avenue of trees whose leaves were all made of silver and glittered and glimmered. You'd better take a piece of evidence with you, the soldier thought, and broke off a branch, but the tree cracked and made a tremendous sound. Again the youngest called out, "Something's wrong! Didn't you hear the noise?"

But the oldest said, "That was just a burst of joy because we'll soon be setting our princes free."

Then they came to another avenue of trees, where all the leaves were made of gold, and finally to one where all the leaves were made of pure diamond. The soldier broke off branches from each kind, and each time there was such a cracking sound that the youngest sister was terrified. But the oldest maintained that they were just bursts of joy. They went on and came to a large lake with twelve boats on it, and in each boat sat a handsome prince. They had been waiting for the twelve princesses, and each one took a princess in his boat, while the soldier went aboard with the youngest princess. Then her prince said, "I don't understand it, but the boat is much heavier today. I'll have to row with all my might to get it moving."

"It's probably due to the warm weather," said the youngest. "I feel quite hot too."

On the other side of the lake stood a beautiful, brightly lit palace, and sounds of merry music with drums and trumpets could be heard from it. They rowed over there, entered the palace, and each prince danced with his sweetheart. The invisible soldier danced along as well, and whenever a princess went to drink a beaker of wine, he would drain it dry before it could reach her lips. The youngest sister was terribly concerned about this too, but the oldest continued to soothe her. They danced until three in the morning, when all the shoes were worn through and they had to stop. The princes rowed them back across the lake, and this time the soldier sat in the first boat with the oldest sister. The princesses took leave of their princes on the bank and promised to return the following night. When they reached the stairs, the soldier ran ahead of them and got into bed, and by the time the twelve princesses came tripping slowly and wearily up the stairs, he was again snoring so loudly that they could all hear it, and they said, "We don't have to worry about him." Then they took off their beautiful clothes, put them away, placed the worn-out shoes under their beds, and lay down to sleep.

The next morning the soldier decided not to say anything but rather to follow and observe their strange life for the next two nights. Everything happened just as it had on the first night: they danced each time until their shoes fell apart. However, the third time he took a beaker with him for evidence. When the time came for him to give his answer, he took along the three branches and beaker and went before the king. The twelve princesses stood behind the door and listened to what he said. When the king asked, "Where did my daughters spend the night?" he answered, "With twelve princes in an underground palace." Then he reported what had taken place and produced the evidence. The king summoned his daughters and asked them whether the soldier had told the truth. When they saw that they had been exposed and that denying would not help, they had to confess everything. Then the king asked the soldier which princess he would like for his wife.

"I'm no longer so young," he answered, "so I'll take the oldest."

The wedding was held that same day, and the king promised to make him his successor to the kingdom after his death. The princes, however, were compelled to remain under a curse for as many nights as they had danced with the princesses.

◆ 134 ◆

The Six Servants

LONG, long ago there lived an old queen who was a sorceress, and her daughter was the most beautiful maiden under the sun. The old woman, however, thought of nothing but how to lure people to their doom. Whenever a suitor came to her asking for her daughter's hand, she said that he would first have to perform a task and would die if he failed. Many men were tempted by the extraordinary beauty of the maiden and actually risked their lives, but none could perform the task given by the old woman, and she showed them no mercy: they had to kneel down, and their heads were cut off.

There was a prince who had also heard of the great beauty of the maiden, and he said to his father, "Let me go and try to win her hand."

"Never," answered the king. "If you go, it will be your death."

The son then withdrew to his bed and became dangerously ill. He lay there seven years, and no doctor could help him. When the king saw that there was no more hope, his heart became filled with sadness, and he said to his son, "Go there, and try your luck. I know of no other way to help you."

When the son heard this, he left his bed, got well again, and went merrily on his way. As he was riding across a heath he happened to see something lying on the ground in the distance. It seemed like a big pile of hay, but as he came closer, he could see that it was the belly of a man who lay stretched out on the heath. However, the belly looked like a small mountain. When the fat man saw the traveler coming toward him, he stood up and said, "If you need someone, then take me into your service."

"What can I do with such a monstrosity as you?" the prince answered.

"Oh," said the fat man, "this is nothing. When I really want to expand, I'm three thousand times as fat."

"If that's the case," the prince said, "then I can use you. Come with me."

The fat man followed the prince, and after a while they found another man, who was lying on the ground with his ear glued to the grass.

"What are you doing there?" asked the prince.

"I'm listening," answered the man.

"What are you listening to so intensely?"

"I'm listening to what's going on in the world right now, for nothing escapes my ears. I can even hear the grass grow."

"Tell me," asked the prince, "what do you hear at the palace of the old queen who has the beautiful daughter?"

"I hear the swishing of a sword," he answered. "A suitor has just had his head cut off."

The prince said, "I can use you. Come with me."

They continued on their way, and suddenly they saw a pair of feet lying on the ground, also part of the legs, but they could not see where they ended. When they had gone a good distance, they came to the body and finally to the head.

"My!" said the prince. "I thought we'd never reach the end of you!"

"Oh," responded the tall man. "You haven't seen anything yet! When I really want to stretch out my limbs, I'm three thousand times as tall, taller than the highest mountain on earth. I'd gladly serve you if you'd have me."

"Come with me," said the prince. "I can use you."

They continued on their way and came across a blindfolded man sitting beside the road.

"Are your eyes so weak that you can't look into the light?" asked the prince.

"No," answered the man. "I don't dare take off the blindfold, for my glance is so powerful that it shatters whatever I gaze upon with my eyes. If something like this can be of use to you, then I'll gladly serve you."

"Come with me," answered the prince. "I can use you."

They continued on their way and came upon a man basking under the hot sun, but he was freezing and shivered so much that his entire body was shaking.

"How can you be freezing when the sun is so warm?" asked the prince.

"Ah," answered the man, "my nature is of a completely different kind. The hotter it is, the more I freeze, and the frost chills me to the bone. The colder it is, the hotter I am. In the midst of ice, I can't stand the heat, and in the midst of hot flames, I can't stand the cold."

"You're a strange fellow," said the prince, "but if you'd like to serve me, then come along."

They continued on their way and saw a man stretching his long neck way out and looking in different directions and over all the mountains.

"What are you looking for so eagerly?" asked the prince.

"I have such sharp eyes," said the man, "that I can see over all the forests and fields, valleys and mountains, and throughout the whole world."

"If you want to," said the prince, "then come with me, for I've been in need of someone just like you."

Now the prince and his six servants entered the city where the old queen lived. He did not reveal his identity to her but said, "If you will give me your beautiful daughter, I'll carry out any task you give me."

The sorceress was happy that she had snared such a handsome young man again and said, "I'll give you three tasks. If you perform them all, you shall be my daughter's lord and master."

"What's the first to be?" he asked.

"To bring back a ring that I dropped in the Red Sea."

Then the prince went home to his servants and said, "The first task isn't easy. A ring must be fetched out of the Red Sea. Now help me think of a way to do it."

Then Sharp Eyes said, "I'll see where it is." After looking down into the sea, he said, "It's caught on a sharp stone."

Tall Man carried them there and said, "I'd get it out if only I could see it."

"If that's all there's to it, don't worry," said Fat Man. He lay down, put his mouth to the water, and the waves rushed into it as if into an abyss. He drank up the entire sea until it was as dry as a meadow. Tall Man bent over a little and picked up the ring with his hand. The prince was happy when he got the ring, and he brought it to the old woman, who was astonished and said, "Yes, that's the ring. You've performed the first task all right, but now comes the second. Do you see the three hundred oxen grazing on the meadow in front of my castle? You must devour them, skin and bones, hair and horns. Then, down in my cellar there are three hundred barrels of wine that you must drink up as well. If one hair is left from the oxen or one little drop from the wine, then your life will be forfeited to me."

"May I invite some guests?" asked the prince. "I don't enjoy my meals without company."

The old woman laughed maliciously and answered, "You may invite one person to keep you company, but no more than that."

The prince then went to his servants and said to Fat Man, "Today you shall be my guest, and for once you'll have your fill to eat."

Fat Man expanded himself and ate the three hundred oxen without leaving a single hair anywhere. After that he asked what came after breakfast, and he proceeded to drink the wine right out of the barrels, without a glass, until the barrels were completely drained. When the meal was finished, the prince went to the old woman and told her he had completed the second task. She was surprised and said, "No one has ever gotten this far, but there's still one task left." And she thought to herself, You won't escape me, nor will you keep your head. Then she said aloud, "Tonight I'm going to bring my daughter into your room, and you're to put your arms around her. While you sit there with her, be sure not to fall asleep. I shall come at midnight, and if she's no longer in your arms, you'll lose your life."

This task is easy, the prince thought. I'll certainly be able to keep my eyes open. Nevertheless, he called his servants to him, told them what the old woman had said, and declared, "Who knows what kinds of tricks she intends to play. It's wise to be cautious. So keep watch and make sure that the maiden doesn't get out of my room."

At nightfall the old woman brought her daughter and put her into the prince's arms. Then Tall Man formed a circle around the two, and Fat Man placed himself in front of the door so that no living soul could enter. The couple sat there, and though the maiden did not say a word, the moon shone through the window on her face so that the prince could gaze at her marvelous beauty. He was content just looking at her. His heart was full of joy and love, and his eyes did not tire at all. All this lasted until eleven o'clock. Then the old woman cast a spell on all of them, so they fell asleep. It was just at that moment that the maiden was carried off.

The others continued to sleep soundly until a quarter of twelve when the magic lost its power and they all awoke.

"Oh, what bad luck and grief!" exclaimed the prince. "Now I'm lost!"

The loyal servants also began to moan, but Listener said, "Be quiet, I want to see if I can hear something." He listened for a minute and then said, "She's being kept in a rock three hundred miles from here and is lamenting her fate. Tall Man, only you can help. If you stand up at your full height, you can be there in a couple of steps."

"All right," Tall Man answered, "but Sharp Eyes must come with me so we can dispose of the rock."

Then Tall Man lifted his blindfolded companion onto his back, and in no time they were in front of the enchanted rock. As soon as Tall Man took off the blindfold, Sharp Eyes needed only to look around, and the rock shattered into a thousand pieces. Tall Man took the maiden in his arms, carried her back to the prince in a split second, and then fetched his companion just as fast. Before the clock struck twelve, they were all seated again as they had previously been, and they were cheerful and in high spirits.

When the clock struck twelve, the old sorceress came creeping into the room with a scornful look on her face, as if she wanted to say, "Now he's mine!" For she thought that her daughter was sitting in the rock three hundred miles away. However, when she saw her daughter in the prince's arms, she became horrified and said, "I've more than met my match." Hence, she could no longer object to the prince's bidding and had to give her daughter to him. Nevertheless, she whispered into her daughter's ear, "It's a disgrace that you must obey a commoner and are not allowed to choose a husband to your own liking."

Then the maiden's proud heart filled with anger, and she sought to avenge herself. The next morning she had three hundred cords of wood gathered together and said to the prince that, even though he had performed the three tasks, she would not become his wife until someone was ready to sit in the middle of the woodpile and withstand the fire. She was convinced that none of his servants would let himself be burned for the prince's sake and that the prince would have to sacrifice himself on the woodpile out of love for her. But the servants said, "We've all done something with the exception of Frosty. Now he's got to do his share."

They placed him in the middle of the heap of wood and set fire to it. The flames began to burn, and they burned for three days until all the wood had been consumed, and when the flames died down, Frosty stood in the middle of the ashes trembling like an aspen leaf and said, "Never in my life have I endured such a frost, and if it had lasted much longer, I'd have been frozen stiff."

Now there was no other way out: the beautiful maiden had to marry the young stranger. Still, when they left to drive to the church, the old woman said, "I can't bear the disgrace," and she sent her soldiers after them to bring back her daughter and to strike down anyone that opposed them. However, Listener had pricked up his ears and had heard the words spoken in secret by the old woman.

"What shall we do?" he asked Fat Man, who knew exactly what to do. He spat on the ground once or twice, and part of the sea water he had drunk came flowing out behind the carriage and formed a huge lake that stopped the soldiers, and they drowned. When the sorceress saw this, she sent her knights in armor, but Listener heard the rattling of the armor and undid the blindfold of Sharp Eyes, who took a piercing look at the enemy, and they shattered like glass. Thus the prince and his bride could continue on their way undisturbed, and when the couple had been blessed in church, the six servants took their leave. "Your wishes have been fulfilled," they said. "So you don't need us anymore, and now we want to move on and seek our fortune."

Half an hour from the prince's castle was a village, and outside the village a swineherd was tending his pigs. When the prince and his wife arrived there, he said to her, "Do you know who I really am? I'm not the son of a king but a swineherd, and the man with the pigs over there is my father. You and I must now get to work and help my father look after the pigs."

The prince took lodgings at the inn and secretly told the innkeeper and his wife to take away his wife's royal garments during the night. When she awoke the next morning, she had nothing to put on, and the innkeeper's wife gave her an old skirt and a pair of woolen stockings. At the same time the woman acted as if she were doing the princess a great favor and said, "If it weren't for your husband, I wouldn't have given you a thing."

After that the prince's wife believed that he really was a swineherd, tended the pigs with him, and thought, I've deserved this because of my arrogance and pride. All of this lasted a week, by which time she could no longer stand it, for her feet had become all sore. Then some people came and asked whether she knew who her husband was. "Yes," she answered. "He's a swineherd, and he's gone out to do a little trading with ribbons and laces."

"Just come with us," they said. "We want to take you to him," and they brought her up to the castle.

When they entered the hall, her husband was standing there in his royal attire, but she did not recognize him until he took her into his arms, kissed her, and said, "I suffered a great deal for you, and it was only right that you should also suffer for me."

Now the wedding was truly celebrated, and you can imagine that the person who told this tale would have liked to have been there too.

◆ 135 ◆

The White Bride and the Black Bride

A WOMAN WAS WALKING with her daughter and stepdaughter over the fields to cut fodder when the dear Lord came toward them in the guise of a poor man and asked, "Which is the way to the village?"

"If you want to know," said the mother, "then look for it yourself." And her daughter added, "If you're worried about not finding it, then take a signpost with you."

However, the stepdaughter said, "Poor man, I'll show you the way. Come with me."

Since the mother and daughter had infuriated the dear Lord, he turned his back on them and cursed them so that they became black as night and ugly as sin. But God showed mercy to the poor stepdaughter and went with her to the village. When they drew close to the village, he gave her his blessing and said, "Choose three things for yourself, and I'll grant them to you."

The maiden said, "I'd like to be as beautiful and pure as the sun," and in no time she was as white and beautiful as the day.

"Then I'd like to have a money purse that is never empty," and the dear Lord gave her that as well but said, "Don't forget the best thing of all."

And she replied, "For my third wish, I want to live in the eternal kingdom of heaven after my death."

This wish was also granted, and then the Lord parted from her.

When the stepmother arrived home with her daughter and saw that they were both as black as coal and ugly, while the stepdaughter was white and beautiful, her heart turned even more evil, and she could think of nothing but how she might harm her stepdaughter. However, the stepdaughter had a brother named Reginer, whom she loved very much, and she told him everything that had happened.

One day Reginer said to her, "Dear sister, I want to paint your picture so that I may always see you before my eyes. My love for you is so great that I want to see you constantly."

"All right," she said, "but I beg of you not to let anyone else see the picture."

So he painted a portrait of his sister and hung it in his room, which was in the royal castle because he served the king as coachman. Every day he stood in front of the portrait and thanked God for his dear sister's good fortune.

It happened that the king's wife had just died, and she had been so beautiful that the king was greatly distressed because her equal could not be found anywhere. The court servants had noticed, however, that the coachman stood in front of a beautiful portrait every day, and since they envied him, they reported it to the king, who ordered the portrait to be brought to him. When he saw how the portrait resembled his wife in each and every way and was even more beautiful, he fell desperately in love with it. Consequently, he summoned the coachman and asked him whose picture it was. The coachman said that it was his sister, and the king decided to marry no other woman but her. He gave the coachman a carriage and horses and magnificent golden clothes and sent him to fetch his chosen bride.

When Reginer arrived with the news, his sister rejoiced, but the black maiden was jealous of her good fortune and became terribly annoyed. "What's the good of all your craftiness," she said to her mother, "if you can't bring about such good luck for me?"

"Be quiet," said the old woman. "I'll soon make things turn your way."

And through her witchcraft she clouded the eyes of the coachman so that he became half blind, and she stopped up the ears of the white maiden so that she became half deaf. After this had been done, they climbed into the carriage, first the bride in her splendid royal garments, then the stepmother with her daughter, while Reginer sat on the box to drive. When they had gone some distance, the coachman cried out:

"Cover yourself, my sister dear,
don't let the rain get you too wet.
Don't let the wind blow dust on you.
Take care, for you must look your very best
when you appear at your good king's request."

The bride asked, "What's my dear brother saying?"

"Ah," replied the old woman. "He said you should take off your golden dress and give it to your sister."

Then she took it off and put it on her sister, who gave her a shabby gray gown in return. They continued on their way, and after a while the brother called out again:

"Cover yourself, my sister dear,
don't let the rain get you too wet.
Don't let the wind blow dust on you.
Take care, for you must look your very best
when you appear at your good king's request."

The bride asked, "What's my dear brother saying?"

"Ah," replied the old woman. "He said you should take off your golden bonnet and give it to your sister."

Then she took off the bonnet, put it on the black maiden, and sat with her hair uncovered. They continued on their way, and after a while her brother called out once more:

"Cover yourself, my sister dear,
don't let the rain get you too wet.
Don't let the wind blow dust on you.
Take care, for you must look your very best
when you appear at your good king's request."

The bride asked, "What's my brother saying?"

"Ah," replied the old woman. "He said you should take a look out of the carriage."

Just then they happened to be crossing a bridge over a deep river. When the bride stood up and leaned out the window of the carriage, the other two pushed her out, and she fell into the middle of the water. At the very instant that she sank out of sight, a snow white duck arose out of the smooth glittering water and swam down the river. Since the brother had not noticed a thing, he kept driving until they reached the court. Then he brought the black maiden to the king as his sister and really thought it was her because his eyes were so clouded and he could only go by the glimmer of the golden clothes. When the king saw how abysmally ugly his intended bride was, he became furious and ordered the coachman to be thrown into a pit full of adders and snakes. However, the old witch managed to charm the king and deceive him through witchcraft, so that he allowed her and her daughter to stay. Indeed, the daughter gradually appeared quite nice to him, and thus he actually married her.

One evening, while the black bride was sitting on the king's lap, a white duck swam up the drain to the kitchen and said to the kitchen boy:

"Light a fire, little boy, light it quick,
for I must warm my feathers to not get sick."

The kitchen boy did as he was asked and lit a fire on the hearth. Then the duck came and sat down next to it, shook herself, and cleaned her feathers with her beak. While she sat there and made herself comfortable, she asked, "What's my brother Reginer doing?" The kitchen boy answered:

"With snakes and adders in a pit,
that's where he's been forced to sit."

Then she asked, "What's the black witch doing in the house?" The kitchen boy answered:

"She's nice and warm,
for the king has got her in his arms."

The duck said, "God have mercy!" and swam back down the drain.

The next evening she came again and asked the same questions, and on the third evening as well. The kitchen boy could not bear this any longer, went to the king, and revealed everything to him. The king, however, wanted to see for himself and went to the kitchen on the following evening. When the duck stuck her head out through the drain, he took his sword and cut her head off by the neck. All at once she turned into a most beautiful maiden and looked like the portrait that her brother had made of her. The king rejoiced, and since she was standing there soaking wet, he had fine clothes brought to her, which she put on. Then she told him how she had been betrayed through guile and deceit and how ultimately she had been thrown into the water.

Her first request was to have her brother taken out of the snake pit. When the king had fulfilled this request, he went into the room where the old witch sat and asked, "What kind of punishment does a woman deserve if she does something like the following?" Then he told her all about the past events. Yet, she was so distracted that she did not realize what was going on and said, "She deserves to be stripped naked and put into a barrel studded with nails. Then a horse should be hitched to the barrel and sent running out into the world."

This is what happened to her and her black daughter. But the king married the beautiful white bride and rewarded the faithful brother by making him a rich and respected man.

◆ 136 ◆

Iron Hans

ONCE UPON A TIME there was a king who had a large forest near his castle, and in the forest all sorts of game could be found. One day he sent a huntsman there to shoot a deer, but he did not return. "Perhaps he met with an accident," said the king, and on the following day he sent two other huntsmen into the forest to look for the missing one, but they too did not return. So, on the third day the king assembled all his huntsmen and said to them, "Comb the entire forest and don't stop until you've found all three of them." But these huntsmen were never seen again, nor were the dogs from the pack of hounds that went with them. From that time on nobody dared venture into the forest, and it stood there solemnly and desolately, and only every now and then could an eagle or a hawk be seen flying over it.

This lasted for many years and then a huntsman, a stranger, called on the king seeking employment and offered to go into the dangerous forest. However, the king would not give his consent and said, "The forest is enchanted, and I'm afraid the same thing would happen to you that happened to the others, and you wouldn't return."

"Sire," replied the huntsman, "I'll go at my own risk. I don't know the meaning of fear."

So the huntsman went into the forest with his dog. It was not long before the dog picked up the scent of an animal and wanted to chase it, but after the dog had run just a few steps, it came upon a deep pool and could go no further. Then a long, bare arm reached out of the water, grabbed the dog, and dragged it down. When the huntsman saw that, he went back to the castle and got three men to come with buckets and bale the water out of the pool. When they could see to the bottom, they discovered a wild man lying there. His body was as brown as rusty iron, and his hair hung over his face down to his knees. They bound the wild man with rope and led him away to the castle, where everyone was amazed by him. The king had him put in an iron cage in the castle courtyard and forbade anyone to open the cage under the penalty of death. The queen herself was given the key for safekeeping. From then on the forest was safe, and everyone could go into it again.

One day the king's son, who was eight years old, was playing in the courtyard and as he was playing, his golden ball fell into the cage. The boy ran over to it and said, "Give me back my ball."

"Only if you open the door," answered the man.

"No," said the boy. "I won't do that. The king has forbidden it." And he ran away.

The next day he came again and demanded his ball. The wild man said, "Open my door," but the boy refused.

On the third day, when the king was out hunting, the boy returned and said, "Even if I wanted to, I couldn't because I don't have the key."

"It's under your mother's pillow," said the wild man. "You can get it."

The boy, who wanted to have the ball again, threw all caution to the winds and brought him the key. It was difficult to open the door, and the boy's finger got stuck. When the door was open, the wild man stepped out, gave him the golden ball, and hurried away. But the boy became afraid, screamed, and called after him, "Oh, wild man, don't go away; otherwise, I'll get a beating!"

The wild man turned back, lifted him onto his shoulders, and sped into the forest with swift strides. When the king came home, he noticed the empty cage and asked the queen what had happened. She knew nothing about it and looked for the key, but it was gone. Then she called the boy, but nobody answered. The king sent people out into the fields to search for him, but they did not find him. By then it was not all that difficult for the king to guess what had happened, and the royal court fell into a period of deep mourning.

When the wild man reached the dark forest once again, he set the boy down from his shoulders and said to him, "You won't see your father and mother again, but I'll keep you with me because you set me free, and I feel sorry for you. If you do everything that I tell you, you'll be all right. I have plenty of treasures and gold, more than anyone in the world."

He made a bed out of moss for the boy, and the child fell asleep on it. The next morning the man led him to a spring and said, "Do you see this golden spring? It's bright and crystal clear. I want you to sit there and make sure that nothing falls in; otherwise, it will become polluted. I'll come every evening to see if you've followed my command."

The boy sat down on the edge of the spring, and once in a while he saw a golden fish or a golden snake, but he made sure that nothing fell in. While he was sitting there, his finger began to hurt him so much that he dipped it into the water without meaning to. He pulled it out quickly but saw that it had turned to gold, and no matter how hard he tried, he could not wipe off the gold. It was all in vain.

In the evening Iron Hans returned, looked at the boy, and said, "What happened to the spring?"

"Nothing, nothing," the boy answered, and held his finger behind his back so that the man would not see it.

But Iron Hans said, "You dipped your finger in the water. I'll let it go this time, but make sure that you don't let anything else fall in."

At the crack of dawn the next day the boy was already sitting by the spring and guarding it. His finger began hurting him again, and he brushed his head with it. Unfortunately a strand of his hair fell into the spring. He quickly pulled it out, but it had already turned completely into gold. When Iron Hans came, he already knew what had happened. "You've let a hair fall into the spring," he said. "I'll overlook it once more, but if this happens a third time, the spring will become polluted, and you'll no longer be able to stay with me."

On the third day the boy sat at the spring and did not move his finger even when it hurt him a great deal. However, he became bored and began looking at his face's reflection in the water. As he leaned farther and farther over to look himself straight in the eye, his long hair fell down from his shoulders into the water. He straightened up instantly, but his entire head of hair had already turned golden and shone like the sun. You can imagine how terrified the boy was. He took his handkerchief and tied it around his head so that the man would not be able to see it. When Iron Hans came, he already knew everything and said, "Untie the handkerchief."

The golden hair came streaming out, and no matter how much the boy apologized, it did not help. "You've failed the test and can no longer stay here. Go out into the world, and you'll learn what it means to be poor. However, since you're not bad at heart, and since I wish you well, I'll grant you one thing: whenever you're in trouble, go to the forest and call, 'Iron Hans,' then I'll come and help you. My power is great, greater than you think, and I have more than enough gold and silver."

Then the king's son left the forest and traveled over trodden and untrodden paths until he came to a large city. He looked for work there but could not find any, nor had he been trained in anything that might enable him to earn a living. Finally, he went to the palace and asked for work and a place to stay. The people at the court did not know how they might put him to good use, but they took a liking to him and told him to stay. At length the cook found work for him and had him carry wood and water and sweep away the ashes. Once, when nobody else was available, the cook told him to carry the food to the royal table. Since the boy did not want his golden hair to be seen, he kept his little cap on. The king had never seen anything like this and said, "When you come to the royal table, you must take off your cap."

"Oh, Sire," the boy answered, "I can't. I have an ugly scab on my head." The king summoned the cook, scolded him, and asked him how he could have taken such a boy into his service. He told the cook to dismiss him at once. The cook, however, felt sorry for him and had him exchange places with the gardener's helper.

Now the boy had to plant and water the garden, hoe and dig, and put up with the wind and bad weather. One summer day, while he was working in the garden all alone, it was so hot that he took off his cap to let the breeze cool his head. When the sun shone upon his hair, it glistened and sparkled so much that the rays shot into the room of the king's daughter, and she jumped up to see what it was. Then she spotted the boy and called to him, "Boy, bring me a bunch of flowers."

Hastily he put on his cap, picked a bunch of wildflowers, and tied them together. As he was climbing the stairs he came across the gardener, who said, "How can you bring the king's daughter a bunch of common flowers? Quick, get some others and choose only the most beautiful and rarest you can find."

"Oh, no," answered the boy. "Wildflowers have a stronger scent, and she'll like them better."

When he entered her room, the king's daughter said, "Take off your cap. It's not proper for you to keep it on in my presence."

He replied, as he had before, "I've got a scabby head."

However, she grabbed his cap and pulled it off. Then his hair rolled forth and dropped down to his shoulders. It was a splendid sight to see. He wanted to run away, but the king's daughter seized his arm and gave him a handful of ducats. He went off with them, but since he did not care for the gold, he gave them to the gardener and said, "Here's a gift for your children. They can have fun playing with them."

The next day the king's daughter called to him once again and told him to bring her a bunch of wildflowers, and as he entered her room with them, she immediately lunged for his cap and wanted to take it away from him, but he held it tight with both hands. Again she gave him a handful of ducats, but he did not keep them. Instead he gave them to the gardener, again as playthings for his children. The third day passed just like the previous two: she could not take his cap from him, and he did not want her gold.

Not long after this the country became involved in a war. The king assembled his soldiers but was uncertain whether he would be able to withstand the enemy, who was more powerful and had a large army. Then the gardener's helper said, "I'm grown up now and want to go to war. Just give me a horse."

The others laughed and said, "When we're gone, you can have your horse. We'll leave one for you in the stable."

When they had departed, he went to the stable and led the horse out. One foot was lame, and it limped *hippety-hop, hippety-hop*. Nevertheless, he mounted it and rode toward the dark forest. When he reached the edge of the forest, he yelled "Iron Hans" three times, so loudly that the trees resounded with his call. Immediately the wild man appeared and asked, "What do you want?"

"I want a strong steed, for I want to go to war."

"You shall have what you want and even more."

Then the wild man went back into the forest, and it was not long before a stableboy came out leading a horse that snorted through its nostrils and was so lively that it could barely be controlled. They were followed by a host of knights wearing iron armor and carrying swords that flashed in the sun. The young man gave the stableboy his three-legged horse, mounted the other, and rode at the head of the troop of knights. As he approached the battlefield a good part of the king's men had already fallen, and it would not have taken much to have forced the others to yield as well. So the youth charged forward with his troop of iron knights. They broke like a storm over the enemy soldiers, and the young man struck down everything in his way. The enemy took flight, but the young man remained in hot pursuit and did not stop until there was no one left to fight. However, instead of returning to the king, he led his troop back to the forest by roundabout ways and called Iron Hans.

"What do you want?" asked the wild man.

"Take back your horse and your troop, and give me my three-legged horse again." He got all that he desired and rode home on his three-legged horse.

When the king returned to his castle, his daughter came toward him and congratulated him on his victory.

"I'm not the one who brought about the victory," he said. "It was a strange knight, who came to my aid with his troop."

The daughter wanted to know who the strange knight was, but the king had no idea and said, "He went in pursuit of the enemy, and I never saw him after that."

She asked the gardener about his helper, and he laughed and said, "He's just returned home on his three-legged horse, and the others all made fun of him crying out, 'Here comes *hippety-hop, hippety-hop* again.' Then they asked, 'What hedge were you sleeping behind?' And he replied, 'I did my best, and without me things would have gone badly.' Then they laughed at him even more."

The king said to his daughter, "I'm going to proclaim a great festival that will last three days, and I want you to throw out a golden apple. Perhaps the unknown knight will come."

When the festival was announced, the young man went to the forest and called Iron Hans.

"What do you want?" he asked.

"I want to catch the princess's golden apple."

"It's as good as done," said Iron Hans. "You shall also have a suit of red armor and ride on a lively chestnut horse."

When the day of the festival arrived, the young man galloped forward, took his place among the knights, and went unrecognized. The king's daughter stepped up and threw a golden apple to the knights, but only he could catch it. However, as soon as he had it, he galloped away. On the second day Iron Hans provided him with a suit of white armor and gave him a white horse. Once again only he could catch the apple, and again he did not linger long but galloped away with it. The king became angry and said, "I won't allow this. He must appear before me and tell me his name." The king gave orders that his men were to pursue the knight if he caught the apple again, and if he did not come back voluntarily, they were to use their swords and spears on him.

On the third day the young man received a suit of black armor and a black horse from Iron Hans. Again he caught the apple, but this time the king's men pursued him when he galloped away with it. One of them got near enough to wound him with the point of his sword. Nevertheless, he escaped them, and his horse reared so tremendously high in the air that his helmet fell off his head, and they saw his golden hair. Then they rode back and reported everything to the king.

The next day the king's daughter asked the gardener about his helper.

"He's working in the garden. The strange fellow was at the festival too, and he didn't get back until last night. Incidentally, he showed my children three golden apples that he won there."

The king had the young man summoned, and when he appeared, he had his cap on. But the king's daughter went up to him and took it off. Then his golden hair swooped down to his shoulders, and he was so handsome that everyone was astonished.

"Are you the knight who came to the festival every day in a

different-colored armor and caught the three golden apples?" asked the king.

"Yes," he replied. "And here are the apples." He took them out of his pocket and handed them to the king. "If you want more proof than this, you can have a look at the wound that your men gave me as they pursued me. And I'm also the knight who helped you gain the victory over your enemy."

"If you can perform such deeds, you're certainly no gardener's helper. Tell me, who is your father?"

"My father is a mighty king, and I have all the gold I want."

"I can see that," said the king. "I owe you a debt of gratitude now. Is there any favor that I can do for you?"

"Yes," he replied. "You can indeed. You can give me your daughter for my wife."

Then the maiden laughed and said, "He doesn't stand on ceremony, does he? But I already knew from his golden hair that he wasn't a gardener's helper." Then she went over and kissed him.

The young man's mother and father came to the wedding and were filled with joy, for they had given up all hope of ever seeing their dear son again. And, while they were sitting at the wedding table, the music suddenly stopped, and the doors swung open as a proud king entered with a great retinue. He went to the young man, embraced him, and said, "I am Iron Hans and was turned into a wild man by a magic spell. But you released me from the spell, and now all the treasures that I possess shall be yours."

◆ 137 ◆

The Three Black Princesses

EAST INDIA WAS BESIEGED by an enemy that would not withdraw until it first received a ransom of six hundred talers. So it was announced in public that whoever could provide the money would become mayor. There was at that time a poor fisherman, who was fishing at sea with his son. The enemy came, took the son prisoner, and gave the fisherman six hundred talers for him. The father then went and gave the money to the lords of the city. The enemy departed, and the fisherman became mayor. Thereafter it was proclaimed that whoever did not address him as "Lord Mayor" would be hanged on the gallows.

The son escaped from the enemy and came to a large forest on a high mountain. The mountain opened, and he went into a large enchanted castle, where all the chairs, tables, and benches were draped in black. Then three princesses appeared. They were clad entirely in black but had a little white on their faces. They told him not to be afraid, for they would not harm him, and he could save them. He replied that he would gladly do so if only he knew how. They told him he was not to speak to them for one whole year, nor was he to look at them. If he wanted anything, he just had to ask for it, and if they were permitted to answer his questions, they would do so.

After he had been there for a long time, he said that he would like to go and see his father. They told him that he could go, but he was to take a purse of money with him, put on certain clothes, and return in a week. Then he was lifted into the sky, and before he knew it, he was in East India. However, his father was no longer in the fishing hut, so the son asked some people where the poor fisherman was. They told him that he must not say that or he would be taken to the gallows. Then he went to his father and said, "Fisherman, how did you get here?"

The father replied, "You mustn't say that. If the lords of the city hear you say that, you'll be taken to the gallows."

However, he would not stop saying it and was taken to the gallows. When he got there, he said, "My lords, grant me permission to go to the fishing hut." Once there, he put on his old fisherman garb, and then he returned to the lords and said, "Don't you see now that I'm the poor fisherman's son? This was the way I dressed when I earned a living for my mother and father."

They recognized him then and apologized and took him home with them. The son told them everything that had happened, how he got to the forest on a high mountain, how the mountain had opened and he had entered an enchanted castle where everything was black and where three young princesses had come to him who were all in black except for a little white on their faces, and how the princesses had told him not to be afraid and that he could save them. His mother warned that this might not be a good thing to do and told him to take a consecrated candle with him and to let some of its hot wax drop on their faces.

The son returned to the castle and was so fearful that he let the wax drop on their faces while they slept, and they all turned half white. The three princesses jumped up and cried, "You cursed dog, our blood shall cry out for vengeance! There is no man born now anywhere nor ever will be who can save us. But we still have three brothers bound by seven chains, and they shall tear you to pieces."

Then there was a shrieking throughout the castle, and he jumped out a window and broke his leg. The castle sank back into the earth, the mountain closed, and nobody knows where the castle once stood.

❖ 138 ❖

Knoist and His Three Sons

BETWEEN WERREL AND SOIST there lived a man named Knoist, and he had three sons. One was blind, the other was lame, and the third was stark naked. Once they were walking across a field and saw a hare. The blind one shot it. The lame one caught it, and the naked one stuck it into his pocket. Then they came to a tremendously large lake with three boats on it. One boat leaked, the other sank, and the third had no bottom to it. They went aboard the boat with no bottom. Then they came to a tremendously large forest, where they saw a tremendously large tree. In the tree was a tremendously large chapel, and in the chapel was a hornbeam sexton and a boxwood pastor, who dispensed holy water with cudgels.

Blessed is he who gets away
when the holy water comes his way.

❖ 139 ❖

The Maiden From Brakel

ONCE THERE WAS A MAIDEN FROM BRAKEL who went to Saint Anne's Chapel at the foot of the Hinnenberg. Since she wanted a husband and thought that nobody else was in the chapel, she sang:

Holy Saint Anne,
please help me get my man.
Oh, you know him, I'm sure.
He lives down by the Suttmer Gate;
his hair is yellow and quite pure.
Oh, you know him, I'm sure.

The sexton was standing behind the altar and heard her. So he called out in a shrill voice, "You won't get him, you won't get him!" The maiden thought that it was the child Mary standing beside

Mother Anne who had spoken. Hence, the maiden became angry and replied, "*Tra-la-la,* you stupid brat! Hold your tongue and let your mother speak."

◈ 140 ◈

The Domestic Servants

"WHERE ARE YOU GOING?"

"To Woelpe."

"I'm going to Woelpe, you're going to Woelpe. So then, let's go together."

"Do you also have a husband? What's his name?"

"Cham."

"My husband's named Cham, yours is Cham. I'm going to Woelpe, you're going to Woelpe. So then, let's go together."

"Do you also have a child? What's he called?"

"Scab."

"My child's called Scab. Yours is Scab. My husband's Cham. Yours is Cham. I'm going to Woelpe. You're going to Woelpe. So then, let's go together."

"Do you also have a cradle? What's your cradle called?"

"Hippodeige."

"My cradle's called Hippodeige. Yours is Hippodeige. My child's Scab. Yours is Scab. My husband's Cham. Yours is Cham. You're going to Woelpe. I'm going to Woelpe. So then, let's go together."

"Do you also have a servant? What's your servant called?"

"Do-It-Right."

"My servant's Do-It-Right. Your servant's Do-It-Right. My cradle's Hippodeige, yours is Hippodeige. My child's Scab, yours is Scab. My husband's Cham, your husband's Cham. I'm going to Woelpe, you're going to Woelpe. So then, let's go together."

◈ 141 ◈

The Little Lamb and the Little Fish

ONCE UPON A TIME there was a little brother and a little sister who loved each other with all their hearts. However, their real mother was dead, and they had a stepmother who was not good to them and secretly did all she could to hurt them. It happened that one day the two of them were playing with other children on a meadow in front of the house, and in the meadow was a pond that bordered on one side of the house. The children ran around it, caught each other, and played a counting-out game.

"Eenie, meenie, let me live,
my little bird to you I'll give.
The bird will pick up straw for me.
The straw I'll give the cow to eat.
The cow will make me lots of milk.
I'll give the baker all the milk,
who'll bake my cat a cake so nice,
and then the cat will catch some mice.
The mice I'll hang and let them smoke
before I take one big slice!"

As they played this game they stood in a circle, and when the word "slice" fell on one of them, he had to run away, and the others ran after him until they caught him. While they were merrily running around, the stepmother watched from the window and became annoyed. Since she understood witchcraft, she cast a spell on the brother and sister, and turned the little boy into a fish and the little girl into a lamb. The little fish swam about in the pond and was sad. The little lamb ran about in the meadow and was so distressed that she ate nothing. She would not even touch a blade of grass.

A long time passed, and strangers came as guests to the castle. The treacherous stepmother thought, Now's the time. So she called the cook and said to him, "Go and fetch the lamb from the meadow and slaughter it. Otherwise, we'll have nothing for the guests."

The cook went to the meadow, got the little lamb, led her to the kitchen, and tied her feet. The lamb bore all this patiently. As the cook took his knife and began to sharpen it on the doorstep in order to kill the lamb, she noticed a little fish swimming back and forth in the water in front of the gutter and looking up at her. It was her little brother, for when he had seen the cook leading the little lamb away, he had swum along in the pond up to the house. Then the little lamb called to him:

"Oh, brother in the pond so deep,
my heart is torn, and I must weep.
The cook's about to take his knife
and bring an end to my short life."

The little fish answered:

"Oh, sister way up high,
you make me sad and want to cry,
while in this pond I must swim."

When the cook heard that the little lamb could speak and was uttering such sad words to the little fish down in the pond, he became frightened and concluded that the lamb was not a real one but one that had been bewitched by the wicked woman of the house. Then the cook said, "Don't worry. I won't slaughter you."

So he took another animal and prepared it for the guests. Then he led the little lamb to a kind peasant woman and told her everything he had seen and heard. The woman happened to have been the wet nurse of the little girl and guessed at once who the lamb was and went with her to a wise woman. There the wise woman pronounced a blessing over the lamb and the fish so that they soon regained their human form. Afterward she took both of them to a little cottage in a large forest, where they lived by themselves but were content and happy.

◈ 142 ◈

Simelei Mountain

THERE WERE ONCE TWO BROTHERS, one rich and the other poor. The rich one, however, gave nothing to the poor brother, who barely supported himself by dealing in grain. Things often went so badly for him that his wife and children would have to go without bread.

One day, as he was going through the forest with his wheelbarrow, he noticed a big bald mountain off to the side. Since he had never seen it before, he stopped in amazement and gazed at it. While he was standing there, he saw twelve big, rough men coming toward him. Since he thought that they might be robbers, he pushed his wheelbarrow into the bushes, climbed a tree, and waited to see what would happen. The twelve men went up to the mountain and cried, "*Semsi* Mountain, *Semsi* Mountain, open up."

Immediately the bald mountain opened in the middle, and the twelve men entered. Once they were inside, the mountain closed. After a short while, however, it opened up again, and the men came out carrying heavy sacks on their backs. After they were all out in the open, they said, "*Semsi* Mountain, *Semsi* Mountain, close together." Then the mountain closed, and there was no more sign of an entrance. The twelve men departed, and when they were completely out of sight, the poor man climbed down from the tree, curious to know what secret things might be hidden in the mountain. So he went up to the mountain and said, "*Semsi* Mountain, *Semsi* Mountain, open up," and the mountain opened before him. Then he entered, and the entire mountain was a cavern filled with silver and gold, and in the rear were large piles of pearls and glistening jewels heaped on top of each other like grain. The poor man did not know what to do, nor whether he should take any of the treasure. Finally, he filled his pockets with gold, but he left the pearls and jewels alone. When he came out again, he repeated the words "*Semsi* Mountain, *Semsi* Mountain, close together." Then the mountain closed, and he went home with his wheelbarrow. Now his worries disappeared, and he could buy bread and even wine for his wife and children. He lived happily and honestly, gave to the poor, and was kind to everyone. However, when he ran out of money, he went to his brother, borrowed a bushel measure, and fetched more gold. Yet, he refrained from touching any of the precious jewels. When he needed some more gold a third time, he borrowed the bushel measure from his brother once again. But the rich man had long been jealous of his brother's fortune and the beautiful way he had built up his house. He had also been puzzled by his brother's sudden wealth and his need for the bushel measure. So he thought of a trick, and he covered the bottom of the measure with sticky wax. When the measure was returned to him, there was a gold coin stuck to it. Immediately he went to his brother and asked him, "What have you been doing with the measure?"

"I've been measuring wheat and barley," said the other.

Then the rich one showed him the gold coin and threatened to take him to court about this unless he told him the truth. So the poor brother told him how everything had happened. The rich brother had a wagon hitched up at once and drove to the mountain with the idea of taking more advantage of this wonderful opportunity than had his brother and bringing back quite different treasures. When he arrived at the mountain, he cried out, "*Semsi* Mountain, *Semsi* Mountain, open up." The mountain opened, and he went inside, where he found all the treasures in front of him. For a long time he could not make up his mind what to grab first. Finally, he took as many jewels as he could carry. He was about to leave with his load of jewels, but his heart and mind had become so occupied by the treasures that he had forgotten the name of the mountain and called out, "*Simelei* Mountain, *Simelei* Mountain, open up." But that was not the right name, and the mountain did not budge and remained closed. Then he became frightened, but the more he tried to recall the name, the more confused his thoughts became, and the treasures were of no use to him at all. That evening the mountain opened up, and the twelve robbers entered. When they saw him, they laughed and cried out, "Well, we've finally caught our little bird! Did you think we hadn't noticed that you had slipped in here three times. Maybe we weren't able to catch you then, but you won't escape us now."

The rich man screamed, "It wasn't me, it was my brother!"

But no matter what he said, no matter how he pleaded for his life, they would not listen, and they cut off his head.

◈ 143 ◈

Going Traveling

ONCE UPON A TIME there was a poor woman who had a son. He wanted to go traveling very much, but his mother said, "How can you travel when we have no money whatsoever to give you?"

Then the son said, "I'll get along all right. I'll just keep saying 'not much, not much, not much.' "

So he walked for some time and kept saying, "Not much, not much, not much." Then he came to a group of fishermen and said, "God help you. Not much, not much, not much."

"What did you say, fellow, 'not much'?" And, indeed, when the fishermen pulled in their nets, they had not caught much fish. So one of them beat the young fellow with a stick and said, "Now you've seen how much I can thresh, haven't you?"

"But what should I say?" asked the young man.

"You should say, 'Catch a lot, catch a lot.' "

Then he again walked for some time and kept saying, "Catch a lot, catch a lot," until he came to a gallows, where a poor sinner was about to be hanged. Then he said, "Good morning, catch a lot, catch a lot."

"What did you say, fellow? 'Catch a lot'? Do you think the world needs more wicked people? Aren't there enough?"

Again he was given a good beating.

"But what should I say?"

"You should say, 'May God comfort the poor soul.' "

So the young man continued on his way and kept saying, "May God comfort the poor soul." Now he came to a ditch, where a knacker was standing and skinning a horse. The young man said, "Good morning, may God comfort the poor soul."

"What did you say, you nasty fellow?" And he gave the youth such a blow on the head with his skinning hook that he was dazed and could not see.

"But what should I say?"

"Stay there in the ditch, you carcass."

Then he continued on his way and kept saying, "Stay there in the ditch, you carcass. Stay there in the ditch, you carcass." Soon he came to a wagon carrying a load of people and said, "Good morning, stay there in the ditch, you carcass."

The wagon then fell into a ditch, and the driver took his whip and gave the young fellow such a beating that he had to crawl home to his mother. And he never went traveling again as long as he lived.

◆ 144 ◆

The Donkey

THERE ONCE LIVED A KING AND QUEEN who were rich and had everything they desired except children. The queen lamented day and night because of this, saying, "I'm like a field on which nothing grows."

Finally, God fulfilled her wishes. However, when the baby was born, it did not look like a human child but like a young donkey. When the mother saw it, she really began to lament and screamed that she would rather have had no child at all than to have had a donkey, and she ordered the donkey to be thrown into the water so the fish could eat him up.

But the king said, "No. Since God has given him to us, then he shall be my son and heir. After my death he shall sit on the royal throne and wear the royal crown."

So the donkey was brought up at court. As he got bigger his ears also grew quite high and straight. Otherwise, he had a cheerful disposition, was frisky, played, and was especially fond of music. At one time he went to a famous minstrel and said, "Teach me your art so that I can play the lute as well as you."

"Ah, my dear young lord," answered the minstrel, "this will be difficult for you. Your fingers aren't really made for it. They are much too big, and I'm afraid you'd break the strings."

Yet, the donkey would not be dissuaded, for he was determined to learn how to play the lute. He was diligent and persistent, and at last he learned how to play as well as the master himself.

One day the young lord was in a contemplative mood and went out for a walk. He came to a spring and looked at his donkey shape reflected in water that was as clear as a mirror. He was so distressed by the sight that he decided to go out into the wide world and to take only one trusted companion with him.

So they wandered here and there and finally came to a country ruled by an old king who had just one daughter, but she was exceedingly beautiful. The donkey said, "This is where we shall stay awhile," and he knocked on the gate and cried, "There's a guest out here! Open up and let him in."

When the gate did not open, he sat down, took his lute, and began playing a lovely tune with his two forefeet. The gatekeeper's eyes opened in astonishment, and he ran to the king and said, "There's a young donkey sitting outside the front gate. It's playing the lute like a great expert."

"Then let the musician come in," said the king.

When the donkey entered, however, everyone began to laugh at the lute player. He was directed to sit down and eat with the servants, but he refused and said, "I'm not a common barnyard donkey. I'm of noble birth."

"If this is what you are," they said, "then sit down with the knights."

"No," he said. "I'll sit with the king."

The king laughed and showed his good humor. "Yes, indeed. You may have your way, donkey. Come here to me." And soon after, he asked, "Donkey, how do you like my daughter?"

The donkey turned his head, looked at her, nodded, and said, "Exceptionally well. I've never seen anyone as beautiful as she is."

"Well, you shall sit next to her," said the king.

"That's fine with me," said the donkey, and sat down next to her, ate and drank, and showed that he could conduct himself in a courteous and proper manner.

After the noble animal had spent quite some time at the king's court, he thought, What's the use of all this? You've got to return home. He lowered his head sadly, went before the king, and asked his permission to depart. However, the king had taken a liking to him and said, "My little donkey, what's the matter with you? You look as sour as a jug of vinegar. Stay with me. I'll give you anything your heart requests. Do you want gold?"

"No," said the donkey and shook his head.

"Do you want some fine, valuable things?"

"No."

"Do you want half my kingdom?"

"Ah, no."

"If only I knew what would make you happy," said the king. "Do you want my beautiful daughter for your wife?"

"Oh, yes," said the donkey. "I'd be delighted to have her for my wife," and suddenly he was quite cheerful and in good spirits, for that was exactly what he had desired.

Soon a huge and splendid wedding was held, and that night, when the bride and bridegroom were led to their bedchamber, the king wanted to know whether the donkey would conduct himself in a nice and polite manner, and he ordered a servant to hide himself in their room. When the two were inside, the bridegroom bolted the door and looked around. Once he was convinced that they were completely alone, he threw off the donkey skin, and all at once he stood there as a handsome young prince.

"Now you see who I am," he said, "and you also see that I'm worthy of you."

The bride was happy, gave him a kiss, and loved him with all her heart. When morning came, he jumped up, put on his donkey skin again, and nobody would have guessed what lay beneath it. Soon the old king came along.

"Goodness!" he cried. "The donkey's already wide-awake." Then, turning to his daughter, he said, "You probably regret that you weren't wed to a real man, don't you?"

"Oh, no, Father, I love him as if he were the handsomest man in the world, and I want to keep him for the rest of my life."

The king was puzzled by this, but then the servant, who had concealed himself, came to him and told him everything.

"I don't believe it," said the king.

"Well, keep tonight's watch yourself, and then you shall see it with your own eyes. My advice to you, Your Majesty, is to take his skin away from him and throw it into a fire. Then he'll certainly have to reveal himself in his true form."

"That's good advice," said the king, and that night, while they were sleeping, he crept into their room, and when he came to their bed, he saw a noble-looking young man resting in the moonlight and the skin lying discarded on the ground. So he took it away and ordered a tremendous fire to be made outside. Then he threw the skin into the fire and remained there until it was entirely burned to ashes. Since he wanted to see what the young man would do when he discovered the theft, he stayed awake the whole night and lay in wait. When the young man had slept his fill, he got up with the first rays of the sun and wanted to put on his donkey skin, but he could not find it anywhere. So he was horrified and overcome by sadness and dread. "Now I must find some way to flee," he said.

However, when he left the room, the king was standing there and said, "My son, why are you in such a hurry? What do you intend to do? Stay here. You're such a handsome man, and I don't want you to leave. I'll give you half my kingdom now, and after my death you'll get all of it."

"Well," said the young man, "since I want everything that began well to end well, I'll stay with you."

Then the old man gave him half the kingdom, and when he died a year later, the young man had all of it. Then, after the death of his own father, he received yet another kingdom and lived in great splendor.

◆ 145 ◆

The Ungrateful Son

ONCE A MAN AND HIS WIFE were sitting by the entrance to their house. They had a roasted chicken in front of them and were about to eat it when the man saw his father coming toward them. So the man quickly grabbed the chicken and hid it because he did not want to give him any. The old man came, had a drink, and went away. As the son reached to put the roasted chicken back on the table, he found that it had turned into a toad, which then sprang onto his face, sat there, and would not leave him. If anyone tried to take it off, the toad would look at the person viciously as if it wanted to spring right into his face too. So nobody dared touch it. And the ungrateful son had to feed the toad every day; otherwise, it would have eaten away part of his face. Thus the son wandered about the world without a moment of rest.

◆ 146 ◆

The Turnip

ONCE UPON A TIME there were two brothers, both of whom served as soldiers. One was rich, the other poor. Since the poor brother wanted to improve his circumstances, he left the army and became a farmer. He dug and hoed his little piece of ground and planted turnip seeds. As the turnips began to grow, one became large and strong and noticeably fatter than the others. It seemed as if it would not stop growing at all. Soon it was called the queen of all turnips, because nobody had ever seen one like it, nor will anybody ever see one like it again. At last it became so big that it filled an entire wagon by itself, and two oxen were needed to pull it. The farmer did not know what to do with the turnip, nor did he know whether it would bring him luck or misfortune. Finally, he thought, If you sell it, you won't get anything worth much. And, if you eat it, you might as well eat the small turnips, which are just as good. The best thing would be to bring it to the king. That way you can honor him with a gift.

So he loaded the turnip on his wagon, hitched up two oxen, brought it to court, and gave it to the king.

"What kind of a rarity do we have here?" asked the king. "I've seen many strange things in my life, but I've never seen such a monstrosity as this. What kind of a seed did it grow from? Or do you have a green thumb and are lady fortune's favorite son?"

"Oh, no," the farmer replied. "I'm not fortune's favorite son. I'm just a poor soldier who gave up the army life because I could no longer support myself. Now I've taken up farming. You probably know my brother, Your Majesty. He's rich, but nobody pays attention to me because I have nothing."

Then the king took pity on him and said, "You shall be relieved of your poverty and shall receive such gifts from me that will make you the equal of your brother." So he gave him a great deal of gold, fields, meadows, and herds, and made him so terribly rich that his brother's wealth could no longer match his at all.

When the brother heard what he had acquired with a single turnip, he became jealous and pondered ways to get fortune to smile on him too. However, he wanted to plan everything in a more clever way. So he took gold and horses and brought them to the king, for he was firmly convinced that the king would give him a much larger present in return. After all, if his brother had obtained so much for a turnip, he would certainly get many more beautiful things.

The king accepted his gifts and said that he could think of nothing better or rarer to give him than the large turnip. So the rich brother had the turnip loaded on his wagon and driven to his home. Once there he did not know on whom to vent his anger and frustration. Finally, some evil thoughts came to him, and he decided to kill his brother. He hired murderers and showed them a place where they were to ambush his brother. Afterward he went to his brother and said, "Dear brother, I know where there's a secret treasure. Let's dig it up and divide it among us."

The brother liked the idea and went with him without suspecting a thing. However, when they went out into the fields, the murderers fell upon him, tied him up, and were about to hang him from a tree when they heard loud singing and hoofbeats in the distance. They became frightened for their lives and hastily shoved their prisoner head over heels into a sack. Then they hoisted it up on a branch and took flight. But soon the prisoner was at work and managed to make a hole in the sack through which he could poke his head. Then who should happen upon the way but a wandering scholar, a young fellow, riding along the road through the forest and singing a merry song. When the man up in the tree noticed that someone was passing below, he cried out, "Welcome! You've come just at the right time."

The scholar looked all around him but could not detect where the voice was coming from. Finally, he said, "Who's calling me?"

The man in the tree answered from above, "Lift your head. I'm sitting up here in the sack of wisdom, where I've learned great things in only a short time. Compared to this, all schools are like a bag of hot wind. Soon I shall have learned all there is to know. Then I'll climb down from the tree and be wiser than all other human beings. I understand the stars and the signs of the zodiac, the movements of the wind, the sand in the sea, the curses for sickness, and the power of herbs, birds, and stones. If you could be here in the sack just once, then you'd know the glorious feeling that flows from the sack of wisdom."

When the scholar heard all this, he was astounded and said, "Blessed be this hour in which I have found you! Would it be possible for me to get into the sack for a little while?"

The man in the tree answered as if he did not like this idea. "I'll let you do it for a short time if you pay me and speak sweetly, but you'll have to wait another hour because there's still something more that I have to learn."

The student waited a little while, but he became impatient and begged to be let in because his thirst for knowledge was so over-whelming. The man in the tree pretended to give in to the scholar finally and said, "In order for me to leave the house of wisdom, you must lower the sack by the rope. Then you may climb in."

So the scholar lowered the sack, untied it, and set the man free. Next he cried out, "Now pull me up quickly," and he sought to get into the sack feet first.

"Stop!" said the other. "That's not the way." He grabbed the scholar's head and shoved him upside down into the sack. After that he tied the sack and hoisted the disciple of wisdom up the tree by the rope. Then he swung him back and forth in the air and said, "How's it going, my dear fellow? You see, I'm sure you already feel wisdom coming and are getting valuable experience. Sit there nice and quiet until you get wiser."

Upon saying this, he mounted the scholar's horse and rode away. An hour later, however, he sent somebody to let the scholar down.

❖ 147 ❖

The Rejuvenated Little Old Man

AT THE TIME WHEN our Lord still walked on the earth, he stopped with Saint Peter one evening at the house of a blacksmith and received lodging for the night. Now, it happened that a poor beggar, suffering greatly from old age and illness, entered this house and asked for alms from the blacksmith. Saint Peter took pity on him and said, "Lord and Master, may it please you, cure him of his sufferings so he can earn his own living."

Then the Lord said gently to the blacksmith, "Lend me your forge, and put some coals on the fire. I want to make this sick old man young again."

The blacksmith was quite willing, and Saint Peter pumped the bellows, and when the fire sparkled and was in full blaze, the Lord took the little old man and shoved him into the forge, right in the middle of the glowing fire, so that he became as red as a rosebush and praised God in a loud voice. Afterward the Lord stepped over to the water tub and dunked the glowing little man in it so that he was completely covered by the water, and when he was nice and properly cooled off, the Lord gave him his blessing. Then, lo and behold, the little man jumped out of the tub and was straight, sound, and fit as a young man of twenty. The blacksmith, who had watched everything closely and carefully, invited them all to supper. His old, half-blind, hunchbacked mother-in-law now went over to the rejuvenated man and asked him earnestly whether the fire had burned him badly. He answered that he had never felt better and that the flames had been like the cool morning dew.

The young man's words kept ringing in the ears of the old woman all night, and early the next morning, after the Lord had thanked the blacksmith and had gone on his way, it occurred to the blacksmith that he could make his mother-in-law young since he had watched everything very carefully and since everything involved the skills of a blacksmith. Therefore, he called his mother-in-law to see whether she wanted to walk sprightly again like a girl of eighteen. Well, since everything had turned out so well for the young man, she said, "With all my heart." So the blacksmith made a big fire and shoved the old woman into the forge. She wriggled this way and that and cried bloody murder.

"Sit still! Why are you crying and jumping around? I haven't pumped the bellows enough yet."

Upon saying this, he pumped the bellows again until all her rags caught fire. The old woman would not stop shrieking, and the blacksmith thought, This isn't working out quite right. So he pulled her out and threw her into the water tub. Then she screamed so loudly that the blacksmith's wife and daughter-in-law heard it upstairs in the house. They both ran downstairs and saw the old woman, who was lying doubled-up in pain and howling and groaning. Her wrinkled and shriveled face had lost its shape.

At the sight of this the two women, who were both with child, became so upset that they gave birth that very night to two boys who were not shaped like human beings but like apes. They ran off into the forest, and it is from them that we have the race of apes.

◆ 148 ◆

The Animals of the Lord and the Devil

THE LORD GOD HAD CREATED ALL THE ANIMALS and had selected the wolves for his dogs. However, he had forgotten to create the goat. Then the devil got ready to create as well and made goats with long fine tails. Yet, when they went out to graze, they usually caught their tails in the brier bushes, and the devil always had to go to the trouble of disentangling them from the bushes. Finally, he became so fed up that he went and bit off the tail of each goat, as you can still see today by their stumps.

Now he could let them graze alone. But it happened that the Lord God saw how they soon took to gnawing away at the fruit trees. Then they damaged the precious vines and spoiled other tender plants. He became so disturbed by this that, out of kindness and mercy, he set loose his wolves, and they soon tore apart the goats that went there. When the devil learned of this, he appeared before the Lord and said, "Your creatures have torn mine apart."

The Lord replied, "Why did you create them to do damage?"

"I couldn't help it," said the devil. "Just as my own inclinations tend toward destruction, my own creatures can have no other nature but this. So now you'll have to pay me compensation."

"I'll pay you as soon as the oak leaves fall. Come to me then, and your money will be ready."

When the oak leaves had fallen, the devil came and demanded his due. But the Lord said, "In the Church at Constantinople there's a tall oak tree that still has all its leaves."

The devil departed, cursing in rage, and began to search for the oak tree. He wandered about in the wilderness for six months before he found it, and when he returned, all the other oak trees were covered with green leaves again. So he had to forget about his compensation. In his anger he poked out the eyes of the remaining goats and replaced them with his own.

This is why all goats have devil's eyes and bitten-off tails and why the devil likes to appear in their shape.

◆ 149 ◆

The Beam

ONCE UPON A TIME there was a magician who was standing in the middle of a large crowd of people and performing marvelous tricks. Among other things, he made a rooster appear, lift a heavy beam, and carry it as though it were as light as a feather. However, there was a girl who had just found a four-leaf clover, and it made her so sharp-minded that she could see through any kind of deception. Consequently, she saw that the beam was nothing but a straw, and she cried out, "Don't you people see that the rooster's carrying a mere piece of straw and not a beam?"

As soon as she said this, the magic vanished, and the people saw what was what and chased the magician away, with scorn and contempt. However, he was filled with rage and said, "I'll get my revenge."

Time passed, and the girl was about to be married. She got dressed up and marched through the fields in a large procession to the village where the church was. All at once, the procession came to a brook overflowing its banks, and there was no bridge or plank to cross it. The bride, however, was quick to react. She lifted her skirts and started to wade. When she got to the middle of the water, a man, who was standing nearby, called to her. It was the magician, and he began mocking her. "Hey! What's the matter with your eyes? You don't think that this is actually a brook, do you?"

Her eyes flew wide open, and she saw that she was standing in the middle of a field of blue flax in full bloom with her skirts raised high. Then everyone else saw this too, and their jeers and laughter forced her to flee.

◈ 150 ◈

The Old Beggar Woman

ONCE UPON A TIME there was an old woman. Of course, you've seen old women go begging before. Well, this woman begged too, and whenever she got something, she said, "May God reward you." Now, this beggar woman came to a door where a friendly young rascal was warming himself inside by a fire. As she stood shivering at the door the youngster spoke kindly to the old woman, "Come in, grandma, and warm yourself."

She entered but went too close to the fire so that her old rags began to burn without her noticing it. The youngster stood there and watched. He should have put out the fire, don't you think? And even if there was no water at hand, he should have wept out all the water in his body through his eyes. That would have made for two nice streams of water, and with that he could have extinguished the fire.

◈ 151 ◈

The Three Lazy Sons

A KING HAD THREE SONS, and since he loved them equally, he did not know which to choose to be king after his death. When the time of his death drew near, he summoned them to his bedside and said, "Dear children, I've been contemplating something for a while, and now I want to reveal it to you: I've decided that the laziest among you shall become king after me."

"Then, Father," said the oldest, "the kingdom belongs to me, for I'm so lazy that, when I'm lying on my back and want to sleep and a drop of rain falls on my eyes, I won't even shut them so I can fall asleep."

The second said, "Father, the kingdom belongs to me, for I'm so lazy that, when I'm sitting by the fire to warm myself, I'd sooner let my heels be burned than draw back my feet."

The third said, "Father, the kingdom is mine, for I'm so lazy that, if

I were about to be hanged and the noose were already around my
neck and someone handed me a sharp knife to cut the rope, I'd rather
let myself be hanged than lift my hand to cut the rope."

When the father heard that, he said, "You've outdone the others
and shall be king."

❖ 151a ❖

The Twelve Lazy Servants

TWELVE SERVANTS, who had done nothing all day long, did not want
to exert themselves even by evening. Rather, they lay down in the
grass and boasted about their laziness.

The first one said, "Your laziness doesn't concern me. I'm too busy
with my own. My chief occupation involves looking after my body. I
eat a good deal and drink even more. After I've had four meals, I fast
for a short time until I feel hungry again. This suits me best. I don't
like getting up early. When it gets toward noon, I already begin

looking for a place to rest. If my master calls, I pretend not to hear him, and if he calls a second time, I wait awhile before getting up, and even then I walk very slowly. This way life is bearable."

The second said, "I have to look after a horse, but I leave the bit in his mouth, and if I don't feel like it, then I don't feed him and say that he's already eaten. Instead I lie down in the oat bin and sleep for four hours. Afterward I stretch out one foot and move it a few times over the horse's body so that he's combed and groomed. Why go to more trouble for something like that? Still, my job's too bothersome for me."

The third said, "Why be bothered with work? Nothing comes of it. Once, I lay down in the sun and slept. It began to drizzle, but I didn't get up. I just let it rain and couldn't have cared less. Finally, there was a thunderstorm, and the rain came down so hard that it tore the hair off my head and washed it away, and I got a hole in my skull. I put a bandage over it, and then everything was all right. Since then I've had many injuries like that."

The fourth said, "If I have to take on some work, I first loaf about for an hour to conserve my strength. Then I begin very slowly and ask whether other people might be around to help me. Of course, I let them do most of the work while I just look on. But even that's too much for me."

The fifth said, "That's nothing special. Listen to this: I'm supposed to cart the manure from the stable and load it onto a wagon. I start off slowly, and when I get a little something on the pitchfork, I only lift it halfway up and then rest fifteen minutes before I finish my task. It's more than enough if I do a cartload a day. I have no desire to work myself to death."

The sixth said, "You should be ashamed of yourself. I'm not afraid of any kind of work, but I lie down for three weeks at a time and don't even take off my clothes. Why have buckles on my shoes? Let the shoes fall off my feet—it makes no difference to me. Whenever I want to climb a flight of stairs, I drag one foot slowly after the other onto the first step, and then I count the remaining steps so that I'll know where to rest."

The seventh said, "That won't work in my case. My master oversees my work, only he's away all day. Still, I don't neglect a thing: I creep instead of hurrying. It would take four hefty men to make me move faster, and they would have to push with all their might. Once I came to a place where six men were asleep, lying side by side. I lay down beside them and slept too. It was impossible to wake me up, and when they wanted to get me home, they had to carry me."

The eighth said, "It's clear to me that I'm the brightest here. If I find a stone lying in front of me, I don't take the trouble to lift my feet and step over it. I lie down on the ground, and if I get wet, muddy, and dirty, I continue to lie there until the sun dries me out. At most I turn myself so that it can shine on me."

The ninth said, "Here's something for you! Today my bread was in front of me, but I was too lazy to pick it up and nearly died of hunger. There was also a pitcher standing there, but it was so large and heavy that I refused to lift it and preferred to go thirsty. The thought of turning around was too much for me, and I spent the entire day lying flat on my back like a log."

The tenth said, "Laziness has brought me nothing but injuries, such as a broken leg and swollen calves. Three of us were lying by the roadside, and I stretched out my legs. Then someone came along with a wagon, and the wheels went over me. Of course, I could have pulled in my legs, but I didn't hear the wagon coming. The gnats were buzzing in my ears and crawling in my nose and out of my mouth. Who'd want to take the trouble to chase the vermin away?"

The eleventh said, "Yesterday I quit my job. I no longer wished to fetch heavy books for my master and take them away again. That was all I did the entire day. But to tell the truth, he didn't want to keep me any longer. He gave me my walking papers because I left his clothes lying in the dust, and they were all eaten by moths. It was all right with me."

The twelfth said, "Today I had to drive the wagon across country. I made myself a bed of straw on top of it and fell into a deep sleep. The reins slipped out of my hand, and when I awoke, the horse had nearly broken loose. The harness was gone, and so were the crupper, collar, bridle, and bit. Someone had come along and had made off with everything. Besides this, the wagon had got stuck in a ditch. I let it stay there and stretched myself out on the straw again. Finally, my master himself came and pushed the wagon out, and if he hadn't come, I would be lying not here but out there, sleeping nice and peacefully."

◆ 152 ◆

The Little Shepherd Boy

ONCE UPON A TIME there was a little shepherd boy who was famous far and wide for the wise answers he gave whenever anyone asked a question. The king of the country also heard about this, but he did not believe it and had the little boy summoned to his palace, where he said to him, "If you can answer the three questions that I'm going to put to you, then I shall regard you as my own child, and you shall live with me in my royal palace."

The little boy responded, "What are the three questions?"

The king said, "The first one is, How many drops of water are in the ocean?"

The little shepherd boy answered, "Your Majesty, have all the rivers on the earth dammed up so that no more drops of water can flow into the ocean until I have finished counting them. Then I shall tell you how many drops of water are in the ocean."

Thereupon the king said, "My next question is, How many stars are in the sky?"

The little shepherd boy said, "Give me a large sheet of white paper," and he proceeded to make so many fine dots on it with a pen that they could hardly be seen and were almost impossible to count. One would have gone blind trying to do so. Then the boy spoke. "There are as many stars in the sky as there are dots on this paper. Just count them."

But nobody could, and the king said, "The third question is, How many seconds does eternity have?"

The little shepherd boy said, "The Diamond Mountain is in Lower Pomerania, and it takes an hour to climb it, an hour to go around it, and an hour to go down into it. Every hundred years a little bird comes and sharpens its beak on it, and when the entire mountain is chiseled away, the first second of eternity will have passed."

Then the king spoke, "You have answered the three questions like a wise man, and from now on you shall live with me in my royal palace, and I shall regard you as my own child."

◈ 153 ◈

The Star Coins

THERE WAS ONCE A LITTLE GIRL whose father and mother had died, and she was so poor that she no longer had a room in which to live nor a bed in which to sleep. In the end, she had nothing more than the clothes on her back and a little piece of bread in her hand that some kind soul had given her. To be sure, she was good and pious, and since she had been forsaken by the entire world, she went out into the countryside, trusting that the good Lord would look after her. There she met a poor man, who said, "Ah, give me something to eat. I'm so hungry."

She handed him her entire piece of bread and said, "May God bless you," and continued on her way. Then she encountered a child who moaned and said, "My head is cold. Give me something so I can cover it." The girl took off her cap and gave it to the child. After she had gone a little way farther, she met another child, who had no jacket and was freezing. So she gave him hers, and later on another child asked her for her little dress, and she gave it to her as well. Finally, she reached a forest, and it had already become dark. Then another child came and asked for a little shirt, and the pious girl thought, It's dark, and nobody can see you. So you might as well give away your shirt. She took off the shirt and gave it away too. And, as she stood there, with nothing on whatsoever, the stars fell from the sky all at once, and they turned into hard shining coins. Though she had just given away her little shirt, she now had a new one of the finest linen. Thereupon, she gathered the coins together and was rich for the rest of her life.

❖ 154 ❖

The Stolen Pennies

ONE DAY A FATHER WAS SITTING with his wife and children, and they were having their noonday meal. A good friend, who had come to visit, was also eating with them. As they were sitting there the clock struck twelve, and the visitor saw the door open and a little child enter. He was very pale and clad in snow white clothes. He neither looked around nor said anything but went straight into the next room. Soon he returned and went out the door just as quietly as he had entered. On the second and third day the child came and went in the exact same way. Finally, the visitor asked the father who the beautiful child was that went into the room every day at noon.

"I didn't see it," he answered, "and I have no idea at all whose child it might be."

On the next day, when the child came again, the visitor pointed it out to the father, but he did not see it. Neither did the mother and the children. Then the visitor stood up, went to the door of the room, opened it a little, and looked inside. There he saw the child sitting on the floor, busily digging and rummaging in the cracks of the boards. However, as soon as the child noticed the visitor, he disappeared. Now, the visitor told the family what he had seen and gave an exact description of the child. The mother was then able to recognize the child and said, "Alas, it's my own dear child who died four weeks ago."

They ripped up the boards of the floor and found two pennies that the child had received from his mother at one time to give to a poor man, but the child had thought, You can buy yourself a biscuit for that. He had kept the pennies and had hidden them in the cracks of the floor. However, he had not been able to rest in his grave and had come back every day at noon to look for the pennies. So the parents gave the money to a poor man, and after that the child was never seen again.

❖ 155 ❖

Choosing a Bride

THERE WAS A YOUNG SHEPHERD who wanted very much to get married, and there were three sisters he knew, one just as beautiful as the next, so that it was difficult for him to make a choice. Indeed, he could not decide which one he preferred. So he went to his mother for advice, and she said, "Invite them all here, serve them cheese, and watch carefully how they cut into it."

The young man did as his mother said. The first sister devoured the cheese along with the rind. The second cut the rind from the cheese in haste, but because she was so hasty, she left a good part of the cheese on the rind that was thrown away. The third peeled the rind off neatly, not too much and not too little. The shepherd then told his mother what had happened, and she said, "Take the third one for your wife."

This he did, and they lived together happily and contentedly.

❖ 156 ❖

The Leftovers

ONCE UPON A TIME there was a maiden who was beautiful but lazy and neglectful. Whenever she was supposed to spin and there was a tiny knot, she became so irritated that she would tear out a whole bunch of the flax and throw it on the ground beside her. Now, she had a servant girl who was hardworking, and she collected the leftover flax, cleaned it, spun it fine, and wove it into a pretty dress.

A young man had been wooing the lazy maiden, and the wedding was about to take place. The night before the wedding there was a party, and the industrious servant girl danced merrily in her beautiful dress. Then the bride said:

"Ah, look how that girl does hop and spring,
and she's dressed herself in my leftover things!"

The bridegroom heard her and asked the bride what she had meant by it. Then she told him that the servant girl was wearing a dress made from the flax that she had thrown away. When the bridegroom heard that and realized how lazy the maiden was and how thrifty the servant girl was, he left the maiden standing there, went to the other girl, and chose her for his wife.

❖ 157 ❖

The Sparrow and His Four Children

A SPARROW HAD FOUR YOUNG ONES in a swallow's nest. When they were fledged, some bad boys broke up the nest, but fortunately all the young birds were swept away by a gust of wind. The father sparrow grieved that his sons had gone out into the world before he had been able to warn them about its many dangers or to give them good advice about how to fend for themselves.

In the fall a great many sparrows came together in a wheatfield. It was there that the father came upon his four sons once again, and he joyfully took them home with him.

"Ah, my dear sons, I was terribly concerned about you all summer, especially since you had been carried away by the wind before I could give you my advice. Now listen to my words, obey your father, and keep this in mind: Little birds must face great dangers!" Then he asked his oldest son where he had spent the summer and how he had fed himself.

"I lived in gardens and hunted caterpillars and little worms until the cherries turned ripe."

"Ah, my son," said the father, "such tasty morsels are not bad, but it can be dangerous searching for them. So, from now on, be on your guard, especially when people walk around the gardens carrying long green poles that are hollow inside and have a little hole on top."

"Yes, Father," said the son. "And what should I do when a green leaf is stuck over the little hole with wax?"

"Where have you seen this?"

"In a merchant's garden," the young bird said.

"Oh, my son," responded the father, "merchants are wily people! If you have been among such worldly folk, you have learned enough of their shrewd ways. But see that you use all this shrewdness well and do not become overconfident."

Then he asked the next son, "Where did you set up your home?"

"At court," said the son.

"Sparrows and silly little birds have no business being in such a place. There is too much gold, velvet and silk, armor and harnesses, sparrow hawks, screech owls, and falcons. Keep to the horse stables, where the oats are winnowed and threshed. Then you may be lucky enough to get your daily piece of bread and eat it in peace."

"Yes, Father," said this son, "but what shall I do if the stableboys make traps and set their gins and snares in the straw? Many a bird has gone away limp because of this."

"Where have you seen this?"

"At the court, among the stableboys."

"Oh, my son, those court servants are bad boys! If you have been at court and mixed with the lords and left no feathers behind, you have learned quite a bit and will know how to get by in the world. However, keep your eyes open all around you and above you, for often even the smartest dogs have felt the bite of wolves."

The father now took his third son to account, "Where did you try your luck?"

"I cast my lot on the highways and country roads, and sometimes I managed to find a grain of wheat or barley."

"Indeed, this is a fine meal," said the father, "but keep on the alert for signs of danger and look around carefully, especially when someone bends over and is about to pick up a stone. Then make sure you take off quickly."

"That's true," said the son. "But what should I do when someone may already be carrying a rock, or a stone from a wall, under his shirt or in his pocket?"

"Where have you seen this?"

"Among the miners, dear Father. When they return from work, they generally carry stones with them."

"Miners are workers and resourceful people! If you've been around mining boys, you've seen and learned something.

"Fly there if you will, but this you must know:
Mining boys have killed many a sparrow."

Finally, the father came to the youngest son. "You, my dear little chatterbox, you were always the silliest and weakest. Stay with me. The world is filled with crass and wicked birds that have crooked beaks and long claws. Stick to your own kind and pick up little spiders and caterpillars from the trees or cottages. This way you'll live long and be content."

"My dear Father, he who feeds himself without causing harm to other people will go far, and no sparrow hawk, falcon, eagle, or kite will do him harm if he faithfully commends himself, and his honestly earned food, each morning and evening to merciful God, who is the creator and preserver of all the birds of the forest and village. Likewise, it is He who hears the cries and prayers of the young ravens, for no sparrow or wren shall ever fall to the ground against His will."

"Where have you learned this?"

The son answered, "When the gust of wind tore me from you, I landed in a church. There I picked the flies and spiders from the windows and heard these words during a sermon. Then the Father of all sparrows fed me during the summer and protected me from misfortune and fierce birds."

"Faith, my dear son! If you take refuge in the churches and help clean out the spiders and the buzzing flies, and if you chirp to God like the young ravens and commend yourself to the eternal Creator, you will stay well, even if the entire world be full of wild and malicious birds.

"For he who worships God in every way,
who suffers, waits, is meek, and prays,
who keeps his faith and conscience pure,
God will keep him safe and sure."

◈ 158 ◈

The Tale About the Land of Cockaigne

IN THE DAYS OF THE LAND OF COCKAIGNE I went and saw Rome and the Lateran hanging from a small silk thread. There was also a man without feet who outran a fast horse, and a keen-edged sword that sliced a bridge in two. Then I saw a young ass with a silver nose chasing after two quick hares, and a large linden tree grew hotcakes. I saw a scrawny old goat carrying a hundred cartloads of fat on its body and sixty loads of salt. Now, haven't I lied enough? Then I saw a plow tilling the ground without horse or ox, and a one-year-old child threw four millstones from Regensburg to Trier and from Trier to Strasbourg, and a hawk swam across the Rhine, which he had a perfect right to do. Then I heard some fishes make such a noise together that it reached all the way to heaven, and sweet honey flowed like water from a deep valley to the top of a high mountain. All this was quite strange. Then there were two crows mowing a meadow, and I saw two gnats building a bridge, while two doves tore a wolf to pieces. Two children gave birth to two goats, and two frogs threshed grain together. Then I saw two mice consecrating a bishop and two cats scratching out a bear's tongue. Then a snail came and killed two wild lions. There was also a barber who shaved a woman's beard off, and two sucking babes who told their mother to keep quiet. Then I saw two greyhounds dragging a mill out of the water, and an old, worn-out horse stood there and said that it was all right. And in the courtyard there were four horses threshing grain with all their might, and two goats were heating the stove, and a red cow shoved the bread into the oven. Then a chicken crowed "*Cock-a-doodle doo!* The tale is done, *cock-a-doodle-doo!*"

❖ 159 ❖

A Tall Tale From Ditmarsh

I WANT TO TELL YOU SOMETHING. I saw two roasted chickens flying swiftly with their breasts turned toward heaven, their backs toward hell. An anvil and millstone swam across the Rhine very slowly and softly, and a frog sat on the ice eating a plowshare at Pentecost. There were three fellows on crutches and stilts who wanted to catch a hare. One was deaf, the second blind, the third dumb, and the fourth could not move either foot. Do you want to know how they did it? Well, first the blind one saw the hare trotting over the field. Then the dumb one called to the lame one, and the lame one caught the hare by the collar. There were some men who wanted to sail on land. They set their sails in the wind and sailed across the wide fields. As they sailed over a high mountain they were miserably drowned. A crab chased a hare, making it flee, and high on a roof was a cow who had climbed on top of it. In that country the flies are as large as the goats here. Open the window so the lies can fly out.

❖ 160 ❖

A Tale With a Riddle

THREE WOMEN WERE TRANSFORMED INTO FLOWERS that stood in a field. However, one of them was permitted to spend the night in her own home. Once, as dawn drew near and she had to return to her companions in the field to become a flower again, she said to her husband, "If you come and pick me this morning, I'll be set free, and I'll be able to stay with you forever." And this is exactly what happened.

Now the question is how her husband was able to recognize her, for the three flowers were all the same without any distinguishing mark. Answer: Since she had spent the night in her house and not in the field, the dew had not fallen on her as it had on the other two. This is how her husband was able to recognize her.

❖ 161 ❖

Snow White and Rose Red

A POOR WIDOW LIVED ALL ALONE in a small cottage, and in front of this cottage was a garden with two rosebushes. One bore white roses and the other red. The widow had two children who looked like the rosebushes: one was called Snow White and the other Rose Red. They were more pious and kind, more hardworking and diligent than any other two children in the world. To be sure, Snow White was more quiet and gentle than Rose Red, who preferred to run around in the meadows and fields, look for flowers, and catch butterflies. Snow White stayed at home with her mother, helped her with the housework, or read to her when there was nothing to do. The two children loved each other so much that they always held hands whenever they went out, and when Snow White said, "Let us never leave each other," Rose Red answered, "Never, as long as we live." And their mother added, "Whatever one of you has, remember to share it with the other."

They often wandered in the forest all alone and gathered red berries. The animals never harmed them and, indeed, trusted them completely and would come up to them. The little hare would eat a cabbage leaf out of their hands. The roe grazed by their side. The stag leapt merrily around them. And the birds sat still on their branches and sang whatever tune they knew. Nothing bad ever happened to the girls. If they stayed too long in the forest and night overtook them, they would lie down next to each other on the moss and sleep until morning came. Their mother knew this and did not worry about them.

Once, when they had spent the night in the forest and the morning sun had wakened them, they saw a beautiful child in a white, glistening garment sitting near them. The child stood up, looked at them in a friendly way, but went into the forest without saying anything. When they looked around, they realized that they had been sleeping at the edge of a cliff and would have certainly fallen over it if they had gone a few more steps in the darkness. Their mother told them that the child must have been the angel who watches over good children.

Snow White and Rose Red kept their mother's cottage so clean that it was a joy to look inside. In the summer Rose Red took care of the house, and every morning she placed two flowers in front of her mother's bed before she awoke, a rose from each one of the bushes. In the winter Snow White lit the fire and hung the kettle over the hearth. The kettle was made out of brass but glistened like gold because it was polished so clean. In the evening when the snowflakes fell, the mother said, "Go, Snow White, and bolt the door." Then they sat down at the hearth, and their mother put on her glasses and read aloud from a large book, while the two girls sat and spun as they listened. On the ground next to them lay a little lamb, and behind them sat a white dove with its head tucked under its wing.

One evening, as they were sitting together, there was a knock on the door, as if someone wanted to be let in. The mother said, "Quick, Rose Red, open the door. It must be a traveler looking for shelter." Rose Red pushed back the bolt thinking that it would be some poor man, but instead it was a bear. He stuck his thick black head through the door, and Rose Red jumped back and screamed loudly. The little lamb bleated, the dove fluttered its wings, and Snow White hid herself behind her mother's bed. However, the bear began to speak and said, "Don't be afraid. I won't harm you. I'm half frozen and only want to warm myself here a little."

"You poor bear," the mother said. "Lie down by the fire and take care that it does not burn your fur." Then she called out, "Snow White, Rose Red, come out. The bear won't harm you. He means well."

They both came out, and gradually the lamb and dove also drew near and lost their fear of him. Then the bear said, "Come, children, dust the snow off my coat a little."

So they fetched a broom and swept the fur clean. Afterward he stretched himself out beside the fire and uttered growls to show how content and comfortable he was. It did not take them long to all become accustomed to one another, and the clumsy guest had to put up with the mischievous pranks of the girls. They tugged his fur with their hands, planted their feet upon his back and rolled him over, or they took a hazel switch and hit him. When he growled, they just laughed. The bear took everything in good spirit. Only when they became too rough did he cry out, "Let me live, children.

Snow White, Rose Red,
would you beat your suitor dead?"

When it was time to sleep and the others went to bed, the mother said to the bear, "You're welcome, in God's name, to lie down by the hearth. Then you'll be protected from the cold and bad weather."

As soon as dawn arrived, the two girls let him go outside, and he trotted over the snow into the forest. From then on the bear came every evening at a certain time, lay down by the hearth, and allowed the children to play with him as much as they wanted. And they became so accustomed to him that they never bolted the door until their black playmate had arrived.

One morning, when spring had made its appearance and everything outside was green, the bear said to Snow White, "Now I must go away, and I shall not return the entire summer."

"But where are you going, dear bear?" asked Snow White.

"I must go into the forest and guard my treasures from the wicked dwarfs. In the winter, when the ground is frozen hard, they must remain underground and can't work their way through to the top. But now that the sun has thawed and warmed the earth, they will break through, climb out, search around, and steal. Once they get something in their hands and carry it to their caves, it will not easily see the light of day again."

Snow White was very sad about his departure. She unlocked the door, and when the bear hurried out, he became caught on the bolt and a piece of his fur ripped off, and it seemed to Snow White that she saw gold glimmering through the fur, but she was not sure. The bear hurried away and soon disappeared beyond the trees.

Some time after, the mother sent the girls into the forest to gather firewood. There they found a large tree lying on the ground that had been chopped down. Something was jumping up and down on the grass near the trunk, but they could not tell what it was. As they came closer they saw a dwarf with an old, withered face and a beard that was snow white and a yard long. The tip of the beard was caught in a crack of the tree, and the little fellow was jumping back and forth like a dog on a rope and did not know what to do. He glared at the girls with his fiery red eyes and screamed, "What are you standing there for? Can't you come over here and help me?"

"How did you get into this jam, little man?" asked Rose Red.

"You stupid, nosy goose," answered the dwarf, "I wanted to split the tree to get some wood for my kitchen. We dwarfs need but little food; however, it gets burned fast when we use those thick logs. We don't devour such large portions as you coarse and greedy people. I had just driven in the wedge safely, and everything would have gone all right, but the cursed wedge was too smooth, and it sprang out unexpectedly. The tree snapped shut so rapidly that I couldn't save my beautiful white beard. Now it's stuck there, and I can't get away. And all you silly, creamy-faced things can do is laugh! Uggh, you're just nasty!"

The girls tried as hard as they could, but they could not pull the beard out. It was stuck too tight.

"I'll run and get somebody," Rose Red said.

"Crazy fool!" the dwarf snarled. "Why run and

get someone? The two of you are already enough. Can't you think of something better?"

"Don't be so impatient," said Snow White. "I'll think of something." She took out a pair of scissors from her pocket and cut off the tip of his beard. As soon as the dwarf felt that he was free, he grabbed a sack filled with gold that was lying between the roots of the tree. He lifted it out and grumbled to himself, "Uncouth slobs! How could you cut off a piece of my fine beard? Good riddance to you!" Upon saying this, he swung the sack over his shoulder and went away without once looking at the girls.

Some time after this Snow White and Rose Red wanted to catch some fish for dinner. As they approached the brook, they saw something like a large grasshopper bouncing toward the water as if it wanted to jump in. They ran to the spot and recognized the dwarf.

"Where are you going?" asked Rose Red. "You don't want to jump into the water, do you?"

"I'm not such a fool as that!" the dwarf screamed. "Don't you see that the cursed fish wants to pull me in?" The little man had been sitting there and fishing, and unfortunately the wind had caught his beard, so that it had become entangled with his line. Just then a large fish had bitten the bait, and the feeble little dwarf did not have the strength to land the fish, which kept the upper hand and pulled him toward the water. To be sure, the dwarf tried to grab hold of the reeds and rushes, but that did not help too much. He was compelled to follow the movements of the fish and was in constant danger of being dragged into the water, but the girls had come just in the nick of time. They held on to him tightly and tried to untangle his beard from the line. However, it was to no avail. The beard and line were meshed together, and there was nothing left to do but to take out the scissors and cut off a small part of his beard. When the dwarf saw this, he screamed at them, "You birdbrains! You've disfigured my face like barbarians. It was not enough that you clipped the tip of my beard. Now you've cut off the best part. I won't be able to show myself among my friends. May you both walk for miles on end until the soles of your shoes are burned off!" Then he grabbed a sack of pearls that was lying in the rushes, and without saying another word, he dragged it away and disappeared behind a rock.

It happened that soon after this the girls were sent by their mother to the city to buy thread, needles, lace, and ribbons. Their way led over a heath which had huge pieces of rock scattered here and there. A large bird circled slowly in the air above them, flying lower and lower until it finally landed on the ground not far from a rock. Right after that they heard a piercing, terrible cry. They ran to the spot and saw with horror that the eagle had seized their old acquaintance the dwarf and intended to carry him away. The girls took pity on him and grabbed hold of the little man as tightly as they could. They tugged against the eagle until finally the bird had to abandon his booty. When the dwarf had recovered from his initial fright, he screeched at them, "Couldn't you have handled me more carefully? You've torn my coat to shreds. It was thin enough to begin with, but now it's got holes and rips all over, you clumsy louts!" Then he took a sack with jewels and once again slipped under a rock into his cave.

The girls were accustomed to his ingratitude and continued on their way. They took care of their chores in the city, and when they crossed the heath again on their way home, they surprised the dwarf, who had dumped his sack of jewels on a clean spot, not thinking that anyone would come by at such a late hour. The evening sun's rays were cast upon the glistening stones, which glimmered and sparkled in such radiant different colors that the girls had to stop and look at them.

"Why are you standing there and gaping like monkeys?" the dwarf screamed, and his ash gray face turned scarlet with rage. He was about to continue his cursing when a loud growl was heard and a black bear came trotting out of the forest. The dwarf jumped up in terror, but he could not reach his hiding place in time. The bear was already too near. Filled with fear, the dwarf cried out, "Dear Mister Bear, spare my life, and I'll give you all my treasures! Look at the beautiful jewels lying there. Grant me my life! What good is a small, measly fellow like me? You wouldn't be able to feel me between your teeth. Those wicked girls over there would be better for you. They're such tender morsels, fat as young quails. For heaven's sake, eat them instead!"

The bear did not pay any attention to the dwarf's words but gave the evil creature a single blow with his paw, and the dwarf did not move again.

The girls had run away, but the bear called after them, "Snow White, Rose Red, don't be afraid! Wait. I'll go with you!"

Then they recognized his voice and stopped. When the bear came up to them, his bearskin suddenly fell off, and there stood a handsome man clad completely in gold. "I am the son of a king," he said, "and I had been cast under a spell by the wicked dwarf who stole my treasures. He forced me to run around the forest as a wild bear, and only his death could release me from the spell. Now he has received his justly earned punishment."

Snow White was married to the prince, and Rose Red to his brother, and they shared the great treasures that the dwarf had collected in his cave. The old mother lived many more peaceful and happy years with her children. Indeed, she took the two rosebushes with her, and they stood in front of her window, and every year they bore the most beautiful roses, white and red.

❖ 162 ❖

The Clever Servant

A MASTER MAY CONSIDER HIMSELF FORTUNATE and may rest assured that his house will be well run if he has a clever servant who listens to his orders, but who then acts according to his own wisdom rather than carrying out his master's commands.

Once there was a servant like this named Hans, who was sent out by his master to look for a lost cow. He was gone a long time, and the master thought, Faithful Hans, he always does his utmost when I give him a task. However, when Hans still had not returned, his master feared that something might have happened to him and went out himself to look for him. He had to search for a long time. Finally, he spotted his servant running up and down in a large field.

"Well, my dear Hans," said the master when he had caught up with him, "have you found the cow that I sent you to get?"

"No, master," he answered. "I haven't found the cow, but I haven't looked for it either."

"Then what have you been looking for, Hans?"

"Something better, and fortunately I've also found it."

"What's that, Hans?"

"Three blackbirds," answered the servant.

"And where are they?" asked the master.

"One I can see, the other I can hear, and the third one I'm still chasing," answered the clever servant.

Learn a lesson from this. Don't worry about your master and his commands. Do whatever comes into your head and whatever pleases you. Then your actions will be just as wise as those of clever Hans.

❖ 163 ❖

The Glass Coffin

LET NO ONE EVER SAY that a poor tailor cannot advance far in the world and achieve great honors. He needs only to hit upon the right person and, most important, to have good luck. Once there was such a tailor, who was a pleasing and smart apprentice. He set out on his travels and wandered into a large forest, and since he did not know the way, he got lost. Night fell, and there was nothing left for him to do but to search for a place to sleep in this desolate spot. Of course, he could have made a bed on the soft moss, but his fear of wild animals would not have let him rest. Eventually, he decided to spend the night in a tree. He looked for a large oak tree, climbed to the top, and thanked God that he had carried his flatiron with him; otherwise, the wind that blew over the treetops would have swept him away.

After he had spent a few hours in the dark, not without shivering in his shoes, he saw a light shining from a place nearby. Since he thought that people might be living there and that he would feel better off with them than on the branches of a tree, he climbed down carefully and headed toward the light, which led him toward a small cottage made out of reeds and bushes. Bravely he knocked, and the door opened. By the glow of the light that issued forth, he could see an old, gray-haired little man clad in a coat sewn together with brightly colored patches.

"Who are you and what do you want?" the man asked with a snarling voice.

"I'm a poor tailor," the young man replied, "and I was overtaken by the night here in the wilderness. I beseech you to let me stay in your cottage until morning."

"Get on your way," responded the old man in a sullen tone. "I don't want to have anything to do with tramps. Find your lodging somewhere else."

With these words he intended to turn his back on the tailor, but the young man held him so tightly by his coattails and pleaded in such a touching way that the old man, who was not so cruel as he made himself seem, finally softened and took him into his cottage, where he gave the tailor something to eat and then directed him to a very good bed in a corner.

The tired tailor did not need to be rocked to sleep. Indeed, he slept like an angel until morning, and he would not have even considered getting up if he had not been startled by a loud noise, a terrible roaring and bellowing that penetrated the walls of the house. To his surprise, the tailor, moved by his courage, got dressed quickly and hurried outside, where he saw a large black bull and a beautiful stag in the midst of a violent fight near the little house. They charged at each other with such tremendous fury that the ground trembled from their trampling and the air resounded with their cries. For a long time it was unclear who would win the fight. Finally, the stag plunged his antlers into the body of his opponent, whereupon the bull sank to the ground with a horrible groan and was finished off by a few more thrusts from the stag.

The tailor, who had watched the battle with astonishment, continued to stand there motionless when the stag bounded over to him, and then, before he could escape, the stag lifted him up with his huge antlers. The tailor did not have any time to think about what was happening, for he was swiftly carried over hill and dale, mountain and valley, meadow and forest. He clutched the antlers with both hands and resigned himself to his fate. It seemed as if he were flying until finally the stag stopped in front of a rocky cliff and let the tailor slide gently to the ground. The tailor, who was more dead than alive, needed a long time to regain his composure. When he had more or less recovered, the stag, who was standing next to him, knocked his antlers against a door in the cliff with such force that it sprang open. Flames of fire shot out, followed by a great deal of smoke, which made him lose sight of the stag. The tailor did not know what to do or where to turn to escape this desolate spot and get back to people and society again. As he stood there, unable to make a decision, a voice sounded from inside the cliff and called to him, "Enter without fear. No harm will be done to you." To be sure, he wavered, but he was also driven by a mysterious power. So he obeyed the voice and went through an iron door and into a large, spacious hall. The ceiling, walls, and floor were made of glittering polished blocks of stone. Signs were engraved in the stone, which he could not decipher. Full of astonishment, he looked at everything and was just about to leave when the voice sounded once more and said to him, "Step upon the stone that lies in the middle of the hall. Your great fortune awaits you."

His courage had grown so much that he was not afraid to follow the order. The stone began to give way under his feet, and he sank slowly into the depths. When the tailor reached solid ground again and looked around, he found himself in a hall that was the same size as the previous one. However, there was even more to see and admire. In niches carved into the walls stood vases of transparent glass filled with a colored vapor or with blue steam. Two large glass chests sat facing each other on the floor of the hall, and they immediately aroused his curiosity. He walked over to one of them and peeked inside: in it he saw a beautiful dwelling, similar to a castle, surrounded by farmhouses, stables, barns, and a lot of other fine things. Everything was tiny but carefully and delicately made, as though carved with great precision by a skilled hand.

He would not have taken his eyes off this rarity if the voice had not spoken to him once more. It commanded him to turn around and look at the glass chest that stood across from him. His astonishment became even greater when he caught sight of an exceedingly beautiful maiden. She lay as if asleep, wrapped in her long blond hair, which seemed like a precious cloak. Her eyes were tightly shut. However, the bright complexion of her face and a ribbon that bobbed up and down as she breathed left no doubt that she was alive. With a pounding heart, the tailor was regarding the beauty, when suddenly she opened her eyes, gave a start, and then stirred in joy at the sight of him.

"Good heavens!" she exclaimed. "I shall soon be free. Quick, quick, help me out of my prison. If you push back the bolt of this glass coffin, I'll be saved."

The tailor obeyed without hesitating, and she immediately lifted up the glass top, climbed out, and rushed into a corner of the hall, where she wrapped herself in a large cloak. Then she sat down on a stone and called the young man to her. After she gave him a friendly kiss on his lips, she said, "I had been hoping for a long time, my savior, that you'd come. Now God in his mercy has led you to me and put an end to my suffering. And on this very day that my suffering has ended, your happiness shall begin. Heaven has chosen you as my husband, and you shall spend the rest of your life in joy and peace, and you shall be provided with an abundance of earthly possessions. Sit down now and listen to my fateful story.

"I am the daughter of a rich count. My parents died when I was still at a tender age. In accord with their last will I was to be raised by my older brother. We loved each other so dearly and were so much alike in our ideas and inclinations that we both decided never to marry but to remain together for the rest of our lives. There was never a lack of company in our house. Neighbors and friends visited us frequently, and we were most hospitable to everyone. Well, one evening it happened that a stranger came riding to our castle and requested a night's lodging because he had been unable to reach the next town. We granted his request cordially and politely, and during dinner he entertained us with his conversation that was elegantly mixed with stories. My brother took such a great liking to him that he asked him to spend a few days with us, and after some hesitation, he agreed. We got up from the table very late at night, and the stranger was shown to his room.

"Tired as I was, I hurried to spread my limbs on a soft bed, but no sooner had I fallen asleep than I was wakened by the sound of soft and lovely music. Since I had no idea where it was coming from, I wanted to call my chambermaid, who slept in the next room. Yet, to my astonishment, I found that I was deprived of my speech by a mysterious power, and I felt as if overcome by a nightmare, unable to utter the slightest sound. In the meantime, by the light of my night lamp I saw the stranger enter my room through two doors that had been tightly locked. He approached me and said that through magic arts that stood at his command he had caused the lovely music to sound in order to wake me. He had then forced his way through all the locks with the intention of offering me his heart and hand. However, his magic arts repulsed me so much that I did not deem his offer worthy of a reply.

"He stood there awhile without moving, probably with the expectation of receiving a favorable answer, but when I continued to remain silent, he declared angrily that he would revenge himself and find some means to punish my arrogance. Then he left the room. I slept a most restless night and could manage to fall asleep only toward morning. When I awoke, I rushed to my brother to tell him what had happened, but I didn't find him in his room. His servant told me that he had gone out hunting with the stranger at daybreak.

"Immediately I sensed that something was wrong. I got dressed quickly, had my palfrey saddled, and rode in a full gallop toward the forest in the company of a servant. However, my servant's horse stumbled and broke its leg, so he could not follow me. I continued on my way without stopping, and in a few minutes I saw the stranger heading toward me and leading a beautiful stag by a rope. I asked him where he had left my brother and how he had come upon this stag, whose eyes were filled with large tears. Instead of answering me, he began to laugh loudly. I became furious, pulled out a pistol, and fired it at the monster, but the bullet bounced off his chest and rebounded into the head of my horse. I fell to the ground, and the stranger mumbled some words that robbed me of my consciousness.

"When I regained my senses, I found myself in a glass coffin in this underground cavern. The magician appeared once more and told me that he had turned my brother into a stag. Moreover, he had reduced my castle with all its surroundings to such a tiny size that they could be put into the other glass chest along with my people, who had all been transformed into vapor and were confined in glass bottles. However, he said, if I would comply with his desire, it would be easy for him to return everything to its original condition. He had only to open the containers and everything would regain its natural form. I refused to answer him, just as I had done before. He disappeared and left me lying in my prison, and I fell into a deep sleep. Among the many things I envisioned in my sleep, that which consoled me most, was the image of a young man who came and set me free. And, today, when I opened my eyes, I saw you and knew that my dream had been fulfilled. Now I want you to help me make the other things I saw come true. First we must lift the other glass chest that contains my castle and move it to that broad stone."

As soon as the glass chest was moved to the stone slab, the stone began to rise and carried the maiden and young man up through an opening into the upper hall. From there they could easily reach the open air. Then the maiden opened the top of the chest, and it was wonderful to see how the castle, houses, and farms expanded and grew rapidly back to their natural size. The maiden and young man returned to the underground cavern and had the vapor-filled containers carried up by the stone. No sooner did the maiden open the bottles than the blue steam shot out and transformed itself into living creatures, whom the maiden recognized as her people and servants. Her joy became even greater when her brother, who had killed the magician in the form of a bull, came out of the forest in his human form. And, on that very same day, the maiden kept her promise and gave her hand at the altar to the lucky tailor.

❖ 164 ❖

Lazy Heinz

HEINZ WAS LAZY, and even though he had nothing else to do but drive his goat to pasture every day, he still groaned when he came home at night after a full day's work. "Truthfully," he said, "it's a heavy burden and hard job driving a goat into the field year after year up till the end of fall. If only I could lie down during work and sleep! But no, I've got to keep my eyes open so that the goat won't damage the young trees, break through a hedge into a garden, or even run away. How could anyone get any rest or enjoy life this way!" He sat down, collected his thoughts, and pondered the ways he might lift this burden from his shoulders. For a long time all his thinking was in vain. Then suddenly an idea occurred to him. "I know what I'll do!" he exclaimed. "I'll marry fat Trina. She has a goat too, and she can drive mine and hers out to pasture. Then I won't have to torment myself anymore."

So Heinz lifted himself up, set his weary legs in motion, and went straight across the road, for he had to go no further than that to get to the house of Trina's parents, where he asked for the hand of their diligent and virtuous daughter. The parents did not have to think long about this offer. Birds of a feather flock together, they thought, and gave their consent. So Fat Trina became Heinz's wife and drove the two goats to the pasture. Heinz now had good times and did not need to recuperate from anything more strenuous than his own laziness. Only every now and then did he go out with Trina, and he would explain, "I'm merely doing this so that I can enjoy my rest afterward even more. Otherwise, I might lose all feeling for it."

However, Fat Trina was no less lazy. "Dear Heinz," she said one day, "why should we make our lives so dreary and ruin the best years of our youth when there's no need for it? Wouldn't we be better off if we traded our two goats to our neighbor? They disturb our sweetest sleep each morning with their bleating, and I'm sure that our neighbor would give us his beehive for them. We can place the hive on a sunny spot behind the house and not have to concern ourselves about it. Bees don't have to be tended or taken out to pasture. They fly out and find their own way home again. Moreover, they gather honey by themselves, and we won't have to exert ourselves in the least."

"You've spoken like a sensible woman," Heinz replied. "Let's carry out your plan without delay. Besides, honey tastes better and is more nourishing than goat milk, and it also keeps longer."

The neighbor was glad to give them his beehive for the two goats. The bees flew tirelessly in and out of the hive from early morning until late in the evening, and they filled the hive with the finest honey. By fall Heinz was able to take out an entire jugful. They placed the jug on a shelf high on the wall in their bedroom. Since they feared that it could be stolen or that mice could get at it, Trina fetched a sturdy hazel stick and laid it next to their bed so that she could reach it and, without getting up unnecessarily, could chase away uninvited guests.

Lazy Heinz did not like to get out of bed before noon. "The earlier you rise, the sooner you sap your strength," he said. One morning, while he was still lying in bed on a bright sunny day, resting from his long sleep, he said to his wife, "Women love sweets, and you like to nibble away at the honey. So, before you eat up everything, I think it's best that we exchange it for a goose with a young gander."

"But not before we have a child to look after them," replied Trina. "Do you want me to wear myself out and waste away my strength for no reason at all?"

"Do you think our son will tend the geese?" asked Heinz. "Nowadays children no longer obey. They do as they please because they think they're smarter than their parents, just like that servant who was supposed to search for the cow and went hunting for three blackbirds."

"Oh," Trina answered, "he'll really get it from me if he doesn't do what I say. I'll take a switch and tan his hide but good. Look, Heinz!" she exclaimed. "You see! This is the way I'll hit him." She swung out her arm to demonstrate, but unfortunately she hit the honey jug over the bed. The jug smashed against the wall and broke into pieces, and the beautiful honey flowed all over the floor.

"Well, there goes the goose with the gander," said Heinz. "They won't need tending now. Anyway, it's lucky that the jug did not fall on my head. We have every reason to be grateful for the way things are." And, as he noticed that there was still some honey in a piece of the jug, he reached for it and said with delight, "Let us enjoy this leftover, my wife, and then we shall rest a little after the fright we've just had. What harm is it if we get up a little later than usual. The day is indeed long enough."

"Yes," answered Trina. "We'll always get to the end of it in due time. You know, the snail was once invited to a wedding and set upon its way, but it only arrived in time for the christening. In front of the house it fell over the fence and said, 'Haste makes waste.' "

◈ 165 ◈

The Griffin

THERE WAS ONCE A KING, but where he ruled and what his name was, I do not know. He had no sons, only a daughter, who was always sick, and no doctor had been able to cure her. Then the king learned through a fortune-teller that his daughter would regain her health by eating apples. So he let it be proclaimed throughout the entire land that whoever brought his daughter apples that would make her well again would wed her and become king.

This news was heard by a peasant who had three sons, and he said to the oldest, "Go into the garden and take a basket full of those beautiful apples with red cheeks and bring them to the court. Maybe the king's daughter will regain her health by eating them, and you'll be able to marry her and become king."

The young fellow did his father's bidding and set upon his way. After he had gone a short while, he met a little, gray-haired man, who asked him what he had in the basket. In reply, Ule—for that was his name—said, "Frog's legs."

Upon hearing this, the little man said, "Well, so be it, and so shall it remain," and he moved on.

When Ule finally reached the castle, he let it be known that he had apples for the daughter that would make her well if she ate them. The king was tremendously pleased to hear this and ordered Ule to come before him, but alas, when he opened the basket, there were frog's legs wriggling about in it instead of apples. The king became angry and had Ule chased out of his house.

Then the father sent the next son, whose name was Saeme, but the same thing happened to him. He met the little, gray-haired man, who asked him what he had in the basket, and Saeme said, "Hog's bristles," and the man replied, "Well, so be it, and so shall it remain."

When he arrived at the king's castle and said that he had apples that could make the king's daughter regain her health, they did not want to let him enter and said that someone else had already been there and had made fools out of them. However, Saeme insisted that his were real apples and that they should let him in. At last they believed him and led him to the king. But when he opened the basket, there were only hog's bristles. This made the king terribly angry, so he had Saeme whipped out of the house.

When Saeme returned home, he related what had happened to him. Then the youngest son, who was called Dumb Hans, asked his father whether he might also go to the castle with some apples. "Come now," said the father, "do you really think you're the right fellow for the job? If the smart ones can't succeed, what do you think you'll be able to accomplish?"

However, the boy would not give up. "I want to, Father. I want to go."

"Get away from me, you dumb thing. You must wait until you're smarter," his father said, and turned his back on Hans.

But Hans tugged at the back of his father's jacket and said, "I want to go, Father. I want to go."

"Well, as far as I'm concerned, you may go, but I'm sure you'll be coming back soon," responded the father in a nasty tone. His son, however, was exceedingly pleased and jumped for joy. "Now, don't act like a fool. You're getting more and more stupid every day," the father said. But this did not upset Hans. Nothing could spoil his pleasure.

Now, since it was almost dark, Hans thought that it would be better to wait until the next day because he could never reach the court that same day. At night as he lay in bed he could not sleep, and even when he dozed for a while, he dreamed of beautiful maidens, castles, gold and silver, and all kinds of things like that. Early the next morning he set out on his way, and as soon as he was out in the open, he met the shabby little man in gray clothes, who asked him what he had in the basket. In reply, Hans said that he had apples for the king's daughter to help her regain her health.

"Well," said the little man, "then so be it, and so shall it remain."

But at the court nobody would let Hans in because two fellows had already come and said that they were bringing apples and one had frog's legs and the other hog's bristles. However, Hans insisted earnestly that he did not have frog's legs but had the most beautiful apples in the whole kingdom. Since he spoke so forthrightly, the gatekeeper thought that he could not be lying and let him in. And he was right, because there were nothing but golden apples to be seen when Hans opened the basket before the king. Now, the king was overjoyed and ordered some of them to be taken to his daughter, and he waited anxiously for news about their effect to be brought to him. It was not long before he received the news, and who do you think it was who brought the news to him? It was his daughter herself. As soon

as she had eaten
some of the apples,
she had leapt out of bed
in perfect health. It is
impossible to describe the
joy that the king felt. But now he did not want to give Hans his
daughter in marriage and told Hans he had to make a boat that goes
faster on dry land than in water. Hans accepted the condition, went
home, and related what had happened.

The father sent Ule into the woods to make such a boat. He worked
hard and whistled away. At noon, when the sun is at its highest, the
little, gray-haired man came and asked him what he was making. In
reply Ule said, "Wooden dishes."

Then the gray little man said, "Well, so be it, and so shall it
remain."

By evening Ule thought he had finished the boat, but when he
wanted to get into it, there was nothing there but wooden dishes. The
next day Saeme went into the woods, but the exact same thing
happened to him. On the third day Dumb Hans went and worked so
assiduously that the whole forest resounded from his powerful blows,
and all the while he sang and whistled merry tunes. Then the little
man again came at noon, the hottest time of the day, and asked what
he was making.

"I'm making a boat that will go faster on dry land than in water, and when I'm finished, I'm to get the king's daughter for my bride."

"Well," said the little man, "so be it, and so shall it remain."

In the evening, when the sun turned gold, Hans was finished with his boat, oars, and rudder. He sat down in it and sailed away to the palace. The boat went as swiftly as the wind, and from afar the king saw this but still did not want to give his daughter to Hans. So he said that Hans must first tend a hundred hares from early in the morning until late in the evening, and if one of them got away, Hans would not get his daughter. Hans was satisfied with this, and the very next day he went to the meadow with the hares and kept on the alert so that none of them would run away. After a while a maid came from the castle and said to Hans that he should give her a hare quickly because visitors had come to the castle. Yet, Hans knew perfectly well what was going on and said that he would not give her one but that the king could give his visitors jugged hare the next day. The maid, however, would not take no for an answer and eventually began to fight with him. Then Hans said that if the king's daughter herself would come he would give her a hare. The maid reported this back at the castle, and the daughter decided to go herself. In the meantime, the little man reappeared and asked Hans what he was doing there. Hans said that he had to look after a hundred hares and make sure that not a single one ran away. Then he might marry the king's daughter and become king.

"Good," said the little man. "Here's a whistle for you, and if one runs away, just blow on the whistle until it returns."

When the daughter came, Hans put a hare in her apron. But after she had gone a hundred feet, Hans whistled, and the hare sprang from the apron and immediately rejoined the other hares. When evening came, Hans whistled once more and looked to see if all the hares were there, and then he drove them to the castle. The king was astounded to see that Hans had been able to look after a hundred hares without any of them getting lost. Nevertheless, he still did not want to give his daughter to Hans and said that he must now bring him a feather from the Griffin's tail.

Hans set out right away and marched at a fast pace. Toward evening he came to a castle, where he asked for a night's lodging because there were still no inns in those days. The lord of the castle granted his request with pleasure and asked him where he was going. In reply Hans said, "To the Griffin."

"So, you're off to see the Griffin. They say that he knows everything, and since I've just lost the key to my iron money chest, perhaps you'd be so kind as to ask him where it is."

"Yes, of course," said Hans. "I'll certainly do that."

Early the next morning he continued his journey and came to

another castle, where he also spent the night. When the people there learned he was going to the Griffin, they told him that the daughter in the house was sick, and they had tried everything to cure her, but nothing had worked. So they asked Hans if he would be so kind as to ask the Griffin what might make the daughter well again. Hans said that he would be pleased to do this and continued his journey. Then he came to a lake and, instead of a ferry, there was a big man who had to carry everyone across the water. The man asked where he was heading.

"To the Griffin," said Hans.

"Well, when you meet him," said the man, "ask him why I must carry everyone across the lake."

Then the man lifted him on his shoulders and carried him across. Finally, Hans arrived at the Griffin's house, but only the Griffin's wife was at home and not the Griffin himself. The woman asked him what he wanted, so Hans told her everything: how he had to get the feather from the Griffin's tail, about the castle where the key to the money chest was lost and he was supposed to ask where it was, about the other castle where the daughter was sick and he was supposed to learn what might make her well again, and finally about the lake not far from there with a man beside it who had to carry people across and who would like to know why he had to do this. Then the wife said to him, "Look here, my good friend, there's not a Christian who can talk to the Griffin. He eats them all up. However, if you like, you can lie down under his bed before he returns, and at night, when he is fast asleep, you can reach out and pull a feather from his tail. As for those other things that you want to know, I'll ask him myself."

Hans was satisfied with this and lay down underneath the bed. In the evening the Griffin came home, and as he entered the room he said, "I smell a Christian."

"Yes," said his wife, "there was one here today, but he continued on his way."

Upon hearing this, the Griffin said nothing more. At midnight, when he began snoring loudly, Hans reached out and yanked a feather from his tail. Suddenly the Griffin jumped up and said, "Wife, I smell a Christian, and it seemed to me that someone was pulling at my tail."

"You've surely been dreaming," replied his wife. "I told you already that a Christian had been here today, but he continued on his way. He told me all sorts of things. In one castle the key to the money chest has been lost, and the people there can't find it anywhere."

"Oh, those fools!" said the Griffin. "The key is in the woodshed lying under a log behind the door."

"And then he also said that there was a sick daughter in another castle, and they didn't know how to cure her."

"Oh, those fools!" said the Griffin. "There's a toad under the cellar steps, and it's made a nest out of her hair. If she went and got her hair back, she'd regain her health."

"He told me too that there was a lake where a man had to carry everyone across."

"Oh, the fool," said the Griffin. "All he must do is set someone down right in the middle just once and he'd never have to carry anyone across again."

Early the next morning the Griffin got up and departed. Then Hans crawled out from under the bed carrying a beautiful feather. He had also heard what the Griffin had said in regard to the key, the daughter, and the man. But the Griffin's wife repeated everything to him so that he would not forget a thing, and Hans set upon his way home again. First he came to the man at the lake, who asked him right away what the Griffin had said. Hans replied that he would tell him only after the man had first carried Hans across the lake. Then Hans told him that all he had to do was set someone down in the middle of the lake, and he'd never have to carry anyone across it again. The man was tremendously pleased and said to Hans that he would carry him across the lake and back again to show him his gratitude, but Hans said no, it was not worth the trouble. He was already satisfied. So he continued along his way. Then he came to the castle where the daughter was sick. He lifted her onto his shoulders and carried her down the cellar stairs. Then he pulled out the toad's nest from under the bottom step and handed it to the daughter, who sprang from his shoulders and ran up the stairs ahead of him and showed herself to be in perfect health again. Now the father and mother were overjoyed and gave Hans gold and silver and whatever else he desired. Afterward Hans moved on to the other castle, where he went directly to the woodshed and found the key under the log behind the door and brought it to the lord of the castle, who was more than delighted. As a reward, he gave Hans much of the gold that was in the chest and many other things, such as cows and sheep and goats.

When Hans came to the king with all these things—the money, the gold and silver, and the cows, sheep, and goats—the king asked him how he had obtained them. Then Hans told him that the Griffin had given him everything he had desired. Upon hearing this, the king thought that he too could use such things and set out to seek the Griffin, but when he came to the lake, it so happened that he was the first one to reach it since Hans had been there. So the man set him down in the middle and continued on his way. The king drowned, but Hans married his daughter and became the king.

❖ 168 ❖

Strong Hans

ONCE UPON A TIME there was a husband and wife who had an only child, and they lived all alone in a remote valley. One day it happened that the mother went into the woods to gather branches of fir, and she took little Hans, who was only two years old, with her. Since spring was in full bloom and her child took great delight in the many-hued flowers, she went with him farther and farther into the forest. Suddenly two robbers jumped out of the bushes, grabbed the mother and her child, and carried them off, deep into the black forest, where nobody had ever gone in the course of a year. The poor woman pleaded desperately with the robbers to let her and her child go free. But their hearts were made of stone. They were deaf to all her pleas and prayers and drove her on by force. She and her son were compelled to work their way through shrubs and brier bushes for two hours, and then they came to a rock with a door on it. The robbers knocked, and the door opened immediately. They went through a long dark passage and finally came to a large cave illuminated by a fire that burned on the hearth. On the wall hung swords, sabers, and other murderous weapons, which glittered in the light, and in the middle stood a black table at which four other robbers sat and gambled. At the head of the table was their chief, and when he saw the woman, he went to her and told her to relax and not to worry. They would not harm her, but she would have to do the housekeeping, and if she kept everything in order, she would be treated well. Upon saying this, he gave her something to eat and showed her a bed, where she could sleep with her child.

The woman remained with the robbers for many years, and Hans grew big and strong. His mother told him stories and taught him how to read from an old book about knights, which she had found in the cave. When Hans was nine years old, he made a sturdy club out of a branch of fir and hid it behind his bed. Then he went to his mother and said, "Dear Mother, tell me now, once and for all, who my father is. I've got to and want to know."

The mother remained silent. She did not want to tell him because he might become homesick. Besides, she knew that the godless robbers would not let Hans leave. Yet, it nearly broke her heart knowing that Hans could not go and see his father. That night, when the robbers returned from their robbing expedition, Hans took out his club, went up to the chief, and said, "Now I want to know who my father is, and if you don't tell me right away, I'll knock you down."

The chief laughed and gave Hans such a slap on the face that he rolled over like a ball and slid under the table. Hans got up again, but kept quiet and thought to himself, I'll wait another year, and then I'll try again. Perhaps things will go better next time.

When three years had passed, he took his club out again, wiped off the dust, inspected it carefully, and said, "It's a good, strong club." At night when the robbers came home, they drank one jug of wine after another until their heads began to droop. Then Hans took out his club, placed himself in front of the chief, and asked him who his father was. Once again the chief gave him such a powerful slap on the face that Hans rolled under the table. But this time Hans bounced back up on his feet immediately and gave the chief and the robbers such a beating with his club that they could no longer move their arms and legs. His mother stood in a corner and was astounded by his bravery and strength. When Hans was finished with his work, he went to his mother and said, "Now you see that I'm serious. I want to know who my father is."

"Dear Hans," replied his mother, "let us go and search until we find him."

She took the key to the entrance of the cave from the chief, and Hans fetched a large flour sack, which he filled with gold, silver, and whatever other beautiful things he could find until it was full. Then he lifted the sack on his back and left the cave. When he stepped out of the darkness into the daylight and saw the green forest, flowers, birds, and the morning sun in the sky, his eyes opened wide. Hans stood there and gaped at everything as if he were not quite right in his head. His mother looked for the way home, and after they had journeyed a few hours, they came safely to their little house in the remote valley. The father was sitting in the doorway, and he wept for joy when he recognized his wife and learned that Hans was his son, for he had long since given them up for dead. Even though Hans had just turned twelve years old, he was a head taller than his father. They went into the living room together, but no sooner had Hans set the sack on the bench by the stove than the entire house began to crack loudly. The bench collapsed and the floor as well, and the heavy sack fell down into the cellar.

"God help us!" the father exclaimed. "What's that? Now you've demolished our little house!"

"Father dear, you needn't get gray hairs over this," replied Hans. "There's more than we need in that sack to build a new house."

Right after this Hans and his father began to build a new house. They bought cattle and land and set up a farm. Hans plowed the fields, and when he walked behind the plow and pushed it into the soil, the oxen hardly needed to pull. The next spring Hans said, "Father, I want you to keep all the money and make me a walking staff that weighs a hundred pounds, so that I may go and travel about the world."

When the staff he had requested was finished, Hans left his father's house, journeyed forth, and arrived in a deep, dark forest. There he heard something crackle and crunch, and he looked around and saw a fir tree that was twisted like a rope, from bottom to top. And as his eyes gazed upward, he caught sight of a large fellow who had grabbed hold of the tree and was twisting it around like a willow switch.

"Hey," yelled Hans. "What are you doing up there?"

The fellow replied, "I gathered together some branches yesterday, and I'm twisting a rope so that I can carry them."

There's a man after my own heart, thought Hans. He's got some power. And Hans called to him, "Forget the rope and come with me!"

The fellow climbed down the tree. He was taller than Hans by a whole head, and Hans was by no means small. "From now on your name is Fir-Twister," Hans said to him.

They continued on their way and soon heard something chopping and hammering so hard that the earth trembled with each blow. Shortly after, they came to a mighty rock. A giant stood in front of it and was chopping off large chunks of it with his fist. When Hans asked him why he was doing this, he answered, "Whenever I want to sleep at night, the bears, wolves, and other vermin of that kind come and sniff and snoop around me, and I can't get any sleep. So I'm going to build myself a house here and lie down inside so I can have my peace and quiet."

Yes, indeed, thought Hans. You can use him too. And he said to him, "Forget that house building and come with me. Your name shall be Rock-Chopper."

He agreed, and all three of them roamed through the forest, and wherever they went, they terrified the animals, who would run away from them. In the evening they came to an old, abandoned castle, went into it, and laid themselves down in the hall to sleep. The next morning Hans went down into the garden, which was completely wild and overgrown with bushes and briers. As he was walking around, a wild boar jumped out and charged at him. However, he gave the beast a blow with his staff, and it fell down dead on the spot. Then he lifted it onto his shoulders and carried it up into the castle, where they put it on a spit, roasted it well, and began to enjoy themselves. Then they agreed that they should take turns cooking and hunting every day: two of them were to go out and hunt, and one was to remain home and cook, nine pounds of meat for each of them.

On the first day Fir-Twister stayed at home, and Hans and Rock-Chopper went out hunting. While Fir-Twister was busy cooking, a small, shriveled old man came to him in the castle and demanded some meat.

"Get out of here, you little sneak!" Fir-Twister answered. "You don't need any meat."

Fir-Twister, however, was very surprised when the puny little dwarf sprang at him and beat him so hard with his fists that he could not protect himself and fell to the ground, gasping for breath. The dwarf did not leave until he had thoroughly vented his anger on him. When the two others returned home from hunting, Fir-Twister told them nothing about the dwarf and the blows he had received, for he thought, When they stay at home, then they can try their luck with the quick-tempered little imp, and just the thought of this already gave him pleasure.

The following day Rock-Chopper stayed home, and he fared just as badly as Fir-Twister. He was battered terribly by the dwarf because he was unwilling to give him any meat. When the two others came home in the evening, Fir-Twister saw from Rock-Chopper's face what had happened to him, but both kept quiet and thought, Hans should also get a taste of the same medicine.

The next day it was Hans's turn to stay at home, and he did his work in the kitchen, as was customary. While he was standing and skimming the kettle, the dwarf came and, without much ado, demanded a piece of meat. Hans thought to himself, He's a poor wretch. I'll give him part of my meat so that the others will not be short-changed. And he handed the dwarf a piece of meat. After the dwarf had devoured this, he demanded another piece of meat. Good-natured Hans gave it to him and said that this was a very nice piece and that he should be content with it. The dwarf, however, demanded a third piece.

"You're getting impudent," Hans said, and refused to give him any more. Then the nasty dwarf got ready to jump at him and deal with him as he had with Fir-Twister and Rock-Chopper, but he had picked on the wrong man. Without exerting himself, Hans gave him a couple of blows that sent him sprawling down the castle steps. As Hans ran after him he tripped over the dwarf and landed on his face. By the time he had straightened himself up, the dwarf was far ahead of him. Hans pursued him into the forest and saw him slip into a hole in a rock. Hans took note of the spot and then returned home. When the two others came back to the castle, they were astonished to find that Hans was so well. He told them what had happened, and then they revealed their own experiences. Hans laughed and said, "It served you right. Why were you so stingy with your meat? Indeed, it's a disgrace that you two fellows let yourselves be beaten by a dwarf."

The three of them then took a basket and rope and went to the hole in the rock into which the dwarf had slipped, and they let Hans, who was carrying his staff, down in the basket. When he reached the bottom, he found a door, and when he opened it, he saw a maiden so lovely that she seemed to have come right out of a picture book. Indeed, she was so beautiful that words cannot describe her. And next to her sat the dwarf, who grinned at Hans like a monkey. The maiden was bound with chains, however, and looked at Hans so sadly that he felt very sorry for her and thought to himself, You must set her free from the power of this wicked dwarf. So he struck the dwarf with his staff, and the dwarf fell down dead. As soon as this happened, the chains fell from the maiden, and Hans was dazzled by her beauty. She told him that she was the daughter of a king, and a wild count had stolen her from home. He had locked her up in the rock because she would have nothing to do with him, and the dwarf had been posted as a guard and had caused her a great deal of misery and suffering.

Now Hans put the maiden into the basket and ordered his companions to pull her up. The basket came down again, but Hans did not trust his two companions and thought, They have already shown themselves to be untrustworthy by not telling you about the dwarf. Who knows what they have up their sleeve now? So he put his staff into the basket, and it was lucky he did this, for they let the basket drop when it was halfway up, and if Hans had really been sitting in it, he would have died. But now he could not figure out how to get out of the deep hole. Even after he had tossed many ideas back and forth, he still had not found a way. "It's sad, indeed," he said to himself, "that you must perish down here." And as he paced back and forth he came again to the small chamber where the maiden had been sitting and noticed that the dwarf had a ring on his finger that sparkled and glittered. So he took it off and put it on his own finger, and suddenly he heard something hovering above his head. He looked up into the air and saw spirits there, who said that he was now their master, and they asked what his desire might be. At first Hans was completely dumbfounded, but then he said that they should carry him to the top. They obeyed immediately, and it seemed to him as if he were actually flying upward.

When he reached the top, there was nobody in sight. Fir-Twister and Rock-Chopper had left in a hurry and had taken the beautiful maiden with them. But Hans turned the ring, and the spirits came and told him that the two were at sea. Hans ran and ran without stopping until he came to the seashore. Far, far out on the sea he spied a little ship. His rage was great, and without thinking, he plunged into the water with his staff that weighed one hundred pounds. It dragged him down into the depths so that he almost drowned. However, he turned the ring in the nick of time, and the spirits came instantly and carried him quick as lightning to the little ship. Then he swung his staff, giving his wicked companions the punishment they justly deserved and throwing them overboard into the sea.

After this he sailed home with the beautiful maiden, who had been dreadfully frightened by everything. This was the second time that he had set her free, and after he brought her to her mother and father, they were married, and everyone was tremendously delighted.

◈ 167 ◈

The Peasant in Heaven

ONCE UPON A TIME a poor, pious peasant died and arrived at the gate to heaven. At the same time, a very rich man showed up and wanted to enter heaven too. Then Saint Peter came with a key, opened the gate, and let the rich man in. Apparently he did not see the peasant there and shut the gate again. Soon the peasant could hear from outside how the rich man was welcomed with great joy into heaven and how they played music and sang. Finally, it became quiet again, and Saint Peter came, opened up the gate to heaven, and let the peasant in. The peasant thought that there would now be music and singing for him, but everything remained silent. Of course, he was welcomed with a great deal of love, and the angels came to meet him, but nobody sang. Then the peasant asked Saint Peter why nobody had sung for him the way they had for the rich man. It seemed to him that things were exactly the same in heaven as they had been on earth, where certain people were favored.

"Not at all," said Saint Peter. "You're just as dear to us as anybody else, and you are entitled to all the heavenly joys just as much as the rich man. But, look, poor fellows like you come to heaven every day, while a rich man like this one comes to us only once in a hundred years."

❖ 168 ❖

Lean Lisa

LEAN LISA LOOKED UPON LIFE in an entirely different way from Lazy Heinz and Fat Trina, who never let anything disturb their composure. She slaved away from morning till night and burdened her husband, Tall Lenz, with so much work that his load was heavier than an ass with three sacks. However, their labor was all in vain. They had nothing and accomplished nothing.

One night, as Lean Lisa lay in bed and could barely move a limb of her body because she was so exhausted, her thoughts kept her awake. She poked her husband in his side with her elbow and said, "Listen to me, Lenz, I've been thinking. If I found a gulden, and if someone gave me one, then I would borrow another, and I'd also expect you to give me one. Then, after I had collected the four guldens together, I'd buy a young cow."

Her husband liked this idea very much. "To be sure, I don't know where I'd get the gulden that you want me to give you, but if you can manage to gather the money and can buy a cow with it, you'd do well to go ahead with your plans. I'd be happy," he added, "if the cow gives birth to a calf. Then I'd be able to refresh myself at times with a drink of milk."

"The milk's not for you," said his wife. "We must let the calf suck the milk so that it becomes large and fat and then we can sell it."

"Of course," answered her husband, "but we can still take a little milk. That won't do any harm."

"What do you know about cows?" his wife said. "Whether it's harmful or not, I refuse to have milk taken from the cow. Even if you stand on your head, you won't get a drop. Just because you can never satisfy your stomach, Tall Lenz, you think you can gobble up everything that I've worked so hard to earn."

"Wife," said the husband, "be quiet or I'll give you a slap on the face."

"What?" she exclaimed. "You want to threaten me, you glutton, you good-for-nothing, you Lazy Heinz!"

She tried to pull his hair, but Tall Lenz sat up and with one hand grabbed the skinny arms of Lean Lisa and with the other pressed her head into the pillow. He let her curse but held her head in the pillow until she fell asleep out of exhaustion. Whether she continued to quarrel the next morning when she awoke, or whether she went out to search for the gulden that she wanted to find, I do not know.

◈ 169 ◈

The House in the Forest

A POOR WOODCUTTER LIVED WITH HIS WIFE AND THREE DAUGHTERS on the edge of a lonely forest. One morning, before going out to his work again, he said to his wife, "Have our oldest daughter bring me my noonday meal into the forest. Otherwise, I won't be able to finish my work. Just to make sure that she doesn't lose her way," he added, "I'll take a bag of millet with me, and I'll spread the seeds on the path."

When the sun stood directly above the forest, the maiden set upon her way with a pot full of soup. However, the sparrows from the fields and woods, the larks and finches, the blackbirds and siskins had long since pecked and eaten up the millet, and the maiden could not find the way. So she trusted to chance and continued on her way until the sun set and night fell. The trees rustled in the darkness. The owls hooted, and she began to be afraid. Then she caught sight of a light in the distance that glimmered between the trees. There are probably some people living there who'll let me stay overnight, she thought, and she went toward the light. After a short time she came upon a house with brightly lit windows. She knocked, and a rough voice cried out from inside, "Come in." The maiden entered the dark hallway and knocked on the door in the kitchen. "Just come in," the voice cried out, and when she opened the door, she saw an old, gray-haired man sitting at the table with his head propped up by his hands, and his white beard flowed down over the table almost to the ground. Near the stove lay three animals, a chicken, a rooster, and a spotted cow. The maiden told the old man what had happened to her and asked for sleeping quarters for the night. The man said:

"Pretty hen,
pretty rooster,
and you, my pretty spotted cow,
what do you say to this right now?"

"*Duks!*" answered the animals, and that must have meant "That's fine with us!" because the old man continued to speak. "We have everything you can possibly need here. So go out to the hearth and cook us our supper."

The maiden found more than enough in the kitchen and cooked a good meal, but she did not think of the animals. She carried a full bowl to the table, sat down next to the gray-haired man, and ate until she was full. "But now I'm tired. Where's the bed? I want to lie down and sleep."

The animals responded:

"With him you've eaten,
with him you've drunk,
but you haven't dealt with us quite right.
Find out for yourself where you're to spend the night."

Then the old man spoke. "Just go upstairs, and you'll find a room with two beds. Shake them up and put white linen sheets on them. Then I'll come up too and lie down to sleep."

The maiden climbed the stairs, and after she had shaken the beds and put clean sheets on them, she lay down on one of them without waiting any longer for the old man. After some time, however, the gray-haired man came, held a candle over the girl, and shook his head. When he saw that she was fast asleep, he opened a trapdoor and let her drop into the cellar.

The woodcutter came home late in the evening and reproached his wife for letting him go hungry the entire day. "I'm not to blame," she answered. "I sent our daughter out with your noon meal, but she must have gotten lost. She'll probably return home tomorrow."

The woodcutter got up before daybreak, however, and told his wife that he wanted their second daughter to bring him his noon meal this time. "I'll take a bag of lentils with me," he said. "The seeds are larger than millet grains. The girl will see them more easily and won't get lost."

At noon the maiden carried the food for her father into the woods, but the lentils had disappeared. The birds of the forest had eaten them up just as they had the previous day, and none were left over. The maiden wandered around the forest until it became night. She too came upon the old man's house and requested food and shelter. The man with the white beard asked the animals again:

"Pretty hen,
pretty rooster,
and you, my pretty spotted cow,
what do you say to this right now?"

Once more the animals responded with *"Duks,"* and everything happened as on the day before. The maiden cooked a good meal, ate and drank with the old man, and did not take care of the animals. And, when she inquired about her sleeping quarters, they said:

"With him you've eaten,
with him you've drunk,
but you haven't dealt with us quite right.
Find out for yourself where you're to spend the night."

When she was asleep, the old man came up, looked at her, shook his head, and let her down into the cellar.

On the third morning the woodcutter said to his wife, "Today I want you to send our youngest child into the forest with my food. She has always been good and obedient. She'll stay on the right path. She's not like her sisters, who rove around like wild bumble bees."

The mother did not want to send her and said, "Am I to lose my dearest child too?"

"Don't worry," he replied. "The girl won't lose her way. She's too smart and sensible. Besides, I'll take some peas with me and spread them on the ground. They are even larger than lentils and will show her the way."

However, when the girl went into the woods with the basket on her arm, the forest pigeons had already eaten up the peas, and she did not know where to turn. She was very worried and could not stop thinking of how hungry her poor father would be and how her good mother would grieve if she did not return home. Finally, when it became dark, she caught sight of a little light and came to the house in the forest. She asked in a very friendly way if she might spend the night, and the man with the white beard asked his animals again:

"Pretty hen,
pretty rooster,
and you, my pretty spotted cow,
what do you say to this right now?"

"*Duks,*" they said. Then the maiden went to the stove, where the animals were lying. She petted the hen and rooster, stroking their smooth feathers with her hand, and she caressed the spotted cow between its horns. At the old man's request she prepared some good soup, and when the bowl was on the table, she said, "I'm certainly not going to sit down and eat when these good animals have nothing. There's everything I need outside, and I'm going to take care of them first."

So she went outside, fetched some barley, and spread it on the ground for the hen and rooster. Then she brought the cow an armful of delicious-smelling hay. "Enjoy your meal, my dear animals," she said, "and if you get thirsty, I'll bring you a fresh drink of water." Upon saying this, she carried a bucket full of water inside, and the hen and rooster jumped on the edge, dipped their beaks into it, and held their heads high as birds do when they drink, and the spotted cow also took a hearty gulp. When the animals were fed, the maiden sat down at the table next to the old man and ate whatever he had left over. Soon thereafter the hen and rooster stuck their little heads beneath their wings, and the spotted cow blinked its eyes. Then the maiden said, "I believe it's time that we all go to bed.

"Pretty hen,
pretty rooster,
and you, my pretty spotted cow,
what do you say to this right now?"

The animals answered:

"*Duks,*
with us you've eaten,
with us you've drunk,
you've thought about us just right.
So now we wish you a very good night."

The maiden went upstairs, shook the feather pillows, and put on fresh linen sheets. When she was finished, the old man came and lay down on one of the beds, and his white beard spread down to his toes. The maiden lay down on the other bed, said her prayers, and fell asleep.

She slept peacefully until midnight. Then there was so much noise in the house that the maiden awoke. There was a crackling and rattling in every corner. The doors popped open and slammed against the walls. The beams groaned as if they were being ripped out of their sockets, and the stairs also seemed to be collapsing. Finally, there was a crash as if the entire roof had caved in. However, since it soon became quiet again and the maiden had not been harmed, she remained in bed and fell asleep again. When she awoke the next morning and the sun was shining brightly, she could not believe her eyes. She was lying in a huge hall, and everything glistened around her in royal splendor. Golden flowers grew on a background of green silk high on the walls. The bed was made of ivory and the covers of red velvet, and there were a pair of slippers on a nearby stool that were embroidered with pearls. The maiden thought it was a dream, but three richly dressed servants entered and asked her what her orders for the day were.

"Leave me for now," answered the maiden. "I want to get up right away and cook some soup for the old man. Then I'll feed pretty hen, pretty rooster, and pretty spotted cow."

She thought that the old man had already risen and looked over at his bed, but he was not lying in it. Instead there was a stranger. And as she regarded him more closely, she saw that he was young and handsome. Then he awoke, sat up, and said, "I'm the son of a king, and a wicked witch cast a spell over me and changed me into a gray-haired old man and made me live in the forest. Nobody was allowed to be with me except my three servants in the form of a hen, a rooster, and a spotted cow. Only a maiden could break the spell, but she had to show that her heart was good and that she was not only kind toward humans but also toward animals. You've done that, and at midnight you set us free. Consequently, the old house in the forest was changed back again into my royal palace."

When they stood up, the prince told the three servants to go to the maiden's father and mother and to bring them to the wedding celebration.

"But where are my two sisters?" the maiden asked.

"I have locked them in the cellar, and tomorrow they shall be led out into the forest and shall work as servants for a charcoal burner until they show that they have changed for the better and no longer let poor animals go hungry."

❖ 170 ❖

Sharing Joys and Sorrows

ONCE UPON A TIME there was a quarrelsome tailor whose wife was good, industrious, and pious, but she could never do anything to please him. No matter what she did, he was dissatisfied. He grumbled, scolded, cuffed, and beat her. When at last the authorities heard about this, they had him summoned and sent him to prison so that he would reform his ways. For a while he was given nothing but bread and water. Then he was set free again, but he had to promise not to beat his wife anymore and to keep peace with her, to share all the joys as well as the sorrows, as married couples are supposed to do. Everything went well for some time, but then he fell back into his old ways and was surly and quarrelsome. And, since he was not allowed to beat her, he tried to grab her by the hair and yank it out. His wife broke loose from him and jumped out into the courtyard, but he ran after her with his yardstick and scissors. He chased her around and around and threw the yardstick and scissors at her and whatever else he could get his hands on. Whenever he hit her, he laughed, and whenever he missed, he threw a fit and cursed and swore. He carried on like this for so long that the neighbors came to the aid of his wife. The tailor was once again brought before the authorities and was reminded of his promise.

"My dear gentleman," he answered, "I've kept my promise. I didn't beat my wife. Indeed, I've shared all the joys and sorrows."

"How can that be," the judge said, "when she has brought heavy charges against you again?"

"I didn't beat her. I only wanted to comb her hair with my hand because she looked so strange. But she ran away and deserted me out of spite. So I rushed after her to make her do her duty, and I threw anything I could get my hands on to remind her of her duty. I also shared the joys and sorrows with her. You see, whenever I hit her, it was a joy for me and sorrow for her. Whenever I missed her, it was a joy for her and a sorrow for me."

The judges were not at all satisfied with this answer, and so they gave him the punishment that he justly deserved.

❖ 171 ❖

The Wren

IN OLDEN DAYS every sound still had its sense and meaning. When the blacksmith's hammer resounded, it cried forth, "Smite hard! Smite hard!" When the carpenter's plane rasped, it said, "That's it! That, that's it!" If the mill wheels began to clatter, they said, "Help, Lord God! Help, Lord God!" And if the miller was a cheat and set the mill in motion, it spoke High German and slowly asked at first, "Who's there? Who's there?" Then it answered quickly, "The miller! The miller!" And finally, it spoke very rapidly, "Steals boldly, steals boldly, three pecks in a bushel."

At this time even the birds had their own language that everyone understood. Now it sounds like only chirping, screeching, and whistling, and in some instances like music without words. Gradually, the birds began to feel that they wanted someone to rule over them and decided to elect one among their number to be king. Only one of them, the peewit, was against this: he had lived free and wanted to die free. So he grew anxious and flew back and forth crying out, "Where am I to live? Where am I to live?" Finally, he withdrew to a desolate and unfrequented swamp and never showed himself again among his kind.

Now, the birds wanted to discuss the matter, and on a beautiful May morning, they all gathered together from the woods and the fields—the eagles and chaffinches, the owls and crows, the larks and sparrows. It's impossible to name them all. Even the cuckoo came and the hoopoe, his clerk, who was dubbed with this name because he can be heard a few days earlier than the cuckoo. Then there was also a very small bird without a name, who mingled with the entire troop. By chance the hen had heard nothing about the whole matter and was astounded by the huge congregation. "What? What? What's going on?" she cackled, but the rooster calmed his beloved hen and said, "Nothing but rich people," and he informed her what they intended to do. Indeed, it was decided that whoever could fly the highest should be king. When he heard this, the tree frog, who was sitting in the bushes, cried out a warning, "No, no, no! No, no, no!" He felt that many tears would be shed because of this. However, the crow said, "Caw, caw," that everything would pass in a peaceful way.

Then the birds decided to begin the ascent right away on this beautiful morning so that nobody could say later on, "I could have flown even higher, but evening came and I couldn't continue." Upon a given signal the entire troop rose up in the air. Dust soared from the field, and there was a tremendous whirring and fluttering and flapping of wings. It looked like a black cloud was mounting on high. The smaller birds were soon left behind. They could not fly very far and returned to the earth. The larger ones held out longer, but none could equal the eagle, who climbed so high that he could have poked out the eyes of the sun. And when he saw that the others could not match him, he thought, Why should you fly higher? You're already the king, and he began to descend. All at once the birds beneath him cried out to him, "You shall be our king! Nobody has flown higher than you."

"Except me," yelled the little fellow without a name who had crept into the breast feathers of the eagle. And, since he was not tired, he climbed and climbed so high that he could see God seated upon his throne. After he had gone this far, he folded his wings together, dove downward, and called out underneath with a fine, shrill voice, "I'm the king! I'm the king!"

"You, our king?" the birds screamed angrily. "You managed to fly so high only by using tricks and by cheating." So they made another condition: whoever could descend deepest into the earth would be the king. How the goose slapped the ground with her broad breast! How quickly the rooster scraped out a hole! The duck had the worst luck: she jumped into a ditch, sprained her legs, and waddled away to the nearest pond crying, "Fraud! Fraud!" The little bird without a name, however, looked for a mousehole, slipped down into it, and called out with its shrill voice, "I'm the king! I'm the king!"

"You, our king?" the birds screamed even more angrily. "Do you think that your tricks should count?" They decided to keep him prisoner in the hole and to starve him. The owl was posted there as guard: she was not to let the rascal out if she valued her life. However, when evening came and all the birds felt exhausted from the exertion of flying, they went to bed with their wives and children. Only the owl remained alone at the mousehole, staring inside unflinchingly with her large eyes. In the meantime, she too became tired and thought, You can surely close one eye. You can still keep watch with the other, and the little villain won't be able to come out of the hole. So the owl shut one eye and looked straight at the mousehole with the other. The little fellow, thrusting his head forward, peeked outside and intended to scoot away, but the owl immediately stepped forward, and the little bird pulled his head back inside. Then the owl opened the other eye again and closed the one that had been open, and she intended to keep switching like this the entire night. However, when she closed her one eye again, she forgot to open the other, and, as soon as both eyes were closed, she fell asleep. The little fellow soon noticed this and slipped away.

From that time on the owl has not been allowed to show herself during the day. Otherwise, the other birds will fly after her and pluck out her feathers. She flies only during the night, and indeed she hates mice and hunts them because they make such nasty holes. The little bird too does not like to show himself because he fears for his neck if he is caught. He slips in and out of hedges, and when he feels very safe, he sometimes cries out, "I'm the king!" And this is why the other birds mock him by calling him the king of the hedges.

However, nobody was happier than the lark because she did not have to obey the king of the hedges. Whenever the sun appears, she climbs into the air and cries out, "Ah, it's all so beautiful! So beautiful! Beautiful! Beautiful! Ah, it's all so beautiful!"

◆ 172 ◆

The Flounder

THE FISHES HAD BEEN DISSATISFIED for a long time because there was a lack of order in their realm. Nobody heeded anybody else. The fishes swam to the left and the right as they pleased. Some darted through those who wanted to stay together or blocked their way, and the stronger fishes gave the weaker ones blows with their tails to drive them away, or they swallowed the weaker ones without much ado.

"How nice it would be if we had a king who would rule over us with law and justice," they said, and they agreed to elect as their ruler the one fish who could cut through the water the fastest and bring help to the weak. So they lined up at the shore in rank and file, and the pike gave a signal with his tail, whereupon they all surged forward together. Like an arrow the pike shot through the water and with him the herring, the gudgeon, the perch, the carp, and all the rest of them. Even the flounder swam with them and hoped to win the race.

All at once there was a cry, "The herring's ahead! The herring's ahead!"

"Who's ahead?" peevishly screamed the flat, jealous flounder, who had been left far behind.

"The herring, the herring!" came the answer.

"The naked herring?" the jealous one cried out. "The naked herring?"

Ever since then the flounder speaks from just one side of his mouth as punishment.

◆ 173 ◆

The Bittern and the Hoopoe

"WHERE DO YOU LIKE best of all to have your herd graze?" someone asked an old cowherd.

"Here, sir, where the grass is neither too rich nor too lean. Otherwise, it won't be of much good."

"Why not?" asked the man.

"Do you hear that mournful cry from the meadow over there?" the cowherd answered. "That's the bittern. He was once a cowherd, and the hoopoe was one too. I'll tell you the story:

"The bittern let his herd graze on rich green meadows where flowers bloomed abundantly. His cows became wild and uncontrollable from eating there. The hoopoe, on the other hand, drove his animals to high barren mountains where the wind plays with the sand, and his cows became thin and never developed their strength. In the evening, when the cowherds drove their animals homeward, the bittern could not gather together his cows. They were too high-spirited and ran away from him. He would call, 'Come round, cow. Come round!' But it was no use. They did not heed his call. The hoopoe's cows, in contrast, were so weak and feeble that he could not even get them on their feet. 'Up, up, up!' he screamed, but it did not help. They remained lying on the sand. This is what happens when there is no balance in life. Even today, though they no longer watch over their herds, the bittern cries, 'Come round, cow. Come round!' And the hoopoe, 'Up, up, up!' "

◆ 174 ◆

The Owl

A FEW HUNDRED YEARS AGO, when people were not nearly as smart and cunning as they are nowadays, a strange event took place in a small town. By accident one of the large owls, called horned owls, from the neighboring forest landed in the barn of one of the townspeople during the night, and as dawn began to break she did not dare leave her hiding place for fear of the other birds that always screeched terribly whenever she appeared. In the morning, when the stableboy went to the barn to fetch some straw, he was so tremendously frightened by the sight of the owl sitting in a corner that he ran off and reported to his master that a monster was lurking in the barn and never in his life had he seen a one like this, which rolled its eyes around in its head and could certainly devour any human creature without much trouble.

"I know you too well," the master said. "You have courage enough to hunt blackbirds in the fields, but when you see a dead chicken lying on the ground, you first have to fetch a stick before you dare approach it. I must go and see for myself what kind of a monster this is," he added.

Bravely he strode into the barn and looked around, but when he saw the strange, dreadful beast with his own eyes, he was no less terrified than his servant. In two leaps he was outside and ran to his neighbors, whom he fervently implored to help him against the unknown and dangerous beast. He was positive that the entire town would be in danger if it broke out of his barn, where it was now sitting. There was a great hue and cry in all the streets. The townspeople came around with spears, pitchforks, scythes, and axes, as if they were about to march out and confront the enemy. Finally, the councilmen appeared with the mayor in the lead. After they had all assembled at the marketplace, they moved to the barn and surrounded it from all sides. Then one of the most courageous of the townspeople stepped forward and went inside with his spear lowered, but with a cry he immediately came running out again, his face deathly pale and unable to utter a word. Then two others ventured inside, but their luck was no better. Finally, a big strong man, who was famous for his war deeds, stepped forward and said, "You won't drive the monster away by merely looking at it. We must get serious here. But I see that you've all turned into women, and nobody wants to take charge and tame the beast." He ordered them to bring him his armor, sword, and spear, and he dressed himself for battle. Everyone praised his courage, though many feared for his life. The two doors to the barn were opened, and one could see the owl, who in the meantime had perched herself on the middle of a large crossbeam. The war hero had a ladder brought to the spot, and as he leaned it against the beam and got ready to climb, the townspeople cried out to him to conduct himself like a man, and they commended him to Saint George the dragon slayer. Soon he was at the top, and when the owl realized that he was after her and became confused by the shouting of the crowd and did not know how to escape, she rolled her eyes, fluttered her feathers, flapped her wings, snapped her beak, and hooted *"tu-whit, tu-whoo"* with a harsh voice.

"Stab it! Stab it!" the crowd called from outside to the brave hero.

"Anyone standing here where I'm standing," he answered, "would not cry 'Stab it, stab it.' " To be sure, he did move his foot one step higher but began to tremble, and half-unconscious, he set about his retreat.

Now there was nobody left who volunteered to brave the danger. "The monster," they said, "has poisoned the strongest man among us just by snapping and puffing smoke, and it's wounded him mortally. Why should we others risk our lives too?"

The people conferred on what they should do to prevent the entire town from being destroyed. For a long time everything seemed useless until the mayor finally found a solution. "In my opinion," he said, "I think that we should pay the owner for the barn and everything that's in it, including the wheat, straw, and hay, out of our common funds. Then we should burn down the whole building and the terrible beast along with it. This way nobody will have to risk his life. There's no time to lose here, and we can't afford to be stingy."

Everyone agreed with him. So the barn was set on fire from all four corners, and it was burned miserably to the ground along with the owl. If you don't believe this, you can go there and inquire for yourself.

◈ 175 ◈

The Moon

IN ANCIENT TIMES there was a land where the night was always dark and the sky covered it like a black cloth, for the moon never rose there, and not a single star twinkled in the darkness. At the time of the creation of the world the nocturnal glow had been sufficient.

Once, four young fellows from this land set out on a journey and arrived in another kingdom around evening, just as the sun disappeared beyond the mountains. A glistening ball stood on an oak tree and cast a soft light far and wide. The light allowed one to see and distinguish everything clearly, even though it was not as bright as the sun. The travelers stood still and asked a farmer, who happened to be driving by with his wagon, what kind of light it was.

"That's the moon," he replied. "Our mayor bought it for three

talers and stuck it on the oak tree. He must pour oil on it every day and keep it clean so that it always burns brightly. We pay him a taler a week for doing the work."

When the farmer had driven away, one of the travelers said, "We could use this lamp. We have an oak tree at home that's just as large as this one, and we could hang it there. What a joy it would be if we didn't have to grope about in the dark anymore!"

"You know what we'll do," said the second. "We'll get a wagon and horses and cart the moon away. They can buy another one here."

"I'm a good climber," said the third one. "I'll get it down for sure."

The fourth one brought a wagon with horses to the spot, and the third one climbed the tree, drilled a hole in the moon, passed a rope through it, and let it down. When the shining ball lay on top of the wagon, they covered it with a cloth so that nobody could see the theft. They brought it safely to their land and hung it on a tall oak tree. Old and young rejoiced when the new lamp cast its light over all the fields and filled the rooms and chambers with its rays. The dwarfs came out of their mountain caves, and the elves, dressed in their little red coats, danced around and around on the meadows.

The four young fellows took care that the moon was provided with oil. They cleaned the wick and received a taler a week for their work. But they became old men, and when one of them became sick and saw his death approaching, he ordered that a fourth of the moon was to be buried with him in his grave as his property. When he died, the mayor climbed the tree and cut off a fourth of the moon with his hedge clippers, and he placed it in the coffin. The light of the moon decreased but not very noticeably. When the second died, another fourth was given to him, and the light became less. It became even weaker after the death of the third one, who also took his part with him. And, when the fourth one was buried, the old darkness set in again. Whenever the people went out without a lantern in the evening, they continually bumped heads.

However, when the parts of the moon had become reassembled again in the underworld, where darkness had always reigned, the dead became restless and awoke from their sleep. They were astounded to find that they could see again: the moonlight was enough for them, for their eyes had become so weak that they would not have been able to stand the brightness of the sun. They got up, became merry, and assumed their old ways of life again. Some began to play and dance. Others went to the taverns, where they asked for wine, got drunk, brawled and quarreled, and finally raised their canes and pounded each other. The noise became greater and greater until it finally reached as far as heaven.

Saint Peter, who guards the gate of heaven, believed that the underworld had begun to revolt and called the heavenly host together to repel the wicked archenemy if he and his followers were to storm the abode of the blessed. However, since they did not come, he mounted his horse and rode through the gate of heaven down into the underworld. There he made the dead quiet down and ordered them to return to their graves. Then he took the moon away to heaven and hung it up in the sky.

◈ 176 ◈

The Life Span

AFTER GOD HAD CREATED THE WORLD and was about to determine the life span of each and every creature, the ass came to him and asked, "Lord, how long am I to live?"

"Thirty years," answered God. "Is that all right with you?"

"Oh, Lord," replied the ass, "that's a long time. Just consider the hard life I lead. From morning to night I carry heavy loads, drag sacks of grain into the mill so that others can eat bread, and I'm given nothing but blows and kicks to keep me fresh and cheerful. I ask you to relieve me of part of this long time."

God took pity on him and relieved him of eighteen years. The ass felt consoled and went away. Then the dog appeared.

"How long do you want to live?" God asked him. "Thirty years were too many for the ass, but I think you'll be content with that."

"Lord, is that your will? Just consider how much I must run. My feet will never be able to hold out that long. And once my voice for barking and my teeth for biting are gone, I'll just about be able to run from one corner to another and growl."

God saw that the dog was right and relieved him of twelve years of his life. Next came the monkey.

"You'll certainly want to live thirty years, won't you?" the Lord asked him. "You don't have to work like the ass and the dog, and you're always in good spirits."

"Oh, Lord," he answered, "it just looks that way, but it's not so. Even when times are good, I just get to scrape the bottom of the barrel. I'm always supposed to perform merry pranks and make faces. Yet, whenever they hand me an apple and I bite into it, it's sour. My mirth only masks my sadness. I'll never be able to endure all this for thirty years."

God was merciful and took away ten years of his life. Finally, man appeared. He was joyful, healthy, and vigorous, and he asked God to determine his life span.

"You shall live thirty years," the Lord said. "Is that enough for you?"

"What a short time!" exclaimed man. "Imagine, when I've built my house and the fire is burning on my own hearth, when I've planted trees that blossom and bear fruit, and when I'm just getting ready to enjoy life, I'll have to die! Oh, Lord, give me more time."

"I shall add on the eighteen years of the ass," God said.

"That's not enough," replied man.

"You shall also have the twelve years of the dog."

"Still too little."

"Very well then," said God. "I shall even give you the ten years of the monkey, but nothing more."

The man went away, but he was not satisfied.

So man lives seventy years. The first thirty are his human years, which pass by rapidly. This is the time when he is healthy and cheerful, works with pleasure and is glad to be alive. After this period come the eighteen years of the ass, when one burden after the next is laid upon him. He must carry the grain that nourishes others, and he receives blows and kicks as reward for his faithful service. Then come the twelve years of the dog, when he lies in a corner, growls, and has no more teeth with which to bite. And when this period is over, the ten years of the monkey round out his life. Then man becomes soft in the head and foolish, does silly things, and becomes the laughingstock of children.

◈ 177 ◈

The Messengers of Death

IN DAYS OF OLD there was once a giant who was traveling on a large country road, when suddenly a stranger jumped out in front of him and cried out, "Stop! Not one step farther!"

"What?" the giant said. "You measly wretch, I can squash you between my fingers, and you want to block my way? Who do you think you are that you dare to speak so boldly to me?"

"I am Death," responded the other. "Nobody can resist me, and even you must obey my commands."

However, the giant refused and began to wrestle with Death. It was a long, violent struggle. Finally, the giant got the better of Death and hit him with his fist so that he collapsed next to a stone. The giant continued on his way, and Death lay there defeated. He was so weak that he could not pull himself up. "What will come of this," he said, "if I'm left to lie here on this spot? There will be no more deaths in the world, and there will be so many people in the world that they'll no longer have enough room to stand next to one another."

Just then a young, vigorous, and healthy man came along. He was singing a song, and his eyes roamed back and forth. When he spotted Death, who was half-unconscious, he went to him out of compassion, propped him up, gave him a drink from a bottle to refresh him, and waited until the stranger regained his strength.

"Do you happen to know," asked the stranger as he stood up, "who I am and who you have helped to his feet?"

"No," answered the young man, "I don't know you."

"I am Death," he said. "I don't spare anyone and cannot make exceptions, even with you. But, just so that you can see that I'm grateful, I'm going to promise you that I won't seize you unexpectedly. Instead I'll send my messengers to you right before I come to fetch you."

"Well," said the young man, "it's still to my advantage that I will know when you are coming, and at least I'll be safe from you during this time."

Then the young man moved on. He was merry and in good spirits and took each day as it came. But youth does not last forever. Soon sickness and sorrows came, and they tormented him during the day and would not let him sleep at night. "I won't die," he said to himself, "until Death first sends his messengers. I only wish that these terrible days of sickness were over with."

As soon as he began to feel well, he began to live with joy again. Then one day somebody tapped him on the shoulder. He looked around, and Death was standing behind him and said, "Follow me, the hour has come for you to take leave of the world."

"What?" responded the man. "Are you going to break your word? Didn't you promise me that you'd send your messengers to me before you came yourself? I haven't seen any messengers."

"Be quiet!" replied Death. "Didn't I send you one messenger after another? Didn't fever come to jolt and shake you up and knock you off your feet? Didn't dizziness numb your head? Didn't gout make all your limbs twitch? Didn't you hear a roaring noise in your ears? Didn't the toothache gnaw at your cheeks? Didn't your eyesight become dim? And, aside from all this, didn't my very own brother, sleep, remind you of me? Didn't you lie there evenings as if you were already dead?"

The man did not know what to reply. So he surrendered to his fate and went away with Death.

◆ 178 ◆

Master Pfriem

MASTER PFRIEM WAS A SMALL, LEAN, BUT LIVELY MAN, who could never sit still for a second. His face was deathly pale and pockmarked, and its most outstanding feature was a turned-up nose. His hair was gray and shaggy and his eyes small, and they shifted quickly and constantly to the left and right. He noticed everything, found fault with everything, knew everything better, and was always right. Whenever he went walking on the street, he steered himself by swinging both arms violently, and one time he hit a maiden who was carrying water. Her pail flew high into the air, and he himself was doused by the water.

"You idiot!" he yelled at her while shaking himself. "Couldn't you see that I was coming behind you?"

He was a shoemaker by trade, and when he worked, he pulled out the thread with such force that his fist pulverized anyone who did not stand far enough away from him. Not a single apprentice remained longer than one month in his employ, for the shoemaker always found something wrong, even with the very best work. Sometimes the stitches were not even, or a shoe was too long, or a heel was higher than another, or the leather was not softened enough. "Wait," he would say to the apprentice, "I'll show you how to pound the skin so that it becomes soft." And he would fetch a strap and give him a couple of blows on his back. He called all the apprentices lazy good-for-nothings. However, he himself did not produce very much because he could not sit still longer than fifteen minutes. His wife generally got up early in the morning and started the fire. Then he would jump out of bed and run with bare feet into the kitchen. "Do you want to set my house on fire?" he would scream. "You can roast an ox with a fire like that. Or, do you think that wood doesn't cost money?" If the maids stood at the washbasin and laughed and told each other the latest gossip, he would scold, "There stand the geese jabbering away and neglecting their work, just so they can gossip. And the fresh soap? What a terrible waste. They're disgracefully lazy besides! They won't give the clothes a good rubbing because they want to keep their hands soft." He would jump around and kick over a bucket full of suds so that the entire kitchen would be covered with water.

When a new house was in the process of being built, he ran over to his window and looked on. "They're building a wall with that red sandstone again!" he exclaimed. "It never dries out, and nobody will stay healthy in that house. And just look at how badly the workers are laying the stones. The cement is worthless. They should be putting gravel in it, not sand. I'll live to see the day when the house collapses on the heads of the people inside." He sat down, sewed a couple of stitches, and then jumped up again. This time he took off his leather apron and cried out, "I'll just go out and appeal to their consciences."

When he came up to the carpenters, he asked, "What's that? You're not chopping along the grain! Do you think the beams will be straight? The entire house will fall apart." He snatched an ax from a carpenter's hand to show him how he should chop, but when a wagon loaded with clay came by, he threw away the ax and sprang toward the farmer who was walking next to it. "You're out of your mind!" he exclaimed. "Nobody should ever harness young horses to pull a wagon with a heavy load. The poor beasts will collapse on the spot." The farmer did not respond, and Pfriem ran back into his workshop full of rage. Just as he was about to settle down and resume working, his apprentice handed him a shoe. "What's this again?" Pfriem yelled at him. "Didn't I tell you not to cut the shoes so wide? Who'll buy a shoe like this, when there's nothing left there but a sole? I demand that you carry out my orders to the letter!"

"Master," the apprentice responded. "You may certainly be right that the shoe is poor, but it's the same one that you yourself were cutting and working on before you jumped up and went outside. You knocked it off the table, and I only kept it for you. But even an angel from heaven couldn't make a shoe to please you."

One night Master Pfriem dreamed that he had died and was on his way to heaven. When he arrived, he knocked loudly at the gate. "I'm surprised," he said, "that they don't have a knocker on the gate. You can knock your knuckles sore this way."

Saint Peter opened the gate to see who wanted to enter and was causing such a commotion. "Oh, it's you, Master Pfriem," he said. "I'll let you enter, of course, but I'm warning you that you had better not act as you usually do and better not try to find fault with things here in heaven. Otherwise, you'll have to pay the consequences."

"You could have spared me the warning," Pfriem responded. "I know what's proper, and besides, everything here is perfect, thank God, and there's nothing to find fault with as there is on earth."

So he entered and wandered all over the vast reaches of heaven. He looked around to his left and right, and sometimes he shook his head or mumbled something to himself. Then he caught sight of two angels carrying a beam. It was the beam that someone had had in his eye while he had been searching for the splinter in the eye of someone else. However, they were not carrying the beam lengthwise, rather crosswise. Did you ever see anything so senseless? thought Master Pfriem. However, he said nothing and kept his peace. Basically it's all the same how they carry a beam, lengthwise or crosswise, just as long as they succeed, and to tell the truth, I didn't see them bump into anything.

Soon he saw two angels drawing water from a well and pouring it into a barrel. At the same time he noticed that the barrel was full of holes, and that the water was trickling through all sides. They were watering the earth with rain. "Confound it!" he exploded, but fortunately he gained control of himself and thought, Perhaps it's just a way to pass the time. If they get some enjoyment out of it, obviously they can do all sorts of useless things here in heaven. I've already realized that people here tend to loaf about for the most part.

Pfriem went farther and saw a wagon that was stuck in a deep ditch. "No wonder," he said to the man who stood nearby. "Who loaded the wagon in such a foolish way? What do you have there?"

"Pious wishes," answered the man. "I couldn't get on the right path with them, but fortunately I've managed to push the wagon this far. I'm sure they won't let me remain stuck here."

Indeed, an angel came and harnessed two horses to the front of the wagon.

"Very good," Pfriem asserted, "but two horses are not enough to drag the wagon out. You need at least four."

Another angel came and brought two more horses, but he did not harness them in front, rather in the rear. This was too much for Master Pfriem.

"You idiot!" he exploded. "What are you doing there? Nobody has ever pulled a wagon this way since the world was created. But these people here, with their mysterious arrogance, think they know how to do everything better!"

He wanted to continue talking, but one of the inhabitants of heaven grabbed him by the collar and with great force shoved him outside the gate. Master Pfriem stuck his head underneath the gate once more to take another look at the wagon, and he saw that it was being lifted by four winged horses.

Just at this moment Master Pfriem awoke. Naturally things are done differently in heaven than they are on earth, he thought to himself. Many things can be excused there, but who can watch patiently when horses are harnessed in the front and rear of a wagon at the same time? Of course, they had wings, but who could have known that? Besides, it's amazingly stupid to fasten wings to horses who already have four legs for running. But I must get up; otherwise, they'll start doing everything wrong in my house. It's just lucky that I didn't really die.

◈ 179 ◈

The Goose Girl at the Spring

ONCE UPON A TIME there was a very old woman who lived with a flock of geese in a lonely place on a mountain. She had a little house in this lonely spot, which was surrounded by a large forest. Every morning the old woman took her crutch and hobbled into the woods, where she was quite busy, much busier than one would have expected of someone her age. She gathered grass for her geese, picked wild fruit from the branches that her hands could still reach, and then carried everything home on her back. One would have thought that she would have collapsed to the ground under the heavy load, but she always brought it home safely. If she met people along the way, she would greet them in a friendly manner, "Good day, dear neighbor. Nice weather we're having today. Ah, you're wondering why I'm carrying the grass. Well, we all have burdens to bear on our backs." However, people did not like to encounter her, and when they had a choice, they took a different path. And, whenever a father chanced to meet her in the company of his son, he would say softly to him, "Beware of the old woman. She has cunning ways. She's a witch."

One morning a handsome young man was going through the forest. The sun shone brightly. The birds sang. A cool breeze caressed the leaves, and he was full of joy and good cheer. He had yet to come across anyone, when suddenly he spotted the old witch, who was kneeling on the ground and cutting grass with a sickle. She had already gathered a full load in her pack, and two baskets filled with wild pears and apples stood next to it.

"My God, old woman," he said, "how can you possibly carry all that away?"

"I must carry it, dear sir," she answered. "Children of the rich don't have to do such things. But the peasants have a saying that goes:

'Watch out but don't look back.
Your spine's curved like a sack.'

"Do you want to help me?" she asked as the young man continued to stand next to her. "You still have a straight back and young legs. It would be easy for you. Besides, my house is not very far from here.

It's on a heath beyond the mountain over there. You could make it up there quickly, in a hop, skip, and a jump."

The young man felt sorry for the old woman. "I'll confess. My father is not a farmer," he answered, "but a rich count. However, so that you will see that farmers are not the only ones who can carry things, I shall take your bundle on my back."

"If that's your will," she responded, "then I am pleased. It will take a good hour of your time, but that should not matter to you. You must also carry the apples and pears over there."

The young count began to have some doubts when the woman mentioned an hour's walk, but she did not let him renege. She lifted the sack on his back and hung two baskets on his arm.

"You see," she said, "there's nothing to it."

"No, it's not all that light," responded the count, who had a pained expression on his face. "The bundle is very heavy. It feels as if it were packed with nothing but bricks, and the apples and pears feel as though they were made of lead. I can hardly breathe." He would have liked to set everything down, but the old woman did not let him.

"Just look," she said mockingly, "the young gentleman won't carry what an old woman like me has so often hauled. You're good with pretty words, but when it comes to serious action, you want to scoot away like the wind. Why are you standing around and dallying?" she continued. "Get a move on. Nobody's going to take the bundle off your back again."

As long as he walked on level ground, he could stand it, but as soon as they came to the mountain and had to climb, and the stones rolled out from under his feet as though they were alive, it was beyond his strength. Beads of sweat appeared on his forehead and trickled down his back, hot and cold.

"Old woman," he said, "I can't go any farther. I want to rest a while."

"Nothing doing," answered the old woman. "Once we've arrived, you can relax, but now you must keep marching. Who knows what good all this may do you?"

"Old woman, you're becoming shameless," said the count, and he wanted to throw off the pack. However, he struggled to no avail. The pack was stuck to his back as tightly as if it grew there. He twisted and turned, but he could not get rid of it. The old woman laughed at him and jumped delightedly with her crutch.

"Don't get mad, dear sir," she said. "Your face is turning as red as a tin rooster. Bear your burden with patience. When we get home, I'll certainly give you a good tip for your service."

What was he to do? He could only resign himself to his fate and plod along patiently after the old woman. She seemed to become more and more nimble, while his load seemed to become heavier and heavier. Then, all at once, she took a leap and landed on top of the pack and sat there. Even though she was as thin as a rail, she weighed more than the plumpest peasant woman. The young man's knees wobbled, and when he did not continue, the old woman hit his legs with a branch and with stinging nettles. He groaned continually as he climbed the mountain, and just as he was about to collapse, he finally reached the old woman's house. When the geese spied the old woman, they stretched their wings and necks in the air, ran toward her, and cackled greetings. The flock was followed by an old, old wench with a stick in her hand. She was big and strong, but ugly as sin.

"Mother," she said to the old woman, "did something happen to you along the way? You were gone so long."

"Heaven forbid, my little daughter," she responded. "Nothing bad happened to me. On the contrary, this kind gentleman here carried my load for me. Just think, he even carried me on his back when I became tired. The journey passed by quickly because we enjoyed ourselves and had fun with one another along the way."

The old woman finally slid off the young man and took the bundle from his back and the basket from his arm. She looked at him in a friendly way and said, "Now, sit down on the bench in front of the door and rest. You've earned your reward fairly, and you shall have it in due time."

Then she said to the goose girl, "Go into the house, my little daughter. It's not proper for you to be alone with a young man. No need to add oil to the fire. He could fall in love with you."

The count did not know whether he should weep or cry. Even if she were thirty years younger, he thought, my heart would never be moved by a treasure like that.

In the meantime, the old woman fondled her geese like children and then went into the house with her daughter. The young man stretched himself out on a bench underneath a wild apple tree. The air was warm and mild. All around him was a green meadow covered with cowslips, wild thyme, and a thousand other flowers. There was a clear brook that glistened with the sun's rays and rippled through the middle of the meadow. The white geese waddled back and forth or paddled in the water. "It's quite lovely here," he said. "But I'm so tired that I can't keep my eyes open. I'm going to sleep for a while. I only hope that a gust of wind doesn't come and blow my feet out from under me. They feel as brittle as tinder wood."

After he had slept awhile, the old woman came and shook him until he awoke. "Get up," she said. "You can't stay here. I confess I gave you a hard time, but it didn't cost you your life. Now you shall have your reward. Since you don't need money or land, I shall give you something else." Upon saying this, she placed a little box carved from a single emerald into his hand. "Take good care of it," she added. "It will bring you luck."

The count jumped up feeling that he had regained his strength and energy. He thanked the old woman for the present and set upon his way without turning around even once to look at the beautiful daughter. When he had gone some distance, he could still hear the merry cries of the geese.

The count must have wandered three days in the wilderness before he could find his way out. Eventually he reached a large city, and since he was a stranger, he was taken to the royal castle to meet the king and queen, who were sitting on their throne. The count knelt down before them, took the emerald box out of his pocket, and laid it at the queen's feet. She beckoned to him to stand up and hand her the little box. No sooner had she opened it and looked inside than she fell to the ground as if she were dead. The count was seized by the king's servants and was about to be taken to the prison when the queen opened her eyes and cried out that they should release him. She ordered everyone to go outside and declared that she wanted to speak with the count in private.

When the queen was alone with him, she began to cry bitterly and said, "What's the use of all these splendors and honors that surround me when I awake every morning troubled and sorrowful! I had three daughters, and the youngest was so beautiful that the entire world considered her a miracle. She was as white as snow, as pink as apple blossoms, and her hair glittered like the rays of the sun. Whenever she cried, it was not tears that dropped from her eyes but pearls and jewels. On her fifteenth birthday the king summoned all three daughters to his throne. You should have seen how everyone gaped when the youngest entered: it was as if the sun had risen. The king said, 'My daughters, I don't know how much longer I have to live. So I shall decide today what each one of you is to receive after my death. You all love me, but whoever loves me most shall be given the best part of my realm.' Each of them said she loved him most of all. 'I want you to describe just how much you love me,' said the king. 'Then I'll be able to tell more clearly what you mean.' The oldest one said, 'I love my father as much as I love the sweetest sugar.' The second said, 'I love my father as much as I love my prettiest dress.' The youngest, however, kept quiet. Then her father asked, 'And you, my dearest child, how much do you love me?' 'I don't know,' she answered. 'I can't compare my love with anything.' Yet, her father insisted. She had to name something. Finally, she said, 'The best food has no taste without salt. Therefore, I love my father as much as I love salt.' When the king heard this, he became enraged and said, 'If you love me as much as you love salt, then your love shall also be rewarded with salt.'

"So he divided his kingdom between the two older daughters. However, he ordered a sack of salt bound to the back of his youngest daughter, and two servants were told to lead her out into the wild forest. We all pleaded and begged for her," the queen said, "but the king's rage could not be calmed. How she cried when she was forced to leave us! The entire way was strewn with pearls that fell from her eyes. Soon after, the king regretted his severity and had the entire forest searched for the poor child, but nobody could find her. When I think that wild animals may have eaten her, I don't know how to contain my grief. Sometimes I console myself with the hope that she is still alive and may have hidden herself in a large cave or has found shelter with merciful people. Now, you can imagine how I felt when I opened the emerald box, and there was a pearl just like the ones that my daughter used to shed from her eyes, and you can also imagine how the sight of this stirred my heart. So you must tell me how you came upon this pearl."

The count told her he had received it from the old woman in the forest who had seemed uncanny to him and who he believed must be a witch. However, he had not seen a sign nor had he heard a thing about the queen's child. Nevertheless, the king and queen decided to seek out the old woman because they thought that they might obtain news of their daughter where the count had been given the pearl.

The old woman sat outside in her lonely place, spinning on her spinning wheel. It had already become dark, and a log burning on the hearth gave off a little light. All of a sudden there was a noise from the outside. The geese were coming home from the meadow, and their merry cries could be heard. Soon the daughter entered, but the old woman thanked her only by nodding her head a bit. The daughter sat down beside her, took her spinning wheel, and twisted the thread as nimbly as a young girl would. Thus they both sat for two hours without exchanging a word. Finally, something rustled at the window, and two fiery eyes glared inside. It was an old nightowl that uttered *"Tu whit-whoo"* three times. The old woman looked up just a little and said, "Now, my little daughter, it's time for you to go outside and do your work."

She stood up and went outside. Where did she go? Over the meadow toward the valley, farther and farther. Finally, she reached a spring surrounded by three old oak trees. In the meantime, the moon was round and large and had risen above the hill. It was so bright that one could easily have found a pin on the ground. The maiden removed the skin that covered her face, leaned over the spring, and began to wash herself. When she was finished, she dipped the skin in the water and laid it out on the ground so it could bleach and dry in the moonlight. But how the maiden was transformed! You've never seen anything like this in your life! After the gray wig had been taken off, her golden hair flared like sunbeams and spread like a cloak over her entire body. Her eyes sparkled like glistening stars in the sky, and her cheeks gleamed with the soft red glow of apple blossoms.

But the beautiful maiden was sad. She sat down and cried bitterly. One tear after another sprang from her eyes and rolled through her long hair down onto the ground. There she sat and would have remained for a long time if she had not heard a cracking and rustling in the branches of a nearby tree. Like a deer jolted by the shot of a hunter, she jumped up, and at the same time a black cloud passed over the moon. So the maiden immediately slipped back into the old skin and vanished like a light blown out by the wind. Trembling like an aspen leaf, she ran all the way home. The old woman was standing in front of the door, and the maiden wanted to tell her what had happened, but the old woman laughed in a friendly way and said, "I know everything already." She led the maiden into the room and started a new fire. However, she did not sit down at the spinning wheel again. Rather she fetched a broom and began to sweep and scrub. "Everything must be clean and neat," she said to the maiden.

"But, Mother," the maiden asked. "Why are you starting to work at such a late hour? What do you have in mind?"

"Do you know what time it is?" responded the old woman.

"Not past midnight yet," answered the maiden, "but it certainly must be past eleven."

"Don't you remember," continued the old woman, "that you came to me three years ago on this day? Your time is up. We can no longer stay together."

The maiden was scared and said, "Oh, Mother dear, do you want to throw me out? Where shall I go? I have neither home nor friends to turn to. I've done everything you've asked of me, and you've always been satisfied with me. Don't send me away."

The old woman did not want to tell the maiden what was in store for her. "My own stay here is over," the old woman said to her. "But before I leave, the house and room must be clean. Therefore, I don't want you to hinder my work, and don't worry on your own account. You shall find a roof to shelter you, and I'm sure that you'll be satisfied with the wages that I'm about to give you."

"But tell me, what is going on?" insisted the maiden.

"And I'm telling you again, do not disturb my work. Don't say one more word. Just go into your room, remove the skin from your face, and put on the silk dress that you were wearing when you came to me. Then wait in your room until I call you."

But now I must say something about the king and queen who had departed with the count to seek out the old woman in her lonely place. The count had strayed from them in the forest during the night and had been forced to continue on his way alone. The next day it seemed to him that he was on the right path. He kept going until it became dark, and then he climbed up a tree and intended to spend the night there, for he was worried that he might get lost. When the moon cast its light on his surroundings, he spotted a shape meandering down the mountain. He could see that it was the goose girl whom he had previously encountered at the old woman's house, even though she was not carrying a stick in her hand. "Oho!" he exclaimed. "Here she comes. Once I catch one of the witches, I'll soon have the other in my hands as well." However, as he watched her go to the spring, take off the skin, and wash herself, his astonishment grew. Then when her golden hair swooped down her sides, he felt that she was more beautiful than anything else he had ever seen in the world. He hardly dared to breathe, but he did stick his head between the leaves as far as he could and looked straight at her. Whether he bent over too far, or whatever the cause, the branch suddenly cracked, and at the very same moment she slipped into the skin, jumped up like a deer, and disappeared from his sight just as the moon was covered by a cloud.

No sooner had she disappeared than the count climbed down from the tree and quickly rushed after her. He had not gone very far, when he noticed two figures wandering across the meadow in the twilight. It was the king and queen, who had glimpsed the light in the old woman's house from the distance and were heading straight for it. When the count told them about the miraculous things he had seen at the spring, they were sure that the goose girl was their lost daughter. Full of joy, they went on and soon arrived at the little house. The geese were sitting all around it with their heads tucked under their wings. Not one of them moved, as they were all fast asleep. The three travelers looked through the window and saw the old woman silently sitting and spinning. She nodded her head but did not look around. Everything was very clean in the room, as if the little fog men whose feet carry no dust lived there. However, the king and queen did not see their daughter. For a while they looked at everything, and finally they summoned up the courage to knock softly on the window. The old woman seemed to have expected them. She stood up and called out in a friendly way, "Come in, I already know who you are."

After they had entered the room, the old woman said, "You could have spared yourself the long journey if you had not unjustly banished your good and lovely child three years ago. Yet, the banishment has not harmed her. She has had to tend the geese for three years. She learned nothing evil in the process and has kept herself pure of heart. You, however, have been punished sufficiently by the anguish you've suffered." Then she went to the door and called, "Come out, my little daughter."

The door opened, and the princess emerged with her golden hair and sparkling eyes. She was dressed in her silk gown, and it was as if an angel had descended from heaven into the room. She went directly to her father and mother and embraced and kissed them. They could not help weeping for joy. The young count was standing next to them, and when she noticed him, her cheeks turned as red as a moss rose. She herself did not know why. Then the king said, "My dear child, I have given away my kingdom. What am I to give you now?"

"She doesn't need anything," the old woman said. "I'm giving her the tears that she shed because of you. They are pure pearls, more beautiful than the ones that can be found in the ocean, and they are worth more than your entire kingdom. And as a reward for her work, I am going to give her my little house."

Just as the old woman said that, she vanished in front of their eyes. The walls rattled a little, and when they looked around, they saw that the little house had been transformed into a splendid palace. A royal table had been set for them, and servants were running all about the place.

The story does not end here, but my grandmother, who told me the tale, was losing her memory, and she forgot the rest. Yet, I believe that the beautiful princess married the count and that they remained together in the palace and lived in bliss as long as it pleased God. Whether the snow white geese that were kept at the little house were really girls that the old woman had taken under her care (nobody need take this amiss) and whether they regained their human shape and stayed on as servants for the young queen, I am not sure, but I suspect that this was the case. One thing is sure: The old woman was not a witch, as people believed, but a wise woman who meant well. It was probably she who was at the birth of the princess and gave her the gift of weeping pearls instead of tears. Nowadays this does not happen anymore. Otherwise, the poor would soon become rich.

◈ 180 ◈

Eve's Unequal Children

WHEN ADAM AND EVE WERE DRIVEN OUT OF PARADISE, they were compelled to build a house on unfertile soil and to earn their food by the sweat of their brow. Adam plowed the field, and Eve spun wool. Every year Eve gave birth to a child, but the children were not alike. Some were beautiful, some ugly. After a considerable amount of time had passed, God sent an angel to Adam and Eve to inform them that he was coming to look at their household. Eve, delighted that the Lord was so gracious, cleaned the house diligently, decorated it with flowers, and spread rushes on the stone floor. Then she gathered her children around her, but only the most handsome. She washed and bathed them, combed their hair, put newly washed shirts on them, and warned them to behave decently and properly in the presence of the Lord. They were to bow politely, offer him their hands, and answer his questions in a modest and sensible way. However, the ugly children were told to keep out of sight. Eve hid one of them under the hay, another under the roof, the third in the straw, the fourth in the oven, the fifth in the cellar, the sixth under a tub, the seventh under the wine barrel, the eighth under an old fur, the ninth and tenth under the cloth from which she generally made their clothes, and the eleventh and twelfth under the leather from which she used to cut their shoes.

No sooner had she done all this than there was a knock at the door of the house. Adam peeped through a slit in the door and saw that it was the Lord. He opened the door respectfully, and the Heavenly Father entered and saw the handsome children standing in a row. They bowed, offered him their hands, and knelt down, and the Lord began to bless them. He placed his hands on the first one and said, "You shall become a powerful king." Likewise, to the second, "You shall become a prince." To the third, "You, a count." To the fourth, "You, a knight." To the fifth, "You, a nobleman." To the sixth, "You, a burgher." To the seventh, "You, a merchant." To the eighth, "You, a scholar." Thus he bestowed all his rich blessings on them.

When Eve saw that the Lord was so mild and merciful, she thought, I'll fetch my misshapen children. Perhaps he'll bestow his blessings on them as well. So she ran and fetched them from the hay, straw, oven, and wherever else she had hidden them. Then the entire band of coarse, dirty, scabby, and grimy children appeared. The Lord smiled, looked at all of them, and said, "I shall bless these children too." So he placed his hands on the first one and said to him, "You shall become a farmer." To the second, "You, a fisherman." To the third, "You, a blacksmith." To the fourth, "You, a tanner." To the fifth, "You, a weaver." To the sixth, "You, a shoemaker." To the seventh, "You, a tailor." To the eighth, "You, a potter." To the ninth, "You, a carter." To the tenth, "You, a sailor." To the eleventh, "You, a messenger." To the twelfth, "You, a house servant for the rest of your life."

When Eve had heard everything, she remarked, "Lord, how unequally you divide your blessings! They're all my children, you know. I gave birth to all of them. You should bestow your blessings on them equally."

But God responded, "Eve, you don't understand. I carry the responsibility, and it is necessary for me to populate the entire world with your children. If they were all princes and lords, who would grow the wheat or thresh, grind, and bake it? Who would be the blacksmiths, weavers, carpenters, bricklayers, shoemakers, and tailors? Each shall do according to his place so that one will sustain the next, just like all the limbs of the body support each other."

Then Eve answered, "Oh, Lord, please forgive my rashness and interference. Let your will be done also with my children."

◈ 181 ◈

The Nixie in the Pond

ONCE UPON A TIME there was a miller who led a pleasant life with his wife. They had money and property, and their prosperity increased from year to year. Calamity, however, can strike overnight. Just as their wealth had increased rapidly, it also began to decrease each year until the miller could hardly call the mill that he inhabited his own. His problems weighed heavily on him, and when he lay down in bed after working all day, he could not rest. Instead he tossed and turned and worried himself sick. One morning he got up before daybreak, went outside into the open air, and hoped that this would ease his heart. As he walked over the dam of the mill the first rays of the sun burst forth, and he heard a rushing sound in the pond. When he turned around, he caught sight of a beautiful woman, who was rising slowly out of the water. Her long hair, which she clasped by her tender hands over her shoulders, flowed down both sides and covered her white body. He realized that this was the nixie of the millpond and became so frightened that he did not know whether to go or stay. But the nixie raised her soft voice, called him by his name, and asked him why he was so sad. At first the miller was distrustful, but when he heard her speak in such a friendly way, he summoned his courage and told her that he had formerly lived in happiness and wealth but was now so poor that he did not know what to do.

"Calm yourself," responded the nixie. "I shall make you richer and happier than you ever were before. But you must promise to give me what has just been born in your house."

That can be nothing but a puppy or a kitten, thought the miller, and he agreed to give her what she desired. The nixie descended into the water again, and he rushed back to his mill feeling consoled and in good spirits. Just as he was about to enter the mill, the maid stepped out of his house and shouted that he should rejoice, for his wife had just given birth to a little boy. The miller stood still, as if struck by lightning. He realized that the sly nixie had known this and had deceived him. So he bowed his head and went to his wife's bedside, and when she asked him, "Why aren't you happy about our fine little boy?" he told her what had happened to him and what he had promised the nixie. "What good are happiness and wealth," he added, "if I must lose my child? But what can I do?" Even the relatives, who had come to visit and wish them happiness, did not know what advice to give him.

In the meantime, prosperity returned to the house of the miller. Whatever he undertook turned into a success. It was as if the coffers and chests filled themselves of their own accord, and the money kept multiplying overnight in the closet. It did not take long before his wealth was greater than it had ever been before. But he could not rejoice about this with an easy conscience. The consent that he had given to the nixie tortured his heart. Whenever he walked by the millpond, he feared that she might surface and remind him about his debt. He never let his son go near the water. "Be careful," he said to him. "If you just touch the water, she will grab your hand and drag you under." However, as the years passed, and the nixie did not reappear, the miller began to relax.

When his boy became a young man, he was given to a huntsman as an apprentice. Once he had learned everything and had become an able huntsman, the lord of the village took him into his service. In the village there was a beautiful and true-hearted maiden who had won the hunter's affection, and when the lord became aware of this, he gave the young man a small house. So the maiden and the huntsman were married, lived peacefully and happily, and loved each other with all their hearts.

Once when the huntsman was pursuing a deer, the animal turned out of the forest and into the open field. The huntsman followed it and finally killed it with one shot. He did not realize that he was close to the dangerous millpond, and after he had skinned and gutted the animal, he went to the water to wash his hands that were covered with blood. No sooner did he dip his hands into the water than the nixie rose up and embraced him laughingly with her sopping wet arms. Then she dragged him down into the water so quickly that only the clapping of the waves above him could be heard.

When evening fell, and the huntsman did not return home, his wife became anxious. She went outside to search for him, and since he had often told her that he had to beware of the nixie's snares and that he was never to venture close to the millpond, she already suspected what had happened. She rushed to the water, and when she found his hunting bag lying on the bank of the pond, she could no longer have any doubts about her husband's misfortune. She wrung her hands and uttered a loud groan. She called her beloved by his name, but it was all in vain. Then she rushed to the other side of the millpond and called him again. She scolded the nixie with harsh words, but she received no response. The water's surface remained as calm as a mirror. Only the face of the half-moon returned her gaze in stillness.

The poor woman did not leave the pond. Time and again she paced around it with quick steps, never resting for a moment. Sometimes she was quiet. Other times she whimpered softly. Finally, she lost her strength, sank to the ground, and fell into a deep sleep. Soon she was seized by a dream.

She was anxiously climbing up a mountain between two huge cliffs. Thorns and briers pricked at her feet. Rain slapped her face, and the wind whipped through her long hair. When she reached the peak, there was an entirely different view. The sky was blue; the air, mild. The ground sloped gently downward, and a neat little hut stood on a green meadow covered by flowers. She went toward the hut and opened the door. There sat an old woman with white hair, who beckoned to her in a friendly way.

At that very moment the poor young woman woke up. The day had already dawned, and she decided to let herself be guided by the dream. So she struggled up the mountain, and everything was exactly as she had seen it in the night. The old woman received her in a friendly way and showed her a chair where she was to sit. "You must have had a terrible experience," the woman said, "for you to have searched out my lonely hut."

The young woman cried as she told her what had happened to her. Then the old woman said, "Console yourself, for I shall help you. Here is a golden comb. Wait until the full moon has risen. Then go to the millpond, sit down on the bank, and comb your long black hair with this comb. When you're finished, set it down on the bank, and you'll see what happens."

The woman returned home, but she felt that the full moon was very slow in coming. Finally, it appeared in the sky. So she went out to the millpond, sat down, and combed her long black hair with the golden comb. And, when she was finished, she set it down on the edge of the water. Soon after, a bubbling from the depths could be heard, and a wave rose up, rolled to the shore, and took the comb away with it. The comb sank to the bottom in no time. Then the surface of the water parted, and the head of the huntsman emerged in the air. He did not speak, but with a sad look he glanced at his wife. At that very moment a second wave rushed toward the man and covered his head. Everything disappeared. The millpond was as peaceful as before, and only the face of the full moon shone upon it.

The young woman returned home disheartened. However, the dream came back to her and showed her the old woman's hut. The next morning she set out on her way once again and related her woes to the wise woman, who gave her a golden flute and said, "Wait until the full moon comes again. Then take this flute, sit down on the bank, play a beautiful tune, and after you're done, lay it down on the sand, and you'll see what happens."

The huntsman's wife did what the old woman told her to do. Just as she set the flute on the sand, there was a sudden bubbling from the depths. A wave rose up, moved toward the bank, and took the flute away with it. Soon after, the water parted, and not only the head of the man became visible but also half his body. He stretched out his arms toward her yearningly, but just as he did this, a second wave rolled by, covered him, and dragged him down into the water again.

"Oh, what's the use!" exclaimed the unfortunate woman. "I'm given glimpses of my dearest only to lose him again!" Grief filled her heart anew, but the dream showed her the old woman's hut for a third time. So she set upon her way again, and the wise woman comforted her, gave her a golden spinning wheel, and said, "Not everything has been completed yet. Wait until the full moon comes, then take the spinning wheel, sit down on the bank, and spin until the spool is full. When you're finished, place the spinning wheel near the water, and you'll see what happens."

The young woman followed the instructions exactly as she had been told. As soon as the full moon appeared, she carried the golden spinning wheel to the bank and spun diligently until there was no more flax left and the spool was completely full of thread. But, no sooner was the spinning wheel standing on the bank than the water bubbled in the depths more violently than ever before. A powerful wave rushed to the shore and carried the spinning wheel away with it. Soon after, the head and entire body of the man rose up high like a water geyser. Quickly he jumped to the shore, took his wife by the hand, and fled. But they had gone barely a short distance when the entire millpond rose up with a horrible bubbling and flowed over the wide fields with such force that it tore everything along with it. The two escapees could already picture their death. Then, in her fear, the wife called to the old woman to help them, and at that very moment they were transformed; she into a toad, he into a frog. When the flood swept over them, it could not kill them, but it did tear them apart from each other and carry them far away.

After the flood had run its course, and both had touched down on dry land, they regained their human shape. But neither one knew where the other was. They found themselves among strange people, who did not know where their homeland was. High mountains and deep valleys lay between them. In order to earn a living, both had to tend sheep. For many years they drove their flocks through fields and forests and were full of sadness and longing.

One day, when spring had made its appearance on earth again, they both set out with their flocks, and as chance would have it, they began moving toward each other. When the huntsman caught sight of another flock on a distant mountain slope, he drove his sheep in that direction. They came together in a valley, but they did not recognize each other. However, they were glad to have each other's company in such a lonely place. From then on they drove their flocks side by side every day. They did not speak much, but they felt comforted. One evening, when the full moon appeared in the sky and the sheep had already retired for the night, the shepherd took a flute from his pocket and played a beautiful but sad tune. When he was finished, he noticed that the shepherdess was weeping bitterly. "Why are you crying?" he asked.

"Oh," she answered, "the full moon was shining just like this when I last played that tune on a flute, and the head of my beloved rose out of the water."

He looked at her, and it was as if a veil had fallen from his eyes, for he recognized his dearest wife. And when she looked at him and the light of the moon fell on his face, she recognized him as well. They embraced and kissed each other. And nobody need ask whether they lived in bliss thereafter.

◈ 182 ◈

The Gifts of the Little Folk

A TAILOR AND A GOLDSMITH WERE TRAVELING TOGETHER, and one evening, after the sun had set behind the mountains, they heard the sound of distant music, which became more and more distinct. The music sounded unusual but so charming that they forgot all about how tired they were and rushed forward. The moon had already risen by the time they reached a hill on which they glimpsed a crowd of little men and women, holding hands and dancing joyfully round and round. As they danced, they sang a lovely tune, and this was the music that the travelers had heard.

In the middle of the circle sat an old man who was somewhat larger than the rest. He wore a brightly colored coat, and a whitish gray beard hung over his chest. The two travelers, who were stunned, stood still and watched the dance. The old man motioned to them to enter the circle, and the little folk willingly let them enter. The goldsmith, who had a hump and, like all hunchbacks, was sassy enough, moved into the ring. At first the tailor was afraid and held himself back. However, when he saw how merry everything was, he mustered up his courage and followed the goldsmith. Just as he did this, the circle closed again, and the little folk continued to sing and dance with the wildest leaps. Meanwhile, the old man took a huge knife, which hung on his belt, whetted it, and when it was sufficiently sharpened, he looked around at the strangers. They were frightened, but they did not have any time to reflect, for the old man grabbed the goldsmith, and, quick as lightning, shaved the hair on his head and his beard clean off. Right after this the same thing happened to the tailor. Yet, their fear vanished when the old man, after his work had been completed, slapped them both on the shoulder in a friendly way, as if he wanted to say that they had conducted themselves well by letting this happen to them willingly and without putting up a struggle. Then he pointed to a heap of coal that lay to one side and indicated to the travelers through gestures that they should fill their pockets with it. Both obeyed, although they did not know what use the coal would be to them. They then continued on their way and sought shelter for the night. By the time they arrived in the valley, the clock of the neighboring cloister was striking twelve. The music from the hill stopped abruptly. Everything vanished, and the hill stood alone in the moonlight.

The two travelers found an inn and covered themselves with their coats on their beds made out of straw. They were so tired, however, that they forgot to take the coal out of their pockets. When they were wakened earlier than usual by a heavy weight on their limbs, they reached into their pockets and could not believe their eyes: the pockets were filled not with coal but with gold. Moreover, much to their happiness, they found the hair on their heads and their beards fully restored. They were now rich people. But the goldsmith had filled his pockets more thoroughly than the tailor, in keeping with his greedy disposition, and possessed twice as much as his companion. Once a greedy man has a great deal, he demands even more. So the goldsmith proposed to the tailor that they spend another day in the region and in the evening go out again to fetch even greater treasures from the old man on the hill. The tailor refused and said, "I have enough and am satisfied. Now I can become a master tailor. I'll marry my darling little thing [as he called his beloved] and be a happy man." Nevertheless, to please the goldsmith, he agreed to remain another day.

In the evening the goldsmith hung a few more bags over his shoulder in order to pack away as much as he could, and set out for the hill. As on the previous night, he found the little folk singing and dancing. Once again the old man shaved him clean and indicated to him to take some coal with him. The goldsmith did not hesitate to stuff his pockets with whatever they could carry. He returned to the inn in seventh heaven and covered himself with his coat. "Even if the gold weighs me down," he said, "I'll gladly bear it." Finally, he fell asleep with a sweet feeling that he would awake the next morning as rich as a king. When he opened his eyes, he stood up quickly to examine his pockets, but he was astonished because he pulled out nothing but pieces of black coal. No matter how often he reached into his pockets, it was always the same.

I still have the gold that I won the night before, he thought, and he went to get it. But he was horrified to see that it had also turned to coal once again. As he hit himself on his forehead with his dusty black hand, he felt that his entire head had become smooth and bald and his chin as well. But his distress was not over yet. Just then he became aware of a second hump that had grown on his chest and was much larger than the one on his back. He then recognized that he had been punished for his greed and began to weep loudly. The good tailor, who was wakened by all this, consoled his unhappy companion as best he could and said, "Since you have been my comrade during our travels, I want you to stay with me and share my treasure."

He kept his word, but the poor goldsmith had to carry the two humps for the rest of his life, and he wore a cap to cover his bald head.

❖ 183 ❖

The Giant and the Tailor

A TAILOR, who was a great braggart but who seldom lived up to his boasts, decided to do a little wandering and look around the forest. As soon as he could, he left his workshop and

wandered one day
across bridge and way,
hither and thither,
farther and farther.

When he was finally out in the woods, he spied a steep mountain in the blue distance, and behind it was a tower that rose amidst a wild, dark forest high into the sky.

"My God!" exclaimed the tailor. "What's that?"

And since his curiosity had got the better of him, he went straight toward it without thinking. As he came closer his mouth and eyes popped wide open, for the tower had legs and jumped over the steep mountain in one leap. Now it stood before the tailor in the form of an enormously powerful giant.

"What do you want here, you tiny flyspeck," roared the giant with a voice that sounded like thunder coming from all sides.

The tailor whispered in reply, "I just wanted to look around to see if I could earn a living in the forest."

"If that's all you want," the giant said, "you can work for me as my servant."

"If that's the way it must be, why not?" said the tailor. "But what shall my wages be?"

"Your wages?" said the giant. "I'll tell you. You shall have three hundred and sixty-five days a year and an extra day added on when it's leap year. Is that all right with you?"

"It will do," the tailor answered, and thought to himself, I've got to make the best of a bad situation. I'll try to get out of this as soon as I can.

Then the giant said to him, "Go, little twirp, and fetch me a jug of water."

"Wouldn't it be better if I brought you the entire spring right away along with the entire well?" asked the boaster, and he carried the jug to the water.

"What? The entire spring along with the well?" the giant growled into his beard. He was somewhat stupid and foolish and began to show signs of fear. "This fellow has some tricks up his sleeve. He has a mandrake in his body. Be on your guard, old Hans. He's not meant to be a servant for you."

When the tailor had brought him the water, the giant ordered him to go into the forest and chop some logs and bring them home.

"Wouldn't it be better to chop down the entire forest with one stroke,

the entire forest,
with young and old,
with all that it has,
gnarled and smooth?"

the little tailor asked, and he went to chop the wood.
"What?

The entire forest,
with young and old,
with all that it has,
gnarled and smooth?

And the entire spring along with the well?" the gullible giant growled into his beard, and became even more afraid. "This fellow has tricks up his sleeve. He has a mandrake in his body. Be on your guard, old Hans. He's not meant to be a servant for you."

When the tailor had brought the wood, the giant ordered him to shoot two or three wild boars for supper.

"Wouldn't it be better to shoot a thousand with one shot instead and bring them all here?" asked the feisty tailor.

"What?" exclaimed the cowardly giant, and he became horror stricken. "That's enough for today. Go to sleep."

The giant was so terribly afraid, he could not catch a wink of sleep the entire night. He threw ideas back and forth, for he wanted to get rid of this cursed sorcerer of a servant—the sooner the better. In time he came upon an idea.

The next day the giant and the tailor went to a swamp surrounded by a group of willow trees. Then the giant said, "Listen to me, tailor. I want you to sit down on one of the willow branches because I want to see whether you can bend it down."

The little tailor quickly went and sat down. He held his breath and made himself heavy, so heavy that the branch bent down to the ground. However, since he had to gather his breath again by exhaling, the branch snapped back and sent him soaring into the air. Unfortunately, he had forgotten to put an ironing rod into his pocket so that he soon disappeared from sight, and the giant rejoiced. If the tailor has not descended to the ground by now, he is probably still floating around in the air.

◆ 184 ◆

The Nail

A MERCHANT HAD DONE GOOD BUSINESS at the fair. All his wares had been sold, and his money bag was lined with gold and silver. Now he wanted to begin the journey homeward so that he could reach his house before nightfall. After he had packed his saddlebags with the money and set them on his horse, he rode away. At noon he rested in a city, and when he wanted to continue on his way, the stableboy brought his horse to him but said, "Sir, there's a nail missing in the shoe of the left hind foot."

"Let it stay missing," responded the merchant. "The shoe will certainly hold during the six hours I have yet to go. I'm in a hurry."

In the afternoon, when he dismounted again and had the horse fed, a stableboy came to him and said, "Sir, there's a shoe missing from the left hind foot of your horse. Should I take the horse to the blacksmith?"

"Let it stay missing," replied the man. "The horse will certainly be able to hold out during the couple of hours that are left. I'm in a hurry."

He rode on, but not for long. The horse began to limp. It did not limp for very long before it began to stumble, and it did not stumble for very long before it fell to the ground and broke a leg. The merchant had to leave the horse lying there, while he took the saddlebags, swung them over his shoulder, and made his way home on foot. It was not until late in the night that he reached his house. "It was the cursed nail," he said to himself, "that caused all my misfortune."

Haste makes waste.

◆ 185 ◆

The Poor Boy in the Grave

ONCE UPON A TIME there was a poor shepherd boy whose father and mother had died, and the authorities placed him in the house of a rich man, who was supposed to feed and raise him. However, the man and his wife had wicked hearts, and even with all their wealth they were miserly and envious of others. When anyone took even a little bite of their food, they became upset. Hence, no matter what the poor boy did, he received more beatings than he received food to eat.

One day he was to look after the hen with her chicks. However, she sneaked through a hedge with her young ones, and a hawk suddenly swooped down upon her and carried her away through the air. The young boy screamed with all his might, "Thief, thief! Scoundrel!" But what good did that do? The hawk did not bring back his prey, but the man heard the noise, ran outside, and when he saw that the hen was gone, he fell into a rage and gave the young boy such a thrashing that the youngster could not move for the next few days. Then he had to watch the chicks without the hen, and that situation was even more difficult because the chicks ran all over the place. So he thought he would do a smart thing and tie them all together with a string so the hawk would not be able to steal any of them away from him. He was very much mistaken, however. A few days later, when he was exhausted from running around and from hunger, he fell asleep. The hawk came then and snatched one of the chicks. Since the others were attached to it, the bird carried off all of them together, and he landed on a tree and swallowed them. Just then the farmer returned home, and when he saw the misfortune, he became angry and beat the young boy so mercilessly that the youngster had to lie in bed for many days.

When he was up on his feet again, the farmer said to him, "You're too stupid for me. I can't use you as a chicken keeper, so you'll have to be my messenger."

Now, the man sent him to carry a basket full of grapes to the judge and a letter as well. Along the way the boy became so terribly overcome by thirst and hunger that he ate two of the grapes. After he brought the judge the basket, the judge read the letter, counted the grapes, and said, "Two are missing." The young boy confessed quite honestly that he had been driven by hunger and thirst to eat the two that were missing. The judge wrote a letter to the farmer and ordered the same amount of grapes again. And again the young boy was given the chore of carrying the grapes with a letter to the judge. When he again became terribly hungry and thirsty, he could not help himself and once again ate two grapes. However, before doing so, he took the letter out of the basket, placed it under a stone, and sat upon it so that the letter could not see and betray him later. Nevertheless, the judge took him to task on account of the missing grapes.

"Ah," said the young boy. "How did you discover this? The letter couldn't know because I placed it under a stone before eating the grapes."

The judge had to laugh at such simplemindedness and sent a letter to the man in which he warned him to treat the poor boy better and to give him more food and drink. Also he advised the man to teach him the difference between right and wrong.

"I'll soon show you the difference," the hard man said. "If you want to eat, you must also work, and if you do something wrong, you'll be taught sufficiently through beatings."

The following day the farmer gave the boy a difficult job to do. He was told to cut several bundles of hay to feed the horses, and the man threatened him by saying, "I'll be back in five hours, and if the hay is not chopped into fine pieces by that time, I'll beat you until you can't move a bone in your body."

The farmer went to the fair with his wife, servant, and maid and left only a small piece of bread for the young boy, who sat down at the seat for chopping hay and began to work with all his might. When he became hot, he took of his little coat and threw it onto the hay. Fearing that he would not be finished on time, he kept on cutting, and in his zeal he mistakenly chopped up his little coat with the hay. He became aware of the mishap much too late and therefore could not repair the damage. "Ah!" he exclaimed. "Now it's over for me! That wicked man doesn't make idle threats. When he returns and sees what I've done, he'll beat me to death. I'd rather take my own life."

The young boy had once overheard the farmer's wife say, "I have a jar of poison underneath the bed." However, she had said this only to keep away people with a sweet tooth, for the jug was filled with honey. The young boy crawled under the bed, brought out the jar, and ate it all up. "I don't know," he said, "people say that death tastes bitter, but I find it sweet. No wonder the farmer's wife has so often wished she were dead." He sat down on a small chair and was prepared to die. But instead of becoming weaker, he felt himself strengthened from the nourishing meal. "It must not have been poison," he said. "But the farmer once said that there was a little bottle of poison for the flies in his clothes closet. That will probably be real poison and will bring about my death." However, it was not poison but Hungarian wine. The young boy took the bottle out and drank it empty. "This death also tasted sweet," said he, but soon after, when the wine began to mount to his brain and make him dizzy, he believed his end was approaching. "I feel I'm going to die," he said. "I'll go out to the churchyard and look for a grave." He staggered forth, and when he reached the churchyard, he lay down in a freshly dug grave and felt he was losing his senses more and more. Nearby was a tavern, where a wedding was being celebrated. When he heard the music, he thought he was in paradise and lost all consciousness. The poor boy never awoke again. The shock of the potent wine and the cold frost of the night took his life, and he remained in the grave in which he had laid himself.

When the farmer received news of the young boy's death, he was terrified and feared he would be taken to court. Indeed, the fear took such a powerful hold on him that he sank to the ground and passed out. His wife, who was standing at the hearth with a pan full of fat, ran out to help him, but the flames spread from the pan and set the entire house on fire. It was but a few hours before the house lay in ashes. During the rest of their lives the farmer and his wife were tormented by a guilty conscience and spent their days in poverty and misery.

♦ 186 ♦

The True Bride

ONCE UPON A TIME there was a maiden who was young and beautiful, but when she was young, her mother died, and her stepmother did all she could to make her life miserable. When the stepmother gave her some work to do, the maiden diligently set about her task and tried her very best, no matter how hard the work was. Yet, nothing could move the wicked woman's heart. She was always dissatisfied and always found something wrong. The harder the maiden worked, the more she was given to do. The stepmother thought of nothing but how to make the maiden's burden heavier and heavier, and her life more and more wretched.

One day she said to the maiden, "Here are twelve pounds of feathers. You're to strip the quills, and if you haven't finished by this evening, you'll get a sound thrashing. Don't think that you can loaf the entire day!"

The poor maiden sat down to work but tears flowed down her cheeks, for she saw that it clearly was impossible to finish the work in one day. When a pile of feathers lay in front of her, if she sighed or threw up her hands in anguish, the feathers would fly about, and she would have to gather them and begin her work all over again. Once, when she propped her elbows on the table, put her face in her hands, and cried out, "Is there no one on God's earth who will take pity on me?" she heard a soft voice.

"Console yourself, my child. I have come to help you."

The maiden looked up, and an old woman was standing next to her. She took the maiden by the hand in a friendly way and said, "Just confide in me and tell me what's disturbing you."

Since she had spoken so sincerely, the maiden told her about her sad life, how one burden was piled on top of the next, and how she could no longer finish the chores assigned her. "If I'm not finished with these feathers by this evening, my stepmother will beat me. That was her threat, and I know she keeps her word."

Her tears began to flow again, but the good old woman said, "Don't worry, my child. Rest awhile and sleep. In the meantime, I'll do your work."

The maiden lay down on her bed and soon fell asleep. The old woman sat down at the table with the feathers and—*whish!*—they flew from the quills, which she barely touched with her withered hands, and soon she was finished with the twelve pounds. When the maiden awoke, there were large snow white stacks, and everything in the room had been neatly cleared away, but the old woman had disappeared. The maiden thanked God and sat still until evening came. Then the stepmother entered and was astonished to find that she had finished the work.

"You see, you wench," the stepmother said, "what one can do when one is industrious? You could have started on something else as well, but there you sit with your hands in your lap." As she left the room she said, "The creature has a trick or two up her sleeve. I've got to give her harder work to do."

The next morning she called the maiden and said, "Here's a spoon. You're to use it to empty the large pond next to the garden. And if you're not finished by nightfall, you know what will happen."

The maiden took the spoon and saw that it was full of holes, and even if it had not been, she still could not have emptied the pond with it. Yet, she went to work right away and knelt down by the pond, which caught her tears. Then the good old woman appeared again, and when she learned the reason for the maiden's distress, she said, "Don't give up hope, my child. Go into the bushes and lie down to sleep. I'll take care of your work."

When the old woman was alone, she had only to touch the pond, and the water rose up high like mist and dissolved itself in the clouds. Gradually the pond became empty, and when the maiden awoke before sunset and went to the pond, she saw nothing but fish flapping in the mud. Then she went to her stepmother and reported that the work had been completed.

"You should have been finished long ago," the stepmother replied, and her face turned pale from anger. However, she thought up something new. On the third morning she said to the maiden, "Over there on the plain you must build me a beautiful castle, and it must be finished by evening."

The maiden was horrified and said, "How can I do something as great as that?"

"Don't give me any of your back talk!" screamed the stepmother. "If you can empty a pond with a spoon full of holes, then you can also build a castle. I want to move in today, and if anything is missing, be it the least little thing in the kitchen or cellar, then you know what to expect."

The stepmother drove her out of the house, and when the maiden went into the valley, she found rocks lying on top of one another in piles. She tried with all her might to move them, but she could not make even the smallest one budge. So she sat down and wept and hoped for aid from the good old woman, who did not keep her waiting long. When she came, she comforted the maiden and said, "Just lie down over there in the shade and sleep. I'll soon build the castle for you. If you want, you'll be able to live in it yourself."

When the maiden had gone away, the old woman touched the gray rocks. Immediately they began moving and slid together until they stood there as if giants had built the walls. The castle was erected on this foundation, and it was as though countless hands were working invisibly, laying stone upon stone. The ground groaned, and huge pillars arose by themselves into the air and aligned themselves next to each other. The tiles lay themselves down on the roof in their proper places, and by noon the large golden weather vane, in the shape of a young woman in flowing robes, had already begun turning on top of the tower. By evening the interior of the castle had been completed. How the old woman did all this, I don't know, but the walls of the rooms were covered with silk and velvet. Brightly colored embroidered chairs stood next to richly ornamented armchairs at marble tables. Crystal chandeliers hung from the ceilings and cast their reflections on the polished floor. Green parrots sat in golden cages, and there were exotic birds singing lovely songs. The entire castle was filled with splendor, as though a king were going to move in.

The sun was just about to set when the maiden awoke, and the gleam from a thousand lights was shining on her. She walked quickly toward the castle and entered it through the open gate. The steps were covered with red carpets, and the golden landing was decked with trees in blossom. When she saw the splendor of the rooms, she stood still, as though turned to stone. Who knows how long she would have stood there if she had not begun to think about her stepmother, "Ah," she said to herself, "if only she would be satisfied now and would stop making my life so miserable."

When the maiden went and informed her that the castle was finished, the stepmother said, "I'll move in immediately," and she got up from her seat. When she entered the castle, she had to hold her hands over her eyes because the brightness dazzled her. "You see," she remarked to the maiden, "how easy it was for you! I should have given you something harder to do." She went through all the rooms and checked all the corners to see if anything was missing or lacking, but she could find nothing wrong.

"Now let's go downstairs," she said, and glared evilly at the maiden. "The kitchen and cellar must still be inspected, and, if you've forgotten anything, you won't escape your punishment."

But the fire was burning on the hearth. The food was cooking in the pots. The tongs and shovel were leaning against one side of the hearth. Nothing was missing, not even the coal box and water bucket.

"Where's the entrance to the cellar?" the stepmother cried out. "If it isn't amply stocked with casks of wine, you'll be in trouble." She lifted the trapdoor herself and climbed down the stairs, but she had barely taken two steps, when the heavy trapdoor, which was only propped up, slammed shut. The maiden heard a scream and lifted the door quickly in order to help her, but the stepmother had tumbled down the stairs, and the maiden found her lying dead on the ground.

Now the splendid castle belonged to the maiden. At first she did not know what to make of her good fortune. Beautiful clothes hung in the closets. The chests were filled with gold and silver or with pearls and jewels, and all of her wishes were fulfilled. Soon news of the maiden's wealth and beauty spread throughout the entire world. Every day suitors presented themselves, but none was able to please her. Finally, a prince arrived who found a way to move her heart, and they became engaged.

In the castle garden there was a green linden tree, and one day, as they were sitting together under it, the prince said, "I want to return home and get my father's consent to marry you. I beg you to wait for me here under this linden tree. I'll be back in a few hours."

The maiden kissed him on the left cheek and said, "Remain true to me and don't let anyone kiss you on this cheek. I'll wait here under the linden tree until you return."

The maiden sat under the linden tree until sunset, but he did not come back. She sat there for three days, from morning till evening, waiting for him, but in vain. On the fourth day, when he still did not appear, she said, "I'm certain he's had an accident. I'll go out and search for him, and I won't return until I've found him."

She packed up three of her most beautiful dresses, one embroidered with glittering stars, the second with silvery moons, the third with golden suns. Then she wrapped a handful of jewels in her kerchief and went forth. Wherever she went, she asked about her bridegroom, but nobody had seen him, and nobody knew anything about him. She wandered far and wide throughout the world, but she did not find him. Finally, she hired herself out as shepherdess to a farmer and buried her dresses and jewels under a rock.

Now she lived as a shepherdess by tending a herd, but she was sad and yearned for her beloved. She made a pet out of a calf that she fed from her hand, and when she would say:

"Little calf, little calf,
kneel and show me tenderness.
Don't forget your shepherdess,
as the prince forgot his bride
under the linden tree,
the maid who sat and cried."

then the calf would kneel down, and she would stroke it with her hand.

After she had lived there a few years in solitude and misery, a report circulated throughout the land that the king's daughter was going to celebrate her wedding. The way to the city passed through the village where the maiden lived, and one day, just as the maiden was driving her herd to pasture, the bridegroom happened to ride by on his horse. He sat proudly in the saddle and did not glance at her, but when she saw him, she recognized her beloved. She felt as if a sharp knife had pierced her heart. "Ah," she said, "I thought he would remain true to me, but he has forgotten me."

The next day he rode along the path again, and as he approached her, she spoke to the little calf:

"Little calf, little calf,
kneel and show me tenderness.

Don't forget your shepherdess,
as the prince forgot his bride,
under the linden tree,
the maid who sat and cried."

When he heard her voice, he reined in his horse and looked down, straight into the maiden's face. He held his hands in front of his eyes as if he wanted to remember something, but then he rode away quickly. As he gradually disappeared from sight her sorrow became even greater.

Soon after, a huge celebration was to be held at the king's court for three whole days, and the entire country was invited to attend. Now I'll make one last try, the maiden thought, and when evening came, she went to the rock under which she had buried her treasures. She took out the dress with the golden suns, put it on, and adorned herself with the jewels. She undid her hair, which she had hidden under her kerchief, and it dropped down in long locks at her sides. Then she went into the city, and nobody noticed her in the darkness. But when she entered the brightly lit hall, everyone was startled and taken aback, yet no one knew who she was. The prince approached her, and again he did not recognize her. He led her out to dance and was so enchanted by her beauty that he no longer thought of the other bride. When the ball was over, she disappeared into the crowd and hurried to return to the village before daybreak, where she put on her shepherdess's clothes once again.

On the next evening she took out the dress with the silver moons and stuck half-moons made of jewels in her hair. When she made her appearance at the ball, all eyes followed her. The prince rushed to her, and since he had fallen completely in love with her, he danced with her alone and had eyes for no other woman. Before the maiden departed, she had to promise him to come to the ball again on the final evening.

When she appeared for the third time, she was wearing the dress with stars that sparkled each time she took a step, and her hair ribbon and belt were edged with starlike jewels. The prince had been waiting for her a long time and pushed his way toward her. "Do tell me who you are," he said. "I feel as if I've already known you a long time."

"Don't you remember," she answered, "what I did when you left me?"

Then she went up to him and kissed him on the left cheek. At that moment his eyes were finally opened, and he recognized his true bride.

"Come," he said to her. "I won't stay here any longer." He took her hand and led her down to the coach. The horses galloped away to the magic castle, and it was as though the wind itself had been harnessed to the coach. From the distance they could already see the gleam of the brightly lit windows. When they drove by the linden tree, countless glowworms were swarming around it, and the tree shook its branches and sent out its fragrant smell. The flowers were blooming on the steps, and the song of the exotic birds resounded from the room. The entire court assembled in the main hall and the priest waited to marry the bridegroom to his true bride.

❖ 187 ❖

The Hare and the Hedgehog

WELL, CHILDREN, this story may seem farfetched to you, but it really is true. I got it from my grandfather, who enjoyed telling it, and before he would begin, he would always say, "It must indeed be true, my son; otherwise, nobody would be able to tell it." Anyway, the story went like this:

It was a Sunday morning at harvest time, just as the buckwheat was ripening. The sun was shining brightly in the sky. The morning breeze was blowing warmly over the fields of stubble. The larks were singing in the air. The bees were buzzing in the buckwheat, and the people were going to church in their Sunday best. All God's creatures were happy, and so was the hedgehog.

Indeed, the hedgehog stood in front of his door with his arms folded. And since he took such delight in the morning breeze, he began humming a little song to himself, no better or worse than a hedgehog is accustomed to sing on a fine Sunday morning. While he continued to sing to himself half aloud, it suddenly occurred to him that while his wife bathed and dressed their children, he could take a little walk in his field to see how his turnips were doing. The turnips were right near his house, and he was accustomed to eating them with his family. This is why he considered them his own. No sooner thought than done. The hedgehog closed the door to his house and made his way to the field. He had not gone very far from his house and was heading around the sloe bush at the edge of the turnip patch when he caught sight of the hare, who had gone out on business of the same sort, namely to look at his cabbage. When the hedgehog came within speaking distance of the hare, he bade him a friendly good morning. But the hare, who was a distinguished gentleman in his own way and terribly arrogant, did not reply to the hedgehog's greeting but assumed a very contemptuous manner and said, "How is it that you are here running around the field so early in the morning?"

"I'm taking a walk," the hedgehog said.

"A walk?" The hare laughed. "It seems to me that you could use your legs for better things."

This answer infuriated the hedgehog, for he could stand almost anything except remarks about his legs since they are crooked by nature.

"Do you really think," the hedgehog now said to the hare, "that you can do more things with your legs than I can with mine?"

"That's what I think," the hare said.

"That depends on the situation," asserted the hedgehog. "I'll bet you that I can beat you in a footrace."

"That's ridiculous! You with your crooked legs!" the hare said. "But, as far as I'm concerned, I'm willing if you're so eager. What should we bet?"

"A gold louis d'or and a bottle of brandy," the hedgehog said.

"Done!" said the hare. "Shake on it, and then we can begin at once."

"No, I'm not in such a great hurry," stated the hedgehog. "I still have an empty stomach. First I want to go home and eat a little breakfast. In half an hour I'll be back here at this place."

Upon saying this, the hedgehog headed home, for the hare was satisfied. Along the way, the hedgehog thought to himself, the hare will rely on his long legs, but I'll beat him. Even though he is indeed a distinguished gentleman, he's also stupid, and he'll pay for what he said to me. When the hedgehog arrived at his house, he said to his wife, "Wife, get dressed quickly. You must go with me to the field."

"What's the matter?" asked his wife.

"I've made a bet with the hare for a gold louis d'or and a bottle of brandy. I'm going to run a race with him, and I want you to be there."

"Oh, my God, man!" his wife screamed at the hedgehog. "Are you going mad? Have you lost your mind? How do you expect to run a race with the hare?"

"Hold your tongue, wife," the hedgehog responded. "That's my affair. Don't mix in men's business. Hurry up and get dressed and come with me!"

What was the hedgehog's wife to do? She had to follow him whether she liked it or not. When they were finally on their way, the hedgehog said to his wife, "Now, pay attention to what I'm going to tell you. Do you see the long field over there? That's where we shall hold our race. The hare will run in that furrow there, and I'll be in another, and we'll start from the upper end. Now, all you have to do is place yourself in the furrow, and when the hare arrives from the other side, you call out to him, 'Here I am already!' "

Just as he finished saying this, they arrived at the field. The hedgehog showed his wife her place and went up the field. When he reached the top, the hare was already there.

"Can we start?" asked the hare.

"Yes, indeed," said the hedgehog. "Let's go."

So they each took a place in a furrow, and the hare began to count, "On your mark, get set, go!" and off he went down the field like a cyclone. However, the hedgehog ran approximately three steps. Then he crouched in the furrow and remained quietly where he was.

When the hare arrived at the bottom of the field at full speed, the hedgehog's wife called out to him, "Here I am already!" The hare was astounded and totally baffled. He thought for sure that it was the hedgehog himself who had called out to him, for it is well known that the hedgehog's wife looks just like her husband. However, the hare thought, Something's wrong here. And he cried, "Let's race again. This time up the field!" And away he went again like a cyclone so that his ears flapped behind his head, while the hedgehog's wife remained quietly in her place. When the hare now reached the top, the hedgehog called out to him, "Here I am already!"

The hare was so enraged that he lost control of himself and screamed, "Let's race again! This time down the field."

"I don't mind," answered the hedgehog. "As far as I'm concerned, we can do this as often as you wish."

So the hare ran seventy-three times more, and the hedgehog always held his own against him. Each time the hare reached the bottom or top of the field, either the hedgehog or his wife would say to him, "Here I am already!" By the seventy-fourth time, however, the hare was not able to finish the race. He fell to the ground in the middle of the field. Blood flowed from his throat, and he lay dead on the spot. So the hedgehog took the louis d'or and the bottle of brandy that he had won, called his wife out of the furrow, and they happily went home together. And if they have not died by now, then they are still alive.

So this is how it came to pass that the hedgehog ran the hare to death on the Buxtehude Heath, and ever since that time, no hare has ever had the inclination to run a race with a Buxtehude hedgehog.

But the moral of this story is: First of all, nobody, no matter how superior he thinks he is, should ever make fun of an inferior even if the person is just a hedgehog. Second of all, it is advisable that, when a man wants to get married, he take a wife from his own class, and one who looks just like him. Thus, whoever is a hedgehog must see to it that his wife is also a hedgehog and so forth.

❖ 188 ❖

Spindle, Shuttle, and Needle

ONCE UPON A TIME there was a girl whose mother and father died when she was still a small child. At the end of the village her god-mother dwelt all alone in a cottage, where she supported herself by spinning, weaving, and sewing. This old woman took the orphaned child into her house, gave her work to do, and raised her in a pious way. When the girl was fifteen years old, the old woman became sick. She called the maiden to her bedside and said, "My dear daughter, I feel that my end is drawing near. I'm going to leave you the cottage so that you'll be protected from the wind and weather. I'm also leaving you the spindle, shuttle, and needle, so that you can earn your living." She placed her hands on the girl's head, blessed her, and said, "Keep the Lord in your heart, and everything will go well for you." With that the woman closed her eyes. When she was carried to her grave, the maiden followed the coffin, wept bitterly, and paid her last respects.

Now the maiden lived all alone in the cottage. She kept herself busy by spinning, weaving, and sewing. The blessings of the good old woman graced everything she did. It seemed as though the flax in the room increased by itself, and whenever she had woven a piece of clothing or a rug or had sewn a shirt, then a buyer immediately appeared and gave her plenty of money. Consequently, she was never in need and could even share some things with others.

At about this time a prince was traveling around the land, looking for a bride. He was not to choose a poor maiden, and he did not want a rich one. Hence, he said, "Whoever is the poorest and at the same time the richest shall be my bride." When he came to the village where the maiden lived, he asked, as he always did, who was the richest and who the poorest in the place. They told him first who the richest was. The poorest, they said, was the maiden who lived in the cottage at the end of the village. The rich maiden sat in front of the door to her house in fancy attire, and when the prince approached her, she stood up, went toward him, and curtsied. He looked at her, did not say a word, and rode on. When he came to the house of the poor maiden, she was not standing at the door but sitting in her room. He stopped his horse, looked through the window into the room that was brightened by the sunlight, and saw the maiden sitting at the spindle and spinning busily. She looked up, and when she noticed that the prince was peering inside, she blushed until her face became red, lowered her eyes, and continued spinning. Whether the thread was entirely even this time, I cannot say, but she did continue to spin until the prince rode off. Then she went to the window, opened it, and said, "Oh, it's so hot in the room," and she kept looking after the prince until she could no longer detect the white feathers on his hat.

The maiden sat down to her work again in her room and continued to weave. Then a saying occurred to her, one that the old woman had spoken at times when the maiden was working beside her, and so the maiden now sang to herself:

"Spindle, spindle, go far and wide,
bring back the suitor who seeks a bride."

Lo and behold! The spindle jumped right out of her hand and went through the door. When she stood up in bewilderment and looked after it, she saw it dancing merrily out into the fields, dragging a glittering golden thread behind it. Before long it disappeared from her sight. Since the maiden no longer had the spindle, she took the shuttle in her hand, sat down at the loom and began to weave. However, the spindle kept dancing along the way, and just as the thread reached its end, it came upon the prince.

"What's this I see?" he exclaimed. "I believe the spindle wants to show me the way!" He turned his horse around and followed the line of the golden thread back toward the cottage. Meanwhile, the maiden was still sitting, working, and singing:

"Shuttle, shuttle, weave things fine,
lead my suitor back down the line."

Suddenly the shuttle jumped out of her hand and through the door. In front of the threshold, however, it began to weave a carpet more beautiful than anyone has ever beheld. Roses and lilies blossomed on both sides, and in the middle, upon a golden ground, shoots of tall green grass arose, and hares and rabbits hopped about in their midst, while stags and deer poked their heads into the scene. Brightly colored birds sat high up in the branches. If they had begun singing, the picture would have been complete. The shuttle jumped back and forth, and it was as though everything grew by itself.

Since the shuttle had run away, the maiden sat down to sew. She held the needle in her hand and sang:

"Needle, needle, so sharp and fine,
get the house ready for my suitor on time."

Then the needle jumped from her fingers and flew back and forth in the room as quick as lightning. It was as if invisible spirits were working. Soon the table and benches were covered with green cloth, the chairs with velvet, and the walls with silk curtains. Barely had the needle finished its last stitch when the maiden saw the three white feathers from the prince's hat through the window. The spindle had brought him there with the golden thread. So he dismounted and stepped across the carpet into the house. As he entered the room the maiden stood there in her pitiful dress, yet she sparkled in it like a rose on a bush.

"You are the poorest and also the richest," he said to her. "Come with me. You shall be my bride."

She did not speak, but she extended her hand to him. Then he gave her a kiss, led her outside, lifted her on his horse, and brought her to the royal castle, where the wedding was celebrated with great rejoicing. The spindle, shuttle, and needle were preserved in the treasure chamber and were treated with great honor.

◈ 189 ◈

The Peasant and the Devil

ONCE UPON A TIME there was a smart and crafty little peasant. His numerous pranks were the talk of the land. The best story, however, concerns how he once tricked the devil and made a fool out of him.

One day when the little peasant had finished plowing his field and it was turning dark, he got ready to go home. Just then he caught sight of a heap of burning coals in the middle of his field, and when he went toward it, filled with amazement, he saw a small black devil sitting on top of the coals.

"Are you sitting on a treasure?" the little peasant asked.

"Yes, indeed," the devil answered, "on a treasure that contains more gold and silver than you've ever seen in your entire life."

"The treasure lies on my field and so belongs to me," said the little peasant.

"It's yours," the devil answered, "if you give me half of what your field produces during the next two years. I have money enough, but I yearn to have the fruits of the earth."

The peasant agreed to the bargain. "Just so that we do not quarrel about how to divide everything," he said, "you shall have everything that grows above the earth, and I shall get everything beneath it."

The devil was quite satisfied with the proposal, but the cunning little peasant had planted turnips. When the time came for the harvest, the devil appeared and wanted to fetch his crop. However, he found nothing but yellow, withered leaves, while the peasant took pleasure in pulling out his turnips.

"You've gotten the better of the deal this time," the devil said, "but this won't be the case next time. You shall have what grows above the earth, and I shall take what lies underneath."

"That's fine with me," the peasant answered. However, when the time came for sowing, the little peasant did not plant turnips again but wheat. When the crop became ripe, the little peasant went to the field and cut the full stalks to the ground. When the devil came, he found nothing but the stumps and went away in a fury to a cleft in the cliffs.

"This is the way to dupe foxes," the little peasant said, and he went and fetched the treasure.

◆ 190 ◆

The Crumbs on the Table

ONE DAY the rooster said to his hens, "Come into the kitchen and pick the bread crumbs from the table. Your mistress has gone out to pay some visits."

Then the hens said, "No, no, we're not going to come in. If the mistress finds out, she'll beat us."

Then the rooster said, "She won't find out. Come and help yourselves. After all, she never gives you anything good."

Again the hens said, "No, no. We won't touch a thing. We're not going to come."

But the rooster continued to pester them until finally they came, sprang on the table, and ate up all the bread crumbs to the last piece. But just at that very moment the mistress returned, and she quickly took a stick, and with it she drove the hens away and walloped them mercilessly. And when they were outside the house, the hens said, "D'd ya, d'd ya, d'd ya, d'd ya see?"

Then the rooster laughed and said to them, "Didn't, didn't, didn't I know it?"

Then they just went away.

◈ 191 ◈

The Little Hamster From the Water

ONCE UPON A TIME there was a king's daughter, and in her castle under the pinnacle she had a large rotunda with twelve windows facing all the directions of the sky. Whenever she climbed up to the pinnacle and looked around, she could survey her entire realm. From the first window she could see things more clearly than any other human being. From the second she could see much better, from the third, even more distinctly, and so it went until the twelfth, from which she could see everything above and beneath the earth. Nothing could be concealed from her, and since she was proud, she refused to allow anyone to govern her and intended to rule the kingdom alone. She let it be known that anyone who wished to become her husband would have to be able to hide himself so well that it would be impossible for her to find him. Whoever attempted this and was discovered by her would have his head cut off and stuck on a pole. Soon there were ninety-seven poles with dead heads in front of the castle, and for a long time, nobody came and endeavored to win her hand. The king's daughter was pleased and thought, I shall now remain free for the rest of my life.

Then three brothers appeared before her and announced that they wanted to try their luck. The oldest thought he would be safe if he crawled into a lime pit, but she saw him right away from the first window and had him pulled out and his head chopped off. The second crept into the cellar of the castle, but she saw him from the first window as well, and he was done for: his head was stuck on the ninety-ninth pole. Then the youngest brother appeared before the princess and requested a day of grace for reflection and also asked that she be so merciful as to grant him two chances if she should discover him. If he failed the third time, then he would forfeit his life. Since he was so handsome and made his request so sincerely, she said, "Yes, I shall grant you your wish, but you will not succeed."

The next day he pondered a long time and tried to think of a way to hide himself, but in vain. Then he took his gun and went out hunting. He saw a raven, took aim, and was just about to pull the trigger, when the raven cried out, "Don't shoot, and I shall reward you!" The youngest brother let go of the trigger and continued on his way until he came to a lake, where he surprised a large fish that had emerged from the depths of the water to the surface. When he aimed his gun, the fish exclaimed, "Don't shoot, and I shall reward you!" He let the fish dive back into the water and went farther until he encountered a fox that was limping. He shot and missed him. Then the fox cried out, "Come over here instead and pull the thorn from my foot." Though he did this, he still wanted to kill the fox and skin it. The fox said, "Don't do it, and I shall reward you." The young man let him run off, and since it was evening, he returned home.

The next day he was supposed to hide himself. Yet, no matter how much he racked his brains, he did not know where to hide. Then he went into the forest to the raven and said, "I let you live. Now tell me where I should hide myself so that the king's daughter won't see me."

The raven lowered its head and thought for a long time. Finally, it said with a rasp, "I've got it!" The raven fetched an egg from its nest, broke it in two, and shut the young man inside. Then he made it whole again and sat down on top of it. When the king's daughter stepped to the first window, she could not discover him, nor could she as she moved from window to window, and she began to feel alarmed. However, from the eleventh window she caught sight of him and had the raven shot. Then the egg was fetched, cracked open, and the young man was obliged to come out.

The princess said, "This first time I shall let you go. But if you don't do better, you will be lost."

The following day he went to the lake, called the fish, and said, "I let you live. Now tell me where I should hide myself so that the king's daughter won't see me."

The fish thought awhile and finally exclaimed, "I've got it! I'll lock you up in my stomach."

The fish swallowed the young man and swam to the bottom of the lake. The king's daughter looked through her windows, and even in the eleventh she did not see him and was troubled. However, she finally discovered him in the twelfth. So she had the fish caught and killed, and the young man emerged. You can imagine how he felt.

The princess said, "This is the second time that I'll let you go, but your head will more than likely be stuck on the hundredth pole."

On the last day he went into the fields with a heavy heart and met the fox. "You know where to find all the hiding places," he said. "I let you live, now tell me where I should hide myself so that the king's daughter won't find me."

"A difficult task," answered the fox, with a doubtful look on its face. Finally, he exclaimed, "I've got it!"

The fox went with him to a spring, dunked itself in the water, and came out as a market vendor who sold animals. The young man had to dunk himself into the water as well and was transformed into a little hamster. The merchant went to the city and displayed the tame

little hamster. Many people came to see it. Eventually, the princess gave the merchant a lot of money for it. Before he handed the hamster to her, he said to it, "When the princess goes to the window, crawl quickly beneath her braids."

Now the time arrived when she was to search for him. She went to the windows, one after the other, from the first until the eleventh, and did not see him. When she did not spot him even through the twelfth, she was full of anxiety and anger and slammed the window shut so violently that the glass in all the windows was smashed into a thousand pieces and the entire castle trembled.

She moved from the window and felt the little hamster beneath her braids. Then she grabbed it, threw it to the ground, and yelled, "Get away! Get out of my sight!"

The hamster ran to the vendor, and both rushed to the spring, where they dunked themselves and regained their true forms. The young man thanked the fox and said, "The raven and the fish are dimwits compared to you. You know the right tricks. That's for sure!"

The young man went straight to the castle. The king's daughter was already expecting him and yielded to her fate. The wedding was celebrated, and he was now king and lord of the entire realm. He never told her where he had hidden himself the third time or who had helped him, and so she believed that he had done everything by virtue of his own skill and had great respect for him. After all, she thought to herself, he can indeed do more than you!

◈ 192 ◈

The Master Thief

ONE DAY an old man and his wife sat in front of a wretched-looking hut and sought to relax awhile from their work. Suddenly a magnificent coach drawn by four black horses drove up to their home, and out stepped a richly clad gentleman. The peasant stood up and approached the gentleman and asked him what he wanted and how the peasant might be of service to him. The stranger extended his hand to the old man and said, "My only desire is for once to enjoy a country dish. Prepare some potatoes for me in your customary way. Then I'll sit down at your table and consume them with pleasure."

The peasant smiled and said, "You must be a count or prince or even a duke. Noble people often have such fancies. Your wish shall be fulfilled."

The woman went into the kitchen and began to wash and scrape the potatoes. She intended to make dumplings out of them, just the way the peasants eat them. While she was working, her husband said to the stranger, "Come into my garden for a while, where I must finish something." In the garden he had dug some holes and wanted to plant trees in them.

"Don't you have any children who could help you with this work?" asked the stranger.

"No," the farmer answered. "Of course, I had a son, but he has long since departed for the wide world. He was a spoiled boy, clever and crafty, but he never wanted to learn anything and was always doing mischievous pranks. Eventually, he ran away, and since then I've heard nothing from him."

The old man took a small tree, placed it in a hole, and stuck a post into the ground next to it. After he had shoveled some dirt into the hole and had stamped it down, he took some twine and tied the stem of the tree below, in the middle, and on top to the post.

"Tell me," the gentleman asked, "why don't you also tie the crooked and gnarled tree lying over there in the corner. It's bent almost to the ground, and, if you tied it to a post, it would grow straight like these here."

The old man smiled and said, "Sir, you speak according to your experience, and it's apparent that you've not had much to do with gardening. The tree over there is old and knotted. Nobody can make it grow straight anymore. Trees must be raised carefully when they are young."

"It's the same with your son," the stranger said. "If you had raised him carefully when he was still young, he would not have run away. By now he too must have become hard and knotted."

"Certainly," the old man answered, "it's been quite a long time since he left us. He's probably changed."

"Would you recognize him if he appeared before you?" the stranger asked.

"Hardly by his face," the farmer replied, "but he has a mark on him, a birthmark on his shoulder that looks like a bean."

As he said this the stranger took off his coat, bared his shoulder, and showed the bean to the peasant.

"My God!" exclaimed the old man. "You are indeed my son," and the love for his child aroused his heart. "But," he added, "how can you be my son? You're a grand gentleman and live in wealth and luxury. How did you come by all of this?"

"Ah, Father," replied the son, "the young tree was not bound to a post and grew up crooked. Now it's too old. It will never become straight again. How did I acquire all this? I became a thief. But don't become alarmed. I am a master thief. There's no such thing as locks or bolts for me. Whatever my heart desires is mine. But I don't want you to think that I steal like a common thief. I only take from the rich, who have more than they need. Poor people are safe. I prefer to give them things rather than to take anything from them. Therefore, I won't touch a thing that doesn't demand effort, cunning, and skill to obtain it."

"Ah, my son," the father said, "I'm not at all pleased by this. Once a thief always a thief. I tell you, nothing good will come of this."

He led him to his mother, and when she heard that he was her son, she wept for joy. However, when he told her that he had become a master thief, two streams of tears flowed down her cheeks. Finally, she said, "Even if he has become a thief, he's still my son, and my eyes are fortunate to behold him one more time."

He sat down at the table with his parents and once again ate the sparse meal that he had not eaten for such a long time. Then the father said, "If our lord, the count over there in the castle, learns about who you are and what you do, he will not take you in his arms and rock you the way he did when he held you at the baptismal font. Instead he'll let you dangle from the gallows."

"Don't worry, Father. He won't harm me, for I know my craft. I'll even go to him myself this very day."

As dusk approached, the master thief climbed into his coach and drove to the castle. The count received him courteously because he thought the thief was a refined gentleman. However, when the stranger identified himself, the count turned pale and was silent for a while. Finally, he said, "You are my godson. Therefore, I shall allow mercy to prevail over justice, and I shall deal leniently with you. Since you pride yourself on being a master thief, I intend to put your art to a test. However, if you fail, you must marry the ropemaker's daughter, and the cawing of the crows will provide you with music at this event."

"My lord," the master thief replied, "think of three things as difficult as you want, and if I don't complete your tasks, you may do with me whatever you wish."

The count reflected for a moment. Then he said, "Well then, for your first task, you are to steal my private horse from the stable. Next you are to take away the sheet from under me and my wife while we are sleeping without our noticing it, and in addition, you are to steal the wedding ring from my wife's finger. For your third and last task, you are to steal the parson and the clerk from the church. Make sure that you have noted all this, for your life depends on it."

The master thief went to the nearest city in the region. There he bought the clothes of an old peasant woman and put them on. Then he stained his face brown and drew wrinkles on it so that nobody would be able to recognize him again. Finally, he filled a small cask with old Hungarian wine and mixed a strong sleeping potion in it. He put the small cask into a basket, which he lifted onto his back. With deliberate steps he walked with a sway to the castle of the count. By the time he arrived, it had already become dark. He sat down on a rock in the courtyard, began to cough like an old asthmatic woman, and rubbed his hands as if he were freezing. In front of the door to the horse stable there were soldiers lying around a fire. One of them noticed the old woman and called out to her, "Come closer, little mother, and warm yourself at our fire. I'm sure you don't have a place to sleep for tonight. So you'd better take what you can get."

The old woman tottered over to them, asked them to take the basket from her back. Then she sat down with them at the fire.

"What do you have in your cask, you old bag?" one of the soldiers asked.

"A good drink of wine," she answered. "I earn my living by selling wine. For money and kind words I'll gladly give you a glass."

"Let me have one then," the soldier said, and after he had tasted the wine, he exclaimed, "When wine is good, I always like to have a second!" He let himself be served a second glass, and the others followed his example.

"Hey, there, comrades!" a soldier called out to those who were in the stable. "We have an old lady here who's got wine as old as she is herself. Have a drink too! It'll warm your stomachs even better than our fire."

The old woman carried the cask into the stable. One of the soldiers was sitting on the saddled private horse of the count. Another held the reins in his hand, and a third had the horse by the tail. She served them as much as they demanded until the cask ran dry. Shortly after, the reins fell out of the hands of one soldier. He sank to the ground and began to snore. The other one let go of the tail, laid himself down on the ground, and snored even louder. The soldier, who sat in the saddle, remained sitting. However, he bent his head forward almost to the horse's neck, and while asleep he blew through his mouth like the bellows of a blacksmith's forge. The soldiers outside had long since fallen asleep on the ground and did not budge. It was as if they were made of stone. When the master thief saw that he had succeeded, he gave one soldier a rope in his hand instead of the reins and the other, who held the tail, a straw wisp. But what was he to do with the one who sat on the back of the horse? He did not want to throw him off; otherwise, he would awaken and let out a cry. Soon, however, the thief had an idea. He unbuckled the straps of the saddle, tied the ends of some rope hanging from a ring on the wall to the saddle, and pulled the sleeping rider with the saddle above the horse. Then he fastened the ends of the rope around the posts. He was soon able to release the horse from the chain, but if he had ridden the horse over the stone pavement of the courtyard, the noise would have been heard in the castle. So he wrapped the hoofs of the horse in old rags and led it carefully out of the courtyard. Then he swung himself on top and galloped away from the castle.

At daybreak the master thief jumped on the stolen horse and rode back to the castle. The count had just gotten up and looked out the window.

"Good morning, my lord," the master thief called to him. "Here's the horse that I successfully took from your stable. Just look at how beautifully your soldiers are lying there asleep, and if you should want to go into the stable, you would see how comfortable your guards have made everything for themselves."

The count had to laugh. Then he said, "Well, you've succeeded this first time, but the second time things will not run as smoothly. And I'm warning you, if I encounter you as a thief, I'll also treat you as a thief."

That night when the countess went to bed, she closed her hand with the marriage ring tightly together, and the count said, "All the doors are locked and barred. I'll stay awake and wait for the thief. If he climbs through the window, I'll shoot him down."

But the master thief went out to the gallows in the darkness and cut down a poor sinner, who had been hanging from the halter, and then he carried him on his back to the castle. There he placed a ladder against the wall that led to the bedroom of the count, put the dead man on his shoulders, and began to climb up the ladder. When he had got high enough so that the head of the dead man appeared at the window, the count, who had been on the lookout in his bed, pulled the trigger of his pistol. As he did this the master thief let the poor sinner fall to the ground. Then he himself jumped down the ladder and hid himself in a corner. The moon was so bright this night that the master thief could clearly see how the count climbed down the ladder and carried the dead man into the garden, where he began to dig a hole in which he intended to lay the dead body.

Now, thought the thief, the right moment has arrived. He slipped nimbly out of his corner and climbed the ladder right into the bedroom of the countess.

"My dear wife"—he began talking in the count's voice—"the thief's dead, but he was nevertheless my godson and was more of a rascal than a villain. I don't want to shame him in public, and I also feel sorry for his poor parents. Therefore, I want to bury him myself in the garden before daybreak to keep the affair from becoming known. Now, give me the bedsheet so I can wrap his corpse in it and cart him away like a dog."

The countess gave him the sheet.

"You know what," the thief added. "I feel a touch of generosity. Give me the ring too. The unfortunate wretch risked his life for it. So let him take it with him into his grave."

She did not want to oppose the count, and though she did it reluctantly, she took the ring from her finger and handed it to him. The thief made off with both things and arrived safely at home before the count had finished his grave-digging work in the garden.

The next day the count made a long face when the master came and brought him the sheet and the ring. "Can you work miracles?" the count asked him. "Who got you out of the grave in which I myself buried you? And who brought you back to life?"

"You didn't bury me," the thief said. "You buried a poor sinner from the gallows," and he told him in detail how everything had happened. The count had to concede that he was a smart and cunning thief. "However, you're not finished yet," he added. "You must still perform the third task, and, if you're not successful, nothing will help you."

The master thief smiled but did not respond. When night fell, he went to the village church with a long sack on his back, a bundle under his arm, and a lantern in his hand. In the sack he had crabs, in the bundle there were very short wax candles. He sat down in the graveyard, took a crab out of the sack, and stuck a wax candle on its back. Then he lit the small candle, set the crab on the ground, and let it crawl around. Next he took a second one out of the sack and did exactly the same thing with this crab and continued working in this manner until he had emptied the sack. After this he put on a long black gown that looked like a monk's cowl, and he pasted a gray beard on his chin. When he was finally unrecognizable, he took the sack in which he had carried the crabs, went into the church, and climbed the pulpit. The tower clock was just about to strike twelve. When the last stroke of the clock had faded, he cried out with a loud, shrill voice, "Hark, you sinful people, the end of everything has come! Judgment Day is near. Hark, hark! Whoever wants to go with me to heaven had better crawl into the sack. I am Peter, who opens and shuts the door to heaven. Behold how the dead ones out there amble and gather their bones together. Come, come and crawl into the sack. The world is going under!"

The cries resounded through the entire village. The parson and clerk, who lived closest to the church, had been the first to hear them, and when they caught sight of the lights that were wandering over the graveyard, they realized that something unusual was happening, and they entered the church. They listened to the sermon awhile, and then the clerk nudged the parson and said, "It wouldn't be a bad idea at all if we were to take advantage of this opportunity and together went to heaven in an easy way before Judgment Day actually arrives."

"Indeed," replied the parson, "these were my very own thoughts. If this is your desire, let's be on our way."

"Yes," the clerk answered, "but you, father, take precedence. So I'll follow after you."

The parson went ahead of the clerk and climbed the pulpit, where the thief opened the sack. First the parson crawled inside, then the clerk. Immediately the master thief tied the sack tightly, grabbed it around the middle, and slid it down the stairs of the pulpit. Whenever the heads of the two fools bumped against the steps, the thief called out, "Now we're going over the mountains." Then he dragged them the same way through the village, and when they went through puddles, he cried out, "Now we're going through wet clouds." And when he finally dragged them up the castle steps, he cried out, "Now we're on the steps to heaven, and we'll soon be in the outer court." When he arrived at the top, he shoved the sack into a pigeon coop, and when the pigeons fluttered about, he said, "Just listen to the way the angels are rejoicing and flapping their wings." Then he bolted the door and went away.

The next morning he went to the count and told him that he had also completed the third task and had abducted the parson and the clerk from the church.

"Where have you left them?" the lord asked.

"They're lying in a sack up in the pigeon coop imagining that they're in heaven."

The count himself went up to the coop and convinced himself that the thief had told the truth. When he freed the parson and the clerk from their prison, he said, "You're an inveterate thief and have won your wager. You've gotten away with everything this time, and you've not been harmed. But see to it that you leave my land, for if you ever set foot on it again, you can count on your advancement to the gallows."

The inveterate thief took leave of his parents and went forth once more into the wide world. Since then nobody has ever heard from him again.

◈ 193 ◈

The Drummer

ONE EVENING a young drummer went for a walk and came to the shore of a lake not far from the city where his parents lived. There he saw three pieces of white linen lying on the sand. "What fine linen," he said, and he put one piece into his pocket and thought nothing more about it. At night, as he was lying in his bed and was about to fall asleep, it seemed to him that someone was calling him. He listened and discerned a soft voice calling, "Drummer, drummer, wake up!" Since it was pitch black, he could not see anyone, but it seemed to him that a figure was hovering above his bed.

"What do you want?" he asked.

"Give me back my little blouse that you took from me this evening by the lake," the voice answered.

"I'll return it to you," the drummer said, "if you tell me who you are."

"Ah," replied the voice. "I'm the daughter of a mighty king, but I've fallen under the spell of a witch and have been sentenced to live on the glass mountain. Every day I must bathe in the lake with my two sisters, but without my little blouse I cannot fly back to the mountain. My sisters have already flown away, but I've been forced to stay behind. I beseech you to give me back my little blouse."

"Calm yourself, poor child," the drummer said. "I'll gladly return it to you." He took it out of his pocket and handed it to her in the darkness. She took it hastily and wanted to leave. However, he asked her to stay awhile and tell him whether he might be able to help her.

"You can help me by climbing the glass mountain and freeing me from the witch's spell. But you'll never come close to the glass mountain, and even if you did, you wouldn't be able to climb it."

"When I set my mind on something, I can always do it," the drummer said. "I feel sorry for you, and I am afraid of nothing. But I don't know the way to the glass mountain."

"There's a path that goes through the large forest in which the man-eaters dwell," she answered. "More than this I'm not allowed to tell you."

Then he heard her whizz away.

The next day the drummer set out early in the morning. He hung his drum around him and marched fearlessly into the forest. After he had walked awhile and did not come across a giant, he thought to himself, I'll have to wake the sleepyheads. He swung his drum in front of him and beat such a roll call that the birds flew from the trees with shrieks. Soon after this a giant, who had been lying asleep in the grass, stood up. He was as tall as a fir tree.

"You brat!" he yelled at the drummer. "You woke me from my sleep! Why are you drumming here?"

"I'm drumming," he answered, "to show the way to the thousands who are following me."

"What do they intend to do here in my forest?" the giant asked.

"They want to put an end to you and clean the forest of any monsters like you."

"Oho," the giant said, "I'll stamp you all to death like ants."

"Do you think you can do something to stop them? If you stoop to grab one, he'll just jump aside and hide himself. Then when you lie down and fall asleep, they'll come out from the bushes and crawl all over you. They all have steel hammers attached to their belts, and they'll use their hammers to bash your skull."

The giant became afraid and thought, If I'm forced to deal with such cunning earthworms, they might harm me in some way. Then he said, "Listen, little fellow, continue on your way. I promise you and your companions that in the future I'll leave you in peace. And if there's anything else you wish, just tell me, for I'd be glad to do you a favor."

"You have long legs," the drummer said, "and you can run faster than I can. Carry me to the glass mountain. Then I'll give my companions the signal to retreat, and they'll leave you in peace this time."

"Come here, worm," said the giant, "and sit down on my shoulder. I'll carry you wherever you want."

The giant lifted him to his shoulder, and the drummer began to bang on the drum to his heart's delight up there. The giant thought, That must be the signal for the others to retreat. After a while they came across a second giant standing along the path. He took the drummer from the first giant and stuck him in his buttonhole. The drummer grabbed hold of the button and merrily looked about. Then they came to a third giant, who took him out of the buttonhole and placed him on the rim of his hat, where he went walking and looked over the trees. When he glimpsed a mountain on the blue horizon, he thought, That's certainly the glass mountain, and so it was. The giant had to march only a few more steps to reach the foot of the mountain, where he set the young man down. The drummer demanded that he carry him to the top of the mountain, but the giant shook his head, mumbled something into his beard, and went back into the forest.

The poor drummer now stood before the mountain, which seemed as though it were as high as three mountains stacked one on top of another, and it also seemed as slick as glass. So he had no idea how he would make it to the top. He began to climb, but it was all in vain because he kept slipping back down. If only I were a bird now, he thought. But what good did wishing do? Wings did not sprout from his shoulders.

While he stood there like this, without knowing what to do, he became aware of the two men nearby who were violently quarreling with one another. He went up to them and saw that they were arguing over a saddle that lay on the ground in front of them and which each desired to have.

"What fools you are," he said, "to fight about a saddle when you don't even have a horse for it."

"The saddle is worth fighting over," answered one of the men. "Whoever sits on it and wishes to be somewhere, even if it were the end of the earth, will arrive there the very same instant he utters his wish. The saddle belongs to both of us. It's now my turn to ride on it, but he won't let me."

"I'll settle this argument soon enough," the drummer said. He paced away a short distance and stuck a white pole in the ground. Then he returned and said, "Now, run to the marker. Whoever gets there first shall ride first."

Both men took off at a sprint, but they had barely gone a few feet, when the drummer swung himself on top of the saddle and wished himself to be on top of the glass mountain. And in the wink of an eye, he was there. On top of the mountain was some level ground on which an old stone house stood. In front of the house was a large fishpond and behind it a dark forest. No human beings or animals could be seen. Everything was quiet. Only the wind rustled through the trees, and the clouds flew by close to the drummer's head. He walked to the door and knocked. After he had knocked a third time, an old woman with a brown face and red eyes opened the door. She had glasses on her long nose and looked sharply at him. Then she asked him what he wanted.

"Entrance, food, and lodging for the night," the drummer answered.

"You may have all this," the old woman said, "if you perform three tasks in return."

"Why not?" he replied. "I'm not afraid of any kind of work, even when it may be difficult."

The old woman let him in and gave him food and a good bed at night. The next morning, after he had had a good night's sleep, the old woman took a thimble from her spindly finger, handed it to the drummer, and said, "Now, go to work, and empty the pond outside with this thimble. However, you must be finished before nightfall, and you must take out all the fish from the pond and lay them next to one another according to their size and kind."

"This is a strange job," the drummer said. But he went to the pond and began to empty it. He baled water the entire morning. But, even if one were able to bale for a thousand years, nobody can empty out so much water with a thimble. When noon came, he sat down and thought, It's all for nothing. It's just the same whether I work or not. So he gave it up and reclined on the ground. Then a maiden came out of the house, set a little basket with food in front of him, and said, "Why are you sitting there so sadly? Is anything wrong?"

"Ah," he said. "I can't finish this task. How shall I be able to do the others? I set out to search for a king's daughter who is supposed to be living here, but I haven't found her. I want to move on."

"Stay here," the maiden said. "I'll help you out of this predicament. Lay your head on my lap and sleep. When you wake up again, your work will be done."

The drummer did not have to be persuaded. As soon as he was asleep, she turned a wishing ring and said, "Water, be gone, fish, jump out."

Right after she uttered those words, the water rose up high like white mist and flew away with the other clouds, and the fish clicked their tongues and sprang on the bank, ordering themselves each according to size and kind. When the drummer awoke, he saw to his astonishment that everything had been done. But the young maiden said, "One of the fish is not lying with its kind but is all alone. When the old woman comes this evening and sees that everything she's demanded has been done, she will say, 'What's this fish doing here all by itself?' Then you are to throw the fish in her face and say, 'This one's for you, old witch.' "

In the evening the old woman came, and when she asked the question, he threw the fish in her face. She acted as though she hadn't noticed a thing and remained silent. But she looked at him with evil eyes. The next morning she said, "Yesterday you had it easy. I shall have to give you harder work. So today you must chop down the entire forest, split the wood into logs, and lay them in piles. Everything must be finished by evening."

She gave him an ax, a sledgehammer, and two wedges. But the ax was made out of lead, and the sledgehammer and wedges, out of tin. When he began to chop, the ax became dull, and the hammer and wedges lost their shape. He did not know what to do, but at noon the maiden came again with his meal and consoled him. "Lay your head on my lap and sleep," she said. "When you awake, your work will be done."

She turned her wishing ring, and the entire forest collapsed in an instant. The wood split itself into logs and arranged itself in piles. It was as if an invisible giant had done all the work. When he woke up, the maiden said, "Look how the wood has been chopped and gathered in piles. There's only the branch left over, but when the old woman comes this evening and asks you what the branch is doing here, then you are to hit her with it and say, 'This one's for you, you witch.' "

The old woman came. "You see," she said, "how easy your work was. But for whom is that branch that's lying there?"

"For you, you witch," he answered, and he hit her with it. But she pretended she hadn't felt a thing, laughed scornfully, and said, "Early tomorrow you're to make a large stack out of the wood. Then you're to set the stack afire and let it burn."

At daybreak he got up and began to fetch the wood, but how can a single person gather together an entire forest? His work made no progress. However, the maiden did not let him down. She brought him his meal at noon, and after he had eaten it, he laid his head on her lap and fell asleep. When he awoke, the entire stack of wood was burning in huge flames that stretched their tongues high into the sky.

"Listen to me," the maiden said. "When the witch comes, she'll tell you to do all sorts of things. Do what she demands without fear. After you've done everything, grab her with both your hands, and throw her right into the middle of the fire."

The old woman came sneaking up to him. "Whew! I'm freezing," she said. "Well, but that's a fire burning there. It will warm up my old bones and make me feel good. But I see a log lying over there that's not burning. Fetch it out for me. Once you've done that, you'll be free to go wherever you please. Just jump right in there."

The drummer did not pause to think. He jumped right into the middle of the flames, which, however, did not harm him. They were not even able to singe his hair. He carried the log out and laid it down. The log had barely touched the ground, when it transformed itself into the beautiful maiden who had helped him in his distress. She

stood before him wearing silk clothes that glittered with gold, and he realized that she was the king's daughter. However, the old woman laughed spitefully and said, "You think you have her, but you don't have her yet."

Just as she was about to attack the maiden, the drummer grabbed the old woman with both his hands, raised her in the air, and threw her into the jaws of the fire, which clapped together as though they were rejoicing over the opportunity to consume a witch.

After this the king's daughter looked at the drummer, and when she saw that he was a handsome young man and took into account that he had risked his life to save her, she extended her hand to him and said, "You've risked everything for my sake, but I shall also venture everything for you. Promise me that you'll remain faithful to me, and you shall become my husband. We shall not be in need of riches, for there's enough left over from the witch's hoard for us to live on."

She led him into the house, where there were chests and trunks filled with treasures. They left the gold and silver lying there and took only the precious gems with them. Since they did not want to stay on the glass mountain any longer, the drummer said to her, "Sit down on my saddle. Then we'll fly from here like birds."

"I don't like the old saddle," she said. "I have only to turn my wishing ring, and then we'll be home."

"Very well," the drummer answered, "then wish that we were in front of the city gate."

Within seconds they were there. Then the drummer wished to go straight to his parents to tell him what had happened. He asked the king's daughter to wait for him in the field.

"Oh," she said, "please be careful; don't kiss your parents on the right cheek when you arrive. Otherwise, you'll forget everything, and I'll remain alone and abandoned here in the field."

"How can I forget you?" he said, and he gave her his oath that he would return very soon.

When he entered his father's house, nobody recognized him, for the three days that he had spent on the glass mountain had been three long years. Then he identified himself, and his parents were so terribly overcome with joy that they embraced him, and he was touched so deeply that he kissed them on both cheeks. He did not remember the words of the maiden. However, just as he gave them each a kiss on the right cheek, his memory of the maiden completely vanished. He emptied out his pockets and laid a handful of the largest gems on the table. His parents did not know what to do with this wealth. But then the father had a splendid castle built with gardens, woods, and meadows fit for a prince. And when it was finished, the mother said, "I've chosen a bride for you. The wedding shall take place in three days." And the son was satisfied with everything his parents desired.

The poor king's daughter had waited for a long time outside the city for the return of the young man. When night fell, she said, "I'm sure that he's kissed his parents on the right cheek and he's forgotten me." Her heart was full of sadness. So she wished herself to be in a solitary cottage in the woods and had no desire to return to her father's court. Every evening she went into the city and passed by the young man's house. Sometimes he saw her, but he did not recognize her. Finally, she heard some people say, "Tomorrow his wedding will be celebrated."

So she said, "I'm going to try and see if I can win back his heart."

On the first day of the wedding festivities, she turned her wishing ring and said, "A dress as glistening as the sun." A split second later the dress lay in front of her, and it was as glistening as if it had been woven from the rays of the sun. When all the guests had gathered, she entered the hall. Everyone admired the beautiful dress, most of all the bride, and since she loved beautiful dresses, she went to the stranger and asked whether she could buy it.

"It's not for money," she answered, "but if I may pass the first night in front of the door to the bridegroom's chambers, I'll give it to you."

The bride could not contain her desire to have the dress and agreed. But she mixed a sleeping potion in the glass of wine that the bridegroom took in the evening so that he fell into a deep sleep. When everything had become quiet, the king's daughter crouched in front of the door of the bedroom, opened it a little, and called inside:

"Drummer, drummer, listen to me.
Have you forgotten all about me?
Didn't you sit with me up on the glass mountain?
Didn't I protect you from the witch and sin?
Didn't you promise to be faithful to me?
Drummer, drummer, listen to me!"

But it was in vain. The drummer did not wake up, and as daybreak came, the king's daughter was obliged to go away without having accomplished a thing. On the second evening she turned the ring and said, "A dress as silvery as the moon." When she appeared at the festivities in the dress that was as soft as the moonlight, she aroused the desire of the bride again and gave the dress to her for permission to spend the second night outside the bedroom door. In the still of the night she called again:

"Drummer, drummer, listen to me.
Have you forgotten all about me?
Didn't you sit with me up on the glass mountain?

Didn't I protect you from the witch and sin?
Didn't you promise to be faithful to me?
Drummer, drummer, listen to me."

But the drummer, who was unconscious due to the sleeping potion, could not be wakened. In the morning the king's daughter returned sadly to her cottage in the woods. However, the people in the house had heard the lament of the unknown maiden and told the bridegroom about this. They also told him that it was impossible for him to hear anything because the bride had mixed a sleeping potion in his wine.

On the third evening the king's daughter turned the wishing ring and said, "A dress as glittering as the stars." When she showed up in this dress at the festivities, the bride could not control herself, for this dress was much more magnificent than the other two. And she said, "I want it, and I shall have it."

The maiden gave it to her, as she had given her the others, for permission to spend the night outside the bridegroom's door. But the bridegroom did not drink the wine that was handed to him before he went to sleep. Instead, he poured it out behind his bed. And when everything in the house had become quiet, he heard a soft voice that called to him:

"Drummer, drummer, listen to me.
Have you forgotten all about me?
Didn't you sit with me up on the glass mountain?
Didn't I protect you from the witch and sin?
Didn't you promise to be faithful to me?
Drummer, drummer, listen to me."

"Oh," he exclaimed, "how could I have acted so unfaithfully! It was the kiss on the right cheek that I gave to my parents out of the joy of my heart. That's what's to blame. That's what dulled my mind."

He jumped up, took the king's daughter by her hand, and led her to the bed of his parents. "This is my true bride," he said. "If I marry the other maiden, I'll be doing a great wrong."

After his parents heard how everything had come to pass, they agreed. The lights in the hall were lit again, and drums and trumpets were fetched. Now the friends and relatives were invited to come again, and the true wedding was celebrated with great joy. The former bride kept the beautiful dresses as compensation and declared that she was thus satisfied.

❖ 194 ❖

The Ear of Corn

IN OLDEN DAYS when God himself still walked upon the earth, the soil was much more fruitful than it is now. At that time the yield of ears of corn was not fifty- or sixty-fold but four to five hundred. The corn grew from the bottom to the top of the stalk, and each ear was as long as the stalk. However, it is human nature that people stop appreciating the Lord's blessings and become indifferent and foolish when they have more than they need.

One day a woman went by a cornfield, and her small child, who was skipping along with her, fell into a puddle and dirtied her little dress. So her mother ripped a handful of the beautiful ears of corn from a stalk and cleaned the little dress with them. As the Lord, who happened to come by at that moment, saw this, he became angry and said, "From now on the stalk of corn shall no longer bear ears. Human beings are no longer worthy of this heavenly gift."

Some people standing nearby heard this and were horrified. They fell upon their knees and pleaded with God to leave something on the stalk. Even if they did not deserve this, they asked him to think of the innocent chickens that would otherwise have to starve.

The Lord, who foresaw their misery, took pity on them and granted the request. Hence, the ear of corn was kept on top, just as it grows in our own day.

❖ 195 ❖

The Grave Mound

ONE DAY a rich farmer stood in his yard and looked over his fields and gardens. The corn sprouted vigorously, and the fruit dangled abundantly from the fruit trees. The grain of the previous year still lay in such large piles in the loft that the rafters could barely support them. Then he went into the stable to look at the well-fed oxen, the fat cows, and the glistening horses. Finally, he returned to his room and took a look at the iron chests in which he kept his money. As he was standing there and surveying his wealth he suddenly heard a loud knocking. However, it was not a knocking at the door of his room but at the door of his heart. It opened up, and he heard a voice that said to him, "Have you done good things with all this for your kindred? Have you been aware of the needs of the poor? Have you shared your food with the hungry? Have you been satisfied with what you have, or have you always demanded even more?"

His heart did not hesitate with the answer: "I've been hard and pitiless and have never done good things for my kindred. If a poor person came my way, I turned my eyes away from him. I haven't cared about God but have thought only about increasing my wealth. Even if everything under the sky had become mine, it would still not have been enough for me."

Upon hearing this answer, the rich man was greatly horrified. His knees began to tremble, and he had to sit down. Once again he heard a knocking, but this time it was a knocking at the door to his room. It was his neighbor, a poor man, who had numerous children and could no longer feed them. I know, the poor man thought, my neighbor is rich, but he is just as hard as he is rich. I don't believe he'll help me, but my children are screaming for food, so I'll have to take the risk. Then he said to the rich man, "You don't readily give away things that belong to you, but I stand before you as one who can barely keep his head above water. My children are starving; lend me four bushels of grain."

The rich man looked at him for a long time. Then the first sunbeam of kindness began to melt part of the ice of greediness. "I won't lend you four bushels," he responded, "instead I'll give you eight as a gift, but there is one condition that you must fulfill."

"What must I do?" the poor man asked.

"When I'm dead, you're to watch over my grave for three nights."

The peasant felt very uneasy when he heard the proposition. However, he would have consented to anything because of his terrible situation. So he agreed to do it and carried the grain home with him.

It was as though the rich man had foreseen what was going to happen, for he suddenly dropped dead three days later. Nobody knew exactly how this had come to pass, but no one cared. When he was buried, the poor man remembered his promise. He would have liked to have been released from it, but he thought, He treated you kindly, and you were able to feed your children with his grain. And even if that hadn't happened, you gave your promise, and you must keep it.

At nightfall he went into the churchyard and sat on top of the grave mound. Everything was quiet. Only the moon was shining over the grave mounds, and at times an owl flew overhead and screeched its doleful sounds. When the sun rose, the poor man went home un-

harmed, and the second night passed just as peacefully as the first. On the third night he felt especially afraid. It seemed to him that something was going to happen. When he arrived at the churchyard, he noticed a man at the wall whom he had never seen before. He was no longer young, had scars on his face, and his eyes darted around sharply and fervidly. He was wrapped completely in an old coat, and only his large riding boots were visible.

"What are you looking for here?" the peasant asked him. "Aren't you afraid of being out here at the lonely churchyard?"

"I'm not looking for anything," he answered, "and I'm afraid of nothing. I'm like the young man who set out to learn how to fear, but who tried in vain and still won a king's daughter as wife and great wealth along with her. However, I've always remained poor. I'm nothing but a discharged soldier and want to spend the night here because I don't have any other shelter."

"If you're fearless," the peasant said, "then stay with me and help me guard the grave mound."

"Keeping guard is a soldier's business," he replied. "Whatever we encounter here, good or evil, let that be our common lot."

The peasant agreed, and they sat down together on the grave. Everything remained quiet until midnight. Then suddenly a shrill whistling could be heard in the air, and the two watchmen became aware of the presence of the Evil One, who then stood in full life before them. "Be gone, you scoundrels," he bellowed at them. "That man lying in the grave is mine. I've come to fetch him, and if you don't turn and leave, I'll twist and wring your necks."

"Sir with the red feather," the soldier said, "you're not my captain. I don't need to obey you, and I've yet to learn how to fear. So, move on, for we're going to remain sitting here."

The devil thought, Gold is the best way to trap these two meddlers. So he used a sweeter tune and asked very confidentially whether they would not like to have a bag of gold that they could take with them.

"That's worth considering," the soldier answered, "but just *one* bag of gold is not of much use to us. If you'll give us as much gold as will go into one of my boots, we'll clear out and retreat."

"I don't have enough gold with me," the devil said, "but I'll get it. There's a good friend of mine who's a money changer in the neighboring city. He'll gladly advance me the gold."

After the devil had disappeared, the soldier took off his left boot and said, "Just wait, we'll soon be leading him around by the nose. Give me your knife, my friend." Then he cut off the sole of the boot and put the boot next to the mound in the high grass on the edge of a grave half covered with weeds. "That's just right," he said. "Now, let the chimney sweep return."

The two men sat down and waited. It was not long before the devil came, carrying a small sack of gold in his hand. "Just pour it in there," the soldier said and raised the boot a little in the air, "but that won't be enough."

The black one emptied the sack. The gold fell through, and the boot remained empty.

"Stupid devil," exclaimed the soldier. "That won't do! Didn't I tell you right off? Now turn around and fetch some more."

The devil shook his head, left, and came back after an hour with a much larger sack under his arm.

"Just fill it up," the soldier cried out, "but I doubt that the boot will become full."

The gold jingled as it dropped into the boot, but the boot remained empty. The devil peered into the boot himself with his glaring eyes and convinced himself of the truth.

"The calves of your legs are ridiculously large," he cried out, and made a wry face.

"Do you think," replied the soldier, "that I have a cloven foot like yours? Since when have you been so stingy? See to it that you get more gold; otherwise, you can forget about our deal."

The demon toddled off once again. This time he stayed away longer than before, and when he finally appeared, he was panting due to the weight of the pack that he was carrying on his shoulders. He poured the gold into the boot, which remained just as empty as before. Then he became furious and wanted to tear the boot from the soldier's hand, but just at that moment the first ray of the rising sun burst from the sky, and the evil spirit ran away shrieking loudly. The poor soul had been saved.

The peasant wanted to divide the gold, but the soldier said, "Give my share to poor people. I'll move in with you in your hut, and together we'll live quietly and peacefully with what's left over of the gold, as long as God permits."

◆ 196 ◆

Old Rinkrank

ONCE UPON A TIME there was a king who had a daughter, and this king had a glass mountain built and said that whoever could climb over the mountain without falling could have his daughter for his wife. A man who loved the king's daughter came and asked the king if he could have her.

"Yes," the king said, "if you can climb over the mountain without falling, you may have her."

Then the king's daughter said that she would go with the man and hold him if he was in danger of falling. So they began climbing over the mountain, and when they were halfway up, the king's daughter slipped and fell through the glass mountain, which opened up and closed so that she became locked inside. The bridegroom could not see what had happened to her, for the mountain had closed too quickly. He felt miserable and wept, and the king, who was sad too, ordered the mountain to be broken to see if he could retrieve her, but they could not find the spot where she had fallen.

In the meantime, the king's daughter had fallen deep down into the earth and landed in a large cave. An old fellow with a very long gray beard had then come to her and told her that he would let her live if she would be his servant and do everything he commanded. If not, he would kill her. So she did everything he ordered.

Every morning he took his ladder out of a pocket and placed it against a wall and climbed to the top of the mountain. Then he pulled the ladder up to him on top. While he was away, she had to cook his dinner, make his bed, and do all his work, and when he returned home, he always brought heaps of gold and silver with him. When she had spent many years with him and had become very old, he called her Mother Mansrot, and she had to call him Old Rinkrank. Then one day, after he had departed and she had made his bed and washed his dishes, she closed all the doors and windows tightly, except for a tiny one, which let the light shine through. This she left open. When Old Rinkrank returned home, he knocked on his door.

"Mother Mansrot, open the door for me."

"No," she said, "I won't open the door for you, Old Rinkrank."

Then he said:

"Here I stand, poor Rinkrank,
seventeen feet long I stand on planks,
on my tired-out feet.
Mother Mansrot, wash my dishes."

"I've washed your dishes already," she replied.
Then he said once more:

"Here I stand, poor Rinkrank,
seventeen feet long I stand on planks,
on my tired-out feet.
Mother Mansrot, make my bed."

"I've already made your bed," she replied.
Then he said once more:

"Here I stand, poor Rinkrank,
seventeen feet long I stand on planks,
on my tired-out feet.
Mother Mansrot, open the door for me."

Then he ran around his house to the other side, where the tiny window was open. He thought to himself, You'd better look inside to see what she's up to and why she won't open the door for you. When he tried to push his head through the window, he found it was impossible because his beard was too long. So he stuck his beard through the window first, but just as he had got it through, Mother Mansrot arrived and pulled the window shut with some rope that had been attached to the window, and the beard was caught tight. Then Old Rinkrank began to whine miserably because he was in pain, and he pleaded with her to let him go. She told him that she would not set him free until he gave her the ladder that he used to climb the mountain. Whether he liked it or not, he had to tell her where the ladder was. So she tied another very long rope to the window, and then she set the ladder against the wall and climbed to the top of the mountain. And when she was on top, she pulled the window open with the rope. Then she went to her father and told him all that had happened to her. The king was very glad, and her bridegroom was still there. They went and dug up the mountain and found Old Rinkrank inside with all this gold and silver there. Then the king had Old Rinkrank put to death and took all his silver and gold. And the king's daughter was still able to marry her bridegroom, and they lived quite happily thereafter in splendor and joy.

◈ 197 ◈

The Crystal Ball

ONCE UPON A TIME there was a sorceress who had three sons, and they loved each other dearly. But the old woman did not trust them and thought they wanted to steal her power. So she changed the oldest son into an eagle. He had to make his home in the mountain cliffs, and sometimes he could be seen gliding up and down in the sky and making circles. The second son was changed into a whale that lived deep in the ocean, and one could see him only when he sometimes sent mighty jets of water high into the air. Both sons reverted to their human shape for just two hours every day. Since the third son feared that his mother might change him also, this time into a wild animal, perhaps a bear or a wolf, he sneaked away in secret. Indeed, he had heard that at the castle of the golden sun there was an enchanted princess who was waiting to be rescued. However, one would have to risk one's life. Twenty-three young men had already suffered a miserable death, and only one more would be allowed to try to rescue her. After that nobody would be permitted to come. Since he had a courageous heart, he decided to search for the castle of the golden sun.

He had already traveled a long time and had not been able to find it, when he got lost in a large forest and could not find his way out. Suddenly he noticed two giants in the distance, who waved to him with their hands, and as he approached them they said, "We're quarreling over this hat and who should get it. Since we're each just as strong as the other, neither one can defeat the other. Now, small people are smarter than we are, so we want you to make the decision."

"How can you quarrel over an old hat?" the young man asked.

"You don't know the powers it has. It's a wishing hat. Whoever puts it on can wish himself to be anywhere he wants, and within seconds he'll be there."

"Give me the hat," the young man said. "I'll go off some distance from here, and when I call you, run to me, and whoever wins the race will get the hat." He put the hat on his head and went off. However, he thought about the king's daughter, forgot the giants, and kept going. Once he sighed with all his heart and cried out, "Oh, if only I were at the castle of the golden sun!" And no sooner had he uttered these words than he was standing on top of a high mountain in front of the castle gate.

He entered the castle and strode through all the rooms until he reached the last one, where he found the king's daughter. However, he was horrified when he saw her: her face was ash gray and full of wrinkles, and she had dreary eyes and red hair. "Are you the king's daughter whose beauty is praised by the entire world?" he exclaimed.

"Ah," she replied, "this is not my real condition. Human eyes can see me only in this ugly form. But look into this mirror so you'll know what I look like. The mirror can't be fooled, and it will show you my image as it truly is."

She handed him the mirror, and he saw the reflection of the most beautiful maiden in the world, and he saw tears rolling down her cheeks out of sadness. Then he said, "How can you be saved? I'm afraid of nothing."

She replied, "Whoever gets the crystal ball and holds it in front of the magician will break his power, and I'll return to my true form. But," she added, "many a man has gone to his death because of this, and you, my young thing, I'd feel sorry if you placed yourself in such great danger."

"Nothing can stop me," he said, "but tell me what I must do."

"I want you to know everything," the king's daughter answered. "When you descend the mountain on which the castle stands, there'll be a wild bison at the bottom next to the spring. You will have to fight it. And, if you should be so fortunate as to slay this beast, a firebird will rise from it. This bird carries a glimmering egg in its body, and the egg has a crystal ball as a yolk. However, the bird will not let go of the egg unless it is forced to. And, if the egg falls onto the earth, it will set everything on fire and destroy everything near it. The egg itself will melt along with the crystal ball, and all your efforts will have been in vain."

The young man descended the mountain and reached the spring, where the bison snorted and roared at him. After a long battle the young man pierced the bison's body with his sword, and the beast sank to the ground. The firebird immediately rose from the bison and tried to fly away, but the eagle, the brother of the young man, who flew through the clouds, dived after the bird and chased it toward the ocean. There the eagle hit the bird so hard with his beak that the bird was forced to let the egg fall. However, it did not fall into the ocean but on top of a fisherman's hut standing on the shore, and the hut began to smoke right away and was about to burst into flames. Then waves as large as houses rose up in the ocean, swept over the hut, and vanquished the flames. The other brother, the whale, had swum toward the shore and driven the water onto the land. When the fire was out, the young man searched for the egg and was fortunate enough to find it. It had not melted yet, but the shell had cracked open due to the sudden cooling from the water, and he could take out the crystal ball, which was undamaged.

When the young man went to the magician and held the ball in front of him, the latter said, "My power is destroyed. From now on you are king of the castle of the golden sun. You can also restore your brothers to their human form."

So the young man hurried back to the king's daughter, and as he entered her room she stood there in all her magnificent beauty, and they exchanged rings with each other in a joyful celebration.

◆ 198 ◆

Maid Maleen

ONCE UPON A TIME there was a king who had a son, and his son wished to wed the daughter of a powerful king. Her name was Maid Maleen, and she was exceedingly beautiful. Since her father wanted her to marry someone else, however, he rejected the prince's offer. Yet, Maleen and this prince loved each other with all their hearts and would not let anything come between them. So Maid Maleen told her father, "I cannot and will not accept anyone else as my husband."

Upon hearing this, her father became furious and ordered a dark tower to be built that prevented the rays of light from the sun and moon from penetrating its walls. When the tower was finished, he said, "You're to sit in this tower for seven years, after which time I shall come and see whether your spiteful spirit has been broken."

Enough food and drink for seven years was carried into the tower. Then the princess and her chambermaid were brought there and walled in and thus cut off from heaven and earth. There they sat in darkness, not knowing whether it was day or night. The prince often went there and circled and recircled the tower calling out Maleen's name, but not a single sound from the outside could penetrate the thick walls. There was nothing the two women could do except sob and lament. Meanwhile, the years passed, and eventually they could tell from how much remained of their food and drink that the seven years were nearing their end. They believed that the moment of their salvation had come, but there were no sounds of a hammer to be heard, nor did they hear stones fall from the wall. It seemed to Maid Maleen that her father had forgotten them. Since they had only enough supplies for a short time longer and imagined themselves suffering a miserable death, Maid Maleen said, "We have just one last resort. We must see if we can break through the wall."

So she took a bread knife, dug into the mortar, and tried to pry a stone from the wall. When she became tired, the chambermaid relieved her. After working for a long time, they finally succeeded in lifting out one stone, then a second and a third, and after three days the first ray of light pierced the darkness. As soon as the opening was large enough, they looked out. The sky was blue, and a breath of fresh air whisked their way, but they were greatly saddened by what they saw around them: the king's castle lay in ruins; the city and villages, as far as they could see, had been burned to the ground; the fields had been devastated. Not a soul could be seen. When the opening in the wall became large enough so that they could slip through, the chambermaid hopped through first and Maid Maleen followed. But where were they to turn? The enemy had ravaged the entire kingdom. The king had been driven away, and all the inhabitants had been slaughtered. So they wandered in search of another country, but they found neither shelter nor people kind enough to give them food. Their need became so great that they had to satisfy their hunger by eating stinging nettles from a bush. When they had gone a great distance, they eventually came to another country, where they went about offering their services. Yet, wherever they knocked, they were turned away. Nobody took pity on them. Finally, they reached a large city and went to the royal court. There too they were told to move on, until the cook came and said that they could work in the kitchen as cinderellas.

The son of the king in whose realm they were now living was none other than the former betrothed of Maid Maleen. In the meantime, his father had chosen another bride for him. She had a face as ugly as sin, and her heart was just as wicked. The wedding day had been set, and the bride-to-be had already arrived, but because of her ugliness she had locked herself in her chambers and would not let anyone see her. Maid Maleen had to bring her all her meals from the kitchen. When the day approached for the bride to go with the bridegroom to church, she felt ashamed of her ugliness and feared that she would be mocked and laughed at by the people if she showed herself on the streets. So she said to Maid Maleen, "Today's your lucky day. I've sprained my foot and cannot walk on the streets very well. Therefore, I want you to put on my wedding dress and take my place. Never in your life will you receive an honor like this."

But Maid Maleen refused the offer and said, "I don't want an honor like this if I haven't earned it."

Then the bride-to-be offered Maid Maleen gold, but this too was in vain. So she became furious and said, "If you don't obey me, it will cost you your life. I need only give the word, and your head will be chopped off."

So Maleen had to obey. She put on the magnificent clothes of the bride-to-be, along with her jewels. When she entered the royal hall, everyone was astonished by her great beauty, and the king said to his son, "This is the bride I've chosen for you, and you shall now lead her to church."

The bridegroom was astonished and thought, She looks just like my Maid Maleen; I'd swear it was really her, but I'm sure she's a prisoner in the tower, or she's dead.

He took her by the hand and led her to church. On the way, there was a bush with stinging nettles, and Maid Maleen said:

"Nettle bush,
nettle bush, so small and so bare,
why are you now standing here?
There was a time, you know,
when I ate you raw, you know,
raw and rough."

"What are you saying?" asked the prince.
"Nothing," she answered. "I was only thinking about Maid Maleen."
He was surprised that she knew about Maid Maleen but kept quiet.
When they came to the footbridge leading to the churchyard, she said:

"Footbridge, please don't break or chide,
for I'll gladly admit I'm not his true bride."

"What are you saying," asked the prince.
"Nothing," she answered. "I was only thinking about Maid Maleen."

"Do you know Maid Maleen?"

"No," she replied. "How should I know her? I've only heard about her."

When they came to the church door, she said:

"Church door, please don't break or chide,
for I'll gladly admit I'm not his true bride."

"What are you saying?" he asked.

"Oh," she answered. "I was only thinking about Maid Maleen."

The prince took out a precious jewel necklace, put it around her neck, and clasped the ends together. Then they entered the church, and the priest joined their hands in wedlock before the altar. Afterward the prince led her back to the castle, but she did not utter a single word the entire way. When they reached the royal castle again, she rushed to the chamber of the bride-to-be, took off the magnificent clothes and jewels, and put on her gray smock. The only thing she kept was the necklace that she had received from the bridegroom.

When night arrived and the bride-to-be was to be led into the prince's chamber, she placed a veil over her face so that he would not notice how she had deceived him. As soon as everyone had left them alone, he said to her, "What did you say to the bush of stinging nettles that stood along the way?"

"What bush?" she replied. "I don't talk to bushes of stinging nettles."

"If it wasn't you, then you're not my true bride," he said.

She thought quickly and said:

"My maid, my maid, I must go and see,
for it's she who keeps my thoughts for me."

So she went out and screamed at Maid Maleen, "Girl, what did you say to the bush of stinging nettles?"

"I said nothing but:

Nettle bush,
nettle bush, so small and so bare,
why are you now standing here?
There was a time, you know,
when I ate you raw, you know,
raw and rough."

The bride-to-be returned to the prince's chamber and said, "Now I know what I told the bush of stinging nettles," and she repeated the words that she had just heard.

"But what did you say to the footbridge as we crossed it?" the prince asked.

"To the footbridge?" she replied. "I don't speak to footbridges."

"Then you're not my true bride."

Again she said:

"My maid, my maid, I must go and see,
for it's she who keeps my thoughts for me."

She ran out and screamed at Maid Maleen, "Girl, what did you say to the footbridge?"

"I said nothing but:

Footbridge, please don't break or chide,
for I'll gladly admit I'm not his true bride."

"That will cost you your life," the bride-to-be exclaimed, but then she rushed back to the prince's chamber and said, "Now I know what I told the footbridge," and she repeated the words.

"But what did you say to the church door?"

"Church door?" she replied. "I don't talk to church doors."

"Then you're not my true bride."

She went out and screamed angrily at Maid Maleen, "Girl, what did you say to the church door?"

"I said nothing but:

Church door, please don't break or chide,
for I'll gladly admit I'm not his true bride."

"I'll break your neck," the bride-to-be yelled furiously, but she rushed back to the prince's chamber and said, "Now I know what I told the church door," and she repeated the words.

"But where's the necklace that I gave you at the church door?"

"What kind of a necklace?" she replied. "You didn't give me a necklace."

"I myself put it around your neck and fastened the clasp as well. If you don't know this, then you're not my true bride." He pulled the veil from her face, and when he saw how terribly ugly she was, he jumped back in fright and said, "How did you get here? Who are you?"

"I'm the bride you were to marry, but I was afraid that the people would have mocked me when they saw me on the streets. So I commanded cinderella to put on my clothes and go to church in my place."

"Where is that girl?" he said. "I want to see her. Go and fetch her."

She went outside and told the servants that the kitchen cinderella was a cheat and that they were to take her into the courtyard and chop off her head. The servants grabbed Maid Maleen and wanted to drag her away, but she screamed for help so loudly that the prince heard her voice. He rushed from his room and ordered them to set her free immediately. Lights were brought, and he was able to see the gold necklace around her neck that he had given her at the church door. "You're my true bride," he said. "You're the one who went to church with me. Come into my room."

When they were finally alone, he said, "At the church door you mentioned Maid Maleen, who was once the woman I was to wed. If I thought it were possible, I'd have to believe that she's standing right before me now. You look exactly like her."

"I am Maid Maleen," she responded. "For seven years, on your account, I was a prisoner in darkness and suffered hunger and thirst. Then I lived for a long time in need and poverty. But today the sun is shining on me once again. We were wed in the church, and I'm your lawful wife."

Then they kissed each other and were happy for the rest of their lives. As payment for her actions, the false bride had her head chopped off.

The tower in which Maid Maleen had been a prisoner remained standing for a long time afterward, and whenever children walked by it, they would sing:

"Cling, clang, clum,
who's sitting there alone and glum?
The princess sits without a key,
the princess I can't see.
The walls are thick and will not break.
The stones won't move for heaven's sake.
Come, little Hans, with your coat so gay,
come follow me this very day."

◈ 199 ◈

The Boots of Buffalo Leather

A SOLDIER WHO FEARS NOTHING will let nothing stand in his way. There was once such a soldier, who had received his discharge, and since he had never learned a craft and could not earn anything, he wandered about and asked for charity from kind people. An old cape hung from his shoulders, and he still wore a pair of riding boots made out of buffalo leather. One day he went deep into the fields without regard to the way he took, and finally he found himself in the forest. He had no idea where he was, but he saw a man sitting on the trunk of a tree that had been chopped down. This man was very well-dressed and wore a huntsman's coat. The soldier shook his hand, sat down next to him on the grass, and stretched his legs.

"I see you're wearing fine, sparkling boots," the soldier said, "but if you were forced to wander about as much as I do, they wouldn't last long. Look at mine. They're made out of buffalo leather and have served me well through thick and thin." After a while the soldier stood up and said, "I can't stay here any longer. My stomach is grumbling. So, Brother Sparkle-Boots, tell me the way out of the forest."

"I don't know myself," the huntsman answered. "I've lost my way."

"So, you're in the same boat as me," the soldier said. "Birds of a feather flock together. Let's stick together and look for the way out."

The huntsman smiled slightly, and together they moved on until it became dusk. "We haven't found the way out of the woods," the soldier said, "but I see a light glimmering in the distance. We'll find something to eat there."

They came upon an old stone house and knocked at the door, and an old woman opened it.

"We're looking for a night's lodging," the soldier said, "and something to line our stomachs. Mine is as empty as an old satchel."

"You can't stay here," the old woman answered. "The house belongs to robbers, and you'd be smart to get along before they return home, because you'll be goners if they find you here."

"It won't be that bad," the soldier replied. "I haven't had a thing to eat for two days, and I don't care whether I die here or die from starvation in the forest. I'm going inside." The huntsman did not want to follow, but the soldier tugged him by the sleeve. "Come, old buddy, it won't cost you your life right away."

The old woman took pity on them and said, "Crawl behind the stove. I'll sneak you some of the leftovers after the robbers have fallen asleep."

The soldier and the huntsman had barely found their hiding place, when twelve robbers stormed inside, sat down at the table that was already set, and boisterously demanded their dinner. The old woman carried out a large piece of meat to the table, and the robbers began to devour it with gusto. As the smell of the meat reached the soldier's nose, he said to the huntsman, "I can't hold out anymore. I'm going to join them and eat my share."

"You'll be the death of us," the huntsman replied and grabbed his arm. But the soldier began to cough loudly. When the robbers heard this, they threw down their knives and forks, jumped up, and discovered the two strangers behind the stove.

"Aha, gentlemen," they cried out, "why are you sitting in the corner? What do you want here? Have you been sent to spy on us? Just wait, you'll learn how to fly on a dead branch."

"Mind your manners," the soldier responded. "I'm hungry. Give me something to eat. Afterward you can do what you want with me."

The robbers were startled, and the leader of the band said, "I see you're not afraid. Good, we'll give you something to eat, but then you must die."

"We'll see about that," the soldier responded, and he sat down at the table and began to hack heartily at the roast meat. "Brother Sparkle-Boots, come and eat!" he beckoned the huntsman. "You must be just as hungry as I am, and you won't find better roast meat at home."

But the huntsman refused to eat, while the robbers watched the soldier with astonishment and said, "Nothing bothers this guy."

Afterward the soldier said, "The food wasn't half bad. Now bring me something good to drink."

The leader was in a good mood, so he tolerated this too and called to the old woman, "Fetch a bottle of wine from the cellar, and make it one of the best."

The soldier pulled the cork from the bottle until it popped. Then he took the bottle to the huntsman and said, "Pay attention, brother, you're going to be amazed. I'm now going to make a toast to the health of the entire band." Next the soldier swung the bottle over the heads of the robbers and cried out, "To your health, but open your mouths wide and raise your right hands in the air," and he took a hearty swig. No sooner had he pronounced those words than the robbers all sat there motionless, as though they had been turned into stone. Their mouths were open and their right arms were raised in the air.

The huntsman said to the soldier, "I see that you know tricks of another kind. But now, come. It's time to go home."

"Oho, old buddy, we don't want to march home too early. We've defeated the enemy, and now we're entitled to collect the booty. They're planted there solidly with their mouths open in astonishment. And they can't move until I let them. Come, eat and drink."

The old woman had to fetch another bottle of the best wine, and the soldier did not get up from the table until he had consumed the equal of three days' food. Finally, when dawn approached, he said, "It's time now to break our tent, and the old woman will tell us the shortest way to the city so that our march won't be too long."

When they reached the city, the soldier went to his former comrades and said, "I've found a nest of nasty birds out there in the forest. Come with me, and we'll clean it out." As the soldier led the way he said to the huntsman, "You've got to come along and watch how they flutter when we grab them by their feet."

He stationed his comrades in a circle around the robbers. Then he took a bottle of wine, drank a swig, swung the bottle over their heads, and cried out, "To your health!" Suddenly the robbers could move again, but they were thrown down on the ground and their hands and feet were bound by rope. Then the soldier commanded his comrades to throw the robbers onto a wagon like sacks. "Take them right to the prison." Meanwhile, the huntsman took one of the company aside and gave him an order as well.

"Brother Sparkle-Boots," the soldier said, "we've taken the enemy by surprise and provided well for ourselves. Now we can take our time and march back to the city as stragglers."

When they approached the city, the soldier saw a crowd of people rush from the city gate, utter a loud cry of joy, and wave green branches in the air. Then he saw that the entire royal bodyguard was bringing up the rear.

"What's the meaning of that?" he asked the huntsman in complete astonishment.

"Don't you know," answered the huntsman, "that the king has been absent from his realm for a long time. He's returning today, and everyone has come out to greet him."

"But where's the king?" the soldier asked. "I don't see him."

"Here he is," the huntsman replied. "I'm the king. I had my arrival announced in advance." Then he opened his huntsman's coat so that his royal dress could be seen. The soldier was horrified. Immediately he knelt down and begged to be forgiven for having unknowingly treated the king as his equal and for having called him by such familiar names.

But the king took his hand and said, "You're a good soldier, and you saved my life. From now on you will have everything you need. I'll make sure of that. And if you ever want a piece of good roast meat, as good as the one in the robbers' house, you just have to go into the royal kitchen. However, if you want to make a toast to anyone's health, you'll first have to get my permission."

◈ 200 ◈

The Golden Key

ONE WINTER, when the snow was very deep, a poor boy had to go outside and gather wood on a sled. After he had finally collected enough wood and had piled it on his sled, he decided not to go home right away because he was so frozen. He thought he would instead make a fire to warm himself up a bit. So he began scraping the snow away, and as he cleared the ground he discovered a small golden key. Where there's a key, he knew, there must also be a lock. So he dug further into the ground and found a little iron casket. If only the key will fit! he thought. There are bound to be precious things in the casket. He searched but could not find a keyhole. Then, finally, he noticed one, but it was so small that he could barely see it. He tried the key, and fortunately it fit. So, he began turning it, and now we must wait until he unlocks the casket completely and lifts the cover. That's when we'll learn what wonderful things he found.

Religious Tales
for Children

❖ 201 ❖

Saint Joseph in the Forest

ONCE UPON A TIME there was a mother who had three daughters. The oldest was mischievous and wicked, while the second was much better, even though she also had her faults. Then there was the youngest who was a pious and kind child. Strange to say, but the mother preferred the oldest daughter most of all and could not stand the youngest. Therefore, she often sent the poor girl into the large forest to get rid of her, for she thought the girl would lose her way and never return. However, the child's guardian angel, which every pious child has, did not allow this to happen and always led the girl back home on the right path. Once the guardian angel pretended not to be there, and the girl could not find her way back out of the forest. So she wandered until it became dark. When she saw a light glowing in the distance, she ran in that direction and came upon a small hut. She knocked, the door opened, and she entered. Then she came to a second door and knocked again. An old man with a beard white as snow and a venerable appearance opened the door. It was none other than Saint Joseph, who said to her in a friendly fashion, "Come, my dear child, sit down in my chair next to the fire and warm yourself. I'll fetch you a glass of clear water if you're thirsty. I have nothing for you to eat except some little roots, which you must first peel before you cook them."

Saint Joseph handed the roots to the girl, who scraped them clean. Then she fetched a piece of pancake and bread, which her mother had given her. She mixed everything together in a kettle on the fire and cooked a stew. When it was finished, Saint Joseph said, "I'm so hungry. Give me some of your food."

The girl did not mind and gave him more than she took for herself. However, God's blessing was with her, so she felt full. After they had eaten, Saint Joseph said, "Let's go to bed now. However, I have only one bed. You lie down on it, and I'll lie down in the straw on the ground."

"No," the girl answered. "The straw is soft enough for me."

However, Saint Joseph lifted the girl in his arms and carried her to the bed. Then she said her prayers and fell asleep. Upon awakening the next day, she wanted to say good morning to Saint Joseph, but she did not see him. She got up and searched for him, but he was nowhere to be found. Finally, she noticed a bag with money behind the door, and it was so heavy that she could barely carry it. A note on the bag said that the money was for the girl who slept there that night. So the girl took the bag and hurried straight home with it to her mother. She gave all the money to her mother as a present, and the woman was totally satisfied with her daughter.

The next day the second daughter felt an urge to go into the forest. Her mother gave her a much larger piece of pancake and bread to take with her. Like her sister, she too became lost. By evening she arrived at the hut of Saint Joseph, who handed her roots to make into a stew. When it was finished, he said to her just as he had to the first girl, "I'm so hungry. Give me some of your food."

The girl answered, "Eat with me."

Afterward, when Saint Joseph offered his bed to her and told her that he would lie down in the straw, she answered, "No, lie down in the bed. There's room enough for the two of us."

Saint Joseph lifted her in his arms, set her down on the bed, and then took his place in the straw. In the morning, when the girl awoke and looked for Saint Joseph, he had disappeared, but she found a bag filled with money behind the door. It was the size of a fist, and there was a note on the bag that said the money was for the girl who had slept there that night. So she took the bag and ran straight home, where she gave most of the money to her mother. However, she secretly kept a few coins for herself.

Now the oldest daughter was curious and wanted to go into the forest the next morning. Her mother gave her as many pancakes as she wanted along with bread and cheese. When the sun set, she found Saint Joseph in his hut, just as her two sisters had. After she made the stew, Saint Joseph said, "I'm so hungry. Give me some of your food."

"Wait until I'm full," she answered. "Then you can have whatever's left over."

She ate almost everything, and Saint Joseph had to scrape the bottom of the bowl. Afterward the kind old man offered his bed to her and said he would lie down in the straw. The girl accepted the offer without objection, lay down in the bed, and let the old man lie down in the straw. When she awoke the next morning, she could not find Saint Joseph anywhere. However, she was not at all concerned about this. Instead, she looked behind the door for a bag of money. It seemed to her that there was something on the ground. Since she could not determine what it was, she leaned over, bumped it with her nose, and there it hung. As she straightened herself up she realized, to her horror, that a second nose had become attached to her own. She began to scream and bawl, but that did no good. Everywhere she looked, she saw her own protruding nose. So she ran away in tears, and when she encountered Saint Joseph, she fell at his feet and pleaded until he took pity on her and removed the nose. He even gave her two pennies as well.

When the girl arrived back home, her mother stood in front of the door and asked, "What did you get as a gift?"

The girl answered with a lie, "A bag full of money, but I lost it on the way home."

"Lost!" the mother cried. "Well, we'll soon find it again." So she took her daughter by the hand to go searching for the bag. At first the girl cried and did not want to go along. But then she agreed. Along the way, however, they were attacked by so many lizards and snakes that they could not protect themselves. The wicked girl was finally stung to death, and the mother was stung all over her feet for not having raised her daughter in a proper way.

❖ 202 ❖

The Twelve Apostles

THREE HUNDRED YEARS before the birth of Our Lord Jesus Christ there lived a woman who had twelve sons. However, she was so poor and needy that she could no longer find a way to keep her sons alive. She prayed to God every day and asked Him to allow all her sons to be with the Savior on earth when the promised day arrived. As her situation grew worse and worse, she sent one after the other into the world to seek his bread. The oldest was called Peter, and after he had left and had completed a long day's journey, he found himself in a large forest. He searched for a way out but could not find one. The farther he went, the more he became lost.

In the meantime, he grew so hungry that he could barely stand. Finally, he became so weak that he was forced to lie down on the ground and believed his death was near. Suddenly a small boy stood next to him. He was as radiant, friendly, and fair as an angel. The boy clapped his hands together so that Peter had to look up and take notice of him. Then the boy said, "Why are you sitting there with such a troubled look?"

"Ah," Peter answered. "I'm wandering about the world seeking bread so that I might be able to see the dear Savior on the promised day. This is my greatest wish."

"Come with me," responded the boy. "Your wish will be granted."

He took Peter by the hand and led him between two cliffs to a large cave. As they entered, everything glistened with gold, silver, and crystal, and in the middle of the cave stood twelve cradles in a row. Then the angel said, "Lie down in the first one and sleep a little. I'm going to rock you."

Peter did as the angel said, and the angel sang to him and rocked him until he fell asleep. As he slept the second brother, who was also guided by his guardian angel, entered and was also rocked to sleep like Peter. Afterward the others came, one after another, until all twelve lay fast asleep in the golden cradles. They slept three hundred years until the night the Savior of the world was born. Then they awoke and were with Him on earth and were called the twelve apostles.

❖ 203 ❖

The Rose

ONCE UPON A TIME there was a poor woman who had two children. The youngest had to go into the forest every day to fetch wood. Once, when he had gone deep into the forest, he met a small child who was nevertheless very strong, and the child helped him diligently gather wood and drag it right up to the house. Then, in the wink of an eye, the child disappeared. The boy told his mother all about this, and at first she would not believe him. Finally, the boy brought his mother a rosebud and told her that the beautiful child had given him the bud and would come again when the rose began to bloom. The mother placed the rosebud in water. One morning her son did not get out of bed. So she went to his bed and found him dead, but he lay there looking very content. And the rose reached full bloom that very same morning.

❖ 204 ❖

Poverty and Humility Lead to Heaven

ONCE UPON A TIME there was a prince who was pensive and sad and went into the fields. When he looked at the sky so pure, beautiful, and blue, he sighed and said, "How wonderful it must be to live up there in heaven!" Then he noticed a poor old man coming his way, and he greeted him with a question, "Can you tell me how to get to heaven?"

"By poverty and humility," the old man answered. "Put on my tattered clothes, wander about the world for seven years, and learn all about its misery. Do not take any money, but when you're hungry, ask for a piece of bread from kindhearted people. This is how you'll find the way to heaven."

So the prince took off his magnificent coat and replaced it with the beggar's garments. Then he went out into the world and suffered great misery. He accepted nothing but a little food and never talked, but he prayed that the Lord might let him enter heaven one day. When the seven years had passed, he returned to his father's castle, where nobody recognized him, and said to the servants, "Go, tell my parents that I have returned." But the servants did not believe him. They laughed and left him standing there.

Then he said, "Go, tell my brothers that they should come down. I'd like to see them once again."

The servants would not do that either, until one of them finally decided to tell the king's children. However, they too did not believe it, nor did they want to concern themselves about it. Then the prince wrote a letter to his mother and described all his misery to her, but he did not say that he was her son. The queen took pity on him and allowed him to have a place underneath the stairs and had two servants bring him food every day. But one of them was wicked and said, "Why should we give the beggar such good food?" So, he kept the food for himself or gave it to the dogs and brought the weak, emaciated prince only water. However, the other servant was honest and brought the prince whatever he received. It was not much, but the prince could keep himself alive on this for a time. All the while he remained patient, but he became weaker and weaker. As his illness got worse, he wanted to receive the last sacrament. It was just at this time that mass was being celebrated, and all the bells in the city and the surrounding area began to ring by themselves. After the mass the priest went to the poor man underneath the stairs, but he lay there dead with a rose in one hand and a lily in the other. Next to him was a paper with his story written on it.

After he was buried, a rose grew on one side of his grave, and on the other, a lily.

◈ 205 ◈

God's Food

ONCE UPON A TIME there were two sisters. The first had no children and was rich. The second was a widow who had five children and was so poor that she no longer had enough food for herself and her children. So she went to her sister in distress and said, "My children and I are suffering a great deal from hunger. Since you're so rich, give us some bread." However, the sister, who was as rich as a gold mine and also had a heart made of stone, replied, "I myself have nothing in the house," and she turned her poor sister away with angry words.

After a while the rich sister's husband came home and wanted to cut a slice of bread for himself. However, as he made the first slice in the loaf, red blood gushed out. When his wife saw it, she became horrified and told him what had happened. He rushed to the widow's house to help her, but as he entered her living room he found her praying and holding the two youngest children in her arms. The three oldest were lying dead on the ground. He offered her some food, but she declined. "We no longer desire earthly food. Thanks to God three of us are already content, and He will answer the rest of our prayers as well." She had barely uttered these words, when her two little ones stopped breathing, whereupon her heart broke, and she sank to the ground dead.

❖ 206 ❖

The Three Green Twigs

ONCE UPON A TIME there was a hermit who lived in the forest at the foot of a mountain, and he passed the time by praying and doing good deeds. To honor God he would carry several pails of water up the mountainside each evening. Since there was always a hard wind that dried out the air and soil at the mountain peak, many an animal was able to quench its thirst because of the water he carried, and many a plant was refreshed. The wild birds, which shy away from human beings, circled there on high and looked for a drink with their sharp eyes. And because the hermit was so pious, an angel of God, visible to the hermit's eyes, would always accompany him to the top of the mountain, count his steps, and bring him food after he had completed his work, just as the prophet of olden times was fed by ravens upon God's command.

When the hermit had reached a ripe old age in his pious life, he chanced one day to see from a distance a poor sinner being led to the gallows. Then he said to himself, "This man is now receiving his just due." In the evening, when he carried the water up the mountain, the angel who usually accompanied him and brought him his food did not appear. The hermit became frightened and searched his heart to see how he might have sinned because God was indeed angry, but he did not know why. He stopped eating and drinking, threw himself on the ground and prayed night and day. And one day, when he was crying rather bitterly in the woods, he heard a little bird singing so beautifully and gloriously that he became even more depressed and said, "How cheerfully you sing! The Lord isn't angry with you. Oh, if you could only tell me how I offended Him, so I could do penance and so my heart could become cheerful once again!"

The little bird began to talk and said, "You did wrong by condemning the poor sinner who was being led to the gallows. That is why God is angry with you. He alone sits in judgment. However, if you do penance and repent your sin, He will forgive you."

Then the angel stood next to him, holding a dry branch in his hand, and said, "You are to carry this dry branch with you until three green twigs sprout from it. At night, when you go to sleep, you are to lay it under your head. You are to go from door to door and beg for food and are never to remain in the same house longer than one night. This is the penance that the Lord commands you to fulfill."

Then the hermit took the piece of wood and went back into the world, which he had not seen for a long time. He ate and drank only what people gave him at their doors. But many of his requests went unheeded, and many a door remained closed so that he often went days on end without receiving a single crumb of bread. Once when he went door to door from sunrise to sunset, nobody gave him anything or let him spend the night. So he went into the forest and finally found a cave that had been made into a home. An old woman sat inside, and he said to her, "Kind lady, allow me to spend this night in your dwelling."

But she answered, "No, I can't even if I wanted to. I have three sons who are wicked and wild. If they return home from their marauding and find you here, they'll kill us both."

Then the hermit said, "Let me stay, please. They won't harm either you or me."

The woman had compassion and let herself be moved by the hermit's plea. So he lay down beneath the stairs and placed the piece of wood under his head. When the old woman saw that, she asked him the reason. Then he told her that he carried it with him to do penance and used it as a pillow each night. He had offended the Lord by saying that a poor sinner who was on his way to the gallows was receiving his just due. Then the woman began to sob and cried out, "Oh, if the Lord punishes you just for these words, what will happen to my sons when they appear before Him on Judgment Day?"

At midnight the robbers returned home, where they began romping and making a lot of noise. They lit a fire, and when the cave was bright and they saw a man lying beneath the stairs, they became furious and yelled at their mother, "Who is this man? Didn't we tell you not to let anyone enter our cave?"

Then the mother said, "Let him be. He's an old sinner who's doing penance for his guilt."

"What did he do?" the robbers asked. "Hey, old man," they cried out, "tell us about your sins."

The old man raised himself and told them how he had sinned with just a few words so that God became angry with him. Now he was trying to atone for his crime. The robbers were deeply moved by his story and became terrified when they thought of the life they had been leading up until that moment. They began to search their souls and to repent their past in a sincere way. After the hermit had converted the three sinners, he lay down again beneath the stairs to sleep. However, the next morning they found him dead, and three green twigs were growing out of the dry wood upon which his head lay. Thus the Lord had pardoned him and taken him into his flock once again.

◈ 207 ◈

The Blessed Virgin's Little Glass

THERE WAS ONCE A CARTER whose cart became stuck because it was carrying so much wine. No matter how much he tried to move it, the cart would not budge. Just then the Blessed Virgin happened to come along, and when she perceived the poor man's problem, she said to him, "I'm tired and thirsty. Give me a glass of wine, and I'll set your wagon free."

"Gladly," answered the driver, "but I don't have a glass in which to pour the wine."

Then the Blessed Virgin plucked a red-striped flower that is called bindweed and which looks very much like a glass. She handed it to the driver, and he filled it with wine. As soon as she drank the wine, the cart was set free, and the driver could continue on his way.

From that time on the little flower was called the Blessed Virgin's Little Glass.

◈ 208 ◈

The Little Old Lady

THERE ONCE WAS A LITTLE OLD LADY who lived in a large city, and one evening she sat alone in her room thinking about how she had lost first her husband, next her two children, then little by little all her relatives, and finally her last friend, who had died that very day. Now she sat there alone and forsaken. Her heart was deeply saddened by all these deaths. In particular, the loss of her sons had hurt her so deeply that she blamed God for their deaths. As she was sitting there silently, lost in her thoughts, she suddenly heard the bells for early mass begin to ring. She thought it strange that her sorrow had caused her to lose track of time, but then she lit her lantern and made her way to church. Upon her arrival she noticed that the church was already illuminated, not by candles, as was usually the case, but by a flickering light. It was already crowded with people, and all the seats were occupied so that when the little old lady came to her regular place it was no longer free. In fact, the entire bench was packed full of people. And when she looked at them, she saw that they were none other than her dead relatives, who sat there in old-fashioned clothes. Their faces were pale, and they neither spoke nor sang, but a soft humming and groaning went through the church. Then a relative stood up, went to the old lady, and said, "Look up at the altar, and there you will see your sons."

The old lady looked and saw her two children there. One was hanging on the gallows, the other broken on the wheel. Then the relative said, "You see, that's what would have happened to them if they had lived longer and God had not taken them to himself as innocent children."

The old lady went home trembling and thanked God on her knees for having shown her more kindness than she had been able to understand.

Three days later she lay down and died.

❖ 209 ❖

The Heavenly Wedding

ONCE THERE WAS A PEASANT BOY who heard a priest talking in church. "Whoever desires to enter the kingdom of heaven must always walk a straight path." So the boy set upon his way and went straight along, always straight ahead without turning, over hill and valley. Finally, his way led into a large city and then into the middle of a church where a holy service was being performed. When he saw all the magnificent pomp, he thought that he had now reached heaven. So he sat down and rejoiced with all his heart. When the holy service was over, and the sexton told him to leave, he answered, "No, I'm never going to leave. I'm happy now that I've finally made it to heaven."

The sexton then went to the priest and told him that there was a boy who did not want to leave the church because he thought he was in heaven.

"If this is what he believes," the priest said, "then let him stay." Later he went to the boy and asked him if he would like some work to do.

"Yes," the little fellow answered. He was used to working, but he never wanted to leave heaven again. So he remained in the church, and when he observed how the people went up to the image of the Virgin Mary with the blessed child Jesus carved in wood and how they knelt down and prayed, he thought, That's our dear Lord, and he said, "Listen, dear Lord, you are much too thin! The people are certainly letting you starve. But I'll bring you half my food every day." From then on he brought the image half of his food every day, and the image began to enjoy the meals. After a few weeks the people noticed that the image had put on weight and had become fat and strong, and they were quite surprised. The priest could not understand it either. So he remained in the church and followed the little boy and saw how he shared his meal with the Virgin Mary and how she also accepted it.

After some time the boy became sick and could not leave his bed for a week. But when he could get out of bed again, the first thing he did was to bring his food to the Blessed Virgin. The priest followed him and heard him say, "Dear God, please don't think wrong of me for not having brought you anything for such a long time, but I was sick and couldn't get up."

Then the image answered him by saying, "I have seen your good intentions, and that's enough for me. Next Sunday I want you to come with me to the wedding."

The boy was glad about this and told the priest, who asked him to go to the image and inquire whether the priest could also come along. "No," replied the image. "You alone."

The priest wanted to prepare the boy first by giving him holy communion. The boy was happy to do this, and on the next Sunday, when he partook of the holy communion, he fell down dead, and thus he went to the eternal wedding.

❖ 210 ❖

The Hazel Branch

ONE AFTERNOON the Christ Child lay down in his cradle and fell asleep. Then his mother approached, looked at him with joy, and said, "Have you gone to sleep, my child? Well, sleep soundly. In the meantime, I'll go into the forest and fetch some strawberries for you. I know you'll be glad to have them when you awake."

Outside in the forest she found a place with the finest strawberries. But just as she bent over to pick one, a viper sprang out of the grass and frightened her. She left the strawberries and rushed away with the viper in pursuit. However, the Blessed Virgin knew exactly what to do, as you can well imagine. She hid behind a hazel bush and stood there until the viper went by. Then she gathered the strawberries, and on her way home she said, "As the hazel bush has protected me this time, so shall it protect others in the future."

That is why a green hazel branch has been the safest protection against vipers, snakes, and all sorts of reptiles since times of old.

The Omitted Tales

◆ 211 ◆

The Nightingale and the Blindworm

ONCE UPON A TIME there was a nightingale and a blindworm, each with one eye. For a long time they lived together peacefully and harmoniously in a house. However, one day the nightingale was invited to a wedding, and she said to the blindworm, "I've been invited to a wedding and don't particularly want to go with one eye. Would you be so kind as to lend me yours? I'll bring it back to you tomorrow."

The blindworm gave her the eye out of the kindness of her heart. But when the nightingale came home the following day, she liked having two eyes in her head and being able to see on both sides. So she refused to return the borrowed eye to the blindworm. Then the blindworm swore that she would revenge herself on the nightingale's children and the children of her children.

"Well," replied the nightingale, "see if you can find me.

I'll build my nest in the linden,
so high, so high, so high.
You'll never be able to find it,
no matter how hard you try."

Since that time all the nightingales have had two eyes, and all the blindworms, none. But wherever the nightingale builds her nest, a blindworm lives beneath it in the bushes and constantly endeavors to crawl up the tree, pierce the eggs of her ~my, and drink them up.

◆ 212 ◆

The Hand With the Knife

THERE ONCE WAS A LITTLE GIRL who had three brothers, and the boys meant the world to her mother. Yet, the little girl was always ne-glected, treated badly, and forced to go out early in the morning every day to dig up peat from the dry ground on the heath, which they used for making fires and cooking. To top it all off, she was given an old, blunt shovel to perform this nasty work.

But the little girl had an admirer who was an elf and lived in a hill near her mother's house. Whenever she went by the hill, he would stretch out his hand from the rocky slope and offer her a knife that had miraculous powers and could cut through anything. She used this knife to cut out the peat and would finish her work quickly. Then she would return home happily with the necessary load, and when she walked by the rocky slope, she would knock twice, and the hand would reach out and take back the knife.

When the mother noticed how swiftly and easily she came back home with the peat, she told the girls' brothers that there must be someone helping her; otherwise, it would be impossible for her to complete the work so fast. So the brothers crept after her and watched her receive the magic knife. They overtook her and forced her to give it to them. Then they returned to the rocky slope, knocked the way she had always done, and when the good elf stretched out his hand, they cut it off with his very own knife. The bloody arm drew back, and since the elf believed that his beloved had betrayed him, he was never seen after that.

◈ 213 ◈

Herr Fix-It-Up

FIX-IT-UP HAD BEEN A SOLDIER for a long time. When the war came to an end, however, and there were nothing but the same old things to do every day, he resigned from the army and decided to become a servant for a great lord. There would be clothes trimmed with gold, a lot to do, and always new things happening. So he set out on his way and came to a foreign court, where he saw a lord taking a walk in the garden. Fix-It-Up did not hesitate. He stepped briskly over to the lord and said, "Sir, I'm looking for employment with a great lord. If Your Majesty is himself such a person, it would give me great pleasure to serve you. There's nothing I don't know or can't do. I know just how to carry out orders, no matter how they are given."

"Fine, my son," the lord said. "I'd be pleased to have you. First tell me, what do I desire right now?"

Without answering, Fix-It-Up spun around, rushed away, and returned with a pipe and tobacco.

"Fine, my son. You are hired as my servant, but now I'm going to command you to get Princess Nomini, the most beautiful maiden in the world. I want to have her for my wife."

"All right," said Fix-It-Up. "That's a trifle for me. Your Majesty shall soon have her. Just give me a coach drawn by six horses, a coachman, guards, couriers, servants, and a cook, all in full dress. I myself must have princely garments, and everyone must obey my commands."

Soon they departed. The servant sat inside the coach, which headed straight toward the court of the beautiful princess. When the road came to an end, they drove into a field and soon reached the edge of a large forest filled with many thousands of birds. A boisterous song soared splendidly into the blue air.

"Stop! Stop!" exclaimed Fix-It-Up. "Don't disturb the birds. They are praising their creator and will serve me some other time. Let's go to the left."

So the coachman had to turn and drive around the forest. Soon after, they came to a large field where close to a thousand million ravens were sitting and crying shrilly for food.

"Stop! Stop!" exclaimed Fix-It-Up. "Untie one of the horses way up front. Lead it into the field and stab it to death so that the ravens can eat. I don't want them to suffer from hunger."

After the ravens had eaten, the journey continued, and they came to a pond with a fish in it. It moaned and groaned, "For God's sake, I have nothing to eat in this terrible swamp. Put me into a running river, and I'll repay your deed one day."

Before it could even finish speaking, Fix-It-Up had exclaimed, "Stop! Stop! Cook, take the fish into your apron. Coachman, drive it to a running river."

Fix-It-Up himself got out and put the fish into the water, and the fish flapped its tail in joy.

"Now, have the horses get going," said Fix-It-Up, "so that we arrive at the designated spot by evening."

When he reached the royal residence, he drove straight to the best inn, where the innkeeper and all his people came out and welcomed him with their best manners, thinking that a foreign king had arrived, though it was only a servant. Fix-It-Up had himself announced at the royal court, endeavored to make a good impression, and courted the princess.

"My son," said the king, "many such suitors have already been turned away because none of them could perform the tasks I gave them to win my daughter."

"All right," said Fix-It-Up, "set me a good task."

"I've ordered a quarter of a liter of poppy seeds to be sown in a field. If you can gather them so that not one kernel is missing, you shall have the princess for your wife."

Hoho! Fix-It-Up thought, that's not much for me. He then took a measure, a sack, and snow white sheets, went out to the field, and spread the sheets next to the field where the seeds had been sown. Soon after came the birds whose singing he had not disturbed in the forest, and they picked up the seeds, kernel for kernel, and carried them to the white sheets. When the birds had picked up all of them, Fix-It-Up poured them into the sack, took the measure under his arm, and went to the king, and measured out the poppy seeds for him. Now he thought the princess was already his—but he was wrong.

"One thing more, my son," said the king. "My daughter has recently lost her golden ring. You must get it back for me before you can have her."

Fix-It-Up did not get upset. "Let Your Majesty show me the river and bridge where the ring was lost, then I shall soon return it to you."

When Fix-It-Up was brought there, he looked down, and there he saw the fish that he had put into the river. It stuck its head out into the air and said, "Wait a moment. I'll dive below. A whale has the ring underneath its fins, and I'll fetch it."

Indeed, the fish soon returned and tossed the ring onto the shore. Fix-It-Up brought it to the king, but the latter replied, "Now, just one more thing. There's a unicorn in the forest, and it's been causing a great deal of damage. If you can kill it, there's nothing more you'll have to do."

Fix-It-Up did not get very upset here either. Instead, he went straight into the forest, where he came across the ravens whom he had once fed.

"Just have a little more patience," they said. "The unicorn is lying down and sleeping, but it's not on the side where you can see its eye. When it turns over, we'll peck out its good eye. Then it'll be blind and run furiously against trees and get itself stuck with its horn. That's when you'll be able to kill it easily."

Soon the beast tossed itself around a few times and lay on its other side. Immediately the ravens swooped down and pecked out its good eye. When it felt the pain, it jumped up and ran wildly around the forest. After it got its horn stuck in a thick oak tree, Fix-It-Up jumped out, cut off its head, and brought it to the king, who could no longer deny him his daughter. She was delivered to Fix-It-Up, who took a seat next to her in the coach. He was in full dress, just as he had come, and immediately drove off and brought the lovely princess to his lord. Fix-It-Up was given a fine reception, and the lord's wedding with the princess was celebrated in great splendor. Then Fix-It-Up was appointed prime minister.

Everyone in the company to whom this tale was told wished to be at the celebration. One wanted to be chambermaid; the other, wardrobe attendant. Someone wanted to be a chamber servant; another, the cook, and so on.

◆ 214 ◆

How Some Children Played at Slaughtering

I

IN A CITY NAMED FRANECKER, located in West Friesland, some young boys and girls between the ages of five and six happened to be playing with one another. They chose one boy to play a butcher, another boy was to be a cook, and a third boy was to be a pig. Then they chose one girl to be a cook and another girl her assistant. The assistant was to catch the blood of the pig in a little bowl so they could make sausages. As agreed, the butcher now fell upon the little boy playing the pig, threw him to the ground, and slit his throat open with a knife, while the assistant cook caught the blood in her little bowl.

A councilman was walking nearby and saw this wretched act. He immediately took the butcher with him and led him into the house of the mayor, who instantly summoned the entire council. They deliberated about this incident and did not know what they should do to the boy, for they realized it had all been part of a children's game. One of the councilmen, an old wise man, advised the chief judge to take a beautiful red apple in one hand and a Rhenish gulden in the other. Then he was to call the boy and stretch out his hands to him. If the boy took the apple, he was to be set free. If he took the gulden, he was to be killed. The judge took the wise man's advice, and the boy grabbed the apple with a laugh. Thus he was set free without any punishment.

II

THERE ONCE WAS A FATHER who slaughtered a pig, and his children saw that. In the afternoon, when they began playing, one child said to the other, "You be the little pig, and I'll be the butcher." He then took a shiny knife and slit his little brother's throat.

Their mother was upstairs in a room bathing another child, and when she heard the cries of her son, she immediately ran downstairs.

Upon seeing what had happened, she took the knife out of her son's throat and was so enraged that she stabbed the heart of the other boy, who had been playing the butcher. Then she quickly ran back to the room to tend to her child in the bathtub, but while she was gone, he had drowned in the tub. Now the woman became so frightened and desperate that she did not allow the neighbors to comfort her and finally hung herself. When her husband came back from the fields and saw everything, he became so despondent that he died soon after.

❖ 215 ❖

Death and the Goose Boy

A POOR GOOSE BOY WENT WALKING along the bank of a large, turbulent river while looking after a flock of white geese. When he saw Death come toward him across the water, the boy asked him where he came from and where he intended to go. Death answered that he came from the water and wanted to leave the world. The poor goose boy asked further how one could actually leave the world. Death said that one must go across the river into the new world that lay on the other side. The goose boy said he was tired of this life and asked Death to take him across the water. Death said it was not time yet, for there were things Death still had to do.

Not far from there lived a greedy man, who at night kept trying to gather together more and more money and possessions. Death led him to the large river and pushed him in. Since he could not swim, he sank to the bottom before he could reach the bank. His cats and dogs, which had run after him, were also drowned. A few days later Death returned to the goose boy and found him singing cheerfully.

"Do you want to come with me now?" he asked.

The goose boy went willingly and crossed the river with his white geese, which were all turned into white sheep. The goose boy looked at the beautiful country and heard that the shepherds of places like that became kings, and as he was looking around, the arch-shepherds, Abraham, Isaac, and Jacob, came toward him, put a royal crown on his head, and led him to the castle of the shepherds, where he can still be found.

◆ 216 ◆

Puss in Boots

A MILLER HAD THREE SONS, a mill, a donkey, and a cat. The sons had to grind grain, the donkey had to haul the grain and carry away the flour, and the cat had to catch the mice. When the miller died, the three sons divided the inheritance: the oldest received the mill, the second the donkey, and nothing was left for the third but the cat. This made the youngest sad, and he said to himself, "I certainly got the worst part of the bargain. My oldest brother can grind wheat, and my second brother can ride on his donkey. But what can I do with the cat? Once I make a pair of gloves out of his fur, it's all over."

The cat, who had understood all he had said, began to speak. "Listen, there's no need to kill me when all you'll get will be a pair of poor gloves from my fur. Have some boots made for me instead. Then I'll be able to go out, mix with people, and help you before you know it."

The miller's son was surprised the cat could speak like that, but since the shoemaker happened to be walking by, he called him inside and had him measure a pair of boots for the cat. When the boots were finished, the cat put them on. After that he took a sack, filled the bottom with grains of wheat, and attached a piece of cord to the top, which he could pull to close it. Then he slung the sack over his back and walked out the door on two legs like a human being.

At that time there was a king ruling the country, and he liked to eat partridges. However, there was a grave situation because no one had been able to catch a single partridge. The whole forest was full of them, but they frightened so easily that none of the huntsmen had been able to get near them. The cat knew this and thought he could do much better than the huntsmen. When he entered the forest, he opened the sack, spread the grains of wheat on the ground, placed the cord in the grass, and strung it out behind a hedge. Then he crawled in back of the hedge, hid himself, and lay in wait. Soon the partridges came running, found the wheat, and hopped into the sack, one after the other. When a good number were inside, the cat pulled the cord. Once the sack was closed tight, he ran over to it and wrung their necks. Then he slung the sack over his back and went straight to the king's castle. The sentry called out, "Halt! Where are you going?"

"To the king," the cat answered curtly.

"Are you crazy? A cat to the king?"

"Oh, let him go," another sentry said. "The king's often very bored. Perhaps the cat will give him some pleasure with his meowing and purring."

When the cat appeared before the king, he bowed and said, "My lord, the Count"—and he uttered a long, distinguished name—"sends you his regards and would like to offer you these partridges, which he recently caught in his traps."

The king was amazed by the beautiful, fat partridges. Indeed, he was so overcome with joy that he commanded the cat to take as much gold from his treasury as he could carry and put it into the sack. "Bring it to your lord and give him my very best thanks for his gift."

Meanwhile, the poor miller's son sat at home by the window, propped his head up with his hand, and wondered why he had given away all he had for the cat's boots when the cat would probably not be able to bring him anything great in return. Suddenly the cat entered, threw down the sack from his back, opened it, and dumped the gold at the miller's feet.

"Now you've got something for the boots. The king also sends his regards and best of thanks."

The miller was happy to have such wealth, even though he did not understand how everything had happened. However, as the cat was taking off his boots he told him everything and said, "Surely you have enough money now, but we won't be content with that. Tomorrow I'm going to put on my boots again, and you shall become even richer. Incidentally, I told the king that you're a count."

The following day the cat put on his boots, as he said he would, went hunting again, and brought the king a huge catch. So it went every day, and every day the cat brought back gold to the miller. At the king's court he became a favorite, so that he was permitted to go and come and wander about the castle wherever he pleased. One day, as the cat was lying by the hearth in the king's kitchen and warming himself, the coachman came and started cursing, "May the devil take the king and princess! I wanted to go to the tavern, have a drink, and play some cards. But now they want me to drive them to the lake so they can go for a walk."

When the cat heard that, he ran home and said to his master, "If you want to be a rich count, come with me to the lake and go for a swim."

The miller did not know what to say. Nevertheless, he listened to the cat and went with him to the lake, where he undressed and jumped into the water completely naked. Meanwhile, the cat took his clothes, carried them away, and hid them. No sooner had he done it than the king came driving by. Now the cat began to wail in a miserable voice, "Ahh, most gracious King! My lord went for a swim in the lake, and a thief came and stole his clothes that were lying on the bank. Now the count is in the water and can't get out. If he stays in much longer, he'll freeze and die."

When the king heard that, he ordered the coach to stop, and one of his servants had to race back to the castle and fetch some of the king's garments. The count put on the splendid clothes, and since the king had already taken a liking to him because of the partridges that, he believed, had been sent by the count, he asked the young man to sit down next to him in the coach. The princess was not in the least angry about this, for the count was young and handsome and pleased her a great deal.

In the meantime, the cat went on ahead of them and came to a large meadow, where there were over a hundred people making hay.

"Who owns this meadow, my good people?" asked the cat.

"The great sorcerer."

"Listen to me. The king will be driving by, and when he asks who the owner of this meadow is, I want you to answer, 'The count.' If you don't, you'll all be killed."

Then the cat continued on his way and came to a wheatfield so enormous that nobody could see over it. There were more than two hundred people standing there and cutting wheat.

"Who owns this wheat, my good people?"

"The sorcerer."

"Listen to me. The king will be driving by, and when he asks who the owner of this wheat is, I want you to answer, 'The count.' If you don't do this, you'll all be killed."

Finally, the cat came to a splendid forest, where more than three hundred people were chopping down large oak trees and cutting them into wood.

"Who owns this forest, my good people?"

"The sorcerer."

"Listen to me. The king will be driving by, and when he asks who the owner of this forest is, I want you to answer, 'The count.' If you don't do this, you'll all be killed."

The cat continued on his way, and the people watched him go. Since he looked so unusual and walked in boots like a human being, they were afraid of him. Soon the cat came to the sorcerer's castle, walked boldly inside, and appeared before the sorcerer, who looked at him scornfully and asked him what he wanted. The cat bowed and said, "I've heard that you can turn yourself into any kind of an animal you desire. Well, I'm sure you can turn yourself into a dog, fox, or even a wolf, but I don't believe you can turn yourself into an elephant. That seems impossible to me, and this is why I've come: I want to be convinced with my own eyes."

"That's just a trifle for me," the sorcerer said arrogantly, and within seconds he turned himself into an elephant.

"That's great, but can you also change yourself into a lion?"

"Nothing to it," said the sorcerer, and he suddenly stood before the cat as a lion. The cat pretended to be terrified and cried out, "That's incredible and unheard of! Never in all my dreams would I have thought this possible! But you'd top all of this if you could turn yourself into a tiny animal, such as a mouse. I'm convinced you can do more than any other sorcerer in the world, but that would be too much for you."

The flattery had made the sorcerer quite friendly, and he said, "Oh, no, dear cat, that's not too much at all," and soon he was running around the room as a mouse.

Then the cat ran after him, caught the mouse in one leap, and ate him up.

While all this was happening, the king had continued driving with the count and princess and had come to the large meadow.

"Who owns that hay?" the king asked.

"The count," the people all cried out, just as the cat had ordered them to do.

"You've got a nice piece of land, Count," the king said.

Afterward they came to the large wheatfield.

"Who owns that wheat, my good people?"

"The count."

"My! You've got quite a large and beautiful estate!"

Next they came to the forest.

"Who owns that wood, my good people?"

"The count."

The king was even more astounded and said, "You must be a rich man, Count. I don't think I have such a splendid forest."

At last they came to the castle. The cat stood on top of the stairs, and when the coach stopped below, he ran down, opened the door, and said, "Your Majesty, you've arrived at the castle of my lord, the count. This honor will make him happy for the rest of his life."

The king climbed out of the coach and was amazed by the magnificent building, which was almost larger and more beautiful than his own castle. The count led the princess up the stairs and into the hall, which was flickering with lots of gold and jewels.

The princess became the count's bride, and when the king died, the count became king, and the puss in boots was his prime minister.

◈ 217 ◈

The Tablecloth, the Knapsack,
the Cannon Hat, and the Horn

ONCE THERE WERE THREE BROTHERS from the region of the Black Mountains. Originally, they were very poor and traveled to Spain, where they came to a mountain completely surrounded by silver. The oldest brother took advantage of the situation by gathering as much silver as he could carry and went back home with his booty. The other two continued traveling and came to a mountain where nothing could be seen but gold. One brother said to the other, "What should we do?"

The second took as much gold as he could carry, as his older brother had done, and went home. However, the third wanted to see if he could have even better luck and continued on his way. After three days he entered an enormous forest. After wandering about for some time he became tired, hungry, and thirsty, and could not find his way out of the forest. So he climbed a tall tree and wanted to see if he could catch a glimpse of the end of the forest. However, he saw nothing but the tops of trees. His only wish now was to fill his body once more, and he began climbing down the tree. When he got to the bottom, he noticed a table covered with many different dishes underneath the tree. He was delighted by this and ate until he was full. After he had finished eating, he took the tablecloth with him and moved on. Whenever he got hungry or thirsty again, he opened the tablecloth, and whatever he wished for would appear on it.

After a day's journey he came upon a charcoal burner, who was burning coals and cooking potatoes. The charcoal burner invited him to be his guest, but he replied, "No thanks, but I want you to be my guest."

"How's that possible?" the charcoal burner asked. "You don't seem to be carrying anything with you."

"That doesn't matter," he said. "Just sit down over here."

Then he opened his tablecloth, and soon there was everything one could possibly wish for. The charcoal burner enjoyed the meal and wanted to have the tablecloth. After they had eaten everything, he said, "How'd you like to trade with me? I'll give you an old soldier's knapsack for the tablecloth. If you tap it with your hand, a corporal and six men armed from top to bottom will come out each time you tap. They're of no help to me in the forest, but I'd certainly like the tablecloth."

They made the trade: the charcoal burner kept the tablecloth, while the man from the Black Mountains took the knapsack. However, no sooner had the man gone some distance than he tapped the knapsack, and out popped the war heroes.

"What does my master want?"

"I want you to march back and fetch my tablecloth that I left behind with the charcoal burner."

So they returned to the charcoal burner and then brought him back the tablecloth. In the evening he came to another charcoal burner, who invited him to supper. He had the same potatoes without grease, but the man from the Black Mountains opened his tablecloth instead and invited him to be his guest. One could not have wished for a better meal. When it was over, this charcoal burner also wanted to make a trade. He gave the man a hat for the tablecloth. If the man turned the hat on his head, cannons would fire as if an entire battery were right on the spot. When the man from the Black Mountains had gone some distance, he tapped the old knapsack again, and the corporal and his six men had to fetch the tablecloth again. Now the man continued his journey in the same forest, and in the evening he came upon a third charcoal burner, who invited him to eat potatoes without grease like the others. Then they negotiated, and the charcoal burner gave the man a little horn for the tablecloth. If the man blew on it, all the cities and villages as well as the fortresses would collapse into heaps of rubble. The charcoal burner did not get to keep the tablecloth any longer than the other two, for the corporal and his six men soon came and fetched it.

Now, when the man from the Black Mountains had everything together, he returned home and intended to visit his brothers, who had become rich from their gold and silver. When he went to them wearing an old tattered coat, they refused to recognize him as their brother. So he immediately tapped his knapsack and had one hundred and fifty men march out and give his brothers a good thrashing on their backs. The entire village came to their aid, but they could do very little in this affair. News of this soon reached the king, who sent a military squad to take the soldiers prisoner, but the man from the Black Mountains kept tapping his knapsack and had an infantry and cavalry march out. They defeated the military squad and forced it to retreat. The following day the king had even more soldiers sent to bring an end to the old fellow. However, he kept tapping his knapsack until he had an entire army. In addition, he turned his hat a few times. The cannons fired, and the enemy was defeated and took flight. Finally, peace was made, and he was appointed viceroy and awarded the princess for his bride.

However, the princess was constantly bothered by the fact that she had to take such an old fellow for her husband. Her greatest wish was to get rid of him. Every day she tried to discover the source of the power that he used to his advantage. Finally, since he was so devoted to her, he revealed everything to her. She managed to talk him into giving her his knapsack, whereupon she forced him out. Afterward, when soldiers came marching against him, his men were defeated. However, he still had his little hat. So he turned it and had the cannons fired. Once again he defeated the enemy, and peace was made. After this he let himself be deceived again, and the princess talked him into giving her his little hat. Now, when the enemy attacked him, he had nothing left but his little horn. So he blew on it, and the villages, cities, and all the fortresses collapsed instantly into heaps of rubble. Then he alone was king and blew his horn until he died.

◆ 218 ◆

The Strange Feast

A BLOOD SAUSAGE AND A LIVER SAUSAGE HAD BEEN FRIENDS for some time, and the blood sausage invited the liver sausage for a meal at her home. At dinnertime the liver sausage merrily set out for the blood sausage's house. But when she walked through the doorway, she saw all kinds of strange things. There were many steps, and on each one of them she found something different. There were a broom and shovel fighting with each other, a monkey with a big wound on his head, and more such things.

The liver sausage was very frightened and upset by this. Nevertheless, she took heart, entered the room, and was welcomed in a friendly way by the blood sausage. The liver sausage began to inquire about the strange things on the stairs, but the blood sausage pretended not to hear her or made it seem it was not worth talking about, or she said something about the shovel and the broom such as, "That was probably my maid gossiping with someone on the stairs." And she shifted the topic to something else.

Then the blood sausage said she had to leave the room to go into the kitchen and look after the meal. She wanted to check to see that everything was in order and nothing had fallen into the ashes. The liver sausage began walking back and forth in the room and kept wondering about the strange things until someone appeared—I don't know who it was—and said, "Let me warn you, liver sausage, you're in a bloody murderous trap. You'd better get out of here quickly if you value your life!"

The liver sausage did not have to think twice about this. She ran out the door as fast as she could. Nor did she stop until she got out of the house and was in the middle of the street. Then she looked around and saw the blood sausage standing high up in the attic window with a long, long knife that was gleaming as though it had just been sharpened. The blood sausage threatened her with it and cried out,

"If I had caught you, I would have had you!"

◆ 219 ◆

Simple Hans

ONCE A KING LIVED HAPPILY with his daughter, who was his only child. Then, all of a sudden she gave birth to a baby, and no one knew who the father was. For a long time the king did not know what to do. At last he ordered the princess to take the child and go to the church. There a lemon was to be given to the child, who was to offer it to anyone around him, and that man was to be the child's father and the princess's husband. Everything was arranged accordingly, and the king also gave orders to allow only highborn people into the church.

However, there was a little, crooked hunchback living in the city who was not particularly smart and was therefore called Simple Hans. He managed to push his way into the church among the others without being noticed, and when the child offered the lemon, he handed it to Simple Hans. The princess was mortified, and the king was so upset that he had his daughter, the child, and Simple Hans stuck into a barrel, which was put into the sea. The barrel soon floated off, and when they were alone on the sea, the princess groaned and said, "You nasty, impudent hunchback! You're to blame for my misfortune! Why did you force your way into the church? My child's of no concern to you."

"That's not true," said Simple Hans. "He does concern me because I once made a wish that you would have a child, and whatever I wish comes true."

"Well, if that's the case, wish us something to eat."

"That's easily done," said Simple Hans, and he wished for a dish full of potatoes. The princess would have liked to have something better. Nevertheless, she was so hungry that she helped him eat the potatoes. After they had stilled their hunger, Simple Hans said, "Now I'll wish us a beautiful ship!"

No sooner had he said this than they were sitting in a splendid ship that contained more than enough to fulfill their desires. The helmsman guided the ship straight toward land, and when they went ashore, Simple Hans said, "Now I want a castle over there!"

Suddenly there was a magnificent castle standing there, along with servants dressed in gold. They led the princess and her child inside, and when they were in the middle of the main hall, Simple Hans said, "Now I wish to be a young and clever prince!"

His hunchback disappeared at once, and he was handsome, upright, and kind. Indeed, the princess took such a great liking to him that she became his wife.

For a long time they lived happily together, and then one day the old king went out riding, lost his way, and arrived at their castle. He was puzzled because he had never seen it before and decided to go inside. The princess recognized her father immediately, but he did not recognize her, for he thought she had drowned in the sea a long time ago. She treated him with a great deal of hospitality, and when he was about to return home, she secretly slipped a golden cup into his pocket. After he had ridden off, she sent a pair of knights after him. They were ordered to stop him and search him to see if he had stolen the golden cup. When they found it in his pocket, they brought him back. He swore to the princess that he had not stolen it and did not know how it had got into his pocket.

"That's why," she said, "one must beware of declaring someone guilty too rashly." And she revealed to him that she was his daughter. The king rejoiced, and they all lived happily together, and after his death, Simple Hans became king.

◆ 220 ◆

Bluebeard

THERE ONCE WAS A MAN who lived in a forest with his three sons and beautiful daughter. One day a golden coach drawn by six horses and attended by several servants came driving up to his house. After the coach stopped, a king stepped out and asked him if he could have his daughter for his wife. The man was happy that his daughter could benefit from such a stroke of good fortune and immediately said yes. There was nothing objectionable about the suitor except for his beard, which was all blue and made one shudder somewhat whenever one looked at it. At first the maiden also felt frightened by it and resisted marrying him. But her father kept urging her, and finally she consented. However, her fear was so great that she first went to her brothers, took them aside, and said, "Dear brothers, if you hear me scream, leave everything standing or lying wherever you are, and come to my aid."

The brothers kissed her and promised to do this. "Farewell, dear sister, if we hear your voice, we'll jump on our horses and soon be at your side."

Then she got into the coach, sat down next to Bluebeard, and drove away with him. When she reached his castle, she found everything splendid, and whatever the queen desired was fulfilled. They would have been very happy together if she could only have accustomed herself to the king's blue beard. However, whenever she saw it, she felt frightened.

After some time had passed, he said to her, "I must go on a great journey. Here are the keys to the entire castle. You can open all the rooms and look at everything. But I forbid you to open one particular room, which this little golden key can unlock. If you open it, you will pay for it with your life."

She took the key and promised to obey him. Once he had departed, she opened one door after another and saw so many treasures and magnificent things that she thought they must have been gathered from all over the world. Soon nothing was left but the forbidden room. Since the key was made of gold, she believed that the most precious things were probably kept there. Her curiosity began to gnaw at her, and she would certainly have passed over all the other rooms if she could only have seen what was in this one. At last her desire became so strong that she took the key and went to the room. "Who can possibly see when I open it?" she said to herself. "I'll just glance inside." Then she unlocked the room, and when the door opened, a stream of blood flowed toward her, and she saw dead women hanging along all the walls, some only skeletons. Her horror was so tremendous that she immediately slammed the door, but the key popped out of the lock and fell into the blood. Swiftly she picked it up and tried to wipe away the blood, but to no avail. When she wiped the blood away on one side, it appeared on the other. She sat down, rubbed the key throughout the day, and tried everything possible, but nothing helped: the bloodstains could not be eliminated. Finally, in the evening she stuck it into some hay, which was supposed to be able to absorb blood.

The following day Bluebeard came back, and the first thing he requested was the bunch of keys. Her heart pounded as she brought the keys, and she hoped he would not notice that the golden one was missing. However, he counted all of them, and when he was finished, he said, "Where's the key to the secret room?"

As he said this he looked straight into her face, causing her to blush red as blood.

"It's upstairs," she answered. "I misplaced it. Tomorrow I'll go and look for it."

"You'd better go now, dear wife. I need it today."

"Oh, I might as well tell you. I lost it in the hay. I'll have to go and search for it first."

"You haven't lost it," Bluebeard said angrily. "You stuck it there so the hay would absorb the bloodstains. It's clear that you've disobeyed my command and entered the room. Now, you will enter the room whether you want to or not."

Then he ordered her to fetch the key, which was still stained with blood.

"Now prepare yourself for your death. You shall die today," Bluebeard declared. He fetched his big knife and took her to the threshold of the house.

"Just let me say my prayers before I die," she said.

"All right. Go ahead, but you'd better hurry. I don't have much time to waste."

She ran upstairs and cried out of the window as loud as she could, "Brothers, my dear brothers! Come help me!"

The brothers were sitting in the forest and drinking some cool wine. The youngest said, "I think I heard our sister's voice. Let's go! We must hurry and help her!"

They jumped on their horses and rode like a turbulent wind. Meanwhile, their sister was on her knees, praying in fear.

"Well, are you almost done?" Bluebeard called from below, and she heard him sharpening his knife on the bottom step. She looked out the window but could see only a cloud of dust as if a herd were coming. So she screamed once again, "Brothers, my dear brothers! Come help me!"

And her fear became greater and greater when Bluebeard called, "If you don't come down soon, I'll be up to get you. My knife's been sharpened!"

She looked out the window again and saw her three brothers riding across the field as though they were birds flying through the air. For the third time she screamed desperately and with all her might, "Brothers, my dear brothers! Come help me!"

The youngest brother was already so near that she could hear his voice. "Calm yourself. Another moment, dear sister, and we'll be at your side!"

But Bluebeard cried out, "That's enough praying! I'm not going to wait any longer. If you don't come, I'm going to fetch you."

"Oh, just let me pray for my three dear brothers!"

However, he would not listen to her. Instead, he went upstairs and dragged her down. Then he grabbed her by the hair and was about to plunge the knife into her heart, when the three brothers knocked at the door, charged inside, and tore their sister out of his hands. They then drew out their sabers and cut him down. Afterward he was hung up in the bloody chamber next to the women he had killed. Later, the brothers took their dear sister home with them, and all Bluebeard's treasures belonged to her.

◈ 221 ◈

Hurleburlebutz

ONCE A KING GOT LOST during a hunt, and suddenly a little white dwarf appeared before him.

"Your Majesty," he said, "if you give me your youngest daughter, I'll show you how to get out of the forest."

The king consented out of fear, and the dwarf helped him find his way. As he took leave of the king he called after him, "I'll be coming to fetch my bride in a week."

When the king reached home, he was sad about his promise, for his youngest daughter was his favorite. His daughters noticed how sad he was and wanted to know what the cause of his worry was. Finally, he had to tell them that he had promised the youngest of them to a little white dwarf in the forest and that the dwarf would be coming to fetch her in a week. However, they told him to cheer up, for they would lead the dwarf on a wild goose chase.

When the day came for the dwarf's arrival, they dressed a cowherd's daughter in their clothes and sat her down in their room.

"If someone comes to fetch you, you're to go with him!" they ordered, and they themselves left the house.

No sooner had they left than a fox entered the castle and said to the maiden, "Sit down on my furry tail, Hurleburlebutz! Off to the forest!"

The maiden sat down on the fox's tail, and he carried her out into the forest. When they came to a beautiful green clearing, where the sun was shining very bright and warm, the fox said, "Get off and take the lice out of my hair!"

The maiden followed his orders, and the fox laid his head on her lap so she could louse him. While she was doing this, the maiden said, "When I was in the forest yesterday about this time, it was more beautiful!"

"What were you doing in the forest?" the fox asked.

"Oh, I was tending the cows with my father."

"So, you're not the princess! Sit down on my furry tail, Hurleburlebutz! Back to the castle!"

The fox carried her back and said to the king, "You deceived me. That was a cowherd's daughter. I'll come again in a week and fetch your daughter."

At the end of the week the princesses dressed a gooseherd's daughter in splendid garments, sat her down, and went away. Then the fox came again and said, "Sit down on my furry tail, Hurlebuletbutz! Off to the forest!"

When they arrived at a sunny spot in the forest, the fox said once more, "Get off and take the lice out of my hair!"

As the maiden was lousing the fox she sighed and said, "I wonder where my geese are now?"

"What do you know about geese?"

"Oh, I take them to the meadow every day with my father."

"So, you're not the king's daughter! Sit down on my furry tail, Hurleburlebutz! Back to the castle!"

The fox carried her back and said to the king, "You deceived me again. That was the gooseherd's daughter. I'm going to come again in a week, and if you don't give me your daughter, you'll be in for trouble."

The king became frightened, and when the fox returned, he gave him the princess.

"Sit down on my furry tail, Hurleburlebutz! Off to the forest!"

She had to ride on the fox's tail, and when they got to a sunny place, he said to her, "Get off and take the lice out of my hair!"

However, when he laid his head in her lap, the princess began to cry and said, "I'm a king's daughter, and yet I must louse a fox! If I were sitting at home now, I'd be looking at the flowers in my garden!"

Then the fox knew that he had the right bride and turned himself into the little white dwarf. He was now her husband, and she had to live with him in a little hut and cook and sew for him. This lasted a good long time, and the dwarf did everything he could to please her.

One day the dwarf said to her, "I've got to go away, but three white doves will soon come flying here. When they swoop down to the ground, catch the middle one. Once you've got it, cut off its head right away. But pay attention and make sure you've got the middle dove, or else there'll be a disaster."

The dwarf departed, and it did not take long for the three white doves to come flying toward her. The princess paid close attention and grabbed the middle one. Then she took a knife and cut off its head. No sooner was the dove lying on the ground than a handsome young prince stood before her and said, "A fairy cast a spell over me causing me to lose my human form for seven years. Then I was to fly by my wife as a dove between two other doves, and she would have to catch me and cut off my head. If she didn't catch me or if she caught another and I flew by, then everything would be lost, and I could never be saved. That's why I asked you to pay attention, for I'm the white dwarf, and you're my wife."

The princess was delighted, and together they went to her father. When he died, they inherited the kingdom.

◈ 222 ◈

Okerlo

A QUEEN PUT HER CHILD out to sea in a golden cradle and let it float away. However, the cradle did not sink but drifted to an island inhabited only by cannibals. When the cradle drifted toward the shore, a cannibal's wife happened to be standing there. Upon seeing the child, who was a beautiful baby girl, she decided to raise her for her son, who would wed her one day. But she had a great deal of trouble hiding the maiden carefully from her husband, Old Okerlo, for if he had laid his eyes on her, he would have eaten her up, skin and bones.

When the maiden had grown up, she was to be married to the young Okerlo, but she could not stand him and cried all day long. Once when she was sitting on the shore, a young, handsome prince came swimming up to her. Since they each took a liking to the other, they exchanged vows. Just then the old cannibal's wife came, and she got tremendously angry at finding the prince with her son's bride. So she grabbed hold of him and said, "Just wait! We'll roast you at my son's wedding."

The young prince, the maiden, and Okerlo's three children had to sleep together in one room. When night came, Old Okerlo began craving human flesh and said, "Wife, I don't feel like waiting until the wedding. I want the prince right now."

However, the maiden had heard everything through the wall, and she got up quickly, took off the golden crown from one of Okerlo's children, and put it on the prince's head. When the old cannibal's wife came in, it was dark. So she had to feel their heads and took the boy that was not wearing a crown and brought him to her husband, who immediately ate him up. Meanwhile, the maiden became terribly frightened, for she thought, As soon as day breaks, everything will be revealed, and we'll be in for trouble. She got up quietly and fetched seven-mile boots, a magic wand, and a cake with a bean that provided answers for everything. After that she departed with the prince. They were wearing the seven-mile boots, and with each step they took, they went a mile. Sometimes they asked the bean, "Bean, are you there?"

"Yes," the bean said. "I'm here, but you'd better hurry. The old cannibal's wife is coming after you in some other seven-mile boots that were left behind!"

The maiden took the magic wand and turned herself into a swan and the prince into a pond for the swan to swim on. The cannibal's wife came and tried to lure the swan to the bank, but she did not succeed and went home in a bad mood. The maiden and the prince continued on their way.

"Bean, are you there?"

"Yes," the bean said. "I'm here, but the old woman's coming again. The cannibal explained to her how you duped her."

The princess took the wand and changed herself and the prince into a cloud of dust. Okerlo's wife could not penetrate it and again had to return empty-handed, while the maiden and the prince continued on their way.

"Bean, are you there?"

"Yes, I'm here, but I see Okerlo's wife coming once more, and she's taking tremendous steps!"

The maiden took the magic wand for the third time and turned herself into a rosebush and the prince into a bee. The old cannibal came and did not recognize them because of their changed forms. So she went home.

But now the maiden and the prince could not regain their human forms, because the maiden, in her fear, had thrown the magic wand too far away. Yet, their journey had taken them such a long distance that the rosebush now stood in a garden that belonged to the maiden's mother. The bee sat on the rose, and he would sting anyone who tried to pluck it. One day the queen herself happened to be walking in the garden and saw the beautiful flower. She was so amazed by it that she wanted to pluck it. But the little bee came and stung her hand so hard that she had to let go of the rose. Yet, she had managed to rip the flower a little, and suddenly she saw blood gushing from the stem. Then she summoned a fairy to break the enchantment of the flower and the bee, and the queen then recognized her daughter again and was very happy and delighted. Now a great wedding was held, and a large number of guests were invited. They came in magnificent array, while thousands of candles flickered in the hall. Music was played, and everyone danced until dawn.

"Were you also at the wedding?"

"Of course I was there. My hairdo was made of butter, and as I was exposed to the sun, it melted and was muddled. My dress was made from a spider's web, and as I went through some thornbushes, they ripped it off my body. My slippers were made of glass, and as I stepped on a stone, they broke in two."

◆ 223 ◆

Princess Mouseskin

A KING HAD THREE DAUGHTERS, and he wanted to know which one loved him most. So he summoned them to him and began asking. The oldest daughter said she loved him more than the whole kingdom. The second said she loved him more than all the jewels and pearls in the world. But the third said she loved him more than salt. The king was furious that she compared her love for him to such a meager thing. Therefore, he handed her over to a servant and ordered him to take her into the forest and kill her.

When they reached the forest, the princess begged the servant to spare her life. Since he was devoted to her, he would not have killed her anyway. Indeed, he said he would go with her and do her bidding. But the princess demanded nothing except a garment made out of a mouse skin. When he fetched it for her, she wrapped herself in the skin and went straight to a neighboring king. Once there she pretended to be a man and asked the king to employ her. The king consented, and she was to be his personal servant. In the evening, whenever she pulled off his boots, he always tossed them at her head. One time he asked her where she came from.

"From the country where one doesn't toss boots at people's heads!"

Her remark made the king suspicious. Finally, the other servants brought him a ring that Mouseskin had lost. It was so precious that they thought she had stolen it. The king called Mouseskin to him and asked how she had obtained the ring. Mouseskin could no longer conceal her true identity. She unwrapped the mouseskin, and her golden hair streamed down. As she stepped out of the skin he could see she was beautiful, indeed so beautiful that he immediately took off his crown, put it on her head, and declared her his wife.

When the wedding was celebrated, Mouseskin's father was also invited to attend. He believed that his daughter had died a long time ago and did not recognize her. However, at the dinner table all the dishes put before him were unsalted, and he became irritated and said, "I'd rather die than eat such food!"

No sooner had he uttered those words than the queen said to him, "Well, now you say you can't live without salt, but when I said I loved you more than salt, you wanted to have me killed."

All at once he recognized his daughter, kissed her, and begged her forgiveness. Now that he had found her again, she was more dear to him than his kingdom and all the jewels in the world.

◈ 224 ◈

The Pear Refused to Fall

THE MASTER WENT to shake the pear,
but the pear refused to fall.
The master sent the servant out
to shake the pear and make it fall.
But the servant did not shake at all,
the pear refused to fall.

The master sent the guard dog out
to bite the servant with his snout.
But the dog did not bite at all,
the servant did not shake at all,
the pear refused to fall.

The master sent the big stick out
to hit the dog right on his snout.
But the stick did not hit at all,
the dog did not bite at all,
the servant did not shake at all,
the pear refused to fall.

The master sent the fire out
to burn the stick down to a crisp.
But the fire did not burn at all,
the stick did not hit at all,
the dog did not bite at all,
the servant did not shake at all,
the pear refused to fall.

The master sent the water out
to snuff the little fire out.

But the water did not snuff at all,
the fire did not burn at all,
the stick did not hit at all,
the dog did not bite at all,
the servant did not shake at all,
the pear refused to fall.

The master sent the little calf out
to lap the water up.
But the calf did not lap at all,
the water did not snuff at all,
the fire did not burn at all,
the stick did not hit at all,
the dog did not bite at all,
the servant did not shake at all,
the pear refused to fall.

The master sent the butcher out
to kill the little calf.
But the butcher did not kill at all,
the calf did not lap at all,
the water did not snuff at all,
the fire did not burn at all,
the stick did not hit at all,
the dog did not bite at all,
the servant did not shake at all,
the pear refused to fall.

The master sent the henchman out
to go and hang the butcher.
Now the butcher wants the calf to kill, you bet,
the calf wants the water to lap, you bet,
the water wants the fire to snuff, you bet,
the fire wants the stick to burn, you bet,
the stick wants the dog to hit, you bet,
the dog wants the servant to bite, you bet,
the servant wants the pear to shake, you bet,
and the pear is ready to fall.

◆ 225 ◆

The Castle of Murder

ONCE UPON A TIME there was a shoemaker who had three daughters. One day when the shoemaker was out, a well-dressed nobleman came with a splendid carriage and servants, and he appeared to be very rich. He fell in love with one of the beautiful daughters, who thought herself fortunate to have found such a rich gentleman, and she gladly agreed to ride off with him. As they were on their way it turned dark, and he asked her:

"The moon's shining very bright.
My horses are dashing into the night.
Sweet love, are you feeling any doubts?"

"No, why should I have any doubts? I'm well taken care of by you," but indeed she did feel a certain uneasiness. When they were in a large forest, she asked him if they would soon be there.

"Yes," he said. "Do you see the light in the distance? That's my castle."

At last they arrived, and everything was very beautiful. The next day he said to her that he had to leave her for a few days because he had to take care of some important and urgent business. However, he wanted to leave all the keys with her so she could see the whole castle and what treasures she, as mistress, now possessed. When he was gone, she went through the entire castle and found that everything was beautiful. She was completely satisfied until she came to the cellar, where an old woman was sitting and scraping out intestines.

"My goodness, granny, what are you doing there?"

"I'm scraping intestines, my child. Tomorrow I'll be scraping yours too!"

The maiden was so terrified by her words that she dropped the key she was holding into a basin of blood, and she could not wash the blood off the key.

"Now your death is certain," said the old woman, "because my master will be able to see you were in the chamber, and no one is allowed to enter here except him and me."

(One must indeed know that this was the way her two sisters had lost their lives before her.)

Just then a hay wagon began to drive away and leave the castle. The old woman told her the only way she could save herself was by hiding under the hay and driving off in the wagon. And this is what the maiden did. In the meantime, the nobleman returned home and asked where the maiden was.

"Oh," said the old woman, "since I had no more work for today, and since she was due to be slaughtered tomorrow, I decided to kill her. Here's a lock of her hair. The dogs ate up the heart, the warm blood, and all the rest. I'm scraping out the intestines."

The nobleman was glad that she was dead. Meanwhile, she arrived in the hay wagon at a nearby castle, where the hay was supposed to be delivered. She climbed out of the hay and told everything she knew. Then she was asked to remain, and after some time had passed, the lord of this castle invited all the gentry of the surrounding region to a great feast. Since the nobleman from the castle of murder had also been invited, the maiden changed her features and clothes so she would not be recognized.

Once they were all there, everyone had to tell a tale. When it was the maiden's turn, she told the particular story that concerned the nobleman and made his heart tremble with fear, and he wanted to force his way out. However, the good lord of this noble house had planned ahead of time to have the authorities ready to take our fine count to prison. His castle was destroyed, and all the treasures were given to the maiden for her own. Afterward she married the lord's son in the house where she had been so well received, and they lived together many, many years.

◆ 226 ◆

The Carpenter and the Turner

A CARPENTER AND A TURNER WANTED TO SEE who could make the best piece of work. The carpenter made a dish that could swim by itself, while the turner made wings that he could use to fly. Everyone said that the carpenter's masterpiece was better. So the turner took his wings, put them on, and flew out of the country. He flew the entire day until he came to another country, where a prince saw him flying and asked to borrow the pair of wings. Since the prince promised to pay him well, the turner gave him the wings, and the prince flew to another kingdom. There he saw a tower illuminated by many lights. He decided to swoop down to the ground and find out what the occasion was. When he learned that the most beautiful princess in the world lived there, he became very curious. In the evening he flew through an open window and was able to be with the princess but not for very long, for they were betrayed, and the prince and princess were sentenced to die at the stake.

However, the prince had taken his wings with him, and as the flames flared he tied the wings on and flew with the princess to his homeland, where he descended to the ground. Since everyone had been sad during his absence, he revealed his true identity and was elected king.

After some time had passed, the father of the maiden who had been carried away by the prince made it known that whoever brought back his daughter would receive half his kingdom. When the prince learned about this, he gathered together an army and brought the princess to her father, who was forced to keep his promise.

◈ 227 ◈

The Blacksmith and the Devil

ONCE UPON A TIME there was a blacksmith who enjoyed life: he squandered his money and carried on many lawsuits. After a few years, he did not have a heller left in his pouch.

Why should I torture myself any longer in this world? he thought. So he went into the forest with the intention of hanging himself from a tree. Just as he was about to stick his head into the noose, a man with a long white beard came out from behind a tree carrying a large book in his hand. "Listen, blacksmith," he said. "Write your name down in this large book, and for ten long years you'll have a good life. But after that you'll be mine, and I'll come and fetch you."

"Who are you?" asked the blacksmith.

"I'm the devil."

"What can you do?"

"I can make myself as tall as a fir tree and as small as a mouse."

"Then show me. Seeing is believing," said the blacksmith.

Thereupon the devil made himself as tall as a fir tree and as small as a mouse.

"That's good," said the blacksmith. "Give me the book, and I'll write down my name."

After the blacksmith had signed his name, the devil said, "Now, just go home, and you'll find chests and boxes filled to the brim, and since you've not made much of a fuss, I'll also visit you once during this time."

The blacksmith went home, where he found all his pockets, boxes, and chests filled with ducats, and no matter how much he took, they never became empty or even reduced in the least. So he began his merry life once again, invited his comrades to join him, and was the happiest fellow in the world. After a few years had passed, the devil stopped by one day, as he had promised, to see how things were going. On his departure he gave the blacksmith a leather sack: whoever jumped into this sack would not be able to get out again until the blacksmith himself took him out. Indeed, the blacksmith had a great deal of fun with it. When the ten years were over, however, the devil returned and said to him, "Your time is up, and now you are mine. Get ready for your trip."

"All right," said the blacksmith, who swung his leather sack over his back and went away with the devil.

When they came to the place in the forest where the blacksmith had wanted to hang himself, he said to the devil, "I want to make sure that you're really the devil. Make yourself as large as a fir tree and as small as a mouse again."

The devil was prepared and performed his feat. But just as he changed himself into a mouse, the blacksmith grabbed him and stuck him into the sack. Then the blacksmith cut off a stick from a nearby tree, threw the sack to the ground, and began beating the devil, who screamed pitifully and ran back and forth in the sack. Yet, it was all in vain: he could not get out. Finally, the blacksmith said, "I'll let you go if you give me the sheet from your large book on which I wrote my name."

The devil refused at first, but eventually he gave in. The sheet was ripped out of the book, and the devil returned home to hell, annoyed that he had let himself be deceived and beaten as well. The blacksmith went home to his smithy and continued to live happily as long as it was God's will. Finally, he became sick, and when he realized death was near, he ordered two long nails and a hammer to be put into his coffin. This was done as he desired, and after he died, he approached the gate of heaven and knocked. However, Saint Peter refused to open the gate because the blacksmith had lived in league with the devil. When the blacksmith heard this, he turned around and went to hell. But the devil would not let him enter, for he had no desire to have the blacksmith in hell, where he would only make a spectacle of himself. The blacksmith was angry and began to make a lot of noise in front of hell's gate. A little demon became curious and wanted to see what the blacksmith was doing. So he opened the gate a little and looked out. Quickly the blacksmith grabbed him by the nose and nailed him solidly to the gate of hell with one of the nails he had with him. The little demon began to screech like a wildcat, so that another demon was drawn to the gate. He too stuck his head out, and the blacksmith was alert: he grabbed this one by the ear and nailed him to the gate next to the first little demon. Now both of them began to let out such terrible cries that the old devil himself came running. When he saw the two little demons nailed solidly to the gate, he became so terribly angry that he wept and jumped about. Then he ran up to the dear Lord in heaven and told the Lord that He had to admit the blacksmith into heaven, for there was nothing the devil could do. The blacksmith would nail all the demons by their noses and ears, and he the devil would no longer be master in hell. If the dear Lord and Saint Peter wanted to get rid of the devil, then they would have to let the blacksmith enter heaven.

So now the blacksmith sits there nicely and peacefully, but I don't know how the two little demons were able to free themselves.

◆ 228 ◆

The Three Sisters

ONCE UPON A TIME there was a rich king who was so rich that he believed his wealth would last forever. Therefore, he wallowed in luxury and gambled on a golden board with silver dice. All this continued for some time until he squandered his wealth and was forced to mortgage his cities and castles one after the other. Finally, nothing was left except an old castle in the forest. He moved there with his queen and three daughters, and their lives were miserable: they had only potatoes to eat for their daily meal.

One day the king decided to go hunting to see if he could perhaps shoot a hare. After filling his pocket full of potatoes, he went off to a nearby forest that nobody dared enter because terrible stories had been told about what one might encounter there, such as bears that ate people, eagles that hacked out eyes, and wolves, lions, and all kinds of cruel beasts. However, the king was not in the least afraid and went straight into the forest. At first he did not see anything except huge and mighty trees, but everything was quiet beneath them. After he had walked around for a while, he became hungry and sat down underneath a tree to eat his potatoes. All of a sudden a bear came out of the thicket, trotted straight toward him, and growled, "How dare you sit under my honey tree! You'll pay for this!"

The king was horrified and handed the bear his potatoes to appease him. But the bear began to speak and said, "I don't want your potatoes. I'm going to eat you yourself. Only if you give me your oldest daughter can you save yourself! If you do this, I'll give you a hundred pounds of gold in the bargain."

Since the king was afraid of being eaten, he said, "You shall have her. Just let me go in peace."

The bear showed him the way out of the forest and growled after him, "In a week's time I'll come and fetch my bride."

As he went home the king felt more at ease and was convinced that the bear would not be able to crawl through a keyhole. So from then on everything at the castle was to be shut tight. He ordered all the gates to be locked, the drawbridges to be lifted, and told his daughter not to worry. But just to be on the safe side and to protect his daughter from the bear bridegroom, he gave her a little room under the pinnacle high up in the castle. She was to hide there until the week was over.

Early on the seventh morning, however, when everyone was still asleep, a splendid coach drawn by six horses came driving up to the castle. It was surrounded by numerous knights clad in gold, and as soon as the coach was in front, the drawbridges dropped down by themselves, and the locks sprung open without keys. The coach drove into the courtyard, and a young, handsome prince stepped out. When the king was wakened by the noise and looked out the window, he saw the prince had already fetched his oldest daughter from the locked room and was lifting her into the coach. He could just call after her:

"Farewell, my maiden dear.
I see you're off to wed the bear."

She waved to him with her little white handkerchief from the coach, and then they sped off into the magic forest as if the coach were harnessed to the wind. The king felt very bad about having given his daughter to a bear. He was so sad that he and the queen wept for three days. But on the fourth day, after he had done enough weeping, he realized that he could not change what had happened and went down into the courtyard. There he found a chest made out of smooth wood, which was tremendously difficult to lift. Immediately he remembered what the bear had promised him. So he opened it and found a hundred pounds of glittering and glistening gold.

When the king saw the gold, he felt consoled. He reacquired his cities and kingdom and began leading his former life of luxury once more. Soon after, he was obliged to mortgage everything all over again, and he retreated to his castle in the forest and had nothing to eat but potatoes. Yet the king still had a falcon, and one day the king took it hunting with him and went out into the field to get something better to eat. The falcon soared high into the sky and flew in the direction of the dark magic forest, which the king no longer dared enter. Right after the falcon entered it, an eagle shot out and pursued the falcon, which flew back to the king, who tried to fend off the eagle with his spear. But the eagle grabbed the spear and broke it like a reed. Then the eagle crushed the falcon with one claw and dug into the king's shoulder with the other.

"Why have you disturbed my kingdom in the sky?" the eagle cried out. "Either you give me your second daughter for my wife, or you shall die!"

"All right," the king said. "You shall have my second daughter, but what will you give me for her?"

"Two hundred pounds of gold," the eagle said. "In seven weeks I'll come to fetch her."

Then the eagle let him go and flew off into the forest. The king felt bad about having also sold his second daughter to a wild beast and did not dare tell her anything about it. Six weeks passed, and in the seventh the princess when out one day on the lawn in front of the castle to water the linseed. All at once a splendid parade of handsome knights came riding up, and at their head was the handsomest knight of all, who dismounted and cried out:

"Swing yourself up, my maiden dear.
Come wed the eagle without fear!"

And before she could answer him, he had already lifted her onto his horse and raced off with her into the forest, flying like a bird. Farewell! Farewell!

They waited a long time for the princess to come back to the castle, but she would not return no matter how long they waited. Then the king finally revealed that he had promised her to an eagle when he had once been in trouble, and the eagle must have fetched her. After the king overcame his sadness somewhat, he recalled the eagle's promise, went down to the lawn, and found two golden eggs, each weighing one hundred pounds. Money is a sign of piety, thought the king, and he dismissed all gloomy thoughts from his mind. He resumed his merrymaking once more and lived luxuriously until he ran through the two hundred pounds of gold. Then the king returned to the castle in the forest, and the last of the princesses had to boil the potatoes.

The king did not want to hunt any more hares in the forest or any more birds in the sky, but he did desire to eat some fish. So the princess had to weave a net, which he took with him to a pond not far from the castle. A small boat was there, and he got in and threw the net into the water. On his very first try he caught a bunch of beautiful flounders with red speckles, but when he wanted to row ashore with his catch, the boat would not budge, and he could not get it to move, no matter how much he tried. All of a sudden an enormous whale came puffing up to him and cried out, "Who said you could catch the subjects of my realm and take them away with you? This will cost you your life!"

As the whale said this, he opened his jaws as if he were going to swallow the king and the little boat as well. When the king saw his terrible jaws, he completely lost his courage and recalled his third daughter.

"Spare my life," he cried out, "and you shall have my third daughter!"

"That's fine with me," roared the whale. "I'll also give you something for her. I don't have gold. That's not good enough for me. But the floor of my sea is plastered with precious pearls. I'll give you three sacks full of them. In the seventh month I'll come and fetch my bride."

Then he dived down into the water, while the king rowed ashore and brought the flounders home. Yet, when they were baked, he did not want to eat any of them, and when he looked at his daughter, the only one left and the most beautiful and loveliest of them all, he felt as if a thousand knives were cutting his heart. Six months passed, and the queen and princess did not know what was wrong with the king, for he did not make one pleasant face during all that time. In the seventh month the princess was in the courtyard in front of a man-made well and was drawing a glass of water. Suddenly a coach with six white horses and men clad entirely in silver came driving up. A prince stepped out of the coach, and he was more handsome than any other prince she had ever seen in her life. He asked her for a glass of water, and when she handed it to him, he embraced her and lifted her into the coach. Then they drove back through the gate over the field toward the pond.

"Farewell, you maiden dear.
You're bound to wed the whale down there."

The queen stood at the window and watched the coach as it moved off in the distance. When she was unable to find her daughter, her heart was saddened, and she called her and looked for her everywhere. But the daughter was nowhere to be seen or heard. When the queen was certain the princess could not be found, she began to weep, and now the king revealed to her that a whale must have fetched their daughter, for he had been forced to promise their daughter to him. Indeed, that was the reason he had been so sad. The king wanted to comfort his wife and told her about the great treasure they would now get for the princess. However, the queen did not want to hear anything about it and said her only child was more dear to her than all the treasures of the world. During the time that the whale prince had carried off the princess, his servants had carried three tremendous sacks into the castle, which the king found at the door. When he opened them, he found they were full of big, beautiful, and precious pearls, just as large as the fattest peas imaginable. All of a sudden he was rich again and richer than he had ever been before. He reacquired his cities and castles, but this time he did not resume his luxurious way of living. Instead, he became quiet and thrifty. Whenever he thought about what had happened to his three dear daughters with the wild beasts and that perhaps they had already been eaten up, he lost all zest for life.

Meanwhile, the queen could not be consoled and wept more tears for her daughters than all the pearls the whale had given them. Finally, she became more calm and peaceful, and after some time she was happy again, for she gave birth to a handsome baby boy. Since God had given them the child so unexpectedly, he was named Reinald the Wonder Child. The boy grew big and strong, and the queen often told him about his three sisters, who were being held prisoners by three beasts in the magic forest. When he turned sixteen, he demanded armor and a sword from the king, and when he received all this, he decided to embark on an adventure, blessed his parents, and set forth.

He went straight toward the magic forest and had only one thing on his mind—to search for his sisters. At first he wandered around in the great forest for a long time without encountering a human being or a beast. But after three days he saw a young woman sitting in front of a cave and playing with a young bear cub, while another very young one was lying on her lap. Reinald thought she must surely be his oldest sister. So he left his horse behind him and approached her.

"Dearest sister," he said, "I'm your brother Reinald, and I've come to visit you."

The princess looked at him, and since he resembled her father very strongly, she did not doubt his words, but she was frightened and said, "Oh, dearest brother, hurry and run away as fast as you can if you value your life. When my husband the bear comes home and finds you here, he'll show you no mercy and will eat you up."

But Reinald said, "I'm not afraid and shall not leave you until I know how you are and what things are like for you."

When the princess saw that he was resolute, she led him into the dark cave that was like the dwelling of a bear. On one side was a heap of leaves and hay on which the old bear and his cubs slept, and on the other side was a magnificent bed with red covers trimmed with gold. That belonged to the princess. She told him to crawl under the bed and handed him something to eat. It did not take long before the bear came home.

"I smell, I smell the flesh of a human being," he said, and wanted to stick his hand under the bed. But the princess cried out, "Be quiet! Who would ever come here?"

"I found a horse in the forest and ate it," he growled, and his nose was still bloody from eating the horse. "Where there's a horse, there's a man, and I smell him."

Again he wanted to look under the bed, but she gave him such a kick in the side that he did a somersault, went back to his place, put his paw in his mouth, and fell asleep.

Every seventh day the bear was restored to his natural form. He became a handsome prince; his cave, a splendid castle; the animals in the forest, his servants. It was on such a day that he had fetched the princess. Beautiful young women had come to meet her from the castle. There had been a glorious festival, and she had gone to sleep full of joy, but when she had awakened, she had found herself lying in the bear's dark cave, and her husband had been turned into a bear growling at her feet. Only the bed and everything she had touched had remained in its natural condition and had not been changed. Thus she lived six days in suffering, but on the seventh she was comforted. She did not become old since only one day a week counted in her life, and she was content with her existence. She had given her husband two sons, who were also bears for six days and regained their human form on the seventh day. She stuffed their straw bed with the most delicious food all the time, including cake and fruit, and they lived off this food the entire week. Moreover, the bear obeyed her and did whatever she wanted.

When Reinald awoke, he lay in a silken bed. Servants waited on him and dressed him in the finest clothes, for his visit fell right on the seventh day. His sister entered with the two handsome princes and his brother-in-law the bear. They were glad about his arrival. Everything was magnificent and glorious, and the entire day was filled with pleasurable and joyous things. But, in the evening the princess said, "Dear brother, now it's time for you to get out of here. At daybreak my husband will become a bear again, and if he finds you here tomorrow, he won't be able to control his natural instincts and will eat you up."

Then the bear prince came and gave him three bear hairs and said, "Whenever you're in trouble, just rub these hairs, and I'll come to your aid."

Then they kissed each other and said farewell. Reinald climbed into a carriage drawn by six horses and drove off. He went over hill and valley, up and down mountains, through deserts and forests, shrubs and hedges without stopping to rest until the sky began turning gray at dusk. Then Reinald suddenly lay on the ground, and the horses and carriage disappeared. At sunrise he saw six ants galloping away, drawing a nutshell behind them.

Reinald realized he was still in the magic forest and wanted to search for his second sister. Again he wandered about aimlessly and lonely for three days without accomplishing anything. But on the fourth day he heard a big eagle come swooping down to settle in a nest. Reinald hid in the bushes and waited for the eagle to fly away. After seven hours it soared into the air again. Then Reinald emerged from the bushes, went over to the tree, and cried out, "Dearest sister, are you up above? If so, let me hear your voice. I'm Reinald, your brother, and I've come to visit you!"

Then he heard a voice calling down to him, "If you're Reinald, my dearest brother, whom I've never seen, come up to me."

Reinald wanted to climb the tree, but the trunk was too thick and slippery. He tried three times in vain. Suddenly a silken rope ladder was dropped down, and he climbed it until he reached the eagle's nest, which was strong and secure like a platform on a linden tree. His sister sat under a canopy made out of rose-colored silk, and an eagle's egg was lying on her lap. She was keeping it warm in order to hatch it. They kissed each other and rejoiced, but after a while the princess said, "Now, hurry and see to it that you get out of here, dearest brother. If the eagle, my husband, sees you, he'll hack your eyes out and eat up your heart as he's already done with three of your servants, who were looking for you in the forest."

"No," said Reinald. "I'm staying here until your husband is transformed."

"That will only happen in six weeks. If you can hold out that long, go and hide in the tree. It's hollow on the inside, and I'll drop food down to you every day."

Reinald crawled into the tree, and the princess let food down to him every day. Whenever the eagle flew away, he climbed up to her. After six weeks the eagle was transformed, and once more Reinald awoke in a bed that was like the one at his brother-in-law the bear's place. Only here it was more splendid, and he lived with the eagle prince in great joy. On the seventh evening they said their farewells. The eagle gave him three eagle feathers and said, "If you're in trouble, rub them, and I'll come to your aid."

Then he gave him servants to show him the way out of the forest. But when morning came, they suddenly disappeared, and Reinald was all alone on top of a high rocky cliff in a terrible wilderness. He looked around him, and in the distance he saw the reflection of a large lake, which glistened from the sun's rays. He thought of his third sister, who might be there. So he began to climb down the cliff and work his way through the bushes and between the rocks. He needed three days to do this, and he often lost sight of the lake, but on the fourth day he succeeded in getting there. Once he was on the bank, he called out, "Dearest sister, if you're in the water, let me hear your voice. I'm Reinald, your brother, and I've come to visit you."

But no one answered, and everything was very quiet. He threw bread crumbs into the water and said to the fish, "Dear fish, go to my sister and tell her that Reinald the Wonder Child is here and wants to see her."

But the red-speckled flounders snapped up the bread and did not listen to his words. Then he saw a little boat and immediately took off his armor. He kept only his sword in his hand as he jumped into the boat and rowed off. After he had gone a long way, he saw a chimney made of rock crystal jutting out of the water, and there was a pleasant smell rising up from it. Reinald rowed toward it and was convinced that his sister was living down below. So he climbed on top of the chimney and slid down. The princess was greatly startled when she suddenly saw a pair of wriggling legs followed shortly by a whole man, who identified himself as her brother. She rejoiced with all her heart, but then she turned sad and said, "The whale has heard that you've wanted to visit me, and he's declared that if you come while he's a whale, he'll not be able to control his desire to eat you up. Moreover, he'll break my crystal house, and I'll also perish in the flood of water."

"Can't you hide me until the time comes when the magic loses its power?"

"Oh, no. How can I do that? Don't you see that the walls are all made out of crystal, and you can see through them?"

Nevertheless, she thought and thought, and finally she remembered the room where the wood was kept. She arranged the wood in such a careful way that nobody could see anything from the outside, and it was there that she hid the Wonder Child. Soon after, the whale came, and the princess trembled like an aspen leaf. He swam around the crystal house a few times, and when he saw a little piece of Reinald's clothing sticking out of the wood, he beat his tail, snorted ferociously, and if he had seen more, he would surely have destroyed the house. He came once a day and swam around it until the magic stopped in the seventh month. Suddenly Reinald found himself in a castle right in the middle of an island, and the castle surpassed even the splendor of the eagle's castle. Now he lived with his sister and brother-in-law for a whole month in the lap of luxury. When the time was over, the whale gave him three scales and said, "When you're in trouble, rub them, and I'll come to your aid."

The whale brought him to the bank, where his armor was still lying on the ground. The Wonder Child moved around in the wilderness for seven more days, and he slept seven nights under the open skies. Then he caught sight of a castle with a steel gate that had a mighty lock on it. In front of the gate was a black bull with flashing eyes. It was guarding the entrance, and Reinald attacked it. He gave the bull a powerful blow on its neck, but the neck was made of steel, and the sword broke as if it were glass. He tried to use his lance, but it broke like a piece of straw. Then the bull grabbed him with its horns and threw him into the air so that he got caught in the branches of a tree. In his desperation Reinald remembered the three bear's hairs and rubbed them in his hand. All at once the bear appeared and fought with the bull. He tore the bull to pieces, but a bird came out of the bull's stomach, flew high into the air, and rushed off. But Reinald rubbed the three eagle's feathers, and suddenly a mighty eagle came flying through the air and pursued the bird, which flew directly toward a pond. The eagle dived at the bird and mangled it, but Reinald saw the bird drop a golden egg into the water. Now he rubbed the three fish scales in his hand, and immediately a whale came swimming up, swallowed the egg, and spat it out onto the shore. Reinald picked it up and cracked it open with a stone. There he found a little key that fit the steel gate. As soon as he just touched the gate with the key, the gate sprang open by itself, and he entered. All the bars on the other doors slid off by themselves, and he went through seven doors into seven splendid and brightly lit rooms. In the last room a maiden was lying asleep on a bed. She was so beautiful that he was completely dazzled by her. He sought to wake her, but in vain. Her sleep was so deep that she seemed to be dead. In his rage he struck a black slate standing next to the bed. At that very moment the maiden awoke but fell right back to sleep. Now he took the slate and threw it on the stone floor, so that it shattered into a thousand pieces. No sooner did this happen than the maiden opened her eyes wide, and the magic spell was broken. She turned out to be the sister of Reinald's three brothers-in-law. Because she had rejected the love of a godless magician, he had sentenced her to a deathlike sleep and changed her brothers into animals. They were to remain that way as long as the black slate remained untouched.

Reinald led the maiden out of the castle, and as they passed through the gate his brothers-in-law came riding up from three different directions. They had been released from the magic spell, and with them came their wives and children. Indeed, the eagle's bride had hatched the egg and carried a beautiful baby girl in her arms. Now all of them traveled to the old king and queen as the Wonder Child brought his three sisters home. Soon he married the beautiful maiden, and this provided great joy and pleasure to everyone.

Now the cat's run home, for my tale is done.

◈ 229 ◈

The Stepmother

ONCE THERE WAS A KING AND A QUEEN, and the queen had a terribly evil mother-in-law. One day the king went to war, and the old queen had her daughter-in-law locked up in a damp cellar along with her two little sons. After some time had passed, the mother-in-law said to herself, "I'd really like to eat one of the children." So she called her cook and ordered him to go down into the cellar, take one of the little sons, slaughter him, and cook him.

"What kind of sauce would you like?" asked the cook.

"A brown one," said the old queen.

The cook then went down into the cellar and said, "Ah, Your Highness, the old queen wants me to slaughter and cook one of your sons this evening."

The young queen was deeply distressed and said, "Well, why don't we take a pig? Cook it the way she wants, and say that it was my child."

The cook did just that and served the pig in a brown sauce to the old queen as though it were a child. Indeed, she ate it with great relish.

Soon thereafter the old queen thought, The child's meat tasted so tender that I'd like to have the second as well. She called the cook and ordered him to go down into the cellar and slaughter the second son.

"What kind of a sauce should I cook him in?"

"Oh, in a white one," said the old queen.

The cook went down into the cellar and said, "Ah, the old queen has ordered me now to slaughter your second little son and cook him too."

"Take a suckling pig," the young queen said, "and cook it exactly as she likes it."

The cook did just that and set it in front of the old queen in a white sauce, and she devoured it with even greater relish than before.

Finally, the old queen thought, Now that the children are in my body I'd like to eat the young queen as well. The old queen called the cook and ordered him to cook the young queen.

(Fragment: The cook slaughters a doe the third time. However, the young queen has trouble preventing her children from screaming. She does not want the old queen to hear them and realize they are still alive, etc.)

◈ 230 ◈

Fragments

a. Snowflower

A YOUNG PRINCESS WAS CALLED SNOWFLOWER because she was white like snow and was born during the winter. One day her mother became sick, and the princess went out to pluck herbs that might heal her. As she went by a big tree, a swarm of bees flew out and covered her entire body from head to foot. But they did not sting or hurt her. Instead, they carried honey to her lips, and her entire body glowed through and through with beauty.

b. Prince Johannes

This is a tale about his melancholy and nostalgic wanderings, about his flight with the spirit, about the red castle, about his numerous trials and tribulations until he was finally allowed to glimpse the beautiful princess of the sun.

c. The Good Cloth

Two daughters of a seamstress inherited a good old cloth, and whenever anything was wrapped in it, the cloth turned the object into gold. This cloth provided them with enough to live on, and they also did some sewing to earn a little extra money. One sister was very smart, the other very stupid. One day the oldest went to church, and a Jew came down the street calling, "Beautiful new cloth for sale! Beautiful cloth to trade for old cloth! Anyone want to trade?"

When the stupid sister heard that, she ran out to him and traded the good old cloth for a new cloth. This was exactly what the Jew had wanted, for he knew all about the power of the old cloth. When the older sister came home, she said, "We're doing poorly with our sewing. I've got to get some money. Where's our cloth?"

"It's good that I've done what I've done," said the stupid sister. "While you were gone, I made a trade for a brand-new cloth."

(After this the Jew was turned into a dog, the two maidens into hens. Eventually, the hens regained their human form and beat the dog to death.)

◈ 231 ◈

The Faithful Animals

ONCE UPON A TIME there was a man who did not have much money, and he went out into the wide world with the little money that he had left. He arrived at a village, where some young boys had gathered together and were making noise and yelling.

"What's going on?" the man asked.

"Oh, we've got a mouse," they answered, "and we're making it dance for us. Just look at the funny way the mouse toddles!"

But the man felt sorry for the poor little animal, and he said, "Let the mouse go, boys, and I'll give you some money if you do."

So he gave them money, and they let the mouse go. The poor animal ran into a hole as fast as it could. The man went off and came to another village. There some boys had a monkey, who was being forced to dance and do somersaults. The boys were laughing at the monkey and would not leave it in peace. Once again the man gave them money to let the monkey go. Afterward the man came to a third village, where some boys had a bear on a chain. The bear had to stand on its hind legs and dance, and when it growled, the boys laughed at it even more. The man bought the bear's freedom as well, and the bear was happy to run on his four feet again and dashed off.

Now the man had given away the last of his money and did not have a red cent left in his pocket. So he said to himself, "The king has so much in his treasure chamber that he doesn't need it all. You can't let yourself die of hunger. You might as well go and take some, and if you make money later, you can replace what you took." He managed to get into the treasure chamber and take some money. However, as he was creeping out, he was caught by the king's men. They accused him of being a thief and took him to the court. Since he had committed a crime, he was sentenced to be put into a box, and the box was cast off into water. The lid of the box was full of holes so that air could get inside. In addition, he had been given a jug of water and a loaf of bread. As he was floating on the water in a state of fright, he heard some fumbling with the lock and then some gnawing and puffing. All of a sudden, the lock sprang open, the lid popped up, and there stood the mouse, the monkey, and the bear, who had opened the box. Since he had helped them, they wanted to repay him. However, they did not know what step to take next and began discussing the matter with one another. While they were doing this, a white stone that looked like a round egg came rolling into the water.

"It's come just at the right moment," said the bear. "That's a miraculous stone. Whoever possesses it can wish for whatever he desires."

The man fetched the stone from the water, and when he held it in his hand, he wished for a castle with a garden and stables. No sooner had he uttered the wish than he sat in a castle with a garden and stables. Everything was so beautiful and splendid that he could not get over his amazement. After some time passed, several merchants came his way.

"Just look!" they exclaimed. "What a glorious castle! The last time we came by here, there was nothing but mere sand."

Since they were curious, they went inside and asked the man how he had managed to build everything so swiftly.

"It wasn't I who did it," he said. "It was my miraculous stone."

"What kind of a stone is it?" they asked.

The man went to fetch it and showed it to the merchants. They had a great desire to buy it and asked him to sell it in exchange for all their beautiful wares. The man took a fancy to the wares, and since the heart can be fickle and yearn for new things, he let himself be fooled and thought the beautiful wares were more valuable than his miraculous stone. So he gave it away, and no sooner did it leave his hands than his good fortune disappeared, and he sat once more in the locked box on the river with nothing but a jug of water and a loaf of bread. When the faithful animals, the mouse, the monkey, and the bear, saw his misfortune, they came again and wanted to help him, but this time they could not get the lock open because it was much stronger than the first one.

"We've got to get the miraculous stone back," said the bear, "or else everything we try will be useless."

Since the merchants had remained in the castle and were still living there, the animals went there together. When they got close to it, the bear said, "Mouse, go look through the keyhole and tell us what we can do. You're small, and nobody will notice you."

The mouse agreed but came back and said, "There's nothing we can do. I looked inside, but the stone is hanging on a red ribbon under the mirror, and all around it are cats with fiery eyes. They're stationed there to guard it."

Then the bear and monkey said, "Go back inside and wait until their master's lying asleep in his bed. Then slip through the hole, crawl on top of his bed, pinch his nose, and bite off some of his hair."

The mouse crawled back inside and did what the others told him to do. The master woke up and rubbed his nose in great annoyance.

"The cats are useless!" he said. "The mice go right by them and bite the hair off my head."

So he chased the cats away, and the mouse won the day. When the master went to sleep the following night, the mouse crept inside, and she nibbled and gnawed on the red ribbon on which the stone was hanging until the ribbon split in two and the stone fell to the ground. Then the mouse dragged it to the house door. However, this was hard work for the mouse, and she said to the monkey, who was keeping a lookout, "Pull it out with your paw."

This was easy for the monkey, and after he took the stone in his hand, they all returned to the river.

"How are we going to get to the box?" the monkey asked.

"We'll handle that soon enough," said the bear. "I'll get into the water and swim. Monkey, you get on my back. Hold on to me tightly and put the stone in your mouth. Mouse, you can sit in my right ear."

So they did what he said and swam down the river. After they had gone some distance, the bear felt that it was too quiet and wanted to talk.

"Listen, monkey," he said. "I think we're good comrades. What do you think?"

However, the monkey kept quiet and did not answer.

"Is that the way to behave?" said the bear. "Won't you give your comrade an answer? You're some lousy fellow if you don't!"

Now the monkey could no longer keep silent. He let the stone fall into the water and cried out, "You stupid fellow! How could I answer you with the stone in my mouth? Now it's lost, and you're to blame."

"Let's not quarrel," said the bear. "We'll think of something."

They discussed the situation and then called together the frogs, the toads, and all the animals that lived in the water and said, "A powerful enemy intends to attack you. Go and collect all the stones you can find, and we'll build a wall to protect you."

The animals were frightened and brought stones from all over the place. Finally, a fat, old croaker of a frog emerged from the bottom carrying the miraculous stone with the red ribbon in his mouth. Now the bear was happy. He relieved the frog of his burden, told the animals that everything was all right, and sent them home with a quick farewell. Then the three swam down the river to the man in the box, opened the lid with the help of the stone, and arrived just at the right moment, for the man had consumed the bread and had drunk the water and was already half dead. When he had the miraculous stone back in his hands, he wished to regain his good health and to be transported to his beautiful castle with the garden and stables.

Then he lived there in happiness, and the three animals stayed with him and had a good life for the rest of their years.

◈ 232 ◈

The Crows

AN HONEST AND DILIGENT SOLDIER HAD EARNED and saved some money because he had been industrious and had not squandered his earnings in the taverns as the other soldiers had. It so happened that two of his comrades were quite devious and wanted to get at his money, and so they pretended to be very friendly with him. One day they said to him, "Listen, why should we stay here in this city? We're locked in as though we were prisoners. Besides, someone such as you could really earn something decent and live happily if you were in your own country."

They kept talking to him like this until finally he agreed to break out and leave with them. However, the other two only intended to steal his money. After they had gone part of the way, the two soldiers said, "We must turn right over there if we want to get to the border."

"No," he replied. "That leads straight back into the city. We've got to keep to our left."

"What!" the other two exclaimed. "You always want to have the last word in everything!"

Then they rushed at him and began hitting him until he fell down, and they took the money out of his pocket. But that was not enough. They poked his eyes out, dragged him to the gallows, and tied him up tightly there. After that they left him behind and went back to the city with his stolen money.

The poor blind man was not aware that he had been left in such a terrible place. He groped about and could feel that he was sitting under a beam of wood. Since he thought it was a cross, he said, "Well, at least it was good of them to tie me up under a cross. God is with me." And he began praying to God. When it was almost night, he heard the fluttering of wings, which turned out to be three crows that landed on the beam. After that he heard one of them speaking, "Sister, what good news have you brought? Oh, if the people knew what we know! The king's daughter is sick, and the old king has promised to give her to anyone who can cure her. But no one can do it, for she'll get well again only if the toad in the pond over there is burned to ashes and she drinks the ashes with some water."

Then the second crow said, "Oh, if the people knew what we know! A dew will fall from heaven tonight, and it will have such miraculous and healing powers that the blind will be able to regain their sight if they rub their eyes with it."

Finally, the third crow said, "Oh, if the people knew what we know! The toad can only help one person, and the dew can only help a few. Meanwhile, there's a great emergency in the city. All the wells are dried out, and nobody knows that if the people removed the square stone in the marketplace and dug beneath that spot, the most beautiful water would gush forth."

After the three crows had finished talking, the blind man heard the fluttering of wings again, and they flew away. Gradually he was able to untie himself, and then he stooped down, pulled out a few blades of grass, and rubbed his eyes with the dew that had fallen on them. All at once he regained his sight. The moon and the stars were in the sky, and he saw that he was standing next to the gallows. After that he looked for some earthenware to gather as much of the precious dew as he could find. When this was done, he went to the pond, dug into the water, grabbed hold of the toad, and burned it to ashes. Next he carried the ashes to the king's court and had the king's daughter take some. When she was restored to health, he demanded her for his wife as the king had promised. However, the king did not take a liking to him, because he was dressed so poorly, and he said that whoever wanted to have his daughter would first have to provide water for the city. In this way the king hoped to get rid of him. But the soldier went to the city and ordered the people to remove the square stone from the marketplace and to dig beneath the spot for water. No sooner had they dug than they hit upon a spring, and a mighty jet of water shot forth. Now the king could no longer refuse to give his daughter to him. After the wedding, they lived together in a happy marriage.

One day, when the soldier was taking a walk through the fields, he met his former comrades who had treated him so disgracefully. They did not recognize him, but he knew them right away and went up to them.

"Look," he said, "this is your former comrade whose eyes you poked out so cruelly. But fortunately the dear Lord has allowed me to prosper."

They fell to his feet and begged for mercy. Since he had a kind heart, he took pity on them and brought them back to his palace. He gave them food and clothes and afterward told them what had happened and how he had gained such honor. When the two heard all that, they were restless and eager to spend a night beneath the gallows to see if they could perhaps hear something good as well. So they went and sat underneath the gallows. Soon they heard the fluttering of wings above their heads, and the three crows arrived. One of them said to the others, "Listen, sisters, someone must have overheard us, for the king's daughter is healthy, the toad is gone from the pond, a blind man has regained his sight, and they've dug a fresh well in the city. Come, let's look for the eavesdropper and punish him."

When they swooped down from the beam, they found the two soldiers, and before the men could defend themselves, the crows sat on their heads and hacked out their eyes, and they kept hacking their faces until they were dead and then left them lying beneath the gallows. After a few days, when the soldiers had not returned, their former comrade thought, Where could the two be wandering about? He went out to look for them but found nothing except their bones, which he took away from the gallows and buried in a grave.

◈ 233 ◈

The Lazy One and the Industrious One

ONCE UPON A TIME there were two journeymen who traveled together, and they swore they would always stick together. However, when they reached a large city, one of them began living loosely and forgot his promise. He left the other, went off by himself, and wandered here and there. Most of all he loved to be at the places where he could find the most excitement. The other journeyman remained committed to his job in the city, worked industriously, and then continued his travels.

One night he passed by the gallows without realizing it, but he saw a man lying asleep on the ground. He was shabby and destitute, and since the stars were so bright, the journeyman recognized him as his former companion. So he laid himself down next to him, covered him with his coat, and fell asleep. However, he was soon wakened by two voices. They were ravens sitting on top of the gallows.

One said, "God provides!"

The other, "Act according to the situation!"

After those words were spoken, one of the ravens fell exhausted to the ground. The other went and sat next to him until it was day. Then he fetched some worms and water, revived him with that, and woke him from the dead.

When the two journeymen saw all this, they were astounded and asked the one raven why the other was so miserable and sick. Then the sick raven said, "It was because I didn't want to do anything, for I believe that all my food will be provided for by heaven."

The two journeymen took the ravens with them to the next village. One of the birds was cheerful and searched for his food. He bathed himself every morning and cleaned himself with his beak. However, the other stayed around the house, was bad-tempered, and always looked shaggy. After a while the landlord's daughter, who was a beautiful maiden, became very fond of the industrious raven. She picked him up from the floor and petted him with her hand, and then one day she pressed him to her face and gave him a kiss out of sheer delight. The bird fell to the ground, rolled over, fluttered, and turned into a handsome man. Then he revealed that the other raven was his brother and that they had both insulted their father, who had put a curse on them by saying, "Fly around as ravens until a beautiful maiden kisses you of her own free will."

So one of the brothers was released from the spell, but nobody wanted to kiss the one who was idle, and he died as a raven.

The journeyman who had been living loosely took a lesson from this, and he became industrious and proper and took good care of his companion.

◈ 234 ◈

The Long Nose

ONCE THERE WERE THREE OLD DISCHARGED SOLDIERS who were so old that they could no longer eat even milk pudding. The king sent them away and did not give them a pension. Consequently, they had nothing to live on and had to go begging. One day they began walking through a large forest, and they could not find the end of it. When night arrived, two of them lay down to sleep, and the third kept watch so that the wild animals would not tear them to pieces. After the two soldiers had fallen asleep and while the third was standing guard, a little dwarf in a red outfit appeared and cried out, "Who's there?"

"Good friends," said the soldier.

"What kind of good friends?"

"Three old discharged soldiers who have nothing to live on."

The dwarf then called him over, saying that he wanted to give him something. If the soldier took care of it, the dwarf explained, he would have enough to live on for the rest of his life. So the soldier went over to him, and the dwarf gave him an old cloak that would grant every wish made by the person wearing it. But the soldier was not to tell his comrades about it until daylight. When day finally came and they woke up, he told them what had happened. They continued to walk deeper into the forest until the second night. When they lay down to sleep, the second soldier had to keep watch and stood guard over the others. Then the red dwarf came and cried out, "Who's there?"

"Good friends."

"What kind of good friends?"

"Three old discharged soldiers."

Then the dwarf gave him an old little pouch that would always remain filled with money no matter how much he took from it. However, he was not to tell his comrades about it until daylight. Once again they continued their walk through the forest for a third day, and that night the third soldier had to keep watch. The red dwarf came to him too and cried out, "Who's there?"

"Good friends."

"What kind of good friends?"

"Three old discharged soldiers."

The red dwarf gave him a horn, and whenever anyone blew it, all the soldiers from all over would gather together. The next morning, when each one now had a gift, the first soldier put on the cloak and wished that they were out of the forest. Immediately they were outside. They then went into an inn and ordered food and drink, the best that the innkeeper could provide. When they had finished, the soldier with the little pouch paid everything and was very generous to the innkeeper.

Soon they became tired from traveling, and the soldier with the pouch said to the one with the cloak, "I'd like you to wish for a castle for us. We've got money enough. Now we can live like princes."

So the soldier with the cloak wished for a castle, and quick as a wink it was standing there with everything that went with a castle. After they had lived there for some time, he wished for a coach with three white horses. They wanted to travel from one kingdom to the next and pass themselves off as three princes. So they drove off with a great retinue of servants, who looked quite regal. They went to a king who had only one daughter, and when they arrived, they had themselves announced. Immediately they were asked to dinner and to spend the night there. They had a merry old time, and after they had eaten and drunk, they began to play cards, which was the princess's favorite game. She played with the soldier who had the pouch, and she saw that no matter how much she won, his pouch never became empty, and she realized that it must be some sort of a magical thing. She said to him then that since he was so warm from playing, he should have something to drink. She gave him a glass but put a sleeping potion in the wine. No sooner had he drunk the wine than he fell asleep, and she took his pouch. She went into her chamber and sewed another pouch that looked just like the old one. Then she stuck some money inside it and put it back in place of the old one.

The next morning the three soldiers resumed their journey, and when the one with the pouch spent the little money that was left and reached inside the pouch for some more, he found it was empty and remained empty. Then he exclaimed, "That deceitful princess has switched my pouch. Now we're poor people!"

But the soldier with the cloak said, "Don't get gray hairs over this. I'll have it back in no time."

He put on the cloak and wished himself to be transported to the princess's chamber. Within seconds he was there, and she was sitting and counting money, which she continually took from the pouch. When she saw him, she screamed that a robber was there. And she screamed so loudly that the entire court came running and tried to catch him. Hastily he jumped through a window and left the cloak hanging there, so that this too was lost.

When the three soldiers came together again, they had nothing left but the horn. The soldier with the horn said, "I'll get help now. Let's start a war!"

And he blew together so many hussar and cavalry regiments that they were impossible to count. Next he sent a messenger to the king to let him know that if the king did not return the pouch and the cloak, not a single stone from his castle would be left standing. The king tried to persuade his daughter to return the cloak and pouch before they suffered a great misfortune. But she would not listen to him and said that she wanted to try something first. So she disguised herself as a poor maiden, carried a basket on her arm, and went out to the soldiers' camp to sell all kinds of drinks. Her chambermaid had to go along with her. When the princess reached the middle of the camp, she began to sing, and her voice was so beautiful that all the soldiers ran out of their tents, and the one with the horn ran out too and listened. When the princess saw him, she gave her chambermaid a signal to crawl into his tent, where the chambermaid took the horn and ran back with it to the castle. Then the princess also went home and now had everything. Once again the three comrades had to go begging.

So they moved on, and the one who had possessed the pouch said, "You know, we can't stay together anymore. You two go in that direction, and I'll take this path."

He set out alone and entered a forest, and since he was tired, he lay down beneath a tree to sleep awhile. When he awoke and looked up, he became aware that he had been sleeping under a beautiful apple tree with splendid apples hanging from the branches. Out of hunger he took one, ate it, and then another. Suddenly his nose began to grow and grow and became so long that he could no longer stand up. His nose grew through the forest and sixty miles beyond. Meanwhile, his comrades were traveling about in the world and looking for him because they felt it was better to be together. However, they had been unable to find him. Suddenly one of them tripped over something and stepped on it. He thought, My, what was that? Then it moved, and he saw that it was a nose. The two soldiers decided to follow the nose, and eventually they reached their comrade in the forest. He was lying there and could not stir or budge. So they took a pole and wrapped the nose around it. They wanted to lift it in the air and carry him away, but the nose was too heavy. Then they looked in the forest for a donkey, and they set their friend and the long nose on two poles and had the donkey carry him away in this manner. They dragged him a short distance, but they found him so heavy that they had to rest. While they were resting, they saw a tree nearby with beautiful pears hanging from the branches. Then the little red dwarf came out from behind the tree and said to the soldier with the long nose that, if he ate one of the beautiful pears, the nose would fall off. So he ate a pear, and right away the long nose fell off, and his nose was exactly the size it had been before. Thereupon the dwarf said, "Break off some apples and pears and make some powder out of them. Whenever you give someone the apple powder, his nose will grow, and whenever you give someone the pear powder, the nose will fall off again. Now, go as a doctor and give the princess some of the apples and also the powder. Then her nose will grow even twenty times longer than yours. But brace yourself for anything that might happen!"

So the soldier took some of the apples and went to the king's court, where he at first pretended to be a gardener's helper. He said he had special apples that could not be found anywhere in the region, and when the princess heard about this, she asked her father to buy some of the apples. The king replied, "Buy as many as you wish."

She bought the apples and ate one. It tasted so good that she was convinced that she had never tasted an apple like it in her entire life. So she ate another one. After all that had happened, the gardener's helper departed, and her nose began to grow. It grew with such force that she could not get up out of her chair and fell over. Her nose grew sixty yards around the table, sixty around the closet, and a hundred yards through the window and around the castle and another twenty miles out toward the city. There she lay. She could not stir or budge, and no doctor could help her. The old king had a proclamation made that any man who could help his daughter would receive a great deal of money.

The old soldier had waited for this moment and announced himself

as a doctor. He promised to save her with God's help. Thereupon he
gave her powder from the apples, and her nose began to grow once
more and became even longer. That evening he gave her powder from
the pears, and the nose became somewhat smaller, but not much. The
next day he gave her powder from the apples again in order to scare
her soundly and punish her. The nose grew again, but not more than
had fallen off the day before. Finally, he said to her, "Your Royal
Highness, you must have stolen something at one time. If you don't
give it up, there'll be no help."

"I don't know what you're talking about," she said.

"You must," he responded. "Otherwise, my powder won't help,
and if you don't give it up, you'll have to die from the long nose."

Then the old king said, "Give up the pouch, the cloak, and the horn
that you've stolen. Otherwise, your nose will never become small
again."

So the chambermaid had to fetch all three things and put them
down. Now the doctor gave the princess powder from the pears. Her
nose fell off, and two hundred and fifty men had to come and chop
the nose into pieces. Meanwhile, the soldier went away with the
pouch, the cloak, and the horn and returned to his comrades. Then
they wished to be back in their castle, where they are probably still
sitting and keeping house.

❖ 235 ❖

The Lion and the Frog

THERE ONCE WERE A KING AND A QUEEN, and they had a son and a
daughter who loved each other dearly. The prince went hunting very
often and sometimes remained in the forest a long time. However,
one day he did not return. His sister almost wept herself blind because
of this. Finally, when she could no longer stand it, she went into the
forest to search for her brother. After she had gone a long way, he
was too tired to go any farther, and when she looked around her, a
lion was standing nearby. He seemed friendly and very kind. So she
sat down on his back, and the lion carried her away. As they went he
kept stroking her with his tail and cooling her cheeks.

After they had traveled a good distance, they came to a cave, and
the lion carried her inside. She did not get frightened, nor did she
want to jump off the lion's back because he was so friendly. They
went deeper into the cave, where it became darker and darker until it

was eventually pitch black. They still proceeded for a while until they reached daylight again and were in a beautiful garden. Everything was fresh and glistened in the sun, and in the middle of the garden was a magnificent palace. When they came to the gate, the lion stopped, and the princess climbed down from his back. Then the lion began to speak and said, "You shall live in the beautiful house and serve me, and if you carry out all my orders, you shall see your brother again."

So the princess served the lion and obeyed all his commands. One day she went for a walk in the garden, where it was very beautiful, but she was still sad because she was alone and forsaken by the world. As she walked here and there she became aware of a pond, and in the middle of the pond was a small island with a tent on it. Underneath the tent she saw a frog, who was as green as grass and had a rose leaf on his head instead of a crown. The frog looked at her and said, "Why are you so sad?"

"Ah," she replied. "Why shouldn't I be sad?" And she told him about her troubles.

Then the frog said to her in a very friendly way, "If you need anything, just come to me, and I'll lend you a helping hand."

"But how shall I pay you back?"

"You don't have to pay me back," said the frog. "Just bring me a fresh rose leaf every day for my crown."

The princess returned to the palace and was somewhat comforted. Whenever the lion demanded something, she ran to the pond, and the frog hopped here and there and soon brought her what she needed. After a while, the lion said, "This evening I'd like to eat a gnat pie, but it must be prepared very well."

The princess wondered how she could ever get something like that. It seemed impossible for her. She ran out and told her woes to the frog. But the frog said, "Don't worry. I'll make sure that you have a gnat pie."

He sat down, opened his mouth to the left and right, and when he snapped it shut, he had caught as many gnats as he needed. Then he hopped here and there, gathered together some wood shavings, and built a fire. When it began burning, he kneaded the dough for the pie and put it over the coals. After two hours, the pie was finished, and one could not have wished for anything better. Then he said to the maiden, "I won't give you the pie until you promise me that, when the lion is asleep, you'll cut off his head with the sword that's hidden behind his bed."

"No," she said. "I won't do it. The lion's always been good to me."

"If you don't do it, you'll never see your brother again," said the frog. "Besides, you won't be harming the lion."

So she summoned her courage, took the pie, and brought it to the lion.

"That looks delicious," the lion said, and after sniffing it, he began to eat it right away and ate it all up. When he was finished, he felt tired and wanted to sleep a little. So he said to the princess, "Come and sit down beside me and scratch behind my ears a bit until I fall asleep."

She sat down beside him, scratched him with her left hand, and with her right hand she reached for the sword that was lying behind the bed. After he had fallen asleep, she drew out the sword, closed her eyes, and chopped off the lion's head with one blow. But when she looked again, the lion had disappeared, and her dear brother stood next to her. He kissed her affectionately and said, "You've released me from the spell, for I was the lion and had been cursed to remain so until a maiden's hand would chop off my head out of love for me as a lion."

They went together into the garden to thank the frog, but when they got there, they saw that he was hopping all around and gathering together wood shavings to build a fire. When the fire was burning brightly, he hopped into it himself, and it burned a little more until it finally went out and a beautiful maiden was standing there. This was the prince's sweetheart, who had also been cast under a magic spell. Now they all returned home to the old king and queen, and a great wedding was held. Whoever attended did not go home with an empty stomach.

◆ 236 ◆

The Soldier and the Carpenter

IN A CITY LIVED TWO CARPENTERS whose houses touched each other. Each carpenter had a son, and their children were always together and played with one another. That is why they were called Little Knife and Little Fork, which likewise are always placed together on the table. When they grew up, they refused to be separated. Since one was courageous and the other timid, one became a soldier, and the other learned carpentry. As the time came for the carpenter to go on his travels as a journeyman, the soldier did not want to be left behind, and so they set out together.

When they reached a city, the carpenter went to work for a master craftsman, and since the soldier wanted to remain there too, he hired himself out as a servant in the same house. That would have gone well, but the soldier had no desire to work. He just loafed about, and it did not take long for the master to send him packing. Out of loyalty to his companion the carpenter decided not to stay. He handed his resignation to the master and departed with the soldier. This was the way things continued to happen. If they had work, it did not last long because the soldier was lazy and would be sent away, and the carpenter did not want to stay without him.

One day they arrived in a large city, but when the soldier refused to lift a finger, he was dismissed the very first evening, and they had to leave that night. Now their way took them to the edge of a large mysterious forest, and the timid carpenter said, "I'm not going to enter. I'm sure there are witches and ghosts jumping all over the place."

But the soldier replied, "Oh, nonsense! I'm not yet afraid of things like that!"

The soldier went ahead, and since the timid carpenter did not want to be separated from him, he went along. In a short time they lost their way and wandered in darkness through the trees. Finally, they saw a light and headed in that direction until they came to a beautiful castle that was brightly lit. In front of the castle was a black dog, and nearby was a red swan on a pond. When they entered the castle, however, they did not encounter a living creature until they went into the kitchen, where they found a gray cat standing by a pot on the fire and cooking. They moved on and found many splendid rooms that were all empty, but in one of them there was a table amply covered with food and drink. Since they were both very hungry, they went over to the table and enjoyed a fine meal. Afterward the soldier said, "Now that we're finished and full, we're entitled to some sleep!"

He opened a room and found two beautiful beds. They lay down in them, but just as they were about to fall asleep, it occurred to the timid carpenter that they had not said their prayers. As he got up he saw a cupboard on the wall. He opened it, and inside there was a crucifix with two prayer books. He immediately woke the soldier and got him up. Then they knelt down and said their prayers and fell asleep once more in peace. The next morning the soldier felt such a violent blow that he jumped into the air.

"Hey, what are you hitting me for?" he yelled at his companion, who had also received a blow and replied, "I didn't hit you. What did *you* hit me for?"

Then the soldier said, "It's probably a signal that we should get up."

When they left the room, breakfast was already on the table. But the timid carpenter said, "Before we touch it, let's first look for some people."

"All right," said the soldier. "I agree. Since the cat prepared and cooked the meal, I've lost my desire to eat it."

So they went from the bottom of the castle to the top but could not find a soul. Finally, the soldier said, "Let's go search down in the cellar too."

As they went down the stairs they saw an old woman sitting in front of the first cellar. They began speaking to her and said, "Good day! Did you cook that good meal for us?"

"Yes, children, did it taste all right?"

They went farther and came to a second cellar, where a young boy of fourteen was sitting. They greeted him too, but he did not answer them. Finally, they came to the third cellar, where a maiden of twelve was sitting, and she too did not answer their greeting. Then they continued walking through all the cellars but did not find anyone else. When they returned, the maiden had already stood up from her seat, and they said to her, "Do you want to go upstairs with us?"

But she asked, "Is the *red swan* still on the pond up there?"

"Yes, we saw it at the entrance."

"That's sad. Then I can't go upstairs with you."

The young boy was also standing when they came to him, and they asked him, "Do you want to come upstairs with us?"

But he said, "Is the *black dog* still in the courtyard?"

"Yes, we saw him at the entrance."

"That's sad. Then I can't go upstairs with you."

When they came to the old woman, she had also stood up.

"Granny," they said. "Do you want to come upstairs with us?"

"Is the *gray cat* still upstairs in the kitchen?"

"Yes, she's sitting at the hearth by a pot and cooking."

"That's sad. Unless you kill the red swan, the black dog, and the gray cat, we can't leave the cellar."

When the two companions went upstairs and into the kitchen again, they wanted to pet the cat, but her fiery eyes began to flash, and she looked very wild. Now, there was still a small room left that they had not explored, and when they opened it, they discovered that it was completely empty except for a bow and arrow, a sword, and iron tongs, which were hanging on the wall. Written over the bow and arrow were the words, "This will kill the red swan." Over the sword, "This will chop off the black dog's head." Over the tongs, "This will pinch off the gray cat's head."

"Ah," said the timid carpenter. "Let's get out of here!"

But the soldier replied, "No, let's go after the animals."

They took the weapons off the wall and went into the kitchen, where the three animals, the swan, the dog, and the cat, were standing together as if they had something evil in mind. When the timid carpenter saw them, he ran away. The soldier followed and tried to give his companion courage, but the carpenter wanted something to eat first. After he had eaten, he said, "I saw some suits of armor in a room, and I want to put one on first."

When he was in the room, he looked for a way to escape and said, "We'd be better off if we climbed through that window. Those animals are not our concern!"

However, when he went over to the window, he found strong iron bars in front of it. Now he no longer had a way out and went over to the suits of armor. He tried to put one on, but they were all too heavy. Then the soldier said, "Stop this! Let's go the way we are."

"All right," said the other, "but I wish there were three of us."

Just as he uttered those words a white dove began flapping its wings on the outside of a window and bumped up against it. The soldier opened the window, and as soon as the dove hopped inside, a handsome young man stood before them and said, "I'll lend you support and help you."

The young man picked up the bow and arrow, but the timid carpenter spoke to him and said that he was taking the best part of the bargain with the bow and arrow because he would be in a good position after he took a shot to run wherever he wanted. On the other hand, the carpenter and the soldier would have to get physically closer to the enchanted animals to use their weapons. So the young man exchanged the bow and arrow for the sword.

Now all three went to the kitchen, where the animals were still together. The young man cut off the dog's head, the soldier grabbed the gray cat with the tongs, and the timid carpenter stood behind and shot the red swan dead. After the three animals had fallen, the old woman and her two children came running from the cellar all at once and let out a great cry, "You've killed my dearest friends! You're traitors!"

They charged at the men and wanted to murder them. But the three men overpowered them and killed them with their weapons. When they were dead, the men suddenly began to hear all around them strange murmuring sounds that came out of all the corners. Then the timid carpenter said, "Let's bury the three bodies. After all, they were Christians. We know this from the crucifix."

They carried the bodies out into the courtyard, dug three graves, and laid them down inside. While they were working, however, the murmuring in the castle increased. It became louder and louder, and when they were finished with their work, they heard real voices among the murmurs, and one called out, "Who are you? Who are you?"

Since the handsome young man had disappeared, they became afraid and ran away. After they had gone off a little way, the soldier said, "Hey, we shouldn't have run away. Let's go back and see what's there."

"No," the other said. "I want nothing to do with those enchanted creatures. I want to go to the city and earn an honest living."

But the soldier gave him no peace until he went back with him. When they got to the front of the castle, everything was full of life. Horses dashed through the courtyard, and servants ran back and forth. They pretended to be two poor journeymen and asked for a little something to eat. One of the people said, "Yes, just come inside. Everyone will be helped today."

They were led into a beautiful room and were given food and wine. Afterward they were asked whether they had seen two young men coming from the castle.

"No," they said.

But when someone saw that they had blood on their hands, he asked where the blood came from.

"I cut my finger," replied the soldier.

However, a servant went and told his master, who came himself to see who they were. Indeed, it was the handsome young man who had come to their aid, and when he laid eyes on them, he cried out, "These are the two who saved the castle!"

He welcomed them with great joy and told them how everything had happened. "A housekeeper was living in the castle with her two children. However, she was really a witch, and once when her masters scolded her, she replied with evil and transformed all living things in the castle into stone. There were three other servants who also knew something about magic, and she had no real power over them and could only turn them into animals. They did their mischief upstairs in the castle, and since she was afraid of them, she fled into the cellar with her children. She had only limited power over me as well. So she changed me so that I was a white dove as long as I was outside the castle. When you two came into the castle, you were supposed to kill the animals so she would be free. As a reward she wanted to kill you, but God had things turn out better. The castle is no longer enchanted, and the very moment that the wicked witch and her children were killed, the people who had been turned into stone became alive again, and the murmuring sounds you heard were the words these people first spoke upon being freed."

The young man then led the two companions to the lord of the castle, who gave them his two beautiful daughters, and they lived happily ever after as great knights until the end of their days.

❖ 237 ❖

The Wild Man

ONCE UPON A TIME there was a wild man who was under a spell, and he went into the gardens and wheatfields of the peasants and destroyed everything. The peasants complained to their lord and told him that they could no longer pay their rent. So the lord summoned all the huntsmen and announced that whoever caught the wild beast would receive a great reward. Then an old huntsman arrived and said he would catch the beast. He took a bottle of brandy, a bottle of wine, and a bottle of beer and set the bottles at the river, where the beast went every day. After doing that the huntsman hid behind a tree. Soon the beast came and drank up all the bottles. He licked his mouth and looked around to make sure everything was all right. Since he was drunk, he lay down and fell asleep. The huntsman went over to him and tied his hands and feet. Then he woke up the wild man and said, "You, wild man, come with me, and you'll get such things to drink every day."

The huntsman took the wild man to the royal castle, and they put him in a cage. The lord then visited the other noblemen and invited them to see what kind of beast he had caught. Meanwhile, one of his sons was playing with a ball, and he let it fall into the cage.

"Wild man," said the child, "throw the ball back out to me."

"You've got to fetch the ball yourself," said the wild man.

"All right," said the child. "But I don't have a key."

"Then see to it that you fetch it from your mother's pocket."

The boy stole the key, opened the cage, and the wild man ran out.

"Oh, wild man!" the boy began to scream. "You've got to stay here, or else I'll get a beating!"

The wild man picked up the boy and carried him on his back into the wilderness. So the wild man disappeared, and the child was lost.

The wild man dressed the boy in a coarse jacket and sent him to the gardener at the emperor's court, where he was to ask whether they could use a gardener's helper. The gardener said yes, but the boy was so grimy and crusty that the others would not sleep near him. The boy replied that he would sleep in the straw. Then early each morning he went into the garden, and the wild man came to him and said, "Now wash yourself, now comb yourself."

And the wild man made the garden so beautiful that even the

gardener himself could not do any better. The princess saw the handsome boy every morning, and she told the gardener to have his little assistant bring her a bunch of flowers. When the boy came, she asked him about his origins, and he replied that he did not know them. Then she gave him a roast chicken full of ducats. When he got back to the gardener, he gave him the money and said, "What should I do with it? You can use it."

Later he was ordered to bring the princess another bunch of flowers, and she gave him a duck full of ducats, which he also gave to the gardener. On a third occasion she gave him a goose full of ducats, which the young man again passed on to the gardener. The princess thought that he had money, and yet he had nothing. They got married in secret, and her parents became angry and made her work in the brewery, and she also had to support herself by spinning. The young man would go into the kitchen and help the cook prepare the roast, and sometimes he stole a piece of meat and brought it to his wife.

Soon there was a mighty war in England, and the emperor and all the great armies had to travel there. The young man said he wanted to go there too and asked whether they had a horse in the stables for him. They told him they had one that ran on three legs that would be good enough for him. So he mounted the horse, and the horse went off, *clippety-clop*. Then the wild man approached him, and he opened a large mountain in which there was a regiment of a thousand soldiers and officers. The young man put on some fine clothes and was given a magnificent horse. Then he set out for the war in England with all his men. The emperor welcomed him in a friendly way and asked him to lend his support. The young man defeated everyone and won the battle, whereupon the emperor extended his thanks to him and asked him where his army came from.

"Don't ask me that," he replied. "I can't tell you."

Then he rode off with his army and left England. The wild man approached him again and took all the men back into the mountain. The young man mounted his three-legged horse and went back home.

"Here comes our hobbley-hop again with his three-legged horse!" the people cried out, and they asked, "Were you lying behind the hedge and sleeping?"

"Well," he said, "if I hadn't been in England, things would not have gone well for the emperor!"

"Boy," they said, "be quiet, or else the gardener will really let you have it!"

The second time, everything happened as it had before, and the third time, the young man won the whole battle, but he was wounded in the arm. The emperor took his kerchief, wrapped the wound, and tried to make the boy stay with him.

"No, I'm not going to stay with you. Who I am does not concern you."

Once again the wild man approached the young man and took all his men back into the mountain. The young man mounted his three-legged horse once more and went back home. The people began laughing and said, "Here comes our hobbley-hop again. Where were you lying asleep this time?"

"Truthfully, I wasn't sleeping," he said. "England is now totally defeated, and there's finally peace."

Now, the emperor talked about the handsome knight who lent him support, and the young man said to the emperor, "If I hadn't been with you, it wouldn't have turned out so well."

The emperor wanted to give him a beating, but the young man said, "Stop! If you don't believe me, let me show you my arm."

When he revealed his arm and the emperor saw the wound, he was amazed and said, "Perhaps you are the Lord Himself or an angel whom God has sent to me," and he asked his pardon for treating him so cruelly and gave him a whole kingdom.

Now the wild man was released from the magic spell and stood there as a great king and told his entire story. The mountain turned into a royal castle, and the young man went there with his wife, and they lived in the castle happily until the end of their days.

◈ 238 ◈

The Children of Famine

ONCE UPON A TIME there was a woman with two daughters, and they had become so poor that they no longer had even a piece of bread to put in their mouths. Their hunger became so great that their mother became unhinged and desperate. Indeed, she said to her children, "I've got to kill you so I can have something to eat!"

"Oh, dear Mother," said one daughter, "spare me, and I'll go out and see if I can get something without begging."

She went out and came back carrying a little piece of bread, which they shared with one another. But it was not enough to still their hunger. Therefore, the mother spoke to the other daughter, "Now it's your turn to die."

"Oh, dear Mother," she answered, "spare me and I'll go and get something to eat from somewhere else without anyone noticing me."

She went away and came back carrying two little pieces of bread.

They shared it with one another, but it was not enough to still their hunger. Therefore, when a few hours had gone by, their mother said to them once more, "You've got to die or else we'll waste away."

To which they responded, "Dear Mother, we'll lie down and sleep, and we won't get up again until the Judgment Day arrives."

So they lay down and fell into a deep sleep, and no one could wake them from it. Meanwhile, their mother departed, and nobody knows where she went.

◈ 239 ◈

Saint Solicitous

ONCE UPON A TIME there was a pious maiden who swore to God she would not marry. Since she was so remarkably beautiful, her father would not accept this and tried to force her to marry. Confronted with this predicament, the maiden implored God to let her grow a beard, and this happened right away. But the king was so enraged that he had her crucified, and she became a saint.

Now, it so happened that a very poor minstrel went into the church where her statue was kept. He knelt down in front of it, and the saint was glad that the minstrel was the first one to recognize her innocence. Consequently, the statue, which was adorned with golden slippers, let one slipper drop to the ground so the pilgrim could have it. He bowed in gratitude and took the gift.

Soon the people in the church became aware that the golden slipper was missing, and questions were asked all around until finally the slipper was found on the poor fiddler. He was now condemned as a wicked thief and led to the gallows to be hanged. The procession went by the church where the statue was standing, and the fiddler requested permission to go inside, pour out his heart to his benefactress with his fiddle, and say his last farewell. His request was granted, but no sooner had he moved his bow than—behold!—the statue let the other golden slipper drop to the ground, and this demonstrated that he had not committed the theft. So the irons and rope were taken off the fiddler, who went merrily on his way. From then on the holy saint was called Solicitous.

◆ 240 ◆

Misfortune

WHEN MISFORTUNE IS AFTER SOMEONE, that person may try to hide in all sorts of places or flee into the open fields, but misfortune will still know where to find him.

Once upon a time there was a man who had become so poor that he did not even have a log of wood to keep the fire going on his hearth. So he went out into the forest to chop down a tree, but they were all too big and strong for him. He went deeper and deeper into the forest until he found one that he thought he could manage. Just as he lifted his ax, he saw a pack of wolves break out of a thicket and charge at him with a great howl. He threw down the ax, dashed off, and got to a bridge. However, high waters had weakened the bridge, and just as he was about to step on it, the bridge cracked and collapsed. What was he to do? If he stayed there and waited for the wolves, they would tear him apart. In desperation he jumped into the water, but since he could not swim, he sank to the bottom. Some fishermen who were on the other side of the river saw the man jump into the water. They swam to him, brought him ashore, and propped him up against an old wall, so the sun could warm him up and he could recover his strength. But after he regained consciousness, thanked the fishermen, and began telling them all about his fate, the wall crumbled on top of him and killed him.

◆ 241 ◆

The Pea Test

ONCE UPON A TIME there was a king whose only son was very eager to get married, and he asked his father for a wife.

"Your wish shall be fulfilled, my son," said the king, "but it's only fitting that you marry no one less than a princess, and there are none to be had in the vicinity. Therefore, I shall issue a proclamation and perhaps a princess will come from afar."

Soon a written proclamation was circulated, and it did not take long before numerous princesses arrived at the court. Almost every day a new one appeared, but when the princesses were asked about their birth and lineage, it always turned out that they were not princesses at all, and they were sent away without having achieved their purpose.

"If everything continues like this," the son said, "I'll never get a wife in the end."

"Calm yourself, my son," said the queen. "Before you know it, she'll be here. Happiness is often standing just outside the door. One only needs to open it."

And it was really just as the queen had predicted.

Soon after, on a stormy evening when the wind and rain were beating on the windows, there was a loud knocking on the gate of the royal palace. The servants opened the gate, and a beautiful maiden entered. She demanded to be led directly before the king, who was surprised by such a late visit and asked her where she had come from, who she was, and what she desired.

"I've come from a distant country," she answered, "and I'm the daughter of a mighty king. When your proclamation with the portrait of your son arrived in my father's kingdom, I felt a strong love for your son and immediately set out on my way with the intention of becoming his bride."

"I'm somewhat skeptical about what you've told me," said the king. "Besides, you don't look like a princess. Since when does a princess travel alone without an escort and in such poor clothes?"

"An escort would have only delayed me," she replied. "The color of my clothes faded in the sun, and the rain washed it out completely. If you don't believe I'm a princess, just send a messenger to my father."

"That's too far and too complicated," said the king. "A delegation cannot ride as fast as you. The people must have the necessary time for such a journey. Years would pass before they returned. If you can't prove in some other way that you're a princess, then fortune will not shine upon you, and you'd do well to head for home, the sooner the better."

"Let her stay," the queen said. "I'll put her to a test and know soon enough whether she's a princess."

The queen herself climbed up into the tower and had a bed made up for the maiden in a splendid room. When the mattress was carried into the room, she placed three peas on it, one on top, one in the middle, and one below. Then six other soft mattresses were stacked on top along with linen sheets and a cover made of eiderdown. When everything was ready, she led the maiden upstairs into the bedroom.

"After such a long trip, you must be tired, my child," she said. "Get some sleep. Tomorrow we'll continue talking."

At the break of day the queen climbed up to the room in the tower. She thought the maiden would still be in a deep sleep, but the maiden was awake.

"How did you sleep, my little daughter?" she asked.

"Miserably," replied the princess. "I couldn't sleep a wink the whole night."

"Why, my child? Wasn't the bed good enough?"

"In all my days I've never lain in such a bed. It was hard from my head to my feet. It seemed as if I were lying on nothing but peas."

"Now I know for sure," said the queen, "that you're a genuine princess. I shall send some royal garments up to you with pearls and jewels. Dress yourself as a bride, for we shall celebrate your wedding this very day."

◆ 242 ◆

The Robber and His Sons

ONCE UPON A TIME a robber lived in a great forest and dwelled in ravines and caves with his companions. Whenever princes, noblemen, or rich merchants traveled on the highway, he ambushed them and robbed them of their gold and possessions. As he grew older his occupation lost its appeal for him, and he regretted all the evil he had done. Consequently, he began to lead a decent and honest life and did good wherever he could. The people were surprised that he had changed so quickly, but they were glad that he had done so.

Now, he had three sons, and when they had grown up, he gathered them around him and said, "Tell me, my dear children, what do you want to become, and how do you intend to earn an honest living?"

His sons discussed this together and gave him the following answer: "Like father, like son. We want to earn our living the way you earned yours and intend to become robbers. We have no desire to work ourselves to the bone in some trade from morning till evening, nor do we want to lead a hard life with very little money."

"Ah, dear children," the father replied, "why don't you want to be content with less and live in peace? Honesty is the best policy. Stealing is an evil and godless affair, and you'll end up in a bad way if you do it. You won't get any pleasure from the wealth that you obtain. I know exactly how I felt. I'm telling you, this won't turn out well for you. You can go only so far, and then you'll tie your own noose. In the end, when you're hanging from the gallows, you'll understand what I mean."

But his sons did not heed his warnings and remained resolute. Indeed, the three youths wanted to test their skill right away. They knew the queen had in her stables a splendid horse that was very valuable, and they intended to steal it. They also knew that the horse would eat nothing but tender grass that grew only in a damp forest. So they went into the forest, cut the grass, and made a large bundle out of it, and then the older sons placed the youngest in it in such a way that he could not be seen. They then carried the bundle to the marketplace, and the queen's stable master bought the grass and had it carried to the stable and thrown into the horse's stall. When midnight came, and everyone was asleep, the youngest son crawled out of the bundle, untied the horse, put on him the golden bridle and the saddle embroidered with gold, and stuffed the bells that hung on it with wax so they would not make any noise. Next he unlocked the stable door, rode away on the horse as fast as he could, and arrived at the place that his brothers had designated. However, the sentries in the city had seen the thief and pursued him. When they found him outside with his brothers, they captured all three and conducted them to the prison.

The next morning they were led before the queen, and when she saw that they were three handsome youths, she inquired about their family background and learned that they were the sons of the old robber who had changed his life and had become one of her loyal subjects. She had the sons returned to the prison and sent a message to the father asking him whether he wanted to obtain their release. The old man came and said, "It's not worth spending a penny for my sons' release."

Then the queen replied, "You were a well-known, notorious robber. Tell me about the most extraordinary adventure you had as a robber, and I'll return your sons to you."

Upon hearing that, the old man began to speak. "Your Highness, listen to my story. I'm going to tell you about an incident that scared me more than anything in the world.

"Once I learned that a giant was living in a wild ravine between two mountains twenty miles from any living person, and this giant possessed a great treasure of thousands of coins, gold, and silver. I chose as many as a hundred men from my band to go and look for the giant. It was a long, hard way between cliffs and deep gulleys. We didn't find the giant at home and were glad about that. Then we took as much gold and silver as we could carry, and just as we were about to set out on our way home and thought we were quite safe, the giant came back unexpectedly with ten other giants, and they took us all prisoner. They divided us among themselves, with each receiving ten men. I and nine of my men fell to the giant whose treasure we had taken. He tied our hands behind our backs and drove us like sheep into a cave. We tried to secure our release with money and possessions, but he answered, 'I don't need your treasures. I'm going to keep you here and make a meal of you. That's more to my liking.' Then he began feeling us and picked out one of the men. 'He's the fattest,' he said. 'So I'll begin with him.'

"After killing him, he threw chunks of his flesh into a kettle with water, which he set over a fire. When the flesh was boiled, he had his meal. Every day he ate one more of us, and since I was the leanest, I was to be the last. When my nine companions had been devoured and my turn arrived, I thought of a trick.

" 'I can see that you have bad eyes,' I said to him, 'and that your sight is suffering. I'm a doctor and have had a great deal of experience in my profession. I'll heal your eyes if you'll spare my life.'

"He promised to spare my life if I could cure him, and he gave me everything I demanded. I put oil in a kettle, mixed in sulfur, pitch, salt, arsenic, and other deadly ingredients. Then I set the kettle over the fire as if I wanted to prepare a plaster for his eyes. As soon as the oil started to boil, the giant had to lie down, and I poured everything in the kettle on his eyes, his neck, and his body, so that he lost his sight completely and the skin on his body burned and shriveled up. He leapt into the air with a horrible cry, threw himself down on the ground, and rolled over and over, screaming and roaring like a lion or an ox. Then he jumped up in rage, grabbed a large club, and ran around the house beating the floor and walls trying to hit me. I couldn't escape because the house was surrounded by high walls and the doors were bolted with iron bars. I sprang from one corner to the next until there was nothing left to do but climb a ladder up to the roof and hang from a beam with both my hands. I hung there a whole day and night, and when I could no longer hold out, I climbed down and mixed among the sheep. I had to be nimble and constantly run with the beasts through his legs so he wouldn't notice me. Finally, I found a ram's skin lying in a corner. I slipped into it and arranged it so that the ram's horns stood on my head. The giant had the habit of making the sheep run through his legs before he let them go out into the pasture. Then he counted them, and whichever was the most plump, he would grab and cook for his meal. I hoped to use this opportunity to escape, and I rushed through his legs as the sheep did. However, he grabbed me, and when he felt how heavy I was, he said, 'Since you're so nice and plump, you'll fill my belly today.'

"I leapt out of his hands, but he grabbed me again. Then I got away from him, but he seized me once more, and so it went seven times. Finally, he became so furious that he said, 'All right, may the wolves eat you! I've had enough of your fooling around!'

"When I was outside, I threw off the skin, yelled, taunted him, and made fun of him, so he knew that I had escaped. Then he pulled a ring from his finger and said, 'Take this golden ring as a gift from me. You've earned it. It's not fitting that such a cunning and nimble man should leave here without a gift.'

"I took the ring and put it on my finger, but I didn't know that it possessed magic. The moment the ring was on my finger, I had to keep crying out, 'Here I am! Here I am!' whether I wanted to or not. Since the giant could tell by this where I was, he ran after me into the forest, but because he was blind, he kept bumping into branches or trees and fell down like a mighty tree. Yet, he lifted himself up quickly, and since he had long legs and could take such large steps, he always caught up to me and was constantly close by, for I kept crying out, 'Here I am! Here I am!' without stopping. I realized that the ring was the reason I was screaming that way and tried to pull it off, but I couldn't do it. So there was nothing left to do but to bite off my finger with my teeth. Then, all at once, I stopped screaming and succeeded in getting away from the giant. To be sure, I lost my finger, but I saved my life.

"Your Highness," the robber said, "I've told you this story to gain the release of one of my sons. Now I'll tell you what happened afterward in order to free my second son.

"When I had escaped from the hands of the giant, I wandered about in the wilderness and didn't know where to turn. I climbed the highest fir trees and the peaks of mountains, but even though I gazed far and wide, I couldn't locate a single house. Nor could I see a field or a trace of human existence, just terrible wilderness. So I descended the mountains that were as high as heaven and entered the valleys that were as deep as the deepest canyons. There I encountered lions, bears, buffalo, mules, poisonous snakes, and gruesome reptiles. I saw wild, hairy forest creatures, people with horns and beaks so horrible that I still shudder whenever I think back on them. I moved on and on and was tormented by hunger and thirst. I was afraid I would collapse at any moment from fatigue. Finally, just as the sun was about to set and I was on top of a high mountain, I saw some smoke rising in a lonely valley as if it were coming from a burning stove. I ran down the mountain toward the smoke as fast as I could. When I got there, I saw three dead men hanging from the branch of a tree. I was terrified, for I thought another giant would soon get me in his hands, and I feared for my life. However, I took heart, went on, and found a cottage where the door stood wide open. A woman was sitting by the fire of the hearth with her child. I entered, greeted her, and asked why she was sitting there so alone and where her husband was. I also asked how far it was to some settlement where people were living. She told me that there were people living in a country that was far away, and with tears in her eyes she revealed that wild forest monsters had come the previous night and had stolen her and her child from her husband's side and had brought them into that wilderness. The monsters had departed that morning, but they had ordered her to kill her child and cook him because they wanted to eat him when they returned. Upon hearing that, I felt great pity for the woman and her child and decided to help her out of her predicament. I ran to the tree on which the three thieves were hanging, took down the middle one, who was stocky, and carried him into the house. I cut him into pieces and told the woman to give him to the giants to eat. Meanwhile, I took the child and hid him in a hollow tree. Then I concealed myself behind the house so that I would be able to tell when the wild creatures were back and whether it would be necessary to rush to the aid of the woman. Just as the sun was about to set, I saw the monsters coming down from the mountain: they were a gruesome and terrible sight and looked like apes. They were dragging a dead boy after them, but I couldn't see who it was. When they entered the house, they lit a large fire, tore apart the bloody body with their teeth, and devoured it. Afterward they took from the fire the kettle in which the thief's flesh had been cooked and divided the pieces among themselves for their supper. When they were done, the one who appeared to be their chief asked the woman whether the flesh that they had eaten was the flesh of her child. The woman said yes. Then the monster said, 'I think you hid your child and cooked one of the thieves who was hanging on the branch.'

"He ordered three of his companions to run over there and bring a piece of meat from each of the three thieves so that he could see if they were all there. When I heard that, I ran ahead of them and hung myself between the two thieves, using my hands and the rope that I had taken from the third thief. When the monsters came, they cut a piece of flesh from the thigh of each thief, and they also cut a piece of my own thigh, but I withstood the pain without uttering a sound. As proof I still have a scar on my body."

The robber paused for a moment and then continued. "Your Highness, I've told you this adventure for my second son. Now I'll tell you the end of the story for my third.

"When the wild men ran back to the house with the three pieces of flesh, I got down from the branch and bandaged my wound with strips from my shirt as best I could. But the blood kept oozing and flowing from the wound. Still, I didn't pay any attention to that but kept thinking about my promise to the woman. I wanted to save her and her child, so I hurried back to the house, kept myself hidden, and listened to what was going on. I could hold myself erect only with great difficulty since my wound hurt me and I was completely exhausted from hunger and thirst. Meanwhile, the giant tasted the three pieces of flesh that had been carried to him, and when he had eaten the piece of flesh that had been cut out of my body and was still bloody, he said, 'Run back and bring me the middle thief. His flesh is still fresh and pleases me.'

"When I heard that, I rushed back to the gallows and hung myself with the rope once more and dangled between the two dead men. Soon after, the monsters came, took me down, and dragged me over thorns and thistles to the house, where they stretched me out on the floor. They sharpened their teeth, whetted their knives, and got ready to slaughter and eat me. Just as they were about to put their hands on me, a sudden storm erupted with lightning, thunder, and wind, so that the monsters themselves got frightened and plunged through the windows, doors, and roof with horrible shrieks. They left me lying on the floor, and after three hours, the day began, and the bright sun rose in the sky. I departed with the woman and the child, and we wandered for forty days through the wilderness and had no other food but roots, berries, and herbs that were growing in the forest. Finally, we found people, and I brought the woman back to her husband. You can surely imagine how great his joy was!"

With that the robber's story came to an end.

"By saving the woman and her child, you made up for many evil deeds," the queen said. "Now I'm going to set your three sons free."

Notes

There were seven major editions of the *Children's and Household Tales* of the Brothers Grimm, known in German as *Die Kinder- und Hausmärchen*. The first edition appeared in two volumes; thereafter the tales were always published in one volume:

1st edition	1812,	vol. I	86 tales
	1815,	vol. II	70 tales
2nd edition	1819		170 tales
3rd edition	1837		177 tales
4th edition	1840		187 tales
5th edition	1843		203 tales
6th edition	1850		203 tales
7th edition	1857		210 tales

There was also a small edition that included 50 of the more popular tales, which went through ten editions from 1825 to 1858. Beginning with the second edition of the complete tales in 1819, Wilhelm Grimm was chiefly responsible for revising and expanding the collection of tales, and most of the additions after 1819 came from literary rather than oral sources.

During the initial stages of their collecting, the Grimms relied mainly on people within the region of Kassel and on the so-called Bökendorfer Circle in Westphalia. Wilhelm Grimm visited the estate of Freiherr Werner Adolf von Haxthausen in Bökendorf and became friendly with a group of young people there who provided him with numerous tales. Contrary to popular belief, the Grimms obtained most of their oral and literary tales from educated members of the middle and aristocratic classes. Indeed, the majority of their informants were women, and the Grimms did not travel widely to collect their tales.

A complete list of contributors can be found at the end of the Notes. The following were the key oral contributors: Dorothea Viehmann (35 tales); Family of Rudolf Wild (altogether they contributed 36 tales); Johann Friedrich Krause (7 tales); Friederike Mannel (8 tales); Ferdinand Siebert (13 tales); Family Hassenpflug (altogether they contributed 41 tales); Bökendorfer Circle (altogether they contributed 66 tales).

In the notes that follow, after each story's German title I have indicated in parentheses the date of a tale's first publication in the Grimms' collection. In those instances where Wilhelm Grimm combined two or three tales, I have indicated that the tale is a mixed version. Wherever possible, I have tried to provide the place and date of publication of the literary sources.

For further information about the sources of the Grimms' tales, one should consult:

Brüder Grimm, *Kinder- und Hausmärchen,* 3 vols. edited by Heinz Rölleke (Stuttgart: Redlam, 1980).
Dieter Hennig and Bernhard Lauer, eds., *Die Brüder Grimm. Dokumente ihres Lebens und ihres Wirkens* (Kassel: Weber & Weidemeyer, 1985).

1. **The Frog King, or Iron Heinrich** "Der Froschkönig oder der eiserne Heinrich" (1812). Source: Family Wild
2. **The Companionship of the Cat and the Mouse** "Katz und Maus in Gesellschaft" (1812). Source: Gretchen Wild
3. **The Virgin Mary's Child** "Marienkind" (1812). Source: Gretchen Wild
4. **A Tale About the Boy Who Went Forth to Learn What Fear Was** "Märchen von einem, der auszog, das Fürchten zu lernen" (1812). Source: Originally published under the title "Gut Kegel- und Kartenspiel" ("A Good Game of Ninepins and Cards"), this tale was revised and expanded in 1819 with material from Ferdinand Siebert, Dorothea Viehmann, and a story from Mecklenburg.
5. **The Wolf and the Seven Young Kids** "Der Wolf und die sieben, jungen Geisslein" (1812). Source: Family Hassenpflug
6. **Faithful Johannes** "Der getreue Johannes" (1819). Source: Dorothea Viehmann
7. **The Good Bargain** "Der gute Handel" (1819). Source: Family von Haxthausen
8. **The Marvelous Minstrel** "Der wunderliche Spielmann" (1819). Source: From Lorsch near Worms. Informant unknown.
9. **The Twelve Brothers** "Die zwölf Brüder" (1812). Source: Julia and Charlotte Ramus
10. **Riffraff** "Das Lumpengesindel" (1812)). Source: August von Haxthausen
11. **Brother and Sister** "Brüderchen und Schwesterchen" (1812). Source: Family Hassenpflug
12. **Rapunzel** "Rapunzel" (1812). Source: Story by Friedrich Schultz in *Kleine Romane* (Leipzig, 1790), which was based on the tale "Persinette," in *Les Fées, Contes des Contes*, (1692) by Mlle. Charlotte-Rose de la Force.
13. **The Three Little Gnomes in the Forest** "Die drei Männlein im Walde" (1812). Source: Dortchen Wild
14. **The Three Spinners** "Die drei Spinnerinnen" (1812). Source: Originally published under the title "Von dem bösen Flachsspinnen" ("A Tale About the Evils of Spinning Flax") conveyed by Jeanette Hassenpflug. In 1819 it was replaced by Paul Wigand's version.
15. **Hansel and Gretel** "Hänsel und Grethel" (1812). Source: Family Wild
16. **The Three Snake Leaves** "Die drei Schlangenblätter" (1819). Source: Johann Friedrich Krause and Family von Haxthausen. Mixed version.
17. **The White Snake** "Die weisse Schlange" (1812). Source: Family Hassenpflug
18. **The Straw, the Coal, and the Bean** "Strohalm, Kohle und Bohne" (1812). Source: Dorothea Catharina Wild
19. **The Fisherman and His Wife** "Von dem Fischer un syner Fru" (1812). Source: Philipp Otto Runge. Written in a Pomeranian dialect (*plattdeutsch*).
20. **The Brave Little Tailor** "Das tapfere Schneiderlein" (1812). Source: Martinus Montanus, *Wegkürtzer* (c. 1557).
21. **Cinderella** "Aschenputtel" (1812). Source: From an anonymous woman in the Elizabeth Hospital in Marburg. Obviously influenced by Charles Perrault's "Cendrillon," in *Contes du Temps passé* (1697). This version from Marburg was mixed with additional versions, in particular, one by Dorothea Viehmann. The term *Aschenputtel*, or Cinderella, appears in other tales to characterize a young woman obliged to do the dirty work in the house.
22. **The Riddle** "Das Rätsel" (1819). Source: Dorothea Viehmann
23. **The Mouse, the Bird, and the Sausage** "Von dem Mäuschen, Vögelchen und der Bratwurst" (1812). Source: Hans Michael Moscherosch, *Gesichte Philanders von Sittewald* (1650).

24. **Mother Holle** "Frau Holle" (1812). Source: Dortchen Wild
25. **The Seven Ravens** "Die Sieben Raben" (1812). Source: Family Hassenpflug
26. **Little Red Cap** "Rotkäppchen" (1812). Source: Jeanette and Marie Hassenpflug. Influenced by Charles Perrault's "Le petit chaperon rouge," in *Contes du Temps passé* (1697), and Ludwig Tieck's drama *Leben und Tod des kleinen Rotkäppchens* (1800).
27. **The Bremen Town Musicians** "Die Bremer Stadtmusikanten" (1819). Source: Family von Haxthausen and Dorothea Viehmann. Mixed version.
28. **The Singing Bone** "Der singende Knochen" (1812). Source: Dortchen Wild
29. **The Devil With the Three Golden Hairs** "Der Teufel mit den drei goldenen Haaren" (1819). Source: Dorothea Viehmann. The German term *Glückskind,* which literally means "fortune's child," is translated here as "fortune's favorite."
30. **The Louse and the Flea** "Läuschen und Flöhchen" (1812). Source: Dorothea Catharina Wild
31. **The Maiden Without Hands** "Das Mädchen ohne Hände" (1812). Source: Marie von Hassenpflug, Dorothea Viehmann, and Johann H. B. Bauer. Mixed version.
32. **Clever Hans** "Der gescheidte Hans" (1812). Source: Family Hassenpflug
33. **The Three Languages** "Die drei Sprachen" (1819). Source: Hans Truffer
34. **Clever Else** "Die kluge Else" (1819). Source: Dortchen Wild
35. **The Tailor in Heaven** "Der Schneider im Himmel" (1819). Source: Jakob Frey, *Gartengesellschaft* (1556), and Hans Wilhelm Kirchhoff, *Wendunmuth* (1563). Mixed version.
36. **The Magic Table, the Gold Donkey, and the Club in the Sack** "Tischendeckdich, Goldesel und Knüppel aus dem Sack" (1812). Source: Jeanette Hassenpflug
37. **Thumbling** "Daumesdick" (1819). Source: From Mühlheim, a town near Cologne. Informant unknown.
38. **The Wedding of Mrs. Fox** "Die Hochzeit der Frau Füchsin" (1812). Source: The first tale is from either Frau Gottschalk or Jacob Grimm himself. The second is from Ludovica Jordis.
39. **The Elves** "Die Wichtelmänner" (1812). Source: Dortchen Wild, all three tales.
40. **The Robber Bridegroom** "Der Räuberbräutigam" (1812). Source: Marie Hassenpflug
41. **Herr Korbes** "Herr Korbes" (1812). Source: Jeanette Hassenpflug. According to a letter written by the Grimms to the first English translator of the tales, Edgar Taylor, the name *Korbes* is supposed to mean "bogeyman."
42. **The Godfather** "Der Herr Gevatter" (1812). Source: Amalie Hassenpflug, expanded by a tale with the same title in Ludwig Aurbacher's *Büchlein für die Jugend* (Stuttgart, 1834). Mixed version.
43. **Mother Trudy** "Frau Trude" (1837). Source: Meier Teddy, "Klein Bäschen und Frau Trude, Ammenmärchen," a poem in *Frauentaschenbuch* (1823).
44. **Godfather Death** "Der Gevatter Tod" (1812). Source: Marie Elisabeth Wild and Friedrich Gustav Schilling. Mixed version.
45. **Thumbling's Travels** "Daumerlings Wanderschaft" (1812). Source: Marie Hassenpflug
46. **Fitcher's Bird** "Fichters Vogel" (1812). Source: Friederike Mannel and Dortchen Wild. Mixed version. The influence of Charles Perrault's "La barbe bleue" ("Bluebeard"), in *Contes du Temps passé* (1697), is also apparent. The

word *Fichter* is taken from the Icelandic *Fitfuglar,* which is a kind of web-footed bird.

47. **The Juniper Tree** "Von dem Machandelboom" (1812). Source: Philipp Otto Runge, written in a Pomeranian dialect (*plattdeutsch*).

48. **Old Sultan** "Der alte Sultan" (1812). Source: Johann Friedrich Krause

49. **The Six Swans** "Die sechs Schwäne" (1812). Source: Dortchen Wild and the tale "Die sieben Schwäne," in *Feenmärchen* (Braunschweig, 1801).

50. **Brier Rose** "Dornröschen" (1812). Source: Marie Hassenpflug. Also influenced by Charles Perrault's "La belle au bois dormant" ("Sleeping Beauty"), in *Contes du Temps passé* (1697).

51. **Foundling** "Fundvogel" (1812). Source: Friederike Mannel. Originally entitled "Fündling." A literal translation of *Fundvogel* would be "The Found Bird."

52. **King Thrushbeard** "König Drosselbart" (1812). Source: Family Hassenpflug

53. **Snow White** "Schneewittchen" (1812). Source: Family Hassenpflug

54. **The Knapsack, the Hat, and the Horn** "Der Ranzen, das Hütlein und das Hörnlein" (1819). Source: From Lower Hessia. Informant unknown.

55. **Rumpelstiltskin** "Rumpelstilzchen" (1812). Source: Dortchen Wild and Lisette Wild. Mixed version.

56. **Sweetheart Roland** "Der liebste Roland" (1812). Source: Dortchen Wild

57. **The Golden Bird** "Der goldene Vogel" (1812). Source: Gretchen Wild

58. **The Dog and the Sparrow** "Der Hund und der Sperling" (1812). Source: Gretchen Wild and Dorothea Viehmann. Mixed version.

59. **Freddy and Katy** "Der Frieder und das Katherlieschen" (1819). Source: Dorothea Viehmann

60. **The Two Brothers** "Die zwei Brüder" (1819). Source: Family von Haxthausen

61. **Little Farmer** "Das Bürle" (1812). Source: Family Hassenpflug and Dorothea Viehmann. Mixed version.

62. **The Queen Bee** "Die Bienenkönigin" (1812). Source: Albert Ludwig Grimm, "Die drei Königssöhne," in *Kindermärchen* (1808).

63. **The Three Feathers** "Die drei Federn" (1812). Source: Family Wild and Family Hassenpflug. Mixed version.

64. **The Golden Goose** "Die goldene Gans" (1812). Source: Family Hassenpflug

65. **All Fur** "Allerleirauh" (1812). Source: Dortchen Wild. A more literal translation of the title would be "All Kinds of Fur."

66. **The Hare's Bride** "Häsichenbraut" (1819). Source: Hans Rudolf von Schröter

67. **The Twelve Huntsmen** "Die zwölf Jäger" (1812). Source: Jeanette Hassenpflug

68. **The Thief and His Master** "De Gaudeif un sien Meester" (1819). Source: Family von Droste-Hülshoff. Written in Münster dialect.

69. **Jorinda and Joringel** "Jorinde und Joringel" (1812). Source: Johann Heinrich Jung-Stilling, *Heinrich Stillings Jugend* (Berlin, 1777).

70. **The Three Sons of Fortune** "Die drei Glückskinder" (1819). Source: Family von Haxthausen

71. **How Six Made Their Way in the World** "Sechse kommen durch die ganze Welt" (1819). Source: Dorothea Viehmann

72. **The Wolf and the Man** "Der Wolf und der Mensch" (1819). Source: Family von Haxthausen

73. **The Wolf and the Fox** "Der Wolf und der Fuchs" (1819). Source: From Hessia. Informant unknown.

74. **The Fox and His Cousin** "Der Fuchs und die Frau Gevatterin" (1819). Source: From Bohemia. Informant unknown.

75. **The Fox and the Cat** "Der Fuchs und die Katze" (1819). Source: From Switzerland. Informant unknown.

76. **The Pink Flower** "Die Nelke" (1819). Source: Dorothea Viehmann. *Die Nelke* can also be translated as "The Carnation."

77. **Clever Gretel** "Das kluge Gretel" (1819). Source: Andreas Strobl, *Ovum paschale oder neugefärbte Oster-Ayr* (Salzburg, 1700).

78. **The Old Man and His Grandson** "Der alte Grossvater und der Enkel" (1812). Source: Johann Heinrich Jung-Stilling, *Heinrich Stillings Jünglings-Jahre* (Berlin, 1778).

79. **The Water Nixie** "Die Wassernixe" (1812). Source: Marie Hassenpflug

80. **The Death of the Hen** "Von dem Tode des Hühnchens" (1812). Source: Clemens Brentano and Wilhelm Engelhardt. Mixed version.

81. **Brother Lustig** "Bruder Lustig" (1819). Source: Georg Passy. Tale from Vienna. The word *Lustig* means "merry" or "funny."

82. **Gambling Hans** "De Spielhansl" (1819). Source: Simon Sechter. Tale from Lower Austria written in dialect.

83. **Lucky Hans** "Hans im Glück" (1819). Source: Oral tale recorded by August Wernicke in the journal *Wünschelruthe* 33 (April 23, 1818).

84. **Hans Gets Married** "Hans heiratet" (1819). Source: Johannes Praetorious, *Wünschelruthe* (Leipzig, 1667).

85. **The Golden Children** "Die Goldkinder" (1812). Source: Friederike Mannel

86. **The Fox and the Geese** "Der Fuchs und die Gänse" (1812). Source: Family von Haxthausen

87. **The Poor Man and the Rich Man** "Der Arme und der Reiche" (1815). Source: Ferdinand Siebert

88. **The Singing, Springing Lark** "Das singende, springende Löweneckerchen" (1815). Source: Dortchen Wild

89. **The Goose Girl** "Die Gänsemagd" (1815). Source: Dorothea Viehmann

90. **The Young Giant** "Der junge Riese" (1815). Source: Georg August Friedrich Goldmann

91. **The Gnome** "Dat Erdmänneken" (1815). Source: Ludowine von Haxthausen. Written in Paderborn dialect.

92. **The King of the Golden Mountain** "Der König vom goldenen Berg" (1815). Source: Based on a tale told by a soldier.

93. **The Raven** "Die Rabe" (1815). Source: Georg August Friedrich Goldmann

94. **The Clever Farmer's Daughter** "Die kluge Bauerntochter" (1815). Source: Dorothea Viehmann

95. **Old Hildebrand** "Der alte Hildebrand" (1819). Source: From Austria, perhaps Georg Passy.

96. **The Three Little Birds** "De drei Vügelkens" (1815). Source: From a shepherd in Köterberg. Written in dialect.

97. **The Water of Life** "Das Wasser des Lebens" (1815). Source: From Hessia and Paderborn. Mixed version.

98. **Doctor Know-It-All** "Doktor Allwissend" (1815). Source: Dorothea Viehmann

99. **The Spirit in the Glass Bottle** "Der Geist im Glass" (1815). Source: From a tailor in Bäkendorf (Paderborn).

100. **The Devil's Sooty Brother** "Des Teufels russiger Bruder" (1815). Source: Dorothea Viehmann

101. **Bearskin** "Der Bärenhäuter" (1815). Source: Family von Haxthausen

and J. J. Christoffel von Grimmelshausen's story *Der erste Bärnhäuter* (1670). Mixed version.

102. **The Wren and the Bear** "Der Zaunkönig und der Bär" (1815). Source: Dorothea Viehmann. The literal translation of *Zaunkönig* is "king of the hedges," and the "royalty" of the wren is often a topic of tales and treated with irony. (See also note for tale 171.)

103. **The Sweet Porridge** "Der süsse Brei" (1815). Source: Dortchen Wild

104. **The Clever People** "Die klugen Leute" (1857). Source: Dortchen Wild

105. **Tales About Toads** "Märchen von der Unke" (1815). Source: The first tale is a mixed version from Dortchen and Lisette Wild. The second tale is from Hessia. The third is from Berlin.

106. **The Poor Miller's Apprentice and the Cat** "Der arme Müllerbursch und das Kätzchen" (1815). Source: Dorothea Viehmann

107. **The Two Travelers** "Die beiden Wanderer" (1843). Source: A student named Mein from Kiel.

108. **Hans My Hedgehog** "Hans mein Igel" (1815). Source: Dorothea Viehmann

109. **The Little Shroud** "Das Totenhemdchen" (1815). Source: From Bavaria. Informant unknown.

110. **The Jew in the Thornbush** "Der Jude im Dorn" (1815). Source: Albrecht Dietrich, *Historia von einem Bauernknecht* (1618).

111. **The Expert Huntsman** "Der gelernte Jäger" (1815). Source: Dorothea Viehmann and Johann Friedrich Krause. Mixed version.

112. **The Fleshing Flail From Heaven** "Der Dreschflegel vom Himmel" (1815). Source: Family von Haxthausen

113. **The Two Kings' Children** "De beiden Künigeskinner" Source: Ludowine von Haxthausen. Written in Paderborn dialect.

114. **The Clever Little Tailor** "Vom klugen Schneiderlein" (1815). Source: Ferdinand Siebert

115. **The Bright Sun Will Bring It to Light** "Die klare Sonne bringt's an den Tag" (1815). Source: Dorothea Viehmann

116. **The Blue Light** "Das blaue Licht" (1815). Source: From Mecklenburg. Informant unknown.

117. **The Stubborn Child** "Das eigensinnige Kind" (1815). Source: From Hessia. Informant unknown.

118. **The Three Army Surgeons** "Die drei Feldscherer" (1815). Source: Dorothea Viehmann

119. **The Seven Swabians** "Die sieben Schwaben" (1819). Source: Song by Hans Sachs from 1545 and a story by Hans Wilhelm Kirchhoff in his book *Wendunmuth* (1563).

120. **The Three Journeymen** "Die drei Handwerksburschen" (1815). Source: Dorothea Viehmann and Georg August Friedrich Goldmann

121. **The Prince Who Feared Nothing** "Der Königssohn, der sich vor nichts fürchtet" (1819). Source: Family von Haxthausen

122. **The Lettuce Donkey** "Der Krautesel" (1819). Source: From Bohemia. Informant unknown.

123. **The Old Woman in the Forest** "Die Alte im Wald" (1815). Source: Family von Haxthausen

124. **The Three Brothers** "Die drei Brüder" (1815). Source: Ferdinand Siebert

125. **The Devil and His Grandmother** "Der Teufel und seine Grossmutter" (1815). Source: Dorothea Viehmann

126. **Faithful Ferdinand and Unfaithful Ferdinand** "Ferenand getrü und Ferenand ungetrü" (1815). Source: Family von Haxthausen. Written in Paderborn dialect.

127. **The Iron Stove** "Der Eisenofen" (1815). Source: Dorothea Viehmann
128. **The Lazy Spinner** "Die faule Spinnerin" (1815). Source: Dorothea Viehmann
129. **The Four Skillful Brothers** "Die vier kunstreichen Brüder" (1819). Source: Family von Haxthausen
130. **One-Eye, Two-Eyes, and Three-Eyes** "Einäuglein, Zweiäuglein und Dreiäuglein" (1819). Source: Theodor Pescheck, tale with the same title in the journal *Wöchentliche Nachrichten für Freunde des Mittelalters* 2 (1816).
131. **Pretty Katrinelya and Pif Paf Poltree** "Die schöne Katrinelje und Pif Paf Poltrie" (1815). Source: Family von Haxthausen. The German words for the members of this family are *Hollenthe* (father), *Malcho* (mother), *Hohenstolz* (brother), and *Käsetraut* (sister).
132. **The Fox and the Horse** "Der Fuchs und das Pferd" (1815). Source: Family von Haxthausen
133. **The Worn-out Dancing Shoes** "Die zertanzten Schuhe" (1815). Source: Jenny von Droste-Hülshoff
134. **The Six Servants** "Die sechs Diener" (1815). Source: Family von Haxthausen
135. **The White Bride and the Black Bride** "Die weisse und die schwarze Braut" (1815). Source: Hans Rudolf von Schröter and Family von Haxthausen. Mixed version.
136. **Iron Hans** "Der Eisenhans" (1850). Source: Family Hassenpflug and "Der eiserne Hans," a tale in Friedmund von Arnim's *Hundert Mährchen im Gebirge gesammelt* (Charlottenburg, 1844). Mixed version.
137. **The Three Black Princesses** "De drei schatten Prinzessinnen" (1815). Source: Jenny von Droste-Hülshoff. Written in Münster dialect.
138. **Knoist and His Three Sons** "Knoist un sine dre Sühne" (1815). Source: Family von Haxthausen. Written in Sauerland dialect.
139. **The Maiden From Brakel** "Dat Mäken von Brakel" (1815). Source: Family von Haxthausen. Written in Paderborn dialect. Saint Anne is the patron saint of the town Brakel, which was near the estate of the Family von Haxthausen.
140. **The Domestic Servants** "Das Hausgesinde" (1815). Source: Family von Haxthausen
141. **The Little Lamb and the Little Fish** "Das Lämmchen und Fischen" (1815). Source: Marianne von Haxthausen
142. **Simelei Mountain** "Simeliberg" (1815). Source: Ludowine von Haxthausen
143. **Going Traveling** "Up Reisen gohn" (1819). Source: Family von Haxthausen. Written in Münster dialect.
144. **The Donkey** "Das Eselein" (1815). Source: Latin poem of the 14th century.
145. **The Ungrateful Son** "Der undankbare Sohn" (1815). Source: Johann Paulis, *Schimpf und Ernst* (1522).
146. **The Turnip** "Die Rübe" (1815). Source: Latin poem of the 14th century. Similar to a tale in Gianfresco Straparola's *Piacevoli notti* (1550).
147. **The Rejuvenated Little Old Man** "Das junggeglühte Männlein" (1815). Source: Hans Sachs, *Ursprung der Affen* (1562).
148. **The Animals of the Lord and the Devil** "Des Herrn und des Teufels Getier" (1815). Source: Hans Sachs, *Der Teufel hat die Geiss erschaffen* (1556).
149. **The Beam** "Der Hahnenbalken" (1815). Source: Friedrich Kind, "Der Hahnenbalken," a poem in the journal *Becker'sches Taschenbuch* (1812).
150. **The Old Beggar Woman** *"Die alte Bettelfrau" (1815).* Source: Johann

Heinrich Jung-Stilling, *Heinrich Stillings Jünglings-Jahre* (Berlin, 1778). Heinrich von Kleist (1777–1811) wrote a similar story.

151. **The Three Lazy Sons** "Die drei Faulen" (1815). Source: Johann Paulis, *Schimpf und Ernst* (1522).

151a. **The Twelve Lazy Servants** "Die zwölf faulen Knechte" (1857). Source: Adelbert von Keller, "Spiel von den zwölf Pfaffenknechten," in *Fastnachtspiele* (Stuttgart, 1853). Wilhelm Grimm considered this tale so important that he added it to the last large edition of the tales. To keep the even number of 200 tales, he designated it as 151a.

152. **The Little Shepherd Boy** "Das Hirtenbüblein" (1819). Source: Ludwig Aurbacher

153. **The Star Coins** "Die Sterntaler" (1812). Source: Based on a story in Jean Paul's novel *Die unsichtbare Loge* (Berlin, 1793). A motif was also taken from Achim von Arnim's novella *Die drei liebreichen Schwestern und der glückliche Färber* (Berlin, 1812).

154. **The Stolen Pennies** "Der gestohlene Heller" (1812). Source: Gretchen Wild

155. **Choosing a Bride** "Die Brautschau" (1819). Source: Johann Rudolf Wyss's poem "Die Brautschau," in *Idyllen, Volkssagen, Legenden und Erzählungen aus der Schweiz* (Bern, 1815).

156. **The Leftovers** "Die Schickerlinge" (1819). Source: From Mecklenburg. Informant unknown.

157. **The Sparrow and His Four Children** "Der Sperling und seine vier Kinder" (1812). Source: From a chapter in Johann Balthasar Schuppius's *Lehrreiche Schriften* (1663).

158. **The Tale About the Land of Cockaigne** "Das Märchen vom Schlaraffenland" (1815). Source: Middle German poem from the 14th century in a volume edited by Christoph Heinrich Myller, *Sammlung deutscher Gedichte aus dem 12.–14. Jahrhundert,* vol. 3 (Berlin, 1784). This type of tale, which depicts the world turned upside down and the desire of the peasants to have their stomachs filled, was common throughout Europe during the Middle Ages.

159. **A Tall Tale from Ditmarsh** "Das Diethmarsische Lügenmärchen" (1815). Source: A Low German song from Anton Viethen's *Beschreibung und Geschichte des Landes Dithmarschen* (Hamburg, 1733).

160. **A Tale With a Riddle** "Rätselmärchen" (1815). Source: Based on a folk song with riddles from the 16th century.

161. **Snow White and Rose Red** "Schneeweisschen und Rosenrot" (1837). Source: Caroline Stahl, "Der undankbare Zwerg" in *Fabeln und Erzählungen für Kinder* (Nürnberg, 1818).

162. **The Clever Servant** "Der kluge Knecht" (1837). Source: Based on the interpretation of the 101st Psalm by Martin Luther in a book edited by Hans Luft, *Auslegung des 101. Psalms* (1534).

163. **The Glass Coffin** "Der gläserne Sarg" (1837). Source: Based on a story within a novel by Sylvanus, *Das verwöhnte Mütter-Söhngen* (Freiburg, 1728).

164. **Lazy Heinz** "Der faule Heinz" (1837). Source: Based on a verse story in Eucharius Eyering's *Proverbiorum Copia* (Eisleben, 1601). The ending was taken from a letter by Elizabeth Charlotte von Orleans. Mixed version.

165. **The Griffin** "Der Vogel Greif" (1837). Source: Wilhelm Wackernagel. Written in Swiss dialect and based on an oral tale by Freidrich Schmid.

166. **Strong Hans** "Der starke Hans" (1837). Source: Wilhelm Wackernagel. From Switzerland.

167. **The Peasant in Heaven** "Das Bürli im Himmel" (1837). Source: Wilhelm Wackernagel. Written in Swiss dialect and based on an oral tale by Friedrich Schmid.

168. **Lean Lisa** "Die hagere Liese" (1840). Source: Hans Wilhelm Kirchhoff, *Wendunmuth* (1563).

169. **The House in the Forest** "Das Waldhaus" (1840). Source: Karl Goedeke

170. **Sharing Joys and Sorrows** "Lieb und Leid teilen" (1840). Source: Jörg Wickram, *Rollwagenbüchlin* (1555).

171. **The Wren** "Der Zaunkönig" (1840). Source: Johann Jakob Nikolaus Musäus, "Die Königswahl unter den Vögeln," in the journal *Jahrbuch des Vereins für mecklenburgische Geschichte und Altertumskunde* 5 (1840), and a Low German tale recorded by Karl Goedeke. The literal translation of *Zaunkönig* is "king of the hedge." (See also note for tale 102.)

172. **The Flounder** "Die Scholle" (1840). Source: Johann Jakob Nikolaus Musäus, "Die Königswahl unter den Fischen," in *Jahrbuch des Vereins für mecklenburgische Geschichte und Altertumskunde* 5 (1840).

173. **The Bittern and the Hoopoe** "Rohrdommel und Wiedehopf" (1840). Source: Johann Jakob Nikolaus Musäus, "Die Kuhhirten," in the journal *Jahrbuch des Vereins für mecklenburgische Geschichte und Altertumskunde* 5 (1840).

174. **The Owl** "Die Eule" (1840). Source: Hans Wilhelm Kirchhoff, *Wendunmuth* (1563).

175. **The Moon** "Der Mond" (1857). Source: Heinrich Pröhle, "Das Mondenlicht," in *Märchen für die Jugend* (Leipzig, 1854).

176. **The Life Span** "Die Lebenszeit" (1840). Source: Carl Friedrich Münscher, recorded from a peasant in Zwehrn near Kassel.

177. **The Messengers of Death** "Die Boten des Todes" (1840). Source: Hans Wilhelm Kirchhoff, *Wendunmuth* (1563).

178. **Master Pfreim** "Meister Pfriem" (1843). Source: Ludwig Aurbacher, "Hans Pfriem," in *Volksbüchlein* (Munich, 1827). A *Pfriem* in German is a shoemaker's awl and is used for piercing holes in leather.

179. **The Goose Girl at the Spring** "Die Gänsehirtin am Brunnen" (1843). Source: Based on Andreas Schumacher's Austrian dialect story *D'Ganshiadarin* (Vienna, 1833) and translated into High German by Hermann Kletke as "Die Gänsehüterin," in *Almanach deutscher Volksmärchen* 2 (Berlin, 1840).

180. **Eve's Unequal Children** "Die ungleichen Kinder Evas" (1843). Source: A witty anecdote by Hans Sachs (1558) with the same title.

181. **The Nixie in the Pond** "Die Nixe im Teich" (1843). Source: Moritz Haupt, tale in the journal *Zeitschrift für deutsches Alterthum* 2 (1842).

182. **The Gifts of the Little Folk** "Die Geschenke des kleinen Volkes" (1850). Source: Emil Sommer, "Der Berggeister," in the anthology *Sagen aus Sachsen und Thüringen* (Halle, 1846).

183. **The Giant and the Tailor** "Der Riese und der Schneider" Source: Franz Ziska, ed., *Österreichische Volksmärchen* (Vienna, 1822).

184. **The Nail** "Der Nagel" (1843). Source: Ludwig Aurbacher, "Vom Reiter and seinem Ross," in *Büchlein für die Jugend* (Stuttgart, 1834).

185. **The Poor Boy in the Grave** "Der arme Junge im Grab" (1843). Source: Ludwig Aurbacher, "Des armen Waisen Leben und Tod," in *Büchlein für die Jugend* (Stuttgart, 1834).

186. **The True Bride** "Die wahre Braut" (1843). Source: Moritz Haupt, tale in the journal *Zeitschrift für deutsches Alterthum* 2 (1842).

187. **The Hare and the Hedgehog** "Der Hase und der Igel" (1843). Source: Wilhelm Schröder, tale in dialect (Low German, from Bexhövede) in the newspaper *Hannoversches Volksblatt* 51 (April 26, 1840).

188. **Spindle, Shuttle, and Needle** "Spindel, Weberschiffchen und Nadel" (1843). Source: Ludwig Aurbacher, "Die Patengeschenke," in *Büchlein für die Jugend* (Stuttgart, 1834).

189. **The Peasant and the Devil** "Der Bauer und der Teufel" (1843). Source:

Ludwig Aurbacher, "Der Teufel und der Bauer," in *Büchlein für die Jugend* (Stuttgart, 1834).

190. **The Crumbs on the Table** "Die Brosamen auf dem Tisch" (1843). Source: Wilhelm Wackernagel, tale in Swiss dialect (Aargau) in the journal *Zeitschrift für deutsches Alterthum* 3 (1843).

191. **The Little Hamster From the Water** "Das Meerhäschen" (1857). Source: "Von der Königstochter, die aus ihrem Schlosse alles in ihrem Reich sah," in Josef Haltrich's anthology *Deutsche Volksmärchen aus dem Sachsenlande in Siebenbürgen* (1856).

192. **The Master Thief** "Der Meisterdieb" (1843). Source: Story by Friedrich Stertzing in the journal *Zeitschrift für deutsches Alterthum* 3 (1843). From Thuringia.

193. **The Drummer** "Der Trommler" (1843). Source: Karl Goedeke, a professor from Celle, who sent the tale to Jacob Grimm with the title "Vom glasernen Berg" ("The Glass Mountain") on December 15, 1838. He recorded the tale from his aunt, a modest bourgeois woman from Alfeld.

194. **The Ear of Corn** "Die Kornähre" (1850). Source: Based on a story with the same title by Philipp Hoffmeister in the journal *Zeitschrift des Vereins für hessische Geschichte* 4 (1847). The original source may have been Ludwig Bechstein's tale "Die Ähre" (1843).

195. **The Grave Mound** "Der Grabhügel" (1850). Source: Based on Philipp Hoffmeister's story "Das Märchen vom dummen Teufel," in the journal *Zeitschrift des Vereins für hessische Geschichte* 4 (1847).

196. **Old Rinkrank** "Oll Rinkrank" (1850). Source: Written in dialect (from the Oestringen region of Germany near Oldenburg) and based on a story with the same title by Heinrich Georg Ehrentraud in the journal *Friesisches Archiv* 1 (1849).

197. **The Crystal Ball** "Die Kristallkugel" (1850). Source: Friedmund von Arnim's tale "Vom Schloss der goldenen Sonne," in *Hundert Märchen im Gebirge gesammelt* (Charlottenburg, 1844).

198. **Maid Maleen** "Jungfrau Maleen" (1850). Source: Karl Müllenhoff, ed., *Sagen, Märchen und Lieder der Herzogthümer Schleswig, Holstein und Lauenburg* (Kiel, 1845).

199. **The Boots of Buffalo Leather** "Der Stiefel von Büffelleder" (1850). Source: Friedmund von Arnim, "Vom Bruder Stiefelschmeer," in *Hundert Märchen im Gebirge gesammelt* (Charlottenburg, 1844).

200. **The Golden Key** "Der goldene Schlüssel" (1815). Source: Marie Hassenpflug

Religious Tales for Children

201. **Saint Joseph in the Forest** "Der heilige Joseph im Walde" (1819). Source: Family von Haxthausen

202. **The Twelve Apostles** "Die zwölf Apostel" (1819). Source: Family von Haxthausen

203. **The Rose** "Die Rose" (1819). Source: Family von Haxthausen

204. **Poverty and Humility Lead to Heaven** "Armut und Demut führen zum Himmel" (1819). Source: Family von Haxthausen

205. **God's Food** "Gottes Speise" (1819). Source: Family von Haxthausen

206. **The Three Green Twigs** "Die drei grünen Zweige" (1819). Source: Family von Haxthausen

207. **The Blessed Virgin's Little Glass** "Muttergottesgläschen" (1819). Source: Family von Haxthausen

208. **The Little Old Lady** "Das alte Mütterchen" (1819). Source: Family von Haxthausen

209. **The Heavenly Wedding** "Die himmlische Hochzeit" (1815). Source: From Mecklenburg. Informant unknown.

210. **The Hazel Branch** "Die Haselrute" (1850). Source: High German translation of "Die Muttergottes und die Natter," from Josef Franz Vonbun, ed., *Volkssagen aus Vorarlberg* (Vienna, 1847).

The Omitted Tales

211. **The Nightingale and the Blindworm** "Von der Nachtigall und der Blindschleiche" was first published as no. 6, in 1812, and omitted in 1819 due to its French origins. Source: M. Legier du Loiret, *Traditions et Usages de la Sologne* (Paris, 1808).

212. **The Hand With the Knife** "Die Hand mit dem Messer" was first published as no. 8, in 1812, and was omitted in 1819 due to its Scottish origins. Source: Mrs. Anne Grant, *Essays on the Superstitions of the Highlanders of Scotland* (London, 1811).

213. **Herr Fix-It-Up** "Herr Fix und Fertig" was first published as no. 16, in 1812, and was omitted in 1819 because Wilhelm Grimm felt it was an unpolished piece. He eventually replaced it with "The Queen Bee" (no. 62). Source: Johann Friedrich Krause. The name of the protagonist is an idiomatic expression meaning "to be all ready" or "worn out."

214. **How Some Children Played at Slaughtering** "Wie Kinder Schlachtens miteinander gespielt haben" was first published in no. 22, in 1812, and was omitted in 1819 because the tales were too gruesome. Source: I. Heinrich von Kleist, *Abendblatt* (October 13, 1810); II. Martin Zeiler, *Miscellen* (Nürnberg, 1661).

215. **Death and the Goose Boy** "Der Tod und der Gänshirt" was first published as no. 27, in 1812, and omitted because of its baroque features and allegorical character. Source: Georg Harsdörffer, *Der grosse Schau-Platz jämmerlicher Mord-Geschichten* (Hamburg, 1663).

216. **Puss in Boots** "Der gestiefelte Kater" was first published as no. 33, in 1812, and was omitted in 1819 due to its French origins, in particular, Charles Perrault's "Le chat botté," *Contes du Temps passé* (1697). Source: Jeanette Hassenpflug.

217. **The Tablecloth, the Knapsack, the Cannon Hat, and the Horn** "Von der Serviette, dem Tornister, dem Kanonenhütlein und dem Horn" was first published as no. 37, in 1812, and was omitted in 1819 due to its close resemblance to "The Knapsack, the Hat, and the Horn" (no. 54). Source: Johann Friedrich Krause

218. **The Strange Feast** "Die wunderliche Gasterei" was first published as no. 43, in 1812, and was omitted in 1837 due to its close resemblance to "The Godfather" (no. 42). Source: Amalie Hassenpflug

219. **Simple Hans** "Hans Dumm" was first published as no. 54, in 1812, and was omitted due to its French origins or similarity to a tale by Christoph Martin Wieland. Source: The Hassenpflug sisters

220. **Bluebeard** "Blaubart" was first published as no. 62, in 1812, and was omitted in 1819 due to its French origins, in particular, Charles Perrault's "La barbe bleue," *Contes du Temps passé* (1697). Source: The Hassenpflug sisters

221. **Hurleburlebutz** "Hurleburlebutz" was first published as no. 66, in 1812, and was omitted in 1819 due to its close resemblance to "The Iron Stove" (no. 127). Source: Jeanette Hassenpflug

222. **Okerlo** "Der Okerlo" was first published as no. 70, in 1812, and was

omitted in 1819 due to its French origins, in particular, Mme. Marie-Catherine D'Aulnoy's "L'oranger et l'abeille," in *Contes nouveaux ou les Fées à la Mode* (Paris, 1697). The word *Okerlo* stems from the Italian *huorco* and French *ogre*, and could be translated as "bogeyman." Source: Jeanette Hassenpflug.

223. **Princess Mouseskin** "Prinzessin Mäusehaut" was first published as no. 71, in 1812, and was omitted in 1819 due to its French origins, in particular, Charles Perrault's "Peau d'ane," in *Contes du Temps passé* (1697). Source: Family Wild

224. **The Pear Refused to Fall** "Das Birnli will nit fallen" was first published as no. 72, in 1812, and omitted in 1819 due to its verse form. Source: Switzerland. Written in Swiss dialect. Informant unknown.

225. **The Castle of Murder** "Das Mordschloss" was first published as no. 73, in 1812, and was omitted in 1819 due to its Dutch origins and similarity to "Bluebeard." Source: Fräulein de Kinsky. Dutch.

226. **The Carpenter and the Turner** "Vom Schreiner und Drechsler" was first published as no. 77, in 1812, and was omitted in 1819 due to its fragmentary condition. Source: Friederike Mannel

227. **The Blacksmith and the Devil** "Der Schmied und der Teufel" was first published as no. 81, in 1812, and was omitted in favor of a similar tale. It was published in the Grimms' *Notes* (*Anmerkungen*) beginning in 1822 as a variant to tale no. 82. Source: Oral tale from Hessia. Informant unknown.

228. **The Three Sisters** "Die drei Schwestern" was first published as no. 82, in 1812, and was omitted because Jacob Grimm did not think it was genuinely within the oral tradition. Source: Johann Karl August Musäus, "Die Bücher der Chronika der drey Schwestern" in *Volksmährchen der Deutschen* (Gotha, 1782).

229. **The Stepmother** "Die Stiefmutter" was first published as no. 84, in 1812, and was omitted because of its fragmentary nature and probably also because of its cruelty. It was moved to the *Fragments* (*Bruchstücke*) of the *Notes* (*Anmerkungen*) in 1822 as no. 5 under the title "Die böse Stiefmutter" or "The Evil Stepmother." Source: Probably Charles Perrault's "La belle au bois dormant" ("Sleeping Beauty") in *Contes du temps passé* (1697).

230. **Fragments:** a. **Snowflower;** b. **Prince Johannes;** c. **The Good Cloth** "Fragmente": a. "Schneeblume"; b. "Vom Prinz Johannes"; c. "Der gute Lappen" These tales were first published as no. 85, in 1812, and were omitted in 1819 due to their fragmentary condition. Source: *Snowflower*—French folk tale; *Prince Johannes*—Karl Gotthard Grass's story in the journal *Erheiterungen* (1812); *The Good Cloth*—the Hassenpflug sisters.

231. **The Faithful Animals** "Die treuen Tiere" was first published as no. 18, in 1815, and omitted in 1850 because it came from the *Siddhi-Kür,* a collection of Mongolian tales. Source: Ferdinand Siebert

232. **The Crows** "Die Krähen" was first published as no. 21, in 1815, and was omitted in 1840 because of its resemblance to "The Two Travelers" (no. 107). Source: August von Haxthausen, who wrote down the tale as told him by a soldier from Mecklenburg.

233. **The Lazy One and the Industrious One** "Der Faule und der Fleissige" was first published as no. 33, in 1815, and was omitted in 1819 because the Grimms thought it was too contrived. Source: Ferdinand Siebert

234. **The Long Nose** "Die lange Nase" was first published as no. 36, volume II, in 1815, and was omitted in favor of "The Lettuce Donkey" (no. 122), which is a variant on the motif of transformation. The Grimms probably preferred the latter story. Since 1822 "The Long Nose" was included as a variant to no. 122 in the *Notes* (*Anmerkungen*). Source: Dorothea Viehmann.

235. **The Lion and the Frog** "Der Löwe und der Frosch" was first pub-

lished as no. 43, in 1815, and was omitted in 1819 because it had too many similarities to other tales. Source: Ludovica Jordis-Brentano

236. **The Soldier and the Carpenter** "Der Soldat und der Schreiner" was first published as no. 44, in 1815, and was omitted in 1819 because it was too fragmentary and confused. Source: Family von Haxthausen

237. **The Wild Man** "De wilde Mann" was first published as no. 50, in 1815, and was omitted in 1843 because of its resemblance to "Iron Hans" (no. 136). Source: Family von Haxthausen. Written in Münster dialect.

238. **The Children of Famine** "Die Kinder in Hungersnot" was first published as no. 57, in 1815, and was omitted in 1819 because it was too cruel and too much like a legend. Source: Johannes Praetorius, *Der abenteuerliche Glückstopf* (1669).

239. **Saint Solicitous** "Die heilige Frau Kummernis" was first published as no. 66, in 1815, and was omitted in 1819 because it was too much like a legend. Source: Andreas Strobl, *Ovum paschale oder neugefärbte Oster-Ayr* (Salzburg, 1700).

240. **Misfortune** "Das Unglück" was first published as no. 175, in 1840, and was omitted in 1857. It is not clear why the tale was omitted. Source: Wilhelm Kirchhoff, *Wendunmuth* (1563).

241. **The Pea Test** "Die Erbsenprobe" was first published as no. 182, in 1843, and was omitted in 1850 because of the similarity to Hans Christian Andersen's "The Princess and the Pea" ("Prindsessan paa aerten," 1835).

242. **The Robber and His Sons** "Der Räuber und seine Söhne" was first published as no. 191, in 1843, and was omitted in 1857 because of its similarity to the classical Greek myth of Polyphemus. Source: Moritz Haupt, translation of a medieval poem, printed in the journal *Altdeutsche Blätter* (1836).

Contributors of Oral and Literary Tales

Wherever possible the dates and professions of the contributors have been indicated.

Achim von Arnim (1781–1831), romantic writer and close friend of the Grimms. It was he who encouraged the Grimms to publish their collection of tales in 1812.

Friedmund von Arnim, author of *Hundert Mährchen im Gebirge gesammelt* (1844).

Ludwig Aurbacher (1784–1847), writer and collector of folk and fairy tales, author of *Büchlein für die Jugend*.

Johann Henrich Balthasar Bauer (1792–1835), friend of the Grimms in Kassel, provided a version of "The Maiden Without Hands."

Albrecht Dietrich, author of *Historia von einem Bawrenknecht* (1618).

Jenny von Droste-Hülshoff (1795–1859), member of the Bökendorfer Circle.

Annette von Droste-Hülshoff (1797–1848), member of the Bökendorfer Circle and Germany's most famous woman poet of the 19th century.

H. Eckstein, Viennese bookdealer.

Heinrich Georg Ehrentraud, author of the "Old Rinkrank" version printed in the journal *Friesisches Archiv* (1849).

Wilhelm Engelhardt (1754–1818), a colonel from Kassel.

Eucharius Eyering, author of *Proverbiorum Copia* (1601).

Jakob Frey, author of *Gartengesellschaft* (1556).

Karl Goedeke (1814–87), professor of German from Celle.

Georg August Friedrich Goldmann (1785–1855), sent the Grimms several different versions of tales from Hannover.

Frau Gottschalk, wife of a doctor in Steinau, used to tell the Grimms folk tales.

Anne Grant, author of *Essays on the Superstitions of the Highlanders of Scotland* (1811).

Karl Gotthard Grass (1767–1814), painter and poet.

Albert Ludwig Grimm, (1786–1872), writer of fairy tales and teacher, author of *Kindermährchen* (1808). No relation to the Brothers Grimm.

Herman Grimm (1828–1901), son of Wilhelm Grimm, became a folklorist.

Eberhard von Groote (1789–1864), acquaintance of Jacob Grimm from Cologne.

Joseph Haltrich, editor of *Deutsche Volksmärchen aus dem Sachsenlande in Siebenbürgen* (1856).

Georg Philipp Harsdörffer, author of *Der grosse Schau-Platz jämmerlicher Mord-Geschichten* (1663).

Family Hassenpflug, a magistrate's family in Kassel with a Huguenot background, very close friends of the Grimms. Dorothea Grimm married Ludwig Hassenpflug, and the Hassenpflugs as a group provided numerous tales for the Grimms, many of which were originally French.

Marie Hassenpflug (1788–1856).

Jeanette Hassenpflug (1791–1860).

Amalie Hassenpflug (1800–1871).

Moriz Haupt, professor of German.

Family von Haxthausen, their estate in Westphalia became the meeting place for the Bökendorfer Circle. Contact was first made with the von Haxthausen Family when Jacob made the acquaintance with Werner von Haxthausen in 1808. A warm friendship developed between the Brothers Grimm and most of the Haxthausens in the ensuing years.

Marianne von Haxthausen (1755–1829).

August von Haxthausen (1792–1866).

Ludowine von Haxthausen (1795–1872).

Anna von Haxthausen (1800–1877).

Philipp Hoffmeister, collector of folk tales from the region of Schmalkalden.

Ludovica Jordis-Brentano (1787–1854), a sister of the German romantic writer Clemens Brentano. She lived in Frankfurt am Main and provided the Grimms with two tales.

Johann Heinrich Jung-Stilling (1740–1817), whose significant autobiography *Heinrich Stillings Jugend* (1777) and *Heinrich Stillings Jünglings-Jahre* (1778) contained tales, which the Grimms used in their collection.

Friedrich Kind (1768–1843), German poet and librettist who wrote the libretto for Carl Maria von Weber's opera *Der Freischütz*.

Fräulein de Kinsky, a young woman from Holland.

Hans Wilhelm Kirchhoff, author of *Wendunmuth* (1563).

Johann Friedrich Krause (1747–1828), a retired soldier who lived near Kassel.

Legier du Loiret, author of *Traditions et Usages de la Sologne* (1808).

Hans Luft, editor of *Auslegung des 101. Psalms* (1534), containing an interpretation by Martin Luther, which served as the basis for *The Clever Servant*.

Friederike Mannel (1783–1833), daughter of a minister in Allendorf.

Karl Hartwig Gregor von Meusebach (1781–1847), an old school friend of Jacob Grimm and later a professor in Berlin.

Martin Montanus, author of *Der Wegkürtzer* (1557).

Hans Michael Moscherosch, author of *Gesichte Philanders von Sittewald* (1650).

Karl Müllenhoff, editor of *Sagen, Märchen und Lieder der Herzogthümer Schleswig, Holstein und Lauenburg* (1845).

Carl Friedrich Münscher (1808–73), informant of "The Life Span."

Johann Karl August Musäus (1735–87), writer and author of one of the first, significant collections containing adapted legends of folk tales, *Volksmährchen der Deutschen* (1782).

Karl Nehrlich, author of the novel *Schilly* (1798).

Elisabeth Charlotte von Orleans, author of *Briefe 1676–1722* (1843), edited by W. Menzel.

Georg Passy (1784–1836), librarian in Vienna.

Jean Paul (1763–1825), renowned German author. Part of his novel *Die unsichtbare Loge* (1793) served as the basis for "The Star Coins."

Johann Pauli, author of *Schimpf und Ernst* (1522).

Theodor Pescheck, author of "One-Eye, Two-Eyes, and Three-Eyes" (1816).

Johannes Praetorius, author of *Wünschelruthe* (1667) and *Der abentheurliche Glückstopf* (1669).

Heinrich Pröhle (1797–1875), minister and writer, primarily of religious books, author of *Märchen für die Jugend* (1854).

Charlotte R. Ramus (1793–1858), friend of the Grimms in Kassel.

Julia R. Ramus (1792–1862), friend of the Grimms in Kassel.

Philipp Otto Runge (1777–1810), famous romantic painter.

Hans Sachs (1494–1576), leader of the Nürnberg Meistersinger and prolific author of folk dramas, tales, and anecdotes.

Friedrich Gustav Schilling (1766–1839), poet and novelist who wrote *Neue Abendgenossen* (1811), a collection of stories.

Friedrich Schmid, teller of two Swiss oral tales, "The Griffin" and "The Peasant in Heaven."

Wilhelm Schröder, recorder of "The Hare and the Hedgehog," told to him by a forester in Bexhövede.

Hans Rudolf von Schröter (1798–1842), professor of old German literature in Rostock.

Andreas Schuhmacher, author of *D'Ganshiardarin* (1833).

Friedrich Schultz, author of *Kleine Romane* (1790).

Johann Balthasar Schuppius, author of *Lehrreiche Schriften* (1663).

Simon Sechter (1788–1867) from Weitra in Lower Austria, recorder of the dialect tale "Gambling Hans."

Ferdinand Siebert (1791–1847), teacher in Kassel.

Emil Sommer, editor of *Sagen aus Sachsen und Thüringen* (1846).

Karoline Stahl (1776–1837), writer of children's books and author of *Fabeln und Erzählungen für Kinder* (1818).

Friedrich Stertzing, author of "The Master Thief" (1843).

August Stöber (1808–84), teacher and researcher of folklore in Alsace, author of *Elsässisches Volksbüchlein* (1842).

Andreas Strobl, author of *Ovum paschale oder neugefärbte Oster-Ayr* (1700).

Sylvanus, author of *Das verwöhnte Mutter-Söhngen* (1728).

Meier Teddy, poet, whose poem "Klein Bäschen und Frau Trude," in the journal *Frauentaschenbuch*, served as the basis for "Mother Trudy."

Hans Truffer (1774–1830), a lawyer from Visp.

Dorothea Viehmann (1755–1815), wife of a village tailor near Kassel.

Anton Viethen, author of *Beschreibung und Geschichte des Landes Dithmarschen* (1733).

Josef Franz Vonbun (1824–1870), folklorist and editor of *Volkssagen aus Vorarlberg* (1847).

Wilhelm Wackernagel (1806–68), professor of German in Switzerland.

Burkard Waldis, author of *Esopus* (1548).

August Wernicke, recorder of the oral tale "Lucky Hans."

Jörg Wickram, author of *Rollwagenbüchlin* (1555).

Paul Wigand (1786–1866), close friend of the Brothers Grimm, who studied with them in Kassel.

Family Wild, a pharmacist's family in Kassel, who were all very close to the Family Grimm. Wilhelm eventually married Dortchen Wild, who supplied the brothers with numerous tales.

Dorothea Catharina Wild (1752–1813).

Lisette Wild (1782–1858).

Gretchen Wild (1787–1819).

Marie Elisabeth Wild (1794–1867).

Dortchen Wild (1795–1867).

Johann Rudolf Wyss (1782–1830), Swiss writer, author of the poem "Die Brautschau" and *The Swiss Family Robinson*.

Martin Zeiler, author of *Miscellen* (1661).

Franz Ziska, editor of *Österreichische Volksmärchen* (1822).

About the Translator

JACK ZIPES is professor of German at the University of Florida, in Gainesville, and has previously held professorships at New York University, the University of Munich, the University of Berlin, the University of Frankfurt, and the University of Wisconsin–Milwaukee. In addition to his scholarly work, he is an active storyteller in public schools and has worked with children's theaters in France, Germany, Canada, and the United States. His major publications include *The Great Refusal: Studies of the Romantic Hero in German and American Literature* (Frankfurt, 1970), *Political Plays for Children* (St. Louis, 1976), *Breaking the Magic Spell: Radical Theories of Folk and Fairy Tales* (London, 1979), *Fairy Tales and the Art of Subversion* (New York, 1983), *The Trials and Tribulations of Little Red Riding Hood* (South Hadley, 1983), and *Don't Bet on the Prince: Contemporary Feminist Fairy Tales in North America and England* (New York, 1986). He coedits *New German Critique*, an interdisciplinary journal of German studies, and has written numerous articles for various journals in the United States, Great Britain, Germany, Canada, and France.

A Note on the Illustrations

John B. Gruelle (1880–1938) is known primarily as the creator of Raggedy Ann and Andy, but in fact, he was one of the more versatile and gifted American illustrators of the first half of the twentieth century. Born in Arcalo, Illinois, Gruelle spent his childhood largely in Indianapolis, and the Midwest took a strong hold on his imagination. Throughout his works there are friendly, openhearted country characters, idyllic farm scenes, and placid natural settings reminiscent of the late nineteenth-century American Midwest. His father, Richard B. Gruelle, a noted landscape painter, also exercised a major influence on the young Gruelle, who developed rapidly as an artist. While still in his teens, Gruelle became a cartoonist for the *Indianapolis Star,* and by the time he turned twenty, he had found a position on the *Cleveland Press.* Gruelle was such a talented artist that he could draw any kind of cartoon or illustration for advertisements or articles, and in his spare time he began writing and illustrating his own children's stories.

In 1910 Gruelle won a contest sponsored by the *New York Herald,* and he soon moved to Connecticut to live in an artists' colony called Silvermine, where he hoped to benefit from the exchange with like-minded painters and writers. It was then that his career as commercial artist, illustrator, and cartoonist suddenly began to soar. Due to his versatility, he was able to produce an incredible amount of material for a variety of newspapers and magazines such as *Physical Culture, Judge,* and *Life,* and he continued to write and illustrate children's stories for *Good Housekeeping* and *Woman's World.*

During this time he was commissioned to illustrate the Margaret Hunt translation of the Grimms' tales by the publishers Cupples & Leon. The book appeared in 1914, and unfortunately Gruelle's artwork did not receive the attention it deserved. Although the color illustrations are often sentimental, Gruelle's black and white drawings—most of which have been reproduced in this volume—add a new dimension to the tales because of his introduction of American motifs and settings that would be familiar to his readers. Gruelle also sought to emphasize the humor and optimism of the Grimms' tales by choosing scenes that captured both the mood of each tale and the manner in which a child might view the scene. As in his Raggedy Ann and Andy books, Gruelle contrasted the figures of good and evil in his line drawings in a way that induced an atmosphere of hope. For Gruelle, a fairy-tale illustration always had to point to the possibility of attaining a happy end.

It is interesting to note that only after he had finished the illustrations for *Grimm's Fairy Tales,* in 1914, did he go on to create the Raggedy Ann stories, in 1918. From this point on until his death, in 1938, Gruelle composed twelve Raggedy Ann and Raggedy Andy books as well as his various original fairy-tale collections. Numerous motifs from the Grimms' tales can be found in Gruelle's own tales and their illustrations, and so it is fitting that, in this new American edition of the Grimms' fairy tales, Johnny Gruelle's artwork is once again exhibited and can receive the attention that it deserves.

J.Z.